GREAT
AMERICAN
SHORT
STORIES

GREAT AMERICAN SHORT STORIES

*Selected
by the Editors
of
The Reader's
Digest*

—

The Reader's Digest Association
Pleasantville, New York
Montreal, Sydney, Cape Town, Hong Kong

The stories in this volume
appear at their original length except
for minor editing in a few instances, and
for the following, which have been condensed:
*A New England Nun, The Yellow Wall Paper,
Hook, Sir Edmund Orme, The Blue Hotel,
Bartleby the Scrivener, The Legend of Sleepy Hollow,
The Minister's Black Veil.*

"Christmas Is a Sad Season for the Poor"
by John Cheever, copyright 1949
The New Yorker Magazine, Inc.
Additional acknowledgments to copyright holders
appear on pages 638 through 640

Library of Congress Catalog Card Number: 76–10933
ISBN 0–89577–033–4
Printed in the United States of America

CONTENTS

WINTER DREAMS

F. SCOTT FITZGERALD

SOME OF THE caddies were poor as sin and lived in one-room houses with a neurasthenic cow in the front yard, but Dexter Green's father owned the second-best grocery store in Black Bear—the best one was The Hub, patronized by the wealthy people from Sherry Island—and Dexter caddied only for pocket money.

In the fall when the days became crisp and gray, and the long Minnesota winter shut down like the white lid of a box, Dexter's skis moved over the snow that hid the fairways of the golf course. At these times the country gave him a feeling of profound melancholy—it offended him that the links should lie in enforced fallowness, haunted by ragged sparrows for the long season. It was dreary, too, that on the tees where the gay colors fluttered in summer there were now only the desolate sandboxes knee-deep in crusted ice. When he crossed the hills the wind blew cold as misery, and if the sun was out he tramped with his eyes squinted up against the hard dimensionless glare.

In April the winter ceased abruptly. The snow ran down into Black Bear Lake, scarcely tarrying for the early golfers to brave the season with red and black balls. Without elation, without an interval of moist glory, the cold was gone.

Dexter knew that there was something dismal about this northern spring, just as he knew there was something gorgeous about the fall. Fall made him clinch his hands and tremble and repeat idiotic sentences to himself, and make brisk abrupt gestures of command to imaginary audiences and armies. October filled him with hope, which November raised to a sort of ecstatic triumph, and in this mood the fleeting brilliant impressions of the summer at Sherry Island were ready grist to his mill. He became a golf champion and defeated Mr. T. A. Hedrick in a marvelous match played a hundred times over the fairways of his imagination, a match each detail of which he changed about untiringly—sometimes he won with almost laughable ease, sometimes he came up magnificently from behind. Again, stepping from a Pierce Arrow automobile, like Mr. Mortimer Jones, he strolled frigidly into the lounge of the Sherry Island Golf Club—or perhaps, surrounded by an admiring crowd, he gave an exhibition of fancy diving from the springboard of the club raft. . . . Among those who watched him in openmouthed wonder was Mr. Mortimer Jones.

And one day it came to pass that Mr. Jones—himself and not his ghost—came up to Dexter with tears in his eyes and said that Dexter was the __ __ best caddie in the club, and wouldn't he decide not to quit if Mr. Jones made it worth his while, because every other __ __ caddie in the club lost one ball a hole for him—regularly.

"No, sir," said Dexter decisively, "I don't want to caddie anymore." Then, after a pause: "I'm too old."

"You're not more than fourteen. Why the devil did you decide just this morning that you wanted to quit? You promised that next week you'd go over to the state tournament with me."

"I decided I was too old."

Dexter handed in his A Class badge, collected what money was due him from the caddie master, and walked home to Black Bear Village.

"The best __ __ caddie I ever saw," shouted Mr. Mortimer Jones over a drink that afternoon. "Never lost a ball! Willing! Intelligent! Quiet! Honest! Grateful!"

The little girl who had done this was eleven—beautifully ugly, as little girls are apt to be who are destined after a few years to be inexpressibly lovely and bring no end of misery to a great number of men. The spark, however, was perceptible. There was a general ungodliness in the way her lips twisted down at the corners when she smiled, and in the—Heaven help us!—in the almost passionate quality of her eyes. Vitality is born early in such women. It was utterly in evidence now, shining through her thin frame in a sort of glow.

She had come eagerly out onto the course at nine o'clock with a white linen nurse and five small new golf clubs in a white canvas bag which the nurse was carrying. When Dexter first saw her she was standing by the caddie house, rather ill at ease and trying to conceal the fact by engaging her nurse in an obviously unnatural conversation graced by startling and irrelevant grimaces from herself.

"Well, it's certainly a nice day, Hilda," Dexter heard her say. She drew down the corners of her mouth, smiled, and glanced furtively around, her eyes in transit falling for an instant on Dexter.

Then to the nurse: "Well, I guess there aren't very many people out here this morning, are there?"

The smile again—radiant, blatantly artificial—convincing.

"I don't know what we're supposed to do now," said the nurse, looking nowhere in particular.

"Oh, that's all right. I'll fix it up."

Dexter stood perfectly still, his mouth slightly ajar. He knew that if he moved forward a step his stare would be in her line of vision—if he moved backward he would lose his full view of her face. For a moment he had not realized how young she was. Now he remembered having seen her several times the year before—in bloomers.

Suddenly, involuntarily, he laughed, a short abrupt laugh—then, startled by himself, he turned and began to walk quickly away.

"Boy!"

Dexter stopped.

"Boy . . ."

Beyond question he was addressed. Not only that, but he was treated to that absurd smile, that preposterous smile—the memory of which at least a dozen men were to carry into middle age.

"Boy, do you know where the golf teacher is?"

"He's giving a lesson."

"Well, do you know where the caddie master is?"

"He isn't here yet this morning."

"Oh." For a moment this baffled her. She stood alternately on her right and left foot.

"We'd like to get a caddie," said the nurse. "Mrs. Mortimer Jones sent us out to play golf, and we don't know how without we get a caddie."

Here she was stopped by an ominous glance from Miss Jones, followed immediately by the smile.

"There aren't any caddies here except me," said Dexter to the nurse, "and I got to stay here in charge until the caddie master gets here."

"Oh."

Miss Jones and her retinue now withdrew, and at a proper distance from Dexter became involved in a heated conversation, which was concluded by Miss Jones taking one of the clubs and hitting it on the ground with violence.

For further emphasis she raised it again and was about to bring it down smartly upon the nurse's bosom, when the nurse seized the club and twisted it from her hands.

"You damn little mean old *thing!*" cried Miss Jones wildly.

Another argument ensued. Realizing that the elements of the comedy were implied in the scene, Dexter several times began to laugh, but each time restrained the laugh before it reached audibility. He could not resist the monstrous conviction that the little girl was justified in beating the nurse.

The situation was resolved by the fortuitous appearance of the caddie master, who was appealed to immediately by the nurse.

"Miss Jones is to have a little caddie, and this one says he can't go."

"Mr. McKenna said I was to wait here till you came," said Dexter quickly.

"Well, he's here now." Miss Jones smiled cheerfully at the caddie master. Then she dropped her bag and set off at a haughty mince toward the first tee.

"Well?" The caddie master turned to Dexter. "What you standing there like a dummy for? Go pick up the young lady's clubs."

"I don't think I'll go out today," said Dexter.

"You don't—"

"I think I'll quit."

The enormity of his decision frightened him. He was a favorite caddie, and the thirty dollars a month he earned through the summer were not to be made elsewhere around the lake. But he had received a strong emotional shock, and his perturbation required a violent and immediate outlet.

It is not so simple as that, either. As so frequently would be the case in the future, Dexter was unconsciously dictated to by his winter dreams.

Now, of course, the quality and the seasonability of these winter dreams varied, but the stuff of them remained. They persuaded Dexter several years later to pass up a business course at the state university— his father, prospering now, would have paid his way—for the precarious advantage of attending an older and more famous university in the East, where he was bothered by his scanty funds. But do not get the impression, because his winter dreams happened to be concerned at first with musings on the rich, that there was anything merely snobbish in the boy. He wanted not association with glittering things and glittering people—he wanted the glittering things themselves. Often he reached out for the best without knowing why he wanted it—and sometimes he ran up against the mysterious denials and prohibitions in which life indulges. It is with one of those denials and not with his career as a whole that this story deals.

He made money. It was rather amazing. After college he went to the city from which Black Bear Lake draws its wealthy patrons. When he was only twenty-three and had been there not quite two years, there were already people who liked to say, "Now *there's* a boy—" All about him rich men's sons were peddling bonds precariously, or investing patrimonies precariously, or plodding through the two dozen volumes of the George Washington Commercial Course, but Dexter borrowed a thousand dollars on his college degree and his confident mouth, and bought a partnership in a laundry.

It was a small laundry when he went into it, but Dexter made a specialty of learning how the English washed fine woolen golf stockings without shrinking them, and within a year he was catering to the trade that wore knickerbockers. Men were insisting that their Shetland hose and sweaters go to his laundry, just as they had insisted on a caddie who could find golf balls. A little later he was doing their wives' lingerie as well—and running five branches in different parts of the city.

Before he was twenty-seven he owned the largest string of laundries in his section of the country. It was then that he sold out and went to New York.

But the part of his story that concerns us goes back to the days when he was making his first big success. When he was twenty-three Mr. Hart—one of the gray-haired men who like to say, "Now *there's* a boy"—gave him a guest card to the Sherry Island Golf Club for a weekend. So he signed his name one day on the register, and that afternoon played golf in a foursome with Mr. Hart and Mr. Sandwood and Mr. T. A. Hedrick. He did not consider it necessary to remark that he had once carried Mr. Hart's bag over this same links, and that he knew every trap and gully with his eyes shut—but he found himself glancing at the four caddies who trailed them, trying to catch a gleam or gesture that would remind him of himself, that would lessen the gap which lay between his present and his past.

It was a curious day, slashed abruptly with fleeting, familiar impressions. One minute he had the sense of being a trespasser—in the next he was impressed by the tremendous superiority he felt toward Mr. T. A. Hedrick, who was a bore and not even a good golfer anymore.

Then, because of a ball Mr. Hart lost near the fifteenth green, an enormous thing happened. While they were searching the stiff grasses of the rough there was a clear call of "Fore!" from behind a hill in their rear. And as they all turned abruptly from their search a bright new ball sliced abruptly over the hill and caught Mr. T. A. Hedrick in the abdomen.

"By Gad!" cried Mr. T. A. Hedrick. "They ought to put some of these crazy women off the course. It's getting to be outrageous."

A head and a voice came up together over the hill: "Do you mind if we go through?"

"You hit me in the stomach!" declared Mr. Hedrick wildly.

"Did I?" The girl approached the group of men. "I'm sorry. I yelled 'Fore!' " Her glance fell casually on each of the men—then scanned the fairway for her ball. "Did I bounce into the rough?"

It was impossible to determine whether this question was ingenuous or malicious. In a moment, however, she left no doubt, for as her partner came up over the hill she called cheerfully, "Here I am! I'd have gone on the green except that I hit something."

As she took her stance for a short mashie shot, Dexter looked at her closely. She wore a blue gingham dress, rimmed at throat and shoulders with a white edging that accentuated her tan. The quality of exaggeration, of thinness, which had made her passionate eyes and down-turning mouth absurd at eleven, was gone now. She was arrestingly beautiful. The color in her cheeks was centered like the color in a picture—it was not a high color, but a sort of fluctuating and feverish warmth, so shaded that it seemed at any moment it would recede and disappear. This color and the mobility of her mouth gave a continual impression of flux, of intense life, of passionate vitality—balanced only partially by the sad luxury of her eyes.

She swung her mashie impatiently and without interest, pitching the ball into a sandpit on the other side of the green. With a quick, insincere smile and a careless "Thank you!" she went on after it.

"That Judy Jones!" remarked Mr. Hedrick on the next tee, as they waited—some moments—for her to play on ahead. "All she needs is to be turned up and spanked for six months and then to be married off to an old-fashioned cavalry captain."

"My God, she's good-looking!" said Mr. Sandwood, who was just over thirty.

"Good-looking!" cried Mr. Hedrick contemptuously. "She always looks as if she wanted to be kissed! Turning those big cow eyes on every calf in town!"

It was doubtful if Mr. Hedrick intended a reference to the maternal instinct.

"She'd play pretty good golf if she'd try," said Mr. Sandwood.

"She has no form," said Mr. Hedrick solemnly.

"She has a nice figure," said Mr. Sandwood.

"Better thank the Lord she doesn't drive a swifter ball," said Mr. Hart, winking at Dexter.

Later in the afternoon the sun went down with a riotous swirl of gold and varying blues and scarlets, and left the dry, rustling night of western summer. Dexter watched from the veranda of the golf club, watched the even overlap of the waters in the little wind, silver molasses under the harvest moon. Then the moon held a finger to her lips and the lake became a clear pool, pale and quiet. Dexter put on his bathing suit and swam out to the farthest raft, where he stretched dripping on the wet canvas of the springboard.

There was a fish jumping and a star shining and the lights around the lake were gleaming. Over on a dark peninsula a piano was playing the songs of last summer and of summers before that—songs from *Chin-Chin* and *The Count of Luxemburg* and *The Chocolate Soldier*—and because the sound of a piano over a stretch of water had always seemed beautiful to Dexter he lay perfectly quiet and listened.

The tune the piano was playing at that moment had been gay and new five years before when Dexter was a sophomore at college. They had played it at a prom once when he could not afford the luxury of proms, and he had stood outside the gymnasium and listened. The sound of the tune precipitated in him a sort of ecstasy and it was with that ecstasy he viewed what happened to him now. It was a mood of intense appreciation, a sense that, for once, he was magnificently attune to life and that everything about him was radiating a brightness and a glamour he might never know again.

A low, pale oblong detached itself suddenly from the darkness of the island, spitting forth the reverberate sound of a racing motorboat. Two white streamers of cleft water rolled themselves out behind it and almost immediately the boat was beside him, drowning out the hot tinkle of the piano in the drone of its spray. Dexter, raising himself on his arms, was aware of a figure standing at the wheel, of two dark eyes regarding him over the lengthening space of water—then the boat had gone by and was sweeping in an immense and purposeless circle of spray round and round in the middle of the lake. With equal eccentricity one of the circles flattened out and headed back toward the raft.

"Who's that?" she called, shutting off her motor. She was so near now that Dexter could see her bathing suit, which consisted apparently of pink rompers.

The nose of the boat bumped the raft, and as the latter tilted rakishly he was precipitated toward her. With different degrees of interest they recognized each other.

"Aren't you one of those men we played through this afternoon?" she demanded.

He was.

"Well, do you know how to drive a motorboat? Because if you do I wish you'd drive this one so I can ride on the surfboard behind. My name is Judy Jones"—she favored him with an absurd smirk—rather, what tried to be a smirk, for, twist her mouth as she might, it was not grotesque, it was merely beautiful—"and I live in a house over there on the island, and in that house there is a man waiting for me. When he drove up at the door I drove out of the dock because he says I'm his ideal."

There was a fish jumping and a star shining and the lights around the lake were gleaming. Dexter sat beside Judy Jones and she explained how her boat was driven. Then she was in the water, swimming to the floating surfboard with a sinuous crawl. Watching her was without effort to the eye, watching a branch waving or a sea gull flying. Her arms, burned to butternut, moved sinuously among the dull platinum ripples, elbow appearing first, casting the forearm back with a cadence of falling water, then reaching out and down, stabbing a path ahead.

They moved out into the lake; turning, Dexter saw that she was kneeling on the low rear of the now uptilted surfboard.

"Go faster," she called, "fast as it'll go."

Obediently he jammed the lever forward and the white spray mounted at the bow. When he looked around again the girl was standing up on the rushing board, her arms spread wide, her eyes lifted toward the moon.

"It's awful cold," she shouted. "What's your name?"

He told her.

"Well, why don't you come to dinner tomorrow night?"

His heart turned over like the flywheel of the boat, and, for the second time, her casual whim gave a new direction to his life.

NEXT EVENING while he waited for her to come downstairs, Dexter peopled the soft deep summer room and the sun porch that opened from it with the men who had already loved Judy Jones. He knew the sort of men they were—the men who when he first went to college had entered from the great prep schools with graceful clothes and the deep tan of healthy summers. He had seen that, in one sense, he was better than these men. He was newer and stronger. Yet in acknowledging to himself that he wished his children to be like them he was admitting that he was but the rough, strong stuff from which they eternally sprang.

When the time had come for him to wear good clothes, he had known who were the best tailors in America, and the best tailors in America had made him the suit he wore this evening. He had acquired that particular reserve peculiar to his university, that set it off from other universities. He recognized the value to him of such a mannerism and he had adopted it; he knew that to be careless in dress and manner required more confidence than to be careful.

But carelessness was for his children. His mother's name had been Krimslich. She was a Bohemian of the peasant class and she had talked broken English to the end of her days. Her son must keep to the set patterns.

At a little after seven Judy Jones came downstairs. She wore a blue silk afternoon dress, and he was disappointed at first that she had not put on something more elaborate. This feeling was accentuated when, after a brief greeting, she went to the door of a butler's pantry and pushing it open called, "You can serve dinner, Martha." He had rather expected that a butler would announce dinner, that there would be a cocktail. Then he put these thoughts behind him as they sat down side by side on a lounge and looked at each other.

"Father and Mother won't be here," she said thoughtfully.

He remembered the last time he had seen her father, and he was glad the parents were not to be here tonight—they might wonder who he was. He had been born in Keeble, a Minnesota village fifty miles farther north, and he always gave Keeble as his home instead of Black Bear Village. Country towns were well enough to come from if they weren't inconveniently in sight and used as footstools by fashionable lakes.

They talked of his university, which she had visited frequently during the past two years, and of the nearby city which supplied Sherry Island with its patrons, and whither Dexter would return next day to his prospering laundries.

During dinner she slipped into a moody depression which gave

Dexter a feeling of uneasiness. Whatever petulance she uttered in her throaty voice worried him. Whatever she smiled at—at him, at a chicken liver, at nothing—it disturbed him that her smile could have no root in mirth, or even in amusement. When the scarlet corners of her lips curved down, it was less a smile than an invitation to a kiss.

Then, after dinner, she led him out on the dark sun porch and deliberately changed the atmosphere.

"Do you mind if I weep a little?" she said.

"I'm afraid I'm boring you," he responded quickly.

"You're not. I like you. But I've just had a terrible afternoon. There was a man I cared about, and this afternoon he told me out of a clear sky that he was poor as a church mouse. He'd never even hinted it before. Does this sound horribly mundane?"

"Perhaps he was afraid to tell you."

"Suppose he was," she answered. "He didn't start right. You see, if I'd thought of him as poor—well, I've been mad about loads of poor men, and fully intended to marry them all. But in this case, I hadn't thought of him that way, and my interest in him wasn't strong enough to survive the shock. As if a girl calmly informed her fiancé that she was a widow. He might not object to widows, but—

"Let's start right," she interrupted herself suddenly. "Who are you, anyhow?"

For a moment Dexter hesitated. Then: "I'm nobody," he announced. "My career is largely a matter of futures."

"Are you poor?"

"No," he said frankly, "I'm probably making more money than any man my age in the Northwest. I know that's an obnoxious remark, but you advised me to start right."

There was a pause. Then she smiled and the corners of her mouth drooped and an almost imperceptible sway brought her closer to him, looking up into his eyes. A lump rose in Dexter's throat, and he waited breathless for the experiment, facing the unpredictable compound that would form mysteriously from the elements of their lips. Then he saw—she communicated her excitement to him, lavishly, deeply, with kisses that were not a promise but a fulfillment. They aroused in him not hunger demanding renewal but surfeit that would demand more surfeit . . . kisses that were like charity, creating want by holding back nothing at all.

It did not take him many hours to decide that he had wanted Judy Jones ever since he was a proud, desirous little boy.

IT BEGAN like that—and continued, with varying shades of intensity, on such a note right up to the denouement. Dexter surrendered a part of himself to the most direct and unprincipled personality with which he had ever come in contact. Whatever Judy wanted, she went after with the full pressure of her charm. There was no divergence of method, no jockeying for position or premeditation of effects—there was very little mental side to any of her affairs. She simply made men conscious to the highest degree of her physical loveliness. Dexter had no desire to change her. Her deficiencies were knit up with a passionate energy that transcended and justified them.

When, as Judy's head lay against his shoulder that first night, she whispered, "I don't know what's the matter with me. Last night I thought I was in love with a man and tonight I think I'm in love with you—" it seemed to him a beautiful and romantic thing to say. It was the exquisite excitability that for the moment he controlled and owned. But a week later he was compelled to view this same quality in a different light. She took him in her roadster to a picnic supper, and after supper she disappeared, likewise in her roadster, with another man. Dexter became enormously upset and was scarcely able to be decently civil to the other people present. When she assured him that she had not kissed the other man, he knew she was lying—yet he was glad that she had taken the trouble to lie to him.

He was, as he found before the summer ended, one of a varying dozen who circulated about her. Each of them had at one time been favored above all others—about half of them still basked in the solace of occasional sentimental revivals. Whenever one showed signs of dropping out through long neglect, she granted him a brief honeyed hour, which encouraged him to tag along for a year or so longer. Judy made these forays upon the helpless and defeated without malice, indeed half unconscious that there was anything mischievous in what she did.

When a new man came to town every one dropped out—dates were automatically canceled.

The helpless part of trying to do anything about it was that she did it all herself. She was not a girl who could be "won" in the kinetic sense—she was proof against cleverness, she was proof against charm; if any of these assailed her too strongly she would immediately resolve the affair to a physical basis, and under the magic of her physical splendor the strong as well as the brilliant played her game and not their own. She was entertained only by the gratification of her desires and by the direct exercise of her own charm. Perhaps from so much youthful love, so many youthful lovers, she had come, in self-defense, to nourish herself wholly from within.

Succeeding Dexter's first exhilaration came restlessness and dissatisfaction. The helpless ecstasy of losing himself in her was opiate rather than tonic. It was fortunate for his work during the winter that those moments of ecstasy came infrequently. Early in their acquaintance it had seemed for a while that there was a deep and spontaneous mutual attraction—that first August, for example—three days of long evenings on her dusky veranda, of strange wan kisses through the late afternoon, in shadowy alcoves or behind the protecting trellises of the garden arbors, of mornings when she was fresh as a dream and almost shy at meeting him in the clarity of the rising day. There was all the ecstasy of an engagement about it, sharpened by his realization that there was no engagement. It was during those three days that, for the first time, he had asked her to marry him. She said "Maybe some day," she said "Kiss me," she said "I'd like to marry you," she said "I love you"—she said—nothing.

The three days were interrupted by the arrival of a New York man who visited at her house for half of September. To Dexter's agony, rumor engaged them. The man was the son of the president of a great trust company. But at the end of a month it was reported that Judy was yawning. At a dance one night she sat all evening in a motorboat with a local beau, while the New Yorker searched the club for her frantically. She told the local beau that she was bored with her visitor, and two days later he left. She was seen with him at the station, and it was reported that he looked very mournful indeed.

On this note the summer ended. Dexter was twenty-four, and he found himself increasingly in a position to do as he wished. He joined two clubs in the city and lived at one of them. Though he was by no means an integral part of the stag lines at these clubs, he managed to be on hand at dances where Judy Jones was likely to appear. He could have gone out socially as much as he liked—he was an eligible young man, now, and popular with downtown fathers. His confessed devotion to Judy Jones had rather solidified his position. But he had no social aspirations and rather despised the dancing men who were always on tap for the Thursday or Saturday parties and who filled in at dinners with the younger married set. Already he was playing with the idea of going east to New York. He wanted to take Judy Jones with him. No disillusion as to the world in which she had grown up could cure his illusion as to her desirability.

Remember that—for only in the light of it can what he did for her be understood.

Eighteen months after he first met Judy Jones he became engaged to another girl. Her name was Irene Scheerer, and her father was one of the men who had always believed in Dexter. Irene was light-haired and sweet and honorable, and a little stout, and she had two suitors whom she pleasantly relinquished when Dexter asked her to marry him.

Summer, fall, winter, spring, another summer, another fall—so much he had given of his active life to the incorrigible lips of Judy Jones. She had treated him with interest, with encouragement, with malice, with indifference, with contempt. She had inflicted on him the innumerable little slights and indignities possible in such a case—as if in revenge for having ever cared for him at all. She had beckoned him and yawned at him and beckoned him again and he had responded often with bitterness and narrowed eyes. She had brought him ecstatic happiness and intolerable agony of spirit. She had caused him untold inconvenience and not a little trouble. She had insulted him, and she had ridden over him, and she had played his interest in her against his interest in his work—for fun. She had done everything to him except to criticize him—this she had not done—it seemed to him only because it might have sullied the utter indifference she manifested and sincerely felt toward him.

When autumn had come and gone again it occurred to him that he could not have Judy Jones. He had to beat this into his mind but he convinced himself at last. He lay awake at night for a while and argued it over. He told himself the trouble and the pain she had caused him, he enumerated her glaring deficiencies as a wife. Then he said to himself that he loved her, and after a while he fell asleep. For a week, lest he imagined her husky voice over the telephone or her eyes opposite him at lunch, he worked hard and late, and at night he went to his office and plotted out his years.

At the end of a week he went to a dance and cut in on her once. For almost the first time since they had met he did not ask her to sit out with him or tell her that she was lovely. It hurt him that she did not miss these things—that was all. He was not jealous when he saw that there was a new man tonight. He had been hardened against jealousy long before.

He stayed late at the dance. He sat for an hour with Irene Scheerer and talked about books and about music. He knew very little about either. But he was beginning to be master of his own time now, and he had a rather priggish notion that he—the young and already fabulously successful Dexter Green—should know more about such things.

That was in October, when he was twenty-five. In January, Dexter and Irene became engaged. It was to be announced in June, and they were to be married three months later.

The Minnesota winter prolonged itself interminably, and it was almost May when the winds came soft and the snow ran down into Black Bear Lake at last. For the first time in over a year Dexter was enjoying a certain tranquillity of spirit. Judy Jones had been in Florida, and afterward in Hot Springs, and somewhere she had been engaged, and somewhere she had broken it off. At first, when Dexter had definitely given her up, it had made him sad that people still linked them together and asked for news of her, but when he began to be placed at dinner next to Irene Scheerer people didn't ask him about her anymore—they told him about her. He ceased to be an authority on her.

May at last. Dexter walked the streets at night when the darkness was damp as rain, wondering that so soon, with so little done, so much of ecstasy had gone from him. May one year back had been marked by Judy's poignant, unforgiveable, yet forgiven turbulence—it had been one of those rare times when he fancied she had grown to care for him. That old penny's worth of happiness he had spent for this bushel of content. He knew that Irene would be no more than a curtain spread behind him, a hand moving among gleaming teacups, a voice calling to children . . . fire and loveliness were gone, the magic of nights and the wonder of the varying hours and seasons . . . slender lips, down-turning, dropping to his lips and bearing him up into a heaven of eyes. . . . The thing was deep in him. He was too strong and alive for it to die lightly.

In the middle of May when the weather balanced for a few days on the thin bridge that led to deep summer he turned in one night at Irene's house. Their engagement was to be announced in a week now— no one would be surprised at it. And tonight they would sit together on the lounge at the University Club and look on for an hour at the dancers. It gave him a sense of solidity to go with her—she was so sturdily popular, so intensely "great."

He mounted the steps of the brownstone house and stepped inside. "Irene," he called.

Mrs. Scheerer came out of the living room to meet him.

"Dexter," she said, "Irene's gone upstairs with a splitting headache. She wanted to go with you but I made her go to bed."

"Nothing serious, I—"

"Oh, no. She's going to play golf with you in the morning. You can spare her for just one night, can't you, Dexter?"

Her smile was kind. She and Dexter liked each other. In the living room he talked for a moment before he said good night.

Returning to the University Club, where he had rooms, he stood in the doorway for a moment and watched the dancers. He leaned against the doorpost, nodded at a man or two—yawned.

"Hello, darling."

The familiar voice at his elbow startled him. Judy Jones had left a man and crossed the room to him—Judy Jones, a slender enameled doll in cloth of gold: gold in a band at her head, gold in two slipper points at her dress's hem. The fragile glow of her face seemed to blossom as she smiled at him. A breeze of warmth and light blew through the room.

His hands in the pockets of his dinner jacket tightened spasmodically. He was filled with a sudden excitement.

"When did you get back?" he asked casually.

"Come here and I'll tell you about it."

She turned and he followed her. She had been away—he could have wept at the wonder of her return. She had passed through enchanted streets, doing things that were like provocative music. All mysterious happenings, all fresh and quickening hopes, had gone away with her, came back with her now.

She turned in the doorway.

"Have you a car here? If you haven't, I have."

"I have a coupe."

In then, with a rustle of golden cloth. He slammed the door. Into so many cars she had stepped—like this—like that—her back against the leather, so—her elbow resting on the door—waiting. She would have been soiled long since had there been anything to soil her—except herself—but this was her own self outpouring.

With an effort he forced himself to start the car and back into the street. This was nothing, he must remember. She had done this before, and he had put her behind him, as he would have crossed a bad account from his books.

He drove slowly downtown and, affecting abstraction, traversed the deserted streets of the business section, peopled here and there where a movie was giving out its crowd or where consumptive or pugilistic youth lounged in front of pool halls. The clink of glasses and the slap of hands on the bars issued from saloons, cloisters of glazed glass and dirty yellow light.

She was watching him closely and the silence was embarrassing, yet in this crisis he could find no casual word with which to profane the hour. At a convenient turning he began to zigzag back toward the University Club.

"Have you missed me?" she asked suddenly.

"Everybody missed you."

He wondered if she knew of Irene Scheerer. She had been back only a day—her absence had been almost contemporaneous with his engagement.

"What a remark!" Judy laughed sadly—without sadness. She looked at him searchingly. He became absorbed in the dashboard.

"You're handsomer than you used to be," she said thoughtfully. "Dexter, you have the most rememberable eyes."

He could have laughed at this, but he did not laugh. It was the sort of thing that was said to sophomores. Yet it stabbed at him.

"I'm awfully tired of everything, darling." She called everyone darling, endowing the endearment with careless, individual comradery. "I wish you'd marry me."

The directness of this confused him. He should have told her now that he was going to marry another girl, but he could not tell her. He could as easily have sworn that he had never loved her.

"I think we'd get along," she continued, on the same note, "unless probably you've forgotten me and fallen in love with another girl."

Her confidence was obviously enormous. She had said, in effect, that she found such a thing impossible to believe, that if it were true he had merely committed a childish indiscretion—and probably to show off. She would forgive him, because it was not a matter of any moment but rather something to be brushed aside lightly.

"Of course you could never love anybody but me," she continued. "I like the way you love me. Oh, Dexter, have you forgotten last year?"

"No, I haven't forgotten."

"Neither have I!"

Was she sincerely moved—or was she carried along by the wave of her own acting?

"I wish we could be like that again," she said, and he forced himself to answer:

"I don't think we can."

"I suppose not. . . . I hear you're giving Irene Scheerer a violent rush." There was not the faintest emphasis on the name, yet Dexter was suddenly ashamed.

"Oh, take me home," cried Judy suddenly; "I don't want to go back to that idiotic dance—with those children."

Then, as he turned up the street that led to the residence district, Judy began to cry quietly to herself. He had never seen her cry before.

The dark street lightened, the dwellings of the rich loomed up around them, he stopped his coupe in front of the great white bulk of the Mortimer Joneses' house, somnolent, gorgeous, drenched with the splendor of the damp moonlight. Its solidity startled him. The strong walls, the steel of the girders, the breadth and beam and pomp of it were there only to bring out the contrast with the young beauty beside him. It was sturdy to accentuate her slightness—as if to show what a breeze could be generated by a butterfly's wing.

He sat perfectly quiet, his nerves in wild clamor, afraid that if he moved he would find her irresistibly in his arms. Two tears had rolled down her wet face and trembled on her upper lip.

"I'm more beautiful than anybody else," she said brokenly, "why can't I be happy?" Her moist eyes tore at his stability—her mouth turned slowly downward with an exquisite sadness. "I'd like to marry you if you'll have me, Dexter. I suppose you think I'm not worth having, but I'll be so beautiful for you, Dexter."

A million phrases of anger, pride, passion, hatred, tenderness fought on his lips. Then a perfect wave of emotion washed over him, carrying off with it a sediment of wisdom, of convention, of doubt, of honor. This was his girl who was speaking, his own, his beautiful, his pride.

"Won't you come in?" He heard her draw in her breath sharply.

Waiting.

"All right"—his voice was trembling—"I'll come in."

IT WAS strange that neither when it was over nor a long time afterward did he regret that night. Looking at it from the perspective of ten years, the fact that Judy's flare for him endured just one month seemed of little importance. Nor did it matter that by his yielding he subjected himself to a deeper agony in the end and gave serious hurt to Irene Scheerer and to Irene's parents, who had befriended him. There was nothing sufficiently pictorial about Irene's grief to stamp itself on his mind.

Dexter was at bottom hard-minded. The attitude of the city on his action was of no importance to him, not because he was going to leave the city, but because any outside attitude on the situation seemed superficial. He was completely indifferent to popular opinion. Nor, when he had seen that it was no use, that he did not possess in himself the power to move fundamentally or to hold Judy Jones, did he bear any malice toward her. He loved her, and he would love her until the day he was too old for loving—but he could not have her. So he tasted the deep pain that is reserved only for the strong, just as he had tasted for a little while the deep happiness.

Even the ultimate falsity of the grounds upon which Judy terminated the engagement, that she did not want to "take him away" from Irene—Judy who had wanted nothing else—did not revolt him. He was beyond any revulsion or any amusement.

He went east in February with the intention of selling out his laundries and settling in New York—but the war came to America in March and changed his plans. He returned to the West, handed over the management of the business to his partner, and went into the first officers' training camp in late April. He was one of those young thousands who greeted the war with a certain amount of relief, welcoming the liberation from webs of tangled emotion.

THIS STORY is not his biography, remember, although things creep into it which have nothing to do with those dreams he had when he was young. We are almost done with them and with him now. There is only one more incident to be related here, and it happens seven years farther on.

It took place in New York, where he had done well—so well that there were no barriers too high for him. He was thirty-two years old, and, except for one flying trip immediately after the war, he had not been west in seven years. A man named Devlin from Detroit came into his office to see him in a business way, and then and there this incident occurred, and closed out, so to speak, this particular side of his life.

"So you're from the Middle West," said the man Devlin. "That's funny—I thought men like you were probably born and raised on Wall Street. You know—wife of one of my best friends in Detroit came from your city. I was an usher at the wedding."

Dexter waited with no apprehension of what was coming.

"Judy Simms," said Devlin with no particular interest; "Judy Jones she was once."

"Yes, I knew her." A dull impatience spread over him. He had heard that she was married—perhaps deliberately he had heard no more.

"Awfully nice girl," brooded Devlin meaninglessly; "I'm sort of sorry for her."

"Why?" Something in Dexter was alert, receptive, at once.

"Oh, Lud Simms has gone to pieces in a way. I don't mean he ill-uses her, but he drinks and runs around—"

"Doesn't she run around?"

"No. Stays at home with her kids."

"Oh."

"She's a little too old for him," said Devlin.

"Too old!" cried Dexter. "Why, man, she's only twenty-seven."

He was possessed with a wild notion of rushing out into the streets and taking a train to Detroit. He rose to his feet spasmodically.

"I guess you're busy," Devlin apologized quickly. "I didn't realize—"

"No, I'm not busy," said Dexter, steadying his voice. "I'm not busy at all. Not busy at all. Did you say she was—twenty-seven? No, I said she was twenty-seven."

"Yes, you did," agreed Devlin dryly.

"Go on, then. Go on."

"What do you mean?"

"About Judy Jones."

Devlin looked at him helplessly.

"Well, that's—I told you all there is to it. He treats her like the devil. Oh, they're not going to get divorced or anything. When he's particularly outrageous she forgives him. In fact, I'm inclined to think she loves him. She was a pretty girl when she first came to Detroit."

A pretty girl! The phrase struck Dexter as ludicrous.

"Isn't she—a pretty girl, anymore?"

"Oh, she's all right."

"Look here," said Dexter, sitting down suddenly. "I don't understand. You say she was a 'pretty girl' and now you say she's 'all right.' I don't understand what you mean—Judy Jones wasn't a pretty girl, at all. She was a great beauty. Why, I knew her, I knew her. She was—"

Devlin laughed pleasantly.

"I'm not trying to start a row," he said. "I think Judy's a nice girl and I like her. I can't understand how a man like Lud Simms could fall madly in love with her, but he did." Then he added, "Most of the women like her."

Dexter looked closely at Devlin, thinking wildly that there must be a reason for this, some insensitivity in the man or some private malice.

"Lots of women fade just like *that*," Devlin snapped his fingers. "You must have seen it happen. Perhaps I've forgotten how pretty she was at her wedding. I've seen her so much since then, you see. She has nice eyes."

A sort of dullness settled down upon Dexter. For the first time in his life he felt like getting very drunk. He knew that he was laughing loudly at something Devlin had said, but he did not know what it was or why it was funny. When, in a few minutes, Devlin went he lay down on his lounge and looked out the window at the New York skyline into which the sun was sinking in dull lovely shades of pink and gold.

He had thought that having nothing else to lose he was invulnerable at last—but he knew that he had just lost something more, as surely as if he had married Judy Jones and seen her fade away before his eyes.

The dream was gone. Something had been taken from him. In a sort of panic he pushed the palms of his hands into his eyes and tried to bring up a picture of the waters lapping on Sherry Island and the moonlit veranda, and gingham on the golf links and the dry sun and the gold color of her neck's soft down. And her mouth damp to his kisses and her eyes plaintive with melancholy and her freshness like new fine linen in the morning. Why, these things were no longer in the world! They had existed and they existed no longer.

For the first time in years the tears were streaming down his face. But they were for himself now. He did not care about mouth and eyes and moving hands. He wanted to care, and he could not care. For he had gone away and he could never go back anymore. The gates were closed, the sun was gone down, and there was no beauty but the gray beauty of steel that withstands all time. Even the grief he could have borne was left behind in the country of illusion, of youth, of the richness of life, where his winter dreams had flourished.

"Long ago," he said, "long ago, there was something in me, but now that thing is gone. Now that thing is gone, that thing is gone. I cannot cry. I cannot care. That thing will come back no more."

WHAT STUMPED
THE BLUEJAYS

MARK TWAIN

[signature: Mark Twain]

ANIMALS TALK to each other, of course. There can be no question about that; but I suppose there are very few people who can understand them. I never knew but one man who could. I knew he could, however, because he told me so himself. He was a middle-aged, simple-hearted miner who had lived in a lonely corner of California, among the woods and mountains, a good many years, and had studied the ways of his only neighbors, the beasts and the birds, until he believed he could accurately translate any remark which they made. This was Jim Baker. According to Jim Baker, some animals have only a limited education, and use only very simple words, and scarcely ever a comparison or a flowery figure; whereas, certain other animals have a large vocabulary, a fine command of language and a ready and fluent delivery; consequently these latter talk a great deal; they like it; they are conscious of their talent, and they enjoy "showing off." Baker said, that after long and careful observation, he had come to the conclusion that the bluejays were the best talkers he had found among birds and beasts. Said he:

There's more *to* a bluejay than any other creature. He has got more moods, and more different kinds of feelings than other creatures; and mind you, whatever a bluejay feels, he can put into language. And no mere commonplace language, either, but rattling, out-and-out book talk—and bristling with metaphor, too—just bristling! And as for command of language—why *you* never see a bluejay get stuck for a word. No man ever did. They just boil out of him! And another thing:

I've noticed a good deal, and there's no bird, or cow, or anything that uses as good grammar as a bluejay. You may say a cat uses good grammar. Well, a cat does—but you let a cat get excited once; you let a cat get to pulling fur with another cat on a shed, nights, and you'll hear grammar that will give you the lockjaw. Ignorant people think it's the *noise* which fighting cats make that is so aggravating, but it ain't so; it's the sickening grammar they use. Now I've never heard a jay use bad grammar but very seldom; and when they do, they are as ashamed as a human; they shut right down and leave.

You may call a jay a bird. Well, so he is, in a measure—because he's got feathers on him, and don't belong to no church, perhaps; but otherwise he is just as much a human as you be. And I'll tell you for why. A jay's gifts, and instincts, and feelings, and interests, cover the whole ground. A jay hasn't got any more principle than a congressman. A jay will lie, a jay will steal, a jay will deceive, a jay will betray; and four times out of five, a jay will go back on his solemnest promise. The sacredness of an obligation is a thing which you can't cram into no bluejay's head. Now, on top of all this, there's another thing; a jay can outswear any gentleman in the mines. You think a cat can swear. Well, a cat can; but you give a bluejay a subject that calls for his reserve powers, and where is your cat? Don't talk to *me*—I know too much about this thing. And there's yet another thing; in the one little particular of scolding—just good, clean, out-and-out scolding—a bluejay can lay over anything, human or divine. Yes, sir, a jay is everything that a man is. A jay can cry, a jay can laugh, a jay can feel shame, a jay can reason and plan and discuss, a jay likes gossip and scandal, a jay has got a sense of humor, a jay knows when he is an ass just as well as you do—maybe better. If a jay ain't human, he better take in his sign, that's all. Now I'm going to tell you a perfectly true fact about some bluejays. When I first begun to understand jay language correctly, there was a little incident happened here. Seven years ago, the last man in this region but me moved away. There stands his house— been empty ever since; a log house, with a plank roof—just one big room, and no more; no ceiling—nothing between the rafters and the floor. Well, one Sunday morning I was sitting out here in front of my cabin, with my cat, taking the sun, and looking at the blue hills, and listening to the leaves rustling so lonely in the trees, and thinking of the home away yonder in the states, that I hadn't heard from in thirteen years, when a bluejay lit on that house, with an acorn in his mouth, and says, "Hello, I reckon I've struck something." When he spoke, the acorn dropped out of his mouth and rolled down the roof, of course, but he didn't care; his mind was all on the thing he had struck. It was a knothole in the roof. He cocked his head to one side, shut one eye and put the other one to the hole, like a possum looking down a jug; then he glanced up with his bright eyes, gave a wink or two with his wings—which signifies gratification, you understand—and says, "It looks like a hole, it's located like a hole—blamed if I don't believe it *is* a hole!"

Then he cocked his head down and took another look; he glances up perfectly joyful, this time; winks his wings and his tail both, and says, "Oh, no, this ain't no fat thing, I reckon! If I ain't in luck!—why it's a perfectly elegant hole!" So he flew down and got that acorn, and fetched it up and dropped it in, and was just tilting his head back, with the heavenliest smile on his face, when all of a sudden he was paralyzed into a listening attitude and that smile faded gradually out of his countenance like breath off 'n a razor, and the queerest look of surprise took its place. Then he says, "Why, I didn't hear it fall!" He cocked his eye at the hole again, and took a long look; raised up and shook his head; stepped around to the other side of the hole and took another look from that side; shook his head again. He studied awhile, then he just went into the *details*—walked round and round the hole and spied into it from every point of the compass. No use. Now he took a thinking attitude on the comb of the roof and scratched the back of his head with his right foot a minute, and finally says, "Well, it's too many for *me*, that's certain; must be a mighty long hole; however, I ain't got no time to fool around here, I got to tend to business; I reckon it's all right—chance it, anyway."

So he flew off and fetched another acorn and dropped it in, and tried to flirt his eye to the hole quick enough to see what become of it, but he was too late. He held his eye there as much as a minute; then he raised up and sighed, and says, "Confound it, I don't seem to understand this thing, no way; however, I'll tackle her again." He fetched another acorn, and done his level best to see what become of it, but he couldn't. He says, "Well, *I* never struck no such a hole as this before; I'm of the opinion it's a totally new kind of a hole." Then he begun to get mad. He held in for a spell, walking up and down the comb of the roof and shaking his head and muttering to himself; but his feelings got the upper hand of him, presently, and he broke loose and cussed himself black in the face. I never see a bird take on so about a little thing. When he got through he walks to the hole and looks in again for half a minute; then he says, "Well, you're a long hole, and a deep hole, and a mighty singular hole altogether—but I've started in to fill you, and I'm d____d if I *don't* fill you, if it takes a hundred years!"

And with that, away he went. You never see a bird work so since you was born. The way he hove acorns into that hole for about two hours and a half was one of the most exciting and astonishing spectacles I ever struck. He never stopped to take a look anymore—he just hove 'em in and went for more. Well, at last he could hardly flop his wings, he was so tuckered out. He comes a-drooping down, once more, sweating like an ice pitcher, drops his acorn in and says, "*Now* I guess I've got the bulge on you by this time!" So he bent down for a look. If you'll believe me, when his head come up again he was just pale with rage. He says, "I've shoveled acorns enough in there to keep the family thirty years, and if I can see a sign of one of 'em I wish I may land in a museum with a belly full of sawdust in two minutes!"

He just had strength enough to crawl up onto the comb and lean his back agin the chimbly, and then he collected his impressions and begun to free his mind. I see in a second that what I had mistook for profanity in the mines was only just the rudiments, as you may say.

Another jay was going by, and heard him doing his devotions, and stops to inquire what was up. The sufferer told him the whole circumstance, and says, "Now yonder's the hole, and if you don't believe me, go and look for yourself." So this fellow went and looked, and comes back and says, "How many did you say you put in there?" "Not any less than two tons," says the sufferer. The other jay went and looked again. He couldn't seem to make it out, so he raised a yell, and three more jays come. They all examined the hole, they all made the sufferer tell it over again, then they all discussed it, and got off as many leather-headed opinions about it as an average crowd of humans could have done.

They called in more jays; then more and more, till pretty soon this whole region 'peared to have a blue flush about it. There must have been five thousand of them; and such another jawing and disputing and ripping and cussing, you never heard. Every jay in the whole lot put his eye to the hole and delivered a more chuckle-headed opinion about the mystery than the jay that went there before him. They examined the house all over, too. The door was standing half open, and at last one old jay happened to go and light on it and look in. Of course, that knocked the mystery galley-west in a second. There lay the acorns, scattered all over the floor. He flopped his wings and raised a whoop. "Come here!" he says. "Come here, everybody; hang'd if this fool hasn't been trying to fill up a house with acorns!" They all came a-swooping down like a blue cloud, and as each fellow lit on the door and took a glance, the whole absurdity of the contract that that first jay had tackled hit him home and he fell over backward suffocating with laughter, and the next jay took his place and done the same.

Well, sir, they roosted around here on the housetop and the trees for an hour, and guffawed over that thing like human beings. It ain't any use to tell me a bluejay hasn't got a sense of humor, because I know better. And memory, too. They brought jays here from all over the United States to look down that hole, every summer for three years. Other birds, too. And they could all see the point, except an owl that come from Nova Scotia to visit the Yosemite, and he took this thing in on his way back. He said he couldn't see anything funny in it. But then he was a good deal disappointed about Yosemite, too.

TO BUILD A FIRE

JACK LONDON

Jack London

DAY HAD BROKEN cold and gray, exceedingly cold and gray, when the man turned aside from the main Yukon trail and climbed the high earth bank, where a dim and little-traveled trail led eastward through the fat spruce timberland. It was a steep bank, and he paused for breath at the top, excusing the act to himself by looking at his watch. It was nine o'clock. There was no sun nor hint of sun, though there was not a cloud in the sky. It was a clear day, and yet there seemed an intangible pall over the face of things, a subtle gloom that made the day dark, and that was due to the absence of sun. This fact did not worry the man. He was used to the lack of sun. It had been days since he had seen the sun, and he knew that a few more days must pass before that cheerful orb, due south, would just peep above the skyline and dip immediately from view.

The man flung a look back along the way he had come. The Yukon lay a mile wide and hidden under three feet of ice. On top of this ice were as many feet of snow. It was all pure white, rolling in gentle undulations where the ice jams of the freeze-up had formed. North and south, as far as his eye could see, it was unbroken white, save for a dark hairline that curved and twisted from around the spruce-covered island to the south, and that curved and twisted away into the north, where it disappeared behind another spruce-covered island. This hairline was the main trail that led south five hundred miles to the Chilcoot Pass, Dyea, and salt water; and that led north seventy miles to Dawson, and still on to the north a thousand miles to Nulato, and finally to St. Michael on Bering Sea, a thousand miles and half a thousand more.

But all this—the mysterious, far-reaching hairline trail, the absence of sun from the sky, the tremendous cold, and the strangeness and weirdness of it all—made no impression on the man. It was not because he was long used to it. He was a newcomer in the land, a cheechako, and this was his first winter. The trouble with him was that he was without imagination. He was quick and alert in the things of life, but only in the things, and not in the significances. Fifty degrees below zero meant eighty-odd degrees of frost. Such fact impressed him as being cold and uncomfortable, and that was all. It did not lead him to meditate upon his frailty as a creature of temperature, and upon man's frailty in general, able only to live within certain narrow limits of heat and cold; and from there on it did not lead him to the conjectural field of immortality and man's place in the universe. Fifty degrees below zero stood for a bite of frost that hurt and that must be guarded against by the use of mittens, earflaps, warm moccasins, and thick socks. Fifty degrees below zero was to him just precisely fifty degrees below zero. That there should be anything more to it than that was a thought that never entered his head.

As he turned to go on, he spat speculatively. There was a sharp, explosive crackle that startled him. He spat again. And again, in the air, before it could fall to the snow, the spittle crackled. He knew that at fifty below spittle crackled on the snow, but this spittle had crackled in the air. Undoubtedly it was colder than fifty below—how much colder he did not know. But the temperature did not matter. He was bound for the old claim on the left fork of Henderson Creek, where the boys were already. They had come over across the divide from the Indian Creek country, while he had come the roundabout way to take a look at the possibilities of getting out logs in the spring from the islands in the Yukon. He would be into camp by six o'clock; a bit after dark, it was true, but the boys would be there, a fire would be going, and a hot supper would be ready. As for lunch, he pressed his hand against the protruding bundle under his jacket. It was also under his shirt, wrapped up in a handkerchief and lying against the naked skin. It was the only way to keep the biscuits from freezing. He smiled agreeably to himself as he thought of those biscuits, each cut open and sopped in bacon grease, and each enclosing a generous slice of fried bacon.

He plunged in among the big spruce trees. The trail was faint. A foot of snow had fallen since the last sled had passed over, and he was glad he was without a sled, traveling light. In fact, he carried nothing but the lunch wrapped in the handkerchief. He was surprised, however, at the cold. It certainly was cold, he concluded, as he rubbed his numb nose and cheekbones with his mittened hand. He was a warm-whiskered man, but the hair on his face did not protect the high cheekbones and the eager nose that thrust itself aggressively into the frosty air.

At the man's heels trotted a dog, a big native husky, the proper wolf dog, gray-coated and without any visible or temperamental difference from its brother, the wild wolf. The animal was depressed by the tremendous cold. It knew that it was no time for traveling. Its instinct told it a truer tale than was told to the man by the man's judgment. In reality, it was not merely colder than fifty below zero; it was colder than sixty below, than seventy below. It was seventy-five below zero. Since the freezing point is thirty-two above zero, it meant that one hundred and seven degrees of frost obtained. The dog did not know anything about thermometers. Possibly in its brain there was no sharp consciousness of a condition of very cold such as was in the man's brain. But the brute had its instinct. It experienced a vague but menacing apprehension that subdued it and made it slink along at the man's heels, and that made it question eagerly every unwonted movement of the man as if expecting him to go into camp or to seek shelter somewhere and build a fire. The dog had learned fire, and it wanted fire, or else to burrow under the snow and cuddle its warmth away from the air.

The frozen moisture of its breathing had settled on its fur in a fine powder of frost, and especially were its jowls, muzzle, and eyelashes whitened by its crystaled breath. The man's red beard and mustache were likewise frosted, but more solidly, the deposit taking the form of ice and increasing with every warm, moist breath he exhaled. Also, the man was chewing tobacco, and the muzzle of ice held his lips so rigidly that he was unable to clear his chin when he expelled the juice. The result was that a crystal beard of the color and solidity of amber was increasing its length on his chin. If he fell down it would shatter itself, like glass, into brittle fragments. But he did not mind the appendage. It was the penalty all tobacco chewers paid in that country, and he had been out before in two cold snaps. They had not been so cold as this, he knew, but by the spirit thermometer at Sixty Mile he knew they had been registered at fifty below and at fifty-five.

He held on through the level stretch of woods for several miles and dropped down a bank to the frozen bed of a small stream. This was Henderson Creek, and he knew he was ten miles from the forks. He looked at his watch. It was ten o'clock. He was making four miles an hour, and he calculated that he would arrive at the forks at half past twelve. He decided to celebrate that event by eating his lunch there.

The dog dropped in again at his heels, with a tail drooping discouragement, as the man swung along the creek bed. The furrow of the old sled trail was visible, but a dozen inches of snow covered the marks of the last runners. In a month no man had come up or down that silent creek. The man held steadily on. He was not much given to thinking, and just then particularly he had nothing to think about save that he would eat lunch at the forks and that at six o'clock he would be in camp with the boys. There was nobody to talk to; and, had there been, speech would have been impossible because of the ice muzzle on his mouth. So he continued monotonously to chew tobacco and to increase the length of his amber beard.

Once in a while the thought reiterated itself that it was very cold and that he had never experienced such cold. As he walked along he rubbed his cheekbones and nose with the back of his mittened hand. He did this automatically, now and again changing hands. But rub as he would, the instant he stopped his cheekbones went numb, and the following instant the end of his nose went numb. He was sure to frost his cheeks; he knew that, and experienced a pang of regret that he had not devised a nose strap of the sort Bud wore in cold snaps. Such a strap passed across the cheeks, as well, and saved them. But it didn't matter much, after all. What were frosted cheeks? A bit painful, that was all; they were never serious.

Empty as the man's mind was of thoughts, he was keenly observant, and he noticed the changes in the creek, the curves and bends and timber jams, and always he sharply noted where he placed his feet. Once, coming around a bend, he shied abruptly, like a startled horse, curved away from the place where he had been walking, and retreated several paces back along the trail. The creek he knew was frozen clear to the bottom—no creek could contain water in that arctic winter—but he knew also that there were springs that bubbled out from the hillsides and ran along under the snow and on top the ice of the creek. He knew that the coldest snaps never froze these springs, and he knew likewise their danger. They were traps. They hid pools of water under the snow that might be three inches deep, or three feet. Sometimes a skin of ice half an inch thick covered them, and in turn was covered by the snow. Sometimes there were alternate layers of water and ice skin, so that when one broke through he kept on breaking through for a while, sometimes wetting himself to the waist.

That was why he had shied in such panic. He had felt the give under his feet and heard the crackle of a snow-hidden ice skin. And to get his feet wet in such a temperature meant trouble and danger. At the very least it meant delay, for he would be forced to stop and build a fire, and under its protection to bare his feet while he dried his socks and moccasins. He stood and studied the creek bed and its banks, and decided that the flow of water came from the right. He reflected a while, rubbing his nose and cheeks, then skirted to the left, stepping gingerly and testing the footing for each step. Once clear of the danger, he took a fresh chew of tobacco and swung along at his four-mile gait.

In the course of the next two hours he came upon several similar traps. Usually the snow above the hidden pools had a sunken, candied appearance that advertised the danger. Once again, however, he had a close call; and once, suspecting danger, he compelled the dog to go on in front. The dog did not want to go. It hung back until the man shoved it forward, and then it went quickly across the white, unbroken surface. Suddenly it broke through, floundered to one side, and got away to firmer footing. It had wet its forefeet and legs, and almost immediately the water that clung to it turned to ice. It made quick efforts to lick the ice off its legs, then dropped down in the snow and began to bite out the ice that had formed between the toes. This was a matter of instinct. To permit the ice to remain would mean sore feet. It did not know this. It merely obeyed the mysterious prompting that arose from the deep crypts of its being. But the man knew, having achieved a judgment on the subject, and he removed the mitten from his right hand and helped tear out the ice particles. He did not expose his fingers more than a minute, and was astonished at the swift numbness that smote them. It certainly was cold. He pulled on the mitten hastily, and beat the hand savagely across his chest.

At twelve o'clock the day was at its brightest. Yet the sun was too far south on its winter journey to clear the horizon. The bulge of the earth intervened between it and Henderson Creek, where the man walked under a clear sky at noon and cast no shadow. At half past twelve, to the minute, he arrived at the forks of the creek. He was pleased at the speed he had made. If he kept it up, he would certainly be with the boys by six. He unbuttoned his jacket and shirt and drew forth his lunch. The action consumed no more than a quarter of a minute, yet in that brief moment the numbness laid hold of the exposed fingers. He did not put the mitten on, but, instead, struck the fingers a dozen sharp smashes against his leg. Then he sat down on a snow-covered log to eat. The sting that followed upon the striking of his fingers against his leg ceased so quickly that he was startled. He had had no chance to take a bite of biscuit. He struck the fingers repeatedly and returned them to the mitten, baring the other hand for the purpose of eating. He tried to take a mouthful, but the ice muzzle prevented. He had forgotten to build a fire and thaw out. He chuckled at his foolishness, and as he chuckled he noted the numbness creeping into the exposed fingers. Also, he noted that the stinging which had first come to his toes when he sat down was already passing away. He wondered whether the toes were warm or numb. He moved them inside the moccasins and decided that they were numb.

He pulled the mitten on hurriedly and stood up. He was a bit frightened. He stamped up and down until the stinging returned into the feet. It certainly was cold, was his thought. That man from Sulphur Creek had spoken the truth when telling how cold it sometimes got in the country. And he had laughed at him at the time! That showed one must not be too sure of things. There was no mistake about it, it *was* cold. He strode up and down, stamping his feet and threshing his arms, until reassured by the returning warmth. Then he got out matches and proceeded to make a fire. From the undergrowth, where high water of the previous spring had lodged a supply of seasoned twigs, he got his firewood. Working carefully from a small beginning, he soon had a roaring fire, over which he thawed the ice from his face and in the protection of which he ate his biscuits. For the moment the cold of space was outwitted. The dog took satisfaction in the fire, stretching out close enough for warmth and far enough away to escape being singed.

When the man had finished, he filled his pipe and took his comfortable time over a smoke. Then he pulled on his mittens, settled the earflaps of his cap firmly about his ears, and took the creek trail up the left fork. The dog was disappointed and yearned back toward the fire. This man did not know cold. Possibly all the generations of his ancestry had been ignorant of cold, of real cold, of cold one hundred and seven degrees below freezing point. But the dog knew; all its ancestry knew, and it had inherited the knowledge. And it knew that it was not good to walk abroad in such fearful cold. It was the time to lie snug in a hole in the snow and wait for a curtain of cloud to be drawn across the face of outer space whence this cold came. On the other hand, there was no keen intimacy between the dog and the man. The one was the toil slave of the other, and the only caresses it had ever received were the caresses of the whiplash and of harsh and menacing throat sounds that threatened the whiplash. So the dog made no effort to communicate its apprehension to the man. It was not concerned in the welfare of the man; it was for its own sake that it yearned back toward the fire. But the man whistled, and spoke to it with the sound of whiplashes, and the dog swung in at the man's heel and followed after.

The man took a chew of tobacco and proceeded to start a new amber beard. Also, his moist breath quickly powdered with white his mustache, eyebrows, and lashes. There did not seem to be so many springs on the left fork of the Henderson, and for half an hour the man saw no signs of any. And then it happened. At a place where there were no signs, where the soft, unbroken snow seemed to advertise solidity beneath, the man broke through. It was not deep. He wet himself halfway to the knees before he floundered out to the firm crust.

He was angry, and cursed his luck aloud. He had hoped to get into camp with the boys at six o'clock, and this would delay him an hour, for he would have to build a fire and dry out his footgear. This was imperative at that low temperature—he knew that much; and he turned aside to the bank, which he climbed. On top, tangled in the underbrush about the trunks of several small spruce trees, was a high-water deposit of dry firewood—sticks and twigs, principally, but also larger portions of seasoned branches and fine, dry, last-year's grasses. He threw down several large pieces on top of the snow. This served for a foundation and prevented the young flame from drowning itself in the snow it otherwise would melt. The flame he got by touching a match to a small shred of birch bark that he took from his pocket. This burned even more readily than paper. Placing it on the foundation, he fed the young flame with wisps of dry grass and with the tiniest dry twigs.

He worked slowly and carefully, keenly aware of his danger. Gradually, as the flame grew stronger, he increased the size of the twigs with which he fed it. He squatted in the snow, pulling the twigs out from their entanglement in the brush and feeding directly to the flame. He knew there must be no failure. When it is seventy-five below zero, a man must not fail in his first attempt to build a fire—that is, if his feet are wet. If his feet are dry, and he fails, he can run along the trail for half a mile and restore his circulation. But the circulation of wet and freezing feet cannot be restored by running when it is seventy-five below. No matter how fast he runs, the wet feet will freeze the harder.

All this the man knew. The old-timer on Sulphur Creek had told him about it the previous fall, and now he was appreciating the advice. Already all sensation had gone out of his feet. To build the fire he had been forced to remove his mittens, and the fingers had quickly gone numb. His pace of four miles an hour had kept his heart pumping blood to the surface of his body and to all the extremities. But the instant he stopped, the action of the pump eased down. The cold of space smote the unprotected tip of the planet, and he, being on that unprotected tip, received the full force of the blow. The blood of his body recoiled before it. The blood was alive, like the dog, and like the dog it wanted to hide away and cover itself up from the fearful cold. So long as he walked four miles an hour, he pumped that blood, willy-nilly, to the surface; but now it ebbed away and sank down into the recesses of his body. The extremities were the first to feel its absence.

His wet feet froze the faster, and his exposed fingers numbed the faster, though they had not yet begun to freeze. Nose and cheeks were already freezing, while the skin of all his body chilled as it lost its blood.

But he was safe. Toes and nose and cheeks would be only touched by the frost, for the fire was beginning to burn with strength. He was feeding it with twigs the size of his finger. In another minute he would be able to feed it with branches the size of his wrist, and then he could remove his wet footgear, and, while it dried, he could keep his naked feet warm by the fire, rubbing them at first, of course, with snow. The fire was a success. He was safe. He remembered the advice of the old-timer on Sulphur Creek, and smiled. The old-timer had been very serious in laying down the law that no man must travel alone in the Klondike after fifty below. Well, here he was; he had had the accident; he was alone; and he had saved himself. Those old-timers were rather womanish, some of them, he thought. All a man had to do was to keep his head, and he was all right. Any man who was a man could travel alone. But it was surprising, the rapidity with which his cheeks and nose were freezing. And he had not thought his fingers could go lifeless in so short a time. Lifeless they were, for he could scarcely make them move together to grip a twig, and they seemed remote from his body and from him. When he touched a twig, he had to look and see whether or not he had hold of it. The wires were pretty well down between him and his finger ends.

All of which counted for little. There was the fire, snapping and crackling and promising life with every dancing flame. He started to untie his moccasins. They were coated with ice; the thick German socks were like sheaths of iron halfway to the knees; and the moccasin strings were like rods of steel all twisted and knotted as by some conflagration. For a moment he tugged with his numb fingers, then, realizing the folly of it, he drew his sheath knife.

But before he could cut the strings, it happened. It was his own fault or, rather, his mistake. He should not have built the fire under the spruce tree. He should have built it in the open. But it had been easier to pull the twigs from the brush and drop them directly on the fire. Now the tree under which he had done this carried a weight of snow on its boughs. No wind had blown for weeks, and each bough was fully freighted. Each time he had pulled a twig he had communicated a slight agitation to the tree—an imperceptible agitation, so far as he was concerned, but an agitation sufficient to bring about the disaster. High up in the tree one bough capsized its load of snow. This fell on the boughs beneath, capsizing them. This process continued, spreading out and involving the whole tree. It grew like an avalanche, and it descended without warning upon the man and the fire, and the fire was blotted out! Where it had burned was a mantle of fresh and disordered snow.

The man was shocked. It was as though he had just heard his own sentence of death. For a moment he sat and stared at the spot where the fire had been. Then he grew very calm. Perhaps the old-timer on Sulphur Creek was right. If he had only had a trail mate, he would have been in no danger now. The trail mate could have built the fire. Well, it was up to him to build the fire over again, and this second time there must be no failure. Even if he succeeded, he would most likely lose some toes. His feet must be badly frozen by now, and there would be some time before the second fire was ready.

Such were his thoughts, but he did not sit and think them. He was busy all the time they were passing through his mind. He made a new foundation for a fire, this time in the open, where no treacherous tree could blot it out. Next, he gathered dry grasses and tiny twigs from the high-water flotsam. He could not bring his fingers together to pull them out, but he was able to gather them by the handful. In this way he got many rotten twigs and bits of green moss that were undesirable, but it was the best he could do. He worked methodically, even collecting an armful of the larger branches to be used later when the fire gathered strength. And all the while the dog sat and watched him, a certain yearning wistfulness in its eyes, for it looked upon him as the fire provider, and the fire was slow in coming.

When all was ready, the man reached in his pocket for a second piece of birch bark. He knew the bark was there, and, though he could not feel it with his fingers, he could hear its crisp rustling as he fumbled for it. Try as he would, he could not clutch hold of it. And all the time, in his consciousness, was the knowledge that each instant his feet were freezing. This thought tended to put him in a panic, but he fought against it and kept calm. He pulled on his mittens with his teeth, and threshed his arms back and forth, beating his hands with all his might against his sides. He did this sitting down, and he stood up to do it; and all the while the dog sat in the snow, its wolf brush of a tail curled around warmly over its forefeet, its sharp wolf ears pricked forward intently as it watched the man. And the man, as he beat and threshed with his arms and hands, felt a great surge of envy as he regarded the creature that was warm and secure in its natural covering.

After a time he was aware of the first faraway signals of sensation in his beaten fingers. The faint tingling grew stronger till it evolved into a stinging ache that was excruciating, but which the man hailed with satisfaction. He stripped the mitten from his right hand and fetched forth the birch bark. The exposed fingers were quickly going numb again. Next he brought out his bunch of sulphur matches. But the tremendous cold had already driven the life out of his fingers. In his effort to separate one match from the others, the whole bunch fell in the snow. He tried to pick it out of the snow, but failed. The dead fingers could neither touch nor clutch. He was very careful. He drove the thought of his freezing feet, and nose, and cheeks, out of his mind, devoting his whole soul to the matches. He watched, using the sense of vision in place of that of touch, and when he saw his fingers on each side the bunch, he closed them—that is, he willed to close them, for the wires were down, and the fingers did not obey. He pulled the mitten on the right hand, and beat it fiercely against his knee. Then, with both mittened hands, he scooped the bunch of matches, along with much snow, into his lap. Yet he was no better off.

After some manipulation he managed to get the bunch between the heels of his mittened hands. In this fashion he carried it to his mouth. The ice crackled and snapped when by a violent effort he opened his mouth. He drew the lower jaw in, curled the upper lip out of the way, and scraped the bunch with his upper teeth in order to separate a match. He succeeded in getting one, which he dropped on his lap. He was no better off. He could not pick it up. Then he devised a way. He picked it up in his teeth and scratched it on his leg. Twenty times he scratched before he succeeded in lighting it. As it flamed he held it with his teeth to the birch bark. But the burning brimstone went up his nostrils and into his lungs, causing him to cough spasmodically. The match fell into the snow and went out.

The old-timer on Sulphur Creek was right, he thought in the moment of controlled despair that ensued: after fifty below, a man should travel with a partner. He beat his hands, but failed in exciting any sensation. Suddenly he bared both hands, removing the mittens with his teeth. He caught the whole bunch between the heels of his hands. His arm muscles not being frozen enabled him to press the hand heels tightly against the matches. Then he scratched the bunch along his leg. It flared into flame, seventy sulphur matches at once! There was no wind to blow them out. He kept his head to one side to escape the strangling fumes, and held the blazing bunch to the birch bark. As he so held it, he became aware of sensation in his hand. His flesh was burning. He could smell it. Deep down below the surface he could feel it. The sensation developed into pain that grew acute. And still he endured it, holding the flame of the matches clumsily to the bark that would not light readily because his own burning hands were in the way, absorbing most of the flame.

At last, when he could endure no more, he jerked his hands apart. The blazing matches fell sizzling into the snow, but the birch bark was alight. He began laying dry grasses and the tiniest twigs on the flame. He could not pick and choose, for he had to lift the fuel between the heels of his hands. Small pieces of rotten wood and green moss clung to the twigs, and he bit them off as well as he could with his teeth. He cherished the flame carefully and awkwardly. It meant life, and it must not perish. The withdrawal of blood from the surface of his body now made him begin to shiver, and he grew more awkward. A large piece of green moss fell squarely on the little fire. He tried to poke it out with his fingers, but his shivering frame made him poke too far, and he disrupted the nucleus of the little fire, the burning grasses and tiny twigs separating and scattering. He tried to poke them together again, but in spite of the tenseness of the effort, his shivering got away with him, and the twigs were hopelessly scattered. Each twig gushed a puff of smoke and went out. The fire provider had failed. As he looked apathetically about him, his eyes chanced on the dog, sitting across the ruins of the fire from him, in the snow, making restless, hunching movements, slightly lifting one forefoot and then the other, shifting its weight back and forth on them with wistful eagerness.

The sight of the dog put a wild idea into his head. He remembered the tale of the man, caught in a blizzard, who killed a steer and crawled inside the carcass, and so was saved. He would kill the dog and bury his hands in the warm body until the numbness went out of them. Then he could build another fire. He spoke to the dog, calling it to him; but in his voice was a strange note of fear that frightened the animal, who had never known the man to speak in such way before. Something was the matter, and its suspicious nature sensed danger—it knew not what danger, but somewhere, somehow, in its brain arose an apprehension of the man. It flattened its ears down at the sound of the man's voice, and its restless, hunching movements and the liftings and shiftings of its forefeet became more pronounced; but it would not come to the man. He got on his hands and knees and crawled toward the dog. This unusual posture again excited suspicion, and the animal sidled mincingly away.

The man sat up in the snow for a moment and struggled for calmness. Then he pulled on his mittens, by means of his teeth, and got upon his feet. He glanced down at first in order to assure himself that he was really standing up, for the absence of sensation in his feet left him unrelated to the earth. His erect position in itself started to drive the webs of suspicion from the dog's mind; and when he spoke peremptorily, with the sound of whiplashes in his voice, the dog rendered its customary allegiance and came to him. As it came within reaching distance, the man lost his control. His arms flashed out to the dog, and he experienced genuine surprise when he discovered that his hands could not clutch, that there was neither bend nor feeling in the fingers. He had forgotten for the moment that they were frozen and that they were freezing more and more. All this happened quickly, and before the animal could get away, he encircled its body with his arms. He sat down in the snow, and in this fashion held the dog, while it snarled and whined and struggled.

But it was all he could do, hold its body encircled in his arms and sit there. He realized that he could not kill the dog. There was no way to do it. With his helpless hands he could neither draw nor hold his sheath knife nor throttle the animal. He released it, and it plunged wildly away, with tail between its legs, and still snarling. It halted forty feet away and surveyed him curiously, with ears sharply pricked forward. The man looked down at his hands in order to locate them, and found them hanging on the ends of his arms. It struck him as curious that one should have to use his eyes in order to find out where his hands were. He began threshing his arms back and forth, beating the mittened hands against his sides. He did this for five minutes, violently, and his heart pumped enough blood up to the surface to put a stop to his shivering. But no sensation was aroused in the hands. He had an impression that they hung like weights on the ends of his arms, but when he tried to run the impression down, he could not find it.

A certain fear of death, dull and oppressive, came to him. This fear quickly became poignant as he realized that it was no longer a mere matter of freezing his fingers and toes, or of losing his hands and feet, but that it was a matter of life and death with the chances against him. This threw him into a panic, and he turned and ran up the creek bed along the old, dim trail. The dog joined in behind and kept up with him. He ran blindly, without intention, in fear such as he had never known in his life. Slowly, as he plowed and floundered through the snow, he began to see things again—the banks of the creek, the old timber jams, the leafless aspens, and the sky. The running made him feel better. He did not shiver. Maybe, if he ran on, his feet would thaw out; and, anyway, if he ran far enough, he would reach camp and the boys. Without doubt he would lose some fingers and toes and some of his face; but the boys would take care of him, and save the rest of him when he got there. And at the same time there was another thought in his mind that said he would never get to the camp and the boys; that it was too many miles away, that the freezing had too great a start on him, and that he would soon be stiff and dead. This thought he kept in the background and refused to consider. Sometimes it pushed itself forward and demanded to be heard, but he thrust it back and strove to think of other things.

It struck him as curious that he could run at all on feet so frozen that he could not feel them when they struck the earth and took the weight of his body. He seemed to himself to skim along above the surface, and to have no connection with the earth. Somewhere he had once seen a winged Mercury, and he wondered if Mercury felt as he felt when skimming over the earth.

His theory of running until he reached camp and the boys had one flaw in it: he lacked the endurance. Several times he stumbled, and finally he tottered, crumpled up, and fell. When he tried to rise, he failed. He must sit and rest, he decided, and next time he would merely walk and keep on going. As he sat and regained his breath, he noted that he was feeling quite warm and comfortable. He was not shivering, and it even seemed that a warm glow had come to his chest and trunk. And yet, when he touched his nose or cheeks, there was no sensation. Running would not thaw them out. Nor would it thaw out his hands and feet. Then the thought came to him that the frozen portions of his body must be extending. He tried to keep this thought down, to forget it, to think of something else; he was aware of the panicky feeling that it caused, and he was afraid of the panic. But the thought asserted itself, and persisted, until it produced a vision of his body totally frozen. This was too much, and he made another wild run along the trail. Once he slowed down to a walk, but the thought of the freezing extending itself made him run again.

And all the time the dog ran with him, at his heels. When he fell down a second time, it curled its tail over its forefeet and sat in front of him, facing him, curiously eager and intent. The warmth and security of the animal angered him, and he cursed it till it flattened down its ears appeasingly. This time the shivering came more quickly upon the man. He was losing in his battle with the frost. It was creeping into his body from all sides. The thought of it drove him on, but he ran no more than a hundred feet, when he staggered and pitched headlong. It was his last panic. When he had recovered his breath and control, he sat up and entertained in his mind the conception of meeting death with dignity. However, the conception did not come to him in such terms. His idea of it was that he had been making a fool of himself, running around like a chicken with its head cut off—such was the simile that occurred to him. Well, he was bound to freeze anyway, and he might as well take it decently. With this newfound peace of mind came the first glimmerings of drowsiness. A good idea, he thought, to sleep off to death. It was like taking an anesthetic. Freezing was not so bad as people thought. There were lots worse ways to die.

He pictured the boys finding his body next day. Suddenly he found himself with them, coming along the trail and looking for himself. And, still with them, he came around a turn in the trail and found himself lying in the snow. He did not belong with himself anymore, for even then he was out of himself, standing with the boys and looking at himself in the snow. It certainly was cold, was his thought. When he got back to the States he could tell the folks what real cold was. He drifted on from this to a vision of the old-timer on Sulphur Creek. He could see him quite clearly, warm and comfortable, and smoking a pipe.

"You were right, old hoss; you were right," the man mumbled to the old-timer of Sulphur Creek.

Then the man drowsed off into what seemed to him the most comfortable and satisfying sleep he had ever known. The dog sat facing him and waiting. The brief day drew to a close in a long, slow twilight. There were no signs of a fire to be made, and, besides, never in the dog's experience had it known a man to sit like that in the snow and make no fire. As the twilight drew on, its eager yearning for the fire mastered it, and with a great lifting and shifting of forefeet, it whined softly, then flattened its ears down in anticipation of being chided by the man. But the man remained silent. Later, the dog whined loudly. And still later it crept close to the man and caught the scent of death. This made the animal bristle and back away. A little longer it delayed, howling under the stars that leaped and danced and shone brightly in the cold sky. Then it turned and trotted up the trail in the direction of the camp it knew, where were the other food providers and fire providers.

A JURY
OF HER PEERS

SUSAN GLASPELL

Susan Glaspell

Wʜᴇɴ Mᴀʀᴛʜᴀ Hᴀʟᴇ opened the storm door and got a cut of the north wind, she ran back for her big woolen scarf. As she hurriedly wound that around her head her eye made a scandalized sweep of her kitchen. It was no ordinary thing that called her away—it was probably further from ordinary than anything that had ever happened in Dickson County. But what her eye took in was that her kitchen was in no shape for leaving: her bread all ready for mixing, half the flour sifted and half unsifted.

She hated to see things half done, but she had been at that when the team from town stopped to get Mr. Hale, and then the sheriff came running in to say his wife wished Mrs. Hale would come too—adding, with a grin, that he guessed she was getting scary and wanted another woman along. So she had dropped everything right where it was.

"Martha!" now came her husband's impatient voice. "Don't keep folks waiting out here in the cold."

She again opened the storm door, and this time joined the three men and the one woman waiting in the big two-seated buggy.

After she had the robes tucked around her she took another look at the woman who sat beside her on the back seat. She had met Mrs. Peters the year before at the county fair, and the thing she remembered about her was that she didn't seem like a sheriff's wife. She was small and thin and didn't have a strong voice. Mrs. Gorman, sheriff's wife before Gorman went out and Peters came in, had a voice that somehow seemed to be backing up the law with every word. But if Mrs. Peters didn't look like a sheriff's wife, Peters made it up in looking like a sheriff. He was to a dot the kind of man who could get himself elected sheriff—a heavy man with a big voice, who was particularly genial with the law-abiding, as if to make it plain that he knew the difference between criminals and noncriminals. And right there it came into Mrs. Hale's mind, with a stab, that this man who was so pleasant and lively with all of them was going to the Wrights' now as a sheriff.

"The country's not very pleasant this time of year," Mrs. Peters at last ventured, as if she felt they ought to be talking as well as the men.

Mrs. Hale scarcely finished her reply, for they had gone up a little hill and could see the Wright place now, and seeing it did not make her feel like talking. It looked very lonesome this cold March morning. It had always been a lonesome-looking place. It was down in a hollow, and the poplar trees around it were lonesome-looking trees. The men were looking at it and talking about what had happened. The county attorney was bending to one side of the buggy, and kept looking steadily at the place as they drew up to it.

"I'm glad you came with me," Mrs. Peters said nervously, as the two women were about to follow the men in through the kitchen door.

Even after she had her foot on the doorstep, her hand on the knob, Martha Hale had a moment of feeling she could not cross that threshold. And the reason it seemed she couldn't cross it now was simply because she hadn't crossed it before. Time and time again it had been in her mind, "I ought to go over and see Minnie Foster"—she still thought of her as Minnie Foster, though for twenty years she had been Mrs. Wright. And then there was always something to do and Minnie Foster would go from her mind. But *now* she could come.

THE MEN went over to the stove. The women stood close together by the door. Young Henderson, the county attorney, turned around and said, "Come up to the fire, ladies."

Mrs. Peters took a step forward, then stopped. "I'm not—cold," she said.

And so the two women stood by the door, at first not even so much as looking around the kitchen.

The men talked for a minute about what a good thing it was the sheriff had sent his deputy out that morning to make a fire for them, and then Sheriff Peters stepped back from the stove, unbuttoned his outer coat, and leaned his hands on the kitchen table in a way that seemed to mark the beginning of official business. "Now, Mr. Hale," he said in a sort of semiofficial voice, "before we move things about, you tell Mr. Henderson just what it was you saw when you came here yesterday morning."

The county attorney was looking around the kitchen.

"By the way," he said, "has anything been moved?" He turned to the sheriff. "Are things just as you left them yesterday?"

Peters looked from cupboard to sink; from that to a small worn rocker a little to one side of the kitchen table.

"It's just the same."

"Somebody should have been left here yesterday," said the county attorney.

"Oh—yesterday," returned the sheriff, with a little gesture as of yesterday having been more than he could bear to think of. "When I had to send Frank to Morris Center for that man who went crazy—let me tell you, I had my hands full *yesterday*. I knew you could get back from Omaha by today, George, and as long as I went over everything here myself . . ."

"Well, Mr. Hale," said the county attorney, in a way of letting what was past and gone go, "tell just what happened when you came here yesterday morning."

Mrs. Hale, still leaning against the door, had that sinking feeling of the mother whose child is about to speak a piece. Lewis often wandered along and got things mixed up in a story. She hoped he would tell this straight and plain, and not say unnecessary things that would just make things harder for Minnie Foster. He didn't begin at once, and she noticed that he looked queer—as if standing in that kitchen and having to tell what he had seen there yesterday morning made him almost sick.

"Yes, Mr. Hale?" the county attorney reminded.

"Harry and I had started to town with a load of potatoes," Mrs. Hale's husband began.

Harry was Mrs. Hale's oldest boy. He wasn't with them now, for the very good reason that those potatoes never got to town yesterday and he was taking them this morning, so he hadn't been home when the sheriff stopped to say he wanted Mr. Hale to come over to the Wright place and tell the county attorney his story there, where he could point it all out. With all Mrs. Hale's other emotions came the fear that maybe Harry wasn't dressed warm enough—they hadn't any of them realized how that north wind did bite.

"We come along this road," Hale was going on, with a motion of his hand to the road over which they had just come, "and as we got in sight of the house I says to Harry, 'I'm goin' to see if I can't get John Wright to take a telephone.' You see," he explained to Henderson, "unless I can get somebody to go in with me they won't come out this branch road except for a price *I* can't pay. I'd spoke to Wright about it once before; but he put me off, saying folks talked too much anyway, and all he asked was peace and quiet—guess you know about how much he talked himself. But I thought maybe if I went to the house and talked about it before his wife, and said all the womenfolks liked the telephones, and that in this lonesome stretch of road it would be a good thing—well, I said to Harry that that was what I was going to say—though I said at the same time that I didn't know as what his wife wanted made much difference to John—"

Now there he was!—saying things he didn't need to say. Mrs. Hale tried to catch her husband's eye, but fortunately the county attorney interrupted with, "Let's talk about that a little later, Mr. Hale. I do want to talk about that, but I'm anxious now to get along to just what happened when you got here."

When he began this time, it was very deliberately and carefully. "I didn't see or hear anything. I knocked at the door. And still it was all quiet inside. I knew they must be up—it was past eight o'clock. So I knocked again, louder, and I thought I heard somebody say, 'Come in.' I wasn't sure—I'm not sure yet. But I opened the door—this door," jerking a hand toward the door by which the two women stood, "and there in that rocker"—pointing to it—"sat Mrs. Wright."

Everyone in the kitchen looked at the rocker. It came into Mrs. Hale's mind that that rocker didn't look in the least like Minnie Foster—the Minnie Foster of twenty years before. It was a dingy red, with wooden rungs up the back, and the middle rung was gone, and the chair sagged to one side.

"How did she—look?" the county attorney was inquiring.

"Well," said Hale, "she looked—queer."

"How do you mean—queer?"

As he asked it he took out a notebook and pencil. Mrs. Hale did not like the sight of that pencil. She kept her eye fixed on her husband, as if to keep him from saying unnecessary things that would go into that notebook and make trouble.

Hale did speak guardedly, as if the pencil had affected him too.

"Well, as if she didn't know what she was going to do next. And kind of—done up."

"How did she seem to feel about your coming?"

"Why, I don't think she minded—one way or other. She didn't pay much attention. I said, 'Ho' do, Mrs. Wright? It's cold, ain't it?' And she said, 'Is it?'—and went on pleatin' at her apron. Well, I was surprised. She didn't ask me to come up to the stove, or to sit down, but just set there, not even lookin' at me. And I said, 'I want to see John.'

"And then she—laughed. I guess you would call it a laugh.

"I thought of Harry and the team outside, so I said, a little sharp, 'Can I see John?' 'No,' says she—kind of dull like. 'Ain't he home?' says I. Then she looked at me. 'Yes,' says she, 'he's home.' 'Then why can't I see him?' I asked her, out of patience with her now. 'Cause he's dead,' says she, just as quiet and dull—and fell to pleatin' her apron. 'Dead?' says I, like you do when you can't take in what you've heard.

"She just nodded her head, not getting a bit excited, but rockin' back and forth.

" 'Why—where is he?' says I, not knowing *what* to say.

"She just pointed upstairs—like this"—pointing to the room above. "By this time I didn't know what to do. I walked from there to here; then I says, 'Why, what did he die of?'

" 'He died of a rope round his neck,' says she; and just went on pleatin' at her apron."

HALE STOPPED speaking, and stood staring at the rocker, as if he were still seeing the woman who had sat there the morning before. Nobody spoke; it was as if everyone were seeing the woman who had sat there the morning before.

"And what did you do then?" the county attorney at last broke the silence.

"I went out and called Harry. I thought I might—need help. I got Harry in, and we went upstairs." His voice fell almost to a whisper. "There he was—lying over the—"

"I think I'd rather have you go into that upstairs," the county attorney interrupted, "where you can point it all out. Just go on now with the rest of the story."

"Well, my first thought was to get that rope off. It looked—"

He stopped, his face twitching.

"But Harry, he went up to him, and he said, 'No, he's dead all right, and we'd better not touch anything.' So we went downstairs.

"She was still sitting that same way. 'Has anybody been notified?' I asked. 'No,' says she, unconcerned.

" 'Who did this, Mrs. Wright?' said Harry. He said it businesslike, and she stopped pleatin' at her apron. 'I don't know,' she says. 'You don't *know?*' says Harry. 'Weren't you sleepin' in the bed with him?' 'Yes,' says she, 'but I was on the inside.' 'Somebody slipped a rope round his neck and strangled him, and you didn't wake up?' says Harry. 'I didn't wake up,' she said after him.

"We may have looked as if we didn't see how that could be, for after a minute she said, 'I sleep sound.'

"Harry was going to ask her more questions, but I said maybe that weren't our business; maybe we ought to let her tell her story first to the coroner or the sheriff. So Harry went fast as he could over to High Road—the Rivers' place, where there's a telephone."

"And what did she do when she knew you had gone for the coroner?" The attorney got his pencil in his hand all ready for writing.

"She moved from that chair to this one over here"—Hale pointed to a small chair in the corner—"and just sat there with her hands held together and looking down. I got a feeling that I ought to make some conversation, so I said I had come in to see if John wanted to put in a telephone; and at that she started to laugh, and then she stopped and looked at me—scared."

At sound of a moving pencil the man who was telling the story looked up.

"I dunno—maybe it wasn't scared," he hastened; "I wouldn't like to say it was. Soon Harry got back, and then Dr. Lloyd came, and you, Mr. Peters, and so I guess that's all I know that you don't."

HE SAID that last with relief, and moved a little, as if relaxing. Everyone moved a little. The county attorney walked toward the stair door.

"I guess we'll go upstairs first—then out to the barn and around there."

He paused and looked around the kitchen.

"You're convinced there was nothing important here?" he asked the sheriff. "Nothing that would—point to any motive?"

The sheriff too looked all around, as if to reconvince himself.

"Nothing here but kitchen things," he said, with a little laugh for the insignificance of kitchen things.

The county attorney was looking at the cupboard—a peculiar, ungainly structure, half closet and half cupboard, the upper part of it being built in the wall, and the lower part just the old-fashioned kitchen cupboard. As if its queerness attracted him, he got a chair and opened the upper part and looked in. After a moment he drew his hand away sticky.

"Here's a nice mess," he said resentfully.

The two women had drawn nearer, and now the sheriff's wife spoke.

"Oh—her fruit," she said, looking to Mrs. Hale for sympathetic understanding. She turned back to the county attorney and explained. "She worried about that when it turned so cold last night. She said the fire would go out and her jars might burst."

Mrs. Peters' husband broke into a laugh. "Well, can you beat the women! Held for murder, and worrying about her preserves!"

The young attorney set his lips.

"I guess before we're through with her she may have something more serious than preserves to worry about."

"Oh, well," said Mrs. Hale's husband, with good-natured superiority, "women are used to worrying over trifles."

The two women moved a little closer together. Neither of them spoke. The county attorney seemed suddenly to remember his manners—and think of his future.

"And yet," said he, with the gallantry of a young politician, "for all their worries, what would we do without the ladies?"

The women did not speak, did not unbend. He went to the sink and began washing his hands. He turned to wipe them on the roller towel—whirled it for a cleaner place.

"Dirty towels! Not much of a housekeeper, would you say, ladies?"

He kicked his foot against some dirty pans under the sink.

"There's a great deal of work to be done on a farm," said Mrs. Hale stiffly.

"To be sure. And yet"—with a little bow to her—"I know there are some Dickson County farmhouses that do not have such roller towels." He gave it a pull to expose its full length again.

"Those towels get dirty awful quick. Men's hands aren't always as clean as they might be."

"Ah, loyal to your sex, I see," he laughed. He stopped and gave her a keen look. "But you and Mrs. Wright were neighbors. I suppose you were friends, too."

Martha Hale shook her head.

"I've seen little enough of her of late years. I've not been in this house—it's more than a year."

"And why was that? You didn't like her?"

"I liked her well enough," she replied with spirit. "Farmers' wives have their hands full, Mr. Henderson. And then—" She looked around the kitchen.

"Yes?" he encouraged.

"It never seemed a very cheerful place," said she, more to herself than to him.

"No," he agreed. "I don't think anyone would call it cheerful. I shouldn't say she had the homemaking instinct."

"Well, I don't know as Wright had, either," she muttered.

"You mean they didn't get on very well?" he was quick to ask.

"No. I don't mean anything," she answered, with decision. As she turned a little away from him, she added, "But I don't think a place would be any the cheerfuller for John Wright's bein' in it."

"I'd like to talk to you about that a little later, Mrs. Hale," he said. "I'm anxious to get the lay of things upstairs now."

He moved toward the stair door, followed by the two men.

"I suppose anything Mrs. Peters does'll be all right?" the sheriff inquired. "She was to take in some clothes for her, you know—and a few little things. We left in such a hurry yesterday."

The county attorney looked at the two women whom they were leaving alone there among the kitchen things.

"Yes—Mrs. Peters," he said, his glance resting on the woman who was not Mrs. Peters, the big farmer woman who stood behind the sheriff's wife. "Of course Mrs. Peters is one of us," he said, in a manner of entrusting responsibility. "And keep your eye out, Mrs. Peters, for anything that might be of use. No telling; you women might come upon a clue to the motive—and that's the thing we need."

Mr. Hale rubbed his face after the fashion of a showman getting ready for a pleasantry.

"But would the women know a clue if they did come upon it?" he said; and, having delivered himself of this, he followed the others through the stair door.

THE WOMEN stood motionless and silent, listening to the footsteps, first upon the stairs, then in the room above them.

Then, as if releasing herself from something strange, Mrs. Hale began to arrange the dirty pans under the sink, which the county attorney's disdainful push of the foot had deranged.

"I'd hate to have men comin' into my kitchen," she said testily— "snoopin' round and criticizin'."

"Of course it's no more than their duty," said the sheriff's wife, in her manner of timid acquiescence.

"Duty's all right," replied Mrs. Hale bluffly, "but I guess that deputy sheriff that come out to make the fire might have got a little of this on." She gave the roller towel a pull. "Wish I'd thought of that sooner! Seems mean to talk about her for not having things slicked up, when she had to come away in such a hurry."

She looked around the kitchen. Certainly it was not "slicked up." Her eye was held by a bucket of sugar on a low shelf. The cover was off the wooden bucket, and beside it was a paper bag—half full.

Mrs. Hale moved toward it.

"She was putting this in there," she said to herself—slowly.

She thought of the flour in her kitchen at home—half sifted, half not sifted. She had been interrupted, and had left things half done. What had interrupted Minnie Foster? Why had that work been left half done? She made a move as if to finish it—unfinished things always bothered her—and then she glanced around and saw that Mrs. Peters was watching her—and she didn't want Mrs. Peters to get that feeling she had got of work begun and then—for some reason—not finished.

"It's a shame about her fruit," she said, and walked toward the cupboard that the county attorney had opened, and got on the chair, murmuring, "I wonder if it's all gone."

It was a sorry enough looking sight, but "Here's one that's all right," she said at last. She held it toward the light. "This is cherries, too." She looked again. "I declare I believe that's the only one."

With a sigh, she got down from the chair, went to the sink, and wiped off the bottle.

"She'll feel awful bad, after all her hard work in the hot weather. I remember the afternoon I put up my cherries last summer."

She set the bottle on the table, and, with another sigh, started to sit down in the rocker. But she did not sit down. Something kept her from sitting down in that chair. She straightened—stepped back, and, half turned away, stood looking at it, seeing the woman who had sat there "pleatin' at her apron."

The thin voice of the sheriff's wife broke in upon her. "I must be getting those things from the front-room closet." She opened the door into the other room, started in, stepped back. "You coming with me, Mrs. Hale?" she asked nervously. "You—you could help me get them."

They were soon back—the stark coldness of that shut-up room was not a thing to linger in.

"My!" said Mrs. Peters, dropping the things on the table and hurrying to the stove.

Mrs. Hale stood examining the clothes the woman who was being detained in town had said she wanted.

"Wright was close!" she exclaimed, holding up a shabby black skirt that bore the marks of much making over. "I think maybe that's why she kept so much to herself. I s'pose she felt she couldn't do her part;

and then, you don't enjoy things when you feel shabby. She used to wear pretty clothes and be lively—when she was Minnie Foster, one of the town girls, singing in the choir. But that—oh, that was twenty years ago."

With a carefulness in which there was something tender, she folded the shabby clothes and piled them at one corner of the table. She looked up at Mrs. Peters, and there was something in the other woman's look that irritated her.

"She don't care," she said to herself. "Much difference it makes to her whether Minnie Foster had pretty clothes when she was a girl."

Then she looked again, and she wasn't so sure; in fact, she hadn't at any time been perfectly sure about Mrs. Peters. She had that shrinking manner, and yet her eyes looked as if they could see a long way into things.

"This all you was to take in?" asked Mrs. Hale.

"No," said the sheriff's wife. "She said she wanted an apron. Funny thing to want," she ventured in her nervous little way, "for there's not much to get you dirty in jail, goodness knows. But I suppose just to make her feel more natural. If you're used to wearing an apron— She said they were in the bottom drawer of this cupboard. Yes—here they are. And then her little shawl that always hung on the stair door."

She took the small gray shawl from behind the door leading upstairs, and stood a minute looking at it.

Suddenly Mrs. Hale took a quick step toward the other woman.

"Mrs. Peters!"

"Yes, Mrs. Hale?"

"Do you think she—did it?"

A frightened look blurred the other thing in Mrs. Peters' eyes.

"Oh, I don't know," she said, in a voice that seemed to shrink away from the subject.

"Well, I don't think she did," affirmed Mrs. Hale stoutly. "Asking for an apron and her little shawl. Worryin' about her fruit."

"Mr. Peters says—" Footsteps were heard in the room above; she stopped, looked up, then went on in a lowered voice, "Mr. Peters says—it looks bad for her. Mr. Henderson is awful sarcastic in a speech, and he's going to make fun of her saying she didn't—wake up."

For a moment Mrs. Hale had no answer. Then, "Well, I guess John Wright didn't wake up—when they was slippin' that rope under his neck," she muttered.

"No, it's *strange*," breathed Mrs. Peters. "They think it was such a—funny way to kill a man."

She began to laugh; at sound of the laugh, abruptly stopped.

"That's just what Mr. Hale said," said Mrs. Hale, in a resolutely natural voice. "There was a gun in the house. He says that's what he can't understand."

"Mr. Henderson said, coming out, that what was needed for the case was a motive. Something to show anger—or sudden feeling."

"Well, I don't see any signs of anger around here," said Mrs. Hale. "I don't—"

She stopped. It was as if her mind tripped on something. Her eye was caught by a dish towel in the middle of the kitchen table. Slowly she moved toward the table. One half of it was wiped clean, the other half messy. Her eyes made a slow, almost unwilling turn to the bucket of sugar and the half-empty bag beside it. Things begun—and not finished.

After a moment she stepped back, and said, in that manner of releasing herself, "Wonder how they're finding things upstairs? I hope she had it a little more redd up up there. You know"—she paused, and feeling gathered—"it seems kind of *sneaking*, locking her up in town and coming out here to get her own house to turn against her!"

"But, Mrs. Hale," said the sheriff's wife, "the law is the law."

"I s'pose 'tis," answered Mrs. Hale shortly.

She turned to the stove, saying something about that fire not being much to brag of. She worked with it a minute, and when she straightened up she said aggressively, "The law is the law—and a bad stove is a bad stove. How'd you like to cook on this?"—pointing with the poker to the broken lining. She opened the oven door and started to express her opinion of the oven; but she was swept into her own thoughts, thinking of what it would mean, year after year, to have that stove to wrestle with. The thought of Minnie Foster trying to bake in that oven—and the thought of her never going over to see Minnie Foster—

She was startled by hearing Mrs. Peters say, "A person gets discouraged—and loses heart."

The sheriff's wife had looked from the stove to the sink—to the pail of water which had been carried in from outside. The two women stood there silent, above them the footsteps of the men who were looking for evidence against the woman who had worked in that kitchen. That look of seeing into things, of seeing through a thing to something else, was in the eyes of the sheriff's wife now. When Mrs. Hale next spoke to her, it was gently. "Better loosen up your things, Mrs. Peters. We'll not feel them when we go out."

Mrs. Peters went to the back of the room to hang up the fur tippet she was wearing. A moment later she exclaimed, "Why, she was piecing a quilt!" and held up a large sewing basket piled high with quilt pieces.

Mrs. Hale spread some of the blocks on the table.

"It's log-cabin pattern," she said, putting several of them together. "Pretty, isn't it?"

They were so engaged with the quilt that they did not hear the footsteps on the stairs. Just as the stair door opened Mrs. Hale was saying, "Do you suppose she was going to quilt it or just knot it?"

The sheriff threw up his hands.

"They wonder whether she was going to quilt it or just knot it!"

There was a laugh for the ways of women, a warming of hands over the stove, and then the county attorney said briskly, "Well, let's go right out to the barn and get that cleared up."

"I don't see as there's anything so strange," Mrs. Hale said resentfully, after the outside door had closed on the three men—"our taking up our time with little things while we're waiting for them to get the evidence. I don't see as it's anything to laugh about."

"Of course they've got awful important things on their minds," said the sheriff's wife apologetically.

They returned to an inspection of the block for the quilt. Mrs. Hale was looking at the fine, even sewing, and preoccupied with thoughts of the woman who had done that sewing, when she heard the sheriff's wife say, in a queer tone, "Why, look at this one."

She turned to take the block held out to her.

"The sewing," said Mrs. Peters, in a troubled way. "All the rest of them have been so nice and even—but—this one. Why, it looks as if she didn't know what she was about!"

Their eyes met—something flashed to life, passed between them; then, as if with an effort, they seemed to pull away from each other. A moment Mrs. Hale sat there, her hands folded over that sewing which was so unlike all the rest of the sewing. Then she had pulled a knot and drawn the threads.

"Oh, what are you doing, Mrs. Hale?" asked the sheriff's wife, startled.

"Just pulling out a stitch or two that's not sewed very good," said Mrs. Hale mildly.

"I don't think we ought to touch things," Mrs. Peters said, a little helplessly.

"I'll just finish up this end," answered Mrs. Hale, still in that mild, matter-of-fact fashion.

She threaded a needle and started to replace bad sewing with good. For a little while she sewed in silence. Then, in that thin, timid voice, she heard, "Mrs. Hale!"

"Yes, Mrs. Peters?"

"What do you suppose she was so—nervous about?"

"Oh, I don't know," said Mrs. Hale, as if dismissing a thing not important enough to spend much time on. "I don't know as she was—nervous. I sew awful queer sometimes when I'm just tired."

She cut a thread, and out of the corner of her eye looked up at Mrs. Peters. The small, lean face of the sheriff's wife seemed to have tightened up. Her eyes had that look of peering into something. But next moment she moved, and said in her thin, indecisive way, "Well, I must get those clothes wrapped. They may be through sooner than we think. I wonder where I could find a piece of paper—and string."

"In that cupboard, maybe," suggested Mrs. Hale, after a glance around.

ONE PIECE of the crazy sewing remained unripped. Mrs. Peters' back turned, Martha Hale now scrutinized that piece, compared it with the dainty, accurate sewing of the other blocks. The difference was startling. Holding this block made her feel queer, as if the distracted thoughts of the woman who had perhaps turned to it to try and quiet herself were communicating themselves to her.

Mrs. Peters' voice roused her.

"Here's a birdcage," she said. "Did she have a bird, Mrs. Hale?"

"Why, I don't know whether she did or not." She turned to look at the cage Mrs. Peters was holding up. "I've not been here in so long." She sighed. "There was a man round last year selling canaries cheap— but I don't know as she took one. Maybe she did. She used to sing real pretty herself."

Mrs. Peters looked around the kitchen.

"Seems kind of funny to think of a bird here." She half laughed—an attempt to put up a barrier. "But she must have had one—or why would she have a cage? I wonder what happened to it."

"I suppose maybe the cat got it," suggested Mrs. Hale, resuming her sewing.

"No. She didn't have a cat. She's got that feeling some people have about cats—being afraid of them. When they brought her to our house yesterday, my cat got in the room, and she was real upset and asked me to take it out."

"My sister Bessie was like that," laughed Mrs. Hale.

The sheriff's wife did not reply. The silence made Mrs. Hale turn around. Mrs. Peters was examining the birdcage.

"Look at this door," she said slowly. "It's broke. One hinge has been pulled apart."

Mrs. Hale came nearer.

"Looks as if someone must have been—rough with it."

Again their eyes met—startled, questioning, apprehensive. For a moment neither spoke nor stirred. Then Mrs. Hale, turning away, said brusquely, "If they're going to find any evidence, I wish they'd be about it. I don't like this place."

"But I'm awful glad you came with me, Mrs. Hale." Mrs. Peters put the birdcage on the table and sat down. "It would be lonesome for me—sitting here alone."

"Yes, it would, wouldn't it?" agreed Mrs. Hale, a certain determined naturalness in her voice. She had picked up the sewing, but now it dropped in her lap, and she murmured in a different voice, "But I tell you what I *do* wish, Mrs. Peters. I wish I had come over sometimes when she was here. I wish—I had."

"But of course you were awful busy, Mrs. Hale. Your house—and your children."

"I could've come," retorted Mrs. Hale shortly. "I stayed away because it weren't cheerful—and that's why I ought to have come. I"—she looked around—"I've never liked this place. Maybe because it's down in a hollow and you don't see the road. I don't know what it is, but it's a lonesome place, and always was. I wish I had come over to see Minnie Foster sometimes. I can see now—" She did not put it into words.

"Well, you mustn't reproach yourself," counseled Mrs. Peters. "Somehow, we just don't see how it is with other folks till—something comes up."

"Not having children makes less work," mused Mrs. Hale, "but it makes a quiet house—and Wright out to work all day—and no company when he did come in. Did you know John Wright, Mrs. Peters?"

"Not to know him," said Mrs. Peters. "I've seen him in town. They say he was a good man."

"Yes—good," conceded John Wright's neighbor grimly. "He didn't drink, and kept his word as well as most, I guess, and paid his debts. But he was a hard man, Mrs. Peters. Just to pass the time of day with him—" She stopped, shivered a little. "Like a raw wind that gets to the bone." Her eye fell upon the cage on the table before her, and she added, almost bitterly, "I should think she would've wanted a bird!"

Suddenly she leaned forward, looking intently at the cage. "But what do you s'pose went wrong with it?"

"I don't know," returned Mrs. Peters, "unless it got sick and died."

But after she said it she reached over and swung the broken door. Both women watched it as if somehow held by it.

"You didn't know—her?" Mrs. Hale asked, a gentler note in her voice.

"Not till they brought her yesterday," said the sheriff's wife.

"She—come to think of it, she was kind of like a bird herself. Real sweet and pretty, but kind of timid and—fluttery. How—she—did—change."

That held her for a long time. Finally, as if struck with a happy thought and relieved to get back to everyday things, she exclaimed, "Tell you what, Mrs. Peters, why don't you take the quilt in with you? It might take up her mind."

"Why, I think that's a real nice idea, Mrs. Hale," agreed the sheriff's wife, as if she too were glad to come into the atmosphere of a simple kindness. "There couldn't possibly be any objection to that, could there? Now, just what will I take? I wonder if her patches are in here—and her things."

They turned to the sewing basket.

"Here's some red," said Mrs. Hale, bringing out a roll of cloth. Underneath that was a box. "Here, maybe her scissors are in here—and her things." She held it up. "What a pretty box! I'll warrant that was something she had a long time ago—when she was a girl."

She held it in her hand a moment; then, with a little sigh, opened it.

Instantly her hand went to her nose.

"Why—"

Mrs. Peters drew nearer—then turned away.

"There's something wrapped up in this piece of silk," faltered Mrs. Hale.

"This isn't her scissors," said Mrs. Peters, in a shrinking voice.

Her hand not steady, Mrs. Hale raised the piece of silk. "Oh, Mrs. Peters!" she cried. "It's—"

Mrs. Peters bent closer.

"It's the bird," she whispered.

"But, Mrs. Peters!" cried Mrs. Hale. "*Look* at it! Its *neck*—look at its neck! It's all—other side *to*."

She held the box away from her.

The sheriff's wife again bent closer.

"Somebody wrung its neck," said she, in a voice that was slow and deep.

And then again the eyes of the two women met—this time clung together in a look of dawning comprehension, of growing horror. Mrs. Peters looked from the dead bird to the broken door of the cage. Again their eyes met. And just then there was a sound at the outside door.

Mrs. Hale slipped the box under the quilt pieces in the basket, and sank into the chair before it. Mrs. Peters stood holding to the table. The county attorney and the sheriff came in from outside.

"Well, ladies," said the county attorney, as one turning from serious things to little pleasantries, "have you decided whether she was going to quilt it or knot it?"

"We think," began the sheriff's wife in a flurried voice, "that she was going to—knot it."

He was too preoccupied to notice the change that came in her voice on that last.

"Well, that's very interesting, I'm sure," he said tolerantly. He caught sight of the birdcage. "Has the bird flown?"

"We think the cat got it," said Mrs. Hale, in a voice curiously even.

He was walking up and down as if thinking something out.

"Is there a cat?" he asked absently.

Mrs. Hale shot a look up at the sheriff's wife.

"Well, not *now*," said Mrs. Peters. "They're superstitious, you know; they leave."

She sank into her chair.

The county attorney did not heed her. "No sign at all of anyone having come in from the outside," he said to Peters, in the manner of continuing an interrupted conversation. "Their own rope. Now let's go upstairs again and go over it, piece by piece. It would have to have been someone who knew just the—"

The stair door closed behind them and their voices were lost.

The two women sat motionless, not looking at each other, but as if peering into something and at the same time holding back. When they spoke now it was as if they were afraid of what they were saying, but as if they could not help saying it.

"She liked the bird," said Martha Hale, low and slowly. "She was going to bury it in that pretty box."

"When I was a girl," said Mrs. Peters, under her breath, "my kitten—there was a boy took a hatchet, and before my eyes—before I could get there—" She covered her face an instant. "If they hadn't held me back I would have"—she caught herself, looked upstairs where footsteps were heard, and finished weakly—"hurt him."

Then they sat without speaking or moving.

"I wonder how it would seem," Mrs. Hale at last began, as if feeling her way over strange ground—"never to have had any children around?" Her eyes made a slow sweep of the kitchen, as if seeing what that kitchen had meant through all the years. "No, Wright wouldn't like the bird," she said after that—"a thing that sang. She used to sing. He killed that too." Her voice tightened.

Mrs. Peters moved uneasily.

"Of course we don't know who killed the bird."

"I knew John Wright," was Mrs. Hale's answer.

"It was an awful thing was done in this house that night, Mrs. Hale," said the sheriff's wife. "Killing a man while he slept—slipping a thing round his neck that choked the life out of him."

Mrs. Hale's hand went out to the birdcage.

"His neck. Choked the life out of him."

"We don't *know* who killed him," whispered Mrs. Peters wildly. "We don't *know*."

Mrs. Hale had not moved. "If there had been years and years of—nothing, then a bird to sing to you, it would be awful—still—after the bird was still."

It was as if something within her not herself had spoken, and it found in Mrs. Peters something she did not know as herself.

"I know what stillness is," she said, in a queer, monotonous voice. "When we homesteaded in Dakota, and my first baby died—after he was two years old—and me with no other then—"

Mrs. Hale stirred.

"How soon do you suppose they'll be through looking for the evidence?"

"I know what stillness is," repeated Mrs. Peters, in just that same way. Then she too pulled back. "The law has got to punish crime, Mrs. Hale," she said, in her tight little way.

"I wish you'd seen Minnie Foster," was the answer, "when she wore a white dress with blue ribbons, and stood up there in the choir and sang."

The picture of that girl, the fact that she had lived neighbor to that girl for twenty years, and had let her die for lack of life, was suddenly more than she could bear.

"Oh, I *wish* I'd come over here once in a while!" she cried. "That was a crime! That was a crime! Who's going to punish that?"

"We mustn't take on," said Mrs. Peters, with a frightened look toward the stairs.

"I might 'a' *known* she needed help! I tell you, it's *queer*, Mrs. Peters. We live close together, and we live far apart. We all go through the same things—it's all just a different kind of the same thing! If it weren't—why do you and I *understand?* Why do we *know*—what we know this minute?"

She dashed her hand across her eyes. Then, seeing the jar of fruit on the table, she reached for it and choked out, "If I was you I wouldn't *tell* her her fruit was gone! Tell her it *ain't*. Tell her it's all right—all of it. Here—take this in to prove it to her! She—she may never know whether it was broke or not."

She turned away.

Mrs. Peters reached out for the bottle of fruit as if she were glad to take it—as if touching a familiar thing, having something to do, would keep her from something else. She got up, looked about for something to wrap the fruit in, took a petticoat from the pile of clothes she had brought from the front room, and nervously started winding that around the bottle.

"My!" she began, in a high, false voice. "It's a good thing the men couldn't hear us! Getting all stirred up over a little thing like a—dead canary." She hurried over that. "As if that could have anything to do with—with— My, wouldn't they *laugh?*"

Footsteps were heard on the stairs.

"Maybe they would," muttered Mrs. Hale, "maybe they wouldn't."

"No, Peters," said the county attorney incisively, "it's all perfectly clear, except the reason for doing it. But you know juries when it comes to women. If there was some definite thing—something to show. Something to make a story about. A thing that would connect up with this clumsy way of doing it."

In a covert way Mrs. Hale looked at Mrs. Peters. Mrs. Peters was looking at her. Quickly they looked away from each other. The outer door opened and Mr. Hale came in.

"I've got the team round now," he said. "Pretty cold out there."

"I'm going to stay here awhile by myself," the county attorney suddenly announced. "You can send Frank out for me, can't you?" he asked the sheriff. "I want to go over everything. I'm not satisfied we can't do better."

Again, for one brief moment, the two women's eyes found one another.

The sheriff came up to the table.

"Did you want to see what Mrs. Peters was going to take in?"

The county attorney picked up the apron. He laughed.

"Oh, I guess they're not very dangerous things the ladies have picked out."

Mrs. Hale's hand was on the sewing basket in which the box was concealed. She felt that she ought to take her hand off the basket. She did not seem able to. He picked up one of the quilt blocks which she had piled on to cover the box. Her eyes felt like fire. She had a feeling that if he took up the basket she would snatch it from him.

But he did not take it up. With another little laugh, he turned away, saying, "No. Mrs. Peters doesn't need supervising. For that matter, a sheriff's wife is married to the law. Ever think of it that way, Mrs. Peters?"

Mrs. Peters was standing beside the table. Mrs. Hale shot a look up at her, but she could not see her face. Mrs. Peters had turned away. When she spoke, her voice was muffled.

"Not—just that way," she said.

"Married to the law!" chuckled Mrs. Peters' husband. He moved toward the door into the front room, and said to the county attorney, "I just want you to come in here a minute, George. We ought to take a look at these windows."

"Oh—windows," said the county attorney scoffingly.

"We'll be right out, Mr. Hale," said the sheriff to the farmer, who was still waiting by the door.

Hale went to look after the horses. The sheriff followed the county attorney into the other room. Again—for one final moment—the two women were alone in that kitchen.

Martha Hale sprang up, her hands tight together, looking at that other woman, with whom it rested. At first she could not see her eyes, for the sheriff's wife had not turned back since she turned away at that suggestion of being married to the law. But now Mrs. Hale made her turn back. Her eyes made her turn back. Slowly, unwillingly, Mrs. Peters turned her head until her eyes met the eyes of the other woman. There was a moment when they held each other in a steady, burning look in which there was no evasion nor flinching. Then Martha Hale's eyes pointed the way to the basket in which was hidden the thing that would make certain the conviction of the other woman—that woman who was not there and yet who had been there with them all through that hour.

For a moment Mrs. Peters did not move. And then she did it. With a rush forward, she threw back the quilt pieces, got the box, tried to put it in her handbag. It was too big. Desperately she opened it, started to take the bird out. But there she broke—she could not touch the bird. She stood there helpless, foolish.

There was the sound of a knob turning in the inner door. Martha Hale snatched the box from the sheriff's wife, and got it in the pocket of her big coat just as the sheriff and the county attorney came back into the kitchen.

"Well, Henry," said the county attorney facetiously, "at least we found out that she was not going to quilt it. She was going to—what is it you call it, ladies?"

Mrs. Hale's hand was against the pocket of her coat.

"We call it—knot it, Mr. Henderson."

THE STORM

JESSE STUART

Jesse Stuart

"I CAN'T STAND it any longer, Mick," Mom says. "I'm leaving you. I'm going home to Pap. I'll have a rooftree above my head there. Pap will take me in. He'll give me and my children the best he has."

Mom lifts the washrag from the washpan of soapy water. She washes my neck and ears. Mom pushes the warm soft rag against my ears. Drops of warm water ooze down my neck to my shirt collar. Mom's lips are drawn tight. Her long fingers grip the washrag like a chicken's toes clutch a roost limb on a winter night.

"We're different people," says Pa. "I'm sorry about it all, Sal. If I say things that hurt you, I can't help it."

"That's just it," Mom says as she dips the washrag into the pan and squeezes the soapy water between her long brown fingers. "Since we can't get along together, it's better we part now. It's better we part before we have too many children."

Mom has Herbert ready. He is dressed in a white dress. He is lying on the bed playing with a pretty. Mom gave him the pretty to keep him quiet while she dressed me. It is a thread spool that Pa whittled in two and put a stick through for me to spin like a top. I look at the pretty Herbert holds. Herbert looks at it with bright little eyes and laughs.

"Mom, he has the pretty Pa made for me," I say. "I don't want him to have it."

"Quit fussing with your baby brother," Mom says as she puts my hand into the washpan and begins to scrub it.

"Pa made it for me," I say, "and I want to take it with me. I want to keep it."

Pa looks at the top Herbert has clutched in his young mouse-paw-colored fingers. Pa moves in his chair. He crosses one leg above the other. He pulls hard on his pipe. He blows tiny clouds of smoke into the room.

"You're not going to take all the children and leave me alone!" he says.

"They are mine," says Mom, "and I intend to have all three of them or fight everybody in this hollow. They are of my flesh and blood and I gave them birth—and I remember—and—I'm going to hold them." Mom looks hard at Pa as she speaks these words.

"I thought if you'd let Sis stay," says Pa, "she'd soon be old enough to cook for me. If it's anything I hate, it's cooking. I can't cook much. I'll have a time eating the food I cook."

"Serves you right, Mick," says Mom.

"It doesn't serve me right," says Pa. "I intend to stay right here and see that this farm goes on. And if I'm not fooled an awful lot, you'll be back, Sal."

"That's what you think," Mom storms. "I'm not coming back. I do not want ever to see this shack again."

"It's the best roof I can put over your head," Pa says.

"It's not the roof that's over my head," Mom says. "Mick, it's you. You can be laughing one minute and the next minute you can be raising the roof with your vile oaths. Your mind is more changeable than the weather. I never know how to take you, no more than I know how the wind will blow tomorrow."

"We just aren't the same people," Pa says. "That's why I love you, Sal. You're not like I am. You are solid as a mountain. I need you, Sal. I need you more than anyone I know in this world."

"I'm leaving," Mom says. "I'm tired of this. I've been ready to go twice before. I felt sorry for you and my little children that would be raised without a father. This is the third time I've planned to go. Third time is the charm. I'm going this time."

"I'm ready, Mom," says Sis as she climbs down the ladder from the loft. "I'm ready to go to Grandpa's with you."

Sis is dressed in a blue gingham dress. Her ripe-wheat-colored hair falls over her shoulders in two plaits. A blue ribbon is tied on each plait and beneath the ribbons her hair is not plaited. Her hair is bushy as two cottontails.

Pa cranes his autumn-brown neck. He looks at Sis and blows a cloud of smoke slowly from his mouth. Pa's face is brown as a pawpaw leaf in September. His face has caught the spring sunshine as he plowed our mules around the mountain slope.

"Listen," says Pa, "I hear something like April thunder!"

Pa holds his pipe in his hand. He sits silently. He does not speak. Mom squeezes the washrag in the water again. Now she listens.

"I don't hear anything," says Mom. "You just imagined you heard something."

"No, I didn't," Pa answers.

"It can't be thunder, Mick," says Mom. "The sky is blue as the water in the well."

Pa rises from his chair. He walks to the door. He cranes his brown neck like a hen that says *qrrr* when she thinks a hawk is near to swoop down upon her biddies.

"The rains come over the mountain that's to our right," Pa says. "That's the way the rains come, all right. I've seen them come too many times. But the sky is clear—all but a mare-tail in the sky. That's a good sign there'll be rain in three days."

"Rain three days away won't matter much to us," says Mom. "We just have seven miles to walk. We'll be at Pap's place in three hours."

"Listen—it's thunder I hear," Pa says loudly. "I didn't think my ears fooled me a while ago. I can always hear the foxhounds barking in the deep hollows before Kim and Gaylord can. Can't beat my ears for hearing."

"I don't hear it," says Mom as she takes the pan of water across the dogtrot toward the kitchen.

"You will hear it in a few minutes," says Pa. "It's like potato wagons rolling across the far skies."

"Third time is the charm for me," says Mom as she returns from the kitchen without the washpan. "Ever since I can remember, the third time has been the charm for me. I can remember once setting a hen on guinea eggs. A blacksnake that you kept in the corncrib crawled through a crack to my hen's nest. He crawled under the hen and swallowed the eggs. He was so full of eggs that when he tried to crawl out of the nest he fell to the ground. I saw him fall with his sides bulged in and out like wild frostbitten snowballs. I took a hoe and clipped his head. Then I set my hen on goose eggs and soon as they hatched, my old hen pinched their necks with her bill like you'd do with a pair of scissors. I set her on her own kind of eggs—and she hatched every one of the eggs and raised all her biddies. Third time was the charm."

"See the martins hurrying to their boxes," says Pa. "Look out there, Sal! That's the sign of an approaching storm."

The martins fly in circles above our fresh-plowed garden. They cut the bright April air with black fan-shaped wings. They chatter as they fly—circle once and twice around the boxes and alight on the little porches before the twelve doors cut in each of the two big boxes. Martins chatter as they poke their heads in at the doors—draw them out once and chatter again—then silently slip their black-preening feathered bodies in at the small doors.

Mom looks at the long sagging martin boxes—each pole supported by a corner garden post. Mom watches the martins hurrying to the boxes. She listens to their endless chatter to each other and their quarreling from one box of martins to the other box.

"Listen, Sal—listen—"

"It's thunder, Mick! I hear it."

"Will we go, Mom?" Sis asks.

"Yes, we'll go before the storm."

"But it's coming fast, Sal, or the martins wouldn't be coming home to their nests of young ones like they are. Are you going to take our children out in a storm? Don't you know as much as the martin birds?"

I know what Mom is thinking about when she looks at the martin boxes. She remembers the day when Pa made the boxes at the barn. She held the boards while he sawed them with a handsaw. She remembers when he cut the long chestnut poles and peeled them and slid them over the cliffs above the house. They slid to the foot of the mountain like racer snakes before a newground fire. She held the boxes when Pa nailed them to the poles. Mom helped him lift the poles into the deep postholes and Mom helped him wrap the baled-hay wire around the poles and the corner garden posts to hold them steady when the winds blew. I'd just got rid of my dresses then and started wearing rompers.

Mom turns from the front door. She does not speak to Pa. She walks to the dresser in the corner of the room. She opens a dresser drawer. She lifts clothes from the dresser drawer. She stacks them neatly on the bottom of a hickory-split-bottomed chair. She looks at the chair as she stacks the clothes there.

"I know what Mom is thinking," I think as she looks at the chair. "She remembers when she grumbled about the bad bottoms in the chairs and Pa says, 'Wait till spring, Sal—wait until the sap gets up in the hickories until I can skin their bark. I'll fix the chair bottoms.' "

And when the sap got up, that early spring, in the hickories, Pa took a day off from plowing and peeled hickory bark and scraped the green from the rough side of the bark and laced bottoms across the chairs. I know Mom remembers this, for she helped Pa. I held the soft green, tough slats of bark for them and reached them a piece of bark as they needed it.

Pa fills his pipe with bright burley crumbs that he fingers from his hip overall pocket with his rough gnarled hand. His index finger shakes as he tamps the tobacco crumbs into his pipe bowl. Pa takes a match from his hatband and strikes it on his overall leg and lights his pipe. I never saw Pa smoke this much before at one time. I never saw him blow such clouds of smoke from his mouth.

"The sun has gone from the sky, Sal," Pa says. His face beams as he speaks. "See, the air is stilly blue—and yonder is a black cloud racing over the sky faster than a hound dog runs a fox."

Mom does not listen. She lifts clothes from the dresser drawer. She closes the empty dresser drawers. Mom never opens the top dresser drawer. That is where Mom puts Pa's clothes.

"Bring me the basket, Shan," Mom says.

I take the big willow basket off the sewing-machine top where Mom keeps it for an egg basket. When I gather eggs, I put them in this basket.

"Where will Pa put the eggs, Mom?" I ask.

"Never mind that, Shan," she says. "We'll let him find a place to put the eggs."

Mom stacks our washed and ironed clothes neatly into this big willow basket. I see her looking at this basket. I remember when Mom told me how long it took Pa to make this basket. It was when Sis was the baby. Every Saturday Mom and Pa went to town and took this willow basket filled with eggs and traded the eggs at the stores for salt, sugar, coffee, dry goods, thread, and other things we needed.

"Listen to the rain, Sal," Pa says. "Hear it hitting the clapboards!"

Big waves of rain driven by puffs of wind sweep across our garden. We can barely hear the martins chattering in their boxes now. Their chattering sounds like they are hovering their young birds and talking to them about the storm.

Mom has our clothes in the big willow basket. She has Herbert's dresses on top. Herbert is asleep now. He does not hear the big raindrops thumping the dry-sounding clapboard roof. It sounds like you'd thump with your knuckles on the bottom of a washtub.

Mom walks to the door. She looks at the clothesline Pa made from baled-hay wire. He carefully put the pieces of wire together so that they wouldn't hook holes in the clothes Mom hung to dry. Mom watches the water run along the line and beads of water drop into the mouths of the fresh spring-growing grasses. The clothesline is tied to a plum-tree limb on one end and a white oak limb on the other. There is a forked sourwood that Pa cut and peeled for a clothesline prop between the plum tree and the white oak. It is to brace the clothesline when Mom has it loaded with the wet clothes.

The rain pours from the drainpipe in a big sluice into the water barrel Mom keeps at the corner of the house. "You won't wash my hair in rainwater anymore," says Sis. "Will hard water keep my hair from being curly, Mom?"

"I don't know," says Mom.

"You used to say hard water would hurt my hair," Sis says.

"I don't care whether Mom washes my hair in hard water or not," I say. "I'd as soon have it washed in well water as in water from the rain barrel."

Mom walks from the front room to the dogtrot. She looks at the rock cliffs over on the mountainside. I know Mom remembers holding the lantern for Pa on dark winter nights when the ewes were lambing in these cliffs and they had to bring the baby lambs before the big log fire in the house and warm them.

Mom looks at the snow-white patches of bloodroot blooming around these cliffs. She sees the pink sweet Williams growing by the old logs and rotted stumps on the bluffs. Mom is thinking as she looks at these. I know what she is thinking: "Mick has picked bloodroot blossoms and sweet Williams for me many evenings with his big rough hands after he'd plowed the mules day long around the mountain slopes. Yes, Mick, bad as he is to cuss, loves a wild flower."

Mom walks from the dogtrot into the big kitchen.

"Aren't we going to Grandpa's, Mom?" I ask as I follow Mom.

"Bad as it is raining," Mom answers, "you know we're not going."

"If we go, Mom, who'll cook for Pa?"

Mom does not answer. She looks at the clapboard box Pa made for her and filled with black loam he gathered under the big beech trees in the hollow, back of the house. Pa fixed this for a nasturtium-seed box for Mom. Pa put it in the kitchen window where it would catch the early morning sun.

"I have my little basket filled with my dolly's dresses," Sis says as she comes running across the dogtrot to Mom. "I'm ready too, Mom. I'm not going to leave my doll. There won't be anybody left to play with her. You know Pa won't play with her. Pa won't have time. Pa plays with the mules and pets them and calls them his dolls."

"Yes," Mom says, "your pa—"

The sky is low. The rain falls in steady streams. The thin tender oak leaves, the yard grass, the bloodroot, sweet Williams, and the plum-tree leaves drink in the rain. They look clean-washed as Mom washed my face, hands, neck, and ears.

"God must have turned his water bucket over so we couldn't get to Grandpa's, Mom," I say.

It never rained like this before. It's raining so hard now we cannot see the rock cliffs. We cannot see the plum tree and the clothesline wire. We cannot see the martin-box poles at the corners of the garden.

"It's a cyclone, Sal," says Pa as he walks into the kitchen. "I told you a while ago when I saw the martins making it for their boxes a storm was coming. Now you see just how much sense a bird has!"

"Yes, Mick, I see—"

"What if you had taken little Herbert out on the long road to your pap's place—a tree with leaves as thin as they are this time of spring wouldn't have made much of a shelter and there aren't any rock-cliff shelters close along that lonesome road."

Mom looks at the dim blur of wood-ash barrel that Pa put under the big white oak tree where Mom washes our clothes. Pa carries the wood ashes from the kitchen stove and the fireplace and puts them in this barrel for Mom. She makes lye soap from these wood ashes.

"Don't talk about the road," says Mom.

"Where is my pretty, Pa?" I ask.

"Herbert is asleep with it in his hand," Pa answers.

"When we go to Grandpa's, I'm going to take it with me. Pa made it and I intend to keep it."

Damp cool air from the rain sweeps across the dogtrot.

"The rain has chilled that air so," says Pa, "a person needs a coat."

Through the rain-washed windowpane, Mom sees the little bench Pa made. Mom and Pa would sit on this little bench at the end of the grape arbor and string beans, peel potatoes, and shuck roasting ears. They sit here on the long summer evenings when the katydids sing in the garden bean rows and the crickets chirrup in the yard grasses. Pa smokes his pipe and Mom smokes her pipe and we play about them. We hear the whippoorwills singing from mountaintop to mountain-top and we hear the martins chattering to one another in their boxes. We see the lightning bugs lighting their way in the summer evening dusk above the potato rows—and we hear the beetles singing sadly in the dewy evening grass.

"The sun, Mom," I say. "Look—we can go now."

Pa looks at the red ball of sun hanging brightly in the blue April sky above the mountain. It is like a red oak ball hanging from an oak limb by a tiny stem among the green oak leaves. A shadow falls over Pa's brown, weather-beaten face.

"The third time," says Mom, "that I've got ready to go. Something has happened every time. I'm not going."

"Aren't we going to Grandpa's, Mom?" Sis asks.

"No, we're not going."

"What will I do with my basket of doll clothes?"

"Put them back where you got them."

Pa puts his pipe back in his pocket. His face doesn't have a shadow over it now. Pa looks happy. There is a smile on his September pawpaw-leaf-colored face.

"Come, Sal," says Pa. "Let's see if our sweet potatoes have sprouted yet."

Mom and Pa walk from the kitchen to the dogtrot. They walk up the bank where Pa has his sweet-potato bed. Pa has his arm around Mom. They walk over the clean-washed yard grass, as green and pretty as if God had just made it over new.

"I think the potatoes have sprouted," I hear Pa say.

Sis starts upstairs with her basket of doll clothes and her doll. I go into the front room to see if Herbert has my top in his hand. It is my top, for Pa made it for me.

THE PIONEER HEP-CAT

JOHN O'HARA

[signature: John O'Hara]

Every time I come here you all seem to want to hear some more about Red Watson. I declare, if I ever thought there would have been such a demand for stories about Red Watson I would have sat down and written a book about him. I've told you story after story about people that I thought were much more interesting than Reds. Big people. People that made something of themselves instead of a man that nobody ever heard of outside of two or three counties in Pennsylvania, and even here the name Red Watson never meant a thing to people generally considered worthwhile. You young people nowadays, I'd much rather tell you about a mine boy, a young lad that worked in a breaker but was rescued from that and went away to a seminary and became a cardinal. We had one young fellow in this town that most of you don't even know he was born here, but he was. I'm talking about General Henry T. Corrigan. Lieutenant General Corrigan was born right here in this town and sold papers here till his family moved away. I used to play ball with Henny Corrigan, out at the old Fourteenth Street schoolyard. He caught, and I played shortstop on a team we used to have, called the Athletics. I guess *some* of you would be able to guess where we got that name. Those of you that can't guess, we didn't get the name from Kansas City, if that's any hint. And I might mention that a few years ago, when I was attending the newspaper editors' convention in New York City, the principal speaker was none other than Lieutenant General Henry T. Corrigan, all decorated with a chestful of ribbons and surrounded by famous editors and publishers from all over the country, all wanting to ask him questions about the

Strategic Air Command. And there I was, not a very important person I must admit, but when it came my turn to meet the general he looked at me and then he looked at my name on the convention badge we were all wearing and he burst into a big smile. "Winky Breslin!" he said. That was my nickname when I was young. "Winky, you old son of a gun," and with that he took me by the arm and the two of us went over and sat down and you'd be surprised how many local people he remembered, some now dead and gone, but quite a few still living. Some of them the parents and grandparents of you here today. I ran a little story about it at the time, but I guess not many of you saw it. In any case, that's the kind of man I'd rather talk about, but every time I'm asked to speak at one of your Press Club suppers your representative either asks me outright or gives me a strong hint to the effect that the person you'd like me to talk about is Red Watson. I don't understand it.

I'd understand it a lot better if Reds were still alive, and some rock-and-roll idol. But he passed away before you even had swing, let alone rock-and-roll. And it isn't as if there were any of his old records floating around. Reds never made a record in his life. I don't say he wouldn't have been good, or popular. He would have been. If they'd ever heard of him outside of this section of the country, he might have been, well, not as popular as Gene Austin, or the early Crosby. He had a totally different style. As I've told you before, or your predecessors, there's nobody around today to compare him with. The styles of singing have changed so much from when Reds was around. Beginning I'd say with Rudy Vallee and then on to Russ Columbo and Bing, the crooners came in. All toned down as far as the volume was concerned, and running ahead of or behind the beat. Not Reds. When Red Watson let go, he belted out a song in a way that you'd think was going to break every window in the place. And on the beat. Perfectly on the beat. And he was a tenor. The singers nowadays, if you can classify them at all, you'd have to call them baritones. But Reds was a tenor, a high tenor.

I was thinking the other evening, I happened to be watching a show on TV and one of your Tommy Sandses or Bobby Darins came on and those squealing girls, that I suspect are paid, began screeching. And I thought to myself, Red Watson hit a higher note than any of those bobby-soxers, but when he did it it was music. Yes, it was. That's the sad part about it that there aren't any records around to prove it.

When I was the age of some of you, or a little older, the name bands used to come through this region, playing the parks in the summer and the ballrooms in the winter. I notice you don't get many big bands anymore. In fact, I'm told there aren't any, to speak of. But when I was a young fellow there wasn't a name band in the country that didn't play here and all around here. And over and over again. It won't mean anything to you, but I can remember one night when Paul Whiteman, with a thirty-five-piece band, was playing a one-nighter and only two miles away was Vincent Lopez, with *his* big band. How to compare it nowadays, it would be like—I don't know the names of the bands anymore. Ray Conniff and Neal Hefti, I guess. But I can tell you this much, one of the singers with Whiteman was a young practically unknown singer with a trio, named Bing Crosby. And if memory serves, the famous Bix Beiderbecke was also with Whiteman around that time. Those of you that collect records will recognize the name Bix Beiderbecke. First name, Leon. Played cornet. Also piano. You have a musician today, Bushkin, he plays piano and horn, but Bushkin was never idolized the way Bix was. They even wrote a novel about him, and if I'm not mistaken, it was turned into a New York play.

Well, what I don't understand is your interest in Red Watson, because Reds died around the time I've been speaking of. He was popular *before* Whiteman and Lopez started playing the parks and the ballrooms in this section. The big band then was the Sirens. The Scranton Sirens. Of course you've heard about the Sirens. Both Dorseys played with the Sirens. We had that in our paper when Tommy and Jimmy passed on there a little while ago, and I got a lot of letters from some of your mothers and fathers and I guess your grandparents, that still loved the Scranton Sirens. But with all due credit to the Dorsey boys, the real attraction was Red Watson. Mind you, it was a fine band. None better in the whole United States, because I heard them all. All the big ones of that day. Fletcher Henderson. Earl Fuller. The Barbary Coast. Art Hickman. Oh, my, just saying the names takes me back. Ted Weems. The Original Dixieland. Goldkette. Paul Biese. The Coon-Sanders Kansas City Nighthawks. Jack Chapman. I can remember more than once driving all the way to Atlantic City in a friend of mine's flivver, just to hear a band at the Steel Pier, and then *driving back the same night* so I'd be at work in the morning. That was a long trip then. It's still a long trip, but when we made it—I guess there isn't one of you here that would know how to vulcanize an inner tube. I can see you don't even know what I'm talking about. In those days you could go in any five-and-ten and buy an ignition key for your Ford, and it had a square hole cut in the key to turn on the tank for your headlights. No, you don't register. I might as well be talking about whipsockets.

You must bear in mind, when I graduated from this school, in other words the same age as some of you within sound of my voice, jazz was such a new thing that they weren't even sure how to spell it. Some spelled it j, a, s, s, and I've seen Victrola records with Jass Band instead of Jazz Band printed on the label. But I'll tell you one thing. If you ever heard Red Watson sing "Jazz Me" you knew it was spelled with two z's. To be quite frank with you, I'm always hesitant about coming here and speaking about Red Watson, because as the—I hope—respectable editor of a family newspaper, I don't consider Reds a proper subject for a talk before a group of young high school students. If I weren't so convinced that you know as much about some things as I do, I'd have to decline your invitations. Or at least I'd choose another subject. But then I always say to myself, "These young people today, they know a lot more than I did when I was their age, about certain things, and maybe I can sneak over a moral lesson somehow or other." And I can. You see, boys and girls, or young ladies and gentlemen, Red Watson was an example of great talent wasted. He had a God-given voice, completely untrained, but I was told that he was given many offers to go away and take singing lessons. He came from a little town outside of Scranton and several rich people up there wanted to pay for his vocal training, but he'd have no part of it.

The story was—and those of you that were here two years ago must excuse me for repeating it—but according to the story that I always heard, and I could never summon up the courage to ask Reds to verify it—Reds was a breaker boy, too. Like that cardinal. But when he was about thirteen years old, working in the breaker, his arm got caught in the conveyor and was so badly mangled that they had to amputate above the elbow. Thirteen, maybe fourteen years old. You can imagine what dreadful torture he must have gone through. The accident itself, and then the amputation which left him with a stump about, well, he used to fold up his left sleeve and pin it with a safety pin just under the shoulder. He was an orphan, living with relatives, and after he got out of the hospital he tried selling papers, but that wasn't as easy as you might think. A paper route was just about impossible to get, and selling papers on street corners was just as hard. You had to fight for the busy corners, and Reds only had one arm. So he used to get a few papers and go around to the saloons and try to sell them there, but somehow or other they found out that he could sing, and he began to make as much money singing for nickels and dimes, and pennies, as he could selling papers. At the age of fourteen he was known in all the saloons, and sometimes the miners used to get him liquored up, even though he was hardly more than a child. They'd give him whiskey and get him singing, and he told me himself that by the time he was sixteen years of age, he could drink beer all night long without getting intoxicated. Whiskey was another matter, but beer he could drink till the cows came home, and it wouldn't affect him. That much of the story is true, because Reds told me himself.

This part I can't vouch for, but you can take it for whatever you think it's worth. I've never been able to make up my mind one way or the other whether it's just imagination on someone's part, or based on the truth, and I never asked Reds. But according to the story that a lot of people believed, when Reds wanted to hit his high note, he'd think back on the time he lost his arm and the pain would come back to him and he'd scream. I don't know. It wasn't the kind of question I could ever ask Reds, although I got to know him pretty well. But I remember hearing a story about Caruso, too. He was supposed to be the greatest tenor that ever lived, and they say he hit his highest note when he was in pain from an abscess in his lung. Who knows? I have a hard time believing it, but I think Caruso died of an abscessed lung, or the effects of it, so there may be some connection between the pain and the high note. I know that Red Watson's stump always bothered him, and he became a heavy drinker to take his mind off the pain. But he wouldn't see a doctor. Oh, no. He said another operation—well, not to be squeamish about it, the stump was so short that there was hardly anything left of the arm, and where would they go after that? He said to me once that he wasn't like most people, because he knew exactly how long he had to live. He said he didn't have to measure it in years, like most people, but in a few inches of bone.

People ask me what Reds was like, because when I was a young fellow, I confess that it wasn't only my duty as a reporter that took me into the various places where alcoholic beverages were for sale. And I guess I was one of the pioneer hep-cats, although they didn't use that expression, and in fact I'm told by the modern generation that you don't even say hep anymore. Hip? Or is that passé, too? Well, anyway, I know that the musicians used to call us alligators, because we'd stand in front of a band with our mouths open like alligators, so if you ever heard the expression, "Greetings, 'Gate," that's where it came from. The alligators. And I was one back in the early Twenties, just after the first World War. When we wanted to hear a good jazz band, an orchestra that didn't play waltzes all night, we had to go to the public dances on Saturday nights at the Armory, and whenever I hear you young people being called juvenile delinquents, I have to remind myself that there was plenty of it when I was about your age. Those dances at the Armory, I think the admission was fifty cents for ladies and seventy-five for gents. It may have been less. Fifty for gents and twenty-five for ladies. We had a name for those dances. We called them rock fights. In fact, we didn't even bother to call them by the full name, rock fights. We used to say, "Are you going out to the rocky tonight?" And out of that grew another nickname, the quarry. We used to speak of the rock fights as the quarry. In front of our parents we could say, "I'll see you at the quarry," and our fathers and mothers would think we were talking about going for a swim in the quarry dam. Oh, we were just as wild as you think you are, or almost.

You know, I don't often get to see TV in the daytime, but last year when I was laid up with arthritis I watched you kids, or young people of your generation, dancing on an afternoon program. And one great difference between you and us, *you* don't seem to be having a good time. You hardly even smile at each other. It wasn't that way in my youth. Good Lord, everybody was laughing and jumping around, racing all over the floor when they played a one-step. Now you just glare at your partner and she spins around and you pull her towards you. You don't have any fun. Incidentally, I don't think you dance very well, either, but that's a matter of opinion. I remember a fast tune called "Taxi!" When they played that, you moved fast or you got out of the way. That was good exercise, and fun. There'd always be a few fellows pretty well liquored up and they'd take a spill, but that was part of the fun. And there was always at least one fistfight at the rockies. At least one. You see, most of the girls at those dances, they were high school age, but they weren't going to school. They had working permits and a lot of them worked in the silk mill, the box factories, and some of them were servant girls. You hear the expression, going steady, and you think it's new. Well, it isn't. Girls and boys went steady then, and what that meant was that a girl would go to a rock fight and pay her own way in, dance with as many fellows as she wanted to, but she always went home with the boy she was going steady with, and if she tried to go home with somebody else, there'd be a fistfight. That's really where those dances got the name, rock fights. They didn't throw rocks, and they wouldn't have called them rocks anyway. They called them goonies. A gooney was a piece of stone that boys would throw at each other on the way home from school. In some sections of town the boys used to in the winter take a gooney and wrap it up in snow. A snowball with a gooney in it could inflict a lot of damage. See this scar here in back of my ear? That was a gooney wrapped in snow. I never knew who or what hit me at the time, but a bunch of boys from Third Street school were waiting for us boys from Fourteenth Street one afternoon, and I was one of the casualties. My poor mother when they brought me home!

Well, you're very patient with me, and I don't know why it is that the mere mention of Red Watson opens up the floodgates of reminiscence, only it's more about me than about Reds. I started to answer the question, What was he like? Well, in spite of his name being Watson, he had a real Irish face, no doubt about it. He wasn't a very big fellow. In fact, he was on the short side. But he looked a lot older than his real age. When I first knew him he was only about twenty years of age, but he looked easily thirty. Face was almost purple from drink and he was already starting to get bald. He was usually smiling and he was *always* smiling when he got up to sing. He'd flirt with all the girls around the bandstand that gathered around when he took his place to sing. He was a cake-eater. That was slang for fellows that dressed a certain way. They were also called sharpies. A sharpie, or a cake-eater, wore a suit that was padded at the shoulders and tight at the waist, then flared out. It had exaggerated peaked lapels that went all the way up to the shoulders, hence the name sharpie. The coat was buttoned at the waist with link buttons, sometimes three pairs of link buttons. The cuffs flared out and they were divided. The trousers were very wide at the bottom, and if you were really sharp, they were laced at the sides, like Spanish bullfighters'. The sharpies wore either tiny bow ties, on an elastic, or very narrow four-in-hands. And they wore low-cut vests so that the whole shirtfront was exposed. Tiny little collars. Hair was plastered down with Vaseline, and the cake-eaters wore sideburns. And that was the way Reds dressed, with one sleeve pinned up to his shoulder. You boys and girls are even too young to remember the zoot suit of twenty years ago, which was different from the cake-eater's outfit, but if Reds had lived in a later era, he'd have worn a zoot suit. I think.

As to his personality, he had two. One when he was singing, and the other when he wasn't. When he wasn't singing he wasn't a very remarkable young fellow. Good-natured as a rule, although quick-tempered at times. He liked the girls, and they certainly liked him, not because of his looks, you can be sure of that. And not only because of his singing. He had a car, a yellow Marmon roadster it was, and I went on a couple of rides with him after we became friendly, and we'd drive to Reading and Philadelphia, places where they didn't know him at all, and we'd stop someplace to get a sandwich. If they had a waitress that was halfway good-looking, Reds would start to kid her a little, and always end up with a date. Sometimes he had no intention of keeping the date, but he just had to convince himself that he was irresistible. And he usually was. In fact, too much so. I guess I knew him two or three years before he happened to mention that he was married when he was eighteen and had a baby daughter. He supported his wife and child, but he wasn't a good husband or father by any stretch of the imagination. I could understand his not getting along with his wife, but I've never been able to understand why he didn't seem to take the slightest interest in his daughter. But that was a closed subject, and I decided it was none of my business. In my opinion Reds was one of those people that seem to have a talent for certain things, such as music, writing, art, but they're deficient in the common-ordinary, everyday things that you don't hear so much about, but they're an accomplishment nevertheless. I mean the simple, ordinary things like the sacrifices that some of your mothers and fathers make for you boys and girls, that you may not even know of unless you stop to think about it. Forty boys and girls in this room. How many of you girls had a new dress this year? Don't raise your hands, because my next question is, How many of you girls got a new dress this year because your mother got one for you instead of for herself? And you boys. How many of you have cars—and don't *you* raise your hands, either. Because some of you must know, if you stop to think, that you wouldn't have a car if your fathers didn't decide to spend that money on you instead of on themselves. This isn't a lecture. I'm not at all sure what it is except an informal talk by a newspaper editor to some young people that are interested in the field of journalism. And you don't especially want me to talk about the newspaper business. But in fairness to you, if I'm invited to talk about a colorful character whose example I wouldn't want you to follow, in fairness to you I have to call your attention to the fact that you all have fathers and mothers that do set a good example in love and kindness, and patience and understanding. My conscience won't let me talk about Red Watson, and glamorize him, unless I point out to you that Reds only lived to be twenty-five years of age, and as far as I know—and I knew him pretty well—he never did anything for anybody but himself. With that understanding, I'll continue talking about him. But I had to make that clear. He never did anything for anybody but himself, and he died—well, I'll save that till later, inasmuch as half the members of your Press Club probably are hearing about Reds for the first time. The seniors and juniors were here when I spoke two years ago, but the sophomores and freshmen weren't.

So to continue about his two personalities. The one, he was fun to be with, but I only saw him on his visits to town, maybe four times a year.

I don't know how he'd have been as a steady diet. Selfish, and no respect for girls whatsoever, and as I said before, he seemed good-natured, but he had a quick temper, too. I guess if I had to be completely frank about it, I was flattered because he wanted me for a friend. I was just a young fellow starting out in the newspaper business, and I used to enjoy it when some of our local prizefighters and celebrities would call me by my nickname. And in that little world, Red Watson was as big a celebrity as Kid Lefty Williams or Young Packy Corbett, two fighters we had at the time, both since passed on. Made me feel big, even though I had some misgivings about Reds.

But I'll tell you this, you always forgot what he was like when he got up to sing. I mean the things about him that I didn't go along with. It'd come his turn to sing a number and he'd go behind the piano and take a swig out of a pint bottle of whiskey, and a couple of fast drags on his cigarette, and then he'd go to the middle of the bandstand and stand there grinning at the people gathering around while the orchestra played a full chorus. And then he'd close his eyes and put his head back and start singing. It didn't make any difference what the number was. It might be a sort of risqué song like "Jazz Me" or it might be a ballad. But the dancing would stop and everybody would stand still, as close to the bandstand as they could get, and you'd look at their faces and they were hypnotized. They'd be moving in time to the rhythm, but not dancing, and it was almost as though he were singing for them. Not only to them, but for them. I can remember thinking of him as a misplaced choirboy, and the crowd around him some of the toughest characters in the county. The girls just as tough as the young fellows. They'd all stop chewing gum while he was singing, and even when he happened to be singing a dirty song, they'd smile, but they didn't laugh. And if it was a ballad, he could make them cry. There's a high note in "Poor Butterfly"—"but if he don't come *back*"—that *always* made them cry. Then he'd finish his song and open his eyes and smile at them while they yelled and applauded, and he'd wink at them, and they'd start dancing again. One chorus. No encores, one song every half an hour. That was his agreement. He was paid fifty dollars a night with the band. But then after the dance was over we'd all meet at some saloon and after he had enough to drink you couldn't stop him. He'd get up on the bar and sing whatever you asked him, till the joint closed. The next night it'd be the same thing in some other town, six nights a week.

How he kept it up as long as he did, I don't know. He slept all day, but when he had his breakfast, at seven o'clock in the evening, that was often the only meal he ate all day. By eight o'clock he was hitting the bottle, and usually at half past eight, sometimes nine, he'd be with the band, ready to sing his first number. Naturally he couldn't keep that up, and he began failing to show up with the band. The first few times that happened, he got away with it, but then the crowds were disappointed and the managers of the dance halls were afraid to advertise that he was coming. Then the band broke up and for about a year I didn't see Reds at all. I heard he was forming his own band, Red Watson's Syncopators. And he was leading the band, himself. But that didn't last long. Two or three months of that was all he could stand. And all the musicians could stand. He'd order special arrangements, but then he wouldn't pay for them, and he got in trouble with the union about paying his musicians, and the first thing he knew he was put on the unfair list. After that he just disappeared, and whenever I'd ask about him from people around Wilkes-Barre and Scranton they had conflicting reports, probably all true. I heard he'd opened a speakeasy in Wilkes-Barre and someone else told me he was in prison for non-support of his wife and child. The last time I saw him I was in Scranton, covering a United Mine Workers meeting, and I asked around and finally tracked him down. I asked him how things were, and not knowing I knew anything about him, he put on a great show. He said he'd got rid of the yellow Marmon and was buying a Wills-Sainte Clare. That was an expensive car. He had offers to go in vaudeville, et cetera, et cetera. And he wouldn't let me pay the check. We were in a speakeasy where his credit must have been good, because he told the bartender to put it on his tab and the bartender made a face, but said okay, Reds. I had a feeling that the bartender would have much preferred my cash. So I said to Reds, approaching the subject in a roundabout way, I said I was glad things were better. And he asked me what I meant by better, and I said I'd heard he'd a little trouble. Well, such vituperation! Such invective! And all directed at me. I was a cheap newspaper reporter that never made more than thirty dollars a week in my life, which was true, but I was also a snooping so-and-so, probably sent there by his wife's lawyer to find out all I could. He took a beer bottle off the bar and smashed the neck off it. That was a weapon known as a Glasgie Slasher, and he held it up to my face and said I deserved to have my eyes gouged out, snooping around and asking questions. I didn't dare move, for fear I'd get that thing in my face. And then, I guess because I hadn't made any move, he dropped the broken bottle in the gutter in front of the bar, and ran out.

I was given a drink by the bartender, and I needed it after that experience. "He'll murder somebody yet," the bartender said. "He's suspicious of everybody." I asked the bartender how Reds lived, and the man told me. I don't have to go into that here, but Reds was about as low as a man can get to make a living. Any real man would rather dig ditches, but Reds only had one arm and all he ever did was sing. Anyway, he had a place to live and a little cash. And then the bartender, a nice fellow, asked me how well I'd known Reds. Had Reds ever told me that he didn't measure his life by years, but inches of bone? And I said yes, he'd said that to me some years back. And the bartender said, "Well, he's heard the bad news. No more inches, and no more years. Months, and more likely weeks." Then he said he just hoped Reds got through the next couple of months without killing somebody.

Well, he did, boys and girls. The next I heard of Reds was a few weeks later at the office, the city editor handed me a little squib that came in over the UP wire. Patrick Watson, known throughout the coal region as Red Watson, the popular tenor, was found dead on the bandstand of the Alhambra dance hall in Scranton. It was summer, the wrong time of the year for a dance at the Alhambra. So I got Scranton on the phone and checked. Yes, they found Reds at the Alhambra. Nobody else in the place, which was closed for the summer, and the watchman had no idea what Reds had gone there for. There was nothing worth stealing.

But you and I know why he went there, don't we? Yes, I think as I look at you, you know.

Thank you.

THE FURNISHED ROOM

O. HENRY

RESTLESS, shifting, fugacious as time itself is a certain vast bulk of the population of the red brick district of the lower West Side. Homeless, they have a hundred homes. They flit from furnished room to furnished room, transients forever—transients in abode, transients in heart and mind. They sing "Home, Sweet Home" in ragtime; they carry their *lares et penates* in a bandbox; their vine is entwined about a picture hat; a rubber plant is their fig tree.

Hence the houses of this district, having had a thousand dwellers, should have a thousand tales to tell, mostly dull ones, no doubt; but it would be strange if there could not be found a ghost or two in the wake of all these vagrant guests.

One evening after dark a young man prowled among these crumbling red mansions, ringing their bells. At the twelfth he rested his lean hand baggage upon the step and wiped the dust from his hatband and forehead. The bell sounded faint and far away in some remote, hollow depths.

To the door of this, the twelfth house whose bell he had rung, came a housekeeper who made him think of an unwholesome, surfeited worm that had eaten its nut to a hollow shell and now sought to fill the vacancy with edible lodgers.

He asked if there was a room to let.

"Come in," said the housekeeper. Her voice came from her throat; her throat seemed lined with fur. "I have the third-floor-back, vacant since a week back. Should you wish to look at it?"

The young man followed her up the stairs. A faint light from no particular source mitigated the shadows of the halls. They trod noiselessly upon a stair carpet that its own loom would have forsworn. It seemed to have become vegetable; to have degenerated in that rank, sunless air to lush lichen or spreading moss that grew in patches to the staircase and was viscid under the foot like organic matter. At each turn of the stairs were vacant niches in the wall. Perhaps plants had once been set within them. If so, they had died in that foul and tainted air. It may be that statues of the saints had stood there, but it was not difficult to conceive that imps and devils had dragged them forth in the darkness and down to the unholy depths of some furnished pit below.

"This is the room," said the housekeeper, from her furry throat. "It's a nice room. It ain't often vacant. I had some most elegant people in it last summer—no trouble at all, and paid in advance to the minute. The water's at the end of the hall. Sprowls and Mooney kept it three months. They done a vaudeville sketch. Miss B'retta Sprowls—you may have heard of her—oh, that was just the stage names—right there over the dresser is where the marriage certificate hung, framed. The gas is here, and you see there is plenty of closet room. It's a room everybody likes. It never stays idle long."

"Do you have many theatrical people rooming here?" asked the young man.

"They comes and goes. A good proportion of my lodgers is connected with the theaters. Yes, sir, this is the theatrical district. Actor people never stays long anywhere. I get my share. Yes, they comes and they goes."

He engaged the room, paying for a week in advance. He was tired, he said, and would take possession at once. He counted out the money. The room had been made ready, she said, even to towels and water. As the housekeeper moved away he put, for the thousandth time, the question that he carried at the end of his tongue.

"A young girl—Miss Vashner—Miss Eloise Vashner—do you remember such a one among your lodgers? She would be singing on the stage, most likely. A fair girl, of medium height and slender, with reddish gold hair and a dark mole near her left eyebrow."

"No, I don't remember the name. Them stage people has names they change as often as their rooms. No, I don't call that one to mind."

No. Always no. Five months of ceaseless interrogation and the inevitable negative. So much time spent by day in questioning managers, agents, schools and choruses; by night among the audiences of theaters from all-star casts down to music halls so low that he dreaded to find what he most hoped for. He who had loved her best had tried to find her. He was sure that since her disappearance from home this great, water-girt city held her somewhere, but it was like a monstrous quicksand, shifting its particles constantly, with no foundation, its upper granules of today buried tomorrow in ooze and slime.

The furnished room received its latest guest with a first glow of pseudo hospitality, a hectic, haggard, perfunctory welcome like the specious smile of a demirep. The sophistical comfort came in reflected gleams from the decayed furniture, the ragged brocade upholstery of a couch and two chairs, a foot-wide cheap pier glass between the two windows, from one or two gilt picture frames and a brass bedstead in a corner.

The guest reclined, inert, upon a chair, while the room, confused in speech as though it were an apartment in Babel, tried to discourse to him of its divers tenantry.

A polychromatic rug like some brilliant-flowered, rectangular, tropical islet lay surrounded by a billowy sea of soiled matting. Upon the gay-papered wall were those pictures that pursue the homeless one from house to house—*The Huguenot Lovers, The First Quarrel, The Wedding Breakfast, Psyche at the Fountain.* The mantel's chastely severe outline was ingloriously veiled behind some pert drapery drawn rakishly askew like the sashes of the Amazonian ballet. Upon it was some desolate flotsam cast aside by the room's marooned when a lucky sail had borne them to a fresh port—a trifling vase or two, pictures of actresses, a medicine bottle, some stray cards out of a deck.

One by one, as the characters of a cryptograph became explicit, the little signs left by the furnished room's procession of guests developed a significance. The threadbare space in the rug in front of the dresser told that lovely women had marched in the throng. The tiny fingerprints on the wall spoke of little prisoners trying to feel their way to sun and air. A splattered stain, raying like the shadow of a bursting bomb, witnessed where a hurled glass or bottle had splintered with its contents against the wall. Across the pier glass had been scrawled with a diamond in staggering letters the name Marie. It seemed that the succession of dwellers in the furnished room had turned in fury—perhaps tempted beyond forbearance by its garish coldness—and wreaked upon it their passions. The furniture was chipped and bruised; the couch, distorted by bursting springs, seemed a horrible monster that had been slain during the stress of some grotesque convulsion. Some more potent upheaval had cloven a great slice from the marble mantel. Each plank in the floor owned its particular cant and shriek as from a separate and individual agony. It seemed incredible that all this malice and injury had been wrought upon the room by those who had called it for a time their home; and yet it may have been the cheated home instinct surviving blindly, the resentful rage at false household gods that had kindled their wrath. A hut that is our own we can sweep and adorn and cherish.

The young tenant in the chair allowed these thoughts to file, soft-shod, through his mind, while there drifted into the room furnished sounds and furnished scents. He heard in one room a tittering and incontinent, slack laughter; in others the monologue of a scold, the rattling of dice, a lullaby, and one crying dully; above him a banjo tinkled with spirit. Doors banged somewhere; the elevated trains roared intermittently; a cat yowled miserably upon a back fence. And he breathed the breath of the house—a dank savor rather than a smell—a cold, musty effluvium as from underground vaults mingled with the reeking exhalations of linoleum and mildewed and rotten woodwork.

Then suddenly, as he rested there, the room was filled with the strong, sweet odor of mignonette. It came as upon a single buffet of wind with such sureness and fragrance and emphasis that it almost seemed a living visitant. And the man cried aloud, "What, dear?" as if he had been called, and sprang up and faced about. The rich odor clung to him and wrapped him around. He reached out his arms for it, all his senses for the time confused and commingled. How could one be peremptorily called by an odor? Surely it must have been a sound. But was it not the sound that had touched, that had caressed him?

"She has been in this room," he cried, and he sprang to wrest from it a token, for he knew he would recognize the smallest thing that had belonged to her or that she had touched. This enveloping scent of mignonette, the odor that she had loved and made her own—whence came it?

The room had been but carelessly set in order. Scattered upon the flimsy dresser scarf were half a dozen hairpins—those discreet, indistinguishable friends of womankind, feminine of gender, infinite of mood and uncommunicative of tense. These he ignored, conscious of their triumphant lack of identity. Ransacking the drawers of the dresser he came upon a discarded, tiny, ragged handkerchief. He pressed it to his face. It was racy and insolent with heliotrope; he hurled it to the floor. In another drawer he found odd buttons, a theater program, a pawnbroker's card, two lost marshmallows, a book on the divination of dreams. In the last was a woman's black satin hair bow, which halted him, poised between ice and fire. But the black satin hair bow also is femininity's demure, impersonal common ornament and tells no tales.

And then he traversed the room like a hound on the scent, skimming the walls, considering the corners of the bulging matting on his hands and knees, rummaging mantel and tables, the curtains and hangings, the drunken cabinet in the corner, for a visible sign, unable to perceive that she was there beside, around, against, within, above him, clinging to him, wooing him, calling him so poignantly through the finer senses that even his grosser ones became cognizant of the call. Once again he answered loudly, "Yes, dear!" and turned, wild-eyed, to gaze on vacancy, for he could not yet discern form and color and love and outstretched arms in the odor of mignonette. Oh, God! Whence that odor, and since when have odors had a voice to call? Thus he groped.

He burrowed in crevices and corners, and found corks and cigarettes. These he passed in passive contempt. But once he found in a fold of the matting a half-smoked cigar, and this he ground beneath his heel with a green and trenchant oath. He sifted the room from end to end. He found dreary and ignoble small records of many a peripatetic tenant; but of her whom he sought, and who may have lodged there, and whose spirit seemed to hover there, he found no trace.

And then he thought of the housekeeper.

He ran from the haunted room downstairs and to a door that showed a crack of light. She came out to his knock. He smothered his excitement as best he could.

"Will you tell me, madam," he besought her, "who occupied the room I have before I came?"

"Yes, sir. I can tell you again. 'Twas Sprowls and Mooney, as I said. Miss B'retta Sprowls it was in the theaters, but Missis Mooney she was. My house is well known for respectability. The marriage certificate hung, framed, on a nail over—"

"What kind of a lady was Miss Sprowls—in looks, I mean?"

"Why, black-haired, sir, short, and stout, with a comical face. They left a week ago Tuesday."

"And before they occupied it?"

"Why, there was a single gentleman connected with the draying business. He left owing me a week. Before him was Missis Crowder and her two children, that stayed four months; and back of them was old Mr. Doyle, whose sons paid for him. He kept the room six months. That goes back a year, sir, and further I do not remember."

He thanked her and crept back to his room. The room was dead. The essence that had vivified it was gone. The perfume of mignonette had departed. In its place was the old, stale odor of moldy house furniture, of atmosphere in storage.

The ebbing of his hope drained his faith. He sat staring at the yellow, singing gaslight. Soon he walked to the bed and began to tear the sheets into strips. With the blade of his knife he drove them tightly into every crevice around windows and door. When all was snug and taut he turned out the light, turned the gas full on again and laid himself gratefully upon the bed.

IT WAS Mrs. McCool's night to go with the can for beer. So she fetched it and sat with Mrs. Purdy in one of those subterranean retreats where housekeepers forgather and the worm dieth seldom.

"I rented out my third-floor-back this evening," said Mrs. Purdy, across a fine circle of foam. "A young man took it. He went up to bed two hours ago."

"Now, did ye, Mrs. Purdy, ma'am?" said Mrs. McCool, with intense admiration. "You do be a wonder for rentin' rooms of that kind. And did ye tell him, then?" she concluded in a husky whisper laden with mystery.

"Rooms," said Mrs. Purdy, in her furriest tones, "are furnished for to rent. I did not tell him, Mrs. McCool."

" 'Tis right ye are, ma'am; 'tis by renting rooms we kape alive. Ye have the rale sense for business, ma'am. There be many people will rayjict the rentin' of a room if they be tould a suicide has been after dyin' in the bed of it."

"As you say, we has our living to be making," remarked Mrs. Purdy.

"Yis, ma'am; 'tis true. 'Tis just one wake ago this day I helped ye lay out the third-floor-back. A pretty slip of a colleen she was to be killin' herself wid the gas—a swate little face she had, Mrs. Purdy, ma'am."

"She'd a-been called handsome, as you say," said Mrs. Purdy, assenting but critical, "but for that mole she had a-growin' by her left eyebrow. Do fill up your glass again, Mrs. McCool."

I CAN'T BREATHE

RING LARDNER

Ring W. Lardner

July 12

I AM STAYING here at the Inn for two weeks with my Uncle Nat and
Aunt Jule and I think I will keep a kind of diary while I am here to help
pass the time and so I can have a record of things that happen though
goodness knows there isn't likely to anything happen, that is anything
exciting with Uncle Nat and Aunt Jule making the plans as they are
both at least 35 years old and maybe older.

Dad and mother are abroad to be gone a month and me coming here
is supposed to be a recompence for them not taking me with them. A
fine recompence to be left with old people that come to a place like this
to rest. Still it would be a heavenly place under different conditions, for
instance if Walter were here, too. It would be heavenly if he were here,
the very thought of it makes my heart stop.

I can't stand it. I won't think about it.

This is our first separation since we have been engaged, nearly 17
days. It will be 17 days tomorrow. And the hotel orchestra at dinner
this evening played that old thing "Oh, how I miss you tonight" and it
seemed as if they must be playing it for my benefit though of course the
person in that song is talking about how they miss their mother
though of course I miss mother too, but a person gets used to missing
their mother and it isn't like Walter or the person you are engaged to.

But there won't be any more separations much longer, we are going
to be married in December even if mother does laugh when I talk to
her about it because she says I am crazy to even think of getting married
at 18. She got married herself when she was 18, but of course that was
"different," she wasn't crazy like I am, she knew whom she was

marrying. As if Walter were a policeman or a foreigner or something. And she says she was only engaged once while I have been engaged at least five times a year since I was 14, of course it really isn't as bad as that and I have really only been really what I call engaged six times altogether, but is getting engaged my fault when they keep insisting and hammering at you and if you didn't say yes they would never go home.

But it is different with Walter. I honestly believe if he had not asked me I would have asked him. Of course I wouldn't have, but I would have died. And this is the first time I have ever been engaged to be really married. The other times when they talked about when we should get married I just laughed at them, but I hadn't been engaged to Walter ten minutes when he brought up the subject of marriage and I didn't laugh. I wouldn't be engaged to him unless it was to be married. I couldn't stand it.

Anyway mother may as well get used to the idea because it is "No Foolin'" this time and we have got our plans all made and I am going to be married at home and go out to California and Hollywood on our honeymoon. December, five months away. I can't stand it. I can't wait.

There were a couple of awfully nice looking boys sitting together alone in the dining-room tonight. One of them wasn't so much, but the other was cute. And he—

There's the dance orchestra playing "Always," what they played at the Biltmore the day I met Walter. "Not for just an hour, not for just a day." I can't live. I can't breathe.

July 13

THIS HAS BEEN a much more exciting day than I expected under the circumstances. In the first place I got two long night letters, one from Walter and one from Gordon Flint. I don't see how Walter ever had the nerve to send his, there was everything in it and it must have been horribly embarrassing for him while the telegraph operator was reading it over and counting the words to say nothing of embarrassing the operator.

But the one from Gordon was a kind of a shock. He just got back from a trip around the world, left last December to go on it and got back yesterday and called up our house and Helga gave him my address, and his telegram, well it was nearly as bad as Walter's. The trouble is that Gordon and I were engaged when he went away, or at least he thought so and he wrote to me right along all the time he was away and sent cables and things and for a while I answered his letters, but then I lost track of his itinerary and couldn't write to him any more and when I got really engaged to Walter I couldn't let Gordon know because I had no idea where he was besides not wanting to spoil his trip.

And now he still thinks we are engaged and he is going to call me up tomorrow from Chicago and how in the world can I explain things and get him to understand because he is really serious and I like him ever and ever so much and in lots of ways he is nicer than Walter, not really nicer but better looking and there is no comparison between their dancing. Walter simply can't learn to dance, that is really dance. He says it is because he is flat footed, he says that as a joke, but it is true and I wish to heavens it wasn't.

All forenoon I thought and thought and thought about what to say to Gordon when he calls up and finally I couldn't stand thinking about it any more and just made up my mind I wouldn't think about it any more. But I will tell the truth though it will kill me to hurt him.

I went down to lunch with Uncle Nat and Aunt Jule and they were going out to play golf this afternoon and were insisting that I go with them, but I told them I had a headache and then I had a terrible time getting them to go without me. I didn't have a headache at all and just wanted to be alone to think about Walter and besides when you play with Uncle Nat he is always correcting your stance or your swing or something and always puts his hands on my arms or shoulders to show me the right way and I can't stand it to have old men touch me, even if they are your uncle.

I finally got rid of them and I was sitting watching the tennis when that boy that I saw last night, the cute one, came and sat right next to me and of course I didn't look at him and I was going to smoke a cigarette and found I had left my lighter upstairs and I started to get up and go after it when all of a sudden he was offering me his lighter and I couldn't very well refuse it without being rude. So we got to talking and he is even cuter than he looks, the most original and wittiest person I believe I ever met and I haven't laughed so much in I don't know how long.

For one thing he asked me if I had heard Rockefeller's song and I said no and he began singing "Oil alone." Then he asked me if I knew the orange juice song and I told him no again and he said it was "Orange juice sorry you made me cry." I was in hysterics before we had been together ten minutes.

His name is Frank Caswell and he has been out of Darthmouth a year and is 24 years old. That isn't so terribly old, only two years older than Walter and three years older than Gordon. I hate the name Frank, but Caswell is all right and he is so cute.

He was out in California last winter and visited Hollywood and met everybody in the world and it is fascinating to listen to him. He met Norma Shearer and he said he thought she was the prettiest thing he had ever seen. What he said was "I did think she was the prettiest girl in the world, till today." I was going to pretend I didn't get it, but I finally told him to be sensible or I would never be able to believe anything he said.

Well, he wanted me to dance with him tonight after dinner and the next question was how to explain how we had met each other to Uncle Nat and Aunt Jule. Frank said he would fix that all right and sure enough he got himself introduced to Uncle Nat when Uncle Nat came in from golf and after dinner Uncle Nat introduced him to me and Aunt Jule too and we danced together all evening, that is not Aunt Jule. They went to bed, thank heavens.

He is a heavenly dancer, as good as Gordon. One dance we were dancing and for one of the encores the orchestra played "Just a cottage small by a waterfall" and I simply couldn't dance to it. I just stopped still and said "Listen, I can't bear it, I can't breathe" and poor Frank thought I was sick or something and I had to explain that that was the tune the orchestra played the night I sat at the next table to Jack Barrymore at Barney Gallant's.

I made him sit out that encore and wouldn't let him talk till they got through playing it. Then they played something else and I was all right again and Frank told me about meeting Jack Barrymore. Imagine meeting him. I couldn't live.

I promised Aunt Jule I would go to bed at eleven and it is way past that now, but I am all ready for bed and have just been writing this. Tomorrow Gordon is going to call up and what will I say to him? I just won't think about it.

July 14

GORDON CALLED UP this morning from Chicago and it was wonderful to hear his voice again though the connection was terrible. He asked me if I still loved him and I tried to tell him no, but I knew that would mean an explanation and the connection was so bad that I never could make him understand so I said yes, but I almost whispered it purposely, thinking he wouldn't hear me, but he heard me all right and he said that made everything all right with the world. He said he thought I had stopped loving him because I had stopped writing.

I wish the connection had been decent and I could have told him how things were, but now it is terrible because he is planning to get to New York the day I get there and heaven knows what I will do because Walter will be there, too. I just won't think about it.

Aunt Jule came in my room just after I was through talking to Gordon, thank heavens. The room was full of flowers. Walter had sent me some and so had Frank. I got another long night letter from Walter, just as silly as the first one. I wish he would say those things in letters instead of night letters so everybody in the world wouldn't see them. Aunt Jule wanted me to read it aloud to her. I would have died.

While she was still in the room, Frank called up and asked me to play golf with him and I said all right and Aunt Jule said she was glad my headache was gone. She was trying to be funny.

I played golf with Frank this afternoon. He is a beautiful golfer and it is thrilling to watch him drive, his swing is so much more graceful than Walter's. I asked him to watch me swing and tell me what was the matter with me, but he said he couldn't look at anything but my face and there wasn't anything the matter with that.

He told me the boy who was here with him had been called home and he was glad of it because I might have liked him, the other boy, better than himself.

I told him that couldn't be possible and he asked me if I really meant that and I said of course, but I smiled when I said it so he wouldn't take it too seriously.

We danced again tonight and Uncle Nat and Aunt Jule sat with us a while and danced a couple of dances themselves, but they were really there to get better acquainted with Frank and see if he was all right for me to be with. I know they certainly couldn't have enjoyed their own dancing, no old people really can enjoy it because they can't really *do* anything. They were favorably impressed with Frank I think, at least Aunt Jule didn't say I must be in bed at eleven, but just not to stay up too late. I guess it is a big surprise to a girl's parents and aunts and uncles to find out that the boys you go around with are all right, they always seem to think that if I seem to like somebody and the person pays a little attention to me, why he must be a convict or a policeman or a drunkard or something queer.

Frank had some more songs for me tonight. He asked me if I knew the asthma song and I said I didn't and he said "Oh, you must know that. It goes yes, sir, asthma baby." Then he told me about the underwear song, "I underwear my baby is tonight." He keeps you in hysterics and yet he has his serious side, in fact he was awfully serious when he said good night to me and his eyes simply shown. I wish Walter were more like him, but I mustn't think about that.

July 15

I SIMPLY CAN'T live and I know I'll never sleep tonight. I am in a terrible predicament or rather I won't know whether I really am or not till tomorrow and that is what makes it so terrible.

After we had danced two or three dances, Frank asked me to go for a ride with him and we went for a ride in his car and he had had some cocktails and during the ride he had some drinks out of a flask and finally he told me he loved me and I said not to be silly, but he said he was perfectly serious and he certainly acted that way. He asked me if I loved anybody else and I said yes and he asked if I didn't love him more than anybody else and I said yes, but only because I thought he had probably had too much to drink and wouldn't remember it anyway and the best thing to do was humor him under the circumstances.

Then all of a sudden he asked me when I could marry him and I said, just as a joke, that I couldn't possibly marry him before December. He said that was a long time to wait, but I was certainly worth waiting for and he said a lot of other things and maybe I humored him a little too much, but that is just the trouble, I don't know.

I was absolutely sure he was tight and would forget the whole thing, but that was early in the evening, and when we said good night he was a whole lot more sober than he had been and now I am not sure how it stands. If he doesn't remember anything about it, of course I am all right. But if he does remember and if he took me seriously, I will simply have to tell him about Walter and maybe about Gordon, too. And it isn't going to be easy. The suspense is what is maddening and I know I'll never live through this night.

July 16

I CAN'T STAND it, I can't breathe, life is impossible. Frank remembered everything about last night and firmly believes we are engaged and going to be married in December. His people live in New York and he says he is going back when I do and have them meet me.

Of course it can't go on and tomorrow I will tell him about Walter or Gordon or both of them. I know it is going to hurt him terribly, perhaps spoil his life and I would give anything in the world not to have had it happen. I hate so to hurt him because he is so nice besides being so cute and attractive. He sent me the loveliest flowers this morning and called up at ten and wanted to know how soon he could see me and I hope the girl wasn't listening in because the things he said were, well, like Walter's night letters.

And that is another terrible thing, today I didn't get a night letter from Walter, but there was a regular letter instead and I carried it around in my purse all this afternoon and evening and never remembered to read it till ten minutes ago when I came up in the room. Walter is worried because I have only sent him two telegrams and written him one letter since I have been here, he would be a lot more worried if he knew what has happened now, though of course it can't make any difference because he is the one I am really engaged to be married to and the one I told mother I was going to marry in December and I wouldn't dare tell her it was somebody else.

I met Frank for lunch and we went for a ride this afternoon and he was so much in love and so lovely to me that I simply did not have the heart to tell him the truth, I am surely going to tell him tomorrow and telling him today would have just meant one more day of unhappiness for both of us.

He said his people had plenty of money and his father had offered to take him into partnership and he might accept, but he thinks his true vocation is journalism with a view to eventually writing novels and if I was willing to undergo a few hardships just at first we would probably both be happier later on if he was doing something he really liked. I didn't know what to say, but finally I said I wanted him to suit himself and money wasn't everything.

He asked me where I would like to go on my honeymoon and I suppose I ought to have told him my honeymoon was all planned, that I was going to California, with Walter, but all I said was that I had always wanted to go to California and he was enthusiastic and said that is where we would surely go and he would take me to Hollywood and introduce me to all those wonderful people he met there last winter. It nearly takes my breath away to think of it, going there with someone who really knows people and has the entrée.

We danced again tonight, just two or three dances, and then went out and sat in the tennis-court, but I came upstairs early because Aunt Jule had acted kind of funny at dinner. And I wanted to be alone, too, and think, but the more I think the worse it gets.

Sometimes I wish I were dead, maybe that is the only solution and it would be best for everyone concerned. I *will* die if things keep on the way they have been. But of course tomorrow it will be all over, with Frank I mean, for I must tell him the truth no matter how much it hurts us both. Though I don't care how much it hurts me. The thought of hurting him is what is driving me mad. I can't bear it.

July 18

I HAVE SKIPPED a day. I was busy every minute of yesterday and so exhausted when I came upstairs that I was tempted to fall into bed with all my clothes on. First Gordon called me up from Chicago to remind me that he would be in New York the day I got there and that when he comes he wants me all to himself all the time and we can make plans for our wedding. The connection was bad again and I just couldn't explain to him about Walter.

I had an engagement with Frank for lunch and just as we were going in another long distance call came, from Walter this time. He wanted to know why I haven't written more letters and sent him more telegrams and asked me if I still loved him and of course I told him yes because I really do. Then he asked if I had met any men here and I told him I had met one, a friend of Uncle Nat's. After all it was Uncle Nat who introduced me to Frank. He reminded me that he would be in New York on the 25th which is the day I expect to get home, and said he would have theater tickets for that night and we would go somewhere afterwards and dance. Frank insisted on knowing who had kept me talking so long and I told him it was a boy I had known a long while, a very dear friend of mine and a friend of my family's. Frank was jealous and kept asking questions till I thought I would go mad. He was so serious and kind of cross and gruff that I gave up the plan of telling him the truth till some time when he is in better spirits.

I played golf with Frank in the afternoon and we took a ride last night and I wanted to get in early because I had promised both Walter and Gordon that I would write them long letters, but Frank wouldn't bring me back to the Inn till I had named a definite date in December. I finally told him the 10th and he said all right if I was sure that wasn't a Sunday. I said I would have to look it up, but as a matter of fact I know the 10th falls on a Friday because the date Walter and I have agreed on for our wedding is Saturday the 11th.

Today has just been the same thing over again, two more night letters, a long distance call from Chicago, golf and a ride with Frank, and the room full of flowers. But tomorrow I am going to tell Frank and I am going to write Gordon a long letter and tell him, too, because this simply can't go on any longer. I can't breathe. I can't live.

July 21

I WROTE TO Gordon yesterday, but I didn't say anything about Walter because I don't think it is a thing a person ought to do by letter. I can tell him when he gets to New York and then I will be sure that he doesn't take it too hard and I can promise him that I will be friends with him always and make him promise not to do anything silly, while if I told it to him in a letter there is no telling what he would do, there all alone.

And I haven't told Frank because he hasn't been feeling well, he is terribly sunburned and it hurts him terribly so he can hardly play golf or dance, and I want him to be feeling his best when I do tell him, but whether he is all right or not I simply must tell him tomorrow because he is actually planning to leave here on the same train with us Saturday night and I can't let him do that.

Life is so hopeless and it could be so wonderful. For instance how heavenly it would be if I could marry Frank first and stay married to him five years and he would be the one who would take me to Hollywood and maybe we could go on parties with Norman Kerry and Jack Barrymore and Buster Collier and Marion Davies and Lois Moran.

And at the end of five years Frank could go into journalism and write novels and I would only be 23 and I could marry Gordon and he would be ready for another trip around the world and he could show me things better than someone who had never seen them before.

Gordon and I would separate at the end of five years and I would be 28 and I know of lots of women that never even got married the first time till they were 28 though I don't suppose that was their fault, but I would marry Walter then, for after all he is the one I really love and want to spend most of my life with and I wouldn't care whether he could dance or not when I was that old. Before long we would be as old as Uncle Nat and Aunt Jule and I certainly wouldn't want to dance at their age when all you can do is just hobble around the floor. But Walter is so wonderful as a companion and we would enjoy the same things and be pals and maybe we would begin to have children.

But that is all impossible though it wouldn't be if older people just had sense and would look at things the right way.

It is only half past ten, the earliest I have gone to bed in weeks, but I am worn out and Frank went to bed early so he could put cold cream on his sunburn.

Listen, diary, the orchestra is playing "Limehouse Blues." The first tune I danced to with Merle Oliver, two years ago. I can't stand it. And how funny that they should play that old tune tonight of all nights, when I have been thinking of Merle off and on all day, and I hadn't thought of him before in weeks and weeks. I wonder where he is, I wonder if it is just an accident or if it means I am going to see him again. I simply mustn't think about it or I'll die.

July 22

I KNEW IT wasn't an accident. I knew it must mean something, and it did.

Merle is coming here today, here to this Inn, and just to see me. And there can only be one reason. And only one answer. I knew that when I heard his voice calling from Boston. How could I ever had thought I loved anyone else? How could he ever have thought I meant it when I told him I was engaged to George Morse?

A whole year and he still cares and I still care. That shows we were always intended for each other and for no one else. I won't make *him* wait till December. I doubt if we even wait till dad and mother get home. And as for a honeymoon I will go with him to Long Beach or the Bronx Zoo, wherever he wants to take me.

After all this is the best way out of it, the only way. I won't have to say anything to Frank, he will guess when he sees me with Merle. And when I get home Sunday and Walter and Gordon call me up, I will invite them both to dinner and Merle can tell them himself, with two of them there it will only hurt each one half as much as if they were alone.

The train is due at 2:40, almost three hours from now. I can't wait. And what if it should be late? I can't stand it.

THE SHORT HAPPY LIFE OF FRANCIS MACOMBER

ERNEST HEMINGWAY

It was now lunch time and they were all sitting under the double green fly of the dining tent pretending that nothing had happened.

"Will you have lime juice or lemon squash?" Macomber asked.

"I'll have a gimlet," Robert Wilson told him.

"I'll have a gimlet too. I need something," Macomber's wife said.

"I suppose it's the thing to do," Macomber agreed. "Tell him to make three gimlets."

The mess boy had started them already, lifting the bottles out of the canvas cooling bags that sweated wet in the wind that blew through the trees that shaded the tents.

"What had I ought to give them?" Macomber asked.

"A quid would be plenty," Wilson told him. "You don't want to spoil them."

"Will the headman distribute it?"

"Absolutely."

Francis Macomber had, half an hour before, been carried to his tent from the edge of the camp in triumph on the arms and shoulders of the cook, the personal boys, the skinner and the porters. The gun-bearers had taken no part in the demonstration. When the native boys put him down at the door of his tent, he had shaken all their hands, received their congratulations, and then gone into the tent and sat on the bed until his wife came in. She did not speak to him when she came in and he left the tent at once to wash his face and hands in the portable wash basin outside and go over to the dining tent to sit in a comfortable canvas chair in the breeze and the shade.

"You've got your lion," Robert Wilson said to him, "and a damned fine one too."

Mrs. Macomber looked at Wilson quickly. She was an extremely handsome and well-kept woman of the beauty and social position which had, five years before, commanded five thousand dollars as the price of endorsing, with photographs, a beauty product which she had never used. She had been married to Francis Macomber for eleven years.

"He is a good lion, isn't he?" Macomber said. His wife looked at him now. She looked at both these men as though she had never seen them before.

One, Wilson, the white hunter, she knew she had never truly seen before. He was about middle height with sandy hair, a stubby mustache, a very red face and extremely cold blue eyes with faint white wrinkles at the corners that grooved merrily when he smiled. He smiled at her now and she looked away from his face at the way his shoulders sloped in the loose tunic he wore with the four big cartridges held in loops where the left breast pocket should have been, at his big brown hands, his old slacks, his very dirty boots and back to his red face again. She noticed where the baked red of his face stopped in a white line that marked the circle left by his Stetson hat that hung now from one of the pegs of the tent pole.

"Well, here's to the lion," Robert Wilson said. He smiled at her again and, not smiling, she looked curiously at her husband.

Francis Macomber was very tall, very well built if you did not mind that length of bone, dark, his hair cropped like an oarsman, rather thin-lipped, and was considered handsome. He was dressed in the same sort of safari clothes that Wilson wore except that his were new, he was thirty-five years old, kept himself very fit, was good at court games, had a number of big-game fishing records, and had just shown himself, very publicly, to be a coward.

"Here's to the lion," he said. "I can't ever thank you for what you did."

Margaret, his wife, looked away from him and back to Wilson.

"Let's not talk about the lion," she said.

Wilson looked over at her without smiling and now she smiled at him.

"It's been a very strange day," she said. "Hadn't you ought to put your hat on even under the canvas at noon? You told me that, you know."

"Might put it on," said Wilson.

"You know you have a very red face, Mr. Wilson," she told him and smiled again.

"Drink," said Wilson.

"I don't think so," she said. "Francis drinks a great deal, but his face is never red."

"It's red today," Macomber tried a joke.

"No," said Margaret. "It's mine that's red today. But Mr. Wilson's is always red."

"Must be racial," said Wilson. "I say, you wouldn't like to drop my beauty as a topic, would you?"

"I've just started on it."

"Let's chuck it," said Wilson.

"Conversation is going to be so difficult," Margaret said.

"Don't be silly, Margot," her husband said.

"No difficulty," Wilson said. "Got a damn fine lion."

Margot looked at them both and they both saw that she was going to cry. Wilson had seen it coming for a long time and he dreaded it. Macomber was past dreading it.

"I wish it hadn't happened. Oh, I wish it hadn't happened," she said and started for her tent. She made no noise of crying but they could see that her shoulders were shaking under the rose-colored, sun-proofed shirt she wore.

"Women upset," said Wilson to the tall man. "Amounts to nothing. Strain on the nerves and one thing'n another."

"No," said Macomber. "I suppose that I rate that for the rest of my life now."

"Nonsense. Let's have a spot of the giant killer," said Wilson. "Forget the whole thing. Nothing to it anyway."

"We might try," said Macomber. "I won't forget what you did for me though."

"Nothing," said Wilson. "All nonsense."

So they sat there in the shade where the camp was pitched under some wide-topped acacia trees with a boulder-strewn cliff behind them, and a stretch of grass that ran to the bank of a boulder-filled stream in front with forest beyond it, and drank their just-cool lime drinks and avoided one another's eyes while the boys set the table for lunch. Wilson could tell that the boys all knew about it now and when he saw Macomber's personal boy looking curiously at his master while he was putting dishes on the table he snapped at him in Swahili. The boy turned away with his face blank.

"What were you telling him?" Macomber asked.

"Nothing. Told him to look alive or I'd see he got about fifteen of the best."

"What's that? Lashes?"

"It's quite illegal," Wilson said. "You're supposed to fine them."

"Do you still have them whipped?"

"Oh, yes. They could raise a row if they chose to complain. But they don't. They prefer it to the fines."

"How strange!" said Macomber.

"Not strange, really," Wilson said. "Which would you rather do? Take a good birching or lose your pay?"

Then he felt embarrassed at asking it and before Macomber could answer he went on, "We all take a beating every day, you know, one way or another."

This was no better. Good God, he thought. I am a diplomat, aren't I?

"Yes, we take a beating," said Macomber, still not looking at him. "I'm awfully sorry about that lion business. It doesn't have to go any further, does it? I mean no one will hear about it, will they?"

"You mean will I tell it at the Mathaiga Club?" Wilson looked at him now coldly. He had not expected this. So he's a bloody four-letter man as well as a bloody coward, he thought. I rather liked him too until today. But how is one to know about an American?

"No," said Wilson. "I'm a professional hunter. We never talk about our clients. You can be quite easy on that. It's supposed to be bad form to ask us not to talk though."

He had decided now that to break would be much easier. He would eat, then, by himself and could read a book with his meals. They would eat by themselves. He would see them through the safari on a very formal basis—what was it the French called it? Distinguished consideration—and it would be a damn sight easier than having to go through this emotional trash. He'd insult him and make a good clean break. Then he could read a book with his meals and he'd still be drinking their whisky. That was the phrase for it when a safari went bad. You ran into another white hunter and you asked, "How is everything going?" and he answered, "Oh, I'm still drinking their whisky," and you knew everything had gone to pot.

"I'm sorry," Macomber said and looked at him with his American face that would stay adolescent until it became middle-aged, and Wilson noted his crew-cropped hair, fine eyes only faintly shifty, good nose, thin lips and handsome jaw. "I'm sorry I didn't realize that. There are lots of things I don't know."

So what could he do, Wilson thought. He was all ready to break it off quickly and neatly and here the beggar was apologizing after he had just insulted him. He made one more attempt. "Don't worry about me talking," he said. "I have a living to make. You know in Africa no woman ever misses her lion and no white man ever bolts."

"I bolted like a rabbit," Macomber said.

Now what in hell were you going to do about a man who talked like that, Wilson wondered.

Wilson looked at Macomber with his flat, blue, machine-gunner's eyes and the other smiled back at him. He had a pleasant smile if you did not notice how his eyes showed when he was hurt.

"Maybe I can fix it up on buffalo," he said. "We're after them next, aren't we?"

"In the morning if you like," Wilson told him. Perhaps he had been wrong. This was certainly the way to take it. You most certainly could not tell a damned thing about an American. He was all for Macomber again. If you could forget the morning. But, of course, you couldn't. The morning had been about as bad as they come.

"Here comes the Memsahib," he said. She was walking over from her tent looking refreshed and cheerful and quite lovely. She had a very perfect oval face, so perfect that you expected her to be stupid. But she wasn't stupid, Wilson thought, no, not stupid.

"How is the beautiful red-faced Mr. Wilson? Are you feeling better, Francis, my pearl?"

"Oh, much," said Macomber.

"I've dropped the whole thing," she said, sitting down at the table. "What importance is there to whether Francis is any good at killing lions? That's not his trade. That's Mr. Wilson's trade. Mr. Wilson is really very impressive killing anything. You do kill anything, don't you?"

"Oh, anything," said Wilson. "Simply anything." They are, he thought, the hardest in the world; the hardest, the cruelest, the most predatory and the most attractive and their men have softened or gone to pieces nervously as they have hardened. Or is it that they pick men they can handle? They can't know that much at the age they marry, he thought. He was grateful that he had gone through his education on American women before now because this was a very attractive one.

"We're going after buff in the morning," he told her.

"I'm coming," she said.

"No, you're not."

"Oh, yes, I am. Mayn't I, Francis?"

"Why not stay in camp?"

"Not for anything," she said. "I wouldn't miss something like today for anything."

When she left, Wilson was thinking, when she went off to cry, she seemed a hell of a fine woman. She seemed to understand, to realize, to be hurt for him and for herself and to know how things really stood. She is away for twenty minutes and now she is back, simply enamelled in that American female cruelty. They are the damnedest women. Really the damnedest.

"We'll put on another show for you tomorrow," Francis Macomber said.

"You're not coming," Wilson said.

"You're very mistaken," she told him. "And I want *so* to see you perform again. You were lovely this morning. That is if blowing things' heads off is lovely."

"Here's the lunch," said Wilson. "You're very merry, aren't you?"

"Why not? I didn't come out here to be dull."

"Well, it hasn't been dull," Wilson said. He could see the boulders in the river and the high bank beyond with the trees and he remembered the morning.

"Oh, no," she said. "It's been charming. And tomorrow. You don't know how I look forward to tomorrow."

"That's eland he's offering you," Wilson said.

"They're the big cowy things that jump like hares, aren't they?"

"I suppose that describes them," Wilson said.

"It's very good meat," Macomber said.

"Did you shoot it, Francis?" she asked.

"Yes."

"They're not dangerous, are they?"

"Only if they fall on you," Wilson told her.

"I'm so glad."

"Why not let up on the bitchery just a little, Margot," Macomber said, cutting the eland steak and putting some mashed potato, gravy and carrot on the down-turned fork that tined through the piece of meat.

"I suppose I could," she said, "since you put it so prettily."

"Tonight we'll have champagne for the lion," Wilson said. "It's a bit too hot at noon."

"Oh, the lion," Margot said. "I'd forgotten the lion!"

So, Robert Wilson thought to himself, she *is* giving him a ride, isn't she? Or do you suppose that's her idea of putting up a good show? How should a woman act when she discovers her husband is a bloody coward? She's damned cruel but they're all cruel. They govern, of course, and to govern one has to be cruel sometimes. Still, I've seen enough of their damn terrorism.

"Have some more eland," he said to her politely.

That afternoon, late, Wilson and Macomber went out in the motor car with the native driver and the two gun-bearers. Mrs. Macomber stayed in the camp. It was too hot to go out, she said, and she was going with them in the early morning.

As they drove off Wilson saw her standing under the big tree, looking pretty rather than beautiful in her faintly rosy khaki, her dark hair drawn back off her forehead and gathered in a knot low on her neck, her face as fresh, he thought, as though she were in England. She waved to them as the car went off through the swale of high grass and curved around through the trees into the small hills of orchard bush.

In the orchard bush they found a herd of impala, and leaving the car they stalked one old ram with long, wide-spread horns and Macomber killed it with a very creditable shot that knocked the buck down at a good two hundred yards and sent the herd off bounding wildly and leaping over one another's backs in long, leg-drawn-up leaps as unbelievable and as floating as those one makes sometimes in dreams.

"That was a good shot," Wilson said. "They're a small target."

"Is it a worth-while head?" Macomber asked.

"It's excellent," Wilson told him. "You shoot like that and you'll have no trouble."

"Do you think we'll find buffalo tomorrow?"

"There's a good chance of it. They feed out early in the morning and with luck we may catch them in the open."

"I'd like to clear away that lion business," Macomber said. "It's not very pleasant to have your wife see you do something like that."

I should think it would be even more unpleasant to do it, Wilson thought, wife or no wife, or to talk about it having done it. But he said, "I wouldn't think about that any more. Any one could be upset by his first lion. That's all over."

But that night after dinner and a whisky and soda by the fire before going to bed, as Francis Macomber lay on his cot with the mosquito bar over him and listened to the night noises it was not all over. It was neither all over nor was it beginning. It was there exactly as it happened with some parts of it indelibly emphasized and he was miserably ashamed at it. But more than shame he felt cold, hollow fear in him. The fear was still there like a cold slimy hollow in all the emptiness where once his confidence had been and it made him feel sick. It was still there with him now.

It had started the night before when he had wakened and heard the lion roaring somewhere up along the river. It was a deep sound and at the end there were sort of coughing grunts that made him seem just outside the tent, and when Francis Macomber woke in the night to hear it he was afraid. He could hear his wife breathing quietly, asleep. There was no one to tell he was afraid, nor to be afraid with him, and, lying alone, he did not know the Somali proverb that says a brave man is always frightened three times by a lion; when he first sees his track, when he first hears him roar and when he first confronts him. Then while they were eating breakfast by lantern light out in the dining tent, before the sun was up, the lion roared again and Francis thought he was just at the edge of camp.

"Sounds like an old-timer," Robert Wilson said, looking up from his kippers and coffee. "Listen to him cough."

"Is he very close?"

"A mile or so up the stream."

"Will we see him?"

"We'll have a look."

"Does his roaring carry that far? It sounds as though he were right in camp."

"Carries a hell of a long way," said Robert Wilson. "It's strange the way it carries. Hope he's a shootable cat. The boys said there was a very big one about here."

"If I get a shot, where should I hit him," Macomber asked, "to stop him?"

"In the shoulders," Wilson said. "In the neck if you can make it. Shoot for bone. Break him down."

"I hope I can place it properly," Macomber said.

"You shoot very well," Wilson told him. "Take your time. Make sure of him. The first one in is the one that counts."

"What range will it be?"

"Can't tell. Lion has something to say about that. Don't shoot unless it's close enough so you can make sure."

"At under a hundred yards?" Macomber asked.

Wilson looked at him quickly.

"Hundred's about right. Might have to take him a bit under. Shouldn't chance a shot at much over that. A hundred's a decent range. You can hit him whenever you want at that. Here comes the Memsahib."

"Good morning," she said. "Are we going after that lion?"

"As soon as you deal with your breakfast," Wilson said. "How are you feeling?"

"Marvellous," she said. "I'm very excited."

"I'll just go and see that everything is ready." Wilson went off. As he left the lion roared again.

"Noisy beggar," Wilson said. "We'll put a stop to that."

"What's the matter, Francis?" his wife asked him.

"Nothing," Macomber said.

"Yes, there is," she said. "What are you upset about?"

"Nothing," he said.

"Tell me." She looked at him. "Don't you feel well?"

"It's that damned roaring," he said. "It's been going on all night, you know."

"Why didn't you wake me?" she said. "I'd love to have heard it."

"I've got to kill the damned thing," Macomber said, miserably.

"Well, that's what you're out here for, isn't it?"

"Yes. But I'm nervous. Hearing the thing roar gets on my nerves."

"Well then, as Wilson said, kill him and stop his roaring."

"Yes, darling," said Francis Macomber. "It sounds easy, doesn't it?"

"You're not afraid, are you?"

"Of course not. But I'm nervous from hearing him roar all night."

"You'll kill him marvellously," she said. "I know you will. I'm awfully anxious to see it."

"Finish your breakfast and we'll be starting."

"It's not light yet," she said. "This is a ridiculous hour."

Just then the lion roared in a deep-chested moaning, suddenly guttural, ascending vibration that seemed to shake the air and ended in a sigh and a heavy, deep-chested grunt.

"He sounds almost here," Macomber's wife said.

"My God," said Macomber. "I hate that damned noise."

"It's very impressive."

"Impressive. It's frightful."

Robert Wilson came up then carrying his short, ugly, shockingly big-bored .505 Gibbs and grinning.

"Come on," he said. "Your gun-bearer has your Springfield and the big gun. Everything's in the car. Have you solids?"

"Yes."

"I'm ready," Mrs. Macomber said.

"Must make him stop that racket," Wilson said. "You get in front. The Memsahib can sit back here with me."

They climbed into the motor car and, in the gray first daylight, moved off up the river through the trees. Macomber opened the breech of his rifle and saw he had metal-cased bullets, shut the bolt and put the rifle on safety. He saw his hand was trembling. He felt in his pocket for more cartridges and moved his fingers over the cartridges in the loops of his tunic front. He turned back to where Wilson sat in the rear seat of the doorless, box-bodied motor car beside his wife, them both grinning with excitement, and Wilson leaned forward and whispered,

"See the birds dropping. Means the old boy has left his kill."

On the far bank of the stream Macomber could see, above the trees, vultures circling and plummeting down.

"Chances are he'll come to drink along here," Wilson whispered. "Before he goes to lay up. Keep an eye out."

They were driving slowly along the high bank of the stream which here cut deeply to its boulder-filled bed, and they wound in and out through big trees as they drove. Macomber was watching the opposite bank when he felt Wilson take hold of his arm. The car stopped.

"There he is," he heard the whisper. "Ahead and to the right. Get out and take him. He's a marvellous lion."

Macomber saw the lion now. He was standing almost broadside, his great head up and turned toward them. The early morning breeze that blew toward them was just stirring his dark mane, and the lion looked huge, silhouetted on the rise of bank in the gray morning light, his shoulders heavy, his barrel of a body bulking smoothly.

"How far is he?" asked Macomber, raising his rifle.

"About seventy-five. Get out and take him."

"Why not shoot from where I am?"

"You don't shoot them from cars," he heard Wilson saying in his ear. "Get out. He's not going to stay there all day."

Macomber stepped out of the curved opening at the side of the front seat, onto the step and down onto the ground. The lion still stood looking majestically and coolly toward this object that his eyes only showed in silhouette, bulking like some super-rhino. There was no man smell carried toward him and he watched the object, moving his great head a little from side to side. Then watching the object, not afraid, but hesitating before going down the bank to drink with such a thing opposite him, he saw a man figure detach itself from it and he turned his heavy head and swung away toward the cover of the trees as he heard a cracking crash and felt the slam of a .30-06 220-grain solid bullet that bit his flank and ripped in sudden hot scalding nausea through his stomach. He trotted, heavy, big-footed, swinging wounded, full-bellied, through the trees toward the tall grass and cover, and the crash came again to go past him ripping the air apart. Then it crashed again and he felt the blow as it hit his lower ribs and ripped on through, blood sudden hot and frothy in his mouth, and he galloped toward the high grass where he could crouch and not be seen and make them bring the crashing thing close enough so he could make a rush and get the man that held it.

Macomber had not thought how the lion felt as he got out of the car. He only knew his hands were shaking and as he walked away from the car it was almost impossible for him to make his legs move. They were stiff in the thighs, but he could feel the muscles fluttering. He raised the rifle, sighted on the junction of the lion's head and shoulders and pulled the trigger. Nothing happened though he pulled until he thought his finger would break. Then he knew he had the safety on and as he lowered the rifle to move the safety over he moved another frozen pace forward, and the lion seeing his silhouette now clear of the silhouette of the car, turned and started off at a trot, and, as Macomber fired, he heard a whunk that meant that the bullet was home; but the lion kept on going. Macomber shot again and every one saw the bullet throw a spout of dirt beyond the trotting lion. He shot again, remembering to lower his aim, and they all heard the bullet hit, and the lion went into a gallop and was in the tall grass before he had the bolt pushed forward.

Macomber stood there feeling sick at his stomach, his hands that held the Springfield still cocked, shaking, and his wife and Robert Wilson were standing by him. Beside him too were the two gun-bearers chattering in Wakamba.

"I hit him," Macomber said. "I hit him twice."

"You gut-shot him and you hit him somewhere forward," Wilson said without enthusiasm. The gun-bearers looked very grave. They were silent now.

"You may have killed him," Wilson went on. "We'll have to wait a while before we go in to find out."

"What do you mean?"

"Let him get sick before we follow him up."

"Oh," said Macomber.

"He's a hell of a fine lion," Wilson said cheerfully. "He's gotten into a bad place though."

"Why is it bad?"

"Can't see him until you're on him."

"Oh," said Macomber.

"Come on," said Wilson. "The Memsahib can stay here in the car. We'll go to have a look at the blood spoor."

"Stay here, Margot," Macomber said to his wife. His mouth was very dry and it was hard for him to talk.

"Why?" she asked.

"Wilson says to."

"We're going to have a look," Wilson said. "You stay here. You can see even better from here."

"All right."

Wilson spoke in Swahili to the driver. He nodded and said, "Yes, Bwana."

Then they went down the steep bank and across the stream, climbing over and around the boulders and up the other bank, pulling up by some projecting roots, and along it until they found where the lion had been trotting when Macomber first shot. There was dark blood on the short grass that the gun-bearers pointed out with grass stems, and that ran away behind the river bank trees.

"What do we do?" asked Macomber.

"Not much choice," said Wilson. "We can't bring the car over. Bank's too steep. We'll let him stiffen up a bit and then you and I'll go in and have a look for him."

"Can't we set the grass on fire?" Macomber asked.

"Too green."

"Can't we send beaters?"

Wilson looked at him appraisingly. "Of course we can," he said. "But it's just a touch murderous. You see, we know the lion's wounded. You can drive an unwounded lion—he'll move on ahead of a noise—but a wounded lion's going to charge. You can't see him until you're right on him. He'll make himself perfectly flat in cover you wouldn't think would hide a hare. You can't very well send boys in there to that sort of a show. Somebody bound to get mauled."

"What about the gun-bearers?"

"Oh, they'll go with us. It's their *shauri*. You see, they signed on for it. They don't look too happy though, do they?"

"I don't want to go in there," said Macomber. It was out before he knew he'd said it.

"Neither do I," said Wilson very cheerily. "Really no choice though." Then, as an afterthought, he glanced at Macomber and saw suddenly how he was trembling and the pitiful look on his face.

"You don't have to go in, of course," he said. "That's what I'm hired for, you know. That's why I'm so expensive."

"You mean you'd go in by yourself? Why not leave him there?"

Robert Wilson, whose entire occupation had been with the lion and the problem he presented, and who had not been thinking about Macomber except to note that he was rather windy, suddenly felt as though he had opened the wrong door in a hotel and seen something shameful.

"What do you mean?"

"Why not just leave him?"

"You mean pretend to ourselves he hasn't been hit?"

"No. Just drop it."

"It isn't done."

"Why not?"

"For one thing, he's certain to be suffering. For another, some one else might run onto him."

"I see."

"But you don't have to have anything to do with it."

"I'd like to," Macomber said. "I'm just scared, you know."

"I'll go ahead when we go in," Wilson said, "with Kongoni tracking. You keep behind me and a little to one side. Chances are we'll hear him growl. If we see him we'll both shoot. Don't worry about anything. I'll keep you backed up. As a matter of fact, you know, perhaps you'd better not go. It might be much better. Why don't you go over and join the Memsahib while I just get it over with?"

"No, I want to go."

"All right," said Wilson. "But don't go in if you don't want to. This is my *shauri* now, you know."

"I want to go," said Macomber.

They sat under a tree and smoked.

"Want to go back and speak to the Memsahib while we're waiting?" Wilson asked.

"No."

"I'll just step back and tell her to be patient."

"Good," said Macomber. He sat there, sweating under his arms, his mouth dry, his stomach hollow feeling, wanting to find courage to tell Wilson to go on and finish off the lion without him. He could not know that Wilson was furious because he had not noticed the state he was in earlier and sent him back to his wife. While he sat there Wilson came up. "I have your big gun," he said. "Take it. We've given him time, I think. Come on."

Macomber took the big gun and Wilson said:

"Keep behind me and about five yards to the right and do exactly as I tell you." Then he spoke in Swahili to the two gun-bearers who looked the picture of gloom.

"Let's go," he said.

"Could I have a drink of water?" Macomber asked. Wilson spoke to the older gun-bearer, who wore a canteen on his belt, and the man unbuckled it, unscrewed the top and handed it to Macomber, who took it noticing how heavy it seemed and how hairy and shoddy the felt covering was in his hand. He raised it to drink and looked ahead at the high grass with the flat-topped trees behind it. A breeze was blowing toward them and the grass rippled gently in the wind. He looked at the gun-bearer and he could see the gun-bearer was suffering too with fear.

Thirty-five yards into the grass the big lion lay flattened out along the ground. His ears were back and his only movement was a slight twitching up and down of his long, black-tufted tail. He had turned at bay as soon as he had reached this cover and he was sick with the wound through his full belly, and weakening with the wound through his lungs that brought a thin foamy red to his mouth each time he breathed. His flanks were wet and hot and flies were on the little openings the solid bullets had made in his tawny hide, and his big yellow eyes, narrowed with hate, looked straight ahead, only blinking when the pain came as he breathed, and his claws dug in the soft baked earth. All of him, pain, sickness, hatred and all of his remaining strength, was tightening into an absolute concentration for a rush. He could hear the men talking and he waited, gathering all of himself into this preparation for a charge as soon as the men would come into the grass. As he heard their voices his tail stiffened to twitch up and down, and, as they came into the edge of the grass, he made a coughing grunt and charged.

Kongoni, the old gun-bearer, in the lead watching the blood spoor, Wilson watching the grass for any movement, his big gun ready, the second gun-bearer looking ahead and listening, Macomber close to Wilson, his rifle cocked, they had just moved into the grass when Macomber heard the blood-choked coughing grunt, and saw the swishing rush in the grass. The next thing he knew he was running; running wildly, in panic in the open, running toward the stream.

He heard the *ca-ra-wong!* of Wilson's big rifle, and again in a second crashing *carawong!* and turning saw the lion, horrible-looking now, with half his head seeming to be gone, crawling toward Wilson in the edge of the tall grass while the red-faced man worked the bolt on the short ugly rifle and aimed carefully as another blasting *carawong!* came from the muzzle, and the crawling, heavy, yellow bulk of the lion stiffened and the huge, mutilated head slid forward and Macomber, standing by himself in the clearing where he had run, holding a loaded rifle, while two black men and a white man looked back at him in contempt, knew the lion was dead. He came toward Wilson, his tallness all seeming a naked reproach, and Wilson looked at him and said:

"Want to take pictures?"

"No," he said.

That was all any one had said until they reached the motor car. Then Wilson had said:

"Hell of a fine lion. Boys will skin him out. We might as well stay here in the shade."

Macomber's wife had not looked at him nor he at her and he had sat by her in the back seat with Wilson sitting in the front seat. Once he had reached over and taken his wife's hand without looking at her and she had removed her hand from his. Looking across the stream to where the gun-bearers were skinning out the lion he could see that she had been able to see the whole thing. While they sat there his wife had reached forward and put her hand on Wilson's shoulder. He turned and she had leaned forward over the low seat and kissed him on the mouth.

"Oh, I say," said Wilson, going redder than his natural baked color.

"Mr. Robert Wilson," she said. "The beautiful red-faced Mr. Robert Wilson."

Then she sat down beside Macomber again and looked away across the stream to where the lion lay, with uplifted, white-muscled, tendon-marked naked forearms, and white bloating belly, as the black men fleshed away the skin. Finally the gun-bearers brought the skin over, wet and heavy, and climbed in behind with it, rolling it up before they got in, and the motor car started. No one had said anything more until they were back in camp.

That was the story of the lion. Macomber did not know how the lion had felt before he started his rush, nor during it when the unbelievable smash of the .505 with a muzzle velocity of two tons had hit him in the mouth, nor what kept him coming after that, when the second ripping crash had smashed his hind quarters and he had come crawling on toward the crashing, blasting thing that had destroyed him. Wilson knew something about it and only expressed it by saying, "Damned fine lion," but Macomber did not know how Wilson felt about things either. He did not know how his wife felt except that she was through with him.

His wife had been through with him before but it never lasted. He was very wealthy, and would be much wealthier, and he knew she would not leave him ever now. That was one of the few things that he really knew. He knew about that, about motor cycles—that was earliest—about motor cars, about duck-shooting, about fishing, trout, salmon and big-sea, about sex in books, many books, too many books, about all court games, about dogs, not much about horses, about hanging on to his money, about most of the other things his world dealt in, and about his wife not leaving him. His wife had been a great beauty and she was still a great beauty in Africa, but she was not a great enough beauty any more at home to be able to leave him and better herself and she knew it and he knew it. She had missed the chance to leave him and he knew it. If he had been better with women she would probably have started to worry about him getting another new, beautiful wife; but she knew too much about him to worry about him either. Also, he had always had a great tolerance which seemed the nicest thing about him if it were not the most sinister.

All in all they were known as a comparatively happily married couple, one of those whose disruption is often rumored but never occurs, and as the society columnist put it, they were adding more than a spice of *adventure* to their much envied and ever-enduring *Romance* by a *Safari* in what was known as *Darkest Africa* until the Martin Johnsons lighted it on so many silver screens where they were pursuing *Old Simba* the lion, the buffalo, *Tembo* the elephant and as well collecting specimens for the Museum of Natural History. This same columnist had reported them *on the verge* at least three times in the past and they had been. But they always made it up. They had a sound basis of union. Margot was too beautiful for Macomber to divorce her and Macomber had too much money for Margot ever to leave him.

It was now about three o'clock in the morning and Francis Macomber, who had been asleep a little while after he had stopped thinking about the lion, wakened and then slept again, woke suddenly, frightened in a dream of the bloody-headed lion standing over him, and listening while his heart pounded, he realized that his wife was not in the other cot in the tent. He lay awake with that knowledge for two hours.

At the end of that time his wife came into the tent, lifted her mosquito bar and crawled cozily into bed.

"Where have you been?" Macomber asked in the darkness.

"Hello," she said. "Are you awake?"

"Where have you been?"

"I just went out to get a breath of air."

"You did, like hell."

"What do you want me to say, darling?"

"Where have you been?"

"Out to get a breath of air."

"That's a new name for it. You *are* a bitch."

"Well, you're a coward."

"All right," he said. "What of it?"

"Nothing as far as I'm concerned. But please let's not talk, darling, because I'm very sleepy."

"You think that I'll take anything."

"I know you will, sweet."

"Well, I won't."

"Please, darling, let's not talk. I'm so very sleepy."

"There wasn't going to be any of that. You promised there wouldn't be."

"Well, there is now," she said sweetly.

"You said if we made this trip that there would be none of that. You promised."

"Yes, darling. That's the way I meant it to be. But the trip was spoiled yesterday. We don't have to talk about it, do we?"

"You don't wait long when you have an advantage, do you?"

"Please let's not talk. I'm so sleepy, darling."

"I'm going to talk."

"Don't mind me then, because I'm going to sleep." And she did.

At breakfast they were all three at the table before daylight and Francis Macomber found that, of all the many men that he had hated, he hated Robert Wilson the most.

"Sleep well?" Wilson asked in his throaty voice, filling a pipe.

"Did you?"

"Topping," the white hunter told him.

You bastard, thought Macomber, you insolent bastard.

So she woke him when she came in, Wilson thought, looking at them both with his flat, cold eyes. Well, why doesn't he keep his wife where she belongs? What does he think I am, a bloody plaster saint? Let him keep her where she belongs. It's his own fault.

"Do you think we'll find buffalo?" Margot asked, pushing away a dish of apricots.

"Chance of it," Wilson said and smiled at her. "Why don't you stay in camp?"

"Not for anything," she told him.

"Why not order her to stay in camp?" Wilson said to Macomber.

"You order her," said Macomber coldly.

"Let's not have any ordering, nor," turning to Macomber, "any silliness, Francis," Margot said quite pleasantly.

"Are you ready to start?" Macomber asked.

"Any time," Wilson told him. "Do you want the Memsahib to go?"

"Does it make any difference whether I do or not?"

The hell with it, thought Robert Wilson. The utter complete hell with it. So this is what it's going to be like. Well, this is what it's going to be like, then.

"Makes no difference," he said.

"You're sure you wouldn't like to stay in camp with her yourself and let me go out and hunt the buffalo?" Macomber asked.

"Can't do that," said Wilson. "Wouldn't talk rot if I were you."

"I'm not talking rot. I'm disgusted."

"Bad word, disgusted."

"Francis, will you please try to speak sensibly?" his wife said.

"I speak too damned sensibly," Macomber said. "Did you ever eat such filthy food?"

"Something wrong with the food?" asked Wilson quietly.

"No more than with everything else."

"I'd pull yourself together, laddybuck," Wilson said very quietly. "There's a boy waits at table that understands a little English."

"The hell with him."

Wilson stood up and puffing on his pipe strolled away, speaking a few words in Swahili to one of the gun-bearers who was standing waiting for him. Macomber and his wife sat on at the table. He was staring at his coffee cup.

"If you make a scene I'll leave you, darling," Margot said quietly.

"No, you won't."

"You can try it and see."

"You won't leave me."

"No," she said. "I won't leave you and you'll behave yourself."

"Behave myself? That's a way to talk. Behave myself."

"Yes. Behave yourself."

"Why don't *you* try behaving?"

"I've tried it so long. So very long."

"I hate that red-faced swine," Macomber said. "I loathe the sight of him."

"He's really *very* nice."

"Oh, *shut up*," Macomber almost shouted. Just then the car came up and stopped in front of the dining tent and the driver and the two gun-bearers got out. Wilson walked over and looked at the husband and wife sitting there at the table.

"Going shooting?" he asked.

"Yes," said Macomber, standing up. "Yes."

"Better bring a woolly. It will be cool in the car," Wilson said.

"I'll get my leather jacket," Margot said.

"The boy has it," Wilson told her. He climbed into the front with the driver and Francis Macomber and his wife sat, not speaking, in the back seat.

Hope the silly beggar doesn't take a notion to blow the back of my head off, Wilson thought to himself. Women *are* a nuisance on safari.

The car was grinding down to cross the river at a pebbly ford in the gray daylight and then climbed, angling up the steep bank, where Wilson had ordered a way shovelled out the day before so they could reach the parklike wooded rolling country on the far side.

It was a good morning, Wilson thought. There was a heavy dew and as the wheels went through the grass and low bushes he could smell the odor of the crushed fronds. It was an odor like verbena and he liked this early morning smell of the dew, the crushed bracken and the look of the tree trunks showing black through the early morning mist, as the car made its way through the untracked, parklike country. He had put the two in the back seat out of his mind now and was thinking about buffalo. The buffalo that he was after stayed in the daytime in a thick swamp where it was impossible to get a shot, but in the night they fed out into an open stretch of country and if he could come between them and their swamp with the car, Macomber would have a good chance at them in the open. He did not want to hunt buff with Macomber in thick cover. He did not want to hunt buff or anything else with Macomber at all, but he was a professional hunter and he had hunted with some rare ones in his time. If they got buff today there would only be rhino to come and the poor man would have gone through his dangerous game and things might pick up. He'd have nothing more to do with the woman and Macomber would get over that too. He must have gone through plenty of that before by the look of things. Poor beggar. He must have a way of getting over it. Well, it was the poor sod's own bloody fault.

He, Robert Wilson, carried a double size cot on safari to accommodate any windfalls he might receive. He had hunted for a certain clientele, the international, fast, sporting set, where the women did not feel they were getting their money's worth unless they had shared that cot with the white hunter. He despised them when he was away from them although he liked some of them well enough at the time, but he made his living by them; and their standards were his standards as long as they were hiring him.

They were his standards in all except the shooting. He had his own standards about the killing and they could live up to them or get some one else to hunt them. He knew, too, that they all respected him for this. This Macomber was an odd one though. Damned if he wasn't. Now the wife. Well, the wife. Yes, the wife. Hm, the wife. Well he'd dropped all that. He looked around at them. Macomber sat grim and furious. Margot smiled at him. She looked younger today, more innocent and fresher and not so professionally beautiful. What's in her heart God knows, Wilson thought. She hadn't talked much last night. At that it was a pleasure to see her.

The motor car climbed up a slight rise and went on through the trees and then out into a grassy prairie-like opening and kept in the shelter of the trees along the edge, the driver going slowly and Wilson looking carefully out across the prairie and all along its far side. He stopped the car and studied the opening with his field glasses. Then he motioned to the driver to go on and the car moved slowly along, the driver avoiding wart-hog holes and driving around the mud castles ants had built. Then, looking across the opening, Wilson suddenly turned and said,

"By God, there they are!"

And looking where he pointed, while the car jumped forward and Wilson spoke in rapid Swahili to the driver, Macomber saw three huge, black animals looking almost cylindrical in their long heaviness, like big black tank cars, moving at a gallop across the far edge of the open prairie. They moved at a stiff-necked, stiff-bodied gallop and he could see the upswept wide black horns on their heads as they galloped heads out; the heads not moving.

"They're three old bulls," Wilson said. "We'll cut them off before they get to the swamp."

The car was going a wild forty-five miles an hour across the open and as Macomber watched, the buffalo got bigger and bigger until he could see the gray, hairless, scabby look of one huge bull and how his neck was a part of his shoulders and the shiny black of his horns as he galloped a little behind the others that were strung out in that steady plunging gait; and then, the car swaying as though it had just jumped a road, they drew up close and he could see the plunging hugeness of the bull, and the dust in his sparsely haired hide, the wide boss of horn and his outstretched, wide-nostrilled muzzle, and he was raising his rifle when Wilson shouted, "Not from the car, you fool!" and he had no fear, only hatred of Wilson, while the brakes clamped on and the car skidded, plowing sideways to an almost stop and Wilson was out on one side and he on the other, stumbling as his feet hit the still speeding-by of the earth, and then he was shooting at the bull as he moved away, hearing the bullets whunk into him, emptying his rifle at him as he moved steadily away, finally remembering to get his shots forward into the shoulder, and as he fumbled to re-load, he saw the bull was down. Down on his knees, his big head tossing, and seeing the other two still galloping he shot at the leader and hit him. He shot again and missed and he heard the *carawonging* roar as Wilson shot and saw the leading bull slide forward onto his nose.

"Get that other," Wilson said. "Now you're shooting!"

But the other bull was moving steadily at the same gallop and he missed, throwing a spout of dirt, and Wilson missed and the dust rose in a cloud and Wilson shouted, "Come on. He's too far!" and grabbed his arm and they were in the car again, Macomber and Wilson hanging on the sides and rocketing swayingly over the uneven ground, drawing up on the steady, plunging, heavy-necked, straight-moving gallop of the bull.

They were behind him and Macomber was filling his rifle, dropping shells onto the ground, jamming it, clearing the jam, then they were almost up with the bull when Wilson yelled "Stop," and the car skidded so that it almost swung over and Macomber fell forward onto his feet, slammed his bolt forward and fired as far forward as he could aim into the galloping, rounded black back, aimed and shot again, then again, then again, and the bullets, all of them hitting, had no effect on the buffalo that he could see. Then Wilson shot, the roar deafening him, and he could see the bull stagger. Macomber shot again, aiming carefully, and down he came, onto his knees.

"All right," Wilson said. "Nice work. That's the three."

Macomber felt a drunken elation.

"How many times did you shoot?" he asked.

"Just three," Wilson said. "You killed the first bull. The biggest one. I helped you finish the other two. Afraid they might have got into cover. You had them killed. I was just mopping up a little. You shot damn well."

"Let's go to the car," said Macomber. "I want a drink."

"Got to finish off that buff first," Wilson told him. The buffalo was on his knees and he jerked his head furiously and bellowed in pig-eyed, roaring rage as they came toward him.

"Watch he doesn't get up," Wilson said. Then, "Get a little broadside and take him in the neck just behind the ear."

Macomber aimed carefully at the center of the huge, jerking, rage-driven neck and shot. At the shot the head dropped forward.

"That does it," said Wilson. "Got the spine. They're a hell of a looking thing, aren't they?"

"Let's get the drink," said Macomber. In his life he had never felt so good.

In the car Macomber's wife sat very white faced. "You were marvellous, darling," she said to Macomber. "What a ride."

"Was it rough?" Wilson asked.

"It was frightful. I've never been more frightened in my life."

"Let's all have a drink," Macomber said.

"By all means," said Wilson. "Give it to the Memsahib." She drank the neat whisky from the flask and shuddered a little when she swallowed. She handed the flask to Macomber who handed it to Wilson.

"It was frightfully exciting," she said. "It's given me a dreadful headache. I didn't know you were allowed to shoot them from the cars though."

"No one shot from cars," said Wilson coldly.

"I mean chase them from cars."

"Wouldn't ordinarily," Wilson said. "Seemed sporting enough to me though while we were doing it. Taking more chance driving that way across the plain full of holes and one thing and another than hunting on foot. Buffalo could have charged us each time we shot if he liked. Gave him every chance. Wouldn't mention it to any one though. It's illegal if that's what you mean."

"It seemed very unfair to me," Margot said, "chasing those big helpless things in a motor car."

"Did it?" said Wilson.

"What would happen if they heard about it in Nairobi?"

"I'd lose my licence for one thing. Other unpleasantnesses," Wilson said, taking a drink from the flask. "I'd be out of business."

"Really?"

"Yes, really."

"Well," said Macomber, and he smiled for the first time all day. "Now she has something on you."

"You have such a pretty way of putting things, Francis," Margot Macomber said. Wilson looked at them both. If a four-letter man marries a five-letter woman, he was thinking, what number of letters would their children be? What he said was, "We lost a gun-bearer. Did you notice it?"

"My God, no," Macomber said.

"Here he comes," Wilson said. "He's all right. He must have fallen off when we left the first bull."

Approaching them was the middle-aged gun-bearer, limping along in his knitted cap, khaki tunic, shorts and rubber sandals, gloomy-faced and disgusted-looking. As he came up he called out to Wilson in Swahili and they all saw the change in the white hunter's face.

"What does he say?" asked Margot.

"He says the first bull got up and went into the bush," Wilson said with no expression in his voice.

"Oh," said Macomber blankly.

"Then it's going to be just like the lion," said Margot, full of anticipation.

"It's not going to be a damned bit like the lion," Wilson told her. "Did you want another drink, Macomber?"

"Thanks, yes," Macomber said. He expected the feeling he had had about the lion to come back but it did not. For the first time in his life he really felt wholly without fear. Instead of fear he had a feeling of definite elation.

"We'll go and have a look at the second bull," Wilson said. "I'll tell the driver to put the car in the shade."

"What are you going to do?" asked Margaret Macomber.

"Take a look at the buff," Wilson said.

"I'll come."

"Come along."

The three of them walked over to where the second buffalo bulked blackly in the open, head forward on the grass, the massive horns swung wide.

"He's a very good head," Wilson said. "That's close to a fifty-inch spread."

Macomber was looking at him with delight.

"He's hateful-looking," said Margot. "Can't we go into the shade?"

"Of course," Wilson said. "Look," he said to Macomber, and pointed. "See that patch of bush?"

"Yes."

"That's where the first bull went in. The gun-bearer said when he fell off the bull was down. He was watching us helling along and the other two buff galloping. When he looked up there was the bull up and looking at him. Gun-bearer ran like hell and the bull went off slowly into that bush."

"Can we go in after him now?" asked Macomber eagerly.

Wilson looked at him appraisingly. Damned if this isn't a strange one, he thought. Yesterday he's scared sick and today he's a ruddy fire eater.

"No, we'll give him a while."

"Let's please go into the shade," Margot said. Her face was white and she looked ill.

They made their way to the car where it stood under a single, wide-spreading tree and all climbed in.

"Chances are he's dead in there," Wilson remarked. "After a little we'll have a look."

Macomber felt a wild unreasonable happiness that he had never known before.

"By God, that was a chase," he said. "I've never felt any such feeling. Wasn't it marvellous, Margot?"

"I hated it."

"Why?"

"I hated it," she said bitterly. "I loathed it."

"You know I don't think I'd ever be afraid of anything again," Macomber said to Wilson. "Something happened in me after we first saw the buff and started after him. Like a dam bursting. It was pure excitement."

"Cleans out your liver," said Wilson. "Damn funny things happen to people."

Macomber's face was shining. "You know something did happen to me," he said. "I feel absolutely different."

His wife said nothing and eyed him strangely. She was sitting far back in the seat and Macomber was sitting forward talking to Wilson who turned sideways talking over the back of the front seat.

"You know, I'd like to try another lion," Macomber said. "I'm really not afraid of them now. After all, what can they do to you?"

"That's it," said Wilson. "Worst one can do is kill you. How does it go? Shakespeare. Damned good. See if I can remember. Oh, damned good. Used to quote it to myself at one time. Let's see. 'By my troth, I care not; a man can die but once; we owe God a death and let it go which way it will he that dies this year is quit for the next.' Damned fine, eh?"

He was very embarrassed, having brought out this thing he had lived by, but he had seen men come of age before and it always moved him. It was not a matter of their twenty-first birthday.

It had taken a strange chance of hunting, a sudden precipitation into action without opportunity for worrying beforehand, to bring this about with Macomber, but regardless of how it had happened it had most certainly happened. Look at the beggar now, Wilson thought. It's that some of them stay little boys so long, Wilson thought. Sometimes all their lives. Their figures stay boyish when they're fifty. The great American boy-men. Damned strange people. But he liked this Macomber now. Damned strange fellow. Probably meant the end of cuckoldry too. Well, that would be a damned good thing. Damned good thing. Beggar had probably been afraid all his life. Don't know what started it. But over now. Hadn't had time to be afraid with the buff. That and being angry too. Motor car too. Motor cars made it familiar. Be a damn fire eater now. He'd seen it in the war work the same way. More of a change than any loss of virginity. Fear gone like an operation. Something else grew in its place. Main thing a man had. Made him into a man. Women knew it too. No bloody fear.

From the far corner of the seat Margaret Macomber looked at the two of them. There was no change in Wilson. She saw Wilson as she had seen him the day before when she had first realized what his great talent was. But she saw the change in Francis Macomber now.

"Do you have that feeling of happiness about what's going to happen?" Macomber asked, still exploring his new wealth.

"You're not supposed to mention it," Wilson said, looking in the other's face. "Much more fashionable to say you're scared. Mind you, you'll be scared too, plenty of times."

"But you *have* a feeling of happiness about action to come?"

"Yes," said Wilson. "There's that. Doesn't do to talk too much about all this. Talk the whole thing away. No pleasure in anything if you mouth it up too much."

"You're both talking rot," said Margot. "Just because you've chased some helpless animals in a motor car you talk like heroes."

"Sorry," said Wilson. "I have been gassing too much." She's worried about it already, he thought.

"If you don't know what we're talking about why not keep out of it?" Macomber asked his wife.

"You've gotten awfully brave, awfully suddenly," his wife said contemptuously, but her contempt was not secure. She was very afraid of something.

Macomber laughed, a very natural hearty laugh. "You know I *have*," he said. "I really have."

"Isn't it sort of late?" Margot said bitterly. Because she had done the best she could for many years back and the way they were together now was no one person's fault.

"Not for me," said Macomber.

Margot said nothing but sat back in the corner of the seat.

"Do you think we've given him time enough?" Macomber asked Wilson cheerfully.

"We might have a look," Wilson said. "Have you any solids left?"

"The gun-bearer has some."

Wilson called in Swahili and the older gun-bearer, who was skinning out one of the heads, straightened up, pulled a box of solids out of his pocket and brought them over to Macomber, who filled his magazine and put the remaining shells in his pocket.

"You might as well shoot the Springfield," Wilson said. "You're used to it. We'll leave the Mannlicher in the car with the Memsahib. Your gun-bearer can carry your heavy gun. I've this damned cannon. Now let me tell you about them." He had saved this until the last because he did not want to worry Macomber. "When a buff comes he comes with his head high and thrust straight out. The boss of the horns covers any sort of a brain shot. The only shot is straight into the nose. The only other shot is into his chest or, if you're to one side, into the neck or the shoulders. After they've been hit once they take a hell of a lot of killing. Don't try anything fancy. Take the easiest shot there is. They've finished skinning out that head now. Should we get started?"

He called to the gun-bearers, who came up wiping their hands, and the older one got into the back.

"I'll only take Kongoni," Wilson said. "The other can watch to keep the birds away."

As the car moved slowly across the open space toward the island of brushy trees that ran in a tongue of foliage along a dry water course that cut the open swale, Macomber felt his heart pounding and his mouth was dry again, but it was excitement, not fear.

"Here's where he went in," Wilson said. Then to the gun-bearer in Swahili, "Take the blood spoor."

The car was parallel to the patch of bush. Macomber, Wilson and the gun-bearer got down. Macomber, looking back, saw his wife, with the rifle by her side, looking at him. He waved to her and she did not wave back.

The brush was very thick ahead and the ground was dry. The middle-aged gun-bearer was sweating heavily and Wilson had his hat down over his eyes and his red neck showed just ahead of Macomber. Suddenly the gun-bearer said something in Swahili to Wilson and ran forward.

"He's dead in there," Wilson said. "Good work," and he turned to grip Macomber's hand and as they shook hands, grinning at each other, the gun-bearer shouted wildly and they saw him coming out of the bush sideways, fast as a crab, and the bull coming, nose out, mouth tight closed, blood dripping, massive head straight out, coming in a charge, his little pig eyes bloodshot as he looked at them. Wilson, who was ahead, was kneeling shooting, and Macomber, as he fired, unhearing his shot in the roaring of Wilson's gun, saw fragments like slate burst from the huge boss of the horns, and the head jerked, he shot again at the wide nostrils and saw the horns jolt again and fragments fly, and he did not see Wilson now and, aiming carefully, shot again with the buffalo's huge bulk almost on him and his rifle almost level with the on-coming head, nose out, and he could see the little wicked eyes and the head started to lower and he felt a sudden white-hot, blinding flash explode inside his head and that was all he ever felt.

Wilson had ducked to one side to get in a shoulder shot. Macomber had stood solid and shot for the nose, shooting a touch high each time and hitting the heavy horns, splintering and chipping them like hitting a slate roof, and Mrs. Macomber, in the car, had shot at the buffalo with the 6.5 Mannlicher as it seemed about to gore Macomber and had hit her husband about two inches up and a little to one side of the base of his skull.

Francis Macomber lay now, face down, not two yards from where the buffalo lay on his side and his wife knelt over him with Wilson beside her.

"I wouldn't turn him over," Wilson said.

The woman was crying hysterically.

"I'd get back in the car," Wilson said. "Where's the rifle?"

She shook her head, her face contorted. The gun-bearer picked up the rifle..

"Leave it as it is," said Wilson. Then, "Go get Abdulla so that he may witness the manner of the accident."

He knelt down, took a handkerchief from his pocket, and spread it over Francis Macomber's crew-cropped head where it lay. The blood sank into the dry, loose earth.

Wilson stood up and saw the buffalo on his side, his legs out, his thinly-haired belly crawling with ticks. Hell of a good bull, his brain registered automatically. A good fifty inches, or better. Better. He called to the driver and told him to spread a blanket over the body and stay by it. Then he walked over to the motor car where the woman sat crying in the corner.

"That was a pretty thing to do," he said in a toneless voice. "He *would* have left you too."

"Stop it," she said.

"Of course it's an accident," he said. "I know that."

"Stop it," she said.

"Don't worry," he said. "There will be a certain amount of unpleasantness but I will have some photographs taken that will be very useful at the inquest. There's the testimony of the gun-bearers and the driver too. You're perfectly all right."

"Stop it," she said.

"There's a hell of a lot to be done," he said. "And I'll have to send a truck off to the lake to wireless for a plane to take the three of us into

Nairobi. Why didn't you poison him? That's what they do in England."

"Stop it. Stop it. Stop it," the woman cried.

Wilson looked at her with his flat blue eyes.

"I'm through now," he said. "I was a little angry. I'd begun to like your husband."

"Oh, please stop it," she said. "Please, please stop it."

"That's better," Wilson said. "Please is much better. Now I'll stop."

A NEW ENGLAND NUN

MARY E. WILKINS

I T WAS late in the afternoon, and the light was waning. There was a difference in the look of the tree shadows out in the yard. Somewhere in the distance cows were lowing and a little bell was tinkling; now and then a farm wagon tilted by, and the dust flew; some blue-shirted laborers with shovels over their shoulders plodded past; little swarms of flies were dancing up and down before the people's faces in the soft air. There seemed to be a gentle stir arising over everything—a very premonition of rest and hush and night.

This soft commotion was over Louisa Ellis also. She had been peacefully sewing at her sitting-room window all the afternoon. Now she quilted her needle carefully into her work, which she laid in a basket with her thimble and thread and scissors. Louisa Ellis could not remember that ever in her life she had mislaid one of these little feminine appurtenances.

She tied a green apron around her waist, and went into the garden with a little blue crockery bowl, to pick some currants for her tea. After the currants were picked she sat on the back doorstep and stemmed them, collecting the stems carefully in her apron, and afterward throwing them into the hen coop.

Louisa was slow and still in her movements; it took her a long time to prepare her tea; but when ready it was set forth with as much grace as if she had been her own guest. The little square table stood exactly in the center of the kitchen, and was covered with a starched linen cloth. Louisa had a damask napkin on her tea tray, a cut-glass tumbler full of teaspoons, a silver cream pitcher, a china sugar bowl, and one pink china cup and saucer. She used china every day. Her neighbors' daily tables were laid with common crockery, their sets of best china stayed in the parlor closet, and Louisa Ellis was no richer nor better bred than they. Still she would use the china.

After tea she filled a plate with nicely baked thin corn cakes, and carried them out into the backyard.

"Caesar!" she called. "Caesar! Caesar!"

There was a little rush, and the clank of a chain, and a large yellow-and-white dog appeared at the door of his tiny hut, which was half hidden among the tall grasses. Louisa patted him and gave him the corn cakes. Then she returned to the house and carefully washed the tea things. The twilight had deepened; the chorus of frogs floated in at the open window wonderfully loud and shrill.

Louisa took off her green gingham apron, disclosing a shorter one of pink-and-white print. She lighted her lamp, and sat down again with her sewing.

In about half an hour Joe Dagget came. She heard his heavy step on the walk, and rose and took off her pink-and-white apron, folding it and laying it in a table drawer. Under that apron was still another—white linen with a little cambric edging on the bottom; that was Louisa's company apron.

When the door opened and Joe Dagget entered, he seemed to fill up the whole room. A little yellow canary that had been asleep in his green cage woke up and fluttered wildly, beating his little yellow wings against the wires. He always did so when Joe Dagget came in-to the room.

"Good evening," said Louisa. She extended her hand with a kind of solemn cordiality.

"Good evening, Louisa," returned the man in a loud voice.

She placed a chair for him, and they sat facing each other, with the table between them. He sat bolt upright, toeing out his heavy feet squarely, glancing with a good-humored uneasiness around the room. She sat gently erect, folding her slender hands in her white linen lap.

"Been a pleasant day," remarked Dagget.

"Real pleasant," Louisa assented softly. "Have you been haying?" she asked after a little while.

"Yes, I've been haying all day, down in the ten-acre lot. Pretty hot work."

"It must be."

"Yes, it's pretty hot work in the sun."

"Is your mother well today?"

"Yes, Mother's pretty well."

"I suppose Lily Dyer's with her now?"

Dagget colored. "Yes, she's with her," he answered slowly.

He was not very young, but there was a boyish look about his large face. Louisa was not quite as old as he, her face was fairer and smoother, but she gave people the impression of being older.

"I suppose she's a good deal of help to your mother," she said further.

"I guess she is; I don't know how Mother'd get along without her," said Dagget with a sort of embarrassed warmth.

Presently he began taking up the books on the table and opening them. There was a square red autograph album, and a Young Lady's Gift-Book which had belonged to Louisa's mother. He laid them down again, the album on the gift book.

Louisa kept eyeing them with mild uneasiness. Finally she rose and changed the position of the books, putting the album underneath.

Dagget gave an awkward little laugh. "Now what difference did it make which book was on top?" said he.

"I always keep them that way," murmured Louisa.

"You do beat everything," said Dagget, trying to laugh again.

He remained about an hour longer, then rose to take leave. Going out, he stumbled over a rug, and, trying to recover himself, hit Louisa's workbasket on the table, and knocked it on the floor. He looked at Louisa, then at the rolling spools; he ducked himself awkwardly toward them, but she stopped him. "Never mind," she said with a mild stiffness. "I'll pick them up after you're gone."

When Joe Dagget was outside he drew in the sweet evening air with a sigh, and felt much as an innocent and perfectly well intentioned bear might after his exit from a china shop.

Louisa, on her part, tied on the pink, then the green apron, picked up all the scattered treasures and replaced them in her workbasket. Then she set the lamp on the floor, and began sharply examining the carpet. "He's tracked in a good deal of dust," she murmured.

If Joe Dagget could have known that she then swept the carpet carefully, it would have increased his perplexity and uneasiness, although it would not have disturbed his loyalty in the least. He came twice a week to see Louisa Ellis, and every time, sitting there in her delicately sweet room, he felt as if surrounded by a hedge of lace. He was afraid to stir lest he should put a clumsy foot or hand through the fairy web.

Still the lace and Louisa commanded his perfect respect. They were to be married in a month, after a singular courtship which had lasted for a matter of fifteen years. For fourteen out of the fifteen years the two had not once seen each other. Joe had been all those years in Australia, where he had gone to make his fortune. He would have stayed fifty years if it had taken so long, and come home feeble and tottering to marry Louisa.

Shortly after they were engaged he had announced to Louisa his determination to strike out into new fields and secure a competency before they should be married. She had assented with the sweet serenity which never failed her. Joe broke down a little at the last, but Louisa kissed him with a mild blush and said good-by.

"It won't be for long," Joe had said huskily. But it was for fourteen years.

In that time Louisa's mother and brother had died, and she was all alone in the world. Louisa's feet had turned into a path, smooth maybe under a calm, serene sky, but so straight and so narrow that there was no room for anyone at her side.

Louisa's first emotion when Joe Dagget came home was consternation, although she would not admit it to herself. Fifteen years ago she had been in love with him—at least she considered herself to be. Just at that time, gently falling into the natural drift of girlhood, acquiescing with calm docility to her mother's views upon the subject, she had seen marriage as a reasonable feature of life. When Joe Dagget presented himself, Louisa accepted him with no hesitation.

She had never dreamed of the possibility of marrying anyone else. She had never felt discontented nor impatient over her lover's absence;

still for fourteen years she had looked forward to his return and their marriage as the inevitable conclusion of things. Yet when Joe came home, she was as much surprised and taken aback as if she had never thought of it.

As for Joe, his stint was done; he had turned his face away from fortune seeking, and the old winds of romance whistled as loud and sweet as ever through his ears. All the song which he had been wont to hear in them was Louisa; he had for a long time a loyal belief that he heard it still. Finally it seemed to him that although the winds sang always that one song, it had another name. For Louisa the wind had never more than murmured; now it had gone down, and everything was still. She listened for a little while with half-wistful attention; then she turned quietly away and went to work on her wedding clothes.

Joe had made some quite magnificent alterations in his old homestead. The newly married couple would live there, for Joe could not desert his feeble but domineering old mother. Every morning, going about among her neat possessions, Louisa felt as one looking her last upon the faces of dear friends. It was true that in a measure she could take them with her, but, robbed of their old environments, they would almost cease to be themselves. Then there were some features of her happy solitary life which she would probably be obliged to relinquish altogether. Sterner tasks would devolve upon her. There would be a large house to care for, company to entertain, Joe's mother to wait upon; and it would be contrary to all thrifty village traditions for her to keep more than one servant.

Louisa dearly loved to sew a linen seam, not always for use, but for the pleasure which she took in it. Sitting at her window during long sweet afternoons, drawing her needle gently through the dainty fabric, was peace itself. But there was small chance of such foolish comfort in the future. Joe's mother, and very likely even Joe himself, with his honest masculine rudeness, would laugh and frown down such pretty maiden ways.

Louisa had almost the enthusiasm of an artist over the mere order and cleanliness of her solitary home. She gloated gently over her orderly bureau drawers, with their exquisitely folded contents redolent with lavender and sweet clover. Could she be sure of the endurance of even this? She had visions of masculine belongings strewn about in endless litter; of dust and disorder arising from a coarse masculine presence in the midst of all this delicate harmony.

Among her forebodings of disturbance, not the least was with regard to the dog Caesar. For the greater part of his life he had dwelt in his secluded hut, shut out from the society of his kind. Never had Caesar since his early youth watched at a woodchuck's hole; never had he known the delights of a stray bone. And it was all on account of a sin committed when hardly out of his puppyhood. Old Caesar seldom lifted up his voice; he was fat and sleepy; there were yellow rings which looked like spectacles around his dim old eyes; but there was a neighbor who bore on his hand the imprint of Caesar's youthful teeth. The neighbor had demanded either Caesar's death or complete ostracism. So Louisa's brother, to whom the dog had belonged, had built him his little kennel and tied him up.

It was now fourteen years since Caesar had inflicted that memorable bite, and with the exception of short excursions, always at the end of the chain, the old dog had remained a close prisoner. He was regarded by the village as a very monster of ferocity. Mothers charged their children not to go too near to him, and the children listened and believed, with a fascinated appetite for terror; they ran by Louisa's house stealthily, with many sidelong glances at the terrible dog. Joe Dagget, however, saw Caesar as he was. He strode up to him and patted him on the head, in spite of Louisa's soft clamor of warning, and even attempted to set him loose. Louisa grew so alarmed that he desisted, but kept announcing his opinion in the matter quite forcibly at intervals. "There ain't a better-natured dog in town," he would say, "and it's downright cruel to keep him tied up there. Someday I'm going to take him out."

Louisa was herself very fond of the old dog, and he was always very gentle with her; still she pictured to herself Caesar on the rampage through the quiet village, innocent children bleeding in his path. She looked at the old dog munching his ascetic fare of corn mush and cakes, and thought of her approaching marriage and trembled.

Still no anticipation of disorder and confusion, no forebodings of Caesar on the rampage, no wild fluttering of her little yellow canary were sufficient to turn her a hairsbreadth. Joe Dagget had been fond of her and working for her all these years. It was not for her, whatever came to pass, to break his heart. She put the exquisite little stitches into her wedding garments, and the time went on until it was only a week before her wedding day.

There was a full moon that night. About nine o'clock Louisa strolled down the road a little way. There were harvest fields on either hand, bordered by low stone walls. Luxuriant clumps of bushes grew beside the wall, and trees—wild cherry and old apple trees—at intervals. Presently Louisa sat down on the wall and looked about her with mildly sorrowful reflectiveness. Tall shrubs of blueberry and meadow-sweet shut her in on either side. The road was bespread with a beautiful shifting dapple of silver and shadow; the air was full of a mysterious sweetness. "I wonder if it's wild grapes?" murmured Louisa. She sat there some time, and was just thinking of rising, when she heard footsteps and low voices. It was a lonely place, and she felt a little timid. She thought she would keep still in the shadow and let the persons, whoever they might be, pass her.

But just before they reached her the voices and the footsteps ceased. She understood that their owners had also found seats upon the stone wall. She was wondering if she could steal away unobserved, when a voice broke the stillness. It was Joe Dagget's. She sat still and listened.

"Well," said Dagget, "you've made up your mind, then, I suppose?"

"Yes," returned another voice. "I'm going day after tomorrow."

"That's Lily Dyer," thought Louisa. The voice embodied itself in her mind. She saw a girl tall and full-figured, with a firm, fair face, her strong yellow hair braided in a close knot. A girl full of a calm rustic strength and bloom, Lily Dyer was a favorite with the village folk. She was good and handsome and smart, and Louisa had often heard her praises sounded.

"Well," said Joe Dagget, "I ain't got a word to say." Then there was a silence. "I ain't sorry," he began at last, drawing out the words heavily, "that that happened yesterday—that we kind of let on how we felt to each other. I guess it's just as well we knew. Of course, I'm going right on an' get married next week. I ain't going back on a woman that's waited for me fourteen years."

"If you should jilt her tomorrow, I wouldn't have you. You'd find that out, Joe Dagget," spoke up the girl, with sudden vehemence. "Honor's honor, an' right's right."

"Well, you'll find out fast enough that I ain't going against 'em for you or any other girl," returned he. Their voices sounded almost as if they were angry with each other. "I'm sorry you feel as if you must go away," said Joe, "but I don't know but it's best."

"Of course it's best. I hope you and I have got common sense."

Suddenly Joe's voice got an undertone of tenderness. "Say, Lily," said he, "I'll get along well enough myself, but I hope—one of these days—you'll—come across somebody else—"

"I don't see any reason why I shouldn't." Suddenly her tone changed. She spoke in a sweet, clear voice, so loud that she could have been heard across the street. "No, Joe Dagget," said she. "I've got good sense, an' I ain't going to break my heart nor make a fool of myself; but I'm never going to be married, you can be sure of that. I ain't that sort of a girl to feel this way twice."

Louisa heard an exclamation and a soft commotion behind the bushes; then Lily spoke again—the voice sounded as if she had risen. "This must be put a stop to," said she. "We've stayed here long enough. I'm going home."

Louisa sat there in a daze, listening to their retreating steps. After a while she got up and slunk softly home herself.

The next day she did her housework methodically; that was as much a matter of course as breathing; but she did not sew on her wedding clothes. She sat at her window and meditated. Even now she could hardly believe that she had heard aright, and that she would not do Joe a terrible injury should she break her troth plight.

In the evening Joe came. Louisa Ellis had never known that she had any diplomacy in her, but when she came to look for it that night she found it among her little feminine weapons.

She never mentioned Lily Dyer. She simply said that while she had no cause of complaint against him, she had lived so long in one way that she shrank from making a change.

"Well, I never shrank, Louisa," said Dagget. "I'm going to be honest enough to say that I think maybe it's better this way; but if you'd wanted to keep on, I'd have stuck to you till my dying day. I hope you know that."

"Yes, I do," said she.

That night she and Joe parted more tenderly than they had done for a long time. Standing in the door, holding each other's hands, a last great wave of regretful memory swept over them.

"Well, this ain't the way we've thought it was all going to end, is it, Louisa?" said Joe.

She shook her head. There was a little quiver on her placid face.

"You let me know if there's ever anything I can do for you," said he. "I ain't ever going to forget you, Louisa." Then he kissed her, and went down the path. Louisa wept a little that night, she hardly knew why; but the next morning, on waking, she felt like a queen who, after fearing lest her domain be wrested away from her, sees it firmly ensured in her possession.

That afternoon she sat with her needlework at the window. Lily Dyer, tall and erect and blooming, went past; but Louisa felt no qualm. She gazed ahead through a long reach of future days strung together like pearls in a rosary, every one like the others, and all smooth and flawless and innocent. Outside was the fervid summer afternoon; the air was filled with the sounds of the busy harvest of men and birds and bees; there were halloos, metallic clatterings, sweet calls, and long hummings. Louisa sat, prayerfully numbering her days.

THE
CHRYSANTHEMUMS
JOHN STEINBECK

John Steinbeck

THE HIGH gray-flannel fog of winter closed off the Salinas Valley from the sky and from all the rest of the world. On every side it sat like a lid on the mountains and made of the great valley a closed pot. On the broad, level land floor the gangplows bit deep and left the black earth shining like metal where the shares had cut. On the foothill ranches across the Salinas River, the yellow stubble fields seemed to be bathed in pale cold sunshine, but there was no sunshine in the valley now in December. The thick willow scrub along the river flamed with sharp and positive yellow leaves.

It was a time of quiet and of waiting. The air was cold and tender. A light wind blew up from the southwest so that the farmers were mildly hopeful of a good rain before long; but fog and rain do not go together.

Across the river, on Henry Allen's foothill ranch there was little work to be done, for the hay was cut and stored and the orchards were plowed up to receive the rain deeply when it should come. The cattle on the higher slopes were becoming shaggy and rough-coated.

Elisa Allen, working in her flower garden, looked down across the yard and saw Henry, her husband, talking to two men in business suits. The three of them stood by the tractor shed, each man with one foot on the side of the little Fordson. They smoked cigarettes and studied the machine as they talked.

Elisa watched them for a moment and then went back to her work. She was thirty-five. Her face was lean and strong and her eyes were as clear as water. Her figure looked blocked and heavy in her gardening costume, a man's black hat pulled low down over her eyes, clodhopper shoes, a figured print dress almost completely covered by a big corduroy apron with four big pockets to hold the snips, the trowel and scratcher, the seeds and the knife she worked with. She wore heavy leather gloves to protect her hands while she worked.

She was cutting down the old year's chrysanthemum stalks with a pair of short and powerful scissors. She looked down toward the men by the tractor shed now and then. Her face was eager and mature and handsome; even her work with the scissors was overeager, overpowerful. The chrysanthemum stems seemed too small and easy for her energy.

She brushed a cloud of hair out of her eyes with the back of her glove, and left a smudge of earth on her cheek in doing it. Behind her stood the neat white farmhouse with red geraniums banked around it as high as the windows. It was a hard-swept looking little house, with hard-polished windows, and a clean mud mat on the front steps.

Elisa cast another glance toward the tractor shed. The strangers were getting into their Ford coupe. She took off a glove and put her strong fingers down into the forest of new green chrysanthemum sprouts that were growing around the old roots. She spread the leaves and looked down among the close-growing stems. No aphids were there, no sow bugs or snails or cutworms. Her terrier fingers destroyed such pests before they could get started.

Elisa started at the sound of her husband's voice. He had come near quietly, and he leaned over the wire fence that protected her flower garden from cattle and dogs and chickens.

"At it again," he said. "You've got a strong new crop coming."

Elisa straightened her back and pulled on the gardening glove again. "Yes. They'll be strong this coming year." In her tone and on her face there was a little smugness.

"You've got a gift with things," Henry observed. "Some of those yellow chrysanthemums you had this year were ten inches across. I wish you'd work out in the orchard and raise some apples that big."

Her eyes sharpened. "Maybe I could do it, too. I've a gift with things, all right. My mother had it. She could stick anything in the ground and make it grow. She said it was having planters' hands that knew how to do it."

"Well, it sure works with flowers," he said.

"Henry, who were those men you were talking to?"

"Why, sure, that's what I came to tell you. They were from the Western Meat Company. I sold those thirty head of three-year-old steers. Got nearly my own price, too."

"Good," she said. "Good for you."

"And I thought," he continued, "I thought how it's Saturday afternoon, and we might go into Salinas for dinner at a restaurant, and then to a picture show—to celebrate, you see."

"Good," she repeated. "Oh, yes. That will be good."

Henry put on his joking tone. "There's fights tonight. How'd you like to go to the fights?"

"Oh, no," she said breathlessly. "No, I wouldn't like fights."

"Just fooling, Elisa. We'll go to a movie. Let's see. It's two now. I'm going to take Scotty and bring down those steers from the hill. It'll take us maybe two hours. We'll go in town about five and have dinner at the Cominos Hotel. Like that?"

"Of course I'll like it. It's good to eat away from home."

"All right, then. I'll go get up a couple of horses."

She said, "I'll have plenty of time to transplant some of these sets, I guess."

She heard her husband calling Scotty down by the barn. And a little later she saw the two men ride up the pale yellow hillside in search of the steers.

There was a little square sandy bed kept for rooting the chrysanthemums. With her trowel she turned the soil over and over, and smoothed it and patted it firm. Then she dug ten parallel trenches to receive the sets. Back at the chrysanthemum bed she pulled out the little crisp shoots, trimmed off the leaves of each one with her scissors and laid it on a small orderly pile.

A squeak of wheels and plod of hoofs came from the road. Elisa looked up. The country road ran along the dense bank of willows and cottonwoods that bordered the river, and up this road came a curious vehicle, curiously drawn. It was an old spring wagon, with a round canvas top on it like the cover of a prairie schooner. It was drawn by an old bay horse and a little gray-and-white burro. A big stubble-bearded man sat between the cover flaps and drove the crawling team. Underneath the wagon, between the hind wheels, a lean and rangy mongrel dog walked sedately. Words were painted on the canvas, in clumsy, crooked letters. "Pots, pans, knives, sisors, lawn mores, Fixed." Two rows of articles, and the triumphantly definitive "Fixed" below. The black paint had run down in little sharp points beneath each letter.

Elisa, squatting on the ground, watched to see the crazy, loose-jointed wagon pass by. But it didn't pass. It turned into the farm road in front of her house, crooked old wheels skirling and squeaking. The rangy dog darted from between the wheels and ran ahead. Instantly the two ranch shepherds flew out at him. Then all three stopped, and with stiff and quivering tails, with taut straight legs, with ambassadorial dignity, they slowly circled, sniffing daintily. The caravan pulled up to Elisa's wire fence and stopped. Now the newcomer dog, feeling outnumbered, lowered his tail and retired under the wagon with raised hackles and bared teeth.

The man on the wagon seat called out, "That's a bad dog in a fight when he gets started."

Elisa laughed. "I see he is. How soon does he generally get started?"

The man caught up her laughter and echoed it heartily. "Sometimes not for weeks and weeks," he said. He climbed stiffly down, over the wheel. The horse and the donkey drooped like unwatered flowers.

Elisa saw that he was a very big man. Although his hair and beard were graying, he did not look old. His worn black suit was wrinkled and spotted with grease. The laughter had disappeared from his face and eyes the moment his laughing voice ceased. His eyes were dark, and they were full of the brooding that gets in the eyes of teamsters and of sailors. The callused hands he rested on the wire fence were cracked, and every crack was a black line. He took off his battered hat.

"I'm off my general road, ma'am," he said. "Does this dirt road cut over across the river to the Los Angeles highway?"

Elisa stood up and shoved the thick scissors in her apron pocket. "Well, yes, it does, but it winds around and then fords the river. I don't think your team could pull through the sand."

He replied with some asperity, "It might surprise you what them beasts can pull through."

"When they get started?" she asked.

He smiled for a second. "Yes. When they get started."

"Well," said Elisa, "I think you'll save time if you go back to the Salinas road and pick up the highway there."

He drew a big finger down the chicken wire and made it sing. "I ain't in any hurry, ma'am. I go from Seattle to San Diego and back every year. Takes all my time. About six months each way. I aim to follow nice weather."

Elisa took off her gloves and stuffed them in the apron pocket with the scissors. She touched the under edge of her man's hat, searching for fugitive hairs. "That sounds like a nice kind of a way to live," she said.

He leaned confidentially over the fence. "Maybe you noticed the writing on my wagon. I mend pots and sharpen knives and scissors. You got any of them things to do?"

"Oh, no," she said quickly. "Nothing like that." Her eyes hardened with resistance.

"Scissors is the worst thing," he explained. "Most people just ruin scissors trying to sharpen 'em, but I know how. I got a special tool. It's a little bobbit kind of thing, and patented. But it sure does the trick."

"No. My scissors are all sharp."

"All right, then. Take a pot," he continued earnestly, "a bent pot, or a pot with a hole. I can make it like new so you don't have to buy no new ones. That's a saving for you."

"No," she said shortly. "I tell you I have nothing like that for you to do."

His face fell to an exaggerated sadness. His voice took on a whining undertone. "I ain't had a thing to do today. Maybe I won't have no supper tonight. You see I'm off my regular road. I know folks on the highway clear from Seattle to San Diego. They save their things for me to sharpen up because they know I do it so good and save them money."

"I'm sorry," Elisa said irritably. "I haven't anything for you to do."

His eyes left her face and fell to searching the ground. They roamed about until they came to the chrysanthemum bed where she had been working. "What's them plants, ma'am?"

The irritation and resistance melted from Elisa's face. "Oh, those are chrysanthemums, giant whites and yellows. I raise them every year, bigger than anybody around here."

"Kind of a long-stemmed flower? Looks like a quick puff of colored smoke?" he asked.

"That's it. What a nice way to describe them."

"They smell kind of nasty till you get used to them," he said.

"It's a good bitter smell," she retorted, "not nasty at all."

He changed his tone quickly. "I like the smell myself."

"I had ten-inch blooms this year," she said.

The man leaned farther over the fence. "Look. I know a lady down the road a piece, has got the nicest garden you ever seen. Got nearly every kind of flower but no chrysantheums. Last time I was mending a copper-bottom washtub for her (that's a hard job but I do it good), she said to me, 'If you ever run acrost some nice chrysantheums I wish you'd try to get me a few seeds.' That's what she told me."

Elisa's eyes grew alert and eager. "She couldn't have known much about chrysanthemums. You *can* raise them from seed, but it's much easier to root the little sprouts you see there."

"Oh," he said. "I s'pose I can't take none to her, then."

"Why yes you can," Elisa cried. "I can put some in damp sand, and you can carry them right along with you. They'll take root in the pot if you keep them damp. And then she can transplant them."

"She'd sure like to have some, ma'am. You say they're nice ones?"

"Beautiful," she said. "Oh, beautiful." Her eyes shone. She tore off the battered hat and shook out her dark pretty hair. "I'll put them in a flowerpot, and you can take them right with you. Come into the yard."

While the man came through the picket gate Elisa ran excitedly along the geranium-bordered path to the back of the house. And she returned carrying a big red flowerpot. The gloves were forgotten now. She kneeled on the ground by the starting bed and dug up the sandy soil with her fingers and scooped it into the bright new flowerpot. Then she picked up the little pile of shoots she had prepared. With her strong fingers she pressed them into the sand and tamped around them with her knuckles. The man stood over her. "I'll tell you what to do," she said. "You remember so you can tell the lady."

"Yes, I'll try to remember."

"Well, look. These will take root in about a month. Then she must set them out, about a foot apart in good rich earth like this, see?" She lifted a handful of dark soil for him to look at. "They'll grow fast and tall. Now remember this: in July tell her to cut them down, about eight inches from the ground."

"Before they bloom?" he asked.

"Yes, before they bloom." Her face was tight with eagerness. "They'll grow right up again. About the last of September the buds will start."

She stopped and seemed perplexed. "It's the budding that takes the most care," she said hesitantly. "I don't know how to tell you." She looked deep into his eyes, searchingly. Her mouth opened a little, and she seemed to be listening. "I'll try to tell you," she said. "Did you ever hear of planting hands?"

"Can't say I have, ma'am."

"Well, I can only tell you what it feels like. It's when you're picking off the buds you don't want. Everything goes right down into your fingertips. You watch your fingers work. They do it themselves. You can feel how it is. They pick and pick the buds. They never make a mistake. They're with the plant. Do you see? Your fingers and the plant. You can feel that, right up your arm. They know. They never make a mistake. You can feel it. When you're like that you can't do anything wrong. Do you see that? Can you understand that?"

She was kneeling on the ground looking up at him. Her breast swelled passionately.

The man's eyes narrowed. He looked away self-consciously. "Maybe I know," he said. "Sometimes in the night in the wagon there—"

Elisa's voice grew husky. She broke in on him. "I've never lived as you do, but I know what you mean. When the night is dark—why, the stars are sharp-pointed, and there's quiet. Why, you rise up and up! Every pointed star gets driven into your body. It's like that. Hot and sharp and—lovely."

Kneeling there, her hand went out toward his legs in the greasy black trousers. Her hesitant fingers almost touched the cloth. Then her hand dropped to the ground. She crouched low like a fawning dog.

He said, "It's nice, just like you say. Only when you don't have no dinner, it ain't."

She stood up then, very straight, and her face was ashamed. She held the flowerpot out to him and placed it gently in his arms. "Here. Put it in your wagon, on the seat, where you can watch it. Maybe I can find something for you to do."

At the back of the house she dug in the can pile and found two old and battered aluminum saucepans. She carried them back and gave them to him. "Here, maybe you can fix these."

His manner changed. He became professional. "Good as new I can fix them." At the back of his wagon he set a little anvil, and out of an oily toolbox dug a small machine hammer. Elisa came through the gate to watch him while he pounded out the dents in the kettles. His mouth grew sure and knowing. At a difficult part of the work he sucked his underlip.

"You sleep right in the wagon?" Elisa asked.

"Right in the wagon, ma'am. Rain or shine I'm dry as a cow in there."

"It must be nice," she said. "It must be very nice. I wish women could do such things."

"It ain't the right kind of a life for a woman."

Her upper lip raised a little, showing her teeth. "How do you know? How can you tell?" she said.

"I don't know, ma'am," he protested. "Of course I don't know. Now here's your kettles, done. You don't have to buy no new ones."

"How much?"

"Oh, fifty cents'll do. I keep my prices down and my work good. That's why I have all them satisfied customers up and down the highway."

Elisa brought him a fifty-cent piece from the house and dropped it in his hand. "You might be surprised to have a rival sometime. I can sharpen scissors, too. And I can beat the dents out of little pots. I could show you what a woman might do."

He put his hammer back in the oily box and shoved the little anvil out of sight. "It would be a lonely life for a woman, ma'am, and a scary life, too, with animals creeping under the wagon all night." He climbed over the singletree, steadying himself with a hand on the burro's white rump. He settled himself in the seat, picked up the lines. "Thank you kindly, ma'am," he said. "I'll do like you told me; I'll go back and catch the Salinas road."

"Mind," she called, "if you're long in getting there, keep the sand damp."

"Sand, ma'am? . . . Sand? Oh, sure. You mean around the chrysantheums. Sure I will." He clucked his tongue. The beasts leaned luxuriously into their collars. The mongrel dog took his place between the back wheels. The wagon turned and crawled out the entrance road and back the way it had come, along the river.

Elisa stood in front of her wire fence watching the slow progress of the caravan. Her shoulders were straight, her head thrown back, her eyes half closed, so that the scene came vaguely into them. Her lips moved silently, forming the words "Good-by—good-by." Then she whispered, "That's a bright direction. There's a glowing there." The sound of her whisper startled her. She shook herself free and looked about to see whether anyone had been listening. Only the dogs had heard. They lifted their heads toward her from their sleeping in the dust, and then stretched out their chins and settled asleep again. Elisa turned and ran hurriedly into the house.

In the kitchen she reached behind the stove and felt the water tank. It was full of hot water from the noonday cooking. In the bathroom she tore off her soiled clothes and flung them into the corner. And then she scrubbed herself with a little block of pumice, legs and thighs, loins and chest and arms, until her skin was scratched and red. When she had dried herself she stood in front of a mirror in her bedroom and looked at her body. She tightened her stomach and threw out her chest. She turned and looked over her shoulder at her back.

After a while she began to dress, slowly. She put on her newest underclothing and her nicest stockings and the dress which was the symbol of her prettiness. She worked carefully on her hair, penciled her eyebrows and rouged her lips.

Before she was finished she heard the little thunder of hoofs and the shouts of Henry and his helper as they drove the red steers into the corral. She heard the gate bang shut and set herself for Henry's arrival.

His step sounded on the porch. He entered the house calling, "Elisa, where are you?"

"In my room, dressing. I'm not ready. There's hot water for your bath. Hurry up. It's getting late."

When she heard him splashing in the tub, Elisa laid his dark suit on the bed, and shirt and socks and tie beside it. She stood his polished shoes on the floor beside the bed. Then she went to the porch and sat primly and stiffly down. She looked toward the river road where the willow line was still yellow with frosted leaves so that under the high gray fog they seemed a thin band of sunshine. This was the only color in the gray afternoon. She sat unmoving for a long time. Her eyes blinked rarely.

Henry came banging out of the door, shoving his tie inside his vest as he came. Elisa stiffened and her face grew tight. Henry stopped short and looked at her. "Why—why, Elisa. You look so nice!"

"Nice? You think I look nice? What do you mean by 'nice'?"

Henry blundered on. "I don't know. I mean you look different, strong and happy."

"I am strong? Yes, strong. What do you mean 'strong'?"

He looked bewildered. "You're playing some kind of a game," he said helplessly. "It's a kind of a play. You look strong enough to break a calf over your knee, happy enough to eat it like a watermelon."

For a second she lost her rigidity. "Henry! Don't talk like that. You didn't know what you said." She grew complete again. "I'm strong," she boasted. "I never knew before how strong."

Henry looked down toward the tractor shed, and when he brought his eyes back to her, they were his own again. "I'll get out the car. You can put on your coat while I'm starting."

Elisa went into the house. She heard him drive to the gate and idle down his motor, and then she took a long time to put on her hat. She pulled it here and pressed it there. When Henry turned the motor off, she slipped into her coat and went out.

The little roadster bounced along on the dirt road by the river, raising the birds and driving the rabbits into the brush. Two cranes flapped heavily over the willow line and dropped into the riverbed.

Far ahead on the road Elisa saw a dark speck. She knew.

She tried not to look as they passed it, but her eyes would not obey. She whispered to herself sadly, "He might have thrown them off the road. That wouldn't have been much trouble, not very much. But he kept the pot," she explained. "He had to keep the pot. That's why he couldn't get them off the road."

The roadster turned a bend and she saw the caravan ahead. She swung full around toward her husband so she could not see the little covered wagon and the mismatched team as the car passed them.

In a moment it was over. The thing was done. She did not look back.

She said loudly, to be heard above the motor, "It will be good, tonight, a good dinner."

"Now you're changed again," Henry complained. He took one hand from the wheel and patted her knee. "I ought to take you in to dinner oftener. It would be good for both of us. We get so heavy out on the ranch."

"Henry," she asked, "could we have wine at dinner?"

"Sure we could. Say! That will be fine."

She was silent for a while; then she said, "Henry, at those prizefights, do the men hurt each other very much?"

"Sometimes a little, not often. Why?"

"Well, I've read how they break noses, and blood runs down their chests. I've read how the fighting gloves get heavy and soggy with blood."

He looked around at her. "What's the matter, Elisa? I didn't know you read things like that." He brought the car to a stop, then turned to the right over the Salinas River bridge.

"Do any women ever go to the fights?" she asked.

"Oh, sure, some. What's the matter, Elisa? Do you want to go? I don't think you'd like it, but I'll take you if you really want to go."

She relaxed limply in the seat. "Oh, no. No. I don't want to go. I'm sure I don't." Her face was turned away from him. "It will be enough if we can have wine. It will be plenty." She turned up her coat collar so he could not see that she was crying weakly—like an old woman.

THE TELL-TALE HEART

EDGAR ALLAN POE

TRUE!—NERVOUS—very, very dreadfully nervous I had been and am; but why *will* you say that I am mad? The disease had sharpened my senses—not destroyed—not dulled them. Above all was the sense of hearing acute. I heard all things in the heaven and in the earth. I heard many things in hell. How, then, am I mad? Hearken! and observe how healthily—how calmly I can tell you the whole story.

It is impossible to say how first the idea entered my brain; but once conceived, it haunted me day and night. Object there was none. Passion there was none. I loved the old man. He had never wronged me. He had never given me insult. For his gold I had no desire. I think it was his eye! Yes, it was this! One of his eyes resembled that of a vulture—a pale blue eye, with a film over it. Whenever it fell upon me, my blood ran cold; and so by degrees—very gradually—I made up my mind to take the life of the old man, and thus rid myself of the eye forever.

Now this is the point. You fancy me mad. Madmen know nothing. But you should have seen *me*. You should have seen how wisely I proceeded—with what caution—with what foresight—with what dis-simulation I went to work! I was never kinder to the old man than during the whole week before I killed him. And every night, about midnight, I turned the latch of his door and opened it—oh, so gently! And then, when I had made an opening sufficient for my head, I put in a dark lantern, all closed, closed, so that no light shone out, and then I thrust in my head. Oh, you would have laughed to see how cunningly I thrust it in! I moved it slowly—very, very slowly, so that I might not disturb the old man's sleep. It took me an hour to place my whole head within the opening so far that I could see him as he lay upon his bed. Ha! Would a madman have been so wise as this? And then, when my head was well in the room, I undid the lantern cautiously—oh, so cautiously—cautiously (for the hinges creaked)—I undid it just so much that a single thin ray fell upon the vulture eye. And this I did for seven long nights—every night just at midnight—but I found the eye always closed; and so it was impossible to do the work; for it was not the old man who vexed me, but his Evil Eye. And every morning, when the day broke, I went boldly into the chamber, and spoke courageously to him, calling him by name in a hearty tone, and inquiring how he had passed the night. So you see he would have been a very profound old man, indeed, to suspect that every night, just at twelve, I looked in upon him while he slept.

Upon the eighth night I was more than usually cautious in opening the door. A watch's minute hand moves more quickly than did mine. Never before that night had I *felt* the extent of my own powers—of my sagacity. I could scarcely contain my feelings of triumph. To think that there I was, opening the door, little by little, and he not even to dream of my secret deeds or thoughts. I fairly chuckled at the idea; and perhaps he heard me; for he moved on the bed suddenly, as if startled. Now you may think that I drew back—but no. His room was as black as pitch with the thick darkness (for the shutters were close fastened, through fear of robbers), and so I knew that he could not see the opening of the door, and I kept pushing it on steadily, steadily.

I had my head in, and was about to open the lantern, when my thumb slipped upon the tin fastening, and the old man sprang up in the bed, crying out, "Who's there?"

I kept quite still and said nothing. For a whole hour I did not move a muscle, and in the meantime I did not hear him lie down. He was still sitting up in the bed listening—just as I have done, night after night, hearkening to the deathwatches in the wall.

Presently I heard a slight groan, and I knew it was the groan of mortal terror. It was not a groan of pain or of grief—oh, no!—it was the low stifled sound that arises from the bottom of the soul when overcharged with awe. I knew the sound well. Many a night, just at midnight, when all the world slept, it has welled up from my own bosom, deepening, with its dreadful echo, the terrors that distracted me. I say I knew it well. I knew what the old man felt, and pitied him, although I chuckled at heart. I knew that he had been lying awake ever since the first slight noise, when he had turned in the bed. His fears had been ever since growing upon him. He had been trying to fancy them causeless, but could not. He had been saying to himself, "It is nothing but the wind in the chimney—it is only a mouse crossing the floor," or "it is merely a cricket which has made a single chirp." Yes, he has been trying to comfort himself with these suppositions; but he had found all in vain. *All in vain;* because Death, in approaching him, had stalked with his black shadow before him, and enveloped the victim. And it was the mournful influence of the unperceived shadow that caused him to feel—although he neither saw nor heard—to *feel* the presence of my head within the room.

When I had waited a long time, very patiently, without hearing him lie down, I resolved to open a little—a very, very little crevice in the lantern. So I opened it—you cannot imagine how stealthily, stealthily—until, at length, a single dim ray, like the thread of the spider, shot from out the crevice and full upon the vulture eye.

It was open—wide, wide open—and I grew furious as I gazed upon it. I saw it with perfect distinctness—all a dull blue, with a hideous veil over it that chilled the very marrow in my bones; but I could see nothing else of the old man's face or person: for I had directed the ray as if by instinct, precisely upon the damned spot.

And now have I not told you that what you mistake for madness is but overacuteness of the senses? Now, I say, there came to my ears a low, dull, quick sound, such as a watch makes when enveloped in cotton. I knew *that* sound well too. It was the beating of the old man's heart. It increased my fury, as the beating of a drum stimulates the soldier into courage.

But even yet I refrained and kept still. I scarcely breathed. I held the lantern motionless. I tried how steadily I could maintain the ray upon the eye. Meantime the hellish tattoo of the heart increased. It grew quicker and quicker, and louder and louder every instant. The old man's terror *must* have been extreme! It grew louder, I say, louder every moment! Do you mark me well? I have told you that I am nervous—so I am. And now at the dead hour of the night, amid the dreadful silence of that old house, so strange a noise as this excited me to uncontrollable terror. Yet, for some minutes longer I refrained and stood still. But the beating grew louder, louder! I thought the heart must burst. And now a new anxiety seized me—the sound would be heard by a neighbor! The old man's hour had come! With a loud yell, I threw open the lantern and leaped into the room. He shrieked once—once only. In an instant I dragged him to the floor, and pulled the heavy bed over him. I then smiled gaily, to find the deed so far done. But, for many minutes, the heart beat on with a muffled sound. This, however, did not vex me; it would not be heard through the wall. At length it ceased. The old man was dead. I removed the bed and examined the corpse. Yes, he was stone, stone dead. I placed my hand upon the heart and held it there many minutes. There was no pulsation. He was stone dead. His eye would trouble me no more.

If still you think me mad, you will think so no longer when I describe the wise precautions I took for the concealment of the body. The night waned, and I worked hastily, but in silence. First of all I dismembered the corpse. I cut off the head and the arms and the legs.

I then took up three planks from the flooring of the chamber, and deposited all between the scantlings. I then replaced the boards so cleverly, so cunningly, that no human eye—not even *his*—could have detected anything wrong. There was nothing to wash out—no stain of any kind—no blood spot whatever. I had been too wary for that. A tub had caught all—ha! ha!

When I had made an end of these labors, it was four o'clock—still dark as midnight. As the bell sounded the hour, there came a knocking at the street door. I went down to open it with a light heart—for what had I *now* to fear? There entered three men, who introduced themselves, with perfect suavity, as officers of the police. A shriek had been heard by a neighbor during the night; suspicion of foul play had been aroused; information had been lodged at the police office, and they (the officers) had been deputed to search the premises.

I smiled—for *what* had I to fear? I bade the gentlemen welcome. The shriek, I said, was my own in a dream. The old man, I mentioned, was absent in the country. I took my visitors all over the house. I bade them search—search *well*. I led them, at length, to *his* chamber. I showed them his treasures, secure, undisturbed. In the enthusiasm of my confidence, I brought chairs into the room, and desired them *here* to rest from their fatigues, while I myself, in the wild audacity of my perfect triumph, placed my own seat upon the very spot beneath which reposed the corpse of the victim.

The officers were satisfied. My *manner* had convinced them. I was singularly at ease. They sat, and while I answered cheerily, they chatted familiar things. But, ere long, I felt myself getting pale and wished them gone. My head ached, and I fancied a ringing in my ears; but still they sat and still chatted. The ringing became more distinct—it continued and became more distinct. I talked more freely to get rid of the feeling, but it continued and gained definitiveness—until, at length, I found that the noise was *not* within my ears.

No doubt I now grew *very* pale—but I talked more fluently, and with a heightened voice. Yet the sound increased—and what could I do? It was *a low, dull, quick sound—much such a sound as a watch makes when enveloped in cotton.* I gasped for breath—and yet the officers heard it not. I talked more quickly—more vehemently; but the noise steadily increased. I arose and argued about trifles, in a high key and with violent gesticulations, but the noise steadily increased. Why *would* they not be gone? I paced the floor to and fro with heavy strides, as if excited to fury by the observation of the men—but the noise steadily increased. O God! What *could* I do? I foamed—I raved—I swore! I swung the chair upon which I had been sitting, and grated it upon the boards, but the noise arose over all and continually increased. It grew louder—louder—*louder!* And still the men chatted pleasantly, and smiled. Was it possible they heard not? Almighty God!—no, no! They heard!—they suspected!—they *knew!*—they were making a mockery of my horror! This I thought, and this I think. But anything was better than this agony! Anything was more tolerable than this derision! I could bear those hypocritical smiles no longer! I felt that I must scream or die!—and now—again!—hark! louder! louder! louder! *louder!*—

"Villains!" I shrieked, "dissemble no more! I admit the deed!—tear up the planks!—here, here!—it is the beating of his hideous heart!"

THE MAN
WHO SAW THE FLOOD

RICHARD WRIGHT

A<small>T LAST THE</small> floodwaters had receded. A black father, a black mother, and a black child tramped through muddy fields, leading a tired cow by a thin bit of rope. They stopped on a hilltop and shifted the bundles on their shoulders. As far as they could see the ground was covered with flood silt. The little girl lifted a skinny finger and pointed to a mud-caked cabin.

"Look, Pa! Ain tha our home?"

The man, round-shouldered, clad in blue, ragged overalls, looked with bewildered eyes. Without moving a muscle, scarcely moving his lips, he said, "Yeah."

For five minutes they did not speak or move. The floodwaters had been more than eight feet high here. Every tree, blade of grass, and stray stick had its floodmark: cakey, yellow mud. It clung to the ground, cracking thinly here and there in spiderweb fashion. Over the stark fields came a gusty spring wind. The sky was high, blue, full of white clouds and sunshine. Over all hung a first-day strangeness.

"The henhouse is gone," sighed the woman.

"N the pigpen," sighed the man.

They spoke without bitterness.

"Ah reckon them chickens is all done drowned."

"Yeah."

"Miz Flora's house is gone, too," said the little girl.

They looked at a clump of trees where their neighbor's house had stood.

"Lawd!"

"Yuh reckon anybody knows where they is?"

"Hard t tell."

The man walked down the slope and stood uncertainly.

"There wuz a road erlong here somewheres," he said.

But there was no road now. Just a wide sweep of yellow, scalloped silt.

"Look, Tom!" called the woman. "Here's a piece of our gate!"

The gatepost was half buried in the ground. A rusty hinge stood stiff, like a lonely finger. Tom pried it loose and caught it firmly in his hand. There was nothing particular he wanted to do with it; he just stood holding it firmly. Finally he dropped it, looked up, and said, "C mon. Les go down n see whut we kin do."

Because it sat in a slight depression, the ground about the cabin was soft and slimy.

"Gimme tha bag o lime, May," he said.

With his shoes sucking in mud, he went slowly around the cabin, spreading the white lime with thick fingers. When he reached the front again he had a little left; he shook the bag out on the porch. The fine grains of floating lime flickered in the sunlight.

"Tha oughta hep some," he said.

"Now, yuh be careful, Sal!" said May. "Don yuh go n fall down in all this mud, yuh hear?"

"Yessum."

The steps were gone. Tom lifted May and Sally to the porch. They stood a moment looking at the half-opened door. He had shut it when he left, but somehow it seemed natural that he should find it open. The planks in the porch floor were swollen and warped. The cabin had two colors: near the bottom it was a solid yellow; at the top it was the familiar gray. It looked weird, as though its ghost were standing beside it.

The cow lowed.

"Tie Pat t the pos on the en of the porch, May."

May tied the rope slowly, listlessly.

When they attempted to open the front door, it would not budge. It was not until Tom placed his shoulder against it and gave it a stout shove that it scraped back jerkily. The front room was dark and silent.

The damp smell of flood silt came fresh and sharp to their nostrils. Only one half of the upper window was clear, and through it fell a rectangle of dingy light. The floor swam in ooze. Like a mute warning, a wavering floodmark went high around the walls of the room. A dresser sat catercornered, its drawers and sides bulging like a bloated corpse. The bed, with the mattress still on it, was like a giant casket forged of mud. Two smashed chairs lay in a corner, as though huddled together for protection.

"Les see the kitchen," said Tom.

The stovepipe was gone. But the stove stood in the same place.

"The stove's still good. We kin clean it."

"Yeah."

"But where's the table?"

"Lawd knows."

"It must've washed erway wid the rest of the stuff, Ah reckon."

They opened the back door and looked out. They missed the barn, the henhouse, and the pigpen.

"Tom, yuh bettah try tha ol pump n see ef eny watah's there."

The pump was stiff. Tom threw his weight on the handle and carried it up and down. No water came. He pumped on. There was a dry, hollow cough. Then yellow water trickled. He caught his breath and kept pumping. The water flowed white.

"Thank Gawd! We's got some watah."

"Yuh bettah boil it fo yuh use it," he said.

"Yeah. Ah know."

"Look, Pa! Here's yo ax," called Sally.

Tom took the ax from her. "Yeah. Ah'll need this."

"N here's somethin else," called Sally, digging spoons out of the mud.

"Waal, Ahma git a bucket n start cleanin," said May. "Ain no use in waitin, cause we's gotta sleep on them floors tonight."

When she was filling the bucket from the pump, Tom called from around the cabin. "May, look! Ah done foun mah plow!" Proudly he dragged the silt-caked plow to the pump. "Ah'll wash it n it'll be awright."

"Ahm hongry," said Sally.

"Now, yuh jus wait! Yuh et this mawnin," said May. She turned to Tom. "Now, whutcha gonna do, Tom?"

He stood looking at the mud-filled fields.

"Yuh goin back t Burgess?"

"Ah reckon Ah have to."

"Whut else kin yuh do?"

"Nothin," he said. "Lawd, but Ah sho hate t start all over wid tha white man. Ah'd leave here ef Ah could. Ah owes im nigh eight hundred dollahs. N we needs a hoss, grub, seed, n a lot mo other things. Ef we keeps on like this tha white man'll own us body n soul."

"But, Tom, there ain nothin else t do," she said.

"Ef we try t run erway they'll put us in jail."

"It coulda been worse," she said.

Sally came running from the kitchen. "Pa!"

"Hunh?"

"There's a shelf in the kitchen the flood didn git!"

"Where?"

"Right up over the stove."

"But, chile, ain nothin up there," said May.

"But there's somethin on it," said Sally.

"C mon. Les see."

High and dry, untouched by the floodwater, was a box of matches. And beside it a half-full sack of Bull Durham tobacco. He took a match from the box and scratched it on his overalls. It burned to his fingers before he dropped it.

"May!"

"Hunh?"

"Look! Here's ma bacco n some matches!"

She stared unbelievingly. "Lawd!" she breathed.

Tom rolled a cigarette clumsily.

May washed the stove, gathered some sticks, and after some difficulty, made a fire. The kitchen stove smoked, and their eyes smarted. May put water on to heat and went into the front room. It was getting dark. From the bundles they took a kerosene lamp and lit it. Outside Pat lowed longingly into the thickening gloam and tinkled her cowbell.

"Tha old cow's hongry," said May.

"Ah reckon Ah'll have t be gittin erlong t Burgess."

They stood on the front porch.

"Yuh bettah git on, Tom, fo it gits too dark."

"Yeah."

The wind had stopped blowing. In the east a cluster of stars hung.

"Yuh goin, Tom?"

"Ah reckon Ah have t."

"Ma, Ahm hongry," said Sally.

"Wait erwhile, honey. Ma knows yuh's hongry."

Tom threw his cigarette away and sighed.

"Look! Here comes somebody!"

"Thas Mistah Burgess now!"

A mud-caked buggy rolled up. The shaggy horse was splattered all over. Burgess leaned his white face out of the buggy and spat.

"Well, I see you're back."

"Yessuh."

"How things look?"

"They don look so good, mistah."

"What seems to be the trouble?"

"Waal. Ah ain got no hoss, no grub, nothin. The only thing Ah got is tha ol cow there. . . ."

"You owe eight hundred dollahs down at the store, Tom."

"Yessuh, Ah know. But, Mistah Burgess, can't yuh knock somethin off of tha, seein as how Ahm down n out now?"

"You ate that grub, and I got to pay for it, Tom."

"Yessuh, Ah know."

"It's going to be a little tough, Tom. But you got to go through with it. Two of the boys tried to run away this morning and dodge their debts, and I had to have the sheriff pick em up. I wasn't looking for no trouble out of you, Tom. . . . The rest of the families are going back."

Leaning out of the buggy, Burgess waited. In the surrounding stillness the cowbell tinkled again. Tom stood with his back against a post.

"Yuh got t go on, Tom. We ain got nothin here," said May.

Tom looked at Burgess.

"Mistah Burgess, Ah don wanna make no trouble. But this is jus *too* hard. Ahm worse off now than befo. Ah got to start from scratch."

"Get in the buggy and come with me. I'll stake you with grub. We can talk over how you can pay it back." Tom said nothing. He rested his back against the post and looked at the mud-filled fields.

"Well," asked Burgess. "You coming?" Tom said nothing. He got slowly to the ground and pulled himself into the buggy. May watched them drive off.

"Hurry back, Tom!"

"Awright."

"Ma, tell Pa t bring me some 'lasses," begged Sally.

"Oh, Tom!"

Tom's head came out of the side of the buggy.

"Hunh?"

"Bring some 'lasses!"

"Hunh?"

"Bring some 'lasses for Sal!"

"Awright!"

She watched the buggy disappear over the crest of the muddy hill. Then she sighed, caught Sally's hand, and turned back into the cabin.

BARN BURNING

WILLIAM FAULKNER

Will Faulkner (signature)

THE STORE in which the justice of the peace's court was sitting smelled of cheese. The boy, crouched on his nail keg at the back of the crowded room, knew he smelled cheese, and more: from where he sat he could see the ranked shelves close-packed with the solid, squat, dynamic shapes of tin cans whose labels his stomach read, not from the lettering which meant nothing to his mind but from the scarlet devils and the silver curve of fish—this, the cheese which he knew he smelled and the hermetic meat which his intestines believed he smelled coming in intermittent gusts momentary and brief between the other constant one, the smell and sense just a little of fear because mostly of despair and grief, the old fierce pull of blood. He could not see the table where the justice sat and before which his father and his father's enemy *(our enemy* he thought in that despair; *ourn! mine and hisn both! He's my father!)* stood, but he could hear them, the two of them that is, because his father had said no word yet:

"But what proof have you, Mr. Harris?"

"I told you. The hog got into my corn. I caught it up and sent it back to him. He had no fence that would hold it. I told him so, warned him. The next time I put the hog in my pen. When he came to get it I gave him enough wire to patch up his pen. The next time I put the hog up and kept it. I rode down to his house and saw the wire I gave him still rolled onto the spool in his yard. I told him he could have the hog when he paid me a dollar pound fee. That evening a nigger came with the dollar and got the hog. He was a strange nigger. He said, 'He say to tell you wood and hay kin burn.' I said, 'What?' 'That whut he say to tell you,' the nigger said. 'Wood and hay kin burn.' That night my barn burned. I got the stock out but I lost the barn."

"Where is the nigger? Have you got him?"

"He was a strange nigger, I tell you. I don't know what became of him."

"But that's not proof. Don't you see that's not proof?"

"Get that boy up here. He knows." For a moment the boy thought too that the man meant his older brother until Harris said, "Not him. The little one. The boy," and, crouching, small for his age, small and wiry like his father, in patched and faded jeans even too small for him, with straight, uncombed, brown hair and eyes gray and wild as storm scud, he saw the men between himself and the table part and become a lane of grim faces, at the end of which he saw the justice, a shabby, collarless, graying man in spectacles, beckoning him. He felt no floor under his bare feet; he seemed to walk beneath the palpable weight of the grim turning faces. His father, stiff in his black Sunday coat donned not for the trial but for the moving, did not even look at him. *He aims for me to lie,* he thought, again with that frantic grief and despair. *And I will have to do hit.*

"What's your name, boy?" the justice said.

"Colonel Sartoris Snopes," the boy whispered.

"Hey?" the justice said. "Talk louder. Colonel Sartoris? I reckon anybody named for Colonel Sartoris in this country can't help but tell the truth, can they?" The boy said nothing. *Enemy! Enemy!* he thought; for a moment he could not even see, could not see that the justice's face was kindly nor discern that his voice was troubled when he spoke to the man named Harris: "Do you want me to question this boy?" But he could hear, and during those subsequent long seconds while there was absolutely no sound in the crowded little room save that of quiet and intent breathing it was as if he had swung outward at the end of a grapevine, over a ravine, and at the top of the swing had been caught in a prolonged instant of mesmerized gravity, weightless in time.

"No!" Harris said violently, explosively. "Damnation! Send him out of here!" Now time, the fluid world, rushed beneath him again, the voices coming to him again through the smell of cheese and sealed meat, the fear and despair and the old grief of blood:

"This case is closed. I can't find against you, Snopes, but I can give you advice. Leave this country and don't come back to it."

His father spoke for the first time, his voice cold and harsh, level, without emphasis: "I aim to. I don't figure to stay in a country among people who . . ." he said something unprintable and vile, addressed to no one.

"That'll do," the justice said. "Take your wagon and get out of this country before dark. Case dismissed."

His father turned, and he followed the stiff black coat, the wiry figure walking a little stiffly from where a Confederate provost's man's musket ball had taken him in the heel on a stolen horse thirty years ago, followed the two backs now, since his older brother had appeared from somewhere in the crowd, no taller than the father but thicker, chewing tobacco steadily, between the two lines of grim-faced men and out of the store and across the worn gallery and down the sagging steps and among the dogs and half-grown boys in the mild May dust, where as he passed a voice hissed:

"Barn burner!"

Again he could not see, whirling; there was a face in a red haze, moonlike, bigger than the full moon, the owner of it half again his size, he leaping in the red haze toward the face, feeling no blow, feeling no shock when his head struck the earth, scrabbling up and leaping again, feeling no blow this time either and tasting no blood, scrabbling up to see the other boy in full flight and himself already leaping into pursuit as his father's hand jerked him back, the harsh, cold voice speaking above him: "Go get in the wagon."

It stood in a grove of locusts and mulberries across the road. His two hulking sisters in their Sunday dresses and his mother and her sister in calico and sunbonnets were already in it, sitting on and among the sorry residue of the dozen and more movings which even the boy could remember—the battered stove, the broken beds and chairs, the clock inlaid with mother-of-pearl, which would not run, stopped at some fourteen minutes past two o'clock of a dead and forgotten day and time, which had been his mother's dowry. She was crying, though when she saw him she drew her sleeve across her face and began to descend from the wagon. "Get back," the father said.

"He's hurt. I got to get some water and wash his—"

"Get back in the wagon," his father said. He got in too, over the tailgate. His father mounted to the seat where the older brother already sat, and struck the gaunt mules two savage blows with the peeled willow, but without heat. It was not even sadistic; it was exactly that same quality which in later years would cause his descendants to overrun the engine before putting a motorcar into motion, striking and reining back in the same movement. The wagon went on, the store with its quiet crowd of grimly watching men dropped behind; a curve in the road hid it. *Forever* he thought. *Maybe he's done satisfied now, now that he has* . . . stopping himself, not to say it aloud even to himself. His mother's hand touched his shoulder.

"Does hit hurt?" she said.

"Naw," he said. "Hit don't hurt. Lemme be."

"Can't you wipe some of the blood off before hit dries?"

"I'll wash tonight," he said. "Lemme be, I tell you."

The wagon went on. He did not know where they were going. None of them ever did or ever asked, because it was always somewhere, always a house of sorts waiting for them a day or two days or even three days away. Likely his father had already arranged to make a crop on another farm before he— Again he had to stop himself. He (the father) always did. There was something about his wolflike independence and even courage when the advantage was at least neutral which impressed strangers, as if they got from his latent ravening ferocity not so much a sense of dependability as a feeling that his ferocious conviction in the rightness of his own actions would be of advantage to all whose interest lay with his.

That night they camped, in a grove of oaks and beeches where a spring ran. The nights were still cool and they had a fire against it, of a rail lifted from a nearby fence and cut into lengths—a small fire, neat, niggard almost, a shrewd fire; such fires were his father's habit and custom always, even in freezing weather. Older, the boy might have remarked this and wondered why not a big one; why should not a man who had not only seen the waste and extravagance of war, but who had in his blood an inherent voracious prodigality with material not his own, have burned everything in sight? Then he might have gone a step farther and thought that that was the reason: that niggard blaze was the living fruit of nights passed during those four years in the woods hiding from all men, blue or gray, with his strings of horses (captured horses, he called them). And older still, he might have divined the true reason: that the element of fire spoke to some deep mainspring of his father's being, as the element of steel or of powder spoke to other men, as the one weapon for the preservation of integrity, else breath were not worth the breathing, and hence to be regarded with respect and used with discretion.

But he did not think this now and he had seen those same niggard blazes all his life. He merely ate his supper beside it and was already half asleep over his iron plate when his father called him, and once more he followed the stiff back, the stiff and ruthless limp, up the slope and onto the starlit road where, turning, he could see his father against the stars but without face or depth—a shape black, flat, and bloodless, as though cut from tin in the iron folds of the frock coat which had not been made for him, the voice harsh like tin and without heat like tin: "You were fixing to tell them. You would have told him."

He didn't answer. His father struck him with the flat of his hand on the side of the head, hard but without heat, exactly as he had struck the two mules at the store, exactly as he would strike either of them with any stick in order to kill a horsefly, his voice still without heat or anger: "You're getting to be a man. You got to learn. You got to learn to stick to your own blood or you ain't going to have any blood to stick to you. Do you think either of them, any man there this morning, would? Don't you know all they wanted was a chance to get at me because they knew I had them beat? Eh?" Later, twenty years later, he was to tell himself, "If I had said they wanted only truth, justice, he would have hit me again." But now he said nothing. He was not crying. He just stood there. "Answer me," his father said.

"Yes," he whispered. His father turned.

"Get on to bed. We'll be there tomorrow."

Tomorrow they were there. In the early afternoon the wagon stopped before a paintless two-room house identical almost with the dozen others it had stopped before even in the boy's ten years, and again, as on the other dozen occasions, his mother and aunt got down and began to unload the wagon, although his two sisters and his father and brother had not moved.

"Likely hit ain't fitten for hawgs," one of the sisters said.

"Nevertheless, fit it will and you'll hog it and like it," his father said. "Get out of them chairs and help your ma unload."

The two sisters got down, big, bovine, in a flutter of cheap ribbons; one of them drew from the jumbled wagon bed a battered lantern, the other a worn broom. His father handed the reins to the older son and began to climb stiffly over the wheel. "When they get unloaded, take the team to the barn and feed them." Then he said, and at first the boy thought he was still speaking to his brother, "Come with me."

"Me?" he said.

"Yes," his father said. "You."

"Abner," his mother said. His father paused and looked back—the harsh level stare beneath the shaggy, graying, irascible brows.

"I reckon I'll have a word with the man that aims to begin tomorrow owning me body and soul for the next eight months."

They went back up the road. A week ago—or before last night, that is—he would have asked where they were going, but not now. His father had struck him before last night but never before had he paused afterward to explain why; it was as if the blow and the following calm, outrageous voice still rang, repercussed, divulging nothing to him save the terrible handicap of being young, the light weight of his few years, just heavy enough to prevent his soaring free of the world as it seemed to be ordered but not heavy enough to keep him footed solid in it, to resist it and try to change the course of its events.

Presently he could see the grove of oaks and cedars and the other flowering trees and shrubs where the house would be, though not the house yet. They walked beside a fence massed with honeysuckle and Cherokee roses and came to a gate swinging open between two brick pillars, and now, beyond a sweep of drive, he saw the house for the first time and at that instant he forgot his father and the terror and despair both, and even when he remembered his father again (who had not stopped) the terror and despair did not return. Because, for all the twelve movings, they had sojourned until now in a poor country, a land of small farms and fields and houses, and he had never seen a house like this before. *Hit's big as a courthouse* he thought quietly, with a surge of peace and joy whose reason he could not have thought into words, being too young for that: *They are safe from him. People whose lives are a part of this peace and dignity are beyond his touch, he no more to them than a buzzing wasp: capable of stinging for a little moment but that's all; the spell of this peace and dignity rendering even the barns and stable and cribs which belong to it impervious to the puny flames he might contrive . . .* this, the peace and joy, ebbing for an instant as he looked again at the stiff black back, the stiff and implacable limp of the figure which was not dwarfed by the house, for the reason that it had never looked big anywhere and which now, against the serene columned backdrop, had more than ever that impervious quality of something cut ruthlessly from tin, depthless, as though, sidewise to the sun, it would cast no shadow. Watching him, the boy remarked the absolutely undeviating course which his father held and saw the stiff foot come squarely down in a pile of fresh droppings where a horse had stood in the drive and which his father could have avoided by a simple change of stride. But it ebbed only for a moment, though he could not have thought this into words either, walking on in the spell of the house, which he could even want but without envy, without sorrow, certainly never with that ravening and jealous rage which unknown to him walked in the ironlike black coat before him: *Maybe he will feel it too. Maybe it will even change him now from what maybe he couldn't help but be.*

They crossed the portico. Now he could hear his father's stiff foot as it came down on the boards with clocklike finality, a sound out of all proportion to the displacement of the body it bore and which was not dwarfed either by the white door before it, as though it had attained to a sort of vicious and ravening minimum not to be dwarfed by anything—the flat, wide, black hat, the formal coat of broadcloth which had once been black but which had now that friction-glazed greenish cast of the bodies of old houseflies, the lifted sleeve which was too large, the lifted hand like a curled claw. The door opened so promptly that the boy knew the Negro must have been watching them all the time, an old man with neat grizzled hair, in a linen jacket, who stood barring the door with his body, saying, "Wipe yo foots, white man, fo you come in here. Major ain't home nohow."

"Get out of my way, nigger," his father said, without heat too, flinging the door back and the Negro also and entering, his hat still on his head. And now the boy saw the prints of the stiff foot on the doorjamb and saw them appear on the pale rug behind the machinelike deliberation of the foot which seemed to bear (or transmit) twice the weight which the body compassed. The Negro was shouting, "Miss Lula! Miss Lula!" somewhere behind them; then the boy, deluged as though by a warm wave by a suave turn of carpeted stair and a pendant glitter of chandeliers and a mute gleam of gold frames, heard the swift feet and saw her too, a lady—perhaps he had never seen her like before either—in a gray, smooth gown with lace at the throat and an apron tied at the waist and the sleeves turned back, wiping cake or biscuit dough from her hands with a towel as she came up the hall, looking not at his father at all but at the tracks on the blond rug with an expression of incredulous amazement.

"I tried," the Negro cried. "I tole him to . . ."

"Will you please go away?" she said in a shaking voice. "Major de Spain is not at home. Will you please go away?"

His father had not spoken again. He did not speak again. He did not even look at her. He just stood stiff in the center of the rug, in his hat, the shaggy iron-gray brows twitching slightly above the pebble-colored eyes as he appeared to examine the house with brief deliberation. Then with the same deliberation he turned; the boy watched him pivot on the good leg and saw the stiff foot drag round the arc of the turning, leaving a final long and fading smear. His father never looked at it, he never once looked down at the rug. The Negro held the door. It closed behind them, upon the hysteric and indistinguishable woman-wail. His father stopped at the top of the steps and scraped his boot clean on the edge of it. At the gate he stopped again. He stood for a moment, planted stiffly on the stiff foot, looking back at the house. "Pretty and white, ain't it?" he said. "That's sweat. Nigger sweat. Maybe it ain't white enough yet to suit him. Maybe he wants to mix some white sweat with it."

Two hours later the boy was chopping wood behind the house within which his mother and aunt and the two sisters (the mother and aunt, not the two girls, he knew that; even at this distance and muffled by walls the flat loud voices of the two girls emanated an incorrigible idle inertia) were setting up the stove to prepare a meal, when he heard the hooves and saw the linen-clad man on a fine sorrel mare, whom he recognized even before he saw the rolled rug in front of the Negro youth following on a fat bay carriage horse—a suffused, angry face vanishing, still at full gallop, beyond the corner of the house where his father and brother were sitting in the two tilted chairs; and a moment later, almost before he could have put the ax down, he heard the hooves again and watched the sorrel mare go back out of the yard, already galloping again. Then his father began to shout one of the sisters' names, who presently emerged backward from the kitchen door dragging the rolled rug along the ground by one end while the other sister walked behind it.

"If you ain't going to tote, go on and set up the washpot," the first said.

"You, Sarty!" the second shouted. "Set up the washpot!" His father appeared at the door, framed against that shabbiness, as he had been against that other bland perfection, impervious to either, the mother's anxious face at his shoulder.

"Go on," the father said. "Pick it up." The two sisters stooped, broad, lethargic; stooping, they presented an incredible expanse of pale cloth and a flutter of tawdry ribbons.

"If I thought enough of a rug to have to git hit all the way from France, I wouldn't keep hit where folks coming in would have to tromp on hit," the first said. They raised the rug.

"Abner," the mother said. "Let me do it."

"You go back and git dinner," his father said. "I'll tend to this."

From the woodpile through the rest of the afternoon the boy watched them, the rug spread flat in the dust beside the bubbling washpot, the two sisters stooping over it with that profound and lethargic reluctance, while the father stood over them in turn, implacable and grim, driving them though never raising his voice again. He could smell the harsh homemade lye they were using; he saw his mother come to the door once and look toward them with an expression not anxious now but very like despair; he saw his father turn, and he fell to with the ax and saw from the corner of his eye his father raise from the ground a flattish fragment of fieldstone and examine it and return to the pot, and this time his mother actually spoke: "Abner. Abner. Please don't. Please, Abner."

Then he was done too. It was dusk; the whippoorwills had already begun. He could smell coffee from the room where they would presently eat the cold food remaining from the midafternoon meal, though when he entered the house he realized they were having coffee again probably because there was a fire on the hearth, before which the rug now lay spread over the backs of the two chairs. The tracks of his father's foot were gone. Where they had been were now long, water-cloudy scoriations resembling the sporadic course of a lilliputian mowing machine.

It still hung there while they ate the cold food and then went to bed, scattered without order or claim up and down the two rooms, his mother in one bed, where his father would later lie, the older brother in the other, himself, the aunt and the two sisters on pallets on the floor. But his father was not in bed yet. The last thing the boy remembered was the depthless, harsh silhouette of the hat and coat bending over the rug, and it seemed to him that he had not even closed his eyes when the silhouette was standing over him, the fire almost dead behind it, the stiff foot prodding him awake. "Catch up the mule," his father said.

When he returned with the mule his father was standing in the black door, the rolled rug over his shoulder. "Ain't you going to ride?" he said.

"No. Give me your foot."

He bent his knee into his father's hand, the wiry, surprising power flowed smoothly, rising, he rising with it, onto the mule's bare back (they had owned a saddle once; the boy could remember it though not when or where) and with the same effortlessness his father swung the rug up in front of him. Now in the starlight they retraced the afternoon's path, up the dusty road rife with honeysuckle, through the gate and up the black tunnel of the drive to the lightless house, where he sat on the mule and felt the rough warp of the rug drag across his thighs and vanish.

"Don't you want me to help?" he whispered. His father did not answer and now he heard again that stiff foot striking the hollow portico with that wooden and clocklike deliberation, that outrageous overstatement of the weight it carried. The rug, hunched, not flung (the boy could tell that even in the darkness) from his father's shoulder struck the angle of wall and floor with a sound unbelievably loud, thunderous, then the foot again, unhurried and enormous; a light came on in the house and the boy sat, tense, breathing steadily and quietly and just a little fast, though the foot itself did not increase its beat at all, descending the steps now; now the boy could see him.

"Don't you want to ride now?" he whispered. "We kin both ride now," the light within the house altering now, flaring up and sinking. *He's coming down the stairs now,* he thought. He had already ridden the mule up beside the horse block; presently his father was up behind him and he doubled the reins over and slashed the mule across the neck, but before the animal could begin to trot the hard, thin arm came round him, the hard, knotted hand jerking the mule back to a walk.

In the first red rays of the sun they were in the lot, putting plow gear on the mules. This time the sorrel mare was in the lot before he heard it at all, the rider collarless and even bareheaded, trembling, speaking in a shaking voice as the woman in the house had done, his father merely looking up once before stooping again to the hame he was buckling, so that the man on the mare spoke to his stooping back:

"You must realize you have ruined that rug. Wasn't there anybody here, any of your women . . ." he ceased, shaking, the boy watching him, the older brother leaning now in the stable door, chewing, blinking slowly and steadily at nothing apparently. "It cost a hundred dollars. But you never had a hundred dollars. You never will. So I'm going to charge you twenty bushels of corn against your crop. I'll add it in your contract and when you come to the commissary you can sign it. That won't keep Mrs. de Spain quiet but maybe it will teach you to wipe your feet off before you enter her house again."

Then he was gone. The boy looked at his father, who still had not spoken or even looked up again, who was now adjusting the logger-head in the hame.

"Pap," he said. His father looked at him—the inscrutable face, the shaggy brows beneath which the gray eyes glinted coldly. Suddenly the boy went toward him, fast, stopping as suddenly. "You done the best you could!" he cried. "If he wanted hit done different, why didn't he wait and tell you how? He won't git no twenty bushels! He won't git none! We'll gether hit and hide hit! I kin watch . . ."

"Did you put the cutter back in that straight stock like I told you?"

"No, sir," he said.

"Then go do it."

That was Wednesday. During the rest of that week he worked steadily, at what was within his scope and some which was beyond it, with an industry that did not need to be driven nor even commanded twice; he had this from his mother, with the difference that some at least of what he did he liked to do, such as splitting wood with the half-size ax which his mother and aunt had earned, or saved money somehow, to present him with at Christmas. In company with the two older women (and on one afternoon, even one of the sisters), he built pens for the shoat and the cow which were a part of his father's contract with the landlord, and one afternoon, his father being absent, gone somewhere on one of the mules, he went to the field.

They were running a middlebuster now, his brother holding the plow straight while he handled the reins, and walking beside the straining mule, the rich black soil shearing cool and damp against his bare ankles, he thought, *Maybe this is the end of it. Maybe even that twenty bushels that seems hard to have to pay for just a rug will be a cheap price for him to stop forever and always from being what he used to be;* thinking, dreaming now, so that his brother had to speak sharply to him to mind the mule: *Maybe he even won't collect the twenty bushels. Maybe it will all add up and balance and vanish—corn, rug, fire; the terror and grief, the being pulled two ways like between two teams of horses—gone, done with for ever and ever.*

Then it was Saturday; he looked up from beneath the mule he was harnessing and saw his father in the black coat and hat. "Not that," his father said. "The wagon gear." And then, two hours later, sitting in the wagon bed behind his father and brother on the seat, the wagon accomplished a final curve, and he saw the weathered paintless store with its tattered tobacco and patent-medicine posters and the tethered wagons and saddle animals below the gallery. He mounted the gnawed steps behind his father and brother, and there again was the lane of quiet, watching faces for the three of them to walk through. He saw the man in spectacles sitting at the plank table and he did not need to be told this was a justice of the peace; he sent one glare of fierce, exultant, partisan defiance at the man in collar and cravat now, whom he had seen but twice before in his life, and that on a galloping horse, who now wore on his face an expression not of rage but of amazed unbelief which the boy could not have known was at the incredible circumstance of being sued by one of his own tenants, and came and stood against his father and cried at the justice: "He ain't done it! He ain't burnt . . ."

"Go back to the wagon," his father said.

"Burnt?" the justice said. "Do I understand this rug was burned too?"

"Does anybody here claim it was?" his father said. "Go back to the wagon." But he did not, he merely retreated to the rear of the room, crowded as that other had been, but not to sit down this time, instead, to stand pressing among the motionless bodies, listening to the voices:

"And you claim twenty bushels of corn is too high for the damage you did to the rug?"

"He brought the rug to me and said he wanted the tracks washed out of it. I washed the tracks out and took the rug back to him."

"But you didn't carry the rug back to him in the same condition it was in before you made the tracks on it."

His father did not answer, and now for perhaps half a minute there was no sound at all save that of breathing, the faint, steady suspiration of complete and intent listening.

"You decline to answer that, Mr. Snopes?" Again his father did not answer. "I'm going to find against you, Mr. Snopes. I'm going to find that you were responsible for the injury to Major de Spain's rug and hold you liable for it. But twenty bushels of corn seems a little high for a man in your circumstances to have to pay. Major de Spain claims it cost a hundred dollars. October corn will be worth about fifty cents. I figure that if Major de Spain can stand a ninety-five-dollar loss on something he paid cash for, you can stand a five-dollar loss you haven't earned yet. I hold you in damages to Major de Spain to the amount of ten bushels of corn over and above your contract with him, to be paid to him out of your crop at gathering time. Court adjourned."

It had taken no time hardly, the morning was but half begun. He thought they would return home and perhaps back to the field, since they were late, far behind all other farmers. But instead his father passed on behind the wagon, merely indicating with his hand for the older brother to follow with it, and crossed the road toward the blacksmith shop opposite; pressing on after his father, overtaking him, speaking, whispering up at the harsh, calm face beneath the weathered hat: "He won't git no ten bushels neither. He won't git one. We'll . . ." until his father glanced for an instant down at him, the face absolutely calm, the grizzled eyebrows tangled above the cold eyes, the voice almost pleasant, almost gentle: "You think so? Well, we'll wait till October anyway."

The matter of the wagon—the setting of a spoke or two and the tightening of the tires—did not take long either, the business of the tires accomplished by driving the wagon into the spring branch behind the shop and letting it stand there, the mules nuzzling into the water from time to time, and the boy on the seat with the idle reins, looking up the slope and through the sooty tunnel of the shed where the slow hammer rang and where his father sat on an upended cypress bolt, easily, either talking or listening, still sitting there when the boy brought the dripping wagon up out of the branch and halted it before the door.

"Take them on to the shade and hitch," his father said. He did so and returned. His father and the smith and a third man squatting on his heels inside the door were talking, about crops and animals; the boy, squatting too in the ammoniac dust and hoof parings and scales of rust, heard his father tell a long and unhurried story out of the time before the birth of the older brother even, when he had been a professional horse trader. And then his father came up beside him where he stood before a tattered last year's circus poster on the other side of the store, gazing rapt and quiet at the scarlet horses, the incredible poisings and convolutions of tulle and tights and the painted leers of comedians, and said, "It's time to eat."

But not at home. Squatting beside his brother against the front wall, he watched his father emerge from the store and produce from a paper sack a segment of cheese and divide it carefully and deliberately into three with his pocketknife and produce crackers from the same sack. They all three squatted on the gallery and ate, slowly, without talking; then in the store again, they drank from a tin dipper tepid water smelling of the cedar bucket and of living beech trees. And still they did not go home. It was a horse lot this time, a tall rail fence upon and along which men stood and sat and out of which one by one horses were led, to be walked and trotted and then cantered back and forth along the road while the slow swapping and buying went on and the sun began to slant westward, they—the three of them—watching and listening, the older brother with his muddy eyes and his steady, inevitable tobacco, the father commenting now and then on certain of the animals, to no one in particular.

It was after sundown when they reached home. They ate supper by lamplight, then, sitting on the doorstep, the boy watched the night fully accomplish, listening to the whippoorwills and the frogs, when he heard his mother's voice: "Abner! No! No! Oh, God. Oh, God. Abner!" and he rose, whirled, and saw the altered light through the door where a candle stub now burned in a bottle neck on the table and his father, still in the hat and coat, at once formal and burlesque as though dressed carefully for some shabby and ceremonial violence, emptying the reservoir of the lamp back into the five-gallon kerosene can from which it had been filled, while the mother tugged at his arm until he shifted the lamp to the other hand and flung her back, not savagely or viciously, just hard, into the wall, her hands flung out against the wall for balance, her mouth open and in her face the same quality of hopeless despair as had been in her voice. Then his father saw him standing in the door.

"Go to the barn and get that can of oil we were oiling the wagon with," he said.

The boy did not move. Then he could speak.

"What . . ." he cried. "What are you . . ."

"Go get that oil," his father said. "Go."

Then he was moving, running, outside the house, toward the stable: this the old habit, the old blood which he had not been permitted to choose for himself, which had been bequeathed him willy-nilly and which had run for so long (and who knew where, battening on what of outrage and savagery and lust) before it came to him. *I could keep on,* he thought. *I could run on and on and never look back, never need to see his face again. Only I can't. I can't,* the rusted can in his hand now, the liquid sploshing in it as he ran back to the house and into it, into the sound of his mother's weeping in the next room, and handed the can to his father.

"Ain't you going to even send a nigger?" he cried. "At least you sent a nigger before!"

This time his father didn't strike him. The hand came even faster than the blow had, the same hand which had set the can on the table with almost excruciating care flashing from the can toward him too quick for him to follow it, gripping him by the back of his shirt and onto tiptoe before he had seen it quit the can, the face stooping at him in breathless and frozen ferocity, the cold, dead voice speaking over him to the older brother who leaned against the table, chewing with that steady, curious, sidewise motion of cows:

"Empty the can into the big one and go on. I'll catch up with you."

"Better tie him up to the bedpost," the brother said.

"Do like I told you," the father said. Then the boy was moving, his bunched shirt and the hard, bony hand between his shoulder blades, his toes just touching the floor, across the room and into the other one, past the sisters sitting with spread heavy thighs in the two chairs over the cold hearth, and to where his mother and aunt sat side by side on the bed, the aunt's arms about his mother's shoulders.

"Hold him," the father said. The aunt made a startled movement. "Not you," the father said. "Lennie. Take hold of him. I want to see you do it." His mother took him by the wrist. "You'll hold him better than that. If he gets loose, don't you know what he is going to do? He will go up yonder." He jerked his head toward the road. "Maybe I'd better tie him."

"I'll hold him," his mother whispered.

"See you do then." Then his father was gone, the stiff foot heavy and measured upon the boards, ceasing at last.

Then he began to struggle. His mother caught him in both arms, he jerking and wrenching at them. He would be stronger in the end, he knew that. But he had no time to wait for it. "Lemme go!" he cried. "I don't want to have to hit you!"

"Let him go!" the aunt said. "If he don't go, before God, I am going up there myself!"

"Don't you see I can't?" his mother cried. "Sarty! Sarty! No! No! Help me, Lizzie!"

Then he was free. His aunt grasped at him but it was too late. He whirled, running, his mother stumbled forward onto her knees behind him, crying to the nearer sister: "Catch him, Net! Catch him!" But that was too late too, the sister (the sisters were twins, born at the same time, yet either of them now gave the impression of being, encompassing as much living meat and volume and weight as any other two of the family) not yet having begun to rise from the chair, her head, face, alone merely turned, presenting to him in the flying instant an astonishing expanse of young female features untroubled by any surprise even, wearing only an expression of bovine interest. Then he was out of the room, out of the house, in the mild dust of the starlit road and the heavy rifeness of honeysuckle, the pale ribbon unspooling with terrific slowness under his running feet, reaching the gate at last and turning in, running, his heart and lungs drumming, on up the drive toward the lighted house, the lighted door. He did not knock, he burst in, sobbing for breath, incapable for the moment of speech; he saw the astonished face of the Negro in the linen jacket without knowing when the Negro had appeared.

"De Spain!" he cried, panted. "Where's . . ." then he saw the white man too emerging from a white door down the hall. "Barn!" he cried. "Barn!"

"What?" the white man said. "Barn?"

"Yes!" the boy cried. "Barn!"

"Catch him!" the white man shouted.

But it was too late this time too. The Negro grasped his shirt, but the entire sleeve, rotten with washing, carried away, and he was out that door too and in the drive again, and had actually never ceased to run even while he was screaming into the white man's face.

Behind him the white man was shouting, "My horse! Fetch my horse!" and he thought for an instant of cutting across the park and climbing the fence into the road, but he did not know the park nor how high the vine-massed fence might be and he dared not risk it. So he ran on down the drive, blood and breath roaring; presently he was in the road again though he could not see it. He could not hear either: the galloping mare was almost upon him before he heard her, and even then he held his course, as if the very urgency of his wild grief and need must in a moment more find him wings, waiting until the ultimate instant to hurl himself aside and into the weed-choked roadside ditch as the horse thundered past and on, for an instant in furious silhouette against the stars, the tranquil early summer night sky which, even before the shape of the horse and rider vanished, stained abruptly and violently upward: a long, swirling roar incredible and soundless, blotting the stars, and he springing up and into the road again, running again, knowing it was too late yet still running even after he heard the shot and, an instant later, two shots, pausing now without knowing he had ceased to run, crying "Pap! Pap!", running again before he knew he had begun to run, stumbling, tripping over something and scrabbling up again without ceasing to run, looking backward over his shoulder at the glare as he got up, running on among the invisible trees, panting, sobbing, "Father! Father!"

At midnight he was sitting on the crest of a hill. He did not know it was midnight and he did not know how far he had come. But there was no glare behind him now and he sat now, his back toward what he had called home for four days anyhow, his face toward the dark woods which he would enter when breath was strong again, small, shaking steadily in the chill darkness, hugging himself into the remainder of his thin, rotten shirt, the grief and despair now no longer terror and fear but just grief and despair. *Father. My father,* he thought. "He was brave!" he cried suddenly, aloud but not loud, no more than a whisper: "He was! He was in the war! He was in Colonel Sartoris' cav'ry!" not knowing that his father had gone to that war a private in the fine old European sense, wearing no uniform, admitting the authority of and giving fidelity to no man or army or flag, going to war as Malbrouck himself did: for booty—it meant nothing and less than nothing to him if it were enemy booty or his own.

The slow constellations wheeled on. It would be dawn and then sun-up after a while and he would be hungry. But that would be tomorrow and now he was only cold, and walking would cure that. His breathing was easier now and he decided to get up and go on, and then he found that he had been asleep because he knew it was almost dawn, the night almost over. He could tell that from the whippoorwills. They were everywhere now among the dark trees below him, constant and inflectioned and ceaseless, so that, as the instant for giving over to the day birds drew nearer and nearer, there was no interval at all between them. He got up. He was a little stiff, but walking would cure that too as it would the cold, and soon there would be the sun. He went on down the hill, toward the dark woods within which the liquid silver voices of the birds called unceasing—the rapid and urgent beating of the urgent and quiring heart of the late spring night. He did not look back.

THE YELLOW WALL PAPER

CHARLOTTE PERKINS GILMAN

Charlotte Perkins Gilman

I<small>T IS VERY</small> seldom that mere ordinary people like John and myself secure ancestral halls for the summer.

A colonial mansion, a hereditary estate, I would say a haunted house, and reach the height of romantic felicity—but that would be asking too much of fate!

Still, there is something queer about it. Else, why should it be let so cheaply? And why have stood so long untenanted?

John laughs at me, of course, but one expects that in marriage.

John is a physician, and practical in the extreme. He scoffs openly at any talk of things not to be felt and seen and put down in figures, and *perhaps* (I would not say it to a living soul, of course, but this is dead paper and a great relief to my mind)—*perhaps* that is one reason I do not get well faster.

You see, he does not believe I am sick!

If a physician of high standing, and one's own husband, assures friends and relatives that there is really nothing the matter with one but temporary nervous depression—a slight hysterical tendency—what is one to do? My brother is also a physician, and also of high standing, and he says the same thing.

So I take phosphates, and tonics, and journeys, and air, and exercise and am absolutely forbidden to "work" until I am well again.

I did write for a while in spite of them; but it does exhaust me a good deal—having to be so sly about it, or else meet with heavy opposition.

Personally I sometimes fancy that in my condition if I had less opposition and more society and stimulus—but John says the very worst thing I can do is to think about my condition, and I confess it always makes me feel bad.

So I will let it alone and talk about the house.

The most beautiful place! It is quite alone, standing well back from the road, three miles from the village. There are hedges, and walls and gates that lock, and lots of separate little houses for the gardeners and people.

There is a *delicious* garden! I never saw such a garden—large and shady, full of box-bordered paths, and lined with long grape-covered arbors with seats under them. There were greenhouses, but they are all broken now. There was some legal trouble, I believe, something about the heirs and coheirs; anyhow, the place has been empty for years.

There is something strange and ghostly about the house—I can feel it. I even said so to John one moonlight evening, but he said what I felt was a *draft*, and shut the window. I get unreasonably angry with John sometimes. I think it is due to this nervous condition.

I don't like our room a bit. I wanted one downstairs that opened on the piazza and had roses all over the window, and such pretty, old-fashioned chintz hangings! But John would not hear of it.

He said there was only one window and no room for two beds. He said we came here solely on my account, that I was to have perfect rest and all the air I could get. He is very careful and loving, and hardly lets me stir without special direction. So we took the nursery, at the top of the house.

It is a big, airy room, the whole floor nearly, with windows that look all ways, and air and sunshine galore. It was nursery first and then playroom and gymnasium, I should judge; for the windows are barred for little children, and there are rings and things in the walls.

The paint and paper look as if a boys' school had used it. It is stripped off—the paper—in great patches all around the head of my bed, about as far as I can reach, and in a great place on the other side of the roof, low down.

I never saw a worse paper in my life. One of those sprawling flamboyant patterns committing every artistic sin. It is dull enough to confuse the eye, pronounced enough to constantly irritate, and provoke study. When you follow the lame, uncertain curves for a little distance they suddenly commit suicide—destroy themselves in unheard-of contradictions. The color is repellent, almost revolting; a smoldering, unclean yellow, strangely faded by the slow-turning sunlight. It is a dull yet lurid orange in some places, a sickly sulfur tint in others.

No wonder the children hated it! I should hate it myself if I had to live in this room long.

There comes John, and I must put this away—he hates to have me write a word.

WE HAVE BEEN here two weeks, and I haven't felt like writing since that first day. I am sitting by the window now, up in this atrocious nursery, and there is nothing to hinder my writing as much as I please. John is away all day, and even some nights when his cases are serious.

I am glad my case is not serious!

But these nervous troubles are dreadfully depressing. I meant to be such a help to John, and here I am a comparative burden already! Nobody would believe what an effort it is to do what little I am able.

It is fortunate Mary is so good with the baby. Such a dear baby! And yet I *cannot* be with him, it makes me so nervous.

I suppose John never was nervous in his life. He laughs at me so about this wall paper! At first he meant to repaper the room, but afterward he said that I was letting it get the better of me, and that nothing was worse for a nervous patient than to give way to such fancies. He said that after the wall paper was changed it would be the heavy bedstead, and then the barred windows, and then that gate at the head of the stairs. "You know the place is doing you good," he said, "and really, dear, I don't care to renovate the house just for a three months' rental." Then he took me in his arms and called me a blessed little goose.

But he is right enough about the beds and windows. It is as airy and comfortable a room as anyone need wish, and I'm really getting quite fond of it, all but that horrid wall paper.

It looks to me as if it *knew* what a vicious influence it had!

There is a recurrent spot where the pattern lolls like a broken neck and two bulbous eyes stare at you upside down. I got positively angry at the impertinence of it. In one place the two breadths didn't match, and the eyes go all up and down the line, one a little higher than the other.

I never saw so much expression in an inanimate thing before, and we all know how much expression they have! I used to lie awake as a child and get more entertainment and terror out of blank walls and plain furniture than most children could find in a toy store. I remember what a kindly wink the knobs of our big old bureau used to have, and there was one chair that always seemed like a strong friend.

The furniture in this room is no worse than inharmonious, however, for we had to bring it all from downstairs. I suppose when it was used as a playroom they had to take the nursery things out, and no wonder! I never saw such ravages as the children have made here.

The wall paper, as I said before, is torn off in spots. Then the floor is scratched and gouged and splintered, the plaster itself is dug out here and there, and this great heavy bed, which is all we found in the room, looks as if it had been through the wars.

But I don't mind it a bit—only the paper.

It has a kind of subpattern in a different shade, a particularly irritating one, for you can only see it in certain lights, and not clearly then. But in the places where it isn't faded, and where the sun is just so, I can see a strange, provoking, formless sort of figure that seems to sulk about that silly front design.

There's Jennie, John's sister, on the stairs! Such a dear girl as she is, and so careful of me! I must not let her find me writing. I believe she thinks it is the writing which made me sick!

WELL, THE Fourth of July is over! The people are all gone and I am tired out. John thought it might do me good to see a little company, so we just had Mother and Nellie and the children down for a week.

Of course I didn't do a thing. Jennie sees to everything now. She is a perfect, an enthusiastic housekeeper, and hopes for no better profession. But the visit tired me all the same.

John says if I don't pick up faster he shall send me to Weir Mitchell in the fall. But I don't want to go there at all. I had a friend who was in his hands once, and she says he is just like John and my brother, only more so!

I'm getting dreadfully fretful and querulous. I cry at nothing, and cry most of the time. Of course I don't when John is here, or anybody else, but when I am alone.

And I am alone a good deal just now. John is kept in town very often by serious cases, and Jennie is good and lets me alone when I want her to.

So I walk a little in the garden or sit on the porch under the roses, and lie down up here a good deal.

I'm getting really fond of the room in spite of the wall paper. Perhaps *because* of the wall paper. It dwells in my mind so!

I lie here on this great immovable bed—it is nailed down, I believe—and follow that pattern about by the hour. It is as good as gymnastics, I assure you. I start, we'll say at the bottom, down in the corner over there where it has not been touched, and I determine for the thousandth time that I *will* follow that pointless pattern to some sort of a conclusion.

It is repeated, of course, by the breadths, but not otherwise. Looked at in one way, each breadth stands alone, the bloated curves and flourishes go waddling up and down in isolated columns. But, on the other hand, they connect diagonally, and the sprawling outlines run off in great slanting waves of optic horror, like a lot of wallowing seaweeds in full chase.

It makes me tired to follow it. I will take a nap, I guess.

JOHN SAYS I mustn't lose my strength, and has me take cod-liver oil and tonics, to say nothing of ale and wine and rare meat.

Dear John! He loves me very dearly, and hates to have me sick. I tried to have a reasonable talk with him the other day, and tell him how I wished he would let me go and make a visit to Cousin Henry and Julia. But he said I wasn't able to go, nor able to stand it after I got there; and I did not make out a very good case for myself, for I was crying before I had finished.

And dear John gathered me up in his arms, and just carried me upstairs and laid me on the bed, and sat by me and read to me till he tired my head.

He said I was his darling and his comfort, and that I must take care of myself for his and the baby's sake, and keep well. He says no one but myself can help me out of it, that I must use my will and self-control and not let my silly fancies run away with me.

Of course I never mention the wall paper to him anymore—I am too wise—but I keep watch of it all the same.

There are things in that paper that nobody knows but me, or ever will. Behind that outside pattern the dim shapes get clearer every day. It is always the same shape, only very numerous. And it is like a woman stooping down and creeping about behind that pattern. I don't like it a bit. I wonder—I begin to think—I wish John would take me away from here!

IT IS SO hard to talk with John about my case, because he is so wise, and because he loves me so. But I tried it last night.

John was asleep and I hated to waken him, so I kept still and watched the moonlight on that undulating wall paper till I felt creepy. The faint figure behind seemed to shake the pattern, just as if she wanted to get out.

I got up softly and went to feel and see if the paper *did* move, and when I came back John was awake.

"What is it, little girl?" he said. "Don't go walking about like that— you'll get cold."

I thought it was a good time to talk, so I told him that I really was not gaining here, and that I wished he would take me away.

"Why, darling!" said he. "Our lease will be up in three weeks, and I can't see how to leave before. The repairs are not done at home, and you really are better, dear, whether you can see it or not. You are gaining flesh and color, your appetite is better. I feel really much easier about you."

"I don't weigh a bit more," said I, "nor as much; and my appetite may be better in the evening, when you are here, but it is worse in the morning, when you are away."

"Bless her little heart!" said he with a big hug. "She shall be as sick as she pleases. It is only three weeks more and then we will take a nice little trip while Jennie is getting the house ready. Really, dear, you are better!"

"Better in body, perhaps—" I began, and stopped short, for he sat up straight and looked at me sternly.

"My darling," said he, "I beg that you will never for one instant let that idea enter your mind! There is nothing so dangerous, so fascinating, to a temperament like yours. Can you not trust me as a physician when I tell you so? But now let's sleep, and talk about it in the morning."

So of course I said no more. He thought I was asleep, but I wasn't—I lay there for hours trying to decide whether that front pattern and the back pattern really did move together or separately.

On a pattern like this, by daylight, there is a lack of sequence, a defiance of law, that is a constant irritant to a normal mind. The color is hideous enough, and unreliable enough, and infuriating enough, but the pattern is torturing. It slaps you in the face, knocks you down, and tramples upon you. It is like a bad dream.

The outside pattern is a florid arabesque, reminding one of a fungus. If you can imagine a toadstool in joints, an interminable string of toadstools, budding and sprouting in endless convolutions—why, that is something like it.

That is, sometimes!

There is one marked peculiarity about this paper, a thing nobody seems to notice but myself, and that is that it changes as the light changes. When the first sun shoots in through the east window, it changes so quickly that I never can quite believe it. That is why I watch it always. At night in any kind of light, in twilight, candlelight, lamplight, and worst of all by moonlight, it becomes bars! The outside pattern, I mean, and the woman behind it is as plain as can be.

I didn't realize for a long time what the thing was that showed behind—that dim subpattern—but now I am quite sure it is a woman.

By daylight she is subdued, quiet. I fancy it is the pattern that keeps her so still. It is so puzzling. It keeps me quiet by the hour.

I lie down ever so much now. John started the habit by making me lie down for an hour after each meal. It is a very bad habit, I am convinced, for, you see, I don't sleep. And that cultivates deceit, for I don't tell them I'm awake—oh, no!

The fact is, I am getting a little afraid of John. He seems very queer sometimes, and even Jennie has an inexplicable look. It strikes me occasionally, just as a scientific hypothesis, that perhaps it is the paper! I have watched John when he did not know I was looking, and I've caught him several times *looking at the paper!* And Jennie, too. I caught Jennie with her hand on it once.

She didn't know I was in the room, and when I asked her in a very quiet voice what she was doing with the paper she turned around as if she had been caught stealing, and looked quite angry—asked me why I should frighten her so! Then she said that the paper stained everything it touched, and that she had found yellow smooches on all my clothes and John's, and she wished we would be more careful!

Did not that sound innocent? But I know she was studying that pattern, and I am determined that nobody shall find it out but myself! I don't want to leave now until I have found it out. There is a week more, and I think that will be enough.

I'M FEELING EVER so much better! I don't sleep much at night, for it is so interesting to watch developments; but I sleep a good deal in the daytime.

It is the strangest yellow, that wall paper! It makes me think of all the yellow things I ever saw—not beautiful ones like buttercups, but old foul, bad yellow things.

But there is something else about that paper—the smell! I noticed it the moment we came into the room, but with so much air and sun it was not bad! Now we have had a week of fog and rain, and whether the windows are open or not the smell is here.

It creeps all over the house. I find it hovering in the dining room, skulking in the parlor, hiding in the hall, lying in wait for me on the stairs. It gets into my hair.

Even when I go to ride, if I turn my head suddenly and surprise it— there is that smell! Such a peculiar odor, too! In this damp weather it is awful. I wake up in the night and find it hanging over me.

It used to disturb me at first. I thought seriously of burning the house—to reach the smell.

But now I am used to it. The only thing I can think of that it is like is the *color* of the paper—a yellow smell!

There is a very funny mark on the walls, low down, near the mopboard. A streak that runs around the room. It goes behind every piece of furniture, except the bed, a long, straight, even *smooch,* as if it had been rubbed over and over.

I wonder how it was done and who did it, and what they did it for. Round and round and round—round and round and round—it makes me dizzy!

I REALLY HAVE discovered something at last. Through watching so much at night, I have finally found out. The front pattern *does* move— and no wonder! The woman behind shakes it!

Sometimes I think there are a great many women behind, and sometimes only one, and she crawls around fast, and her crawling shakes it all over. Then in the very bright spots she keeps still, and in the very shady spots she takes hold of the bars and shakes them hard.

And she is all the time trying to climb through. But nobody could climb through that pattern—it strangles so; I think that is why it has so many heads. They get through, and then the pattern strangles them off and turns them upside down, and makes their eyes white!

If those heads were covered or taken off it would not be half so bad.

I THINK THAT woman gets out in the daytime!

And I'll tell you why—privately—I've seen her! I can see her out of every one of my windows! It is the same woman, I know, for she is always creeping, and most women do not creep by daylight. I see her in the long shaded lane, creeping up and down, as fast as a cloud shadow in a high wind. I see her in those dark grape arbors, creeping all around the garden. I see her on that long road under the trees, creeping along, and when a carriage comes she hides under the blackberry vines. I don't blame her a bit. It must be very humiliating to be caught creeping by daylight!

I always lock the door when I creep by daylight. I can't do it at night, for I know John would suspect something at once. And John is so queer, now, that I don't want to irritate him. I wish he would take another room! Besides, I don't want anybody to get that woman out at night but myself.

IF ONLY THAT TOP PATTERN could be gotten off from the under one! I mean to try it, little by little.

There are only two more days to get this wall paper off, and I believe John is beginning to notice. I don't like the look in his eyes. He knows I don't sleep very well at night, for all I'm so quiet! He asked me all sorts of questions, and pretended to be very loving and kind.

As if I couldn't see through him!

Still, I don't wonder he acts so, sleeping under this paper for three months. It only interests me, but I feel sure John and Jennie are secretly affected by it.

HURRAH! THIS is the last day, but it is enough. John is to stay in town overnight, and won't be out until this evening. Jennie wanted to sleep with me—the sly thing! But I told her I should undoubtedly rest better for a night all alone.

That was clever, for really I wasn't alone a bit! As soon as it was moonlight, and that poor thing began to crawl and shake the pattern, I got up and ran to help her.

I pulled and she shook, I shook and she pulled, and before morning we had peeled off yards of that paper. A strip about as high as my head and half around the room. And then when the sun came and that awful pattern began to laugh at me I declared I would finish it today!

We go away tomorrow, and they are moving all my furniture down again to leave things as they were before. Jennie looked at the wall in amazement, but I told her merrily that I did it out of pure spite at the vicious thing. She laughed and said she wouldn't mind doing it herself, but I must not get tired.

How she betrayed herself that time!

But I am here, and no person touches this paper but me—not *alive!*

Jennie tried to get me out of the room. But I said it was so quiet and empty and clean now that I believed I would lie down and sleep all I could; and not to wake me even for dinner—I would call when I woke.

So now she is gone, and the servants are gone, and the things are gone, and there is nothing left but that great bedstead nailed down, with the canvas mattress we found on it. How those children did tear about here! The bedstead is fairly gnawed!

But I must get to work.

I have locked the door and thrown the key down into the front path.

I've got a rope up here that even Jennie did not find. If that woman does get out, and tries to get away, I can tie her!

But I forgot I could not reach far without anything to stand on!

This bed will *not* move!

I tried to lift and push it until I was lame, and then I got so angry I bit off a little piece at one corner—but it hurt my teeth.

Then I peeled off all the paper I could reach standing on the floor. It sticks horribly and the pattern just enjoys it! All those strangled heads and bulbous eyes and the waddling fungus growths just shriek with derision!

I am getting angry enough to do something desperate. To jump out of the window would be admirable exercise, but the bars are too strong even to try.

Besides, I wouldn't do it. Of course not. I know well enough that a step like that is improper and might be misconstrued.

I don't like to *look* out of the windows even—there are so many of those creeping women, and they creep so fast.

I wonder if they all come out of that wall paper, as I did?

But I am securely fastened now by my well-hidden rope—you don't get *me* out in the road there!

I suppose I shall have to get back behind the pattern when it comes night, and that is hard! It is so pleasant to be out in this great room and creep around as I please!

I don't want to go outside. I won't, even if Jennie asks me to.

For outside you have to creep on the ground, and everything is green instead of yellow.

But here I can creep smoothly on the floor, and my shoulder just fits in that long smooch around the wall, so I cannot lose my way.

Why, there's John at the door!

It is no use, young man, you can't open it!

How he does call and pound!

Now he's crying for an ax.

"John, dear," said I in the gentlest voice, "the key is down by the front steps, under a plantain leaf!"

That silenced him for a few moments.

Then he said—very quietly indeed, "Open the door, my darling!"

"I can't," said I. "The key is down by the front door, under a plantain leaf!"

And then I said it again, several times, very gently and slowly, and said it so often that he had to go and see, and he got it, of course, and came in. He stopped short by the door.

"What is the matter?" he cried. "For God's sake, what are you doing?"

I kept on creeping just the same, but I looked at him over my shoulder.

"I've got out at last," said I, "in spite of you and Jennie! And I've pulled off most of the paper, so you can't put me back!"

Now why should that man have fainted? But he did, and right across my path by the wall, so that I had to creep over him every time!

HOOK

WALTER VAN TILBURG CLARK

Walter J. Clark

Hook, the hawks' child, was hatched in a dry spring among the oaks beside the seasonal river, and was struck from the nest early. In the drought his single-willed parents had to extend their hunting ground by more than twice. The range became too great for them to wish to return and feed Hook, and when they had lost interest in each other they drove Hook down into the sand and brush and went back to solitary courses over the bleaching hills.

Unable to fly yet, Hook crept over the ground, challenging all large movements with recoiled head, erected rudimentary wings, and the small rasp of his clattering beak. It was during this time of abysmal ignorance and continual fear that his eyes took on the first quality of hawk, that of being wide, alert and challenging. He dwelt, because of his helplessness, among the rattling brush which grew between the oaks and the river.

Two spacious sounds environed Hook at this time. One was the great rustle of the slopes of yellowed wild wheat, with over it the chattering rustle of the leaves of the California oaks. The other was the distant whisper of the foaming edge of the Pacific, punctuated by the hollow shoring of the waves. But these Hook did not yet hear, for he was attuned by fear and hunger to the small, spasmodic rustlings of live things. Dry, shrunken and nearly starved, and with his plumage delayed, he snatched at beetles, dragging in the sand to catch them. When swifter and stronger birds and animals did not reach them first, which was seldom, he ate the small, silver fish left in the mud by the failing river.

Only one sight and sound not of his world of microscopic necessity was forced upon Hook. That was the flight of the big gulls from the beaches, which sometimes, in quealing play, came spinning back over the foothills and the riverbed. For some inherited reason the big, ship-bodied birds did not frighten Hook, but angered him. Small and chewed-looking, with his wide, already yellowing eyes glaring up at them, he would stand in an open place on the sand in the sun and spread his shaping wings and clatter his bill like shaken dice. Hook was furious about the swift, easy passage of gulls.

His first opportunity to leave off living like a ground owl came accidentally. He was standing in the late afternoon under the thicket when suddenly something beside him moved, and he struck, and killed a field mouse driven out of the wheat by thirst. It was a poor mouse, shriveled and lice-ridden, but in striking, Hook had tasted blood. With started neck plumage and shining eyes, he tore and fed. When the mouse was devoured, Hook had entered hoarse adolescence. He began to seek with a conscious appetite, and to move more readily out of shelter. Impelled by the blood appetite, so glorious after his long preservation upon the flaky and bitter stuff of bugs, he ventured even into the wheat in the open sun beyond the oaks, and discovered the small trails and holes among the roots. With his belly often partially filled with flesh, he grew rapidly in strength and will. His eyes were taking on their final change, their yellow growing deeper and more opaque, their stare more constant, their challenge less desperate.

Once, during this transformation, he surprised a ground squirrel, and although he was ripped and wing-bitten and could not hold his prey, he was not dismayed by the conflict, but exalted. Even while the wing was still drooping and the pinions not grown back, he was excited by other ground squirrels and pursued them futilely, and was angered by their dusty escapes. He realized that his world was a great arena for killing, and felt the magnificence of it.

The two major events of Hook's young life occurred in the same day. A little after dawn he made the customary essay and succeeded in flight. A little before sunset he made his first sustained flight of over two hundred yards, and at its termination struck and slew a great buck squirrel, whose thrashing and terrified gnawing and squealing gave him a wild delight. When he had gorged on the strong meat, Hook stood upright, and in his eyes was the stare of the hawk, never flagging in intensity. He had mastered the first of the three hungers which are fused into the single, flaming will of a hawk, and had experienced the second.

The third and consummating hunger did not awaken in Hook until the following spring, when the exultation of space had grown slow and steady in him, so that he swept freely with the wind over the miles of coastal foothills, using without struggle the warm currents lifting from the slopes.

That spring the rains were long, and Hook sat for hours, hunched and angry under their pelting, glaring into the fogs of the river valley, and killed only small, drenched things flooded up from their tunnels. But when the rains had dissipated and there were sun and sea wind again, the game ran plentiful. Hook then was scorched by the third hunger. Ranging farther, often forgetting to kill and eat, he sailed for days with growing rage, and woke at night clattering on his dead tree limb, and struck and struck and struck at the porous wood of the trunk, tearing it away. After days, in the draft of a coastal canyon miles below his own hills, he came upon the acrid taint he did not know but had expected, and, sailing down it, felt his neck plumes rise and his wings quiver so that he swerved unsteadily. He saw the unmated female perched upon the tall and jagged stump of a tree that had been shorn by storm, and he stooped, as if upon game. But she was older than he, and wary of the gripe of his importunity, and banked off screaming, and he screamed also at the intolerable delay.

At the head of the canyon, the screaming pursuit was crossed by another male with a great wingspread. But his more skillful opening played him false against the ferocity of the twice-balked Hook. His rising maneuver for position was cut short by Hook's wild, upward swoop, and at the blow he raked desperately and tumbled off to the side. Dropping, Hook struck him again, struggled to clutch, but only raked and could not hold, and, diving, struck once more in passage, and then beat up, yelling triumph, and saw the crippled antagonist sideslip away and glide obliquely into the cover of brush. Beating hard and stationary in the wind above the bush that covered his competitor,

Hook waited an instant, but when the bush was still, screamed again, and resought the female.

On a hilltop projection of stone two miles inland, he struck her down, gripping her rustling body with his talons, beating her wings down with his wings, and, when her coy struggles had given way to stillness, succeeded.

In the early summer, Hook drove the three young ones from their nest and went back to lone circling above his own range. He was complete.

THROUGHOUT THAT summer and the cool, growthless weather of the winter, Hook was master of the sky and the hills of his range. His flight became a lovely and certain thing, so that he played with the treacherous currents of the air with a delicate ease surpassing that of the gulls. He could sail for hours, searching the blanched grasses below him with telescopic eyes, gaining height against the wind, and never beating either wing. At the swift passage of his shadow within their vision, gophers, ground squirrels and rabbits froze, or plunged gibbering into their tunnels beneath matted turf. Now, when he struck, he killed easily in one hard-knuckled blow. Occasionally, in sport, he soared up over the river and drove the heavy and weaponless gulls downstream again, until they would no longer venture inland.

There was nothing which Hook feared now, and his spirit was wholly belligerent, swift and sharp, like his gaze. Only the mixed smells and incomprehensible activities of the people at the Japanese farmer's home, inland of the coastwise highway, troubled him. The smells were strong, unsatisfactory and never clear, and the people, though they behaved foolishly, constantly running in and out of their built-up holes, were large and appeared capable, with fearless eyes looking up at him, so that he instinctively swerved aside from them. He cruised over their gardens and their crate-cluttered chicken yard, but he would not alight close to their buildings.

Four times that year he was challenged by other hawks blowing up from behind the coastal hills to scud down his slopes, but two of these he slew in midair and saw hurtle down to thump on the ground and lie still while he circled, and a third, whose wing he tore, he followed closely to earth and beat to death in the grass. The fourth was a strong flier and experienced fighter, and theirs was a long, running battle, with brief, rising flurries of striking and screaming, from which down and plumage soared off.

Here, for the first time, Hook felt doubts and at moments wanted to drop away from the scoring, burning talons and the twisted hammer-strokes of the strong beak, drop away shrieking and take cover and be still. In the end, when Hook, having outmaneuvered his enemy and come above him, wholly in control, and going with the wind, tilted and plunged for the death rap, the other, in desperation, threw over on his back and struck up. Talons locked, beaks raking, they dived earthward. The earth grew and spread under them amazingly, and they were not fifty feet above it when Hook, feeling himself turning toward the underside, tore free and beat up again on heavy, wrenched wings. The other, stroking swiftly, and so close to down that he lost wing plumes to a bush, righted himself and flew away lumberingly between the hills. Hook screamed the triumph and made a brief pretense of pursuit, but was glad to return, slow and victorious, to his dead tree.

In all these encounters Hook was injured, but experienced only the fighter's pride and exultation from the sting of wounds received in successful combat. And in each of them he learned new skill.

In the next spring the third hunger returned upon Hook with a new violence. In this quest he came into the taint of a young hen. Others too were drawn by the unnerving perfume, but only one of them, the same with which Hook had fought his great battle, was a worthy competitor. This hunter drove off two, while two others, game but neophytes, were glad enough that Hook's impatience would not permit him to follow and kill. Then the battle between the two champions fled inland, and was a tactical marvel, but Hook lodged the neck-breaking blow as they dropped past the treetops. The blood had already begun to pool on the gray, fallen foliage as Hook flapped up between branches, too spent to cry his victory. Yet his hunger would not let him rest until, on the second day, he drove the female to ground in a strange river canyon.

When the two fledglings of this second brood had been driven from the nest and Hook had returned to his own range, he was not only complete, but supreme. He slept without concealment on his bare limb, and did not open his eyes when in the night the heavy-billed cranes coughed in the shallows below him.

THE TURNING point of Hook's career came in the autumn, when the brush in the canyons rustled dryly and the hills, mowed close by the cattle, smoked under the wind as if burning. One midafternoon Hook rode the wind diagonally across the river mouth. His great eyes, focused for small things stirring in the dust and leaves, overlooked the large, slow movement of the farmer rising from the brush and lifting the two black eyes of his shotgun. Too late Hook saw and swerved. The surf muffled the reports, and, nearly without sound, Hook felt the minute whips of the first shot, and the astounding, breath-breaking blow of the second.

Beating his good wing, tasting the blood that quickly swelled into his beak, he tumbled off with the wind and struck into the thickets on the far side of the river mouth. The branches tore him. Wild with rage, he thrust up and clattered his beak, challenging, but when he had fallen over twice, he knew that the trailing wing would not carry, and then heard the boots of the hunter among the stones in the riverbed, and, seeing him loom at the edge of the bushes, crept back among the thickest brush and was still. When he saw the boots pause before him, he reared back, his beak open but soundless, his great eyes hard and very shining. The boots passed on.

When Hook could hear nothing but the surf and the wind in the thicket, he let the sickness and shock overcome him. The fine film of the inner lid dropped over his big eyes. His heart beat frantically, so that it made the plumage of his shot-aching breast throb. But this was nothing compared to the lightning of pain in his left shoulder, where the shot had shattered the airy bones so the pinions could not be lifted. Yet, when a sparrow lit in the bush over him, Hook's eyes flew open again, hard and challenging, his good wing was lifted, and his beak strained open. The startled sparrow darted piping out over the river.

Throughout two days and three nights Hook remained stationary, enduring his sickness. At midday of the third day he was so weak that his good wing also trailed to prop him upright, and his eyes were lusterless. But his wounds were hardened and he felt the return of hunger. Beyond his shelter he heard the gulls flying in great numbers and crying their joy. From the fringe of the river came the ecstatic bubblings and chirpings of the small birds.

With the aid of his hunger, and on the crutches of his wings, Hook came down to stand in the sun beside the beach. Through the white foam writing of surf on sand the long-billed pipers twinkled in bevies, escaping each wave, then racing down after it to plunge their fine drills into the minute double holes where the sand crabs bubbled. Among the stones at the foot of the cliff, small red and green crabs made a little, continuous rattling and knocking. The cliff swallows glittered and twanged on aerial forays.

The afternoon began auspiciously. One of two gulls which came squabbling above him dropped a freshly caught fish to the sand. Quickly Hook was upon it. Gripping it, he raised his good wing and cocked his head with open beak at the many gulls which had circled down at once toward the fall of the fish. The gulls sheered off, cursing raucously. Left alone on the sand, Hook devoured the fish and, after resting in the sun, withdrew again to his shelter.

IN THE succeeding days, between rains, he foraged on the beach. He learned to kill and crack the small green crabs. Along the edge of the river mouth, he found the drowned bodies of mice and squirrels and even sparrows. He grew stronger slowly, but the shot sail continued to drag. Often, at the choking thought of soaring and striking and the good, hot-blood kill, he strove to take off, but only the one wing came up, winnowing with a hiss, and drove him over onto his side in the sand. After these futile trials he would rage and clatter. But gradually he learned that he could not fly, that his life must be that of the discharged nestling again. Denied the joy of space, the joy of battle and killing—the bloodlust—became his whole concentration. It was his hope, as he charged feeding gulls, that they would turn and offer battle, but they never did. The sandpipers, at his approach, fled peeping or, like a quiver of arrows shot together, streamed out over the surf in a long curve.

Hook's shame, and hunger too, began to keep him awake at night.

When he became aware that the gulls slept at night in flocks on the sand, each with one leg tucked under him, evil delight filled him at the thought of protracted striking among them.

There was only half of a sick moon in the sky on the night when he managed to stalk into the center of the sleeping gulls. This was light enough, but so great was his vengeful pleasure that there broke from him a shrill scream of challenge as he first struck. Without the power of flight behind it, the blow was not murderous, and this newly discovered impotence made Hook crazy, so that he screamed again and again as he struck and tore at the felled gull. He slew the one, but was twice knocked over by its heavy flounderings, and all the others rose above him, weaving and screaming in the thin moonlight, to settle elsewhere, beyond his pitiful range. He was left alone beside the single kill. It was a disappointing victory. He fed with lowering spirit.

Thereafter he stalked silently. At sunset he would watch where the gulls settled along the miles of beach, and after dark he would come like a sharp shadow among them and drive with his hook on all sides of him. In his best night he killed five, but his ire was so great that he could eat little. It was not the joyous, controlled hunting anger of a sane hawk, but something which made him dizzy and left him unsatisfied with any kill.

One day, when he had very nearly struck a gull while driving it from a gasping yellowfin, the gull's wing rapped against him and he was knocked over. He flurried awkwardly in the sand to regain his feet, but his mastery of the beach was ended. Seeing him, in clear sunlight, struggling after the chance blow, the gulls returned about him in a flashing cloud, circling and pecking on the wing. Hook's plumage showed quick little jets of irregularity here and there. He was forced to turn and dance awkwardly on the sand, trying to clash bills with each tormentor. Again he fell sideways. Before he could right himself he was bowled over, and was struck three times by three successive gulls, shrieking their flock triumph.

Finally he managed to roll to his breast, and to crouch, only his snake head, with its now silent scimitar, erect. One great eye blazed under its level brow, but where the other had been was a shallow hole from which thin blood trickled. In this crouch, by short stages, stopping to turn and drive the gulls up repeatedly, he dragged into the river canyon and under the stiff cover of the bitter-leafed laurel. There the gulls left him, soaring up with great clatter of their valor. Till nearly sunset, Hook, broken-spirited and enduring his hardening eye socket, heard them celebrating over the waves.

When his will was somewhat replenished and his empty eye socket had stopped twitching, Hook ventured from the protective lacings of his thicket. He knew fear again, and the challenge of his remaining eye was once more strident, as in adolescence. He dared not return to the beaches, and with a new weak hunger, the home hunger, made his way by short hunting journeys back to the wild wheat slopes and the crisp oaks. There was in Hook an unwonted sensation now, that of the ever neighboring possibility of death.

At first the familiar surroundings of the bend in the river and the tree with the dead limb to which he could not ascend aggravated his humiliation, but in time, forced to live cunningly and half starved, he lost much of his savage pride. At the first flight of a strange hawk over his realm he was wild at his helplessness, and kept spinning in the grass like a small, feathered dervish to keep the hateful beauty of the wind rider in sight. But in the succeeding weeks, as one after another coasted his beat, his resentment declined and the second of his great hungers was gone. He had no longer the true lust to kill, no joy of battle, but only the poor desire to fill his belly.

Then truly he lived in the wheat and the brush like a ground owl, ridden with ground lice, dusty or muddy, ever half starved, forced to sit for hours by small holes for petty and unsatisfying kills. Only once during the final months before his end did he make a kill where the breath of danger recalled his valor, and then the danger was such as a hawk with wings and eyes would scorn. Waiting beside a gopher hole, surrounded by the high yellow grass, he saw the head emerge, and struck, and was amazed that there writhed in his clutch the neck and dusty coffin skull of a rattlesnake. Holding his grip, Hook saw the great, thick body slither up after, the tip an erect, strident blur, and writhe on the dirt of the gopher's mound. The weight of the snake pushed Hook about, and once threw him down, and the rising and falling whine of the rattles made the moment terrible, but the gaping, vaulted mouth could not reach him. When Hook replaced the grip of his beak with the grip of his talons, and was free to strike again and again at the base of the head, the struggle was over.

THE RAINS returned, and then the season of love and the nesting season, leaving Hook's love hunger shriveled in him. It was during another long period of drought, with Hook starved on dry and fleshless kills, that one night his weary hunting brought him again close to the chicken farm. In the dark he stood outside the wire of the run. The scent of fat and blooded birds reached him from the shelter, and also within the enclosure was water. At the breath of the water, Hook's gorge contracted, and his tongue quivered and clove in its groove of horn. But there was the wire. He stalked its perimeter and found no opening. He beat it with his good wing, wrenched at it with his beak in many places, but could not tear it. Finally, in a fury, he leaped at it, clawed up the wire, and tumbled within.

First he drank at the chill metal trough hung for the chickens. Then he walked stiffly, to stalk down the scent. He trailed it up the runway. Then there was the stuffy, body-warm air, full of soft rustlings as his talons clicked on the board floor. The thick white shapes showed faintly in the darkness. Hook struck quickly, driving a hen to the floor with one blow, its neck broken. He leaped the still pulsing body, and tore it. The rich, streaming blood was overpowering to his dried senses, his starved, leathery body. After a few swallows the flesh choked him. In his rage he struck down another hen. The urge to kill took him again, as on that night on the beach. Clattering, he struck again and again. The henhouse was suddenly filled with the squawking and helpless rushing and buffeting of the terrified, brainless fowls.

Hook reveled in mastery. Here was game big enough to offer weight against a strike, and yet unable to soar away from his blows. When the hens finally discovered the outlet and streamed into the yard to run around the fence, beating and squawking, Hook followed them, scraping down the incline, clumsy and joyous. In the yard, the cock, a bird as large as he and much heavier, found him out and gave valiant battle. In the dark, and both earthbound, there was little skill, but blow upon blow, and only chance parry. While the duel went on, a dog began to bark, running back and forth along the fence on one side. A light flashed on in the farmhouse.

Enthralled by his old battle joy, Hook knew only the burly cock before him. The farmer, with his gun and lantern, was already at the gate when the finish came. The great cock leaped to jab with his spurs, and, toppling forward as he fell, was struck and extinguished. Blood had loosened Hook's throat. Shrilly he cried his triumph. It was a thin and exhausted cry, but within him as good as when he shrilled in midair over the plummeting descent of a fine foe in his best spring.

The light from the lantern partially blinded Hook. He essayed the fence, and, on the second try, in his desperation, was out. But in the open dust the dog was on him, circling, dashing in, snapping. The farmer, who at first had not fired because of the chickens, now did not fire because of the dog, and, when he saw that the hawk was unable to fly, relinquished the sport to the dog, holding the lantern up in order to see better. His wife, in a stained wrapper, joined him hesitantly, but watched, fascinated and a little horrified. Courageous and cruel death, however it may afterward sicken the one who has watched it, is impossible to look away from.

In the circle of the light, Hook turned to keep the dog in front of him. His one eye gleamed with malevolence. Each time the dog pounced, Hook stood ground, raising his good wing, and, at the closest approach, hissed furiously and at once struck. Hit and ripped twice by the whetted horn, the dog recoiled more quickly from several subsequent jumps, and, infuriated by his own cowardice, began to bark wildly.

"Oh, kill the poor thing," the woman begged.

But the man encouraged the dog again, saying, "Sic him; sic him."

The dog rushed bodily. Unable to avoid him, Hook was bowled down, snapping and raking. When the dog leaped away, Hook could not rise to use his talons.

Once again the dog charged, this time throwing the weight of his forepaws against Hook's shoulder and furiously worrying the feathered bulk. Hook's neck went limp, and between his gaping clappers came only a faint chittering, as from some small kill of his own in the grasses.

In this last conflict, however, there had been some minutes of the supreme fire of the hawk whose three hungers are perfectly fused in the one will; enough to burn off a year of shame.

Between the great sails the light body lay caved and perfectly still. The dog, smarting from his cuts, came to the master and was praised. The woman, joining them slowly, looked at the great wingspread, her husband raising the lantern that she might see it better.

"Oh, the brave bird," she said.

THE KEY

EUDORA WELTY

[signature: Eudora Welty]

It was quiet in the waiting room of the remote little station, except for the night sounds of insects. You could hear their embroidering movements in the weeds outside, which somehow gave the effect of some tenuous voice in the night, telling a story. Or you could listen to the fat thudding of the light bugs and the hoarse rushing of their big wings against the wooden ceiling. Some of the bugs were clinging heavily to the yellow globe, like idiot bees to a senseless smell.

Under this prickly light two rows of people sat in silence, their faces stung, their bodies twisted and quietly uncomfortable, expectantly so, in ones and twos, not quite asleep. No one seemed impatient, although the train was late. A little girl lay flung back in her mother's lap as though sleep had struck her with a blow.

Ellie and Albert Morgan were sitting on a bench like the others waiting for the train and had nothing to say to each other. Their names were ever so neatly and rather largely printed on a big reddish tan suitcase strapped crookedly shut, because of a missing buckle, so that it hung apart finally like a stupid pair of lips. "Albert Morgan, Ellie Morgan, Yellow Leaf, Mississippi." They must have been driven into town in a wagon, for they and the suitcase were all touched here and there with a fine yellow dust, like finger marks.

Ellie Morgan was a large woman with a face as pink and crowded as an old-fashioned rose. She must have been about forty years old. One of those black satchel purses hung over her straight, strong wrist. It must have been her savings which were making possible this trip. And to what place? You wondered, for she sat there as tense and solid as a cube, as if to endure some nameless apprehension rising and overflowing within her at the thought of travel. Her face worked and broke into strained, hardening lines, as if there had been a death—that too explicit evidence of agony in the desire to communicate.

Albert made a slower and softer impression. He sat motionless beside Ellie, holding his hat in his lap with both hands—a hat you were sure he had never worn. He looked homemade, as though his wife had self-consciously knitted or somehow contrived a husband when she sat alone at night. He had a shock of very fine sunburned yellow hair. He was too shy for this world, you could see. His hands were like cardboard, he held his hat so still; and yet how softly his eyes fell upon its crown, moving dreamily and yet with dread over its brown surface! He was smaller than his wife. His suit was brown, too, and he wore it neatly and carefully, as though he were murmuring, "Don't look—no need to look—I am effaced." But you have seen that expression too in silent children, who will tell you what they dreamed the night before in sudden, almost hilarious, bursts of confidence.

Every now and then, as though he perceived some minute thing, a sudden alert, tantalized look would creep over the little man's face, and he would gaze slowly around him, quite slyly. Then he would bow his head again; the expression would vanish; some inner refreshment had been denied him. Behind his head was a wall poster, dirty with time, showing an old-fashioned locomotive about to crash into an open touring car filled with women in veils. No one in the station was frightened by the familiar poster, any more than they were aroused by the little man whose rising and drooping head it framed. Yet for a moment he might seem to you to be sitting there quite filled with hope.

Among the others in the station was a strong-looking young man, alone, hatless, red-haired, who was standing by the wall while the rest sat on benches. He had a small key in his hand and was turning it over and over in his fingers, nervously passing it from one hand to the other, tossing it gently into the air and catching it again.

He stood and stared in distraction at the other people; so intent and so wide was his gaze that anyone who glanced after him seemed rocked like a small boat in the wake of a large one. There was an excess of energy about him that separated him from everyone else, but in the motion of his hands there was, instead of the craving for communication, something of reticence, even of secrecy, as the key rose and fell. You guessed that he was a stranger in town; he might have been a criminal or a gambler, but his eyes were widened with gentleness. His look, which traveled without stopping for long anywhere, was a hurried focusing of a very tender and explicit regard.

The color of his hair seemed to jump and move, like the flicker of a match struck in a wind. The ceiling lights were not steady but seemed to pulsate like a living and transient force, and made the young man in his preoccupation appear to tremble in the midst of his size and strength, and to fail to impress his exact outline upon the yellow walls. He was like a salamander in the fire. "Take care," you wanted to say to him, and yet also, "Come here." Nervously, and quite apart in his distraction, he continued to stand tossing the key back and forth from one hand to the other. Suddenly it became a gesture of abandonment: one hand stayed passive in the air, then seized too late: the key fell to the floor.

EVERYONE, EXCEPT Albert and Ellie Morgan, looked up for a moment. On the floor the key had made a fierce metallic sound like a challenge, a sound of seriousness. It almost made people jump. It was regarded as an insult, a very personal question, in the quiet peaceful room where the insects were tapping at the ceiling and each person was allowed to sit among his possessions and wait for an unquestioned departure. Little walls of reproach went up about them all.

A flicker of amusement touched the young man's face as he observed the startled but controlled and obstinately blank faces which turned toward him for a moment and then away. He walked over to pick up his key.

But it had glanced and slid across the floor, and now it lay in the dust at Albert Morgan's feet.

Albert Morgan was indeed picking up the key. Across from him, the young man saw him examine it, quite slowly, with wonder written all over his face and hands, as if it had fallen from the sky. Had he failed to hear the clatter? There was something wrong with Albert. . . .

As if by decision, the young man did not terminate this wonder by claiming his key. He stood back, a peculiar flash of interest or of something more inscrutable, like resignation, in his lowered eyes.

The little man had probably been staring at the floor, thinking. And suddenly in the dark surface the small sliding key had appeared. You could see memory seize his face, twist it and hold it. What innocent, strange thing might it have brought back to life—a fish he had once spied just below the top of the water in a sunny lake in the country when he was a child? This was just as unexpected, shocking, and somehow meaningful to him.

Albert sat there holding the key in his wide-open hand. How intensified, magnified, really vain all attempt at expression becomes in the afflicted! It was with an almost incandescent delight that he felt the unguessed temperature and weight of the key. Then he turned to his wife. His lips were actually trembling.

And still the young man waited, as if the strange joy of the little man took precedence with him over whatever need he had for the key. With sudden electrification he saw Ellie slip the handle of her satchel purse from her wrist and with her fingers begin to talk to her husband.

The others in the station had seen Ellie too; shallow pity washed over the waiting room like a dirty wave foaming and creeping over a public beach. In quick mumblings from bench to bench people said to each other, "Deaf and dumb!" How ignorant they were of all that the young man was seeing! Although he had no way of knowing the words Ellie said, he seemed troubled enough at the mistake the little man must have made, at his misplaced wonder and joy.

Albert was replying to his wife. On his hands he said to her, "I found it. Now it belongs to me. It is something important! Important! It means something. From now on we will get along better, have more understanding. . . . Maybe when we reach Niagara Falls we will even fall in love, the way other people have done. Maybe our marriage was really for love, after all, not for the other reason—both of us being afflicted in the same way, unable to speak, lonely because of that. Now you can stop being ashamed of me, for being so cautious and slow all my life, for taking my own time. . . . You can take hope. Because it was I who found the key. Remember that—I found it." He laughed all at once, quite silently.

Everyone stared at his impassioned little speech as it came from his fingers. They were embarrassed, vaguely aware of some crisis and vaguely affronted, but unable to interfere; it was as though they were the deaf-mutes and he the speaker. When he laughed, a few people laughed unconsciously with him, in relief, and turned away. But the young man remained still and intent, waiting at his little distance.

"This key came here very mysteriously—it is bound to mean something," the husband went on to say. He held the key up just before her eyes. "You are always praying; you believe in miracles; well, now, here is the answer. It came to me."

His wife looked self-consciously around the room and replied on her fingers, "You are always talking nonsense. Be quiet."

But she was secretly pleased, and when she saw him slowly look down in his old manner, she reached over, as if to retract what she had said, and laid her hand on his, touching the key for herself, softness making her worn hand limp. From then on they never looked around them, never saw anything except each other. They were so intent, so very solemn, wanting to have their symbols perfectly understood!

"You must see it is a symbol," he began again, his fingers clumsy and blurring in his excitement. "It is a symbol of something—something that we deserve, and that is happiness. We will find happiness in Niagara Falls."

And then, as if he were all at once shy even of her, he turned slightly away from her and slid the key into his pocket. They sat staring down at the suitcase, their hands fallen in their laps.

The young man slowly turned away from them and wandered back to the wall, where he took out a cigarette and lighted it.

Outside, the night pressed around the station like a pure stone, in which the little room might be transfixed and, for the preservation of this moment of hope, its future killed, an insect in amber. The short little train drew in, stopped, and rolled away, almost noiselessly.

Then inside, people were gone or turned in sleep or walking about, all changed from the way they had been. But the deaf-mutes and the loitering young man were still in their places.

The man was still smoking. He was dressed like a young doctor or some such person in the town, and yet he did not seem of the town. He looked very strong and active; but there was a startling quality, a willingness to be forever distracted, even disturbed, in the very reassurance of his body, some alertness which made his strength fluid and dissipated instead of withheld and greedily beautiful. His youth by now did not seem an important thing about him; it was a medium for his activity, no doubt, but as he stood there frowning and smoking you felt some apprehension that he would never express whatever might be the desire of his life in being young and strong, in standing apart in compassion, in making any intuitive present or sacrifice, or in any way of action at all—not because there was too much in the world demanding his strength, but because he was too deeply aware.

You felt a shock in glancing up at him, and when you looked away from the whole yellow room and closed your eyes, his intensity, as well as that of the room, seemed to have impressed the imagination with a shadow of itself, a blackness together with the light, the negative beside the positive. You felt as though some exact, skillful contact had been made between the surfaces of your hearts to make you aware, in some pattern, of his joy and his despair. You could feel the fullness and the emptiness of this stranger's life.

The railroad man came in swinging a lantern which he stopped suddenly in its arc. Looking uncomfortable, and then rather angry, he approached the deaf-mutes and shot his arm out in a series of violent gestures and shrugs.

Albert and Ellie Morgan were dreadfully shocked. The woman looked resigned for a moment to hopelessness. But the little man—you were startled by a look of bravado on his face.

In the station the red-haired man was speaking aloud—but to himself. "They missed their train!"

As if in quick apology, the trainman set his lantern down beside Albert's foot, and hurried away.

And as if completing a circle, the red-haired man walked over too and stood silently near the deaf-mutes. With a reproachful look at him the woman reached up and took off her hat.

THEY BEGAN AGAIN, TALKING rapidly back and forth, almost as one person. The old routine of their feeling was upon them once more. Perhaps, you thought, staring at their similarity—her hair was yellow, too—they were children together—cousins even, afflicted in the same way, sent off from home to the state institute. . . .

It was the feeling of conspiracy. They were in counterplot against the plot of those things that pressed down upon them from outside their knowledge and their ways of making themselves understood. It was obvious that it gave the wife her greatest pleasure. But you wondered, seeing Albert, whom talking seemed rather to dishevel, whether it had not continued to be a rough and violent game which Ellie, as the older and stronger, had taught him to play with her.

"What do you think he wants?" she asked Albert, nodding at the red-haired man, who smiled faintly. And how her eyes shone! Who would ever know how deep her suspicion of the whole outside world lay in her heart, how far it had pushed her!

"What does he want?" Albert was replying quickly. "The key!"

Of course! And how fine it had been to sit there with the key hidden from the strangers and also from his wife, who had not seen where he had put it. He stole up with his hand and secretly felt the key, which must have lain in some pocket nearly against his heart. He nodded gently. The key had come there, under his eyes on the floor in the station, all of a sudden, but yet not quite unexpected. That is the way things happen to you always. But Ellie did not comprehend this.

Now she sat there as quiet as could be. It was not only hopelessness about the trip. She, too, undoubtedly felt something privately about that key, apart from what she had said or what he had told her. He had almost shared it with her—you realized that. He frowned and smiled almost at the same time. There was something—something he could almost remember but not quite—which would let him keep the key always to himself. He knew that, and he would remember it later, when he was alone.

"Never fear, Ellie," he said, a still little smile lifting his lip. "I've got it safe in a pocket. No one can find it, and there's no hole for it to fall through."

She nodded, but she was always doubting, always anxious. You could look at her troubled hands. How terrible it was, how strange, that Albert loved the key more than he loved Ellie! He did not mind missing the train. It showed in every line, every motion of his body. The key was closer—closer. The whole story began to illuminate them now, as if the lantern flame had been turned up. Ellie's anxious, hovering body could wrap him softly as a cradle, but the secret meaning, that powerful sign, that reassurance he so hopefully sought, so assuredly deserved—that had never come. There was something lacking in Ellie.

Had Ellie, with her suspicions of everything, come to know even things like this, in her way? How empty and nervous her red scrubbed hands were, how desperate to speak! Yes, she must regard it as unhappiness lying between them, as more than emptiness. She must worry about it, talk about it. You could imagine her stopping her churning to come out to his chair on the porch, to tell him that she did love him and would take care of him always, talking with the spotted sour milk dripping from her fingers. Just try to tell her that talking is useless, that care is not needed . . . And sooner or later he would always reply, say something, agree, and she would go away again. . . .

And Albert, with his face so capable of amazement, made you suspect the funny thing about talking to Ellie. Until you do, declared his round brown eyes, you can be peaceful and content that everything takes care of itself. As long as you let it alone everything goes peacefully, like an uneventful day on the farm—chores attended to, woman working in the house, you in the field, crop growing as well as can be expected, the cow giving, and the sky like a coverlet over it all— so that you're as full of yourself as a colt, in need of nothing, and nothing needing you. But when you pick up your hands and start to talk, if you don't watch carefully, this security will run away and leave you. You say something, make an observation, just to answer your wife's worryings, and everything is jolted, disturbed, laid open like the ground behind a plow, with you running along after it.

But happiness, Albert knew, is something that appears to you suddenly, that is meant for you, a thing which you reach for and pick up and hide at your breast, a shiny thing that reminds you of something alive and leaping.

Ellie sat there quiet as a mouse. She had unclasped her purse and taken out a little card with a picture of Niagara Falls on it.

"Hide it from the man," she said. She did suspect him! The red-haired man had drawn closer. He bent and saw that it was a picture of Niagara Falls.

"Do you see the little rail?" Albert began in tenderness. And Ellie loved to watch him tell her about it; she clasped her hands and began to smile and show her crooked tooth; she looked young: it was the way she had looked as a child.

"That is what the teacher pointed to with her wand on the magic-lantern slide—the little rail. You stand right here. You lean up hard against the rail. Then you can hear Niagara Falls."

"How do you hear it?" begged Ellie, nodding.

"You hear it with your whole self. You listen with your arms and your legs and your whole body. You'll never forget what hearing is, after that."

He must have told her hundreds of times in his obedience, yet she smiled with gratitude, and stared deep, deep into the tinted picture of the waterfall.

Presently she said, "By now, we'd have been there, if we hadn't missed the train."

She did not even have any idea that it was miles and days away. She looked at the red-haired man then, her eyes all puckered up, and he looked away at last.

He had seen the dust on her throat and a needle stuck in her collar where she'd forgotten it, with a thread running through the eye—the final details. Her hands were tight and wrinkled with pressure. She swung her foot a little below her skirt, in the new Mary Jane slipper with the hard toe.

Albert turned away too. It was then, you thought, that he became quite frightened to think that if they hadn't missed the train they would be hearing, at that very moment, Niagara Falls. Perhaps they would be standing there together, pressed against the little rail, pressed against each other, with their lives being poured through them, changing. . . . And how did he know what that would be like? He bent his head and tried not to look at his wife. He could say nothing. He glanced up once at the stranger, with almost a pleading look, as if to say, "Won't you come with us?"

"To work so many years, and then to miss the train," Ellie said.

You saw by her face that she was undauntedly wondering, unsatisfied, waiting for the future.

And you knew how she would sit and brood over this as over their conversations together, about every misunderstanding, every discussion, sometimes even about some agreement between them that had been all settled—even about the secret and proper separation that lies between a man and a woman, the thing that makes them what they are in themselves, their secret life, their memory of the past, their childhood, their dreams. This to Ellie was unhappiness.

They had told her when she was a little girl how people who have just been married have the custom of going to Niagara Falls on a wedding trip, to start their happiness; and that came to be where she put her hope, all of it. So she saved money. She worked harder than he did, you could observe, comparing their hands, good and bad years, more than was good for a woman. Year after year she had put her hope ahead of her.

And he—somehow he had never thought that this time would come, that they might really go on the journey. He was never looking so far and so deep as Ellie—into the future, into the changing and mixing of their lives together when they should arrive at last at Niagara Falls. To him it was always something postponed, like the paying off of the mortgage.

But sitting here in the station, with the suitcase all packed and at his feet, he had begun to realize that this journey might, for a fact, take place. The key had materialized to show him the enormity of this venture. And after his first shock and pride he had simply reserved the key; he had hidden it in his pocket.

She looked unblinking into the light of the lantern on the floor. Her face looked strong and terrifying, all lighted and very near to his. But there was no joy there. You knew that she was very brave.

Albert seemed to shrink, to retreat. . . . His trembling hand went once more beneath his coat and touched the pocket where the key was lying, waiting. Would he ever remember that elusive thing about it or be sure what it might really be a symbol of? . . . His eyes, in their quick manner of filming over, grew dreamy. Perhaps he had even decided that it was a symbol not of happiness with Ellie, but of something else—something which he could have alone, for only himself, in peace, something strange and unlooked for which would come to him. . . .

The red-haired man took a second key from his pocket, and in one direct motion placed it in Ellie's red palm. It was a key with a large triangular pasteboard tag on which was clearly printed STAR HOTEL, ROOM 2.

He did not wait to see any more, but went out abruptly into the night. He stood still for a moment and reached for a cigarette. As he held the match close he gazed straight ahead, and in his eyes, all at once wild and searching, there was certainly, besides the simple compassion in his regard, a look both restless and weary, very much used to the comic. You could see that he despised and saw the uselessness of the thing he had done.

THE SHORE LINE
AT SUNSET

RAY BRADBURY

TOM, KNEE-DEEP in the waves, a piece of driftwood in his hand, listened.

The house, up toward the Coast Highway in the late afternoon, was silent. The sounds of closets being rummaged, suitcase locks snapping, vases being smashed, and of a final door crashing shut, all had faded away.

Chico, standing on the pale sand, flourished his wire strainer to shake out a harvest of lost coins. After a moment, without glancing at Tom, he said, "Let her go."

So it was every year. For a week or a month, their house would have music swelling from the windows, there would be new geraniums potted on the porch rail, new paint on the doors and steps. The clothes on the wire line changed from harlequin pants to sheath dresses to handmade Mexican frocks like white waves breaking behind the house. Inside, the paintings on the walls shifted from imitation Matisse to pseudo-Italian Renaissance. Sometimes, looking up, he would see a woman drying her hair like a bright yellow flag on the wind. Sometimes the flag was black or red. Sometimes the woman was tall, sometimes short, against the sky. But there was never more than one woman at a time. And, at last, a day like today came. . . .

Tom placed his driftwood on the growing pile near where Chico sifted the billion footprints left by people long vanished from their holidays.

"Chico. What are we doing here?"

"Living the life of Reilly, boy!"

"I don't feel like Reilly, Chico."

"Work at it, boy!"

Tom saw the house a month from now, the flowerpots blowing dust, the walls hung with empty squares, only sand carpeting the floors. The rooms would echo like shells in the wind. And all night every night bedded in separate rooms he and Chico would hear a tide falling away and away down a long shore, leaving no trace.

Tom nodded, imperceptibly. Once a year he himself brought a nice girl here, knowing she was right at last and that in no time they would be married. But his women always stole silently away before dawn, feeling they had been mistaken for someone else, not being able to play the part. Chico's friends left like vacuum cleaners, with a terrific drag, roar, rush, leaving no lint unturned, no clam unprized of its pearl, taking their purses with them like toy dogs which Chico had petted as he opened their jaws to count their teeth.

"That's four women so far this year."

"Okay, referee." Chico grinned. "Show me the way to the showers."

"Chico—" Tom bit his lower lip, then went on. "I been thinking. Why don't we split up?"

Chico just looked at him.

"I mean," said Tom quickly, "maybe we'd have better luck, alone."

"Well, I'll be damned," said Chico slowly, gripping the strainer in his big fists before him. "Look here, boy, don't you know the facts? You and me, we'll be here come the year 2000. A couple of crazy dumb old gooney birds drying their bones in the sun. Nothing's ever going to happen to us now, Tom, it's too late. Get that through your head and shut up."

Tom swallowed and looked steadily at the other man. "I'm thinking of leaving—next week."

"Shut up, shut up, and get to work!"

Chico gave the sand an angry showering rake that tilled him forty-three cents in dimes, pennies, and nickels. He stared blindly at the coins shimmering down the wires like a pinball game all afire.

Tom did not move, holding his breath.

They both seemed to be waiting for something.

The something happened.

"Hey . . . hey . . . hey . . ."

From a long way off down the coast a voice called.

The two men turned slowly.

"Hey . . . hey . . . oh, hey . . . !"

A boy was running, yelling, waving, along the shore two hundred yards away. There was something in his voice that made Tom feel suddenly cold. He held on to his own arms, waiting.

"Hey!"

The boy pulled up, gasping, pointing back along the shore.

"A woman, a funny woman, by the North Rock!"

"A woman!" The words exploded from Chico's mouth and he began to laugh. "Oh, no, no!"

"What you mean, a funny woman?" asked Tom.

"I don't know," cried the boy, his eyes wide. "You got to come see! Awful funny!"

"You mean drowned?"

"Maybe! She came out of the water, she's lying on the shore, you got to see, yourself . . . funny . . ." The boy's voice died. He gazed off north again. "She's got a fish's tail."

Chico laughed. "Not before supper, please."

"Please!" cried the boy, dancing now. "No lie! Oh, hurry!"

He ran off, sensed he was not followed, and looked back in dismay.

Tom felt his lips move. "Boy wouldn't run this far for a joke, would he, Chico?"

"People have run further for less."

Tom started walking. "All right, son."

"Thanks, mister, oh thanks!"

The boy ran. Twenty yards up the coast, Tom looked back. Behind him, Chico squinted, shrugged, dusted his hands wearily, and followed.

They moved north along the twilight beach, their skin weathered in tiny folds about their burnt pale eyes, looking younger for their hair cut close to the skull so you could not see the gray. There was a fair wind and the ocean rose and fell with prolonged concussions.

"What," said Tom, "what if we get to North Rock and it's true? The ocean *has* washed some *thing* up?"

But before Chico could answer, Tom was gone, his mind racing down coasts littered with horseshoe crabs, sand dollars, starfish, kelp, and stone. From all the times he'd talked on what lives in the sea, the names returned with the breathing fall of waves. Argonauts, they whispered, codlings, pollack, houndfish, tautog, tench, sea elephant, they whispered, gillings, flounder, and beluga, the white whale, and grampus, the sea dog . . . always you thought how these must look from their deep-sounding names. Perhaps you would never in your life see them rise from the salt meadows beyond the safe limits of the shore, but they were there, and their names, with a thousand others, made pictures. And you looked and wished you were a frigate bird that might fly nine thousand miles around to return some year with the full size of the ocean in your head.

"Oh, quick!" The boy had run back to peer in Tom's face. "It might be gone!"

"Keep your shirt on, boy," said Chico.

They came around the North Rock. A second boy stood there, looking down.

Perhaps from the corner of his eye, Tom saw something on the sand that made him hesitate to look straight at it, but fix instead on the face of the boy standing there. The boy was pale and he seemed not to breathe. On occasion he remembered to take a breath, his eyes focused, but the more they saw there on the sand the more they took time off from focusing and turned blank and looked stunned. When the ocean came in over his tennis shoes, he did not move or notice.

Tom glanced away from the boy to the sand.

And Tom's face, in the next moment, became the face of the boy. His hands assumed the same curl at his sides and his mouth moved to open and stay half open and his eyes, which were light in color, seemed to bleach still more with so much looking.

The setting sun was ten minutes above the sea.

"A big wave came in and went out," said the first boy, "and here she was."

They looked at the woman lying there.

Her hair was very long and it lay on the beach like the threads of an immense harp. The water stroked along the threads and floated them up and let them down, each time in a different fan and silhouette. The hair must have been five or six feet long and now it was strewn on the hard wet sand and it was the color of limes.

Her face . . .

The men bent half down in wonder.

Her face was white sand sculpture, with a few water drops shimmering on it like summer rain upon a cream-colored rose. Her face was that moon which when seen by day is pale and unbelievable in the blue sky. It was milk marble veined with faint violet in the temples. The eyelids, closed down upon the eyes, were powdered with a faint water color, as if the eyes beneath gazed through the fragile tissue of the lids and saw them standing there above her, looking down and looking down. The mouth was a pale flushed sea rose, full and closed upon itself. And her neck was slender and white and her breasts were small and white, now covered, uncovered, covered, uncovered in the flow of water, the ebb of water, the flow, the ebb, the flow. And the breasts were flushed at their tips, and her body was startlingly white, almost an illumination, a white-green lightning against the sand. And as the water shifted her, her skin glinted like the surface of a pearl.

The lower half of her body changed itself from white to very pale blue, from very pale blue to pale green, from pale green to emerald green, to moss and lime green, to scintillas and sequins all dark green, all flowing away in a fount, a curve, a rush of light and dark, to end in a lacy fan, a spread of foam and jewel on the sand. The two halves of this creature were so joined as to reveal no point of fusion where pearl woman, woman of a whiteness made of cream water and clear sky merged with that half which belonged to the amphibious slide and rush of current that came up on the shore and shelved down the shore, tugging its half toward its proper home. The woman was the sea, the sea was woman. There was no flaw or seam, no wrinkle or stitch; the illusion, if illusion it was, held perfectly together and the blood from one moved into and through and mingled with what must have been the ice waters of the other.

"I wanted to run get help." The first boy seemed not to want to raise his voice. "But Skip said she was dead and there's no help for that. Is she?"

"She was never alive," said Chico. "Sure," he went on, feeling their eyes on him suddenly. "It's something left over from a movie studio. Liquid rubber skinned over a steel frame. A prop, a dummy."

"Oh, no, it's real!"

"We'll find a label somewhere," said Chico. "Here."

"Don't!" cried the first boy.

"Hell." Chico touched the body to turn it, and stopped. He knelt there, his face changing.

"What's the matter?" asked Tom.

Chico took his hand away and looked at it. "I was wrong." His voice faded.

Tom took the woman's wrist. "There's a pulse."

"You're feeling your own heartbeat."

"I just don't know . . . maybe . . . maybe . . ."

The woman was there and her upper body was all moon pearl and tidal cream and her lower body all slithering ancient green-black coins that slid upon themselves in the shift of wind and water.

"There's a trick somewhere!" cried Chico suddenly.

"No. No!" Just as suddenly, Tom burst out in laughter. "No trick! My God, my God, I feel great! I haven't felt so great since I was a kid!"

They walked slowly around her.

A wave touched her white hand so the fingers faintly, softly waved. The gesture was that of someone asking for another and another wave to come in and lift the fingers and then the wrist and then the arm and then the head and finally the body and take all of them together back down out to sea.

"Tom." Chico's mouth opened and closed. "Why don't you go get our truck?"

Tom didn't move.

"You hear me?" said Chico.

"Yes, but—"

"But what? We could sell this somewhere, I don't know—the university, that aquarium at Seal Beach, or . . . well, hell, why couldn't we just set up a place? Look." He shook Tom's arm. "Drive to the pier. Buy us three hundred pounds of chipped ice. When you take anything out of the water you *need* ice, don't you?"

"I never thought."

"Think about it! Get moving!"

"I don't know, Chico."

"What you mean? She's real, isn't she?" He turned to the boys. *"You* say she's real, don't you? Well, then, what are we waiting for?"

"Chico," said Tom. "You better go get the ice yourself."

"Someone's got to stay and make sure she don't go back out with the tide!"

"Chico," said Tom. "I don't know how to explain. I don't want to get that ice for you."

"I'll go myself, then. Look, boys, build the sand up here to keep the waves back. I'll give you five bucks apiece. Hop to it!"

The sides of the boys' faces were bronze pink from the sun, which was touching the horizon now. Their eyes were a bronze color looking at Chico.

"My God!" said Chico. "This is better than finding ambergris!" He ran to the top of the nearest dune, called, "Get to work!" and was gone.

Now Tom and the two boys were left with the lonely woman by the North Rock and the sun was one-fourth of the way below the western horizon. The sand and the woman were pink gold.

"Just a little line," whispered the second boy. He drew his fingernail along under his own chin, gently. He nodded to the woman. Tom bent again to see the faint line under either side of her firm white chin, the small, almost invisible line where the gills were or had been and were now almost sealed shut, invisible.

He looked at the face and the great strands of hair spread out in a lyre on the shore.

"She's beautiful," he said.

The boys nodded without knowing it.

Behind them, a gull leaped up quickly from the dunes. The boys gasped and turned to stare.

Tom felt himself trembling. He saw the boys were trembling too. A car horn hooted. Their eyes blinked, suddenly afraid. They looked up toward the highway.

A wave poured about the body, framing it in a clear white pool of water.

Tom nodded the boys to one side.

The wave moved the body an inch in and two inches out toward the sea.

The next wave came and moved the body two inches in and six inches out toward the sea.

"But—" said the first boy.

Tom shook his head.

The third wave lifted the body two feet down toward the sea. The wave after that drifted the body another foot down the shingles and the next three moved it six feet down.

The first boy cried out and ran after it.

Tom reached him and held his arm. The boy looked helpless and afraid and sad.

For a moment there were no more waves. Tom looked at the woman, thinking, She's true, she's real, she's mine . . . but . . . she's dead. Or will be if she stays here.

"We can't let her go," said the first boy. "We can't, we just can't!"

The other boy stepped between the woman and the sea. "What would we do with her?" he wanted to know, looking at Tom, "if we kept her?"

The first boy tried to think. "We could—we could—" He stopped and shook his head. "Oh, my gosh."

The second boy stepped out of the way and left a path from the woman to the sea.

The next wave was a big one. It came in and went out and the sand was empty. The whiteness was gone and the black diamonds and the great threads of the harp.

They stood by the edge of the sea, looking out, the man and the two boys, until they heard the truck driving up on the dunes behind them.

The last of the sun was gone.

They heard footsteps running on the dunes and someone yelling.

THEY DROVE back down the darkening beach in the light truck with the big treaded tires in silence. The two boys sat in the rear on the bags of chipped ice. After a long while, Chico began to swear steadily, half to himself, spitting out the window.

"Three hundred pounds of ice. Three hundred *pounds* of ice! What do I do with it now? And I'm soaked to the skin, soaked! You didn't even move when I jumped in and swam out to look around! Idiot, idiot! You haven't changed! Like every other time, like always, you do nothing, nothing, just stand there, stand there, do nothing, nothing, just stare!"

"And what did you do, I ask, what?" said Tom, in a tired voice, looking ahead. "The same as you always did, just the same, no different, no different at all. You should've seen yourself."

They dropped the boys off at their beach house. The younger spoke in a voice you could hardly hear against the wind. "Gosh, nobody'll ever believe . . ."

The two men drove down the coast and parked.

Chico sat for two or three minutes waiting for his fists to relax on his lap, and then he snorted.

"Hell. I guess things turn out for the best." He took a deep breath. "It just came to me. Funny. Twenty, thirty years from now, middle of the night, our phone'll ring. It'll be one of those two boys, grown up, calling long distance from a bar somewhere. Middle of the night, them calling to ask one question. It's *true,* isn't it? they'll say. It *did* happen, didn't it? Back in 1958, it really happened to *us?* And we'll sit there on the edge of the bed, middle of the night, saying, Sure, boy, sure, it really happened to us in 1958. And they'll say, Thanks, and we'll say, Don't mention it, any old time. And we'll all say good night. And maybe they won't call again for a couple of years."

The two men sat on their front-porch steps in the dark.

"Tom?"

"What?"

Chico waited a moment.

"Tom, next week—you're not going away."

It was not a question but a quiet statement.

Tom thought about it, his cigarette dead in his fingers. And he knew that now he could never go away. For tomorrow and the day after the day after that he would walk down and go swimming there in all the green-and-white fires and the dark caverns in the hollows under the strange waves. Tomorrow and tomorrow and tomorrow.

"Yes, Chico. I'm staying here."

Now the silver looking glasses advanced in a crumpling line all along the coast from a thousand miles north to a thousand miles south. The mirrors did not reflect so much as one building or one tree or one highway or one car or even one man himself. The mirrors reflected only the quiet moon and then shattered into a billion bits of glass that spread out in a glaze on the shore. Then the sea was dark awhile, preparing another line of mirrors to rear up and surprise the two men who sat there for a long time never once blinking their eyes, waiting.

THE IDYLL OF
MISS SARAH BROWN

DAMON RUNYON

$Alfred Damon Runyon$

O<small>F ALL</small> the high players this country ever sees, there is no doubt but that the guy they call The Sky is the highest. In fact, the reason he is called The Sky is because he goes so high when it comes to betting on any proposition whatever. He will bet all he has, and nobody can bet any more than this.

His right name is Obadiah Masterson, and he is originally out of a little town in southern Colorado, where he learns to shoot craps, and play cards, and one thing and another, and where his old man is a very well known citizen, and something of a sport himself. In fact, The Sky tells me that when he finally cleans up all the loose scratch around his hometown and decides he needs more room, his old man has a little private talk with him and says to him like this:

"Son," the old guy says, "you are now going out into the wide, wide world to make your own way, and it is a very good thing to do, as there are no more opportunities for you in this burg. I am only sorry," he says, "that I am not able to bankroll you to a very large start, but," he says, "not having any potatoes to give you, I am now going to stake you to some very valuable advice, which I personally collect in my years of experience around and about, and I hope and trust you will always bear this advice in mind.

"Son," the old guy says, "no matter how far you travel, or how smart you get, always remember this: Someday, somewhere," he says, "a guy is going to come to you and show you a nice brand-new deck of cards on which the seal is never broken, and this guy is going to offer to bet you that the jack of spades will jump out of this deck and squirt cider in your ear. But, son," the old guy says, "do not bet him, for as sure as you do you are going to get an ear full of cider."

Well, The Sky remembers what his old man says, and he is always very cautious about betting on such propositions as the jack of spades jumping out of a sealed deck of cards and squirting cider in his ear, and so he makes few mistakes as he goes along. In fact, the only real mistake The Sky makes is when he hits St. Louis after leaving his old hometown, and loses all his potatoes betting a guy St. Louis is the biggest town in the world.

Now of course this is before The Sky ever sees any bigger towns, and he is never much of a hand for reading up on matters such as this. In fact, the only reading The Sky ever does as he goes along through life is in these Gideon Bibles such as he finds in the hotel rooms where he lives, for The Sky never lives anywhere else but in hotel rooms for years.

He tells me that he reads many items of great interest in these Gideon Bibles, and furthermore The Sky says that several times these Gideon Bibles keep him from getting out of line, such as the time he finds himself pretty much frozen-in over in Cincinnati, what with owing everybody in town except maybe the mayor from playing games of chance of one kind and another.

Well, The Sky says he sees no way of meeting these obligations and he is figuring the only thing he can do is to take a runout powder, when he happens to read in one of these Gideon Bibles where it says like this:

Better is it, the Gideon Bible says, *that thou shouldest not vow, than that thou shouldest vow and not pay.*

Well, The Sky says he can see that there is no doubt whatever but that this means a guy shall not welsh, so he remains in Cincinnati until he manages to wiggle himself out of the situation, and from that day to this, The Sky never thinks of welshing.

He is maybe thirty years old, and is a tall guy with a round kisser, and big blue eyes, and he always looks as innocent as a little baby. But The Sky is by no means as innocent as he looks. In fact, The Sky is smarter than three Philadelphia lawyers, which makes him very smart, indeed, and he is well established as a high player in New Orleans, and Chicago, and Los Angeles, and wherever else there is any action in the way of card playing, or crap shooting, or horse racing, or betting on the baseball games, for The Sky is always moving around the country following the action.

But while The Sky will bet on anything whatever, he is more of a short-card player and a crapshooter than anything else, and furthermore he is a great hand for propositions, such as are always coming up among citizens who follow games of chance for a living. Many citizens prefer betting on propositions to anything you can think of, because they figure a proposition gives them a chance to outsmart somebody, and in fact I know citizens who will sit up all night making up propositions to offer other citizens the next day.

A proposition may be only a problem in cards, such as what is the price against a guy getting aces back to back, or how often a pair of deuces will win a hand in stud, and then again it may be some very daffy proposition, indeed, although the daffier any proposition seems to be, the more some citizens like it. And no one ever sees The Sky when he does not have some proposition of his own.

The first time he ever shows up around this town, he goes to a baseball game at the Polo Grounds with several prominent citizens, and while he is at the ball game, he buys himself a sack of Harry Stevens' peanuts, which he dumps in a side pocket of his coat. He is eating these peanuts all through the game, and after the game is over and he is walking across the field with the citizens, he says to them like this:

"What price," The Sky says, "I cannot throw a peanut from second base to the home plate?"

Well, everybody knows that a peanut is too light for anybody to throw it this far, so Big Nig, the crapshooter, who always likes to have a little the best of it running for him, speaks as follows:

"You can have three to one from me, stranger," Big Nig says.

"Two C's against six," The Sky says, and then he stands on second base, and takes a peanut out of his pocket, and not only whips it to the home plate, but on into the lap of a fat guy who is still sitting in the grandstand putting the zing on Bill Terry for not taking Walker out of the box when Walker is getting a pasting from the other club.

Well, naturally, this is a most astonishing throw, indeed, but afterwards it comes out that The Sky throws a peanut loaded with lead, and of course it is not one of Harry Stevens' peanuts, either, as Harry is not selling peanuts full of lead at a dime a bag, with the price of lead what it is.

It is only a few nights after this that The Sky states another most unusual proposition to a group of citizens sitting in Mindy's restaurant when he offers to bet a C note that he can go down into Mindy's cellar and catch a live rat with his bare hands, and everybody is greatly astonished when Mindy himself steps up and takes the bet, for ordinarily Mindy will not bet you a nickel he is alive.

But it seems that Mindy knows that The Sky plants a tame rat in the cellar, and this rat knows The Sky and loves him dearly, and will let him catch it anytime he wishes, and it also seems that Mindy knows that one of his dishwashers happens upon this rat, and not knowing it is tame, knocks it flatter than a pancake. So when The Sky goes down into the cellar and starts trying to catch a rat with his bare hands, he is greatly surprised how inhospitable the rat turns out to be, because it is one of Mindy's personal rats, and Mindy is around afterwards saying he will lay plenty of seven to five against even Strangler Lewis being able to catch one of his rats with his bare hands, or with boxing gloves on.

I am only telling you all this to show you what a smart guy The Sky is, and I am only sorry I do not have time to tell you about many other very remarkable propositions that he thinks up outside of his regular business.

It is well known to one and all that he is very honest in every respect, and that he hates and despises cheaters at cards, or dice, and further-more The Sky never wishes to play with any the best of it himself, or anyway not much. He will never take the inside of any situation, as many gamblers love to do, such as owning a gambling house, and having the percentage run for him instead of against him, for always The Sky is strictly a player, because he says he will never care to settle down in one spot long enough to become the owner of anything.

In fact, in all the years The Sky is drifting around the country, nobody ever knows him to own anything except maybe a bankroll, and when he comes to Broadway the last time, which is the time I am now speaking of, he has a hundred G's in cash money, and an extra suit of clothes, and this is all he has in the world. He never owns such a thing as a house, or an automobile, or a piece of jewelry. He never owns a watch, because The Sky says time means nothing to him.

Of course some guys will figure a hundred G's comes under the head of owning something, but as far as The Sky is concerned, money is nothing but just something for him to play with and the dollars may as well be doughnuts as far as value goes with him. The only time The Sky ever thinks of money as money is when he is broke, and the only way he can tell he is broke is when he reaches into his pocket and finds nothing there but his fingers.

Then it is necessary for The Sky to go out and dig up some fresh scratch somewhere, and when it comes to digging up scratch, The Sky is practically supernatural. He can get more potatoes on the strength of a telegram to some place or other than John D. Rockefeller can get on collateral, for everybody knows The Sky's word is as good as wheat in the bin.

Now one Sunday evening The Sky is walking along Broadway, and at the corner of Forty-ninth Street he comes upon a little bunch of mission workers who are holding a religious meeting, such as mission workers love to do on a Sunday evening, the idea being that they may round up a few sinners here and there, although personally I always claim the mission workers come out too early to catch any sinners on this part of Broadway. At such an hour the sinners are still in bed resting up from their sinning of the night before, so they will be in good shape for more sinning a little later on.

There are only four of these misson workers, and two of them are old guys, and one is an old doll, while the other is a young doll who is tootling on a cornet. And after a couple of ganders at this young doll, The Sky is a goner, for this is one of the most beautiful young dolls anybody ever sees on Broadway, and especially as a mission worker. Her name is Miss Sarah Brown.

She is tall, and thin, and has a first-class shape, and her hair is a light brown, going on blond, and her eyes are like I do not know what, except that they are one-hundred-percent eyes in every respect. Furthermore, she is not a bad cornet player, if you like cornet players, although at this spot on Broadway she has to play against a scat band in a chop-suey joint nearby, and this is tough competition, although at that many citizens believe Miss Sarah Brown will win by a large score if she only gets a little more support from one of the old guys with her who has a big bass drum, but does not pound it hearty enough.

Well, The Sky stands there listening to Miss Sarah Brown tootling on the cornet for quite a spell, and then he hears her make a speech in which she puts the blast on sin very good, and boosts religion quite some, and says if there are any souls around that need saving, the owners of same may step forward at once. But no one steps forward, so The Sky comes over to Mindy's restaurant where many citizens are congregated, and starts telling us about Miss Sarah Brown. But of course we already know about Miss Sarah Brown, because she is so beautiful, and so good.

Furthermore, everybody feels somewhat sorry for Miss Sarah Brown, for while she is always tootling the cornet, and making speeches, and looking to save any souls that need saving, she never seems to find any souls to save, or at least her bunch of mission workers never gets any bigger. In fact, it gets smaller, as she starts out with a guy who plays a very fair sort of trombone, but this guy takes it on the lam one night with the trombone, which one and all consider a dirty trick.

Now from this time on, The Sky does not take any interest in anything but Miss Sarah Brown, and any night she is out on the corner with the other mission workers, you will see The Sky standing around looking at her, and naturally after a few weeks of this, Miss Sarah Brown must know The Sky is looking at her, or she is dumber than seems possible. And nobody ever figures Miss Sarah Brown dumb, as she is always on her toes, and seems plenty able to take care of herself, even on Broadway.

Sometimes after the street meeting is over, The Sky follows the mission workers to their headquarters in an old storeroom around in Forty-eighth Street where they generally hold an indoor session, and I hear The Sky drops many a large coarse note in the collection box while looking at Miss Sarah Brown, and there is no doubt these notes come in handy around the mission, as I hear business is by no means so good there.

It is called the Save-a-Soul Mission, and it is run mainly by Miss Sarah Brown's grandfather, an old guy with whiskers, by the name of

Arvide Abernathy, but Miss Sarah Brown seems to do most of the work, including tootling the cornet, and visiting the poor people around and about, and all this and that, and many citizens claim it is a great shame that such a beautiful doll is wasting her time being good.

How The Sky ever becomes acquainted with Miss Sarah Brown is a very great mystery, but the next thing anybody knows, he is saying hello to her, and she is smiling at him out of her one-hundred-percent eyes, and one evening when I happen to be with The Sky we run into her walking along Forty-ninth Street, and The Sky hauls off and stops her, and says it is a nice evening, which it is, at that. Then The Sky says to Miss Sarah Brown like this:

"Well," The Sky says, "how is the mission dodge going these days? Are you saving any souls?" he says.

Well, it seems from what Miss Sarah Brown says, the soul saving is very slow, indeed, these days.

"In fact," Miss Sarah Brown says, "I worry greatly about how few souls we seem to save. Sometimes I wonder if we are lacking in grace."

She goes on up the street, and The Sky stands looking after her, and he says to me like this:

"I wish I can think of some way to help this little doll," he says, "especially," he says, "in saving a few souls to build up her mob at the mission. I must speak to her again, and see if I can figure something out."

But The Sky does not get to speak to Miss Sarah Brown again, because somebody weighs in the sacks on him by telling her he is nothing but a professional gambler, and that he is a very undesirable character, and that his only interest in hanging around the mission is because she is a good-looking doll. So all of a sudden Miss Sarah Brown plays plenty of chill for The Sky. Furthermore, she sends him word that she does not care to accept any more of his potatoes in the collection box, because his potatoes are nothing but ill-gotten gains.

Well, naturally, this hurts The Sky's feelings no little, so he quits standing around looking at Miss Sarah Brown, and going to the mission, and takes to mingling again with the citizens in Mindy's, and showing some interest in the affairs of the community, especially the crap games.

Of course the crap games that are going on at this time are nothing much, because practically everybody in the world is broke, but there is a head-and-head game run by Nathan Detroit over a garage in Fifty-second Street where there is occasionally some action, and who shows up at this crap game early one evening but The Sky, although it seems he shows up there more to find company than anything else.

In fact, he only stands around watching the play, and talking with the other guys who are also standing around and watching, and many of these guys are very high shots during the gold rush, although most of them are now as clean as a jaybird, and maybe cleaner. One of these guys is a guy by the name of Brandy Bottle Bates, who is known from coast to coast as a high player when he has anything to play with, and who is called Brandy Bottle Bates because it seems that years ago he is a great hand for belting a brandy bottle around.

This Brandy Bottle Bates is a big, black-looking guy, with a large beezer, and a head shaped like a pear, and he is considered a very immoral and wicked character, but he is a pretty slick gambler, and a fast man with a dollar when he is in the money.

Well, finally The Sky asks Brandy Bottle why he is not playing and Brandy laughs, and states as follows:

"Why," he says, "in the first place I have no potatoes, and in the second place I doubt if it will do me much good if I do have any potatoes the way I am going the past year. Why," Brandy Bottle says, "I cannot win a bet to save my soul."

Now this crack seems to give The Sky an idea, as he stands looking at Brandy Bottle very strangely, and while he is looking, Big Nig, the crapshooter, picks up the dice and hits three times hand running, bing, bing, bing. Then Big Nig comes out on a six and Brandy Bottle Bates speaks as follows:

"You see how my luck is," he says. "Here is Big Nig hotter than a stove, and here I am without a bob to follow him with, especially," Brandy says, "when he is looking for nothing but a six. Why," he says, "Nig can make sixes all night when he is hot. If he does not make this six, the way he is, I will be willing to turn square and quit gambling forever."

"Well, Brandy," The Sky says, "I will make you a proposition. I will lay you a G note Big Nig does not get his six. I will lay you a G note against nothing but your soul," he says. "I mean if Big Nig does not get his six, you are to turn square and join Miss Sarah Brown's mission for six months."

"Bet!" Brandy Bottle Bates says right away, meaning the proposition is on, although the chances are he does not quite understand the proposition. All Brandy understands is The Sky wishes to wager that Big Nig does not make his six, and Brandy Bottle Bates will be willing to bet his soul a couple of times over on Big Nig making his six, and figure he is getting the best of it, at that, as Brandy has great confidence in Nig.

Well, sure enough, Big Nig makes the six, so The Sky weeds Brandy Bottle Bates a G note, although everybody around is saying The Sky makes a terrible overlay of the natural price in giving Brandy Bottle a G against his soul. Furthermore, everybody around figures the chances are The Sky only wishes to give Brandy an opportunity to get in action, and nobody figures The Sky is on the level about trying to win Brandy Bottle Bates' soul, especially as The Sky does not seem to wish to go any further after paying the bet.

He only stands there looking on and seeming somewhat depressed as Brandy Bottle goes into action on his own account with the G note, fading other guys around the table with cash money. But Brandy Bottle Bates seems to figure what is in The Sky's mind pretty well, because Brandy Bottle is a crafty old guy.

It finally comes his turn to handle the dice, and he hits a couple of times, and then he comes out on a four, and anybody will tell you that a four is a very tough point to make, even with a lead pencil. Then Brandy Bottle turns to The Sky and speaks to him as follows:

"Well, Sky," he says, "I will take the odds off you on this one. I know you do not want my dough," he says. "I know you only want my soul for Miss Sarah Brown, and," he says, "without wishing to be fresh about it, I know why you want it for her. I am young once myself," Brandy Bottle says. "And you know if I lose to you, I will be over there in Forty-eighth Street in an hour pounding on the door, for Brandy always settles.

"But, Sky," he says, "now I am in the money, and my price goes up.

Will you lay me ten G's against my soul I do not make this four?"

"Bet!" The Sky says, and right away Brandy Bottle hits with a four.

Well, when word goes around that The Sky is up at Nathan Detroit's crap game trying to win Brandy Bottle Bates' soul for Miss Sarah Brown, the excitement is practically intense. Somebody telephones Mindy's, where a large number of citizens are sitting around arguing about this and that, and telling one another how much they will bet in support of their arguments, if only they have something to bet, and Mindy himself is almost killed in the rush for the door.

One of the first guys out of Mindy's and up to the crap game is Regret, the horseplayer, and as he comes in, Brandy Bottle is looking for a nine, and The Sky is laying him twelve G's against his soul that he does not make this nine, for it seems Brandy Bottle's soul keeps getting more and more expensive.

Well, Regret wishes to bet his soul against a G that Brandy Bottle gets his nine, and is greatly insulted when The Sky cannot figure his price any better than a double saw, but finally Regret accepts this price, and Brandy Bottle hits again.

Now many other citizens request a little action from The Sky, and if there is one thing The Sky cannot deny a citizen it is action, so he says he will lay them according to how he figures their word to join Miss Sarah Brown's mission if Brandy Bottle misses out, but about this time The Sky finds he has no more potatoes on him, being now around thirty-five G's loser, and he wishes to give markers.

But Brandy Bottle says that while ordinarily he will be pleased to extend The Sky this accommodation, he does not care to accept markers against his soul, so then The Sky has to leave the joint and go over to his hotel two or three blocks away, and get the night clerk to open his damper so The Sky can get the rest of his bankroll. In the meantime the crap game continues at Nathan Detroit's among the small operators, while the other citizens stand around and say that while they hear of many a daffy proposition in their time, this is the daffiest that ever comes to their attention, although Big Nig claims he hears of a daffier one, but cannot think what it is.

Big Nig claims that all gamblers are daffy anyway, and in fact he says if they are not daffy they will not be gamblers, and while he is arguing this matter, back comes The Sky with fresh scratch, and Brandy Bottle Bates takes up where he leaves off, although Brandy says he is accepting the worst of it, as the dice have a chance to cool off.

Now the upshot of the whole business is that Brandy Bottle hits thirteen licks in a row, and the last lick he makes is on a ten, and it is for twenty G's against his soul, with about a dozen other citizens getting anywhere from one to five C's against their souls, and complaining bitterly of the price.

And as Brandy Bottle makes his ten, I happen to look at The Sky and I see him watching Brandy with a very peculiar expression on his face, and furthermore I see The Sky's right hand creeping inside his coat where I know he always packs a Betsy in a shoulder holster, so I can see something is wrong somewhere.

But before I can figure out what it is, there is quite a fuss at the door, and loud talking, and a doll's voice, and all of a sudden in bobs nobody else but Miss Sarah Brown. It is plain to be seen that she is all steamed up about something. She marches right up to the crap table where Brandy Bottle Bates and The Sky and the other citizens are standing, and one and all are feeling sorry for Dobber, the doorman, thinking of what Nathan Detroit is bound to say to him for letting her in. The dice are still lying on the table showing Brandy Bottle Bates' last throw, which cleans The Sky and gives many citizens the first means they enjoy in several months.

Well, Miss Sarah Brown looks at The Sky, and The Sky looks at Miss Sarah Brown, and Miss Sarah Brown looks at the citizens around and about, and one and all are somewhat dumbfounded, and nobody seems to be able to think of much to say, although The Sky finally speaks up as follows:

"Good evening," The Sky says. "It is a nice evening," he says. "I am trying to win a few souls for you around here, but," he says, "I seem to be about half out of luck."

"Well," Miss Sarah Brown says, looking at The Sky most severely out of her hundred-percent eyes, "you are taking too much upon yourself. I can win any souls I need myself. You better be thinking of your own soul. By the way," she says, "are you risking your own soul, or just your money?"

Well, of course up to this time The Sky is not risking anything but his potatoes, so he only shakes his head to Miss Sarah Brown's question, and looks somewhat disorganized.

"I know something about gambling," Miss Sarah Brown says, "especially about crap games. I ought to," she says. "It ruins my poor papa and my brother Joe. If you wish to gamble for souls, Mister Sky, gamble for your own soul."

Now Miss Sarah Brown opens a small black leather pocketbook she is carrying in one hand, and pulls out a two-dollar bill, and it is such a two-dollar bill as seems to have seen much service in its time, and holding up this deuce, Miss Sarah Brown speaks as follows:

"I will gamble with you, Mister Sky," she says. "I will gamble with you," she says, "on the same terms you gamble with these parties here. This two dollars against your soul, Mister Sky. It is all I have, but," she says, "it is more than your soul is worth."

Well, of course anybody can see that Miss Sarah Brown is doing this because she is very angry, and wishes to make The Sky look small, but right away The Sky's duke comes from inside his coat, and he picks up the dice and hands them to her and speaks as follows:

"Roll them," The Sky says, and Miss Sarah Brown snatches the dice out of his hand and gives them a quick sling on the table in such a way that anybody can see she is not a professional crapshooter, and not even an amateur crapshooter, for all amateur crapshooters first breathe on the dice, and rattle them good, and make remarks to them, such as "Come on, baby!"

In fact, there is some criticism of Miss Sarah Brown afterwards on account of her haste, as many citizens are eager to string with her to hit, while others are just as anxious to bet she misses, and she does not give them a chance to get down.

Well, Scranton Slim is the stick guy, and he takes a gander at the dice as they hit up against the side of the table and bounce back, and then Slim hollers, "Winner, winner, winner," as stick guys love to do, and what is showing on the dice as big as life, but a six and a five, which makes eleven, no matter how you figure, so The Sky's soul belongs to Miss Sarah Brown.

She turns at once and pushes through the citizens around the table without even waiting to pick up the deuce she lays down when she grabs the dice. Afterwards a most obnoxious character by the name of Red Nose Regan tries to claim the deuce as a sleeper and gets the heave-o from Nathan Detroit, who becomes very indignant about this, stating that Red Nose is trying to give his joint a wrong rap.

Naturally, The Sky follows Miss Brown, and Dobber, the doorman, tells me that as they are waiting for him to unlock the door and let them out, Miss Sarah Brown turns on The Sky and speaks to him as follows:

"You are a fool," Miss Sarah Brown says.

Well, at this Dobber figures The Sky is bound to let one go, as this seems to be most insulting language, but instead of letting one go, The Sky only smiles at Miss Sarah Brown and says to her like this:

"Why," The Sky says, "Paul says, *If any man among you seemeth to be wise in this world, let him become a fool, that he may be wise.* I love you, Miss Sarah Brown," The Sky says.

Well, now, Dobber has a pretty fair sort of memory, and he says that Miss Sarah Brown tells The Sky that since he seems to know so much about the Bible, maybe he remembers the second verse of The Song of Solomon, but the chances are Dobber muffs the number of the verse, because I look the matter up in one of these Gideon Bibles, and the verse seems a little too much for Miss Sarah Brown, although of course you never can tell.

Anyway, this is about all there is to the story, except that Brandy Bottle Bates slides out during the confusion so quietly even Dobber scarcely remembers letting him out, and he takes most of The Sky's potatoes with him, but he soon gets batted in against the faro bank out in Chicago, and the last anybody hears of him he gets religion all over again, and is preaching out in San Jose, so The Sky always claims he beats Brandy for his soul, at that.

I see The Sky the other night at Forty-ninth Street and Broadway, and he is with quite a raft of mission workers, including Mrs. Sky, for it seems that the soul-saving business picks up wonderfully, and The Sky is giving a big bass drum such a first-class whacking that the scat band in the chop-suey joint can scarcely be heard. Furthermore, The Sky is hollering between whacks, and I never see a guy look happier, especially when Mrs. Sky smiles at him out of her hundred-percent eyes. But I do not linger long, because The Sky gets a gander at me, and right away he begins hollering:

"I see before me a sinner of deepest dye," he hollers. "Oh, sinner, repent before it is too late. Join with us, sinner," he hollers, "and let us save your soul."

Naturally, this crack about me being a sinner embarrasses me no little, as it is by no means true, and it is a good thing for The Sky there is no copper in me, or I will go to Mrs. Sky, who is always bragging about how she wins The Sky's soul by outplaying him at his own game, and tell her the truth.

And the truth is that the dice with which she wins The Sky's soul, and which are the same dice with which Brandy Bottle Bates wins all his potatoes, are strictly phony, and that she gets into Nathan Detroit's just in time to keep The Sky from killing old Brandy Bottle.

CORONER'S INQUEST

MARC CONNELLY

"WHAT IS your name?"

"Frank Wineguard."

"Where do you live?"

"A hundred and eighty-five West Fifty-fifth Street."

"What is your business?"

"I'm stage manager for *Hello, America.*"

"You were the employer of James Dawle?"

"In a way. We both worked for Mr. Bender, the producer, but I have charge backstage."

"Did you know Theodore Robel?"

"Yes, sir."

"Was he in your company, too?"

"No, sir. I met him when we started rehearsals. That was about three months ago, in June. We sent out a call for midgets and he and Jimmy showed up together, with a lot of others. Robel was too big for us. I didn't see him again until we broke into their room Tuesday."

"You discovered their bodies?"

"Yes, sir. Mrs. Pike, there, was with me."

"You found them both dead?"

"Yes, sir."

"How did you happen to be over in Jersey City?"

"Well, I'd called up his house at curtain time Monday night when I found Jimmy hadn't shown up for the performance. Mrs. Pike told me they were both out, and I asked her to have either Jimmy or Robel call me when they came in. Then Mrs. Pike called me Tuesday morning and said she tried to get into the room but she'd found the door was bolted. She said all her other roomers were out and she was alone and scared.

"I'd kind of suspected something might be wrong. So I said to wait and I'd come over. Then I took the tube over and got there about noon. Then we went up and I broke down the door."

"Did you see this knife there?"

"Yes, sir. It was on the floor, about a foot from Jimmy."

"You say you suspected something was wrong. What do you mean by that?"

"I mean I felt something might have happened to Jimmy. Nothing like this, of course. But I knew he'd been feeling very depressed lately, and I knew Robel wasn't helping to cheer him up any."

"You mean that they had had quarrels?"

"No, sir. They just both had the blues. Robel had had them for a long time. Robel was Jimmy's brother-in-law. He'd married Jimmy's sister—she was a midget, too—about five years ago, but she died a year or so later. Jimmy had been living with them and after the sister died he and Robel took a room in Mrs. Pike's house together."

"How did you learn this?"

"Jimmy and I were pretty friendly at the theater. He was a nice little fellow and seemed grateful that I'd given him his job. We'd only needed one midget for an Oriental scene in the second act and the agencies had sent about fifteen. Mr. Gehring, the director, told me to pick one of them as he was busy and I picked Jimmy because he was the littlest.

"After I got to know him he told me how glad he was I'd given him the job. He hadn't worked for nearly a year. He wasn't little enough to be a featured midget with circuses or in museums so he had to take whatever came along. Anyway, we got to be friendly and he used to tell me about his brother-in-law and all."

"He never suggested that there might be ill feeling between him and his brother-in-law?"

"No, sir. I don't imagine he'd ever had any words at all with Robel. As a matter of fact from what I could gather I guess Jimmy had quite a lot of affection for him and he certainly did everything he could to help him. Robel was a lot worse off than Jimmy. Robel hadn't worked for a couple of years and Jimmy practically supported him. He used to tell me how Robel had been sunk ever since he got his late growth."

"His what?"

"His late growth. I heard it happens among midgets often, but Jimmy told me about it first. Usually a midget will stay as long as he lives at whatever height he reaches when he's fourteen or fifteen, but every now and then one of them starts growing again just before he's thirty, and he can grow a foot or even more in a couple of years. Then he stops growing for good. But of course he don't look so much like a midget anymore.

"That's what had happened to Robel about three years ago. Of course he had trouble getting jobs and it hit him pretty hard.

"From what Jimmy told me and from what Mrs. Pike says, I guess he used to talk about it all the time. Robel used to come over and see his agent in New York twice a week, but there was never anything for him. Then he'd go back to Jersey City. Most of the week he lived alone because after the show started Jimmy often stayed in New York with a cousin or somebody that lived uptown.

"Lately Robel hadn't been coming over to New York at all. But every Saturday night Jimmy would go over to Jersey City and stay till Monday with him, trying to cheer him up. Every Sunday they'd take a walk and go to a movie. I guess as they walked along the street Robel realized most the difference in their heights. And I guess that's really why they're both dead now."

"How do you mean?"

"Well, as I told you, Jimmy would try to sympathize with Robel and cheer him up. He and Robel both realized that Jimmy was working and supporting them and that Jimmy would probably keep right on working, according to the ordinary breaks of the game, while Robel would always be too big. It simply preyed on Robel's mind.

"And then three weeks ago Monday, Jimmy thought he saw the ax fall.

"I was standing outside the stage door—it was about seven thirty—and Jimmy came down the alley. He looked down in the mouth, which I thought was strange seeing that he usually used to come in swinging his little cane and looking pretty cheerful. I said, 'How are you feeling,

Jimmy?' and he said, 'I don't feel so good, Mr. Wineguard.' So I said, 'Why, what's the matter, Jimmy?' I could see there really was something the matter with him by this time.

" 'I'm getting scared,' he said, and I says, 'Why?'

" 'I'm starting to grow again,' he says. He said it the way you'd say you just found out you had some disease that was going to kill you in a week. He looked like he was shivering.

" 'Why, you're crazy, Jimmy,' I says. 'You ain't growing.'

" 'Yes, I am,' he says. 'I'm thirty-one and it's that late growth like my brother-in-law has. My father had it, but his people had money, so it didn't make much difference to him. It's different with me. I've got to keep working.'

"He went on like that for a while and then I tried to kid him out of it.

" 'You look all right to me,' I said. 'How tall have you been all along?'

" 'Thirty-seven inches,' he says. So I says, 'Come on into the prop room and I'll measure you.'

"He backed away from me. 'No,' he says, 'I don't want to know how much it is.' Then he went up to the dressing room before I could argue with him.

"All week he looked awful sunk. When he showed up the next Monday evening he looked almost white.

"I grabbed him as he was starting upstairs to make up.

" 'Come on out of it,' I says. I thought he'd make a break and try to get away from me, but he didn't. He just sort of smiled as if I didn't understand. Finally he says, 'It ain't any use, Mr. Wineguard.'

" 'Listen,' I says, 'you've been over with that brother-in-law of yours, haven't you?' He said yes, he had. 'Well,' I says, 'that's what's bothering you. From what you tell me about him he's talked about his own tough luck so much that he's given you the willies, too. Stay away from him the end of this week.'

"He stood there for a second without saying anything. Then he says, 'That wouldn't do any good. He's all alone over there and he needs company. Anyway, it's all up with me, I guess. I've grown nearly two inches already.'

"I looked at him. He was pretty pathetic, but outside of that there wasn't any change in him as far as I could see.

"I says, 'Have you been measured?' He said he hadn't. Then I said, 'Then how do you know? Your clothes fit you all right, except your pants, and as a matter of fact they seem a little longer.'

" 'I fixed my suspenders and let them down a lot farther,' he says. 'Besides they were always a little big for me.'

" 'Let's make sure,' I says. 'I'll get a yardstick and we'll make absolutely sure.'

"But I guess he was too scared to face things. He wouldn't do it.

"He managed to dodge me all week. Then, last Saturday night, I ran into him as I was leaving the theater. I asked him if he felt any better.

" 'I feel all right,' he says. He really looked scared to death.

"That's the last time I saw him before I went over to Jersey City after Mrs. Pike phoned me Tuesday morning."

"Patrolman Gorlitz has testified that the bodies were in opposite ends of the room when he arrived. They were in that position when you forced open the door?"

"Yes, sir."

"The medical examiner has testified that they were both dead of knife wounds, apparently from the same knife. Would you assume the knife had fallen from Dawle's hand as he fell?"

"Yes, sir."

"Has it been your purpose to suggest that both men were driven to despondency by a fear of lack of employment for Dawle, and that they might have committed suicide?"

"No, sir. I don't think anything of the kind."

"What do you mean?"

"Well, when Mrs. Pike and I went in the room and I got a look at the knife, I said to Mrs. Pike that that was a funny kind of a knife for them to have in the room. You can see it's a kind of a butcher knife. Then Mrs. Pike told me it was one that she'd missed from her kitchen a few weeks before. She'd never thought either Robel or Jimmy had taken it. It struck me as funny Robel or Jimmy had stolen it, too. Then I put two and two together and found out what really happened. Have you got the little broken cane that was lying on the bed?"

"Is this it?"

"Yes, sir. Well, I'd never been convinced by Jimmy that he was really growing. So when Mrs. Pike told me about the knife I started figuring. I figured that about five minutes before that knife came into play Jimmy must have found it, probably by accident."

"Why by accident?"

"Because Robel had gone a little crazy, I guess. He'd stolen it and kept it hidden from Jimmy. And when Jimmy found it he wondered what Robel had been doing with it. Then Robel wouldn't tell him and Jimmy found out for himself. Or maybe Robel did tell him. Anyway, Jimmy looked at the cane. It was the one he always carried. He saw where, when Jimmy wasn't looking, Robel had been cutting little pieces off the end of it."

ROMAN FEVER

EDITH WHARTON

From the table at which they had been lunching two American ladies of ripe but well-cared-for middle age moved across the lofty terrace of the Roman restaurant and, leaning on its parapet, looked first at each other, and then down on the outspread glories of the Palatine and the Forum, with the same expression of vague but benevolent approval.

As they leaned there a girlish voice echoed up gaily from the stairs leading to the court below. "Well, come along, then," it cried, not to them but to an invisible companion, "and let's leave the young things to their knitting"; and a voice as fresh laughed back: "Oh, look here, Babs, not actually *knitting*—" "Well, I mean figuratively," rejoined the first. "After all, we haven't left our poor parents much else to do. . . ." At that point the turn of the stairs engulfed the dialogue.

The two ladies looked at each other again, this time with a tinge of smiling embarrassment, and the smaller and paler one shook her head and colored slightly.

"Barbara!" she murmured, sending an unheard rebuke after the mocking voice in the stairway.

The other lady, who was fuller, and higher in color, with a small determined nose supported by vigorous black eyebrows, gave a good-humored laugh. "That's what our daughters think of us!"

Her companion replied by a deprecating gesture. "Not of us individually. We must remember that. It's just the collective modern idea of Mothers. And you see—" Half guiltily she drew from her handsomely mounted black handbag a twist of crimson silk run through by two fine knitting needles. "One never knows," she murmured. "The new system has certainly given us a good deal of time to kill; and sometimes I get tired just looking—even at this." Her gesture was now addressed to the stupendous scene at their feet.

The dark lady laughed again, and they both relapsed upon the view, contemplating it in silence, with a sort of diffused serenity which might have been borrowed from the spring effulgence of the Roman skies. The luncheon hour was long past, and the two had their end of the vast terrace to themselves. At its opposite extremity a few groups, detained by a lingering look at the outspread city, were gathering up guidebooks and fumbling for tips. The last of them scattered, and the two ladies were alone on the air-washed height.

"Well, I don't see why we shouldn't just stay here," said Mrs. Slade, the lady of the high color and energetic brows. Two derelict basket chairs stood near, and she pushed them into the angle of the parapet, and settled herself in one, her gaze upon the Palatine. "After all, it's still the most beautiful view in the world."

"It always will be, to me," assented her friend Mrs. Ansley, with so slight a stress on the "me" that Mrs. Slade, though she noticed it, wondered if it were not merely accidental, like the random underlinings of old-fashioned letter writers.

"Grace Ansley was always old-fashioned," she thought; and added aloud, with a retrospective smile: "It's a view we've both been familiar with for a good many years. When we first met here we were younger than our girls are now. You remember?"

"Oh, yes, I remember," murmured Mrs. Ansley, with the same undefinable stress. "There's that headwaiter wondering," she interpolated. She was evidently far less sure than her companion of herself and of her rights in the world.

"I'll cure him of wondering," said Mrs. Slade, stretching her hand toward a bag as discreetly opulent looking as Mrs. Ansley's. Signing to the headwaiter, she explained that she and her friend were old lovers of Rome, and would like to spend the end of the afternoon looking down on the view—that is, if it did not disturb the service? The headwaiter, bowing over her gratuity, assured her that the ladies were most welcome, and would be still more so if they would condescend to remain for dinner. A full-moon night, they would remember. . . .

Mrs. Slade's black brows drew together, as though references to the moon were out of place and even unwelcome. But she smiled away her frown as the headwaiter retreated. "Well, why not? We might do worse. There's no knowing, I suppose, when the girls will be back. Do you even know back from *where?* I don't!"

Mrs. Ansley again colored slightly. "I think those young Italian aviators we met at the embassy invited them to fly to Tarquinia for tea. I suppose they'll want to wait and fly back by moonlight."

"Moonlight—moonlight! What a part it still plays. Do you suppose they're as sentimental as we were?"

"I've come to the conclusion that I don't in the least know what they are," said Mrs. Ansley. "And perhaps we didn't know much more about each other."

"No; perhaps we didn't."

Her friend gave her a shy glance. "I never should have supposed you were sentimental, Alida."

"Well, perhaps I wasn't." Mrs. Slade drew her lids together in retrospect; and for a few moments the two ladies, who had been intimate since childhood, reflected how little they knew each other. Each one, of course, had a label ready to attach to the other's name; Mrs. Delphin Slade, for instance, would have told herself, or anyone who asked her, that Mrs. Horace Ansley, twenty-five years ago, had been exquisitely lovely—no, you wouldn't believe it, would you? . . . though, of course, still charming, distinguished. . . . Well, as a girl she had been exquisite; far more beautiful than her daughter, Barbara, though certainly Babs, according to the new standards at any rate, was more effective—had more *edge*, as they say. Funny where she got it, with those two nullities as parents. Yes; Horace Ansley was—well, just the duplicate of his wife. Museum specimens of old New York. Good-looking, irreproachable, exemplary. Mrs. Slade and Mrs. Ansley had lived opposite each other—actually as well as figuratively—for years. When the drawing-room curtains in number 20 East Seventy-third Street were renewed, number 23, across the way, was always aware of it. And of all the movings, buyings, travels, anniversaries, illnesses—the tame chronicle of an estimable pair. Little of it escaped Mrs. Slade. But she had grown bored with it by the time her husband made his big *coup* in Wall Street, and when they bought in upper Park Avenue had already begun to think: "I'd rather live opposite a speakeasy for a change; at least one might see it raided." The idea of seeing Grace raided was so amusing that (before the move) she launched it at a woman's lunch. It made a hit, and went the rounds—she sometimes wondered if it had crossed the street, and reached Mrs. Ansley. She hoped not, but didn't much mind. Those were the days when respectability was at a discount, and it did the irreproachable no harm to laugh at them a little.

A few years later, and not many months apart, both ladies lost their husbands. There was an appropriate exchange of wreaths and condolences, and a brief renewal of intimacy in the half shadow of their mourning; and now, after another interval, they had run across each other in Rome, at the same hotel, each of them the modest appendage of a salient daughter. The similarity of their lot had again drawn them together, lending itself to mild jokes, and the mutual confession that, if in old days it must have been tiring to "keep up" with daughters, it was now, at times, a little dull not to.

No doubt, Mrs. Slade reflected, she felt her unemployment more than poor Grace ever would. It was a big drop from being the wife of Delphin Slade to being his widow. She had always regarded herself (with a certain conjugal pride) as his equal in social gifts, as contributing her full share to the making of the exceptional couple they were: but the difference after his death was irremediable. As the wife of the famous corporation lawyer, always with an international case or two on hand, every day brought its exciting and unexpected obligation: the impromptu entertaining of eminent colleagues from abroad, the hurried dashes on legal business to London, Paris or Rome, where the entertaining was so handsomely reciprocated; the amusement of hearing in her wake: "What, that handsome woman with the good clothes and the eyes is Mrs. Slade—*the* Slade's wife? Really? Generally the wives of celebrities are such frumps."

Yes; being *the* Slade's widow was a dullish business after that. In living up to such a husband all her faculties had been engaged; now she had only her daughter to live up to, for the son who seemed to have inherited his father's gifts had died suddenly in boyhood. She had fought through that agony because her husband was there, to be helped and to help; now, after the father's death, the thought of the boy had become unbearable. There was nothing left but to mother her daughter; and dear Jenny was such a perfect daughter that she needed no excessive mothering. "Now with Babs Ansley I don't know that I *should* be so quiet," Mrs. Slade sometimes half enviously reflected; but Jenny, who was younger than her brilliant friend, was that rare accident, an extremely pretty girl who somehow made youth and prettiness seem as safe as their absence. It was all perplexing—and to Mrs. Slade a little boring. She wished that Jenny would fall in love—with the wrong man, even; that she might have to be watched, outmaneuvered, rescued. And instead, it was Jenny who watched her mother, kept her out of drafts, made sure that she had taken her tonic. . . .

Mrs. Ansley was much less articulate than her friend, and her mental portrait of Mrs. Slade was slighter, and drawn with fainter touches. "Alida Slade's awfully brilliant; but not as brilliant as she thinks," would have summed it up; though she would have added, for the enlightenment of strangers, that Mrs. Slade had been an extremely dashing girl; much more so than her daughter, who was pretty, of course, and clever in a way, but had none of her mother's—well, "vividness," someone had once called it. Mrs. Ansley would take up current words like this, and cite them in quotation marks, as unheard-of audacities. No; Jenny was not like her mother. Sometimes Mrs. Ansley thought Alida Slade was disappointed; on the whole she had had a sad life. Full of failures and mistakes; Mrs. Ansley had always been rather sorry for her. . . .

So these two ladies visualized each other, each through the wrong end of her little telescope.

FOR A LONG time they continued to sit side by side without speaking. It seemed as though, to both, there was a relief in laying down their somewhat futile activities in the presence of the vast Memento Mori which faced them. Mrs. Slade sat quite still, her eyes fixed on the golden slope of the Palace of the Caesars, and after a while Mrs. Ansley ceased to fidget with her bag, and she too sank into meditation. Like many intimate friends, the two ladies had never before had occasion to be silent together, and Mrs. Ansley was slightly embarrassed by what seemed, after so many years, a new stage in their intimacy, and one with which she did not yet know how to deal.

Suddenly the air was full of that deep clangor of bells which periodically covers Rome with a roof of silver. Mrs. Slade glanced at her wristwatch. "Five o'clock already," she said, as though surprised.

Mrs. Ansley suggested interrogatively: "There's bridge at the embassy at five." For a long time Mrs. Slade did not answer. She appeared to be lost in contemplation, and Mrs. Ansley thought the remark had escaped her. But after a while she said, as if speaking out of a dream: "Bridge, did you say? Not unless you want to. . . . But I don't think I will, you know."

"Oh, no," Mrs. Ansley hastened to assure her. "I don't care to at all. It's so lovely here; and so full of old memories, as you say." She settled herself in her chair, and almost furtively drew forth her knitting. Mrs. Slade took sideways note of this activity, but her own beautifully cared for hands remained motionless on her knee.

"I was just thinking," she said slowly, "what different things Rome stands for to each generation of travelers. To our grandmothers, Roman fever; to our mothers, sentimental dangers—how we used to be guarded!—to our daughters, no more dangers than the middle of Main Street. They don't know it—but how much they're missing!"

The long golden light was beginning to pale, and Mrs. Ansley lifted her knitting a little closer to her eyes. "Yes; how we were guarded!"

"I always used to think," Mrs. Slade continued, "that our mothers had a much more difficult job than our grandmothers. When Roman fever stalked the streets it must have been comparatively easy to gather in the girls at the danger hour; but when you and I were young, with such beauty calling us, and the spice of disobedience thrown in, and no worse risk than catching cold during the cool hour after sunset, the mothers used to be put to it to keep us in—didn't they?"

She turned again toward Mrs. Ansley, but the latter had reached a delicate point in her knitting. "One, two, three—slip two; yes, they must have been," she assented, without looking up.

Mrs. Slade's eyes rested on her with a deepened attention. "She can knit—in the face of *this!* How like her. . . ."

Mrs. Slade leaned back, brooding, her eyes ranging from the ruins which faced her to the long green hollow of the Forum, the fading glow of the church fronts beyond it, and the outlying immensity of the Colosseum. Suddenly she thought: "It's all very well to say that our girls have done away with sentiment and moonlight. But if Babs Ansley isn't out to catch that young aviator—the one who's a marchese—then I don't know anything. And Jenny has no chance beside her. I know that too. I wonder if that's why Grace Ansley likes the two girls to go everywhere together? My poor Jenny as a foil!" Mrs. Slade gave a hardly audible laugh, and at the sound Mrs. Ansley dropped her knitting.

"Yes?"

"I—oh, nothing. I was only thinking how your Babs carries everything before her. That Campolieri boy is one of the best matches in Rome. Don't look so innocent, my dear—you know he is. And I was wondering, ever so respectfully, you understand . . . wondering how two such exemplary characters as you and Horace had managed to produce anything quite so dynamic." Mrs. Slade laughed again, with a touch of asperity.

Mrs. Ansley's hands lay inert across her needles. She looked straight out at the great accumulated wreckage of passion and splendor at her feet. But her small profile was almost expressionless. At length she said, "I think you overrate Babs, my dear."

Mrs. Slade's tone grew easier. "No; I don't. I appreciate her. And perhaps envy you. Oh, my girl's perfect; if I were a chronic invalid I'd—well, I think I'd rather be in Jenny's hands. There must be times . . . but there! I always wanted a brilliant daughter . . . and never quite understood why I got an angel instead."

Mrs. Ansley echoed her laugh in a faint murmur. "Babs is an angel too."

"Of course—of course! But she's got rainbow wings. Well, they're wandering by the sea with their young men; and here we sit . . . and it all brings back the past a little too acutely."

Mrs. Ansley had resumed her knitting. One might almost have imagined (if one had known her less well, Mrs. Slade reflected) that, for her also, too many memories rose from the lengthening shadows of those august ruins. But no; she was simply absorbed in her work. What was there for her to worry about? She knew that Babs would almost certainly come back engaged to the extremely eligible Campolieri. "And she'll sell the New York house, and settle down near them in Rome, and never be in their way . . . she's much too tactful. But she'll have an excellent cook, and just the right people in for bridge and cocktails . . . and a perfectly peaceful old age among her grandchildren."

Mrs. Slade broke off this prophetic flight with a recoil of self-disgust. There was no one of whom she had less right to think unkindly than of Grace Ansley. Would she never cure herself of envying her? Perhaps she had begun too long ago.

She stood up and leaned against the parapet, filling her troubled eyes with the tranquilizing magic of the hour. But instead of tranquilizing her the sight seemed to increase her exasperation. Her gaze turned toward the Colosseum. Already its golden flank was drowned in purple shadow, and above it the sky curved crystal clear, without light or color. It was the moment when afternoon and evening hang balanced in midheaven.

Mrs. Slade turned back and laid her hand on her friend's arm. The gesture was so abrupt that Mrs. Ansley looked up, startled.

"The sun's set. You're not afraid, my dear?"

"Afraid?"

"Of Roman fever or pneumonia? I remember how ill you were that winter. As a girl you had a very delicate throat, hadn't you?"

"Oh, we're all right up here. Down below, in the Forum, it does get deathly cold, all of a sudden . . . but not here."

"Ah, of course you know because you had to be so careful." Mrs. Slade turned back to the parapet. She thought: "I must make one more effort not to hate her." Aloud she said: "Whenever I look at the Forum from up here, I remember that story about a great-aunt of yours, wasn't she? A dreadfully wicked great-aunt?"

"Oh, yes; Great-aunt Harriet. The one who was supposed to have sent her young sister out to the Forum after sunset to gather a night-blooming flower for her album. All our great-aunts and grandmothers used to have albums of dried flowers."

Mrs. Slade nodded. "But she really sent her because they were in love with the same man—"

"Well, that was the family tradition. They said Aunt Harriet confessed it years afterward. At any rate, the poor little sister caught the fever and died. Mother used to frighten us with the story when we were children."

"And you frightened *me* with it, that winter when you and I were here as girls. The winter I was engaged to Delphin."

Mrs. Ansley gave a faint laugh. "Oh, did I? Really frightened you? I don't believe you're easily frightened."

"Not often; but I was then. I was easily frightened because I was too happy. I wonder if you know what that means?"

"I—yes . . ." Mrs. Ansley faltered.

"Well, I suppose that was why the story of your wicked aunt made such an impression on me. And I thought: 'There's no more Roman fever, but the Forum is deathly cold after sunset—especially after a hot day. And the Colosseum's even colder and damper.' "

"The Colosseum?"

"Yes. It wasn't easy to get in, after the gates were locked for the night. Far from easy. Still, in those days it could be managed; it *was* managed, often. Lovers met there who couldn't meet elsewhere. You knew that?"

"I—I daresay. I don't remember."

"You don't remember? You don't remember going to visit some ruins or other one evening, just after dark, and catching a bad chill? You were supposed to have gone to see the moonrise. People always said that expedition was what caused your illness."

There was a moment's silence; then Mrs. Ansley rejoined: "Did they? It was all so long ago."

"Yes. And you got well again—so it didn't matter. But I suppose it struck your friends—the reason given for your illness. I mean—because everybody knew you were so prudent on account of your throat, and your mother took such care of you. . . . You *had* been out late sightseeing, hadn't you, that night?"

"Perhaps I had. The most prudent girls aren't always prudent. What made you think of it now?"

Mrs. Slade seemed to have no answer ready. But after a moment she broke out: "Because I simply can't bear it any longer!"

Mrs. Ansley lifted her head quickly. Her eyes were wide and very pale. "Can't bear what?"

"Why—your not knowing that I've always known why you went."

"Why I went?"

"Yes. You think I'm bluffing, don't you? Well, you went to meet the man I was engaged to—and I can repeat every word of the letter that took you there."

While Mrs. Slade spoke Mrs. Ansley had risen unsteadily to her feet. Her bag, her knitting and gloves, slid in a panic-stricken heap to the ground. She looked at Mrs. Slade as though she were looking at a ghost.

"No, no—don't," she faltered out.

"Why not? Listen, if you don't believe me. 'My one darling, things can't go on like this. I must see you alone. Come to the Colosseum immediately after dark tomorrow. There will be somebody to let you in. No one whom you need fear will suspect'—but perhaps you've forgotten what the letter said?"

Mrs. Ansley met the challenge with an unexpected composure. Steadying herself against the chair she looked at her friend, and replied, "No; I know it by heart too."

"And the signature? 'Only *your* D.S.' Was that it? I'm right, am I? That was the letter that took you out that evening after dark?"

Mrs. Ansley was still looking at her. It seemed to Mrs. Slade that a slow struggle was going on behind the voluntarily controlled mask of her small quiet face. "I shouldn't have thought she had herself so well in hand," Mrs. Slade reflected, almost resentfully. But at this moment Mrs. Ansley spoke. "I don't know how you knew. I burned that letter at once."

"Yes; you would, naturally—you're so prudent!" The sneer was open now. "And if you burned the letter you're wondering how on earth I know what was in it. That's it, isn't it?"

Mrs. Slade waited, but Mrs. Ansley did not speak.

"Well, my dear, I know what was in that letter because I wrote it!"

"You wrote it?"

"Yes."

The two women stood for a minute staring at each other in the last golden light. Then Mrs. Ansley dropped back into her chair. "Oh," she murmured, and covered her face with her hands.

Mrs. Slade waited nervously for another word or movement. None came, and at length she broke out: "I horrify you."

Mrs. Ansley's hands dropped to her knees. The face they uncovered was streaked with tears. "I wasn't thinking of you. I was thinking—it was the only letter I ever had from him!"

"And I wrote it. Yes; I wrote it! But I was the girl he was engaged to. Did you happen to remember that?"

Mrs. Ansley's head drooped again. "I'm not trying to excuse myself.... I remembered. . . ."

"And still you went?"

"Still I went."

Mrs. Slade stood looking down on the small bowed figure at her side. The flame of her wrath had already sunk, and she wondered why she had ever thought there would be any satisfaction in inflicting so purposeless a wound on her friend. But she had to justify herself.

"You do understand? I'd found out—and I hated you, hated you. I knew you were in love with Delphin—and I was afraid; afraid of you, of your quiet ways, your sweetness . . . your . . . well, I wanted you out of the way, that's all. Just for a few weeks; just till I was sure of him. So in a blind fury I wrote that letter. . . . I don't know why I'm telling you now."

"I suppose," said Mrs. Ansley slowly, "it's because you've always gone on hating me."

"Perhaps. Or because I wanted to get the whole thing off my mind." She paused. "I'm glad you destroyed the letter. Of course I never thought you'd die."

Mrs. Ansley relapsed into silence, and Mrs. Slade, leaning above her, was conscious of a strange sense of isolation, of being cut off from the warm current of human communion. "You think me a monster!"

"I don't know. . . . It was the only letter I had, and you say he didn't write it?"

"Ah, how you care for him still!"

"I cared for that memory," said Mrs. Ansley.

Mrs. Slade continued to look down on her. She seemed physically reduced by the blow—as if, when she got up, the wind might scatter her like a puff of dust. Mrs. Slade's jealousy suddenly leaped up again at the sight. All these years the woman had been living on that letter. How she must have loved him, to treasure the mere memory of its ashes! The letter of the man her friend was engaged to. Wasn't it she who was the monster?

"You tried your best to get him away from me, didn't you? But you failed; and I kept him. That's all."

"Yes. That's all."

"I wish now I hadn't told you. I'd no idea you'd feel about it as you do; I thought you'd be amused. It all happened so long ago, as you say; and you must do me the justice to remember that I had no reason to think you'd ever taken it seriously. How could I, when you were married to Horace Ansley two months afterward? As soon as you could get out of bed your mother rushed you off to Florence and married you. People were rather surprised—they wondered at its being done so quickly; but I thought I knew. I had an idea you did it out of *pique*—to be able to say you'd got ahead of Delphin and me. Girls have such silly reasons for doing the most serious things. And your marrying so soon convinced me that you'd never really cared."

"Yes. I suppose it would," Mrs. Ansley assented.

The clear heaven overhead was emptied of all its gold. Dusk spread over it, abruptly darkening the Seven Hills. Here and there lights began to twinkle through the foliage at their feet. Steps were coming and going on the deserted terrace—waiters looking out of the doorway at the head of the stairs, then reappearing with trays and napkins and flasks of wine. Tables were moved, chairs straightened. A feeble string of electric lights flickered out. Some vases of faded flowers were carried away, and brought back replenished. A stout lady in a dustcoat suddenly appeared, asking in broken Italian if anyone had seen the elastic band which held together her tattered Baedeker. She poked with her stick under the table at which she had lunched, the waiters assisting.

The corner where Mrs. Slade and Mrs. Ansley sat was still shadowy and deserted. For a long time neither of them spoke. At length Mrs. Slade began again: "I suppose I did it as a sort of joke—"

"A joke?"

"Well, girls are ferocious sometimes, you know. Girls in love especially. And I remember laughing to myself all that evening at the idea that you were waiting around there in the dark, dodging out of sight, listening for every sound, trying to get in— Of course I was upset when I heard you were so ill afterward."

Mrs. Ansley had not moved for a long time. But now she turned slowly toward her companion. "But I didn't wait. He'd arranged everything. He was there. We were let in at once," she said.

Mrs. Slade sprang up from her leaning position. "Delphin there? They let you in? Ah, now you're lying!" she burst out with violence.

Mrs. Ansley's voice grew clearer, and full of surprise. "But of course he was there. Naturally he came—"

"Came? How did he know he'd find you there? You must be raving!"

Mrs. Ansley hesitated, as though reflecting. "But I answered the letter. I told him I'd be there. So he came."

Mrs. Slade flung her hands up to her face. "Oh, God—you answered! I never thought of your answering. . . ."

"It's odd you never thought of it, if you wrote the letter."

"Yes. I was blind with rage."

Mrs. Ansley rose, and drew her fur scarf about her. "It is cold here. We'd better go. . . . I'm sorry for you," she said, as she clasped the fur about her throat.

The unexpected words sent a pang through Mrs. Slade. "Yes; we'd better go." She gathered up her bag and cloak. "I don't know why you should be sorry for me," she muttered.

Mrs. Ansley stood looking away from her toward the dusky secret mass of the Colosseum. "Well—because I didn't have to wait that night."

Mrs. Slade gave an unquiet laugh. "Yes; I was beaten there. But I oughtn't to begrudge it to you, I suppose. At the end of all these years. After all, I had everything; I had him for twenty-five years. And you had nothing but that one letter that he didn't write."

Mrs. Ansley was again silent. At length she turned toward the door of the terrace. She took a step, and turned back, facing her companion.

"I had Barbara," she said, and began to move ahead of Mrs. Slade toward the stairway.

THE OUTCASTS OF
POKER FLAT

BRET HARTE

As Mr. John Oakhurst, gambler, stepped into the main street of Poker Flat on the morning of the twenty-third of November, 1850, he was conscious of a change in its moral atmosphere since the preceding night. Two or three men, conversing earnestly together, ceased as he approached, and exchanged significant glances. There was a Sabbath lull in the air, which, in a settlement unused to Sabbath influences, looked ominous.

Mr. Oakhurst's calm, handsome face betrayed small concern in these indications. Whether he was conscious of any predisposing cause was another question. "I reckon they're after somebody," he reflected; "likely it's me." He returned to his pocket the handkerchief with which he had been whipping away the red dust of Poker Flat from his neat boots, and quietly discharged his mind of any further conjecture.

In point of fact, Poker Flat was "after somebody." It had lately suffered the loss of several thousand dollars, two valuable horses, and a prominent citizen. It was experiencing a spasm of virtuous reaction, quite as lawless and ungovernable as any of the acts that had provoked it. A secret committee had determined to rid the town of all improper persons. This was done permanently in regard to two men who were then hanging from the boughs of a sycamore in the gulch, and temporarily in the banishment of certain other objectionable characters. I regret to say that some of these were ladies. It is but due to the sex, however, to state that their impropriety was professional, and it was only in such easily established standards of evil that Poker Flat ventured to sit in judgment.

Mr. Oakhurst was right in supposing that he was included in this category. A few of the committee had urged hanging him as a possible example and a sure method of reimbursing themselves from his pockets of the sums he had won from them. "It's agin justice," said Jim Wheeler, "to let this yer young man from Roaring Camp—an entire stranger—carry away our money." But a crude sentiment of equity residing in the breasts of those who had been fortunate enough to win from Mr. Oakhurst overruled this narrower local prejudice.

Mr. Oakhurst received his sentence with philosophic calmness, none the less coolly that he was aware of the hesitation of his judges. He was too much of a gambler not to accept fate. With him life was at best an uncertain game, and he recognized the usual percentage in favor of the dealer.

A body of armed men accompanied the deported wickedness of Poker Flat to the outskirts of the settlement. Besides Mr. Oakhurst, who was known to be a coolly desperate man, and for whose intimidation the armed escort was intended, the expatriated party consisted of a young woman familiarly known as "the Duchess"; another who had won the title of "Mother Shipton"; and "Uncle Billy," a suspected sluice-robber and confirmed drunkard. The cavalcade provoked no comments from the spectators, nor was any word uttered by the escort. Only when the gulch which marked the uttermost limit of Poker Flat was reached, the leader spoke briefly and to the point. The exiles were forbidden to return at the peril of their lives.

As the escort disappeared, their pent-up feelings found vent in a few hysterical tears from the Duchess, some bad language from Mother Shipton, and a Parthian volley of expletives from Uncle Billy. The philosophic Oakhurst alone remained silent. He listened calmly to Mother Shipton's desire to cut somebody's heart out, to the repeated statements of the Duchess that she would die in the road, and to the alarming oaths that seemed to be bumped out of Uncle Billy as he rode forward. With the easy good humor characteristic of his class, he insisted upon exchanging his own riding horse, Five-Spot, for the sorry mule which the Duchess rode. But even this act did not draw the party into any closer sympathy. The young woman readjusted her somewhat draggled plumes with a feeble, faded coquetry; Mother Shipton eyed the possessor of Five-Spot with malevolence, and Uncle Billy included the whole party in one sweeping anathema.

The road to Sandy Bar—a camp that, not having as yet experienced the regenerating influences of Poker Flat, consequently seemed to offer some invitation to the emigrants—lay over a steep mountain range. It was distant a day's severe travel. In that advanced season the party soon passed out of the moist, temperate regions of the foothills into the dry, cold, bracing air of the Sierras. The trail was narrow and difficult. At noon the Duchess, rolling out of her saddle upon the ground, declared her intention of going no farther, and the party halted.

The spot was singularly wild and impressive. A wooded amphitheater, surrounded on three sides by precipitous cliffs of naked granite, sloped gently toward the crest of another precipice that overlooked the valley. It was, undoubtedly, the most suitable spot for a camp, had camping been advisable. But Mr. Oakhurst knew that scarcely half the journey to Sandy Bar was accomplished, and the party were not equipped or provisioned for delay. This fact he pointed out to his companions curtly, with a philosophic commentary on the folly of "throwing up their hand before the game was played out." But they were furnished with liquor, which in this emergency stood them in place of food, fuel, rest, and prescience. In spite of his remonstrances, it was not long before they were more or less under its influence. Uncle Billy passed rapidly from a bellicose state into one of stupor, the Duchess became maudlin, and Mother Shipton snored. Mr. Oakhurst alone remained erect, leaning against a rock, calmly surveying them.

Mr. Oakhurst did not drink. It interfered with a profession which required coolness, impassiveness, and presence of mind, and, in his own language, he "couldn't afford it." As he gazed at his recumbent fellow exiles, the loneliness begotten of his pariah trade, his habits of life, his very vices, for the first time seriously oppressed him. He bestirred himself in dusting his black clothes, washing his hands and face, and other acts characteristic of his studiously neat habits, and for a moment forgot his annoyance. The thought of deserting his weaker and more pitiable companions never perhaps occurred to him. Yet he could not help feeling the want of that excitement which, singularly enough, was most conducive to that calm equanimity for which he was notorious. He looked at the gloomy walls that rose a thousand feet sheer above the circling pines around him, at the sky ominously clouded, at the valley below, already deepening into shadow; and doing so, suddenly he heard his own name called.

A HORSEMAN slowly ascended the trail. In the fresh, open face of the newcomer Mr. Oakhurst recognized Tom Simson, otherwise known as "the Innocent," of Sandy Bar. He had met him some months before over a "little game," and had, with perfect equanimity, won the entire fortune—amounting to some forty dollars—of that guileless youth. After the game was finished, Mr. Oakhurst drew the youthful speculator behind the door and thus addressed him: "Tommy, you're a good little man, but you can't gamble worth a cent. Don't try it ever again." He then handed him his money back, pushed him gently from the room, and so made a devoted slave of Tom Simson.

THERE WAS A remembrance of this in his boyish and enthusiastic greeting of Mr. Oakhurst. He had started, he said, to go to Poker Flat to seek his fortune. "Alone?" No, not exactly alone; in fact (a giggle), he had run away with Piney Woods. Didn't Mr. Oakhurst remember Piney? She that used to wait on the table at the Temperance House? They had been engaged a long time, but old Jake Woods had objected, and so they had run away, and were going to Poker Flat to be married, and here they were. And they were tired out, and how lucky it was they had found a place to camp, and company. All this the Innocent delivered rapidly, while Piney, a stout, comely damsel of fifteen, emerged from behind the pine tree, where she had been blushing unseen, and rode to the side of her lover.

Mr. Oakhurst seldom troubled himself with sentiment, still less with propriety; but he had a vague idea that the situation was not fortunate. He retained, however, his presence of mind sufficiently to kick Uncle Billy, who was about to say something, and Uncle Billy was sober enough to recognize in Mr. Oakhurst's kick a superior power that would not bear trifling. He then endeavored to dissuade Tom Simson from delaying further, but in vain. He even pointed out the fact that there was no provision, nor means of making a camp. But, unluckily, the Innocent met this objection by assuring the party that he was provided with an extra mule loaded with provisions, and by the discovery of a rude attempt at a log house near the trail. "Piney can stay with Mrs. Oakhurst," said the Innocent, pointing to the Duchess, "and I can shift for myself."

Nothing but Mr. Oakhurst's admonishing foot saved Uncle Billy from bursting into a roar of laughter. As it was, he felt compelled to retire up the canyon until he could recover his gravity. There he confided the joke to the tall pine trees, with many slaps of his leg, contortions of his face, and the usual profanity. But when he returned to the party, he found them seated by a fire—for the air had grown strangely chill and the sky overcast—in apparently amicable conversation. Piney was actually talking in an impulsive girlish fashion to the Duchess, who was listening with an interest and animation she had not shown for many days. The Innocent was holding forth, apparently with equal effect, to Mr. Oakhurst and Mother Shipton, who was actually relaxing into amiability.

"Is this yer a d——d picnic?" said Uncle Billy, with inward scorn, as he surveyed the sylvan group, the glancing firelight, and the tethered animals in the foreground. Suddenly an idea mingled with the alcoholic fumes that disturbed his brain. It was apparently of a jocular nature, for he felt impelled to slap his leg again and cram his fist into his mouth.

As the shadows crept slowly up the mountain, a slight breeze rocked the tops of the pine trees and moaned through their long and gloomy aisles. The ruined cabin, patched and covered with pine boughs, was set apart for the ladies. As the lovers parted, they unaffectedly exchanged a kiss, so honest and sincere that it might have been heard above the swaying pines. The frail Duchess and the malevolent Mother Shipton were probably too stunned to remark upon this last evidence of simplicity, and so turned without a word to the hut. The fire was replenished, the men lay down before the door, and in a few minutes were asleep.

Mr. Oakhurst was a light sleeper. Toward morning he awoke benumbed and cold. As he stirred the dying fire, the wind, which was now blowing strongly, brought to his cheek that which caused the blood to leave it—snow!

He started to his feet with the intention of awakening the sleepers, for there was no time to lose. But turning to where Uncle Billy had been lying, he found him gone. A suspicion leaped to his brain, and a curse to his lips. He ran to the spot where the mules had been tethered—they were no longer there. The tracks were already rapidly disappearing in the snow.

The momentary excitement brought Mr. Oakhurst back to the fire with his usual calm. He did not waken the sleepers. The Innocent slumbered peacefully, with a smile on his good-humored, freckled face; the virgin Piney slept beside her frailer sisters as sweetly as though attended by celestial guardians; and Mr. Oakhurst, drawing his blanket over his shoulders, stroked his mustaches and waited for the dawn. It came slowly in a whirling mist of snowflakes that dazzled and confused the eye. What could be seen of the landscape appeared magically changed. He looked over the valley, and summed up the present and future in two words, "Snowed in!"

A careful inventory of the provisions, which, fortunately for the party, had been stored within the hut, and so escaped the felonious fingers of Uncle Billy, disclosed the fact that with care and prudence they might last ten days longer. "That is," said Mr. Oakhurst *sotto voce* to the Innocent, "if you're willing to board us. If you ain't—and perhaps you'd better not—you can wait till Uncle Billy gets back with provisions." For some occult reason, Mr. Oakhurst could not bring himself to disclose Uncle Billy's rascality, and so offered the hypothesis that he had wandered from the camp and had accidentally stampeded the animals. He dropped a warning to the Duchess and Mother Shipton, who of course knew the facts of their associate's defection. "They'll find out the truth about us *all* when they find out anything," he added significantly, "and there's no good frightening them now."

Tom Simson not only put all his worldly store at the disposal of Mr. Oakhurst, but seemed to enjoy the prospect of their enforced seclusion. "We'll have a good camp for a week, and then the snow'll melt, and we'll all go back together." The cheerful gaiety of the young man and Mr. Oakhurst's calm infected the others. The Innocent, with the aid of pine boughs, extemporized a thatch for the roofless cabin, and the Duchess directed Piney in the rearrangement of the interior with a taste and tact that opened the blue eyes of that provincial maiden to their fullest extent. "I reckon now you're used to fine things at Poker Flat," said Piney. The Duchess turned away sharply to conceal something that reddened her cheeks through their professional tint, and Mother Shipton requested Piney not to "chatter." But when Mr. Oakhurst returned from a weary search for the trail, he heard the sound of happy laughter echoed from the rocks. He stopped in some alarm, and his thoughts first naturally reverted to the whiskey, which he had prudently cached. "And yet it don't somehow sound like whiskey," said the gambler. It was not until he caught sight of the blazing fire through the still blinding storm, and the group around it, that he settled to the conviction that it was "square fun."

Whether Mr. Oakhurst had cached his cards with the whiskey as something debarred the free access of the community, I cannot say. It was certain that, in Mother Shipton's words, he "didn't say 'cards' once" during that evening. Haply the time was beguiled by an accordion, produced somewhat ostentatiously by Tom Simson from his pack. Notwithstanding some difficulties attending the manipulation of this instrument, Piney Woods managed to pluck several reluctant melodies from its keys, to an accompaniment by the Innocent on a pair of bone castanets. But the crowning festivity of the evening was reached in a rude camp-meeting hymn, which the lovers, joining hands, sang with great earnestness and vociferation. I fear that a certain defiant tone and covenanter's swing to its chorus, rather than any devotional quality, caused it speedily to infect the others, who at last joined in the refrain:

> *"I'm proud to live in the service of the Lord,*
> *And I'm bound to die in His army."*

The pines rocked, the storm eddied and whirled above the miserable group, and the flames of their altar leaped heavenward, as if in token of the vow.

At midnight the storm abated, the rolling clouds parted, and the stars glittered keenly above the sleeping camp. Mr. Oakhurst, whose professional habits had enabled him to live on the smallest possible amount of sleep, in dividing the watch with Tom Simson somehow managed to take upon himself the greater part of that duty. He excused himself to the Innocent by saying that he had "often been a week without sleep." "Doing what?" asked Tom. "Poker!" replied Oakhurst sententiously. "When a man gets a streak of luck, he don't get tired. The luck gives in first. Luck," continued the gambler reflectively, "is a mighty queer thing. All you know about it for certain is that it's bound to change. And it's finding out when it's going to change that makes you. We've had a streak of bad luck since we left Poker Flat—you come along, and slap you get into it, too. If you can hold your cards right along you're all right. For," added the gambler, with cheerful irrelevance—

> *"I'm proud to live in the service of the Lord,*
> *And I'm bound to die in His army."*

The third day came, and the sun, looking through the white-curtained valley, saw the outcasts divide their slowly decreasing store of provisions for the morning meal. It was one of the peculiarities of that mountain climate that its rays diffused a kindly warmth over the wintry landscape, as if in regretful commiseration of the past. But it revealed drift on drift of snow piled high around the hut—a hopeless, uncharted, trackless sea of white lying below the rocky shores to which the castaways still clung. Through the marvelously clear air the smoke of the pastoral village of Poker Flat rose miles away. Mother Shipton saw it, and from a remote pinnacle of her rocky fastness hurled in that direction a final malediction. It was her last vituperative attempt, and perhaps for that reason was invested with a certain degree of sublimity. It did her good, she privately informed the Duchess. "Just you go out there and cuss, and see." She then set herself to the task of amusing "the child," as she and the Duchess were pleased to call Piney. Piney was no chicken, but it was a soothing and original theory of the pair thus to account for the fact that she didn't swear and wasn't improper.

When night crept up again through the gorges, the reedy notes of the accordion rose and fell in fitful spasms and long-drawn gasps by the flickering campfire. But music failed to fill entirely the aching void left by insufficient food, and a new diversion was proposed by Piney—storytelling. Neither Mr. Oakhurst nor his female companions caring to relate their personal experiences, this plan would have failed, too, but for the Innocent. Some months before, he had chanced upon a stray copy of Mr. Pope's ingenious translation of the *Iliad*. He now proposed to narrate the principal incidents of that poem—having thoroughly mastered the argument and fairly forgotten the words—in the current vernacular of Sandy Bar. And so for the rest of that night the Homeric demigods again walked the earth. Trojan bully and wily Greek wrestled in the winds, and the great pines in the canyon seemed to bow to the wrath of the son of Peleus. Mr. Oakhurst listened with quiet satisfaction. Most especially was he interested in the fate of "Ash-heels," as the Innocent persisted in denominating the "swift-footed Achilles."

So, with small food and much of Homer and the accordion, a week passed over the heads of the outcasts. The sun again forsook them, and again from leaden skies the snowflakes were sifted over the land. Day by day closer around them drew the snowy circle, until at last they looked from their prison over drifted walls of dazzling white that towered twenty feet above their heads. It became more and more difficult to replenish their fires, even from the fallen trees beside them, now half hidden in the drifts. And yet no one complained. The lovers turned from the dreary prospect and looked into each other's eyes, and were happy. Mr. Oakhurst settled himself coolly to the losing game before him. The Duchess, more cheerful than she had been, assumed the care of Piney.

Only Mother Shipton—once the strongest of the party—seemed to sicken and fade. At midnight on the tenth day she called Oakhurst to her side. "I'm going," she said, in a voice of querulous weakness, "but don't say anything about it. Don't waken the kids. Take the bundle from under my head, and open it." Mr. Oakhurst did so. It contained Mother Shipton's rations for the last week, untouched. "Give 'em to the child," she said, pointing to the sleeping Piney. "You've starved yourself," said the gambler. "That's what they call it," said the woman querulously, as she lay down again, and, turning her face to the wall, passed quietly away.

The accordion and the bones were put aside that day, and Homer was forgotten. When the body of Mother Shipton had been committed to the snow, Mr. Oakhurst took the Innocent aside and showed him a pair of snowshoes, which he had fashioned from the old packsaddle. "There's one chance in a hundred to save her yet," he said, pointing to Piney; "but it's there," he added, pointing toward Poker Flat. "If you can reach there in two days she's safe." "And you?" asked Tom Simson. "I'll stay here," was the curt reply.

The lovers parted with a long embrace. "You are not going, too?" said the Duchess, as she saw Mr. Oakhurst apparently waiting to accompany him. "As far as the canyon," he replied. He turned suddenly and kissed the Duchess, leaving her pallid face aflame, and her trembling limbs rigid with amazement.

Night came, but not Mr. Oakhurst. It brought the storm again and the whirling snow. Then the Duchess, feeding the fire, found that someone had quietly piled beside the hut enough fuel to last a few days longer. The tears rose to her eyes, but she hid them from Piney.

The women slept but little. In the morning, looking into each other's faces, they read their fate. Neither spoke, but Piney, accepting the position of the stronger, drew near and placed her arm around the Duchess's waist. They kept this attitude for the rest of the day. That night the storm reached its greatest fury, and, rending asunder the protecting vines, invaded the very hut.

Toward morning they found themselves unable to feed the fire, which gradually died away. As the embers slowly blackened, the Duchess crept closer to Piney, and broke the silence of many hours: "Piney, can you pray?" "No, dear," said Piney simply. The Duchess, without knowing exactly why, felt relieved, and, putting her head upon Piney's shoulder, spoke no more. And so reclining, the younger and purer pillowing the head of her soiled sister upon her virgin breast, they fell asleep.

The wind lulled as if it feared to waken them. Feathery drifts of snow, shaken from the long pine boughs, flew like white-winged birds and settled about them as they slept. The moon through the rifted clouds looked down upon what had been the camp. But all human stain, all trace of earthly travail, was hidden beneath the spotless mantle mercifully flung from above.

They slept all that day and the next, nor did they waken when voices and footsteps broke the silence of the camp. And when pitying fingers brushed the snow from their wan faces, you could scarcely have told from the equal peace that dwelt upon them which was she that had sinned. Even the law of Poker Flat recognized this, and turned away, leaving them still locked in each other's arms.

But at the head of the gulch, on one of the largest pine trees, they found the deuce of clubs pinned to the bark with a bowie knife. It bore the following, written in pencil in a firm hand:

BENEATH THIS TREE

LIES THE BODY

OF

JOHN OAKHURST,

WHO STRUCK A STREAK OF BAD LUCK

ON THE 23D OF NOVEMBER, 1850,

AND

HANDED IN HIS CHECKS

ON THE 7TH OF DECEMBER, 1850.

And pulseless and cold, with a derringer by his side and a bullet in his heart, though still calm as in life, beneath the snow lay he who was at once the strongest and yet the weakest of the outcasts of Poker Flat.

THE LAST
GAS STATION

SHIRLEY ANN GRAU

WE HAVE lived here with our father for years and years. Joe, who's the
oldest—then Mark, then me—says he can remember our other place
real well: the house we used to live in, and the kitchen with yellow
roses on the wallpaper. He says there were tall trees, real tall trees where
you could lie on your back and watch the sun spin in the leaves.
(There's no trees that big around here.) He says that there was a high
bluff where you could look down on a river that was twenty feet across.
He caught crawfish in the pools there sometimes.

Joe tells that our father had a whole pack of spotted hounds, and
when they went hunting you could hear them for hours, our father
shouting and the dogs fighting and howling. Joe says on nights when
the moon was full the country was plain crowded with animals
running.

Joe says all of that—only thing he won't talk about is our mother.
Now, I know we got to have had one, but Joe won't answer, and Mark,
being younger, don't remember more than some old black lady who
took care of us for a while.

Of course I don't even remember that, being the youngest. For all I
know, I never been anywhere but here. Our gas station. Our house
next door, sitting high on its foundations against the damp and the
snakes. The highway, four lanes straight down from the north and
straight off to the south, not a curve nor a bend in it. And all around
everywhere, far as you can see, palmettos. Low and yellow green, and
good for nothing except making fans. There's a fair number of snakes
out there and some mice and rabbits but not much else. You can see

it—the scrub's no higher than a man's shoulder—and that's all there is.

Once Mark told me that if I climbed to the very top of the roof and looked to the west, I'd see a big lake shining. But he was just fooling. All I saw was heat haze, and I don't have to climb a roof for that.

In one way it's a good thing we don't have our father's hunting pack anymore. The scrub's full of sinkholes, and dogs are pretty like to fall in. I suppose that's what happened to Lucky—he was a dog we had for a while. He came off a Buick sedan—the people, they slowed down and threw him out a window. He bounced two or three times and landed on his back, but he wasn't any more than scared. That's why we called him Lucky. He was small and long-haired and he suffered from ticks during the spring and ear infections the rest of the year. Never was a time when both his ears stood up straight—always something draining out one or the other. But he sure did like running in the palmettos. And one day he never came back.

We went looking, Joe and Mark and me, but there was too many holes and too much ground. We never even found a sign of him.

We had a cat too, you know that? She got killed on the highway by a big semi, name of Beatons Long Distance Moving.

When Joe scraped her up with a shovel and tossed her way back in the scrub, I started crying. I really did love that cat. I kept on crying until Joe and our father beat the tears out of me. They said it wasn't decent.

After that I felt different about the highway. Before, I used to like it, especially the sounds: the tires whistling and singing on the wet, and hissing on the dry. The soft growling sound—kind of like a sigh— when some trucker tested his air brakes. The way horns echo way off in the distance. The thin little screech of car brakes, too, almost like a laugh. And something else—a steady even whisper. Day and night, no different. It ran along the whole length of highway, like electric wires singing. Or maybe kind of like breathing.

And I got to admit that sometimes the highway was a pretty thing too. When the moon was on it. When quick summer rains fell and clouds of steam rose up and cleared away leaving just a heat mirage in the distance. The wind was nice too. On a hot August day, those passing cars and trucks really stirred up a nice little breeze for you.

But I didn't like the highway anymore. Not at all. There just wasn't no getting away from it. If I didn't hear it or see it, if I closed my eyes and stuck my fingers in my ears, I still could smell it. The different exhausts, gas and diesel. The smell of oil that's burning clean and oil that's not. The paint smell of engines overheating with the load of their air conditioners.

Like Joe would say, the highway brought everything to us, and took it away too. Joe's always been the religious one around here, the one who put a Bible on the top shelf in the kitchen. He used to read a little from it now and then. It was a comfort to him, I guess, specially after Bruce left.

You see, when we first came here, there were four boys, not three. The oldest was Bruce. And this was how he come to leave.

Every December there was a big increase in southbound traffic. Out of that crowd there'd always be some who'd made the trip before, and who always made a point of coming back to the same places.

Take this one car now; it had stopped every winter for four or five years. It was a man and his wife and their girl. She got prettier each year, her blond hair hanging long and loose down her back. The last time the man wasn't with them. They stayed quite a while, parked off to one side of the station, talking to Bruce. Afterward, Bruce was very excited: he smashed his thumb with a tire iron, something he don't ever do.

Anyhow, right after they left, he marked a date on the wall calendar with a big red star, and on that day he packed his clothes in a paper bag and told us he was going north with them. Then he walked across the highway to wait.

I remember that: Bruce walking across the road, putting his feet down heavily, as if they hurt him, crossing the wide median, kicking at the pine trees the state planted there. (Funny thing, those trees, been there five or six years and don't hardly reach to your knee.) He waited a long time, swatting at the flies and slapping at the mosquitoes—they're both pretty bad sometimes.

Joe and Mark and me, we sat on the curb by the gas pumps and watched and waited with him. We only moved when a car came in. Then the three of us rushed to fill the tank, clean the windshield, and

check the tires. (I always checked the tires because I was the smallest.)
We worked so fast we even got a couple of tips.

The sun got hotter and hotter. Bruce kept taking off his hat to fan
himself with it, and now and then he'd spit to clear the dust out his
mouth.

Along toward the middle of the afternoon, Joe said, "Maybe he
won't get to go after all." And he went in the house to tell our father.
Minute or two later he was back. "He said it don't matter none about
Bruce."

Then a Mercedes pulled in, a 220 with special order extra green
glass—made the people with their big sunglasses look just like frogs.

They wanted diesel fuel, which we never had.

"We may not make it," the man said accusingly to us. Like we had
let his tank run low. "We just may not."

"She won't burn gas, mister," Joe said firmly. He figures he knows a
lot about cars because he's filled so many tanks.

"How far to the next station?"

"I don't know," Joe said. "I never been down that way."

They pulled out very slowly to avoid wasting any fuel. With a shrug
Joe moved the sign that said LAST GAS a little closer to the road. It was
one of those folding tripod things that we had to take in at night so the
big trucks wouldn't backwind it over. It could make an awful racket in
the middle of the night.

All of a sudden the three of us remembered and looked across the
highway. Bruce was gone. We never even saw the car that stopped
for him.

YOU'D THINK we'd be lonely living in a place like this. But we weren't.
There was the cars stopping for gas. And once a week the company
truck came to fill the underground tanks. That man always stayed to
pass the time of day with us. Sometimes he'd bring the newspapers, and
he'd always bring our groceries and take our order for the next week.
We didn't ever go to town. Our father's car was parked behind the
house, next to the cistern, a '59 Pontiac. It was up on blocks, nice and
neat, and the hens liked to nest under it. Used to be, too, that the
school bus picked us up, and made a big U-turn through the highway

median. But we stopped going to school, and the big tracks filled in and grass grew over them.

We had plenty to do what with running the station, and keeping house, and doing the cooking, and feeding the chickens, and hunting after their eggs, and repairing the roof, and keeping the screens patched. Our father, he didn't do anything. He was so tired that he could only sit all day long on the front porch. He used to chew tobacco, but finally he even stopped fooling with the plug.

One day Joe and Mark told me he was dead. "You come see for yourself."

I'd seen dead things before but never a man. Even so, just the way he sat there, head a little on one side—and the big blue-and-green flies banging away at the porch screen to get at him—I'd have known by myself.

That night Joe and Mark (they wouldn't let me go with them) carried our father way far out into the scrub and dropped him into one of the sinkholes there. They took a couple of tire irons and a piece or two of rusted junk from the backyard—to make sure he stayed down.

Nothing changed after his death. Joe went on signing his name on the receipts from the company. He'd been doing it so long that nobody, not the driver of the gas truck nor the company office, seemed to notice the difference.

So, like I said, things went on, quiet except for that one busy season in the winter when all the campers and the trailers and the baggage-packed cars poured south over the road.

"Look at that," Joe said one day when four Pace Arrows and six Winnebagos passed, bumper to bumper. All the Winnebagos had little Christmas trees in the back windows. "Don't it look like something's chasing them?"

And that was exactly the way it looked: drivers scowling, staring hard ahead, concentrating on the road, just like something awful was right behind them.

FEW MONTHS after that, Joe and Mark got in a fight. I didn't see the start; when I walked in the kitchen Mark had ahold of a broken bottle and Joe had his knife out, the big switchblade he kept from our father. I could tell that Mark was beginning to have second thoughts; he'd have turned and run only he was scared of getting that knife in his back. He just kept moving in the general direction of the door. Me, I was too scared to say anything.

Mark managed to back around the table, past the stove, and down the steps leading to the yard, pushing open the screen as he went. He had his left hand on the rail and he was trying to get down the three steps without taking his eyes off Joe. Well, we all knew that the railing was loose, been loose for years I guess, but neither Joe nor I knew that all you had to do was pick it up.

And that was very lucky for Mark. Because once he got to the steps, Joe closed on him, holding the knife low and flat, just the right position.

Well, Mark faked a stumble and Joe moved in. Joe was so busy watching the broken bottle he wasn't paying no attention to Mark's left hand. The long piece of two-by-two rail caught him square alongside the head. And he slid face down the steps into the yard.

Mark watched Joe for a long time. But whatever he was waiting for, it didn't come. Slowly, in an easy underhand, Mark tossed the broken bottle at Joe's back, the way you'd throw something on a pile of garbage. The railing he dropped right where he stood.

He came back inside, walked straight by me into the bedroom. He pushed the mattress off his bed so that the whole set of springs showed. He kept his special secret things hidden in a black plastic zipper case stuffed down in one of the center coils. He took that case, and his good jacket from where it hung on a nail by his bed, and his special clean cap from the shelf.

"Cain killed Abel," he said to me as he left. And, "The end of the world is coming."

You see that he was really the religious one in the family.

He got a hitch almost immediately, a big truck with a load of cattle, going south. I never saw him again.

LIKE I SAID, Mark used his left hand. I guess that's why the side of Joe's head wasn't caved in. But he looked pretty terrible lying there, not moving, bleeding into the gravel, half his ear knocked off. I pulled him up the steps and inside; took me a long time and I couldn't hardly do it: he was a big man. I stopped the bleeding and kept ice on his head, but it was days before he came around. And then he couldn't do nothing but talk foolishness and vomit all over the kitchen floor.

He got well after a while and was just like always. Except for the headaches and the limp in his left leg. That never did feel right, he said.

Now I was really busy. I had to do the cars all by myself and of course I had to take care of him. That's why lots of things that should have been done, didn't get done. Like the light bulb over the round orange sign GAS. I wasn't tall enough to reach it, not even with our ladder; Joe didn't feel like fooling with it; and the sign stayed dark. I took to leaving the porch light on, so people could see where we were in all that empty stretch of road. I even found some reflectors and put them along the highway too.

We got along, one season after the other. Just Joe and me.

THEN SOMETHING changed, really changed. All of a sudden there was too much traffic on the highway. Now, it gets pretty busy during the holiday season, but this was fifty times more. Thousands and thousands of cars, and this was the middle of the summer. The ground was shaking with their weight, all the windows were rattling in the back draft, like a storm blowing up.

We'd have four, five cars in the gas station at once. They weren't the usual crowd, wanting to get out and stretch, complaining because we didn't have a Coke machine or any rest rooms. They wanted gas and they wanted oil, forget the windshield, they wanted to be gone.

"Something's going on up north there," Joe said.

Nobody would stop long enough to talk. They were in that much a hurry.

Pretty soon our tanks were empty, regular and super both. And the truck from the company, the one that always came on Wednesdays, it didn't come. So I took in the sign that said LAST GAS and leaned it against the house wall, and at night I turned off the porch light.

Now the traffic raced by us without stopping. And on the sides of the road abandoned cars began to appear. Nothing wrong with them, they were just out of gas.

The people from those cars, they'd thumb a ride if they could. If they couldn't, they'd start walking—not talking, nor anything like that—just following the highway.

Soon the roadsides were lined solid with empty cars, and then the left lane was closed completely by an eight-car smashup. And then, well, then it began slowing down. Just as suddenly as it started, it was stopping.

This upset Joe, really upset him. "I know it ain't right," he said. He got more and more nervous, and that brought on his headaches, like it always did. In a couple of hours he was limping up and down by the empty gas pumps, holding his head with both hands.

All of a sudden he spun around, rubber heel squealing on the asphalt. "Now look"—he jabbed me right in the middle of the chest with his finger. "If they're going, we're going too. Let's get together right now. Before we miss the last car."

While his back was turned, I took off, running. There was this one particular sinkhole I'd known about for years—I'd found it myself. You could climb down into it (limestone is nothing but layers) to a nice wide shelf, under the overhanging ground. You were out of sight unless somebody happened to climb down after you. And I didn't think Joe was going to look for me in every single sink, not with the pain he had in his leg.

He sure did look for quite a while. He yelled and he cursed after me for hours and hours, before he finally gave up.

Even when I knew he was gone, I stayed hidden, just to be sure. I'd rather met a coral snake where I was than run into Joe on the surface, mad as he was. So I waited a long, long time. When I came out, it was late evening and the highway was empty and I thought, Maybe Joe really did get the last car. Maybe he really did.

THAT WAS yesterday. And there's things I didn't think about before that's bothering me now. Like, when I went to turn on the light, there wasn't any electricity. And food. Joe left everything for me, but it isn't all that much. And the quiet. I'm not used to the quiet. Nor the way winds sound in the dark, hollow and big. And most of all, being alone.

I should have gone with him. Sometimes I think I'll walk along after him, but it's got to be too far. I climbed on the roof to look off that way; I could see for miles and miles, and there wasn't a single thing moving.

And I wonder if there's anything there either, in that direction where all the people were rushing.

I sure wish I'd gone with Joe.

When the next car passes I think I'm going to run out in the highway so they have to hit me or stop for me. I know that's what I'm going to do.

If there ever is another car.

THE FIFTY-FIRST DRAGON

HEYWOOD BROUN

Of all the pupils at the knight school Gawaine le Coeur-Hardy was among the least promising. He was tall and sturdy, but his instructors soon discovered that he lacked spirit. He would hide in the woods when the jousting class was called, although his companions and members of the faculty sought to appeal to his better nature by shouting to him to come out and break his neck like a man. Even when they told him that the lances were padded, the horses no more than ponies and the field unusually soft for late autumn, Gawaine refused to grow enthusiastic. The Headmaster and the Assistant Professor of Pleasaunce were discussing the case one spring afternoon and the Assistant Professor could see no remedy but expulsion.

"No," said the Headmaster, as he looked out at the purple hills which ringed the school, "I think I'll train him to slay dragons."

"He might be killed," objected the Assistant Professor.

"So he might," replied the Headmaster brightly, but he added, more soberly, "we must consider the greater good. We are responsible for the formation of this lad's character."

"Are the dragons particularly bad this year?" interrupted the Assistant Professor. This was characteristic. He always seemed restive when the head of the school began to talk ethics and the ideals of the institution.

"I've never known them worse," replied the Headmaster. "Up in the hills to the south last week they killed a number of peasants, two cows and a prize pig. And if this dry spell holds there's no telling when they may start a forest fire simply by breathing around indiscriminately."

"Would any refund on the tuition fee be necessary in case of an accident to young Coeur-Hardy?"

"No," the principal answered, judicially, "that's all covered in the contract. But as a matter of fact he won't be killed. Before I send him up in the hills I'm going to give him a magic word."

"That's a good idea," said the Professor. "Sometimes they work wonders."

From that day on Gawaine specialized in dragons. His course included both theory and practice. In the morning there were long lectures on the history, anatomy, manners and customs of dragons. Gawaine did not distinguish himself in these studies. He had a marvelously versatile gift for forgetting things. In the afternoon he showed to better advantage, for then he would go down to the South Meadow and practice with a battle-ax. In this exercise he was truly impressive, for he had enormous strength as well as speed and grace. He even developed a deceptive display of ferocity. Old alumni say that it was a thrilling sight to see Gawaine charging across the field toward the dummy paper dragon which had been set up for his practice. As he ran he would brandish his ax and shout, "A murrain on thee!" or some other vivid bit of campus slang. It never took him more than one stroke to behead the dummy dragon.

Gradually his task was made more difficult. Paper gave way to papier-mâché and finally to wood, but even the toughest of these dummy dragons had no terrors for Gawaine. One sweep of the ax always did the business. There were those who said that when the practice was protracted until dusk and the dragons threw long, fantastic shadows across the meadow, Gawaine did not charge so impetuously nor shout so loudly. It is possible there was malice in this charge. At any rate, the Headmaster decided by the end of June that it was time for the test. Only the night before, a dragon had come close to the school grounds and had eaten some of the lettuce from the garden. The faculty decided that Gawaine was ready. They gave him a diploma and a new battle-ax and the Headmaster summoned him to a private conference.

"Sit down," said the Headmaster. "Have a cigarette."

Gawaine hesitated.

"Oh, I know it's against the rules," said the Headmaster. "But after all, you have received your preliminary degree. You are no longer a boy. You are a man. Tomorrow you will go out into the world, the great world of achievement."

Gawaine took a cigarette. The Headmaster offered him a match, but he produced one of his own and began to puff away with a dexterity which quite amazed the principal.

"Here you have learned the theories of life," continued the Headmaster, resuming the thread of his discourse, "but after all, life is not a matter of theories. Life is a matter of facts. It calls on the young and the old alike to face these facts, even though they are hard and sometimes unpleasant. Your problem, for example, is to slay dragons."

"They say that those dragons down in the South Wood are five hundred feet long," ventured Gawaine, timorously.

"Stuff and nonsense!" said the Headmaster. "The curate saw one last week from the top of Arthur's Hill. The dragon was sunning himself down in the valley. The curate didn't have an opportunity to look at him very long because he felt it was his duty to hurry back to make a report to me. He said the monster—or shall I say, the big lizard?— wasn't an inch over two hundred feet. But the size has nothing at all to do with it. You'll find the big ones even easier than the little ones. They're far slower on their feet and less aggressive, I'm told. Besides, before you go I'm going to equip you in such fashion that you need have no fear of all the dragons in the world."

"I'd like an enchanted cap," said Gawaine.

"What's that?" asked the Headmaster, testily.

"A cap to make me disappear," explained Gawaine.

The Headmaster laughed indulgently. "You mustn't believe all those old wives' stories," he said. "There isn't any such thing. A cap to make you disappear, indeed! What would you do with it? You haven't even appeared yet. Why, my boy, you could walk from here to London, and nobody would so much as look at you. You're nobody. You couldn't be more invisible than that."

Gawaine seemed dangerously close to a relapse into his old habit of whimpering. The Headmaster reassured him: "Don't worry; I'll give you something much better than an enchanted cap. I'm going to give you a magic word. All you have to do is to repeat this magic charm once and no dragon can possibly harm a hair of your head. You can cut off his head at your leisure."

He took a heavy book from the shelf behind his desk and began to run through it. "Sometimes," he said, "the charm is a whole phrase or even a sentence. I might, for instance, give you 'To make the'—no, that might not do. I think a single word would be best for dragons."

"A short word," suggested Gawaine.

"It can't be too short or it wouldn't be potent. There isn't so much hurry as all that. Here's a splendid magic word: 'Rumplesnitz.' Do you think you can learn that?"

Gawaine tried and in an hour or so he seemed to have the word well in hand. Again and again he interrupted the lesson to inquire, "And if I say 'Rumplesnitz' the dragon can't possibly hurt me?" And always the Headmaster replied, "If you only say 'Rumplesnitz,' you are perfectly safe."

Toward morning Gawaine seemed resigned to his career. At daybreak the Headmaster saw him to the edge of the forest and pointed him to the direction in which he should proceed. About a mile away to the southwest a cloud of steam hovered over an open meadow in the woods and the Headmaster assured Gawaine that under the steam he would find a dragon. Gawaine went forward slowly. He wondered whether it would be best to approach the dragon on the run as he did in his practice in the South Meadow or to walk slowly toward him, shouting "Rumplesnitz" all the way.

The problem was decided for him. No sooner had he come to the fringe of the meadow than the dragon spied him and began to charge. It was a large dragon and yet it seemed decidedly aggressive in spite of the Headmaster's statement to the contrary. As the dragon charged it released huge clouds of hissing steam through its nostrils. It was almost as if a gigantic teapot had gone mad. The dragon came forward so fast and Gawaine was so frightened that he had time to say "Rumplesnitz" only once. As he said it, he swung his battle-ax and off popped the head of the dragon. Gawaine had to admit that it was even easier to kill a real dragon than a wooden one if only you said "Rumplesnitz."

Gawaine brought the ears home and a small section of the tail. His schoolmates and the faculty made much of him, but the Headmaster wisely kept him from being spoiled by insisting that he go on with his work. Every clear day Gawaine rose at dawn and went out to kill dragons. The Headmaster kept him at home when it rained, because he said the woods were damp and unhealthy at such times and that he didn't want the boy to run needless risks. Few good days passed in which Gawaine failed to get a dragon. On one particularly fortunate day he killed three, a husband and wife and a visiting relative. Gradually he developed a technique. Pupils who sometimes watched him from the hilltops a long way off said that he often allowed the dragon to come within a few feet before he said "Rumplesnitz." He came to say it with a mocking sneer. Occasionally he did stunts. Once when an excursion party from London was watching him he went into action with his right hand tied behind his back. The dragon's head came off just as easily.

As Gawaine's record of killings mounted higher the Headmaster found it impossible to keep him completely in hand. He fell into the habit of stealing out at night and engaging in long drinking bouts at the village tavern.

It was after such a debauch that he rose a little before dawn one fine August morning and started out after his fiftieth dragon. His head was heavy and his mind sluggish. He was heavy in other respects as well, for he had adopted the somewhat vulgar practice of wearing his medals, ribbons and all, when he went out dragon hunting. The decorations began on his chest and ran all the way down to his abdomen. They must have weighed at least eight pounds.

Gawaine found a dragon in the same meadow where he had killed the first one. It was a fair-sized dragon, but evidently an old one. Its face was wrinkled and Gawaine thought he had never seen so hideous a countenance. Much to the lad's disgust, the monster refused to charge and Gawaine was obliged to walk toward him. He whistled as he went. The dragon regarded him hopelessly, but craftily. Of course it had heard of Gawaine. Even when the lad raised his battle-ax the dragon made no move. It knew that there was no salvation in the quickest thrust of the head, for it had been informed that this hunter was protected by an enchantment. It merely waited, hoping something would turn up.

Gawaine raised the battle-ax and suddenly lowered it again. He had grown very pale and he trembled violently.

The dragon suspected a trick. "What's the matter?" it asked, with false solicitude.

"I've forgotten the magic word," stammered Gawaine.

"What a pity," said the dragon. "So that was the secret. It doesn't seem quite sporting to me, all this magic stuff, you know. Not cricket, as we used to say when I was a little dragon; but after all, that's a matter of opinion."

Gawaine was so helpless with terror that the dragon's confidence rose immeasurably and it could not resist the temptation to show off a bit.

"Could I possibly be of any assistance?" it asked. "What's the first letter of the magic word?"

"It begins with an 'r,' " said Gawaine weakly.

"Let's see," mused the dragon, "that doesn't tell us much, does it? What sort of a word is this? Is it an epithet, do you think?"

Gawaine could do no more than nod.

"Why, of course," said the dragon, " 'reactionary Republican.' "

Gawaine shook his head.

"Well, then," said the dragon, "we'd better get down to business. Will you surrender?"

With the suggestion of a compromise Gawaine mustered up enough courage to speak.

"What will you do if I surrender?" he asked.

"Why, I'll eat you," said the dragon.

"And if I don't surrender?"

"I'll eat you just the same."

"Then it doesn't mean any difference, does it?" moaned Gawaine.

"It does to me," said the dragon with a smile. "I'd rather you didn't surrender. You'd taste much better if you didn't."

The dragon waited for a long time for Gawaine to ask "Why?" but the boy was too frightened to speak. At last the dragon had to give the explanation without his cue line. "You see," he said, "if you don't surrender you'll taste better because you'll die game."

This was an old and ancient trick of the dragon's. By means of some such quip he was accustomed to paralyze his victims with laughter and then to destroy them. Gawaine was sufficiently paralyzed as it was, but laughter had no part in his helplessness. With the last word of the joke the dragon drew back his head and struck. In that second there flashed into the mind of Gawaine the magic word "Rumplesnitz," but there was no time to say it. There was time only to strike and, without a word, Gawaine met the onrush of the dragon with a full swing. He put all his back and shoulders into it. The impact was terrific and the head of the dragon flew almost a hundred yards and landed in a thicket.

Gawaine did not remain frightened very long after the death of the dragon. His mood was one of wonder. He was enormously puzzled. He cut off the ears of the monster almost in a trance. Again and again he thought to himself, "I didn't say 'Rumplesnitz'!" He was sure of that and yet there was no question that he had killed the dragon. In fact, he had never killed one so utterly. Never before had he driven a head for anything like the same distance. Twenty-five yards was perhaps his best previous record. All the way back to the knight school he kept rumbling about in his mind seeking an explanation for what had occurred. He went to the Headmaster immediately and after closing the door told him what had happened. "I didn't say 'Rumplesnitz,' " he explained with great earnestness.

The Headmaster laughed. "I'm glad you've found out," he said. "It makes you ever so much more of a hero. Don't you see that? Now you know that it was you who killed all these dragons and not that foolish little word 'Rumplesnitz.' "

Gawaine frowned. "Then it wasn't a magic word after all?" he asked.

"Of course not," said the Headmaster, "you ought to be too old for such foolishness. There isn't any such thing as a magic word."

"But you told me it was magic," protested Gawaine. "You said it was magic and now you say it isn't."

"It wasn't magic in a literal sense," answered the Headmaster, "but it was much more wonderful than that. The word gave you confidence. It took away your fears. If I hadn't told you that, you might have been killed the very first time. It was your battle-ax did the trick."

Gawaine surprised the Headmaster by his attitude. He was obviously distressed by the explanation. He interrupted a long philosophic and ethical discourse by the Headmaster with, "If I hadn't of hit 'em all mighty hard and fast any one of 'em might have crushed me like a, like a—" He fumbled for a word.

"Eggshell," suggested the Headmaster.

"Like a eggshell," assented Gawaine, and he said it many times. All through the evening meal people who sat near him heard him muttering, "Like a eggshell, like a eggshell."

The next day was clear, but Gawaine did not get up at dawn. Indeed, it was almost noon when the Headmaster found him cowering in bed, with the clothes pulled over his head. The principal called the Assistant Professor of Pleasaunce, and together they dragged the boy toward the forest.

"He'll be all right as soon as he gets a couple more dragons under his belt," explained the Headmaster.

The Assistant Professor of Pleasaunce agreed. "It would be a shame to stop such a fine run," he said. "Why, counting that one yesterday, he's killed fifty dragons."

They pushed the boy into a thicket above which hung a meager cloud of steam. It was obviously quite a small dragon. But Gawaine did not come back that night or the next. In fact, he never came back. Some weeks afterward brave spirits from the school explored the thicket, but they could find nothing to remind them of Gawaine except the metal parts of his medals. Even the ribbons had been devoured.

The Headmaster and the Assistant Professor of Pleasaunce agreed that it would be just as well not to tell the school how Gawaine had achieved his record and still less how he came to die. They held that it might have a bad effect on school spirit. Accordingly, Gawaine has lived in the memory of the school as its greatest hero. No visitor succeeds in leaving the building today without seeing a great shield which hangs on the wall of the dining hall. Fifty pairs of dragons' ears are mounted upon the shield and underneath in gilt letters is "Gawaine le Coeur-Hardy," followed by the simple inscription, "He killed fifty dragons." The record has never been equaled.

SIR EDMUND ORME

HENRY JAMES

The statement appears to have been written, though the fragment is undated, long after the death of his wife. When I took possession of his effects I found these pages, in a locked drawer, among papers relating to the unfortunate lady's too brief career (she died in childbirth a year after her marriage), letters, memoranda, accounts, faded photographs, cards of invitation. I cannot vouch that it is a report of a real occurrence—I can only vouch for his general veracity. In any case it was written for himself, not for others. I have altered nothing but the names.

It began on a soft, still Sunday noon in November, just after church, on the sunny Parade at Brighton. I was leaning over the rail which separates the King's Road from the beach when I became conscious of a light walking stick laid across my shoulders. It was Teddy Bostwick, of the Rifles. We strolled together and looked at the people, and bowed to some of them, and differed in opinion as to the prettiness of the girls. About Charlotte Marden we agreed, however, as we saw her coming toward us with her mother. The Brighton air was rare for complexions, and Miss Marden's was one that made people turn round. It made *us* stop, heaven knows—at least, it was one of the things, for we already knew the ladies.

They were only going to the end and back—they had just come out of church. Teddy got immediate possession of Charlotte, leaving me to walk with her mother. However, I was not unhappy; the girl was before me and I had her to talk about. Presently Mrs. Marden said she was tired and must sit down. We two found a place on a sheltered bench—we gossiped as the people passed. It had already struck me that the resemblance between the mother and the daughter was wonderful. One often hears mature mothers spoken of as warnings—signposts, more or less discouraging, of the way daughters may go. But there was nothing deterrent in the idea that Charlotte, at fifty-five, should be as beautiful, even though as pale and preoccupied, as Mrs. Marden. At twenty-two Charlotte was admirably handsome. Her head had the charming shape of her mother's, and her features the same fine order. Then there were looks and movements and tones, which, between the two personalities, were a reflection, a recall.

These ladies had a small fortune and a cheerful little house at Brighton, full of portraits and tokens and trophies to which Mrs. Marden professed herself attached by pious memories. Her husband had been "ordered" there in ill health, to spend the last years of his life, and she had already mentioned to me that it was a place in which she felt herself still under the protection of his goodness. His goodness appeared to have been great, and she sometimes had the air of defending it against mysterious imputations. Some sense of protection, of an influence invoked and cherished, was evidently necessary to her; she had a dim wistfulness, a longing for security.

On the Parade the stream of strollers held its course, and Charlotte presently came by with Teddy Bostwick, who positively declined to go in. He said the occasion was too jolly—might they therefore take another turn? Her mother dropped a "Do as you like," and the girl gave me an impertinent smile over her shoulder as they quitted us.

"She's a bit of a coquette, you know," I observed to my companion, laughing.

"Don't say that—don't say that!" Mrs. Marden murmured.

"The nicest girls always are—just a little."

"Then why are they always punished?"

The intensity of the question startled me. "What do you know about it?" I inquired.

"I was a bad girl myself."

"And were you punished?"

"I carry it through life," said Mrs. Marden, looking away from me.

"Ah!" She suddenly panted, rising to her feet and staring at her daughter. She stood a few seconds, with the queerest expression in her face; then she sank upon the seat again and I saw that she had blushed crimson. Charlotte, who had observed her movement, came straight up to her and, taking her hand, seated herself on the other side of her. The girl had turned pale—she gave her mother a fixed, frightened look. Mrs. Marden sat quiet and inexpressive, gazing at the indifferent crowd. My eye happened to fall, however, on the interlocked hands of the two ladies, and the grasp of the elder one was violent.

Bostwick stood before them, wondering what was the matter and asking me if *I* knew; which led Charlotte to say to him after a moment, with a certain irritation, "Don't stand there that way, Captain Bostwick; go away—*please* go away."

I got up at this, but Mrs. Marden immediately begged that we would *not* go away, and that we would presently come home to lunch. She drew me down beside her and for a moment I felt her hand pressing my arm in a way that might have been an involuntary betrayal of distress and might have been a private signal. What she might have wished to point out to me I couldn't divine—perhaps she had seen somebody or something abnormal in the crowd. She explained to us in a few minutes that she was all right, that she was only liable to palpitations—they came as quickly as they went. The incident was felt to be closed. Bostwick and I lunched with our sociable friends, and when I walked away with him he declared that he had never seen such dear, kind creatures.

Mrs. Marden had made us promise to come back the next day to tea. Yet the next day, when at five o'clock I knocked at the door of the pretty house, it was to learn that the ladies had gone up to town. They had left a message for us with the butler that they had suddenly been called—were very sorry. They would be absent a few days. I went again three days later, but they were still away; and it was not till the end of a week that I got a note from Mrs. Marden, saying, "We are back; do come and forgive us." It was on this occasion, I remember (the occasion of my going just after getting the note), that she told me she had intuitions and that some of these uncanny promptings were connected with me. There were other people present and I had but a few minutes' talk with Charlotte; but the day after this I met them both at dinner and had the satisfaction of sitting next to Miss Marden. I recall that hour as the hour on which it first completely came over me that she was a beautiful, liberal creature. I had seen her personality in patches and gleams, like a song sung in snatches, but now it was before me in a large rosy glow, as if it had been a full volume of sound—I heard the whole of the air. It was sweet, fresh music.

After dinner I had a few words with Mrs. Marden; it was at the moment, late in the evening, when tea was handed about. A servant passed near us with a tray, I asked her if she would have a cup and, on her assenting, took one and handed it to her. She put out her hand for it; but as she was in the act of receiving it she started and faltered, so that the cup and saucer dropped with a crash of porcelain and without, on the part of Mrs. Marden, the usual woman's movement to save her dress. I stooped to pick up the fragments, and when I raised myself Mrs. Marden was looking across the room at her daughter, who looked back at her smiling, but with an anxious light in her eyes. Dear Mama, what on earth *is* the matter with you? the silent question seemed to say.

Mrs. Marden colored, just as she had done after her strange movement on the Parade the other week, and I was therefore surprised when she said to me with unexpected assurance, "You should really have a steadier hand!" I began to stammer a defense of my hand when I became aware that she had fixed her eyes upon me with an intense appeal. I understood, as plainly as if she had murmured, Make believe it was you—make believe it was you. The servant came to wipe up the spilled tea, and while I was in the midst of making believe, Mrs. Marden brushed away from me and went into another room. I noticed that she gave no heed to the state of her dress.

I saw nothing more of either of them that evening, but the next morning, in the King's Road, I met Miss Marden with a roll of music in her muff. She told me she had been to practice duets with a friend, and gave me leave to attend her to her door. As we stood before it I inquired if I might go in. "No, not today—I don't want you," she said, candidly though not roughly; while the words caused me to direct a wistful, disconcerted gaze at one of the windows of the house. It fell upon the white face of Mrs. Marden, who was looking out at us from the drawing room. She stood there for a moment, then vanished before her daughter had observed her. As I had been told they didn't want me, I left them alone a little, and shortly thereafter I went up to London. While there I received a pressing invitation to come immediately down to Tranton, a pretty place in Sussex belonging to a couple whose acquaintance I had lately made.

On arriving at Tranton I found the Mardens, with a dozen other people, in the house. The first thing Mrs. Marden said was, "Will you forgive me for throwing my tea over you?" I replied that it had gone over herself; whereupon she said, "At any rate I was very rude; but someday I think you'll understand, and then you'll make allowances for me." The first day I was there she dropped two or three references to the mystic initiation that was in store for me. Didn't I remember she had told me she had intuitions? From the first time of her seeing me she had been sure there were things I should not escape knowing. Meanwhile there was nothing to do but wait and I was not to be nervous, she said—one got used to everything. I couldn't imagine what she meant. I might have said to myself that she was a little wrong in the upper story, but that never occurred to me.

There were other girls in the house, but Charlotte Marden was generally felt to be the most charming. There were two or three men, including Teddy Bostwick (who had come over from Brighton), and she was kind to all of us.

The third day I was at Tranton was a Sunday, and there was a very pretty walk to morning service over the fields. It was gray, windless weather, and the bell of the little old church that nestled in the hollow of the Sussex down sounded near and domestic. We were a straggling procession, in the mild damp air, and I managed to fall a good way behind with Miss Marden. I remember entertaining a strong impulse to say something intensely personal, such as that I had never seen her so lovely, or that that particular moment was the sweetest of my life. But always, in youth, such words have been on the lips many times before they are spoken; and I had the sense, not that I didn't know her well enough (I cared little for that), but that she didn't know *me* well enough.

In the church, the big Tranton pew was full. Several of us were scattered, and I found a seat for Miss Marden and another for myself beside it, at a distance from her mother and from most of our friends. There were two or three decent rustics on the bench, who moved in farther to make room for us, and I took my place first, to cut off my companion from our neighbors. After she was seated there was still a space left, which remained empty till service was about half over.

This at least was the moment at which I became aware that another person had entered and had taken the seat. When I noticed him he had already settled himself and put down his hat beside him and, with his hands crossed on the nob of his cane, was gazing before him at the altar. He was a pale young man in black, with the air of a gentleman. I was slightly startled on perceiving him, for Miss Marden had not attracted my attention to his entrance by moving to make room for him.

Observing that he had no prayer book, I reached across my neighbor and placed mine before him, on the ledge of the pew. The moment I offered him the book, however, the intruder rose from his place without thanking me, stepped noiselessly out of the pew and, so discreetly as to attract no attention, passed down the center of the church. I noticed, and with surprise, that Mrs. Marden had been so affected by his withdrawal as to rise, involuntarily, an instant, in her place. She stared at him as he passed, but he passed very quickly, and she as quickly dropped down again, though not too soon to catch my eye across the church. I then asked Miss Marden, in a low voice, if she would kindly pass me back my prayer book. She restored it to me, saying as she did so, "Why on earth did you put it there?" I was on the point of answering her when she dropped on her knees, and I held my tongue. I had only been going to say, "To be decently civil."

After the benediction, as we were leaving our places, Mrs. Marden came up the aisle to join us, having apparently something to say to her daughter. She said it, but in an instant I observed that it was only a pretext—her real business was with me. She pushed Charlotte forward and suddenly murmured to me, "Did you see him?"

"The gentleman who sat down here? How could I help seeing him?"

"Hush!" she said, with the intensest excitement. "Don't *speak* to her—don't tell her!" She slipped her hand into my arm, to keep me, it seemed, away from her daughter. The precaution was unnecessary, for

Teddy Bostwick had already taken possession of Miss Marden. "Don't speak to anyone—don't tell anyone!" Mrs. Marden went on.

"I don't understand. Tell them what?"

"Why, that you saw him."

"Surely they saw him for themselves."

"Not one of them, not one of them. You're the only person, the only person in the world."

"But *you*, dear madam?"

"Oh me—of course. That's my curse!" And with this she moved rapidly away from me to join the body of the party. I hovered on its outskirts on the way home, for I had food for rumination. Whom had I seen and why was the apparition invisible to the others? If an exception had been made for Mrs. Marden, why did it constitute a curse, and why was I to share so questionable an advantage?

After luncheon I went out on the old terrace to smoke a cigarette, but I had only taken a couple of turns when I perceived Mrs. Marden at a window, motioning me to come in. She was in a little reception room, known as the Indian room, which had a decoration vaguely Oriental—lacquered screens, lanterns with long fringes, and strange idols in cabinets. The place was little used, and when I went round to her we had it to ourselves. As soon as I entered she said to me, "Please tell me this—are you in love with my daughter?"

I hesitated a moment. "Before I answer your question will you kindly tell me what gives you the idea? I don't consider that I have been very forward."

Mrs. Marden gave me no satisfaction on the point I mentioned; she only went on strenuously, "Did you say nothing to her on the way to church?"

"What makes you think I said anything?"

"The fact that you saw him."

"Saw whom, dear Mrs. Marden? Do you mean the gentleman who came into the pew?"

"You saw him, you saw him!" she panted, with a strange mixture of dismay and relief. "Did you feel it to be inevitable?"

I was puzzled again. "Inevitable?"

"That you *should* see him?"

"Certainly, since I'm not blind."

"You might have been; everyone else is." I was wonderfully at sea, and I frankly confessed it, but the case was not made clearer by her presently exclaiming, "I knew you would see him from the moment you should be really in love with her! You'll see him again."

"I've no objection," I said, "but I shall take more interest in him if you'll kindly tell me who he is."

She hesitated, looking down a moment; then she said, raising her eyes, "I'll tell you if you'll tell me first what you said to her on the way to church."

"I'm afraid your intuitions are at fault this time. I said nothing to your daughter that was the least out of the way."

"Then you consider that you're not in love with her?"

"That's another affair!" I laughed.

"You are—you *are!* You wouldn't have seen him if you hadn't been."

"Who the deuce *is* he, then, madam?" I inquired with some irritation.

She would still only answer me with another question. "Didn't you at least *want* to say something to her—didn't you come very near it?"

The question justified the famous intuitions. "Very near it—it was the turn of a hair. I don't know what kept me quiet."

"That was quite enough," said Mrs. Marden. "It isn't what you say that determines it; it's what you feel. *That's* what he goes by."

I clasped my hands with an air of supplication which covered much real impatience, a sharper curiosity and even a certain dread. "I entreat you to tell me whom you're talking about."

She threw up her arms, as if to shake off both reserve and responsibility. "Sir Edmund Orme."

"And who is Sir Edmund Orme?"

She gave a start. "Hush, here they come." Then as, following the direction of her eyes, I saw Charlotte Marden on the terrace, at the window, she added, "Don't notice him—*never!*"

Charlotte made a sign that she was to be admitted, on which I went and opened the long window. The girl came in laughing. "What plot are you two hatching here?"

I was flurried, because I saw that Mrs. Marden was flurried, and to pass it off I said, fancifully, to Charlotte, "I've been asking your mother for your hand."

"Oh, indeed, and has she given it?" Miss Marden answered, gaily.

"She was just going to when you appeared there."

"Do you like him, Charlotte?" Mrs. Marden asked, with a candor I scarcely expected.

"It's difficult to say it *before* him, isn't it?" the girl replied, entering into the humor of the thing, but looking at me as if she didn't like me.

At that moment there stepped into the room from the terrace (the window had been left open) a gentleman who had come into sight, at least into mine, only within the instant. Mrs. Marden had said, "Here *they* come," but he appeared to have followed her daughter at a certain distance. I immediately recognized him as the personage who had sat beside us in church. This time I saw him better, saw that his face and his whole air were strange. I speak of him as a personage, because one felt, indescribably, as if a reigning prince had come into the room. He held himself with a kind of habitual majesty, as if he were different from us. Yet he looked fixedly and gravely at me, till I wondered what he expected of me.

He turned his eyes in the same way on Mrs. Marden, but she knew what to do. After the first agitation produced by his approach she took no notice of him whatever; it made me remember her passionate adjuration to me. I had to achieve a great effort to imitate her, for though I knew nothing about him but that he was Sir Edmund Orme, I felt his presence as a strong appeal, almost as an oppression. He stood there without speaking—young, pale, handsome, clean-shaven, decorous, with extraordinary light blue eyes and something old-fashioned, like a portrait of years ago, in his head, his manner of wearing his hair. He was in complete mourning, and he carried his hat in his hand. He looked again strangely hard at me, and I remember feeling rather cold and wishing he would say something. No silence had ever seemed to me so soundless.

Charlotte Marden stared from her mother to me and back again, and then broke out with, "What on earth is the matter with you? You've such odd faces! One would think you had seen a ghost!"

"Don't be impertinent; and go and tell them all that I'll join them," said Mrs. Marden with much dignity, but with a quaver in her voice.

"And will you come—*you?*" the girl asked, turning away. I made no answer, taking the question as meant for her companion. But he was more silent than I, and when she reached the door she stopped, with her hand on the knob, and looked at me, repeating it. I assented, springing forward to open the door for her, and as she went out she exclaimed to me mockingly, "You haven't got your wits about you—you shan't have my hand!"

I closed the door and turned round to find that Sir Edmund Orme had gone. Mrs. Marden and I looked at each other long. It had only then come home to me that her daughter was unconscious of what had happened. She had been equally unaware in church, and the two facts together set my heart more sensibly beating. I wiped my forehead, and Mrs. Marden broke out with a low distressful wail, "Now you know my life—now you know my life!"

"In God's name who is he—*what* is he?"

"He's a man I wronged."

"How did you wrong him?"

"Oh, awfully—years ago."

"Years ago? Why, he's very young."

"Young—young?" cried Mrs. Marden. "He was born before *I* was!"

"Then why does he look so?"

She came nearer to me, she laid her hand on my arm, and there was something in her face that made me shrink a little. "Don't you understand—don't you *feel?*" she murmured.

"I feel very queer!" I laughed, and I was conscious that my laugh betrayed it.

"He's dead!" said Mrs. Marden, from her white face.

"Dead?" I panted. "Then that gentleman was—"

"Call him what you like—he's a perfect presence."

"He's a splendid presence!" I cried. "The place is haunted—*haunted!*"

"It isn't the place—more's the pity! That has nothing to do with it!"

"Then it's you, dear lady?"

"No, nor me either. I wish it were!"

"Perhaps it's me," I suggested with a sickly smile.

"It's nobody but my child—my innocent, innocent child!" And with this Mrs. Marden broke down—she dropped into a chair and burst into tears. I stammered some question, I pressed on her some bewildered appeal, but she waved me off. I persisted—couldn't I help her, couldn't I intervene? "You *have* intervened," she sobbed. "You're *in* it, you're *in* it."

"I'm very glad to be in anything so curious," I boldly declared.

"I'm glad you like it. Go away."

"But I want to know more about it."

"You'll see all you want. Go away!"

"But I want to understand what I see."

"How can you, when I don't understand myself?"

"We'll do so together—we'll make it out."

At this she got up, doing what she could to obliterate her tears. "Yes, it will be better together—that's why I've liked you. But go and join them. I'll come in a moment."

I passed out to the terrace and I felt that I had a part to play. So far from dreading another encounter with the "perfect presence," as Mrs. Marden called it, I was filled with an excitement that was positively joyous. I went round the house as quickly as if I expected to overtake Sir Edmund Orme. I didn't overtake him just then, but the day was not to close without my recognizing that, as Mrs. Marden had said, I should see all I wanted of him.

Most of us took the collective sociable walk which, in the English country house, is the consecrated pastime on Sunday afternoons, and by five o'clock we were restored to the fireside in the hall for tea. Mrs. Marden had said she would join us, but she had not appeared; her daughter, who had seen her again before we went out, only explained that she was tired.

Afternoon tea was a friendly hour at Tranton; the firelight played into the wide white last-century hall; sympathies almost confessed themselves, lingering together before dressing, on deep sofas, in muddy boots, for last words. I watched my moment and went over to Charlotte Marden when I saw she was about to withdraw. The ladies had left the place one by one, and after I had addressed myself particularly to Miss Marden, the three men who were near her gradually dispersed. We had a little vague talk—she appeared preoccupied, and heaven knows *I* was—after which she said she must go up to see her mother; she was afraid she was unwell.

"On the contrary, she's better than she has been for a long time," I said. "She has found out that she can have confidence in me, and that has done her good." Miss Marden had dropped into her chair again. I was standing before her, and she looked up at me without a smile—with a dim distress in her beautiful eyes; not exactly as if I were hurting her, but as if she were no longer disposed to treat as a joke what had passed between her mother and myself. But I could answer her inquiry in all kindness and candor, for I was really conscious that the poor lady had put off a part of her burden on me and was proportionately relieved and eased. "I'm sure she has slept all the afternoon as she hasn't slept for years," I went on. "You have only to ask her."

Charlotte got up again. "You make yourself out very useful."

"There's no hurry," I said. "Haven't I a right to talk to you a little this way, alone, when your mother has given me your hand?"

"And is it *your* mother who has given me yours? I'm much obliged to her, but I don't want it. I think our hands are not our mothers'— they happen to be our own!" The girl laughed.

"Sit down, sit down and let me tell you!" I pleaded.

I still stood before her, urgently, to see if she wouldn't oblige me. She hesitated a moment, looking vaguely this way and that, as if under a compulsion that was slightly painful. The empty hall was quiet; we heard the loud ticking of the great clock. Then she slowly sank down and I drew a chair close to her. This made me face round to the fire again, and with the movement I perceived, disconcertedly, that we were not alone. The next instant, more strangely than I can say, my discomposure, instead of increasing, dropped, for the person before the fire was Sir Edmund Orme. He stood there as I had seen him in the Indian room, looking at me with expressionless attention. I knew so much more about him now that I had to check a movement of recognition, an acknowledgment of his presence. Charlotte evidently saw nothing to look at, and I made a tremendous and very nearly successful effort to conceal from her that my own situation was different. I say very nearly, because she watched me an instant in a way that made me fear she was going to say again, as she had said in the Indian room, "What on earth is the matter with you?"

The matter with me was that in the presence of this extraordinary portent I was taken up with the idea of protecting *her*. As she sat there, innocent and charming, my heart beat high with this idea; and I had become more aware than of anything else that I loved her. The way to protect her was to love her, and the way to love her was to tell her, now and here, that I did so. Sir Edmund Orme didn't prevent me; he turned his back to us and stood looking discreetly at the fire. At the end of another moment he leaned his head on his arm, against the chimney-piece, with an air of dejection.

Charlotte Marden was startled by what I said to her, and she jumped up; but she took no offense—my tenderness was too real. She only moved about the room with a deprecating murmur, and I was so busy following up any little advantage that I might have obtained that I didn't notice in what manner Sir Edmund Orme disappeared. I only observed presently that he had gone.

"I don't ask for an answer now," I said. "I only want you to be sure—to know how much depends on it."

"Oh, I don't want to give it to you, now or ever!" she replied with a slow, sweet, sad headshake. "I hate the subject, please—I wish one could be let alone." And she added, vaguely, kindly, as she left the room, "Thank you, thank you—thank you so much!"

At dinner I was placed on the same side of the table with her, where she couldn't see me. Her mother was nearly opposite to me, and just after we had sat down Mrs. Marden gave me a long look, in which all our strange communion was expressed. It meant, of course, She has told me, but it meant other things besides. At any rate I know what my answering look to her conveyed: I've seen him again—I've seen him again! This didn't prevent Mrs. Marden from treating her neighbors with her usual scrupulous blandness.

After dinner, when, in the drawing room, the men joined the ladies and I went straight up to her to tell her how I wished we could have some private conversation, she said in a low tone, "He's here—he's here."

"Here?" I looked round the room, but I was disappointed.

"Look where *she* is," said Mrs. Marden. Charlotte was not in the main saloon, but in the morning room, into which it opened. I took a few steps and saw her, through a doorway, upright in the middle of the room, talking with three gentlemen, whose backs were practically turned to me. One of them—the middle one—was Sir Edmund Orme. This time it *was* surprising that the others didn't see him. Charlotte seemed to be looking straight at him, addressing her conversation to him. She saw me after an instant, however, and immediately turned her eyes away. I went back to her mother with an annoyed sense that the girl would think I was watching *her*, which would be unjust. Mrs. Marden had found a small sofa, a little apart, and I sat down beside her.

"Oh, yes, he's there," I said, "and at about a quarter past seven he was in the hall."

"I knew it at the time, and I was so glad that it was your affair, this time, and not mine. It's a rest for me."

"Did you sleep all the afternoon?" I asked.

"As I haven't done for months. It's a blessing, the way you take it."

"I take it as a man who's in love with your daughter."

"I believe it will all pass—if she loves you," Mrs. Marden said.

"It will all pass?"

"We shall never see him again."

"Oh, if she loves me I don't care how often I see him!"

"Ah, you take it better than I could," said my companion. "You have the happiness not to know—not to understand."

"I don't indeed. What on earth does he want?"

"He wants to make me suffer." She turned her wan face upon me with this, and I saw how perfectly, if this had been Sir Edmund Orme's purpose, he had succeeded. "For what I did to him," Mrs. Marden explained.

"And what did you do to him?"

She looked at me a moment. "I killed him." As I had seen him fifty yards away only five minutes before, the words gave me a start. "Yes, I make you jump; be careful. He's there still, but he killed himself. I broke his heart. We were to have been married, but I broke it off—just at the last. I saw someone I liked better; I had no reason but that. It

315

wasn't for money or position. *Those* things were his. It was simply that I fell in love with Captain Marden. When I saw him I felt that I couldn't marry anyone else. I wasn't in love with Edmund Orme—my mother had brought it about. But he did love me. I told him I didn't care, that I couldn't. I threw him over, and he took some abominable drug that proved fatal. It was dreadful; he died in agony. I married Captain Marden, but not for five years. I was happy, perfectly happy; time obliterates. But when my husband died I began to see him."

"To see your husband?"

"Never, never *that* way, thank God! To see *him*, with Chartie—always with Chartie. The first time it nearly killed me—about seven years ago, when she first came out. Never when I'm by myself, only with her. Sometimes not for months, then every day for a week. I've tried everything to break the spell—doctors and *régimes* and climates; I've prayed to God on my knees. That day at Brighton, on the Parade with you, when you thought I was ill, that was the first for an age. And then, in the evening, when I knocked my tea over you, and the day you were at the door with Charlotte and I saw you from the window—each time he was there."

"I see, I see." I was more thrilled than I could say. "It's a tremendously interesting case."

"Oh, you're the right one!" she exclaimed. "I was right when I trusted you."

"I'm devoutly grateful you did, but what made you do it?"

"I had thought the whole thing out in those dreadful years, while he was punishing me in my daughter."

"Hardly that," I objected, "if she never knew."

"That has been my terror, that she *will*, from one occasion to another. I've an unspeakable dread of the effect on her."

"She shan't, she shan't!" I declared, so loud that several people looked round. Mrs. Marden made me get up, and I had no more talk with her that evening. The next day I told her I must take my departure from Tranton; it was neither comfortable nor considerate to remain as a rejected suitor. She accepted my reasons, but said to me out of her mournful eyes, You'll leave me alone then with my burden? It was understood between us that for many weeks to come there would be no discretion in "worrying poor Charlotte"; such were the terms in which, with odd feminine and maternal inconsistency, she alluded to an attitude on my part that she favored.

I was prepared to be heroically considerate, but it seemed to me that even this delicacy permitted me to say a word to Miss Marden before I went. I begged her, after breakfast, to take a turn with me on the terrace, and as she hesitated, I informed her that it was only to ask her a question and to say good-by.

She came out with me, and we passed slowly round the house three or four times. Nothing is finer than this great airy platform, from which every look is a sweep of the country, with the sea on the farthest edge. It might have been that as we passed the windows we were conspicuous to our friends in the house, but I didn't care. I only wondered whether they wouldn't really this time make out Sir Edmund Orme, who joined us and strolled slowly on the other side of my companion.

Of what transcendent essence he was composed I knew not; I have no theory about him. I should no more have thought of practicing an experiment with him, of touching him, for instance, or speaking to him, since he set the example of silence, than I should have thought of committing any other social grossness. He had always the perfect propriety of his position—had always the appearance of being dressed and of comporting himself as the occasion demanded. I very soon came to attach an idea of beauty to his unmentionable presence, the beauty of an old story of love and pain. What I ended by feeling was that he was watching over my interest, that he was looking to it that my heart shouldn't be broken.

Oh, he had taken it seriously, his own catastrophe; he had certainly proved that in his day. If poor Mrs. Marden, as she told me, had thought it out, I also subjected the case to the finest analysis of which my intellect was capable. It was a case of retributive justice. The mother was to pay, in suffering, for the suffering she had inflicted, and as the disposition to jilt a lover might have been transmitted to the daughter, the daughter was to be watched, so that *she* might be made to suffer should she do an equal wrong. She might reproduce her mother in character as vividly as she did in face. On the day she should transgress, her eyes would be opened to the "perfect presence." I had no great fear for her, because I didn't believe she was, in any cruel degree, a coquette. We should have a good deal of ground to get over before I, at least, should be in a position to be sacrificed by her.

The question I asked her on the terrace that morning was whether I might continue, during the winter, to come to Mrs. Marden's house. I promised not to come too often and not to speak to her for three months of the question I had raised the day before. She replied that I might, and on this we parted.

I carried out my vow and held my tongue for three months. Unexpectedly to myself there were moments of this time when she struck me as capable of playing with a man. I wanted so to make her like me that I became subtle and ingenious, wonderfully alert, patiently diplomatic. Sometimes I thought I had brought her to the point of saying, "Well, well, you're the best of them all—you may speak to me now." And on certain days a mocking light in her eyes, of which the meaning seemed to be, If you don't take care, I *will* accept you, to have done with you the more effectually.

After our visit to Tranton, Sir Edmund Orme gave us a holiday, and I confess it was at first a disappointment to me. I felt less designated, less connected with Charlotte. "Oh, don't cry till you're out of the wood," her mother said. "He has let me off sometimes for six months. He'll break out again when you least expect it." For her these weeks were happy, and she was wise enough not to talk about me to the girl. She assured me that I was taking the right way, that I looked as if I felt secure and that in the long run women give way to that. For herself she was better than she had been for years, and she had me to thank for it. The sense of visitation was light upon her; she wasn't in anguish every time she looked round.

That winter was a wonder of mildness, and we often sat out in the sun. I walked up and down with Charlotte, and Mrs. Marden, sometimes on a bench, sometimes in a bath chair, waited for us and smiled at us as we passed. I always looked out for a sign in her face—He's with you, he's with you (she would see him before I should), but nothing came. Toward the end of April the air was so like June that, meeting my two friends one night at some Brighton sociability—an evening party with amateur music—I drew Miss Marden unresistingly out upon a balcony to which a window in one of the rooms stood open. The night was close and thick, the stars were dim, and below us, under the cliff, we heard the regular rumble of the sea. We listened to it a little and we heard mixed with it, from within the house, the sound of a violin accompanied by a piano.

"Do you like me a little better?" I asked, abruptly, after a minute. "Could you listen to me again?"

I had no sooner spoken than she laid her hand quickly, with a certain force, on my arm. "Hush! Isn't there someone there?" She was looking into the gloom of the far end of the balcony. This balcony ran the whole width of the house, a width very great in the best of the old houses at Brighton. We were lighted a little by the open window behind us, but the other windows, curtained within, left the darkness undiminished, so that I made out but dimly the figure of a gentleman standing there and looking at us.

He was in evening dress, like a guest—I saw the vague shine of his white shirt and the pale oval of his face—and he might have been a guest who had stepped out to take the air. Miss Marden took him for one at first; then evidently, even in a few seconds, she saw that the intensity of his gaze was unconventional. What else she saw I couldn't determine; I was too taken up with my own impression to do more than feel the quick contact of her uneasiness. My own impression was a sensation of horror, for what could the thing mean but that the girl at last *saw?* I heard her give a sudden, gasping "Ah!" and move quickly into the house. It was only afterward that my horror passed into anger, and my anger into a stride along the balcony with a gesture of reprobation. The case was simplified to the vision of a frightened girl whom I loved. I advanced to vindicate her security, but I found nothing there to meet me. Sir Edmund Orme had vanished.

I followed Miss Marden immediately, but there were symptoms of confusion in the drawing room when I passed in. A lady had fainted, the music had stopped; there was a shuffling of chairs and a pressing forward. The lady was Mrs. Marden. She revived shortly and insisted on going home, after which I uneasily withdrew.

I called the next morning, but when I asked if Miss Marden would see me, the message sent down was that it was impossible. Toward evening I received a line in pencil, brought by hand—"Please come; Mother wishes you." Five minutes afterward I was at the door again and ushered into the drawing room. Mrs. Marden lay upon the sofa, and as soon as I looked at her I saw the shadow of death in her face. But the first thing she said was that she was better, ever so much better; her poor old heart had been behaving queerly again, but now it was quiet. She gave me her hand and I bent over her with my eyes on hers, and in this way I was able to read what she didn't speak—I'm really very ill, but appear to take what I say exactly as I say it. Charlotte stood there beside her, looking intensely grave, and not meeting my eyes. "She has told me—she has told me!" her mother went on.

"She has told you?" I stared from one of them to the other, wondering if Mrs. Marden meant that the girl had spoken to her of the circumstances on the balcony.

"That you spoke to her again—that you're admirably faithful."

I felt a thrill of joy at this; it showed me that Charlotte had wished to say the thing that would soothe her mother most. Yet I now knew, myself, as well as if Mrs. Marden had told me, that she knew what her daughter had seen. "I spoke; I spoke, but she gave me no answer," I said.

"She will now. Won't you, Chartie? I want it so, I want it!" the poor lady murmured, with ineffable wistfulness.

"You're very good to me," Charlotte said to me, seriously and sweetly, looking fixedly on the carpet. There was something different in her. She had recognized something, she felt a coercion. I could see that she was trembling.

"Ah, if you would let me show you *how* good I can be!" I exclaimed, holding out my hands to her. As I uttered the words I was touched with the knowledge that something had happened. A form had constituted itself on the other side of the bed, and the form leaned over Mrs. Marden. My whole being went forth into a mute prayer that Charlotte shouldn't see it and that I should be able to betray nothing. Charlotte got up to give me her hand, and with the definite act she saw. She gave, with a shriek, one stare of dismay, and another sound, like a wail of one of the lost, fell at the same instant on my ear. But I had already sprung toward the girl to cover her, to veil her face. She had already thrown herself into my arms. I held her there a moment; then, all of a sudden, coldly, I gathered that we were alone. She released herself.

The figure beside the sofa had vanished, but Mrs. Marden lay in her place with closed eyes, with something in her stillness that gave us both another terror. Charlotte expressed it in the cry of "Mother, Mother!" with which she flung herself down. I fell on my knees beside her. Mrs. Marden had passed away.

Was the sound I heard when Chartie shrieked—the other and still more tragic sound, I mean—the despairing cry of the poor lady's death shock, or the articulate sob of the exorcised and pacified spirit? Possibly the latter, for that was, mercifully, the last of Sir Edmund Orme.

THE DAEMON LOVER

SHIRLEY JACKSON

Shirley Jackson

SHE HAD NOT slept well; from one thirty, when Jamie left and she went lingeringly to bed, until seven, when she at last allowed herself to get up and make coffee, she had slept fitfully, stirring awake to open her eyes and look into the half-darkness, remembering over and over, slipping again into a feverish dream. She spent almost an hour over her coffee—they were to have a real breakfast on the way—and then, unless she wanted to dress early, had nothing to do. She washed her coffee cup and made the bed, looking carefully over the clothes she planned to wear, worried unnecessarily, at the window, over whether it would be a fine day. She sat down to read, thought that she might write a letter to her sister instead, and began, in her finest handwriting, "Dearest Anne, by the time you get this I will be married. Doesn't it sound funny? I can hardly believe it myself, but when I tell you how it happened, you'll see it's even stranger than that. . . ."

Sitting, pen in hand, she hesitated over what to say next, read the lines already written, and tore up the letter. She went to the window and saw that it was undeniably a fine day. It occurred to her that perhaps she ought not to wear the blue silk dress; it was too plain, almost severe, and she wanted to be soft, feminine. Anxiously she pulled through the dresses in the closet, and hesitated over a print she had worn the summer before; it was too young for her, and it had a ruffled neck, and it was very early in the year for a print dress, but still . . .

She hung the two dresses side by side on the outside of the closet door and opened the glass doors carefully closed upon the small closet that was her kitchenette. She turned on the burner under the coffeepot, and went to the window; it was sunny. When the coffeepot began to crackle she came back and poured herself coffee, into a clean cup. I'll have a headache if I don't get some solid food soon, she thought, all this coffee, smoking too much, no real breakfast. A headache on her wedding day; she went and got the tin box of aspirin from the bathroom closet and slipped it into her blue pocketbook. She'd have to change to a brown pocketbook if she wore the print dress, and the only brown pocketbook she had was shabby. Helplessly, she stood looking from the blue pocketbook to the print dress, and then put the pocketbook down and went and got her coffee and sat down near the window, drinking her coffee, and looking carefully around the one-room apartment. They planned to come back here tonight and everything must be correct. With sudden horror she realized that she had forgotten to put clean sheets on the bed; the laundry was freshly back and she took clean sheets and pillowcases from the top shelf of the closet and stripped the bed, working quickly to avoid thinking consciously of why she was changing the sheets. The bed was a studio bed, with a cover to make it look like a couch, and when it was finished no one would have known she had just put clean sheets on it. She took the old sheets and pillowcases into the bathroom and stuffed them down into the hamper, and put the bathroom towels in the hamper too, and clean towels on the bathroom racks. Her coffee was cold when she came back to it, but she drank it anyway.

When she looked at the clock, finally, and saw that it was after nine, she began at last to hurry. She took a bath, and used one of the clean towels, which she put into the hamper and replaced with a clean one. She dressed carefully, all her underwear fresh and most of it new; she put everything she had worn the day before, including her nightgown, into the hamper. When she was ready for her dress, she hesitated before the closet door. The blue dress was certainly decent, and clean, and fairly becoming, but she had worn it several times with Jamie, and there was nothing about it which made it special for a wedding day. The print dress was overly pretty, and new to Jamie, and yet wearing such a print this early in the year was certainly rushing the season. Finally she thought, This is my wedding day, I can dress as I please, and she took the print dress down from the hanger. When she slipped it on over her head it felt fresh and light, but when she looked at herself in the mirror she remembered that the ruffles around the neck did not show her throat to any great advantage, and the wide swinging skirt looked irresistibly made for a girl, for someone who would run freely, dance, swing it with her hips when she walked. Looking at herself in the mirror she thought with revulsion, It's as though I was trying to make myself look prettier than I am, just for him; he'll think I want to look younger because he's marrying me; and she tore the print dress off so quickly that a seam under the arm ripped. In the old blue dress she felt comfortable and familiar, but unexciting. It isn't what you're wearing that matters, she told herself firmly, and turned in dismay to the closet to see if there might be anything else. There was nothing even remotely suitable for her marrying Jamie, and for a minute she thought of going out quickly to some little shop nearby, to get a dress. Then she saw that it was close on ten, and she had no time for more than her hair and her makeup. Her hair was easy, pulled back into a knot at the nape of her neck, but her makeup was another delicate balance between looking as well as possible, and deceiving as little. She could not try to disguise the sallowness of her skin, or the lines around her eyes, today, when it might look as though she were only doing it for her wedding, and yet she could not bear the thought of Jamie's bringing to marriage anyone who looked haggard and lined. You're thirty-four years old after *all*, she told herself cruelly in the bathroom mirror. Thirty, it said on the license.

It was two minutes after ten; she was not satisfied with her clothes, her face, her apartment. She heated the coffee again and sat down in the chair by the window. Can't do anything more now, she thought, no sense trying to improve anything the last minute.

Reconciled, settled, she tried to think of Jamie and could not see his face clearly, or hear his voice. It's always that way with someone you love, she thought, and let her mind slip past today and tomorrow, into the farther future, when Jamie was established with his writing and she had given up her job, the golden house-in-the-country future they had been preparing for the past week. "I used to be a wonderful cook," she had promised Jamie; "with a little time and practice I could remember how to make angel food cake. And fried chicken," she said, knowing how the words would stay in Jamie's mind, half tenderly. "And hollandaise sauce."

Ten thirty. She stood up and went purposefully to the phone. She dialed, and waited, and the girl's metallic voice said, ". . . the time will be exactly ten twenty-nine." Half consciously she set her clock back a minute; she was remembering her own voice saying last night, in the doorway, "Ten o'clock then. I'll be ready. Is it really *true?*"

And Jamie laughing down the hallway.

By eleven o'clock she had sewn up the ripped seam in the print dress and put her sewing box away carefully in the closet. With the print dress on, she was sitting by the window drinking another cup of coffee. I could have taken more time over my dressing after all, she thought; but by now it was so late he might come any minute, and she did not dare try to repair anything without starting all over. There was nothing to eat in the apartment except the food she had carefully stocked up for their life beginning together: the unopened package of bacon, the dozen eggs in their box, the unopened bread and the unopened butter; they were for breakfast tomorrow. She thought of running downstairs to the drugstore for something to eat, leaving a note on the door. Then she decided to wait a little longer.

By eleven thirty she was so dizzy and weak that she had to go downstairs. If Jamie had had a phone she would have called him then. Instead, she opened her desk and wrote a note: "Jamie, have gone downstairs to the drugstore. Back in five minutes." Her pen leaked onto her fingers and she went into the bathroom and washed, using a clean towel which she replaced. She tacked the note on the door, surveyed the apartment once more to make sure that everything was perfect, and closed the door without locking it, in case he should come.

In the drugstore she found that there was nothing she wanted to eat except more coffee, and she left it half finished because she suddenly realized that Jamie was probably upstairs waiting and impatient, anxious to get started.

But upstairs everything was prepared and quiet, as she had left it, her note unread on the door, the air in the apartment a little stale from too many cigarettes. She opened the window and sat down next to it until she realized that she had been asleep and it was twenty minutes to one.

Now, suddenly, she was frightened. Waking without preparation into the room of waiting and readiness, everything clean and untouched since ten o'clock, she was frightened, and felt an urgent need to hurry. She got up from the chair and almost ran across the room to the bathroom, dashed cold water on her face, and used a clean towel; this time she put the towel carelessly back on the rack without changing it; time enough for that later. Hatless, still in the print dress with a coat thrown on over it, the wrong blue pocketbook with the aspirin inside in her hand, she locked the apartment door behind her, no note this time, and ran down the stairs. She caught a taxi on the corner and gave the driver Jamie's address.

It was no distance at all; she could have walked it if she had not been so weak, but in the taxi she suddenly realized how imprudent it would be to drive brazenly up to Jamie's door, demanding him. She asked the driver, therefore, to let her off at a corner near Jamie's address and, after paying him, waited till he drove away before she started to walk down the block. She had never been here before; the building was pleasant and old, and Jamie's name was not on any of the mailboxes in the vestibule, nor on the doorbells. She checked the address; it was right, and finally she rang the bell marked SUPERINTENDENT. After a minute or two the door buzzer rang and she opened the door and went into the dark hall where she hesitated until a door at the end opened and someone said, "Yes?"

She knew at the same moment that she had no idea what to ask, so she moved forward toward the figure waiting against the light of the open doorway. When she was very near, the figure said, "Yes?" again and she saw that it was a man in his shirt sleeves, unable to see her any more clearly than she could see him.

With sudden courage she said, "I'm trying to get in touch with someone who lives in this building and I can't find the name outside."

"What's the name you wanted?" the man asked, and she realized that she would have to answer.

"James Harris," she said. "Harris."

The man was silent for a minute and then he said, "Harris." He turned around to the room inside the lighted doorway and said, "Margie, come here a minute."

"What now?" a voice said from inside, and after a wait long enough for someone to get out of a comfortable chair a woman joined him in the doorway, regarding the dark hall. "Lady here," the man said. "Lady looking for a guy name of Harris, lives here. Anyone in the building?"

"No," the woman said. Her voice sounded amused. "No men named Harris here."

"Sorry," the man said. He started to close the door. "You got the wrong house, lady," he said, and added in a lower voice, "or the wrong guy," and he and the woman laughed.

When the door was almost shut and she was alone in the dark hall she said to the thin lighted crack still showing, "But he *does* live here; I know it."

"Look," the woman said, opening the door again a little, "it happens all the time."

"Please don't make any mistake," she said, and her voice was very dignified, with thirty-four years of accumulated pride. "I'm afraid you don't understand."

"What did he look like?" the woman said wearily, the door still only part open.

"He's rather tall, and fair. He wears a blue suit very often. He's a writer."

"No," the woman said, and then, "Could he have lived on the third floor?"

"I'm not sure."

"There was a fellow," the woman said reflectively. "He wore a blue suit a lot, lived on the third floor for a while. The Roysters lent him their apartment while they were visiting her folks upstairs."

"That might be it; I thought, though . . ."

"This one wore a blue suit mostly, but I don't know how tall he was," the woman said. "He stayed there about a month."

"A month ago is when—"

"You ask the Roysters," the woman said. "They come back this morning. Apartment 3B."

The door closed, definitely. The hall was very dark and the stairs looked darker.

On the second floor there was a little light from a skylight far above.

The apartment doors lined up, four on the floor, uncommunicative and silent. There was a bottle of milk outside 2C.

On the third floor, she waited for a minute. There was the sound of music beyond the door of 3B, and she could hear voices. Finally she knocked, and knocked again. The door was opened and the music swept out at her, an early afternoon symphony broadcast. "How do you do," she said politely to this woman in the doorway. "Mrs. Royster?"

"That's right." The woman was wearing a housecoat and last night's makeup.

"I wonder if I might talk to you for a minute?"

"Sure," Mrs. Royster said, not moving.

"About Mr. Harris."

"*What* Mr. Harris?" Mrs. Royster said flatly.

"Mr. James Harris. The gentleman who borrowed your apartment."

"Oh, Lord," Mrs. Royster said. She seemed to open her eyes for the first time. "What'd he do?"

"Nothing. I'm just trying to get in touch with him."

"Oh, Lord," Mrs. Royster said again. Then she opened the door wider and said, "Come in," and then, "Ralph!"

Inside, the apartment was still full of music, and there were suitcases half unpacked on the couch, on the chairs, on the floor. A table in the corner was spread with the remains of a meal, and the young man sitting there, for a minute resembling Jamie, got up and came across the room.

"What about it?" he said.

"Mr. Royster," she said. It was difficult to talk against the music. "The superintendent downstairs told me that this was where Mr. James Harris has been living."

"Sure," he said. "If that was his name."

"I thought you lent him the apartment," she said, surprised.

"I don't know anything about him," Mr. Royster said. "He's one of Dottie's friends."

"Not *my* friends," Mrs. Royster said. "No friend of mine." She had gone over to the table and was spreading peanut butter on a piece of bread. She took a bite and said thickly, waving the bread and peanut butter at her husband. "Not *my* friend."

"You picked him up at one of those damn meetings," Mr. Royster said. He shoved a suitcase off the chair next to the radio and sat down, picking up a magazine from the floor next to him. "I never said more'n ten words to him."

"You said it was okay to lend him the place," Mrs. Royster said before she took another bite. "You never said a word against him, after *all*."

"*I* don't say anything about *your* friends," Mr. Royster said.

"If he'd of been a friend of mine you would have said *plenty*, believe me," Mrs. Royster said darkly. She took another bite and said, "Believe me, he would have said *plenty*."

"That's all I want to hear," Mr. Royster said, over the top of the magazine. "No more, now."

"You see." Mrs. Royster pointed the bread and peanut butter at her husband. "That's the way it is, day and night."

There was silence except for the music bellowing out of the radio next to Mr. Royster, and then she said, in a voice she hardly trusted to be heard over the radio noise, "Has he gone, then?"

"Who?" Mrs. Royster demanded, looking up from the peanut butter jar.

"Mr. James Harris."

"Him? He must've left this morning, before we got back. No sign of him anywhere."

"Gone?"

"Everything was fine, though, perfectly fine. I told you," she said to Mr. Royster, "I told you he'd take care of everything fine. I can always tell."

"You were lucky," Mr. Royster said.

"Not a thing out of place," Mrs. Royster said. She waved her bread and peanut butter inclusively. "Everything just the way we left it," she said.

"Do you know where he is now?"

"Not the slightest idea," Mrs. Royster said cheerfully. "But, like I said, he left everything fine. Why?" she asked suddenly. "You looking for *him?*"

"It's very important."

"I'm sorry he's not here," Mrs. Royster said. She stepped forward politely when she saw her visitor turn toward the door.

"Maybe the super saw him," Mr. Royster said into the magazine.

When the door was closed behind her the hall was dark again, but the sound of the radio was deadened. She was halfway down the first flight of stairs when the door was opened and Mrs. Royster shouted down the stairwell, "If I see him I'll tell him you were looking for him."

What can I do? she thought, out on the street again. It was impossible to go home, not with Jamie somewhere between here and there. She stood on the sidewalk so long that a woman, leaning out of a window across the way, turned and called to someone inside to come and see. Finally, on an impulse, she went into the small delicatessen next door to the apartment house, on the side that led to her own apartment. There was a small man reading a newspaper, leaning against the counter; when she came in he looked up and came down inside the counter to meet her.

Over the glass case of cold meats and cheese she said, timidly, "I'm trying to get in touch with a man who lived in the apartment house next door, and I just wondered if you know him."

"Whyn't you ask the people there?" the man said, his eyes narrow, inspecting her.

It's because I'm not buying anything, she thought, and she said, "I'm sorry. I asked them, but they don't know anything about him. They think he left this morning."

"I don't know what you want *me* to do," he said, moving a little back toward his newspaper. "I'm not here to keep track of guys going in and out next door."

She said quickly, "I thought you might have noticed, that's all. He would have been coming past here, a little before ten o'clock. He was rather tall, and he usually wore a blue suit."

"Now how many men in blue suits go past here every day, lady?" the man demanded. "You think I got nothing to do but—"

"I'm sorry," she said. She heard him say, "For God's sake," as she went out the door.

As she walked toward the corner, she thought, He must have come this way, it's the way he'd go to get to my house, it's the only way for him to walk. She tried to think of Jamie: Where would he have crossed the street? What sort of person was he actually—would he cross in front of his own apartment house, at random in the middle of the block, at the corner?

On the corner was a newsstand; they might have seen him there. She hurried on and waited while a man bought a paper and a woman asked directions. When the newsstand man looked at her she said, "Can you possibly tell me if a rather tall young man in a blue suit went past here this morning around ten o'clock?" When the man only looked at her, his eyes wide and his mouth a little open, she thought, He thinks it's a joke, or a trick, and she said urgently, "It's very important, please believe me. I'm not teasing you."

"*Look*, lady," the man began, and she said eagerly, "He's a writer. He might have bought magazines here."

"What you want him for?" the man asked. He looked at her, smiling, and she realized that there was another man waiting in back of her and the news dealer's smile included him. "Never mind," she said, but the news dealer said, "Listen, maybe he did come by here." His smile was knowing and his eyes shifted over her shoulder to the man in back of her. She was suddenly horribly aware of her overyoung print dress, and pulled her coat around her quickly. The news dealer said, with vast thoughtfulness, "Now I don't know for sure, mind you, but there might have been someone like your gentleman friend coming by this morning."

"About ten?"

"About ten," the news dealer agreed. "Tall fellow, blue suit. I wouldn't be at all surprised."

"Which way did he go?" she said eagerly. "Uptown?"

"Uptown," the news dealer said, nodding. "He went uptown. That's just exactly it. What can I do for you, sir?"

She stepped back, holding her coat around her. The man who had been standing behind her looked at her over his shoulder and then he and the news dealer looked at one another. She wondered for a minute whether or not to tip the news dealer, but when both men began to laugh she moved hurriedly on across the street.

Uptown, she thought, that's right, and she started up the avenue, thinking, He wouldn't have to cross the avenue, just go up six blocks and turn down my street, so long as he started uptown. About a block farther on she passed a florist's shop; there was a wedding display in the window and she thought, This is my wedding day after all, he might have gotten flowers to bring me, and she went inside. The florist came out of the back of the shop, smiling and sleek, and she said, before he could speak, so that he wouldn't have a chance to think she was buying anything, "It's *terribly* important that I get in touch with a gentleman who may have stopped in here to buy flowers this morning. *Terribly* important."

She stopped for breath, and the florist said, "Yes, what sort of flowers were they?"

"I don't know," she said, surprised. "He never—" She stopped and said, "He was a rather tall young man, in a blue suit. It was about ten o'clock."

"I see," the florist said. "Well, *really*, I'm afraid . . ."

"But it's *so* important," she said. "He may have been in a hurry," she added helpfully.

"Well," the florist said. He smiled genially, showing all his small teeth. "For a *lady*," he said. He went to a stand and opened a large book. "Where were they to be sent?" he asked.

"Why," she said, "I don't think he'd have sent them. You see, he was coming—that is, he'd *bring* them."

"Madam," the florist said; he was offended. His smile became deprecatory, and he went on, "Really, you must realize that unless I have *something* to go on . . ."

"*Please* try to remember," she begged. "He was tall, and had a blue suit, and it was about ten this morning."

The florist closed his eyes, one finger to his mouth, and thought deeply. Then he shook his head. "I simply *can't*," he said.

"Thank you," she said despondently, and started for the door, when the florist said, in a shrill, excited voice, "Wait! Wait just a moment, madam." She turned and the florist, thinking again, said finally, "Chrysanthemums?" He looked at her inquiringly.

"Oh, *no*," she said; her voice shook a little and she waited for a minute before she went on. "Not for an occasion like this, I'm sure."

The florist tightened his lips and looked away coldly. "Well, of *course* I don't know the *occasion*," he said, "but I'm almost certain that the gentleman you were inquiring for came in this morning and purchased one dozen chrysanthemums. No delivery."

"You're *sure?*" she asked.

"Positive," the florist said emphatically. "That was absolutely the man." He smiled brilliantly, and she smiled back and said, "Well, thank you very much."

He escorted her to the door. "Nice corsage?" he said, as they went through the shop. "Red roses? Gardenias?"

"It was very kind of you to help me," she said at the door.

"Ladies always look their best in flowers," he said, bending his head toward her. "Orchids, perhaps?"

"No, thank you," she said, and he said, "I hope you find your young man," and gave it a nasty sound.

Going on up the street she thought, Everyone thinks it's so *funny:* and she pulled her coat tighter around her, so that only the ruffle around the bottom of the print dress was showing.

There was a policeman on the corner, and she thought, Why don't I go to the police—you go to the police for a missing person. And then thought, What a fool I'd look like.

She had a quick picture of herself standing in a police station, saying, "Yes, we were going to be married today, but he didn't come," and the policemen, three or four of them standing around listening, looking at her, at the print dress, at her too-bright makeup, smiling at one another. She couldn't tell them any more than that, could not say, "Yes, it looks silly, doesn't it, me all dressed up and trying to find the young man who promised to marry me, but what about all of it you don't know? I have more than this, more than you can see: talent, perhaps, and humor of a sort, and I'm a lady and I have pride and affection and delicacy and a certain clear view of life that might make a man satisfied and productive and happy; there's more than you think when you look at me."

The police were obviously impossible, leaving out Jamie and what he might think when he heard she'd set the police after him. "No, no," she said aloud, hurrying her steps, and someone passing stopped and looked after her.

On the coming corner—she was three blocks from her own street—was a shoeshine stand, an old man sitting almost asleep in one of the chairs. She stopped in front of him and waited, and after a minute he opened his eyes and smiled at her.

"Look," she said, the words coming before she thought of them, "I'm sorry to bother you, but I'm looking for a young man who came up this way about ten this morning, did you see him?" And she began her description, "Tall, blue suit, carrying a bunch of flowers?"

The old man began to nod before she was finished. "I saw him," he said. "Friend of yours?"

"Yes," she said, and smiled back involuntarily.

The old man blinked his eyes and said, "I remember I thought, You're going to see your girl, young fellow. They all go to see their girls," he said, and shook his head tolerantly.

"Which way did he go? Straight on up the avenue?"

"That's right," the old man said. "Got a shine, had his flowers, all dressed up, in an awful hurry. You got a girl, I thought."

"Thank you," she said, fumbling in her pocket for her loose change.

"She sure must of been glad to see him, the way he looked," the old man said.

"Thank you," she said again, and brought her hand empty from her pocket.

For the first time she was really sure he would be waiting for her, and she hurried up the three blocks, the skirt of the print dress swinging under her coat, and turned into her own block. From the corner she could not see her own windows, could not see Jamie looking out, waiting for her, and going down the block she was almost running to get to him. Her key trembled in her fingers at the downstairs door, and as she glanced into the drugstore she thought of her panic, drinking coffee there this morning, and almost laughed. At her own door she could wait no longer, but began to say, "Jamie, I'm here, I was so worried," even before the door was open.

Her own apartment was waiting for her, silent, barren, afternoon shadows lengthening from the window. For a minute she saw only the empty coffee cup, thought, *He has been here waiting*, before she recognized it as her own, left from the morning. She looked all over the room, into the closet, into the bathroom.

"I never saw him," the clerk in the drugstore said. "I know because I would of noticed the flowers. No one like that's been in."

The old man at the shoeshine stand woke up again to see her standing in front of him. "Hello again," he said, and smiled.

"Are you *sure?*" she demanded. "Did he go on up the avenue?"

"I watched him," the old man said, dignified against her tone. "I thought, *There's a young man's got a girl*, and I watched him right into the house."

"What house?" she said remotely.

"Right there," the old man said. He leaned forward to point. "The next block. With his flowers and his shine and going to see his girl. Right into her house."

"Which one?" she said.

"About the middle of the block," the old man said. He looked at her with suspicion, and said, "What you trying to do, anyway?"

She almost ran, without stopping to say "Thank you." Up on the next block she walked quickly, searching the houses from the outside to see if Jamie looked from a window, listening to hear his laughter somewhere inside.

A woman was sitting in front of one of the houses, pushing a baby carriage monotonously back and forth the length of her arm. The baby inside slept, moving back and forth.

The question was fluent, by now. "I'm sorry, but did you see a young man go into one of these houses about ten this morning? He was tall, wearing a blue suit, carrying a bunch of flowers."

A boy about twelve stopped to listen, turning intently from one to the other, occasionally glancing at the baby.

"Listen," the woman said tiredly, "the kid has his bath at ten. Would I see strange men walking around? I ask you."

"Big bunch of flowers?" the boy asked, pulling at her coat. "Big bunch of flowers? I seen him, missus."

She looked down and the boy grinned insolently at her. "Which house did he go in?" she asked wearily.

"You gonna divorce him?" the boy asked insistently.

"That's not nice to ask the lady," the woman rocking the carriage said.

"Listen," the boy said, "I seen him. He went in there." He pointed to the house next door. "I followed him," the boy said. "He give me a quarter." The boy dropped his voice to a growl, and said, " 'This is a big day for me, kid,' he says. Give me a quarter."

She gave him a dollar bill. "Where?" she said.

"Top floor," the boy said. "I followed him till he give me the quarter. Way to the top." He backed up the sidewalk, out of reach, with the dollar bill. "You gonna divorce him?" he asked again.

"Was he carrying flowers?"

"Yeah," the boy said. He began to screech. "You gonna divorce him, missus? You got something on him?" He went careening down the street, howling, "She's got something on the poor guy," and the woman rocking the baby laughed.

The street door of the apartment house was unlocked; there were no bells in the outer vestibule, and no lists of names. The stairs were narrow and dirty; there were two doors on the top floor. The front one was the right one; there was a crumpled florist's paper on the floor outside the door, and a knotted paper ribbon, like a clue, like the final clue in the paper chase.

She knocked, and thought she heard voices inside, and she thought, suddenly, with terror, What shall I say if Jamie is there, if he comes to the door? The voices seemed suddenly still. She knocked again and there was silence, except for something that might have been laughter far away. He could have seen me from the window, she thought, it's the front apartment and that little boy made a dreadful noise. She waited, and knocked again, but there was silence.

Finally she went to the other door on the floor, and knocked. The door swung open beneath her hand and she saw the empty attic room, bare lath on the walls, floorboards unpainted. She stepped just inside, looking around; the room was filled with bags of plaster, piles of old newspapers, a broken trunk. There was a noise which she suddenly realized was a rat, and then she saw it, sitting very close to her, near the wall, its evil face alert, bright eyes watching her. She stumbled in her haste to be out with the door closed, and the skirt of the print dress caught and tore.

She knew there was someone inside the other apartment, because she was sure she could hear low voices and sometimes laughter. She came back many times, every day for the first week. She came on her way to work, in the mornings; in the evenings, on her way to dinner alone, but no matter how often or how firmly she knocked, no one ever came to the door.

THE BLUE HOTEL
STEPHEN CRANE

Stephen Crane

THE PALACE Hotel at Fort Romper was painted a light blue, a shade that is on the legs of a kind of heron, causing the bird to declare its position against any background. The Palace Hotel, then, was always screaming and howling in a way that made the dazzling winter landscape of Nebraska seem only a gray swampish hush. It stood alone on the prairie, and when the snow was falling the town two hundred yards away was not visible. But when the traveler alighted at the railway station he was obliged to pass the Palace Hotel before he could come upon the company of low clapboard houses which composed Fort Romper, and it was not to be thought that any traveler could pass the Palace Hotel without looking at it. Pat Scully, the proprietor, had proved himself a master of strategy when he chose his paints. It is true that on clear days, when the great transcontinental expresses swept through Fort Romper, passengers were overcome at the sight, and the cult that knows the brown reds and the dark greens of the East expressed shame, pity, horror, in a laugh. But to the citizens of this prairie town and to the people who would naturally stop there, Pat Scully had performed a feat.

As if the displayed delights of such a blue hotel were not sufficiently enticing, it was Scully's habit to go every morning and evening to meet the leisurely trains that stopped at Romper and work his seductions upon any man that he might see wavering, gripsack in hand.

One morning, when a snow-crusted engine dragged its long string of freight cars and its one passenger coach to the station, Scully performed the marvel of catching three men. One was a shaky and quick-eyed Swede, with a great shining cheap valise; one was a tall bronzed cowboy, who was on his way to a ranch near the Dakota line; one was a little silent man from the East, who didn't look it, and didn't announce it. Scully practically made them prisoners. He was so merry and kind that each probably felt it would be the height of brutality to try to escape. They trudged off over the creaking board sidewalks in the wake of the eager little Irishman.

At last, Scully, with boisterous hospitality, conducted them through the portals of the blue hotel. The room which they entered was small. It seemed to be merely a temple for an enormous iron stove, which glowed yellow from the heat. Beside the stove Scully's son Johnnie was playing high five with an old farmer. They were quarreling. With a loud flourish of words Scully destroyed the game of cards and bustled his son upstairs with the baggage of the new guests.

Afterward, sitting about the stove, the three travelers listened to Scully's officious clamor at his daughters, who were preparing the midday meal. The old farmer, invincible in his chair near the warmest part of the stove, frequently addressed a commonplace to the strangers. Usually he was answered in short but adequate sentences by either the cowboy or the Easterner. The Swede said nothing. He seemed to be occupied in making furtive estimates of each man in the room.

Later, at dinner, the Swede spoke a little, addressing his conversation entirely to Scully. He volunteered that he had come from New York, where for ten years he had worked as a tailor. These facts seemed to strike Scully as fascinating. The Swede asked about the crops and the price of labor. He seemed barely to listen to Scully's extended replies. His eyes continued to rove from man to man. Finally, with a laugh and a wink, he said that some of these western communities were very dangerous; and after his statement he tilted his head and laughed again, loudly. The others looked at him wondering and in silence.

As the men trooped heavily back into the front room, the two little windows presented views of a turmoiling sea of snow. The huge arms of the wind were making attempts—mighty, circular, futile—to embrace the flakes as they sped. In a hearty voice Scully announced the presence of a blizzard. The guests of the blue hotel, lighting their pipes, assented with grunts of lazy masculine contentment.

Johnnie, son of Scully, challenged the old farmer to another game of high five. The farmer agreed with a contemptuous scoff. They sat close to the humming stove, and squared their knees under a wide board. The cowboy and the Easterner watched the game with interest. The Swede remained near the window, aloof, but with a countenance that showed signs of an inexplicable excitement.

The play was suddenly ended by another quarrel. The old man arose while casting a look of heated scorn at his adversary. He slowly buttoned his coat, and then stalked with fabulous dignity from the room. In the discreet silence of all the other men the Swede laughed. His laughter rang somehow childish. Men by this time had begun to look at him askance, as if they wished to inquire what ailed him.

A new game was formed. The cowboy volunteered to become the partner of Johnnie, and they all then turned to ask the Swede to throw in his lot with the little Easterner. The Swede, learning that high five wore many names, and that he had played it when it was under an alias, accepted the invitation. He strode toward the men nervously, as if he expected to be assaulted. Finally, seated, he gazed from face to face and laughed shrilly. This laugh was so strange that the Easterner looked up quickly, the cowboy sat intent and with his mouth open, and Johnnie paused, holding the cards with still fingers.

Afterward there was a short silence. Then Johnnie said, "Well, let's get at it." They pulled their chairs forward until their knees were bunched under the board, and began to play.

The cowboy was a board whacker. Each time that he held superior cards he whanged them, one by one, with exceeding force, down upon the improvised table. A game with a board whacker in it is sure to become intense. The countenances of the Easterner and the Swede were miserable whenever the cowboy thundered down his aces and kings.

Because of the absorbing play none considered the strange ways of the Swede. Finally, during a lull caused by a new deal, the Swede suddenly addressed Johnnie: "I suppose there have been a good many men killed in this room." The jaws of the others dropped and they looked at him.

"What in hell are you talking about?" said Johnnie.

The Swede laughed again his blatant laugh, full of a kind of false courage and defiance. "Oh, you know what I mean all right," he answered.

"I'm a liar if I do!" Johnnie protested.

The Swede winked at him. It was a wink full of cunning. "Oh, maybe you think I have been to nowheres. Maybe you think I'm a tenderfoot?"

"I don't know nothin' about you," answered Johnnie. "All I got to say is that I don't know what you're driving at. There hain't never been nobody killed in this room."

The cowboy, who had been steadily gazing at the Swede, then spoke: "What's wrong with you, mister?"

Apparently it seemed to the Swede that he was formidably menaced. He sent an appealing glance in the direction of the little Easterner. "They say they don't know what I mean," he remarked mockingly.

The Easterner answered after prolonged and cautious reflection. "I don't understand you," he said impassively.

The Swede had encountered treachery from the only quarter where he had expected sympathy, if not help. "Oh, I see you are all against me. I see—"

The cowboy was in a state of deep stupefaction. "Say," he cried as he tumbled the deck violently down upon the board, "say, what are you gittin' at, hey?"

The Swede sprang up. "I don't want to fight!" he shouted.

The cowboy stretched his long legs indolently and deliberately. His hands were in his pockets. "Well, who the hell thought you did?" he inquired.

The Swede backed rapidly toward a corner of the room. His hands were out protectingly in front of his chest, but he was making an obvious struggle to control his fright. "Gentlemen," he quavered, "I suppose I am going to be killed before I can leave this house!" Through the windows could be seen the snow turning blue in the shadow of dusk.

A door opened and Scully himself entered. He paused in surprise as he noted the tragic attitude of the Swede. Then he said, "What's the matter here?"

The Swede answered him swiftly, "These men are going to kill me."

"Kill you!" ejaculated Scully. "Kill you! What are you talkin'?" He wheeled sternly upon his son. "What is this, Johnnie?"

The lad had grown sullen. "Damned if I know," he answered. "I can't make no sense to it." He began to shuffle the cards, fluttering them together with an angry snap. "He says a good many men have been killed in this room, or something like that. And he says he's goin' to be killed here too. I don't know what ails him. He's crazy, I shouldn't wonder."

"Kill you?" said Scully again to the Swede. "Kill you? Man, you're off your nut."

"Yes, I'm crazy—yes," burst out the Swede. "But I know one thing—" There was a sort of sweat of misery and terror upon his face. "I know I won't get out of here alive."

The cowboy drew a deep breath. "Well, I'm doggoned," he whispered to himself.

Scully faced his son. "You've been troublin' this man!"

Johnnie's voice was loud with its burden of grievance. "Why, good Gawd, I ain't done nothin' to 'im."

The Swede broke in. "Never mind, Mr. Scully; never mind. I will leave this house. I will go away, because"—he accused them dramatically with his glance—"I do not wish to be killed. Yes, of course, I am crazy—yes. But I know one thing! I will go away. I will leave this house."

"You will not go way," said Scully. "You will not go way until I hear the reason of this business. You are under my roof, and I will not allow any peaceable man to be troubled here." He cast a terrible eye upon Johnnie, the cowboy, and the Easterner.

"Never mind, Mr. Scully, I will go away." The Swede moved toward the door which opened upon the stairs, and disappeared. It was evidently his intention to go at once for his baggage.

"Now," said Scully severely, "what does this mean?"

Johnnie and the cowboy cried together, "Why, we didn't do nothin' to 'im!"

Scully began to howl. "But what does it mean?" He stared ferociously at his son. "I have a mind to lather you for this, me boy."

Johnnie swore a deep oath. "Why, this is the wildest loon I ever see.

We didn't do nothin' at all. We were jest sittin' here playin' cards, and he—"

"I think you are tongue-tied," said Scully to his son, the cowboy, and the Easterner; and at the end of this scornful sentence he left the room.

Upstairs the Swede was swiftly fastening the straps of his great valise. His back was toward the door, and, hearing a noise there, he wheeled, uttering a loud cry. Scully's wrinkled visage showed grimly in the light of the small lamp he carried.

"Man! Man!" he exclaimed. "Have you gone daffy?" He placed the light on the table and sat himself on the edge of the bed. "It's a complete muddle. I can't, for the soul of me, think how you ever got this idea into your head." Presently he lifted his eyes and asked, "And did you sure think they were going to kill you?"

The Swede scanned the old man as if he wished to see into his mind. "I did," he said at last.

Scully banged his hand impressively on the footboard of the bed. "Why, man, we're goin' to have a line of ilictric streetcars in this town next spring."

"A line of electric streetcars," repeated the Swede stupidly.

"And," said Scully, "there's a new railroad goin' to be built down from Broken Arm to here. Not to mintion the four churches and the smashin' big brick schoolhouse. Then there's the big factory, too. Why, in two years Romper'll be a met-tro-*pol*-is."

Having finished the preparation of his baggage, the Swede straightened himself. "Mr. Scully," he said with sudden hardihood, "how much do I owe you?"

"You don't owe me anythin'," said the old man angrily. "I'll not take your money. Not after what's been goin' on here." Then a plan seemed to strike him. He picked up his lamp and moved toward the door. "Here," he cried. "Come with me—just across the hall—in my room."

The Swede must have concluded that his hour was come. His jaw dropped and his teeth showed like a dead man's. He ultimately followed Scully, but he had the step of one hung in chains.

In his own chamber, Scully dropped to the floor and thrust his head beneath the bed. The Swede could hear his muffled voice. "I'd keep it under me piller if it wasn't for that boy Johnnie. Then there's the old woman— Where is it now? I never put it twice in the same place. Ah, now come out with you!"

Presently he backed clumsily from under the bed, dragging with him an old coat rolled into a bundle. Kneeling on the floor, he unrolled the coat and extracted a large yellow-brown whiskey bottle. Holding the bottle up to the light to see that nobody had been tampering with it, he thrust it with a generous movement toward the Swede.

The weak-kneed Swede was about to eagerly clutch this element of strength, but he suddenly jerked his hand away and cast a look of horror upon Scully.

"Drink," said the old man affectionately. He had risen to his feet, and now stood facing the Swede.

The Swede laughed wildly. He grabbed the bottle, put it to his mouth; and as his lips curled absurdly around the opening and his throat worked, he kept his glance, burning with hatred, upon the old man's face.

Downstairs, after the departure of Scully, the three men preserved for a long time an astounded silence. Then Johnnie said, "That's the doddangedest Swede I ever see."

"Well, what do you think makes him act that way?" asked the cowboy.

"Why, he's frightened." The Easterner knocked his pipe against a rim of the stove. "He's clear frightened out of his boots."

"What at?" cried Johnnie and the cowboy together.

"Oh, I don't know, but it seems to me this man has been reading dime novels, and he thinks he's right out in the middle of it—the shootin' and stabbin' and all."

"But," said the cowboy, deeply scandalized, "this ain't Wyoming, ner none of them places. This is Nebrasker."

The traveled Easterner laughed. "It isn't different in Wyoming even—not in these days. But he thinks he's right in the middle of hell."

Johnnie and the cowboy mused long.

"It's awful funny," remarked Johnnie at last. "I wish Pop would throw him out."

Presently they heard a loud stamping on the stairs, and laughter, evidently from the Swede. The door flew open and old Scully came into the room. He was jabbering at the Swede, who followed him, laughing bravely. It was the entry of two roisterers from a banquet hall.

"Come now," said Scully sharply to the three seated men, "move up and give us a chance at the stove." The cowboy and the Easterner obediently sidled their chairs to make room for the newcomers. Johnnie, however, simply arranged himself in a more indolent attitude, and then remained motionless.

"Come! Git over there," said Scully.

"Plenty of room on the other side of the stove," said Johnnie.

"Do you think we want to sit in the draft?" roared the father.

But the Swede here interposed with a grandeur of confidence. "No, no. Let the boy sit where he likes," he cried in a bullying voice to the father.

"All right! All right!" said Scully deferentially. The cowboy and the Easterner exchanged glances of wonder.

The five chairs were formed in a crescent about one side of the stove. The Swede began to talk; he talked arrogantly, profanely, angrily. Johnnie, the cowboy, and the Easterner maintained a morose silence, while old Scully appeared to be receptive and eager, breaking in constantly with sympathetic ejaculations.

Finally the Swede announced that he was thirsty. He moved in his chair, and said that he would go for a drink of water.

"I'll git it for you," cried Scully at once.

"No," said the Swede contemptuously. "I'll get it for myself." He arose and stalked with the air of an owner off into the executive parts of the hotel.

As soon as the Swede was out of hearing Scully sprang to his feet and whispered to the others, "Upstairs he thought I was tryin' to poison 'im."

"Say," said Johnnie, "this makes me sick. Why don't you throw 'im out in the snow?"

"Why, he's all right now," declared Scully. "It was only that he was from the East, and he thought this was a tough place."

The cowboy looked with admiration upon the Easterner. "You were straight," he said. "You were on to that there Swede."

"Well," said Johnnie to his father, "he may be all right now, but I don't see it. Other time he was scared, but now he's too fresh."

"What do I keep?" demanded Scully in a voice of thunder. "I keep a hotel. A hotel, do you mind? A guest under my roof has sacred privileges. Not one word shall he hear that would prejudice him in favor of goin' away. I'll not have it." He wheeled suddenly upon the cowboy and the Easterner. "Am I right?"

"Yes, Mr. Scully," said the cowboy, "I think you're right."

"Yes, Mr. Scully," said the Easterner, "I think you're right."

AT SIX-O'CLOCK supper, the Swede fizzed like a fire wheel. He sometimes seemed on the point of bursting into riotous song, and in all his madness he was encouraged by old Scully. The Easterner was encased in reserve; the cowboy sat in widemouthed amazement, forgetting to eat, while Johnnie wrathily demolished great plates of food. The daughters of the house, when they were obliged to replenish the biscuits, approached as warily as Indians, and fled with ill-concealed trepidation. The Swede gave the whole feast the appearance of a cruel bacchanal. He gazed, brutally disdainful, into every face. His voice rang through the room. Once when he jabbed out harpoon-fashion with his fork to pinion a biscuit, the weapon nearly impaled the hand of the Easterner.

After supper, as the men filed toward the other room, the Swede smote Scully ruthlessly on the shoulder. "Well, old boy, that was a good, square meal." Johnnie looked hopefully at his father; he knew that shoulder was tender from an old fall; and, indeed, it appeared for a moment as if Scully was going to flame out over the matter, but in the end he smiled a sickly smile and remained silent.

Johnnie addressed his parent in an aside. "Why don't you license somebody to kick you downstairs?" Scully scowled darkly by way of reply.

When they were gathered about the stove, the Swede insisted on another game of high five. Scully gently deprecated the plan at first, but the Swede turned a wolfish glare upon him. He canvassed the others. In his tone there was always a great threat. The cowboy and the Easterner both remarked indifferently that they would play. Scully said that he would presently have to go to meet the 6:58 train, and so the Swede turned menacingly upon Johnnie. For a moment their glances crossed like blades, and then Johnnie smiled and said, "Yes, I'll play."

They formed a square, with the little board on their knees. The Easterner and the Swede were again partners. As the play went on, it was noticeable that the cowboy was not board whacking as usual. Scully went out to meet the train, and a gust of polar wind whirled into the room as he opened the door, scattering the cards. The Swede cursed frightfully. When Scully returned, his entrance disturbed a cozy and friendly scene. The Swede again cursed. But presently the players were once more intent, their heads bent forward and their hands moving swiftly. The Swede had adopted the cowboy's fashion of board whacking.

Scully took up his paper and for a long time remained immersed in matters which were extraordinarily remote from him. The lamp burned badly, and once he stopped to adjust the wick. Then suddenly he heard three terrible words: "You are cheatin'!"

The little room was now hideous. The new faces of the men themselves had changed it upon the instant. The Swede held a huge fist in front of Johnnie's face, while the latter looked steadily over it into the blazing orbs of his accuser. The Easterner had grown pallid; the cowboy's jaw had dropped. Scully stared at the cardplayers. Probably a second elapsed. Then the five men projected themselves headlong toward a common point.

It happened that Johnnie, in rising to hurl himself upon the Swede, had stumbled slightly. The loss of the moment allowed time for the arrival of Scully, and also allowed the cowboy time to give the Swede a great push which sent him staggering back. Hoarse shouts of rage, appeal, or fear burst from every throat. Through the smoky air, above the swaying bodies, the eyes of the two warriors sought each other in glances of challenge that were at once hot and steely.

The board had been overturned, and now the whole company of cards was scattered over the floor, where the boots of the men trampled the fat and painted kings and queens as they gazed with their silly eyes at the war that was waging above them.

Scully's voice was dominating the yells. "Stop now! Stop, I say! Stop, now—"

Johnnie, as he struggled to burst through the rank formed by Scully and the Easterner, was crying, "He says I cheated! I won't allow no man to say I cheated! If he says I cheated, he's a—"

The cowboy was telling the Swede, "Quit, now! Quit, d'ye hear—"

The screams of the Swede never ceased: "He did cheat! I saw him! I saw him—"

As for the Easterner, he was importuning, "Wait a moment, can't you? What's the good of a fight over a game of cards? Wait a moment—"

Then suddenly there was a great cessation. It was as if each man had paused for breath; and although the room was still lighted with anger, it could be seen that there was no danger of immediate conflict, and at once Johnnie, shouldering his way forward, almost succeeded in confronting the Swede. "What did you say I cheated for? I don't cheat, and I won't let no man say I do!"

The Swede said, "I saw you! I saw you!"

"Ah, be still, can't you?" said Scully, coming between them.

Johnnie, his red face appearing above his father's shoulder, hailed the Swede again. "Did you say I cheated?"

The Swede showed his teeth. "Yes."

"Then," said Johnnie, "we must fight."

"Yes, fight!" roared the Swede. "I'll show you what kind of a man I am! Maybe you think I can't fight! I'll show you, you cardsharp! Yes, you cheated! You cheated! You cheated!"

"Well, let's go at it, then, mister," said Johnnie coolly.

The cowboy turned in despair to Scully. "What are you goin' to do now?"

A change had come over the Celtic visage of the old man. He now seemed all eagerness; his eyes glowed.

"We'll let them fight," he answered stalwartly. "I can't put up with it any longer. I've stood this damned Swede till I'm sick. We'll let them fight."

Without words, the men prepared to go outside. Scully threw open the door. "Well, come on," he said. Instantly a terrific wind caused the flame of the lamp to struggle at its wick. The men lowered their heads and plunged into the tempest as into a sea. No snow was falling now, but great whirls and clouds of flakes, swept up from the ground by the frantic winds, were streaming southward with the speed of bullets. The covered land was blue with the sheen of an unearthly satin, and there was no other hue save where, at the low, black railway station—which seemed incredibly distant—one light gleamed like a tiny jewel.

Immediately turning their backs upon the wind, the men had swung around a corner to the sheltered side of the hotel. When the party reached the comparative peace of this spot, the Swede began bellowing.

"Oh, I know what kind of a thing this is! I know you'll all pitch on me. I can't lick you all!"

Scully turned upon him panther-fashion. "You'll not have to whip all of us. You'll have to whip my son Johnnie. An' the man what troubles you durin' that time will have me to deal with."

The arrangements were swiftly made. The two men faced each other, obedient to the harsh commands of Scully. They had not stripped off any clothing. Their fists were up, and they eyed each other in a calm that had the elements of leonine cruelty in it.

"Now!" said Scully.

The two combatants leaped forward and crashed together like bullocks. There was heard the cushioned sound of blows, and of a curse squeezing out from between the tight teeth of one. As for the spectators, the Easterner's pent-up breath exploded from him with a pop of relief, absolute relief from the tension of the preliminaries. The cowboy bounded into the air with a yowl. Scully was immovable as from supreme amazement and fear at the fury of the fight which he himself had permitted and arranged.

For a time the encounter in the darkness presented no more detail than would a swiftly revolving wheel. Occasionally a face, as if illumined by a flash of light, would shine out. A moment later the men might have been known as shadows, if it were not for the involuntary utterance of oaths that came from them in whispers.

Suddenly a holocaust of warlike desire caught the cowboy, and he bolted forward. "Go it, Johnnie! Go it! Kill him! Kill him!"

To the Easterner it was a monotony of unchangeable fighting that was an abomination, seeming eternal to his sense, which was concentrated in a longing for the end, the priceless end. Once the fighters lurched near him, and as he scrambled hastily backward he heard them breathe like men on the rack.

"Kill him, Johnnie! Kill him! Kill him! Kill him!"

"Keep still," said Scully to the cowboy icily.

Then there was a sudden loud grunt, incomplete, cut short, and Johnnie's body swung away from the Swede and fell with sickening heaviness to the grass. The cowboy was barely in time to prevent the mad Swede from flinging himself upon his prone adversary. "No, you don't," said the cowboy, interposing an arm. "Wait a second."

Scully was at his son's side. "Johnnie! Johnnie, me boy!" His voice had a quality of melancholy tenderness. "Johnnie! Can you go on with it?" He looked anxiously down into the bloody, pulpy face of his son.

There was a moment of silence, and then Johnnie answered in his ordinary voice, "Yes, I—it—yes."

Assisted by his father he struggled to his feet. "Wait a bit now till you git your wind," said the old man.

A few paces away the cowboy was lecturing the Swede. "No, you don't! Wait a second!"

The Easterner was plucking at Scully's sleeve. "Oh, this is enough," he pleaded. "Let it go as it stands. This is enough!"

"Bill," said Scully, "git out of the road." The cowboy stepped aside. "Now." The combatants were actuated by a new caution as they advanced toward collision. They glared at each other, and then the Swede aimed a lightning blow that carried with it his entire weight. Johnnie was evidently half stupid from weakness, but he miraculously dodged, and his fist sent the overbalanced Swede sprawling.

The cowboy, Scully, and the Easterner burst into a cheer, but before its conclusion the Swede had scuffled agilely to his feet and come in berserk abandon at his foe. Johnnie's body again swung away and fell, even as a bundle might fall from a roof. The Swede instantly staggered to a little wind-waved tree and leaned upon it, breathing like an engine, while his savage eyes roamed from face to face as the men bent over Johnnie. There was a splendor of isolation in his situation at this time which the Easterner felt once when, lifting his eyes from the man on the ground, he beheld that mysterious and lonely figure, waiting.

"Are you any good yet, Johnnie?" asked Scully in a broken voice.

The son gasped and opened his eyes languidly. After a moment he answered, "No—I ain't—any good—any—more." Then, from shame and bodily ill, he began to weep, the tears furrowing down through the bloodstains on his face. "He was too—too—too heavy for me."

Scully straightened and addressed the waiting figure. "Stranger," he said evenly, "it's all up with our side." Then his voice changed into that vibrant huskiness which is commonly the tone of the most simple and deadly announcements. "Johnnie is whipped."

Without replying, the victor moved off on the route to the front door of the hotel.

"Johnnie, can you walk?" asked Scully.

"Did I hurt—hurt him any?" asked the son. His voice was suddenly strong. There was a robust impatience in it.

"Yes, yes, Johnnie," answered the cowboy consolingly; "he's hurt a good deal."

They raised him from the ground, and as soon as he was on his feet he went tottering off, rebuffing all attempts at assistance. When the party rounded the corner they were fairly blinded by the pelting of the snow. It burned their faces like fire. The cowboy carried Johnnie through the drift to the door. As they entered, some cards rose from the floor and beat against the wall.

The Easterner rushed to the stove. The Swede was not in the room. Johnnie sank into a chair and, folding his arms on his knees, buried his face in them. Scully, warming one foot and then the other at a rim of the stove, muttered to himself with Celtic mournfulness. The cowboy had removed his fur cap, and with a dazed and rueful air he was running one hand through his tousled locks. From overhead they could hear the creaking of boards as the Swede tramped here and there in his room.

The sad quiet was broken by the sudden flinging open of a door that led toward the kitchen. It was instantly followed by an inrush of women. They precipitated themselves upon Johnnie amid a chorus of lamentation. Before they carried their prey off to the kitchen, there to be bathed and harangued with a mixture of sympathy and abuse, the mother straightened herself and fixed old Scully with an eye of stern reproach. "Shame be upon you, Patrick Scully!" she cried. "Your own son, too. Shame be upon you!"

"There, now! Be quiet, now!" said the old man weakly.

The girls sniffed disdainfully in the direction of those trembling accomplices, the cowboy and the Easterner. Presently they bore Johnnie away, and left the three men to dismal reflection.

"I'd like to fight this here Swede myself," said the cowboy, breaking the long silence.

"No," answered Scully, with mournful heroism. "It wouldn't be right. It was Johnnie's fight, and now we mustn't whip the man just because he whipped Johnnie."

"Yes, that's true enough," said the cowboy; "but—he better not get fresh with me, because I couldn't stand no more of it."

"You'll not say a word to him," commanded Scully, and even then they heard the tread of the Swede on the stairs. He swept the door back with a bang and swaggered to the middle of the room, dressed for departure, with his valise in his hand.

"Well," he cried insolently at Scully, "I s'pose you'll tell me now how much I owe you?"

The old man remained stolid. "You don't owe me nothin'."

"Huh!" said the Swede. "Huh! Don't owe 'im nothin'."

The cowboy addressed the Swede. "Stranger, I don't see how you come to be so gay around here."

Old Scully was instantly alert. "Stop!" he shouted, holding his hand forth, fingers upward. "Bill, you shut up!"

"Huh!" said the Swede. "I guess you're right. I guess if it was any way at all, you'd owe me somethin'." He turned to the cowboy. "Kill him! Kill him!" he mimicked, and then guffawed victoriously.

But he might have been jeering the dead. The three men were immovable and silent, staring with glassy eyes at the stove.

The Swede opened the door and passed into the storm, giving one derisive glance backward at the still group.

As soon as the door was closed, Scully and the cowboy leaped to their feet and began to curse. They trampled to and fro, waving their arms and smashing into the air with their fists. "Oh, but that was a hard minute!" wailed Scully. "Him there leerin' and scoffin'! One bang at his nose was worth forty dollars to me that minute! How did you stand it, Bill?"

The cowboy groaned. "I'd like to git him by the neck and ha-ammer him"—he brought his hand down on a chair with a noise like a pistol shot—"hammer him until he couldn't tell himself from a dead coyote!"

"I'd beat 'im until he—"

"I'd show *him* some things—"

And then together they raised a yearning, fanatic cry—"Oh-o-oh! If we only could—"

THE SWEDE, tightly gripping his valise, tacked across the face of the storm. He was following a line of little naked, gasping trees which, he knew, must mark the way of the road. His face, fresh from the pounding of Johnnie's fists, felt more pleasure than pain in the wind and the driving snow. A number of square shapes loomed upon him finally, and he knew them as the houses of the main body of the town. Here, with the bugles of the tempest pealing, it was hard to imagine a peopled earth. However, the Swede found a saloon.

In front of it an indomitable red light was burning, and the snowflakes were made blood color as they flew through the lamp's shining. The Swede pushed open the door of the saloon and entered. A sanded expanse was before him, and at the end of it four men sat about a table drinking. Down one side of the room extended a radiant bar, and its guardian was leaning upon his elbows listening to the talk of the men at the table.

The Swede dropped his valise upon the floor and, smiling fraternally upon the barkeeper, said, "Gimme some whiskey, will you?" The man placed a bottle, a whiskey glass, and a glass of water upon the bar. The Swede poured himself an abnormal portion of whiskey and drank it in three gulps.

"Pretty bad night," remarked the bartender indifferently, but furtively studying the half-erased bloodstains on the face of the Swede. "Bad night," he said again.

"Oh, it's good enough for me," replied the Swede hardily as he poured himself some more whiskey. The barkeeper took his coin and maneuvered it through the highly nickeled cash machine.

The copious drams made the Swede's eyes swim, and he breathed a trifle heavier. "Yes, I like this weather. It suits me." It was apparently his design to impart a deep significance to these words.

"So?" murmured the bartender languidly.

"Well, I guess I'll take another drink," said the Swede presently. "Have something?"

"No, thanks. I'm not drinkin'," answered the bartender. Afterward he asked, "How did you hurt your face?"

The Swede immediately began to boast loudly. "Why, in a fight. I thumped the soul out of a man down here at Scully's hotel."

The interest of the four men at the table was at last aroused.

"Who was it?" said one.

"Johnnie Scully," blustered the Swede. "Son of the man what runs it. He will be pretty near dead for some weeks, I can tell you. I made a nice thing of him, I did. He couldn't get up. They carried him in the house. Have a drink?"

Instantly the men in some subtle way encased themselves in reserve. "No, thanks," said one. The group was of curious formation. Two were prominent local businessmen; one was the district attorney; and one was a professional gambler of the kind known as "square." But a scrutiny of the group would not have enabled an observer to pick the gambler from the men of more reputable pursuits. He was, in fact, a man so delicate in manner, when among people of fair class, and so judicious in his choice of victims, that in the strictly masculine part of the town's life he had come to be explicitly trusted and admired. People called him a thoroughbred.

The Swede continued to drink raw whiskey, meanwhile babbling at the barkeeper. "Come on. Have a drink. What—no? By Gawd, I've whipped a man tonight, and I want to celebrate. Gentlemen," the Swede cried to the men at the table, "have a drink?"

"Ssh!" said the barkeeper.

The group at the table had been pretending to be deep in talk, but now a man lifted his eyes toward the Swede and said shortly, "Thanks. We don't want any more."

At this reply the Swede ruffled out his chest like a rooster. "Well," he exploded, "it seems I can't get anybody to drink with me in this town. Seems so, don't it? Well!"

"Ssh!" said the barkeeper.

"Say," snarled the Swede, "don't you try to shut me up. I won't have it. I'm a gentleman, and I want people to drink with me. And I want 'em to drink with me now. *Now*—do you understand?" He rapped the bar with his knuckles.

Years of experience had calloused the bartender. He merely grew sulky. "I hear you," he answered.

"Well," cried the Swede, "listen hard then. See those men over there? Well, they're going to drink with me, and don't you forget it. Now you watch." He stalked over to the table, and by chance laid his hand upon the shoulder of the gambler. "How about this?" he asked wrathfully. "I asked you to drink with me."

The gambler simply twisted his head and spoke over his shoulder. "My friend, I don't know you."

"Oh, hell!" answered the Swede. "Come and have a drink."

"Now, my boy," advised the gambler kindly, "take your hand off my shoulder and go way and mind your own business." He was a little, slim man, and it seemed strange to hear him use this tone of heroic patronage to the burly Swede. The other men at the table said nothing.

"What! You won't drink with me, you little dude? I'll make you, then! I'll make you!"

The Swede grasped the gambler frenziedly at the throat, and was dragging him from his chair. The other men sprang up. The barkeeper dashed around the corner of his bar. There was a great tumult, and then was seen a long blade in the hand of the gambler. It shot forward, and a human body was pierced as easily as if it had been a melon. The Swede fell with a cry of supreme astonishment.

The prominent merchants and the district attorney must have at once tumbled out of the place backward. The bartender found himself hanging limply to the arm of a chair and gazing into the eyes of a murderer.

"Henry," said the gambler as he wiped his knife on one of the towels that hung beneath the bar rail, "you tell 'em where to find me. I'll be home, waiting for 'em." Then he vanished. A moment afterward the barkeeper was in the street dinning through the storm for help and, moreover, companionship.

The corpse of the Swede, alone in the saloon, had its eyes fixed upon a dreadful legend that dwelt atop the cash machine: "This registers the amount of your purchase."

MONTHS LATER, the cowboy was frying pork over the stove of a little ranch near the Dakota line, when there was a quick thud of hoofs outside, and presently the Easterner entered with the letters and the papers.

"Well," said the Easterner at once, "the chap that killed the Swede has got three years. Wasn't much, was it?"

"He has?" The cowboy poised his pan of pork while he ruminated upon the news. "Three years. That ain't much."

"No. It was a light sentence," replied the Easterner as he unbuckled his spurs. "Seems there was a good deal of sympathy for him in Romper."

"If the bartender had been any good," observed the cowboy thoughtfully, "he would have gone in and cracked that there Swede on the head with a bottle in the beginnin' of it."

"Yes, a thousand things might have happened," said the Easterner tartly.

The cowboy returned his pan of pork to the fire, but his philosophy continued. "It's funny, ain't it? If that Swede hadn't said Johnnie was cheatin' he'd be alive this minute. He was an awful fool. Game played for fun, too. Not for money. I believe he was crazy."

"I feel sorry for that gambler," said the Easterner.

"Oh, so do I," said the cowboy. "He don't deserve none of it for killin' who he did."

"The Swede might not have been killed if everything had been square."

"Might not have been killed?" exclaimed the cowboy. "Everythin' square? Why, when he said that Johnnie was cheatin' and acted like such a jackass? And then in the saloon he fairly walked up to git hurt?" With these arguments the cowboy reduced the Easterner to rage.

"You're a fool!" cried the Easterner viciously. "You're a bigger jackass than the Swede by a million majority. Now let me tell you one thing. Listen! Johnnie *was* cheating!"

"Johnnie," said the cowboy blankly. There was a minute of silence, and then he said robustly, "Why, no. The game was only for fun."

"Fun or not," said the Easterner, "Johnnie was cheating. I saw him. And I refused to stand up and be a man. I let the Swede fight it out alone. And you—you were simply puffing around the place and wanting to fight. And then old Scully himself! We are all in it! Every sin is the result of a collaboration. We have collaborated in the murder of this Swede. Usually there are from a dozen to forty women really involved in every murder, but in this case it seems to be only five men—you, I, Johnnie, old Scully; and that fool of an unfortunate gambler came merely as a culmination, the apex of a human movement, and gets all the punishment."

The cowboy, injured and rebellious, cried out blindly into this fog of mysterious theory, "Well, I didn't do anythin', did I?"

YOU'LL NEVER KNOW, DEAR,
HOW MUCH I LOVE YOU

JOHN UPDIKE

CARNIVAL! IN the vacant lot beyond the old ice plant! Trucks have been unloading all afternoon; the Whirlo-Gig has been unfolded like a giant umbrella, they assembled the baby Ferris wheel with an Erector Set. Twice the trucks got stuck in the mud. Straw has been strewn everywhere. They put up a stage and strung lights. Now, now, gather your pennies; supper is over and an hour of light is left in the long summer day. See, Sammy Hunnenhauser is running; Gloria Gring and her gang have been there all afternoon, they never go home, oh hurry, let me go; how awful it is to have parents that are poor, and slow, and sad!

Fifty cents. The most Ben could beg. A nickel for every year of his life. It feels like plenty. Over the roof of crazy Mrs. Moffert's house, the Ferris wheel tints the air with pink, and the rim of this pink mixes in excitement with the great notched rim of the coin sweating in his hand. This house, then this house, and past the ice plant, and he will be there. Already the rest of the world is there, he is the last, hurrying, hurrying, the balloon is about to take off, the Ferris wheel is lifting; only he will be left behind, on empty darkening streets.

Then there, what to buy? There are not so many people here. Grown-ups carrying babies mosey glassily on the straw walks. All the booth people, not really Gypsies, stare at him, and beckon weakly. It hurts him to ignore the man with the three old softballs, and the old cripple at the merry-go-round, and the fat lady with her plaster Marys, and the skeleton suspended behind a fountain of popcorn. He feels his walking past them as pain. He wishes there were more people here; he feels a fool. All of this machinery assembled to extract from him his pathetic fifty cents.

He watches at a distance a thickset man in earnestly rolled-up shirt sleeves twirl a great tinseled wheel with a rubber tongue that patters slower and slower on a circle of nails until it stops between two, and the number there wins. Only a sailor and two boys in yellow silk high-school athletic jackets play. None win. The thick tattooed arm below the rolled-up shirt sleeve carefully sweeps their nickels from a long board divided and numbered as if for hopscotch. The high-school boys, with sideburns and spotty whiskers on their bright pink jaws, put down nickels again leadenly, and this time the man spinning the wheel shouts when it stops, seems more joyful than they, and reaches into his deep apron pocket and pours before them, without counting, a perfect little slipping stack of nickels. Their gums showing as if at a dirty joke, the two boys turn—the shimmer on their backs darts and shifts in cool *z*'s—and walk away, while the man is shouting, "Hey, uh winneh. Hey, uh winneh, evvybody wins." His table is bare, and as his mouth continues to form the loud words his eyes lock Ben into a stare of heartbreaking brown blankness that seems to elucidate with paralyzing clarity Ben's state: his dungarees, his fifty cents, his ten years, his position in space, and above the particulars the immense tinted pity, the waste, of being at one little place instead of everywhere, at any time. Then the man looks away, and twirls the wheel for his own amusement.

The fifty-cent piece feels huge to Ben's fingers, a wide oppressive rigidity that must be broken, shattered into twinkling fragments, to merge in the tinsel and splinters of strewn straw. He buys, at the first stand he strikes, a cone of cotton candy, and receives, with the furry pink pasty uncoiling thing, a quarter, a dime, and a nickel: three coins, tripling his wealth.

Now people multiply, crowd in from the houses of the town, that stand beyond the lot on all sides in black forbidding silhouettes like the teeth of a saw. The lights go on; the faces of the houses flee. There is nothing in the lot but light, and at its core, on the stage, three girls wearing white cowboy hats and white spangled skirts and white boots appear, and a man also in white and bearing a white guitar strung with gold. The legs around Ben crush him toward the stage; the smell of mud mingles with the bright sight there. One of the girls coughs into the microphone and twists its neck, so a sharp whine pierces from the loudspeakers and cuts a great crescent through the crowd, leaving silence as harvest. The girls sing, toe-tapping gingerly, "The other *night*, dear, as I lay *sleep*ing, I dreamed I *held* you in my *arms*." The spangles on their swishing skirts spring prickles like tears in Ben's eyes. The three voices sob, catch, twang, distend his heart like a rubber band at the highest pitch of their plaint. "—I was mis*tak*en and I *hung* my *head* and *cried*." And then the unbearable rising sugar of the chorus that makes his scalp so tight he fears his head will burst from sweet fullness.

The girls go on to sing other songs, less good, and then they give way to a thin old man in suspenders and huge pants he keeps snapping and looking down and whooping into. He tells horrible jokes that make the nice fat ladies standing around Ben—nice fat factory and dust-mop women that made him feel protected—shake with laughter. He fears their quaking, feels threatened from beneath, as if there is a treacherous stratum under this mud and straw. He wanders away, to let the words of "You Are My Sunshine" revolve in his head. "Please don't *take* my *sun*shine *away*." Only the money in his pocket weights him; get rid of it, and he will sail away like a dandelion seed.

He goes to the booth where the wheel is turning, and puts his nickel on the board in a square marked 7, and loses it.

He puts the dime there and it too is taken away.

Squeezed, almost hidden, between the crusty trousered haunches of two adults, he puts down his quarter, as they do, on the inner edge, to be changed. The tattooed man comes along picking up the quarters and pouring, with his wonderfully automatic fingers, the little slipping stacks of five nickels; Ben holds his breath, and to his horror feels his low face catch in the corner of the man's absentminded eyes. The thick solemn body snags in its smooth progress, and Ben's five nickels are raggedly spaced. Between the second and third there is a gap. A blush cakes Ben's cheeks; his gray-knuckled fingers, as they push out a nickel, are trembling sideways at each other. But the man goes back, and spins the wheel, and Ben loses three nickels one after another. The twittering wheel is a moonfaced god; but Ben feels humanity clouding the space between them, that should be unobstructed.

When the tattooed arm—a blue fish, an anchor, the queer word PEACE—comes to sweep in his nickels, he feels the stippled skin breathing thought, and lowers his head against the expected fall of words. Nothing is said, the man moves on, returns to the wheel; but Ben feels puzzled pressure radiating from him, and the pointed eyes of a man in a suit with chalk stripes, who has come to stand at the far side of the stand, intersect this expanding circle, and Ben, hurrying to pour his money down a narrowing crack, puts down his last two nickels, still on 7.

The rubber tongue leaps into pattering and as the wheel whirls the tattooed man leans backward to hear the one in chalk stripes talk; his tongue patterns silently but a tiny motion of his polished hand, simultaneous with a sideways stab of his eyes, is toward Ben.

The rubber tongue slows, flops, stops at 7—no, 8. He lost, and can leave. The floor of his stomach lifts queerly. "Hey kid." The man with stenciled arms comes over. Ben feels that no matter how fast he would run, those arms would stretch and snare him.

"Huh?"

"How old are you, kid?"

"Ten."

"Whatsamatta with ya, ya daddy rich?"

A titter moves stiffly through the immense adult heads all around. Ben understands the familiar role, that he has undergone a hundred times with teachers and older boys, of being a comic prop. He understands everything, and wants to explain that he knows his eyes are moist and his cheeks red but that it's because of joy, freedom, not because of losing. But this would be too many words; even the one-word answer "No" sticks to the roof of his mouth and comes loose with a faint tearing noise.

"Here." With his exciting expert touch, the man flicks Ben's two coins back across the painted number. Then he digs into his pocket. He comes up with the usual little stack of five, drops four, but holds the fifth delicately between the tips of two fingers and a thumb, hesitates so that Ben can reread PEACE in blue above his wrist, and then flips the fifth nickel up into his palm and thence down with a plunge into his dirty sagging apron pouch.

"Now move away from the board, kid, move away. Don't come back."

Ben fumbles the coins into his hands and pushes away, his eyes screwed to the sharp edge of painted wood, and shoulders blindly backward through the legs. Yet all the time, in the midst of the heat and water welling up from springs all over his body, he is figuring, and calculates he's been gypped. Forty: he had the quarter and dime and nickel and they gave him back only six nickels: thirty. The injustice, they pretend he's too little to lose and then keep a dime; the waste. The lost dime seems a tiny hole through which everything in existence is draining. As he moves away, his wet knees jarring, trying to hide forever from every sailor and fat woman and high schooler who witnessed his disgrace, the six nickels make a knobbed weight bumping his thigh through his pocket. The spangles, the splinters of straw and strings of light, the sawtooth peaks of houses showing behind the scattered white heads scented sweetly with mud, are hung like the needles of a Christmas tree with the transparent, tinted globes confusing his eyelashes.

Thus the world, like a bitter coquette, spurns our attempts to give ourselves to her wholly.

THE BEAUTY

PEARL S. BUCK

Pearl S. Buck

M RS. OMURA glanced at the kitchen clock. The hour was five, but the winter darkness had already fallen upon the city of Tokyo. The children would be home now at any moment, and let it be hoped that Setsu's feet were not wet. Though she was twelve and should know better, she was always in a dream, the way girls were nowadays. In the old days it could not happen that a child left school without her shoes, for she would have taken them off at the door and could not step outside until she had slipped her feet into geta. Now that schools were Western in their habits the children wore their shoes indoors and outdoors. There were no distinctions anywhere.

Her son's voice shouted at this moment from the garden gate. "Mama-san!"

"Here I am, Toru!"

He ran in, kicking off his shoes at the door. At least the house was still Japanese. She did not allow shoes in here. She went to the faucet and wet a clean towel in the gush of hot water.

"Come here, Toru."

He stood before her, books hanging in a strap from his right hand while she wiped his face thoroughly with the warm cloth.

"Now your hands. How dirty you are!"

"It's the chalk. Is Father here?"

He asked the same question every day until it had become a dagger in her heart. The boy was growing up and wanted his father.

"You know your father is very busy. He cannot come home just because you are here."

"Where does he go?"

"I have told you."

"The bar. That is where he goes."

"Put away your books. We will eat our supper as soon as Setsu comes."

He went out and she heard him in the next room behind the sliding paper-covered shoji. He was a good child, quiet for his ten years, and too thoughtful. She must speak to her husband tonight.

"Good evening, Mother."

It was Setsu. The tall slender young girl had come silently into the kitchen, her shoes off, and her hair brushed neatly behind her ears.

"You are late, Setsu."

"The traffic was bad. Our bus stopped again and again."

"Worse than usual?"

She asked the question as carelessly as she could, but she glanced sharply at the pretty girl who was her only daughter. Twelve was still to be a child, but Setsu was maturing early. All the girls grew up too soon in this new Tokyo. They went out freely, they saw Western films, they imitated American young people. Thus far, however, she had been able to refuse to allow Setsu to go to the rock-and-roll theater. She had gone there herself one day, when Setsu had first begged to go.

"All the girls go," Setsu had pouted.

"I will go," she had said. "I will see."

What she had seen had frightened her. There in a huge theater she had found herself surrounded by thousands of young people—mostly girls, she had been shocked to see. On the stage the singers, young men, stood behind a microphone and sang, if it could be called singing, the wailing of Western music, cowboy music, love songs that made her blush, old as she was. Yet the music was nothing in comparison to the screams and moans that came from the girls. Were they indeed Japanese? She saw that they were, for when the songs ended, first one girl, then twenty and more, rushed to the stage to hang garlands of flowers on the necks of the singers and even to kiss their cheeks. She had covered her eyes with her hands and stolen away.

"No, Setsu," she had said firmly. "Never will I allow you to go to that place."

She was not sure whether Setsu did go, in spite of this command. No mother could be sure of her children in this new Tokyo—or of her husband. She thrust aside the disloyal thought of her husband. "A woman may not be disloyal to her husband even in thought," her mother had taught her.

She looked up from the stove, where she was turning the fish in a pan. Setsu was washing her hands. Now she set the bowls on the table, and the chopsticks.

"Shall I set a place for Father?" she asked.

"You know he will not be here."

Silence fell between mother and daughter. It was broken again by Setsu.

"I don't see why you let Father go to the bar every evening."

Mrs. Omura paused in her task. She was slicing a raw carrot into flower shapes for the clear soup with which the meal began. "I let him? I have nothing to do with it. He has always gone to bars."

"Not before the war."

"Before the war it was a geisha house. Nowadays the geisha are the bar girls. You know that."

"Mother, why do you stand it?"

Mrs. Omura put down the knife. "But men must go to bars now that we have no geisha houses. Where else would they go?"

"They could stay home."

Mrs. Omura allowed herself a bit of pretended laughter, stifled behind her palm, denying the pain of hearing her daughter speak aloud what she herself had only dared in thought.

"Mother, I wish you wouldn't giggle behind your hand! It is so old-fashioned." Setsu's cry was strangely passionate.

Mrs. Omura's hand dropped. "Your father stay home? He stopped that as soon as you children were born. He couldn't endure the crying and noise. Besides, he does have business."

Setsu was scornful. "Business! In bars? Such business!"

Mrs. Omura took up the knife. She spoke with regained dignity. "I do not allow this manner toward your father. The men go to bars to talk business over a cup of sake. All big business deals, your father says, are—"

Setsu broke in, "And he comes home at two in the morning and expects you to be waiting for him with smiles and pity. 'My poor one, you are so tired. You have been working for our family all these hours. Here is your tea. I have drawn the hot water for your bath. Sleep late until the children are gone to school—' "

Setsu's imitation of her mother's voice was so perfect that Mrs. Omura was aghast. The child had lain awake to listen!

"You are a very naughty girl," she said severely.

Setsu stamped her foot. "Think of us, if you won't think of yourself! He is our father, isn't he? When do we see him? A few hours, perhaps, on Sunday, or on a holiday. Is that good for Toru? It doesn't matter about me, of course—"

She shrugged. "I don't know what he looks like anymore. I could pass him on the street and not know him."

She turned and left the room, but Mrs. Omura called after her. "Setsu, come back!"

The girl came back reluctantly and stood in the half-open shoji.

Mrs. Omura walked toward her shyly. The girl looked a woman— and a stranger.

"What would you do if you were I?"

"I would go to the bar with him," Setsu said firmly.

"I?" Mrs. Omura said faintly. She was aware of appearing absurd as she stood there, knife in one hand and carrot in the other.

"Young women do go to bars," Setsu said. "They go with their husbands. Then the husbands stop going."

"How do you know this?"

"We talk about it at school. Some of the girls have older sisters who are married."

Mrs. Omura was horrified. "Such talk in school!"

"Yes," Setsu said. "Why not? It is only a few years until we are grown up and we will not allow our husbands to go to bars as you do."

Mrs. Omura looked at her daughter's round pretty face. She had not noticed before how firm were the lines of the childish mouth, how direct the gaze of the dark eyes. Girls were different nowadays, very different. She sighed and returned to the kitchen sink.

"Change your clothes and call Toru. We will have our supper and then you must both do your homework. I have almost finished your pink dress."

The evening proceeded as usual. They ate in silence and Mrs. Omura cleared away. The children, wearing their home kimono, sat down at the low table with their books. Mrs. Omura sat at the table, too, with the pink dress she was making for Setsu. The girl was pretty in pink, her eyes and hair so dark. Let it be hoped that Setsu would not want someday to dye her hair in rusty blond streaks, as young girls were doing nowadays. Strange fashion, when only a few years ago beauty lay in the darkness of a woman's hair! But everything was strange these days. The bars, for example—she preferred the old geisha houses, where women were of one class and wives of another. These bar girls—

At this moment she thought of what Setsu had said. Perhaps the child was right. Why should she not go and see for herself what took place in bars? She had the right, surely, to know how her husband spent his evenings, these long evenings, endless after the children had gone to bed. It seemed, of a sudden, that she could not sit through one more evening waiting for his return, watching the hours pass until midnight and counting two more hours to wait. And as Setsu had said, so sharply true, when at two o'clock, or even half past, he came home at last, she must force a smile, she must bravely lie, she must welcome him tenderly and speak no word to him of her weariness or of the problems of her life in the home. He must be spared everything, as men are always spared.

The young girl's words had sunk into her long-wounded heart. Perhaps she was old-fashioned. Perhaps there was no reason why she should go on living this stupid life. Thus it came about that when the children were in bed and asleep, she amazed herself by what she did. She went to the closet where her clothes were folded and she took out her one Western dress, bought during the Occupation. "You should have one Western dress," her husband had said, "to please the Americans." So she had bought a two-piece suit of blue silk, but after the Occupation ended she had not worn it. The skirt was short and revealed her slightly bowed legs. She put it on now and combed her hair freshly, knotting it at the back, and clasped her string of pearls about her neck. After a moment, she even touched her lips with lipstick and looked at herself in the glass. She was neither pretty nor ugly, as such words go, but she looked as she wished to look, a woman of breeding and delicacy in spite of the grotesque costume. Kimono was far more flattering, but it would be conspicuous in a bar. She had once asked her husband if the bar girls wore kimono and he had answered shortly no, they did not.

She let herself out of the garden gate quietly, fastening the padlock since the children were alone. Then she stopped a taxicab.

"The Golden Moon Bar," she said.

It was one of the three best bars in the city and the taxi driver swung his cab into the heart of the night traffic. As usual with cabdrivers he talked.

"You go alone, miss?"

"I am meeting my husband there," she said. She was astonished at the calmness with which she spoke such words.

The man laughed.

"Old Japan is gone," he said, turning abruptly in order to avoid collision with a crowded bus. "Women go to bars with the men. What becomes of the children?"

She did not answer the question. It was none of his business.

He continued his prattle. "Everything is changed. The homes are empty and the offices and bars are full of women. All the women are looking for men. A man can have any woman he wants nowadays, except the old ones. Who wants them anyway? It's a great new world for the men."

He gave a coarse laugh and she shrank into deeper silence. When he perceived that she was not willing to talk, he began to sing raucously and she had not the courage to protest. She had never before been alone in a taxicab. After a few minutes he turned sharply to the left and squeezed his way through a long alley. She knew at once when they reached the bar, for three girls in fluffy red dresses stood outside the door, smiling and waving. They crowded to the cab and fell back when they saw a woman.

"She is coming to find her husband," the driver explained. "Look out, you three!"

The girls tittered. Mrs. Omura paid no heed to them or to the man.

She was stupefied with fright and could only go doggedly on. She paid off the man and turned to the girls, who stood across the doorway.

"Excuse me," she said. "I have come to meet my husband."

"Who is he?" the tallest girl inquired.

"He is Mr. Omura, vice-president of the Sakura Manufacturing Company."

The girls fell back. "Ah, Mr. Omura—we know him very well. A fine man—"

At the mention of her husband's name they changed. They looked at her with respect, they led her into the entrance hall of the bar and called, "Mama, here is Mrs. Omura!"

Madame came out at once. She was a pretty woman, perhaps thirty-five, but still slender and vivid. She wore a yellow satin dress of Western style, low in the neck, without sleeves, and full-skirted. She put out both hands warmly. "Mrs. Omura," she cried in a hearty voice. "We are so glad to see you. Mr. Omura is having a drink at the bar. He enjoys whiskey very much. We always give him what he likes. Is he expecting you?"

Mrs. Omura did not answer at once. She would have liked to lie, but she was not accustomed to doing so, and she was afraid she might blush and betray herself. She could only tell the truth.

"He does not expect me. I just—I just came."

Madame understood. "Ah yes. We welcome ladies, too. Would you like to sit in the other room and have a quiet drink before you go into the main bar?"

"I would like that very much," Mrs. Omura faltered. Now that she was here she was glad to delay the meeting with her husband. She followed Madame into a small room, quite empty, where there were only a table and two chairs.

"Sit down," Madame said cheerfully. "I will have one of our girls bring you something nice to drink, something sweet, and she will keep you company for a while. I have just the girl for you—our very best."

She smiled brightly and bustled away, her full skirt swinging. Mrs. Omura sat motionless and waiting. She had not long to wait. In less than five minutes a beautiful woman came in. That was what Mrs. Omura noticed instantly—she was a beauty. Then she saw that she was not a young woman—not a young girl, that is. She was perhaps twenty-eight. She wore a red Western dress, but her hair was long and smoothly coiffed into a high knot instead of cut short and brushed into every which way. She set down on the table a tray bearing two tall glasses. Then she bowed deeply. Mrs. Omura rose and bowed only slightly less deeply and they sat down. The beauty began the conversation.

"Mrs. Omura?"

"I am she."

"Our Mama asked me to sit with you."

"Thank you."

"When you are ready, I will ask Mr. Omura to join us. Or you can join him at the bar."

"Are there other ladies at the bar? Like me, I mean."

The beauty smiled. She had a pale oval face in the classic style, and her mouth was small and exquisitely shaped. When her lips parted, her teeth showed even and white.

"Not quite like you, but the young wives sometimes come with their husbands. It is a new custom."

"Why do they come?" Mrs. Omura asked.

She was surprised to find that she was drawn to this woman. This was a warm beauty, a friend by intention, and not an enemy, as she had supposed all women in bars must be.

The beauty laughed softly. "Ask yourself why you have come."

Mrs. Omura was surprised to discover at this moment that she wanted to weep.

"You—you cannot imagine," she stammered, "what it is to sit alone evening after evening, year after year, to wait for two o'clock, when he comes home. And then to be compelled to smile and pretend to welcome him, never asking a question, for fear he will be angry and not come home at all!"

The beauty nodded. "I know. Other wives have told me. And yet count yourself fortunate. Mr. Omura never makes an assignation. He comes here, he drinks and tells a few jokes, he talks to businessmen now and then. That is all."

At this point the beauty seemed somewhat embarrassed and invited

Mrs. Omura, by a graceful gesture of her right hand, to drink a sip of wine. They drank and the beauty continued.

"Of course Mr. Omura has a favorite and it is understood that she sits by him and keeps his glass full and watches that he does not become drunk. But that is all. He never takes her to an hotel."

"An hotel?"

The beauty spoke with dignity. "This is a very decent bar, Mrs. Omura. Mama never allows assignations to take place here. Such arrangements are made after hours and in some hotel. We always close at two. Mama is very strict."

Mrs. Omura listened, gazing at the beautiful face.

"It is not fair," she said at last. "It is not at all fair."

"What is not fair, Mrs. Omura?"

"That women like you—"

"Women like me?"

"So beautiful—"

"Can I help that? You are quite pretty yourself."

"I have no chance—in comparison to you."

"Mrs. Omura, I promise you—"

"No, don't promise. I am only asking you—a question."

"Yes?"

"What shall I do?"

And then before Mrs. Omura could stop herself it all came pouring out, the sadness, the wounded love, repressed by long habit and ancient tradition. The soft face, the tender dark eyes, the gentle hands, these attributes of the beauty drew it out from her, and she sobbed as she talked.

"How can women like you—you should think of us, you women— It's we who have all the weariness—the housekeeping—bearing the children— We are like servants, but we are not servants. We are women and we long for our husbands. But you steal him from me. You take his best—his thoughts—his talk—his laughter. He comes home silent, empty. I am even more lonely when he comes home."

The beautiful face changed from surprise to defense, to pain. The rose lips trembled, tears hung on the long dark lashes, the delicate hands fluttered and clasped themselves together under the soft chin.

Above these hands the beauty looked at the sobbing wife as though she had never before seen a woman weep.

"I didn't think— Mrs. Omura, it has not occurred to me to imagine— You see, dear Mrs. Omura, I hate him!"

Mrs. Omura wiped her eyes and swallowed a sob. "How can you hate him?" she demanded indignantly. "He is good."

"He is a man," the beauty said. *"I hate all men."*

Mrs. Omura stared into the dark eyes. "You hate *men?*"

The beauty nodded. Her hands fell to her lap and lay there like loosely petaled flowers. "There are—so many of them and they are all the same. They are quite stupid. Each thinks himself—irresistible."

Mrs. Omura began to feel angry with the beauty. "It is you who make him believe this," she retorted. For her there was only one man, Mr. Omura.

The beauty drew a fan from her sleeve and fanned herself. "Can he not see that we behave the same toward any man who pays us? Why does he think it is only for him? I am so tired of them all. Do you know how many years I have been in this bar? Twelve years! Will you believe that I was only sixteen when I first came here? But it is true. Twelve years of flattering and coaxing and pretending and listening to stupid jokes! You have known only one man. I have known hundreds. There is not a straw's difference between them—vain, conceited, selfish, stupid—"

Mrs. Omura interrupted. "It is because you have no children."

The beauty shrugged. "For this one thing I give thanks."

She folded the fan and put it in her sleeve again. She leaned her elbows on the table and spoke earnestly, her face close to Mrs. Omura's. "If I were free, as you are, I would have a little shop—a dress shop. I would employ six girls, four to sew the dresses I design, two to tend the shop. I would never receive a man—never!"

"Why don't you do what you want to do?" Mrs. Omura asked. She could feel anger rising hot under her breastbone. "Why do you make women like me miserable? Have your dress shop—leave my husband alone! We need him, the children and I. As a matter of fact—"

Here she felt suddenly shy. She had never used the word "love." There are no such words as "I love you" in Japanese, but she knew them from English, because she had been to American motion pictures. There also she had heard such words as "sweetheart" and "darling," for which also there are no words in Japanese. Love for a husband, her mother had taught her, was too deep to be spoken. It can only be shown through tender and unselfish actions.

"As a matter of fact," she went on bravely, "we—love him."

The beauty sighed. She seemed not to notice Mrs. Omura's emotion. "I should do what you say, Mrs. Omura, but the truth is—I am very lazy. After all these years I have learned to sleep late in the day. When I have eaten a little food, my maid bathes me and dresses me. Then I have nothing to do except to look—as I am—and pretend that I admire a man. It is an easy way to earn a living. It is too late now for me to change."

"So because you are lazy," Mrs. Omura said bitterly, "I am to spend my evenings alone and my children without a father."

The beauty rose and began to walk back and forth as gracefully as a lazy cat. She smoothed her soft dark hair away from her cheeks, she bit her lip, she shrugged, smiled and sighed again. Then she sat down across the room from Mrs. Omura.

"Why don't you have the dress shop? You rise early every day. Your children go to school, you are alone in the evening."

"I don't want a dress shop," Mrs. Omura said.

"Then something else," the beauty urged. "Let him see that you have your own life, and therefore whether he comes home is of no importance."

"And compel him to turn more than ever to you? No, thank you! At least I am not stupid."

With this Mrs. Omura rose indignantly and left the room and the bar. In the alleyway she turned once to look back, uncertain whether she should let Mr. Omura know. The beauty was standing in the doorway, gazing wistfully toward her. When she saw Mrs. Omura turn, she smiled and waved, but Mrs. Omura did not wave back or smile. Instead she went into the street, summoned a cab, and sat silent in the back seat. Two sentences remained clearly in her mind, one that the beauty hated all men, and the second that she, Mrs. Omura, could live a life of her own.

This life became so quickly clear to her, so possible, that when Mr. Omura entered the house at a quarter past two, she met him with a real smile. "The tea is fresh," she said. "You look tired. You should not have to do business at night as well as in the day. You are so faithful to your conscience."

He groaned mildly and sat down before the low table while she poured tea for him and went on talking.

"I have not been a good wife to you. I enjoy myself here at home when I should be working at something to earn money so you need not go to bars."

"What could you do?" he inquired without interest.

"I have been thinking of a dress shop," she said. She knelt on the mat across the table from him.

"A dress shop," he repeated. "Where would you get the capital? It is an absurd idea, the sort of thing a bar girl does with her savings when she grows old. But you have no savings."

"True," she said thoughtfully. "I have no savings. I am not so fortunate as a bar girl."

He raised his eyebrows. "What does that mean?"

"Nothing," she said, "nothing at all."

The evening proceeded as usual. He yawned and went to bed and she put away the teapot and bowls and went to bed, also.

Nevertheless the idea persisted that she could have a life of her own, although nothing changed. Mr. Omura continued to go to the bar and she continued to spend her evenings in solitude after the children were in bed. After about two months once more she sought out the beauty. This time she did not feel at all strange about going to the bar. She could even refuse to increase the tip to the cabdriver and she entered the bar with assurance. "If you please," she said to the girls fluttering on the doorstep. This time Madame did not appear, and the beauty came immediately.

"Mrs. Omura," she said warmly. "I am so happy. You have come on a good day. Do you know how you helped me? After you left I began to think how shameful that I am so lazy while you slave in your household, and your husband always here in the evenings and leaving you alone. The result is I have taken my savings and I have bought a dress shop. It is small, only one room for the shop and behind it a smaller room for me to live in. Now I need someone to help me. Will you be that one? I am afraid to begin alone."

Mrs. Omura was startled. She sat down at the table in the same room where she had sat before and considered.

"I cannot leave my house," she said at last.

"While Mr. Omura comes to the bar, you could come to my shop," the beauty suggested.

She looked so touchingly helpless, so exquisitely beautiful, that Mrs. Omura was moved. Seeing this, the beauty put out her little hand and took Mrs. Omura's hand. "It would only be for a short while, until I am accustomed to being alone. Then one by one I can find my six girls, as the business grows. It is not forever. Nothing is forever."

"Have you no mother?" Mrs. Omura inquired. "No older sister or friend?"

"None," the beauty said sadly. "They are far away in Hokkaido. I have lost them. They are only farm people and they sold me in a hungry winter. I do not belong to them now."

A long look passed between the two women. Mrs. Omura was the one to speak.

"Then I will help you."

In this way, simply and swiftly, Mrs. Omura's life changed. For a few weeks and then into months she went every evening to the dress shop. The beauty had chosen the site well. The shop was on the edge of the Ginza, where many people came and went. The beauty herself was a good saleswoman. She had only to linger in the doorway or to be busy at the window to have people stop to watch what she was doing. Men stopped because she was so beautiful and women stopped to see what the men were looking at. Then, forgetting the men, they went into the shop to buy the dresses. The beauty was clever and the dresses were unusual and very soon the shop was doing so well that the first two girls were employed, one to sew and one to serve.

Meanwhile Mrs. Omura and the beauty had become like sisters, elder and younger. For a while Mr. Omura was ignorant and innocent. One evening, however, he did not go to the bar. Mrs. Omura was first surprised and then impatient. She was especially eager to get to the shop. Some new fashion books had come in from America and she had planned to study them this evening with the beauty. There Mr. Omura sat, smoking a cigar while he read the newspaper.

"Are you not going to the bar?" Mrs. Omura inquired at last.

"No," Mr. Omura said.

"Is there something wrong?" she asked.

He put down the paper. "Can I not spend the evening quietly in my own house?"

"Certainly," she said, alarmed at his frown. "But it is so unusual."

To this he said nothing. He was reading his paper again. She glanced at the clock. She was half an hour late, and she could not telephone, for the instrument was on the small table at Mr. Omura's elbow. She grew desperate and brave.

"Since you are at home," she said, "may I go out?"

He looked over the top of the paper. "Where?"

"To see a friend."

He stared at her. "The first evening I am at home you go out?"

"When you are not here, I must stay with the children. Now that you are here—"

"Go on," he said shortly, "go on—go on. Leave me to solitude. I will be the nursemaid. Suit yourself first."

She knew that he was asking for pity and her heart hardened against him. How many evenings through the years had she not sat here alone?

"Thank you," she said and went away.

In the shop she confided the whole conversation to the beauty, who listened with profound interest. Observing the enchanting face, it now occurred to Mrs. Omura why Mr. Omura no longer went to the bar.

"It is because you are not there," she said. She felt guilty as she spoke. Here she was, enjoying the company of the woman whom perhaps her husband loved.

"Hush," the beauty said. "I never want to see a man again. I need not lie, I need not tell him how wonderful he is—"

Mrs. Omura interrupted. "In some ways he is wonderful."

The beauty laughed. "How funny you are! But let us waste no more time talking about men. Let us look at the new fashions from America."

The rest of the evening they spent in delightful discussion of American women and how they looked, and from the pictures the beauty designed several dresses suited to the Japanese female figure, combining the daring of the American and the subtlety of the Japanese. "To reveal innocently," the beauty said, "without seeming to reveal—"

Mrs. Omura received these words of wisdom gratefully. "I learn so much from you," she told the beauty.

The two women exchanged a look of sisterly affection and continued their work. It was two o'clock before Mrs. Omura reached home. She had hoped that the house would be dark, but no, the light was still burning in the living room. When she entered, Mr. Omura was waiting for her without a smile and certainly without a pot of hot tea. He sat on his folded legs beside the low table in the middle of the room, and he looked at her with accusing eyes.

"While you have been gone," he announced with majesty, "your son Toru has nearly died of a stomachache. He says the fish was not fresh."

She gasped and fled into the next room. Toru lay asleep on the tatami mat, his hand on his cheek. She felt his forehead. It was cool, but at her touch he opened his eyes.

"Does your stomach ache?" she asked anxiously.

"It did," he said, "but my father made me some hot ginseng tea and I am well."

"Oh, what a good father," she murmured.

The boy smiled and his eyes closed.

Mrs. Omura went back into the living room. "It was very good of you to make the ginseng tea— How did you know to make it?"

"I am not a fool," Mr. Omura said. He rose with a loud sigh. "But I am exhausted with waiting for you."

"You should not have waited," she said apologetically.

"Of course I should," he declared. "I was anxious about you at this time of night—a woman still young and good-looking." He did not look at her as he spoke these astounding words. He rearranged the folds of his kimono and looked at her sidewise.

Mrs. Omura stared at him. She did not know what to say. In all the years of their marriage he had never praised her looks or her behavior and she yearned now to thank him, to speak a few words, perhaps even of love. But there are still no such words in Japanese, and if she said "I love you" in English he would be startled and suspicious. Where could she have learned such English words? Impulsively she decided to tell him the truth. "You remember the dress shop?"

He was sliding back the shoji and he paused, he turned and looked at her. "What dress shop?"

"You said I had no capital for a dress shop."

"Have you capital?"

She shook her head and looked back at him bravely.

"So there is no dress shop," he said.

"Yes, there is."

He returned to face her across the table. "How can you be at a dress shop until two o'clock in the morning?"

"I was designing dresses—with my business partner."

"Business partner!" He was suddenly furious. He strode to her side and seized her by the arm. "Who is the man?"

She stared at him, astounded. "What man?" she asked.

"Your business partner!"

He glared into her wide eyes and seizing her by both arms he shook her. "I might have known! No woman is to be trusted. But you, my wife—coming home at two in the morning—"

She wrenched herself free of his arms. A lifetime of anger rushed through her memory. Now was the moment for revenge. Now she could pour it all out on him like acid. You, you who came home year after year at two o'clock in the morning, you who went to geisha houses as soon as we were married and then to bars, always to bars, giving your time, your thought, to other women. It was all there to be said, but she did not speak it. Who was there to love him if she did not—he, poor man, who had wasted so many evenings of his life at a bar where no one loved him!

"Dear sir," she said softly and in deep pity. "Dear sir, my business partner is a woman. She had the capital."

"How could a woman have capital?" Mr. Omura demanded.

"She used to be a bar girl," Mrs. Omura said simply.

Husband and wife looked at each other, she with the pity, he with a dawning comprehension.

"How did you two meet?" he demanded.

"I was so lonely in the evenings. I missed you. One evening I went to—to find you."

"You went to the bar?" Mr. Omura asked, unbelieving.

"Yes."

"I never saw you."

"No, but a beautiful woman came to entertain me."

"What did she say?"

"She said she wanted to start a dress shop."

"Why?"

"Because she hates all men."

Mr. Omura seemed suddenly to collapse. He sat down on the table and held his head in his hands. "So that is why she went away."

"Yes."

"Of course I knew she did not care for—for any of us. None of them do."

"Why did you keep going there, year after year?"

"It was pleasant," he muttered. "Very pleasant. So pleasant to be surrounded by pretty women, hearing only pleasant things—a man can almost believe himself to be what he knows he is not—"

Too much was being said and Mrs. Omura knew it. A wife must not allow her husband to humiliate himself before her. She knelt beside him. "I cannot believe that she did not love you. To me it is impossible that any woman could be near you, night after night, and not—love you."

His hands dropped away from his face. "You think so?"

"Impossible," she repeated.

He coughed, he got up, he walked around the table and stopped to look down at her. She continued to kneel before him as she had been taught that a wife should kneel before her husband. When he did not speak, however, she lifted her head to look up at him, and suddenly they both smiled. For a moment they looked at each other in silence. Then he spoke.

"From now on you need not kneel in my presence. In these modern times it is no longer the fashion."

And putting out his hands he took hers and lifted her to her feet.

THE DEVIL
AND DANIEL WEBSTER

STEPHEN VINCENT BENÉT

Stephen Vincent Benét

I T'S A STORY they tell in the border country, where Massachusetts joins Vermont and New Hampshire.

Yes, Dan'l Webster's dead—or, at least, they buried him. But every time there's a thunderstorm around Marshfield, they say you can hear his rolling voice in the hollows of the sky. And they say that if you go to his grave and speak loud and clear, "Dan'l Webster—Dan'l Webster!" the ground'll begin to shiver and the trees begin to shake. And after a while you'll hear a deep voice saying, "Neighbor, how stands the Union?" Then you better answer the Union stands as she stood, rock-bottomed and copper-sheathed, one and indivisible, or he's liable to rear right out of the ground. At least, that's what I was told when I was a youngster.

You see, for a while, he was the biggest man in the country. He never got to be President, but he was the biggest man. There were thousands that trusted in him right next to God Almighty, and they told stories about him that were like the stories of patriarchs and such. They said, when he stood up to speak, stars and stripes came right out in the sky, and once he spoke against a river and made it sink into the ground. They said, when he walked the woods with his fishing rod, Killall, the trout would jump out of the streams right into his pockets, for they knew it was no use putting up a fight against him; and, when he argued a case, he could turn on the harps of the blessed and the shaking of the earth underground. That was the kind of man he was, and his big farm up at Marshfield was suitable to him. The chickens he raised were all white meat down through the drumsticks, the cows were tended like children, and the big ram he called Goliath had horns with a curl like a morning-glory vine and could butt through an iron door. But Dan'l wasn't one of your gentlemen farmers; he knew all the ways of the land, and he'd be up by candlelight to see that the chores got done. A man with a mouth like a mastiff, a brow like a mountain, and eyes like burning anthracite—that was Dan'l Webster in his prime. And the biggest case he argued never got written down in the books, for he argued it against the devil, nip and tuck and no holds barred. And this is the way I used to hear it told.

There was a man named Jabez Stone, lived at Cross Corners, New Hampshire. He wasn't a bad man to start with, but he was an unlucky man. If he planted corn, he got borers; if he planted potatoes, he got blight. He had good-enough land, but it didn't prosper him; he had a decent wife and children, but the more children he had, the less there was to feed them. If stones cropped up in his neighbor's field, boulders boiled up in his; if he had a horse with the spavins, he'd trade it for one with the staggers and give something extra. There's some folks bound to be like that, apparently. But one day Jabez Stone got sick of the whole business.

He'd been plowing that morning and he'd just broke the plowshare on a rock that he could have sworn hadn't been there yesterday. And, as he stood looking at the plowshare, the off horse began to cough—that ropy kind of cough that means sickness and horse doctors. There were two children down with the measles, his wife was ailing, and he had a whitlow on his thumb. It was about the last straw for Jabez Stone. "I vow," he said, and he looked around him kind of desperate—"I vow it's enough to make a man want to sell his soul to the devil! And I would, too, for two cents!"

Then he felt a kind of queerness come over him at having said what he'd said; though, naturally, being a New Hampshireman, he wouldn't take it back. But, all the same, when it got to be evening and, as far as he could see, no notice had been taken, he felt relieved in his mind, for he was a religious man. But notice is always taken, sooner or later, just like the Good Book says. And, sure enough, next day, about supper-time, a soft-spoken, dark-dressed stranger drove up in a handsome buggy and asked for Jabez Stone.

Well, Jabez told his family it was a lawyer, come to see him about a legacy. But he knew who it was. He didn't like the looks of the stranger, nor the way he smiled with his teeth. They were white teeth, and plentiful—some say they were filed to a point, but I wouldn't vouch for that. And he didn't like it when the dog took one look at the stranger and ran away howling, with his tail between his legs. But having passed his word, more or less, he stuck to it, and they went out behind the barn and made their bargain. Jabez Stone had to prick his finger to sign, and the stranger lent him a silver pin. The wound healed clean, but it left a little white scar.

After that, all of a sudden, things began to pick up and prosper for Jabez Stone. His cows got fat and his horses sleek, his crops were the envy of the neighborhood, and lightning might strike all over the valley, but it wouldn't strike his barn. Pretty soon, he was one of the prosperous people of the county; they asked him to stand for selectman, and he stood for it; there began to be talk of running him for state senate. All in all, you might say the Stone family was as happy and contented as cats in a dairy. And so they were, except for Jabez Stone.

He'd been contented enough, the first few years. It's a great thing when bad luck turns; it drives most other things out of your head. True, every now and then, especially in rainy weather, the little white scar on his finger would give him a twinge. And once a year, punctual as clockwork, the stranger with the handsome buggy would come driving by. But the sixth year, the stranger lighted, and, after that, his peace was over for Jabez Stone.

The stranger came up through the lower field, switching his boots with a cane—they were handsome black boots, but Jabez Stone never liked the look of them, particularly the toes. And, after he'd passed the time of day, he said, "Well, Mr. Stone, you're a hummer! It's a very pretty property you've got here, Mr. Stone."

"Well, some might favor it and others might not," said Jabez Stone, for he was a New Hampshireman.

"Oh, no need to decry your industry!" said the stranger, showing his teeth in a smile. "After all, we know what's been done, and it's been according to contract and specifications. So when—ahem—the mortgage falls due next year, you shouldn't have any regrets."

"Speaking of that mortgage, mister," said Jabez Stone, and he looked around for help to the earth and the sky, "I'm beginning to have one or two doubts about it."

"Doubts?" said the stranger, not quite so pleasantly.

"Why, yes," said Jabez Stone. "This being the U.S.A. and me always having been a religious man." He cleared his throat and got bolder. "Yes, sir," he said, "I'm beginning to have considerable doubts as to that mortgage holding in court."

"There's courts and courts," said the stranger, clicking his teeth. "Still, we might as well have a look at the original document." And he hauled out a big black pocketbook, full of papers. "Sherwin, Slater, Stevens, Stone," he muttered. "I, Jabez Stone, for a term of seven years— Oh, it's quite in order, I think."

But Jabez Stone wasn't listening, for he saw something else flutter out of the black pocketbook. It was something that looked like a moth, but it wasn't a moth. And as Jabez Stone stared at it, it seemed to speak to him in a small sort of piping voice, terrible small and thin, but terrible human. "Neighbor Stone!" it squeaked. "Neighbor Stone! Help me! For God's sake, help me!"

But before Jabez Stone could stir hand or foot, the stranger whipped out a big bandanna handkerchief, caught the creature in it, just like a butterfly, and started tying up the ends of the bandanna.

"Sorry for the interruption," he said. "As I was saying—"

But Jabez Stone was shaking all over like a scared horse.

"That's Miser Stevens' voice!" he said, in a croak. "And you've got him in your handkerchief!"

The stranger looked a little embarrassed.

"Yes, I really should have transferred him to the collecting box," he said with a simper, "but there were some rather unusual specimens there and I didn't want them crowded. Well, well, these little contretemps will occur."

"I don't know what you mean by contertan," said Jabez Stone, "but that was Miser Stevens' voice! And he ain't dead! You can't tell me he is! He was just as spry and mean as a woodchuck, Tuesday!"

"In the midst of life—" said the stranger, kind of pious. "Listen!" Then a bell began to toll in the valley and Jabez Stone listened, with the sweat running down his face. For he knew it was tolled for Miser Stevens and that he was dead.

"These long-standing accounts," said the stranger with a sigh; "one really hates to close them. But business is business."

He still had the bandanna in his hand, and Jabez Stone felt sick as he saw the cloth struggle and flutter.

"Are they all as small as that?" he asked hoarsely.

"Small?" said the stranger. "Oh, I see what you mean. Why, they vary." He measured Jabez Stone with his eyes, and his teeth showed. "Don't worry, Mr. Stone," he said. "You'll go with a very good grade. I wouldn't trust you outside the collecting box. Now, a man like Dan'l Webster, of course—well, we'd have to build a special box for him, and even at that, I imagine the wingspread would astonish you. But, in your case, as I was saying—"

"Put that handkerchief away!" said Jabez Stone, and he began to beg and to pray. But the best he could get at the end was a three years' extension, with conditions.

But till you make a bargain like that, you've got no idea of how fast four years can run. By the last months of those years, Jabez Stone's known all over the state and there's talk of running him for governor— and it's dust and ashes in his mouth. For every day, when he gets up, he thinks, "There's one more night gone," and every night when he lies down, he thinks of the black pocketbook and the soul of Miser Stevens, and it makes him sick at heart. Till, finally, he can't bear it any longer, and, in the last days of the last year, he hitches up his horse and drives off to seek Dan'l Webster. For Dan'l was born in New Hampshire, only a few miles from Cross Corners, and it's well known that he has a particular soft spot for old neighbors.

It was early in the morning when he got to Marshfield, but Dan'l was up already, talking Latin to the farmhands and wrestling with the ram, Goliath, and trying out a new trotter and working up speeches to make against John C. Calhoun. But when he heard a New Hampshire-man had come to see him, he dropped everything else he was doing, for that was Dan'l's way. He gave Jabez Stone a breakfast that five men couldn't eat, went into the living history of every man and woman in Cross Corners, and finally asked him how he could serve him.

Jabez Stone allowed that it was a kind of mortgage case.

"Well, I haven't pleaded a mortgage case in a long time, and I don't generally plead now, except before the Supreme Court," said Dan'l, "but if I can, I'll help you."

"Then I've got hope for the first time in ten years," said Jabez Stone, and told him the details.

Dan'l walked up and down as he listened, hands behind his back, now and then asking a question, now and then plunging his eyes at the floor, as if they'd bore through it like gimlets. When Jabez Stone had finished, Dan'l puffed out his cheeks and blew. Then he turned to Jabez Stone and a smile broke over his face like the sunrise over Monadnock. "You've certainly given yourself the devil's own row to hoe, Neighbor Stone," he said, "but I'll take your case."

"You'll take it?" said Jabez Stone, hardly daring to believe.

"Yes," said Dan'l Webster. "I've got about seventy-five other things to do and the Missouri Compromise to straighten out, but I'll take your case. For if two New Hampshiremen aren't a match for the devil, we might as well give the country back to the Indians."

Then he shook Jabez Stone by the hand and said, "Did you come down here in a hurry?"

"Well, I admit I made time," said Jabez Stone.

"You'll go back faster," said Dan'l Webster, and he told 'em to hitch up Constitution and Constellation to the carriage. They were matched grays with one white forefoot, and they stepped like greased lightning.

Well, I won't describe how excited and pleased the whole Stone family was to have the great Dan'l Webster for a guest, when they finally got there. Jabez Stone had lost his hat on the way, blown off when they overtook a wind, but he didn't take much account of that. But after supper he sent the family off to bed, for he had most particular business with Mr. Webster. Mrs. Stone wanted them to sit in the front parlor, but Dan'l Webster knew front parlors and said he preferred the kitchen. So it was there they sat, waiting for the stranger, with a jug on the table between them and a bright fire on the hearth—the stranger being scheduled to show up on the stroke of midnight, according to specifications.

Well, most men wouldn't have asked for better company than Dan'l

Webster and a jug. But with every tick of the clock Jabez Stone got sadder and sadder. His eyes roved round, and though he sampled the jug you could see he couldn't taste it. Finally, on the stroke of eleven thirty he reached over and grabbed Dan'l Webster by the arm.

"Mr. Webster, Mr. Webster!" he said, and his voice was shaking with fear and a desperate courage. "For God's sake, Mr. Webster, harness your horses and get away from this place while you can!"

"You've brought me a long way, neighbor, to tell me you don't like my company," said Dan'l Webster, quite peaceable, pulling at the jug.

"Miserable wretch that I am!" groaned Jabez Stone. "I've brought you a devilish way, and now I see my folly. Let him take me if he wills. I don't hanker after it, I must say, but I can stand it. But you're the Union's stay and New Hampshire's pride! He mustn't get you, Mr. Webster! He mustn't get you!"

Dan'l Webster looked at the distracted man, all gray and shaking in the firelight, and laid a hand on his shoulder.

"I'm obliged to you, Neighbor Stone," he said gently. "It's kindly thought of. But there's a jug on the table and a case in hand. And I never left a jug or a case half finished in my life."

And just at that moment there was a sharp rap on the door.

"Ah," said Dan'l Webster, very coolly, "I thought your clock was a trifle slow, Neighbor Stone." He stepped to the door and opened it. "Come in!" he said.

The stranger came in—very dark and tall he looked in the firelight. He was carrying a box under his arm—a black, japanned box with little air holes in the lid. At the sight of the box, Jabez Stone gave a low cry and shrank into a corner of the room.

"Mr. Webster, I presume," said the stranger, very polite, but with his eyes glowing like a fox's deep in the woods.

"Attorney of record for Jabez Stone," said Dan'l Webster, but his eyes were glowing too. "Might I ask your name?"

"I've gone by a good many," said the stranger carelessly. "Perhaps Scratch will do for the evening. I'm often called that in these regions."

Then he sat down at the table and poured himself a drink from the jug. The liquor was cold in the jug, but it came steaming into the glass.

"And now," said the stranger, smiling and showing his teeth, "I shall call upon you, as a law-abiding citizen, to assist me in taking possession of my property."

Well, with that the argument began—and it went hot and heavy. At first, Jabez Stone had a flicker of hope, but when he saw Dan'l Webster being forced back at point after point, he just scrunched in his corner, with his eyes on that japanned box. For there wasn't any doubt as to the deed or the signature—that was the worst of it. Dan'l Webster twisted and turned and thumped his fist on the table, but he couldn't get away from that. He offered to compromise the case; the stranger wouldn't hear of it. He pointed out the property had increased in value, and state senators ought to be worth more; the stranger stuck to the letter of the law. He was a great lawyer, Dan'l Webster, but we know who's the King of Lawyers, as the Good Book tells us, and it seemed as if, for the first time, Dan'l Webster had met his match.

Finally, the stranger yawned a little. "Your spirited efforts on behalf of your client do you credit, Mr. Webster," he said, "but if you have no more arguments to adduce, I'm rather pressed for time"—and Jabez Stone shuddered.

Dan'l Webster's brow looked dark as a thundercloud.

"Pressed or not, you shall not have this man!" he thundered. "Mr. Stone is an American citizen, and no American citizen may be forced into the service of a foreign prince. We fought England for that in '12 and we'll fight all hell for it again!"

"Foreign?" said the stranger. "And who calls me a foreigner?"

"Well, I never yet heard of the dev—of your claiming American citizenship," said Dan'l Webster with surprise.

"And who with better right?" said the stranger, with one of his terrible smiles. "When the first wrong was done to the first Indian, I was there. When the first slaver put out for the Congo, I stood on her deck. Am I not in your books and stories and beliefs, from the first settlements on? Am I not spoken of, still, in every church in New England? 'Tis true the North claims me for a Southerner and the South for a Northerner, but I am neither. I am merely an honest American like yourself—and of the best descent—for, to tell the truth, Mr. Webster, though I don't like to boast of it, my name is older in this country than yours."

"Aha!" said Dan'l Webster, with the veins standing out in his forehead. "Then I stand on the Constitution! I demand a trial for my client!"

"The case is hardly one for an ordinary court," said the stranger, his eyes flickering. "And, indeed, the lateness of the hour—"

"Let it be any court you choose, so it is an American judge and an American jury!" said Dan'l Webster in his pride. "Let it be the quick or the dead; I'll abide the issue!"

"You have said it," said the stranger, and pointed his finger at the door. And with that, and all of a sudden, there was a rushing of wind outside and a noise of footsteps. They came, clear and distinct, through the night. And yet, they were not like the footsteps of living men.

"In God's name, who comes by so late?" cried Jabez Stone, in an ague of fear.

"The jury Mr. Webster demands," said the stranger, sipping at his boiling glass. "You must pardon the rough appearance of one or two; they will have come a long way."

And with that the fire burned blue and the door blew open and twelve men entered, one by one.

If Jabez Stone had been sick with terror before, he was blind with terror now. For there was Walter Butler, the loyalist, who spread fire and horror through the Mohawk Valley in the times of the Revolution; and there was Simon Girty, the renegade, who saw white men burned at the stake and whooped with the Indians to see them burn. His eyes were green, like a catamount's, and the stains on his hunting shirt did not come from the blood of the deer. King Philip was there, wild and proud as he had been in life, with the great gash in his head that gave him his death wound, and cruel Governor Dale, who broke men on the wheel. There was Morton of Merry Mount, who so vexed the Plymouth Colony, with his flushed, loose, handsome face and his hate of the godly. There was Teach, the bloody pirate, with his black beard curling on his breast. The Reverend John Smeet, with his strangler's hands and his Geneva gown, walked as daintily as he had to the gallows. The red print of the rope was still around his neck, but he carried a perfumed handkerchief in one hand. One and all, they came into the room with the fires of hell still upon them, and the stranger named their names and their deeds as they came, till the tale of twelve was told. Yet the stranger had told the truth—they had all played a part in America.

"Are you satisfied with the jury, Mr. Webster?" said the stranger mockingly, when they had taken their places.

The sweat stood upon Dan'l Webster's brow, but his voice was clear.

"Quite satisfied," he said. "Though I miss General Arnold from the company."

"Benedict Arnold is engaged upon other business," said the stranger, with a glower. "Ah, you asked for a justice, I believe."

He pointed his finger once more, and a tall man, soberly clad in Puritan garb, with the burning gaze of the fanatic, stalked into the room and took his judge's place.

"Justice Hathorne is a jurist of experience," said the stranger. "He presided at certain witch trials once held in Salem. There were others who repented of the business later, but not he."

"Repent of such notable wonders and undertakings?" said the stern old justice. "Nay, hang them—hang them all!" and he muttered to himself in a way that struck ice into the soul of Jabez Stone.

Then the trial began, and, as you might expect, it didn't look anyways good for the defense. And Jabez Stone didn't make much of a witness in his own behalf. He took one look at Simon Girty and screeched, and they had to put him back in his corner in a kind of swoon.

It didn't halt the trial, though; the trial went on, as trials do. Dan'l Webster had faced some hard juries and hanging judges in his time, but this was the hardest he'd ever faced, and he knew it. They sat there with a kind of glitter in their eyes, and the stranger's smooth voice went on and on. Every time he'd raise an objection, it'd be "Objection sustained," but whenever Dan'l objected, it'd be "Objection denied." Well, you couldn't expect fair play from a fellow like this Mr. Scratch.

It got to Dan'l in the end, and he began to heat, like iron in the forge. When he got up to speak he was going to flay that stranger with every trick known to the law, and the judge and jury too. He didn't care if it was contempt of court or what would happen to him for it. He didn't care anymore what happened to Jabez Stone. He just got madder and madder, thinking of what he'd say. And yet, curiously enough, the more he thought about it, the less he was able to arrange his speech in his mind.

Till, finally, it was time for him to get up on his feet, and he did so, all ready to bust out with lightnings and denunciations. But before he started he looked over the judge and jury for a moment, such being his custom. And he noticed the glitter in their eyes was twice as strong as before, and they all leaned forward. Like hounds just before they get the fox, they looked, and the blue mist of evil in the room thickened as he watched them. Then he saw what he'd been about to do, and he wiped his forehead, as a man might who's just escaped falling into a pit in the dark.

For it was him they'd come for, not only Jabez Stone. He read it in the glitter of their eyes and in the way the stranger hid his mouth with one hand. And if he fought them with their own weapons, he'd fall into their power; he knew that, though he couldn't have told you how. It was his own anger and horror that burned in their eyes; and he'd have to wipe that out or the case was lost. He stood there for a moment, his black eyes burning like anthracite. And then he began to speak.

He started off in a low voice, though you could hear every word. They say he could call on the harps of the blessed when he chose. And this was just as simple and easy as a man could talk. But he didn't start out by condemning or reviling. He was talking about the things that make a country a country, and a man a man.

And he began with the simple things that everybody's known and felt—the freshness of a fine morning when you're young, and the taste of food when you're hungry, and the new day that's every day when you're a child. He took them up and he turned them in his hands. They were good things for any man. But without freedom, they sickened. And when he talked of those enslaved, and the sorrows of slavery, his voice got like a big bell. He talked of the early days of America and the men who had made those days. It wasn't a spread-eagle speech, but he made you see it. He admitted all the wrong that had ever been done. But he showed how, out of the wrong and the right, the suffering and the starvations, something new had come. And everybody had played a part in it, even the traitors.

Then he turned to Jabez Stone and showed him as he was—an ordinary man who'd had hard luck and wanted to change it. And, because he'd wanted to change it, now he was going to be punished for all eternity. And yet there was good in Jabez Stone, and he showed that good. He was hard and mean, in some ways, but he was a man. There was sadness in being a man, but it was a proud thing too. And he showed what the pride of it was till you couldn't help feeling it. Yes, even in hell, if a man was a man, you'd know it. And he wasn't pleading for any one person anymore, though his voice rang like an organ. He was telling the story and the failures and the endless journey of mankind. They got tricked and trapped and bamboozled, but it was a great journey. And no demon that was ever foaled could know the inwardness of it—it took a man to do that.

The fire began to die on the hearth and the wind before morning to blow. The light was getting gray in the room when Dan'l Webster finished. And his words came back at the end to New Hampshire ground, and the one spot of land that each man loves and clings to. He painted a picture of that, and to each one of that jury he spoke of things long forgotten. For his voice could search the heart, and that was his gift and his strength. And to one, his voice was like the forest and its secrecy, and to another like the sea and the storms of the sea; and one heard the cry of his lost nation in it, and another saw a little harmless scene he hadn't remembered for years. But each saw something. And when Dan'l Webster finished he didn't know whether or not he'd saved Jabez Stone. But he knew he'd done a miracle. For the glitter was gone from the eyes of judge and jury, and, for the moment, they were men again, and knew they were men.

"The defense rests," said Dan'l Webster, and stood there like a mountain. His ears were still ringing with his speech, and he didn't hear anything else till he heard Judge Hathorne say, "The jury will retire to consider its verdict."

Walter Butler rose in his place and his face had a dark, gay pride on it. "The jury has considered its verdict," he said, and looked the stranger full in the eye. "We find for the defendant, Jabez Stone."

With that, the smile left the stranger's face, but Walter Butler did not flinch.

"Perhaps 'tis not strictly in accordance with the evidence," he said, "but even the damned may salute the eloquence of Mr. Webster."

With that, the long crow of a rooster split the gray morning sky, and judge and jury were gone from the room like a puff of smoke and as if they had never been there. The stranger turned to Dan'l Webster.

"Major Butler was always a bold man," he said, smiling wryly. "I had not thought him quite so bold. Nevertheless, my congratulations, as between two gentlemen."

"I'll have that paper first, if you please," said Dan'l Webster, and he took it and tore it into four pieces. It was queerly warm to the touch. "And now," he said, "I'll have you!" and his hand came down like a bear trap on the stranger's arm. For he knew that once you bested anybody like Mr. Scratch in fair fight, his power on you was gone. And he could see that Mr. Scratch knew it too.

The stranger twisted and wriggled, but he couldn't get out of that grip. "Come, come, Mr. Webster," he said, smiling palely. "This sort of thing is ridic—ouch!—is ridiculous. If you're worried about the costs of the case, naturally, I'd be glad to pay—"

"And so you shall!" said Dan'l Webster, shaking him till his teeth rattled. "For you'll sit right down at that table and draw up a document, promising never to bother Jabez Stone nor his heirs or assigns nor any other New Hampshireman till doomsday! For any hades we want to raise in this state, we can raise ourselves, without assistance from strangers."

"Ouch!" said the stranger. "Ouch! Well, they never did run very big to the barrel, but—ouch!—I agree!"

So he sat down and drew up the document. But Dan'l Webster kept his hand on his coat collar all the time.

"And, now, may I go?" said the stranger, quite humble, when Dan'l'd seen the document was in proper and legal form.

"Go?" said Dan'l, giving him another shake. "I'm still trying to figure out what I'll do with you. For you've settled the costs of the case, but you haven't settled with me. I think I'll take you back to Marshfield," he said, kind of reflective. "I've got a ram there named Goliath that can butt through an iron door. I'd kind of like to turn you loose in his field and see what he'd do."

Well, with that the stranger began to beg and to plead. And he begged and he pled so humble that finally Dan'l, who was naturally kindhearted, agreed to let him go. The stranger seemed terrible grateful for that and said, just to show they were friends, he'd tell Dan'l's fortune before leaving. So Dan'l agreed to that, though he didn't take much stock in fortune-tellers ordinarily. But, naturally, the stranger was a little different.

Well, he pried and he peered at the lines in Dan'l's hands. And he told him one thing and another that was quite remarkable. But they were all in the past.

"Yes, all that's true, and it happened," said Dan'l Webster. "But what's to come in the future?"

The stranger grinned, kind of happily, and shook his head.

"The future's not as you think it," he said. "It's dark. You have a great ambition, Mr. Webster."

"I have," said Dan'l firmly, for everybody knew he wanted to be President.

"It seems almost within your grasp," said the stranger, "but you will not attain it. Lesser men will be made President and you will be passed over."

"And, if I am, I'll still be Daniel Webster," said Dan'l. "Say on."

"You have two strong sons," said the stranger, shaking his head. "You look to found a line. But each will die in war and neither reach greatness."

"Live or die, they are still my sons," said Dan'l Webster. "Say on."

"You have made great speeches," said the stranger. "You will make more."

"Ah," said Dan'l Webster.

"But the last great speech you make will turn many of your own against you," said the stranger. "They will call you Ichabod; they will call you by other names. Even in New England, some will say you have turned your coat and sold your country, and their voices will be loud against you till you die."

"So it is an honest speech, it does not matter what men say," said Dan'l Webster. Then he looked at the stranger and their glances locked.

"One question," he said. "I have fought for the Union all my life. Will I see that fight won against those who would tear it apart?"

"Not while you live," said the stranger, grimly, "but it will be won. And after you are dead, there are thousands who will fight for your cause, because of words that you spoke."

"Why, then, you long-barreled, slab-sided, lantern-jawed, fortune-telling note shaver!" said Dan'l Webster, with a great roar of laughter, "be off with you to your own place before I put my mark on you! For, by the thirteen original colonies, I'd go to the Pit itself to save the Union!" And with that he drew back his foot for a kick that would have stunned a horse. It was only the tip of his shoe that caught the stranger, but he went flying out of the door with his collecting box under his arm.

"And now," said Dan'l Webster, seeing Jabez Stone beginning to rouse from his swoon, "let's see what's left in the jug, for it's dry work talking all night. I hope there's pie for breakfast, Neighbor Stone."

But they say that whenever the devil comes near Marshfield, even now, he gives it a wide berth. And he hasn't been seen in the state of New Hampshire from that day to this. I'm not talking about Massachusetts or Vermont.

WINTER NIGHT

KAY BOYLE

THERE IS A time of apprehension which begins with the beginning of
darkness, and to which only the speech of love can lend security. It is
there, in abeyance, at the end of every day, not urgent enough to be
given the name of fear but rather of concern for how the hours are to be
reprieved from fear, and those who have forgotten how it was when
they were children can remember nothing of this. It may begin around
five o'clock on a winter afternoon when the light outside is dying in
the windows. At that hour the New York apartment in which Felicia
lived was filled with shadows, and the little girl would wait alone in the
living room, looking out at the winter-stripped trees that stood black in
the park against the isolated ovals of unclean snow. Now it was
January, and the day had been a cold one; the water of the artificial lake
was frozen fast, but because of the cold and the coming darkness, the
skaters had ceased to move across its surface. The street that lay between
the park and the apartment house was wide, and the two-way streams of
cars and buses, some with their headlamps already shining, advanced
and halted, halted and poured swiftly on to the tempo of the traffic
signals' altering lights. The time of apprehension had set in, and Felicia,
who was seven, stood at the window in the evening and waited before
she asked the question. When the signals below would change from
red to green again, or when the double-decker bus would turn the
corner below, she would ask it. The words of it were already there, tentative in her mouth, when the answer came from the far end of
the hall.

"Your mother," said the voice among the sound of kitchen things, "she telephoned up before you came in from nursery school. She won't be back in time for supper. I was to tell you a sitter was coming in from the sitting parents' place."

Felicia turned back from the window into the obscurity of the living room, and she looked toward the open door, and into the hall beyond it where the light from the kitchen fell in a clear yellow angle across the wall and onto the strip of carpet. Her hands were cold, and she put them in her jacket pockets as she walked carefully across the living-room rug and stopped at the edge of light.

"Will she be home late?" she said.

For a moment there was the sound of water running in the kitchen, a long way away, and then the sound of the water ceased, and the high, Southern voice went on:

"She'll come home when she gets ready to come home. That's all I have to say. If she wants to spend two dollars and fifty cents and ten cents' carfare on top of that three or four nights out of the week for a sitting parent to come in here and sit, it's her own business. It certainly ain't nothing to do with you or me. She makes her money, just like the rest of us does. She works all day down there in the office, or whatever it is, just like the rest of us works, and she's entitled to spend her money like she wants to spend it. There's no law in the world against buying your own freedom. Your mother and me, we're just buying our own freedom, that's all we're doing. And we're not doing nobody no harm."

"Do you know who she's having supper with?" said Felicia from the edge of dark. There was one more step to take, and then she would be standing in the light that fell on the strip of carpet, but she did not take the step.

"Do I know who she's having supper with?" the voice cried out in what might have been derision, and there was the sound of dishes striking the metal ribs of the drainboard by the sink. "Maybe it's Mr. Van Johnson, or Mr. Frank Sinatra, or maybe it's just the Duke of Wincers for the evening. All I know is you're having soft-boiled egg and spinach and applesauce for supper, and you're going to have it quick now because the time is getting away."

The voice from the kitchen had no name. It was as variable as the faces and figures of the women who came and sat in the evenings.

Month by month the voice in the kitchen altered to another voice, and the sitting parents were no more than lonely aunts of an evening or two who sometimes returned and sometimes did not to this apartment in which they had sat before. Nobody stayed anywhere very long anymore, Felicia's mother told her. It was part of the time in which you lived, and part of the life of the city, but when the fathers came back, all this would be miraculously changed. Perhaps you would live in a house again, a small one, with fir trees on either side of the short brick walk, and Father would drive up every night from the station just after darkness set in. When Felicia thought of this, she stepped quickly into the clear angle of light, and she left the dark of the living room behind her and ran softly down the hall.

The drop-leaf table stood in the kitchen between the refrigerator and the sink, and Felicia sat down at the place that was set. The voice at the sink was speaking still, and while Felicia ate it did not cease to speak until the bell of the front door rang abruptly. The girl walked around the table and went down the hall, wiping her dark palms in her apron, and, from the drop-leaf table, Felicia watched her step from the angle of light into darkness and open the door.

"You put in an early appearance," the girl said, and the woman who had rung the bell came into the hall. The door closed behind her, and the girl showed her into the living room, and lit the lamp on the bookcase, and the shadows were suddenly bleached away. But when the girl turned, the woman turned from the living room too and followed her, humbly and in silence, to the threshold of the kitchen. "Sometimes they keep me standing around waiting after it's time for me to be getting on home, the sitting parents do," the girl said, and she picked up the last two dishes from the table and put them in the sink. The woman who stood in the doorway was a small woman, and when she undid the white silk scarf from around her head, Felicia saw that her hair was black. She wore it parted in the middle, and it had not been cut, but was drawn back loosely into a knot behind her head. She had very clean white gloves on, and her face was pale, and there was a look of sorrow in her soft black eyes. "Sometimes I have to stand out there in the hall with my hat and coat on, waiting for the sitting parents to turn up," the girl said, and, as she turned on the water in the sink, the contempt she had for them hung on the kitchen air. "But you're ahead of time," she said, and she held the dishes, first one and then the other, under the flow of steaming water.

The woman in the doorway wore a neat black coat, not a new-looking coat, and it had no fur on it, but it had a smooth velvet collar and velvet lapels. She did not move, or smile, and she gave no sign that she had heard the girl speaking above the sound of water at the sink. She simply stood looking at Felicia, who sat at the table with the milk in her glass not finished yet.

"Are you the child?" she said at last, and her voice was low, and the pronunciation of the words a little strange.

"Yes, this here's Felicia," the girl said, and the dark hands dried the dishes and put them away. "You drink up your milk quick now, Felicia, so's I can rinse your glass."

"I will wash the glass," said the woman. "I would like to wash the glass for her," and Felicia sat looking across the table at the face in the doorway that was filled with such unspoken grief. "I will wash the glass for her and clean off the table," the woman was saying quietly. "When the child is finished, she will show me where her night things are."

"The others, they wouldn't do anything like that," the girl said, and she hung the dishcloth over the rack. "They wouldn't put their hand to housework, the sitting parents. That's where they got the name for them," she said.

Whenever the front door closed behind the girl in the evening, it would usually be that the sitting parent who was there would take up a book of fairy stories and read aloud for a while to Felicia; or else would settle herself in the big chair in the living room and begin to tell the words of a story in drowsiness to her, while Felicia took off her clothes in the bedroom, and folded them, and put her pajamas on, and brushed her teeth, and did her hair. But this time, that was not the way it happened. Instead, the woman sat down on the other chair at the kitchen table, and she began at once to speak, not of good fairies or bad, or of animals endowed with human speech, but to speak quietly, in spite of the eagerness behind her words, of a thing that seemed of singular importance to her.

"It is strange that I should have been sent here tonight," she said, her eyes moving slowly from feature to feature of Felicia's face, "for you look like a child that I knew once, and this is the anniversary of that child."

"Did she have hair like mine?" Felicia asked quickly, and she did not keep her eyes fixed on the unfinished glass of milk in shyness anymore.

"Yes, she did. She had hair like yours," said the woman, and her glance paused for a moment on the locks which fell straight and thick on the shoulders of Felicia's dress. It may have been that she thought to stretch out her hand and touch the ends of Felicia's hair, for her fingers stirred as they lay clasped together on the table, and then they relapsed into passivity again. "But it is not the hair alone, it is the delicacy of your face, too, and your eyes the same, filled with the same spring lilac color," the woman said, pronouncing the words carefully. "She had little coats of golden fur on her arms and legs," she said, "and when we were closed up there, the lot of us in the cold, I used to make her laugh when I told her that the fur that was so pretty, like a little fawn's skin on her arms, would always help to keep her warm."

"And did it keep her warm?" asked Felicia, and she gave a little jerk of laughter as she looked down at her own legs hanging under the table, with the bare calves thin and covered with a down of hair.

"It did not keep her warm enough," the woman said, and now the mask of grief had come back upon her face. "So we used to take everything we could spare from ourselves, and we would sew them into cloaks and other garments for her and for the other children. . . ."

"Was it a school?" said Felicia when the woman's voice had ceased to speak.

"No," said the woman softly, "it was not a school, but still there were a lot of children there. It was a camp—that was the name the place had; it was a camp. It was a place where they put people until they could decide what was to be done with them." She sat with her hands clasped, silent a moment, looking at Felicia. "That little dress you have on," she said, not saying the words to anybody, scarcely saying them aloud. "Oh, she would have liked that little dress, the little buttons shaped like hearts, and the white collar—"

"I have four school dresses," Felicia said. "I'll show them to you. How many dresses did she have?"

"Well, there, you see, there in the camp," said the woman, "she did not have any dresses except the little skirt and the pullover. That was all she had. She had brought just a handkerchief of her belongings with her, like everybody else—just enough for three days away from home was what they told us, so she did not have enough to last the winter. But she had her ballet slippers," the woman said, and her clasped fingers did not move. "She had brought them because she thought during her three days away from home she would have the time to practice her ballet."

"I've been to the ballet," Felicia said suddenly, and she said it so eagerly that she stuttered a little as the words came out of her mouth. She slipped down from the chair and went around the table to where the woman sat. She took one of the woman's hands away from the other that held it fast, and she pulled her toward the door. "Come into the living room and I'll do a pirouette for you," she said, and then she stopped speaking, her eyes halted on the woman's face. "Did she—did the little girl—could she do a pirouette very well?" she said.

"Yes, she could. At first she could," said the woman, and Felicia felt uneasy now at the sound of sorrow in her words. "But after that she was hungry. She was hungry all winter," she said in a low voice. "We were all hungry, but the children were the hungriest. Even now," she said, and her voice went suddenly savage, "when I see milk like that, clean, fresh milk standing in a glass, I want to cry out loud, I want to beat my hands on the table, because it did not have to be . . ." She had drawn her fingers abruptly away from Felicia now, and Felicia stood before her, cast off, forlorn, alone again in the time of apprehension. "That was three years ago," the woman was saying, and one hand was lifted, as in weariness, to shade her face. "It was somewhere else, it was in another country," she said, and behind her hand her eyes were turned upon the substance of a world in which Felicia had played no part.

"Did—did the little girl cry when she was hungry?" Felicia asked, and the woman shook her head.

"Sometimes she cried," she said, "but not very much. She was very quiet. One night when she heard the other children crying, she said to me, 'You know, they are not crying because they want something to eat. They are crying because their mothers have gone away.' "

"Did the mothers have to go out to supper?" Felicia asked, and she watched the woman's face for the answer.

"No," said the woman. She stood up from her chair, and now that she put her hand on the little girl's shoulder, Felicia was taken into the sphere of love and intimacy again. "Shall we go into the other room, and you will do your pirouette for me?" the woman said, and they went from the kitchen and down the strip of carpet on which the clear light fell. In the front room, they paused hand in hand in the glow of the shaded lamp, and the woman looked about her, at the books, the low tables with the magazines and ashtrays on them, the vase of roses on the piano, looking with dark, scarcely seeing eyes at these things that had no reality at all. It was only when she saw the little white clock on the mantelpiece that she gave any sign, and then she said quickly: "What time does your mother put you to bed?"

Felicia waited a moment, and in the interval of waiting the woman lifted one hand and, as if in reverence, touched Felicia's hair.

"What time did the little girl you knew in the other place go to bed?" Felicia asked.

"Ah, God, I do not know, I do not remember," the woman said.

"Was she your little girl?" said Felicia softly, stubbornly.

"No," said the woman. "She was not mine. At least, at first she was not mine. She had a mother, a real mother, but the mother had to go away."

"Did she come back late?" asked Felicia.

"No, ah, no, she could not come back, she never came back," the woman said, and now she turned, her arm around Felicia's shoulders, and she sat down in the low soft chair. "Why am I saying all this to you, why am I doing it?" she cried out in grief, and she held Felicia close against her. "I had thought to speak of the anniversary to you, and that was all, and now I am saying these other things to you. Three years ago today, exactly, the little girl became my little girl because her mother went away. That is all there is to it. There is nothing more."

Felicia waited another moment, held close against the woman, and listening to the swift, strong heartbeats in the woman's breast.

"But the mother," she said then in the small, persistent voice, "did she take a taxi when she went?"

"This is the way it used to happen," said the woman, speaking in hopelessness and bitterness in the softly lighted room. "Every week they used to come into the place where we were and they would read a list of names out. Sometimes it would be the names of children they would read out, and then a little later they would have to go away. And sometimes it would be the grown people's names, the names of the mothers or big sisters, or other women's names. The men were not with us. The fathers were somewhere else, in another place."

"Yes," Felicia said. "I know."

"We had been there only a little while, maybe ten days or maybe not so long," the woman went on, holding Felicia against her still, "when they read the name of the little girl's mother out, and that afternoon they took her away."

"What did the little girl do?" Felicia said.

"She wanted to think up the best way of getting out so that she could go find her mother," said the woman, "but she could not think of anything good enough until the third or fourth day. And then she tied her ballet slippers up in the handkerchief again, and she went up to the guard standing at the door." The woman's voice was gentle, controlled now. "She asked the guard please to open the door so that she could go out. 'This is Thursday,' she said, 'and every Tuesday and Thursday I have my ballet lessons. If I miss a ballet lesson, they do not count the money off, so my mother would be just paying for nothing, and she cannot afford to pay for nothing. I missed my ballet lesson on Tuesday,' she said to the guard, 'and I must not miss it again today.' "

Felicia lifted her head from the woman's shoulder, and she shook her hair back and looked in question and wonder at the woman's face.

"And did the man let her go?" she said.

"No, he did not. He could not do that," said the woman. "He was a soldier and he had to do what he was told. So every evening after her mother went, I used to brush the little girl's hair for her," the woman went on saying. "And while I brushed it, I used to tell her the stories of the ballets. Sometimes I would begin with *Narcissus*," the woman said, and she parted Felicia's locks with her fingers, "so if you will go and get your brush now, I will tell it while I brush your hair."

"Oh, yes," said Felicia, and she made two whirls as she went quickly to the bedroom. On the way back, she stopped and held on to the piano with the fingers of one hand while she went up on her toes. "Did you see me? Did you see me standing on my toes?" she called to the woman, and the woman sat smiling in love and contentment at her.

"Yes, wonderful, really wonderful," she said. "I am sure I have never seen anyone do it so well." Felicia came spinning toward her, whirling in pirouette after pirouette, and she flung herself down in the chair close to her, with her thin bones pressed against the woman's soft, wide hip. The woman took the silver-backed, monogrammed brush and the tortoiseshell comb in her hands, and now she began to brush Felicia's hair. "We did not have any soap at all and not very much water to wash in, so I never could fix her as nicely and prettily as I wanted to," she said, and the brush stroked regularly, carefully down, caressing the shape of Felicia's head.

"If there wasn't very much water, then how did she do her teeth?" Felicia said.

"She did not do her teeth," said the woman, and she drew the comb through Felicia's hair. "There were not any toothbrushes or toothpaste, or anything like that."

Felicia waited a moment, constructing the unfamiliar scene of it in silence, and then she asked the tentative question.

"Do I have to do my teeth tonight?" she said.

"No," said the woman, and she was thinking of something else, "you do not have to do your teeth."

"If I am your little girl tonight, can I pretend there isn't enough water to wash?" said Felicia.

"Yes," said the woman, "you can pretend that if you like. You do not have to wash," she said, and the comb passed lightly through Felicia's hair.

"Will you tell me the story of the ballet?" said Felicia, and the rhythm of the brushing was like the soft, slow rocking of sleep.

"Yes," said the woman. "In the first one, the place is a forest glade with little pale birches growing in it, and they have green veils over their faces and green veils drifting from their fingers, because it is the springtime. There is the music of a flute," said the woman's voice softly, softly, "and creatures of the wood are dancing—"

"But the mother," Felicia said as suddenly as if she had been awaked from sleep. "What did the little girl's mother say when she didn't do her teeth and didn't wash at night?"

"The mother was not there, you remember," said the woman, and the brush moved steadily in her hand. "But she did send one little letter back. Sometimes the people who went away were able to do that. The mother wrote it in a train, standing up in a car that had no seats," she said, and she might have been telling the story of the ballet still, for her voice was gentle and the brush did not falter on Felicia's hair. "There were perhaps a great many other people standing up in the train with her, perhaps all trying to write their little letters on the bits of paper they had managed to hide on them, or that they had found in forgotten corners as they traveled. When they had written their letters, then they must try to slip them out through the boards of the car in which they journeyed, standing up," said the woman, "and these letters fell down on the tracks under the train, or they were blown into the fields or onto the country roads, and if it was a kind person who picked them up, he would seal them in envelopes and send them to where they were addressed to go. So a letter came back like this from the little girl's mother," the woman said, and the brush followed the comb, the comb the brush in steady pursuit through Felicia's hair. "It said good-by to the little girl, and it said please to take care of her. It said: 'Whoever reads this letter in the camp, please take good care of my little girl for me, and please have her tonsils looked at by a doctor if this is possible to do.' "

"And then," said Felicia softly, persistently, "what happened to the little girl?"

"I do not know. I cannot say," the woman said. But now the brush and comb had ceased to move, and in the silence Felicia turned her thin, small body on the chair, and she and the woman suddenly put their arms around each other. "They must all be asleep now, all of them," the woman said, and in the silence that fell on them again, they held each other closer. "They must be quietly asleep somewhere, and not crying all night because they are hungry and because they are cold. For three years I have been saying, 'They must all be asleep, and the cold and the hunger and the seasons or night or day or nothing matters to them. . . .' "

IT WAS AFTER MIDNIGHT WHEN Felicia's mother put her key in the lock of the front door, and pushed it open, and stepped into the hallway. She walked quickly to the living room, and just across the threshold she slipped the three blue fox skins from her shoulders and dropped them, with her little velvet bag, upon the chair. The room was quiet, so quiet that she could hear the sound of breathing in it, and no one spoke to her in greeting as she crossed toward the bedroom door. And then, as startling as a slap across her delicately tinted face, she saw the woman lying sleeping on the divan, and Felicia, in her school dress still, asleep within the woman's arms.

BARTLEBY
THE SCRIVENER
HERMAN MELVILLE

Herman Melville.

I AM A rather elderly man. The nature of my avocations for the last thirty years has brought me into more than ordinary contact with an interesting and somewhat singular set of men, of whom, as yet, nothing that I know of has ever been written—I mean the law copyists, or scriveners. I have known very many of them, professionally and privately, and, if I pleased, could relate divers histories at which good-natured gentlemen might smile and sentimental souls might weep. But I waive the biographies of all other scriveners for a few passages in the life of Bartleby, who was a scrivener, the strangest I ever saw or heard of. While of other law copyists I might write the complete life, of Bartleby nothing of that sort can be done. What my own astonished eyes saw of Bartleby, *that* is all I know of him, except, indeed, one vague report which will appear in the sequel.

I am a man who, from his youth upwards, has been filled with a profound conviction that the easiest way of life is the best. Though I belong to a profession proverbially energetic and nervous, yet I am one of those unambitious lawyers who never address a jury or in any way draw public applause, but in the cool tranquillity of a snug retreat do a snug business among rich men's bonds and mortgages and title deeds. All who know me consider me an eminently *safe* man. The late John Jacob Astor, a personage little given to poetic enthusiasm, had no hesitation in pronouncing my first grand point to be prudence; my next, method. I do not speak it in vanity, but simply record the fact that I was employed in my profession by the late John Jacob Astor, a name which, I admit, I love to repeat, for it hath a rounded and orbicular sound to it, and rings like unto bullion. I will add that I was not insensible to the late John Jacob Astor's opinion.

Some time prior to the period at which this little history begins, the office of a Master in Chancery had been conferred upon me. It was not a very arduous office, but very pleasantly remunerative. My chambers were upstairs at No. —— Wall Street. At one end they looked upon the white wall of the interior of a spacious skylight shaft penetrating the building from top to bottom. The view from the other end of my chambers offered, at least, a contrast, if nothing more. In that direction my windows commanded an unobstructed view of a lofty brick wall, black by age and everlasting shade, pushed up to within ten feet of my windowpanes.

At the period just preceding the advent of Bartleby, I had two persons as copyists in my employment, and a promising lad as an office boy. First, Turkey; second, Nippers; third, Ginger Nut. These were nicknames conferred upon each other by my three clerks, expressive of their respective persons or characters.

Turkey was a short, pursy Englishman of about my own age—that is, somewhere not far from sixty. In the morning his face was of a fine florid hue, but after twelve o'clock—his dinner hour—it blazed like a grate full of Christmas coals. When Turkey displayed his fullest beams from his red and radiant countenance, just then, too, began the daily period when I considered his business capacities as seriously disturbed for the remainder of the day. Not that he was absolutely idle, or averse to business then; far from it. He was apt to be altogether too energetic. There was a strange, inflamed, flurried, flighty recklessness of activity about him. He made an unpleasant racket with his chair; spilled his sandbox; in mending his pens, impatiently split them all to pieces, and threw them on the floor in a sudden passion; stood up and leaned over his table, boxing his papers about in a most indecorous manner, very sad to behold in an elderly man like him. Nevertheless, as he was in many ways a most valuable person to me, and all the time before twelve o'clock was the quickest, steadiest creature, I was willing to overlook his eccentricities, though, indeed, occasionally I remonstrated with him. I did this very gently, however, because, though the civilest, nay, the blandest and most reverential of men in the morning, yet, in the afternoon, he was disposed, upon provocation, to be slightly rash with his tongue—in fact, insolent.

Nippers was a whiskered, sallow, rather piratical-looking young man of about five-and-twenty. I always deemed him the victim of two evil powers—ambition and indigestion. The ambition was evinced by a certain impatience of the duties of a mere copyist, an unwarrantable usurpation of strictly professional affairs. The indigestion seemed betokened in an occasional nervous testiness and grinning irritability, causing the teeth to audibly grind together over mistakes committed in copying; unnecessary maledictions, hissed rather than spoken, in the heat of business, and especially by a continual discontent with the height of the table where he worked. Though of a very ingenious mechanical turn, Nippers could never get this table to suit him. He put chips under it, blocks of various sorts, and at last went so far as to attempt an exquisite adjustment by final pieces of folded blotting paper. But no invention would answer. The truth of the matter was, Nippers knew not what he wanted. Or, if he wanted anything, it was to be rid of a scrivener's table altogether. Among the manifestations of his diseased ambition was a fondness he had for receiving visits from certain ambiguous-looking fellows in seedy coats, whom he called his clients. Indeed, I was aware that not only was he, at times, considerable of a ward politician, but he occasionally did a little business at the justices' courts, and was not unknown on the steps of the Tombs.

But with all his failings, and the annoyances he caused me, Nippers, like his compatriot Turkey, was a very useful man to me, wrote a neat, swift hand, and, when he chose, was not deficient in a gentlemanly sort of deportment. Though concerning the self-indulgent habits of Turkey I had my own private surmises, yet, touching Nippers, I was well persuaded that he was, at least, a temperate young man. But, indeed, nature herself seemed to have charged him at his birth so thoroughly with an irritable, brandylike disposition, that all subsequent potations were needless.

It was fortunate for me that, owing to its cause—indigestion—the irritability and consequent nervousness of Nippers were mainly observable in the morning, while in the afternoon he was comparatively mild. So that, Turkey's paroxysms only coming on about twelve o'clock, I never had to do with their eccentricities at one time. Their fits relieved each other, like guards.

Ginger Nut, the third on my list, was a lad some twelve years old. His father, a carman, sent him to my office as student at law, errand boy, cleaner and sweeper, at the rate of one dollar a week. He had a little desk to himself, but he did not use it much. Upon inspection, the drawer exhibited a great array of the shells of various sorts of nuts. Indeed, to this quick-witted youth the whole noble science of the law was contained in a nutshell. Not the least among his employments was his duty as cake and apple purveyor for Turkey and Nippers. Copying law papers being a dry, husky sort of business, my two scriveners were fain to moisten their mouths very often with Spitzenbergs, to be had at the numerous stalls nigh the customhouse and post office. Also, they sent Ginger Nut very frequently for that peculiar cake—small, flat, round, and very spicy—after which he had been named by them. Of all the fiery afternoon blunders of Turkey was his once moistening a ginger cake between his lips and clapping it onto a mortgage, for a seal. I came within an ace of dismissing him then.

Now my original business—that of a conveyancer and title hunter, and drawer-up of documents of all sorts—was considerably increased by receiving the Master's office. There was now great work for scriveners. Not only must I push the clerks already with me, but I must have additional help.

In answer to my advertisement, a motionless young man one morning stood upon my office threshold, the door being open, for it was summer. I can see that figure now—pallidly neat, pitiably respectable, incurably forlorn! It was Bartleby.

After a few words touching his qualifications, I engaged him, glad to have among my corps of copyists a man of so singularly sedate an aspect, which I thought might operate beneficially upon the flighty temper of Turkey and the fiery one of Nippers.

I should have stated before that ground-glass folding doors divided my premises into two parts, one of which was occupied by my scriveners, the other by myself. According to my humor, I threw open these doors, or closed them. I resolved to assign Bartleby a corner by the folding doors, but on my side of them, so as to have this quiet man within easy call, in case any trifling thing was to be done. I placed his desk close up to a small side window, which commanded no view at all, though it gave some light. Within three feet of the panes was a wall, and the light came down from far above, between two lofty buildings. I procured a high green folding screen, which might entirely isolate Bartleby from my sight, though not remove him from my voice. And thus, in a manner, privacy and society were conjoined.

At first Bartleby did an extraordinary quantity of writing. As if long famishing for something to copy, he seemed to gorge himself on my documents. I should have been quite delighted with his application had he been cheerfully industrious. But he wrote on silently, palely, mechanically.

It is, of course, an indispensable part of a scrivener's business to verify the accuracy of his copy, word by word. Where there are two or more scriveners in an office, they assist each other in this examination, one reading from the copy, the other holding the original. It is a very dull, wearisome, and lethargic affair.

Now and then, in the haste of business, it had been my habit to assist in comparing some brief document myself, calling Turkey or Nippers for this purpose. One object I had in placing Bartleby so handy to me behind the screen was to avail myself of his services on such trivial occasions. It was on the third day, I think, of his being with me that, being hurried to complete an affair, I abruptly called Bartleby to examine a paper with me. Imagine my surprise when, without moving from his privacy, Bartleby, in a singularly mild, firm voice, replied, "I would prefer not to."

I sat awhile in perfect silence, rallying my stunned faculties. Immediately it occurred to me that Bartleby had entirely misunderstood my meaning. I repeated my request in the clearest tone I could assume; but in quite as clear a one came the previous reply, "I would prefer not to."

"Prefer not to," echoed I, rising in high excitement and crossing the room with a stride. "What do you mean? Are you moonstruck? I want you to help me compare this sheet here—take it," and I thrust it towards him.

"I would prefer not to," said he.

I looked at him steadfastly. His face was leanly composed; his gray eyes dimly calm. Had there been the least uneasiness, anger, impatience, or impertinence in his manner; in other words, had there been anything ordinarily human about him, doubtless I should have violently dismissed him from the premises. But as it was, I should have as soon thought of turning my pale plaster of paris bust of Cicero out of doors.

I reseated myself at my desk. This is very strange, thought I. What had one best do? But my business hurried me. I concluded to forget the matter for the present, reserving it for my future leisure. So, calling Nippers from the other room, the paper was speedily examined.

A few days after this, Bartleby concluded four lengthy documents, being quadruplicates of a week's testimony taken before me in my High Court of Chancery. It was an important suit, and great accuracy was imperative. Having all things arranged, I called Turkey, Nippers, and Ginger Nut from the next room, meaning to place the four copies in the hands of my four clerks, while I should read from the original. Accordingly, Turkey, Nippers, and Ginger Nut had taken their seats in a row, each with his document in his hand, when I called to Bartleby to join this interesting group.

"Bartleby! Quick, I am waiting."

I heard a slow scrape of his chair legs on the uncarpeted floor, and soon he appeared, standing at the entrance of his hermitage.

"What is wanted?" said he mildly.

"The copies, the copies," said I hurriedly. "We are going to examine them. There"—and I held towards him the fourth quadruplicate.

"I would prefer not to," he said, and gently disappeared behind the screen.

For a few moments I was turned into a pillar of salt, standing at the head of my seated column of clerks. Recovering myself, I advanced towards the screen.

"*Why* do you refuse?"

"I would prefer not to."

There was something about Bartleby that not only strangely disarmed me, but, in a wonderful manner, touched and disconcerted me. I began to reason with him.

"These are your own copies we are about to examine. It is labor saving to you, because one examination will answer for your four papers. It is common usage. Every copyist is bound to help examine his copy. Is it not so? Will you not speak? Answer!"

"I prefer not to," he replied in a flutelike tone. It seemed to me that he had carefully revolved every statement that I made and could not gainsay the irresistible conclusion; but, at the same time, some paramount consideration prevailed with him to reply as he did.

"You are decided, then, not to comply with my request—a request made according to common usage and common sense?"

He briefly gave me to understand that on that point my judgment was sound. Yes: his decision was irreversible.

It is not seldom the case that when a man is browbeaten in some violently unreasonable way, he begins to stagger in his own plainest faith. Accordingly, if any disinterested persons are present, he turns to them for some reinforcement for his own faltering mind.

"Turkey," said I, "what do you think of this? Am I not right?"

"With submission, sir," said Turkey in his blandest tone, "I think that you are."

"Nippers," said I, "what do *you* think of it?"

"I think I should kick him out of the office."

(The reader of nice perceptions will here perceive that, it being morning, Nipper's ugly mood was on duty, and Turkey's off.)

"Ginger Nut," said I, willing to enlist the smallest suffrage in my behalf, "what do *you* think of it?"

"I think, sir, he's a little *loony*," replied Ginger Nut, with a grin.

"You hear what they say," said I, turning towards the screen, "come forth and do your duty."

But he vouchsafed no reply. Once more business hurried me. I determined again to postpone the consideration of this dilemma to my future leisure. With a little trouble we made out to examine the papers without Bartleby, who sat in his hermitage, oblivious to everything but his own peculiar business there.

Some days passed, the scrivener being employed upon another lengthy work. His late remarkable conduct led me to regard his ways narrowly. I observed that he never went to dinner; indeed, that he never went anywhere. As yet I had never, of my personal knowledge, known him to be outside of my office. At about eleven o'clock, though, in the morning, I noticed that Ginger Nut would advance towards the opening in Bartleby's screen, as if silently beckoned thither by a gesture invisible to me. The boy would then leave the office, jingling a few pence, and reappear with a handful of ginger nuts, which he delivered in the hermitage, receiving two of the cakes for his trouble. Bartleby lives, then, on ginger nuts, thought I; never eats a dinner, properly speaking.

Poor fellow! thought I. He means no mischief; his eccentricities are involuntary. He is useful to me. I can get along with him. If I turn him away, the chances are he will fall in with some less indulgent employer, and then he will be rudely treated, and perhaps driven forth miserably to starve. Yes. Here I can cheaply purchase a delicious self-approval. To befriend Bartleby, to humor him in his strange willfulness, will cost me little or nothing, while I lay up in my soul what will eventually prove a sweet morsel for my conscience.

But this mood was not invariable with me. The passiveness of Bartleby sometimes irritated me. One afternoon I felt strangely goaded to encounter him in new opposition—to elicit some angry spark from him answerable to my own.

"Bartleby," said I, "Ginger Nut is away; just step around to the post office, won't you" (it was but a three minutes' walk) "and see if there is anything for me?"

"I would prefer not to."

"You *will* not?"

"I *prefer* not."

I staggered to my desk, and sat there in a deep study. Was there any other thing in which I could procure myself to be ignominiously repulsed by this lean, penniless wight—my hired clerk? What added thing is there, perfectly reasonable, that he will be sure to refuse to do?

"Bartleby!"

No answer.

"Bartleby," in a louder tone.

No answer.

"Bartleby," I roared.

Like a ghost he appeared at the entrance of his hermitage.

"Go to the next room and tell Nippers to come to me."

"I prefer not to," he respectfully and slowly said, and mildly disappeared.

"Very good, Bartleby," said I in a quiet, self-possessed tone, intimating some terrible retribution very close at hand. At the moment I half intended something of the kind. But upon the whole, as it was drawing towards my dinner hour, I thought it best to put on my hat and walk home for the day, suffering much from perplexity and distress of mind.

Shall I acknowledge it? The conclusion of this whole business was that it soon became a fixed fact of my chambers that a pale young scrivener by the name of Bartleby had a desk there; that he copied for me at the usual rate of four cents for one hundred words, but was permanently exempt from examining the work done by him, and was never, on any account, to be dispatched on the most trivial errand of any sort.

As days passed on, I became considerably reconciled to Bartleby. His steadiness, his freedom from all dissipation, his incessant industry (except when he chose to throw himself into a standing reverie behind his screen), his great stillness, his unalterableness of demeanor under all circumstances, made him a valuable acquisition. One prime thing was this—*he was always there*—first in the morning, continually through the day, and the last at night.

ONE SUNDAY morning I happened to go to Trinity Church to hear a celebrated preacher, and finding myself rather early, I thought I would walk round to my chambers for a while. Upon applying my key to the lock, I found it resisted by something inserted from the inside. Quite surprised, I called out, when to my consternation a key was turned from within; and thrusting his lean visage at me, and holding the door ajar, Bartleby appeared, in his shirt sleeves and otherwise in a strangely tattered dishabille, saying quietly that he was sorry, but he was deeply engaged just then and preferred not admitting me at present. In a brief word or two he moreover added that perhaps I had better walk round the block two or three times, and by that time he would probably have concluded his affairs.

Now, the utterly unsurmised appearance of Bartleby, tenanting my law chambers of a Sunday morning, with his cadaverously gentlemanly nonchalance, had such a strange effect upon me that I slunk away from my own door and did as desired. But not without sundry twinges of impotent rebellion against Bartleby's mild effrontery. Indeed, it was his wonderful mildness chiefly, which not only disarmed me, but un-manned me, as it were. For I consider that one, for the time, is unmanned when he tranquilly permits his hired clerk to dictate to him and order him away from his own premises. Furthermore, I was uneasy as to what Bartleby could possibly be doing in my office in his shirt sleeves and in an otherwise dismantled condition of a Sunday morning. Was anything amiss going on? Nay, that was out of the question. It was not to be thought of for a moment that Bartleby was an immoral person. But what could he be doing there—copying? Nay again, whatever might be his eccentricities, Bartleby was an eminently decorous person. He would be the last man to sit down to his desk in any state approaching to nudity.

Nevertheless, my mind was not pacified, and full of a restless curiosity, at last I returned to the door. Without hindrance I inserted my key, opened it, and entered. I looked round anxiously, peeped behind Bartleby's screen; but it was very plain that he was gone. Upon more closely examining the place, I surmised that for an indefinite period Bartleby must have eaten, dressed, and slept in my office, and that too without plate, mirror, or bed. The cushioned seat of a rickety old sofa in one corner bore the faint impress of a lean, reclining form. Rolled away under his desk was a blanket; on a chair, a tin basin, with soap and a ragged towel; in a newspaper, a few crumbs of ginger nuts and a morsel of cheese. Yes, thought I, it is evident enough that Bartleby has been making his home here, keeping bachelor's hall all by himself. Immediately then the thought came sweeping across me, What miserable friendlessness and loneliness are here revealed! Think of it. Of a Sunday, Wall Street is deserted, and every night of every day it is an emptiness.

For the first time in my life a feeling of overpowering stinging melancholy seized me. The bond of a common humanity drew me irresistibly to gloom. I remembered the bright silks and sparkling faces

I had seen that day, and I contrasted them with the pallid copyist, and thought to myself, Ah, happiness courts the light, so we deem the world is gay; but misery hides aloof, so we deem that misery there is none. Presentiments of strange discoveries hovered round me. The scrivener's pale form appeared to me laid out, among uncaring strangers, in its shivering winding-sheet.

Suddenly I was attracted by Bartleby's closed desk, the key in open sight left in the lock.

I mean no mischief, seek the gratification of no heartless curiosity, thought I; besides, the desk is mine, and its contents, too, so I will make bold to look within. Everything was methodically arranged, the papers smoothly placed. The pigeonholes were deep, and removing the files of documents, I groped into their recesses. Presently I felt something there, and dragged it out. It was an old bandanna handkerchief, heavy and knotted. I opened it, and saw it was a savings bank.

I now recalled all the quiet mysteries which I had noted in the man. I remembered that he never spoke but to answer; that, though at intervals he had considerable time to himself, yet I had never seen him reading—no, not even a newspaper; that for long periods he would stand looking out, at his pale window behind the screen, upon the dead brick wall; I was quite sure he never visited any refectory or eating house; that he never went out for a walk; that though so thin and pale, he never complained of ill health. And more than all, I remembered a certain unconscious air of pallid—how shall I call it?—of pallid haughtiness, say, or rather an austere reserve about him, which had positively awed me into my tame compliance with his eccentricities.

As the forlornness of Bartleby grew and grew to my imagination, so did melancholy merge into fear, pity into repulsion. Up to a certain point misery enlists our best affections, but in certain special cases beyond that point it does not. To a sensitive being, pity is not seldom pain. And when at last it is perceived that such pity cannot lead to effectual succor, common sense bids the soul be rid of it. What I saw that morning persuaded me that the scrivener was the victim of innate and incurable disorder. I might give alms to his body, but it was his soul that suffered, and his soul I could not reach.

I did not accomplish the purpose of going to Trinity Church.

Somehow, the things I had seen disqualified me. I walked homeward, thinking what I would do with Bartleby. Finally, I resolved upon this—I would put certain calm questions to him the next morning, touching his history, etc., and if he declined to answer them openly and unreservedly (and I supposed he would prefer not), then to give him a twenty-dollar bill over and above whatever I might owe him, and tell him his services were no longer required; but that if in any other way I could assist him, I would be happy to do so, especially if he desired to return to his native place, wherever that might be. Moreover, if after reaching home he found himself at any time in want of aid, a letter from him would be sure of a reply.

The next morning came.

"Bartleby," said I, gently calling to him behind his screen.

No reply.

"Bartleby," said I in a still gentler tone, "come here; I am not going to ask you to do anything you would prefer not to do—I simply wish to speak to you."

Upon this he noiselessly slid into view.

"Will you tell me, Bartleby, where you were born?"

"I would prefer not to."

"Will you tell me *anything* about yourself?"

"I would prefer not to."

"But what reasonable objection can you have to speak to me? I feel friendly towards you."

He did not look at me while I spoke, but kept his glance fixed upon my bust of Cicero, which, as I then sat, was directly behind me, some six inches above my head.

"What is your answer, Bartleby?" said I, after waiting a considerable time for a reply.

"At present I prefer to give no answer," he said, and retired into his hermitage.

Mortified as I was at his behavior, and resolved as I had been to dismiss him when I entered my office, nevertheless I strangely felt something superstitious knocking at my heart, denouncing me for a villain if I dared to breathe one bitter word against this forlornest of mankind. At last, familiarly drawing my chair behind his screen, I sat down and said, "Bartleby, never mind, then, about revealing your history; but let me entreat you, as a friend, to comply as far as may be with the usages of this office. Say now, you will help to examine papers tomorrow or next day: in short, say now that in a day or two you will begin to be a little reasonable. Say so, Bartleby."

"At present I would prefer not to be a little reasonable," was his mildly cadaverous reply.

Just then the folding doors opened and Nippers approached. He seemed suffering from an unusually bad night's rest, induced by severer indigestion than common. He overheard Bartleby's answer.

"*Prefer not*, eh?" gritted Nippers. "I'd *prefer* him, if I were you, sir"—addressing me—"I'd give him preferences, the stubborn mule! What is it, sir, pray, that he *prefers* not to do now?"

Bartleby moved not a limb.

"Mr. Nippers," said I, "I'd prefer that you would withdraw for the present."

Somehow, of late, I had got into the way of involuntarily using this word prefer upon all sorts of not exactly suitable occasions. And I trembled to think that my contact with the scrivener had already and seriously affected me in a mental way. What further and deeper aberration might it not yet produce? Surely I must get rid of this demented man. But I thought it prudent not to break the dismissal at once.

The next day I noticed that Bartleby did nothing but stand at his window in his dead-wall reverie. Upon asking him why he did not write, he said that he had decided upon doing no more writing.

"Why, how now? What next!" exclaimed I. "Do no more writing?"

"No more."

"And what is the reason?"

"Do you not see the reason for yourself?" he indifferently replied.

I looked steadfastly at him, and perceived that his eyes looked dull and glazed. Instantly it occurred to me that his diligence in copying by his dim window might have temporarily impaired his vision.

I was touched. I said something in condolence with him. I hinted that of course he did wisely in abstaining from writing for a while, and urged him to embrace that opportunity of taking wholesome exercise in the open air. This, however, he did not do.

A few days went by. Whether Bartleby's eyes improved or not, I could not say. To all appearance, I thought they did. But when I asked him if they did, he vouchsafed no answer. At all events, he would do no copying. At last, in reply to my urgings, he informed me that he had permanently given up copying.

"What!" exclaimed I. "Suppose your eyes should get entirely well—better than ever before—would you not copy then?"

"I have given up copying," he answered, and slid aside.

He remained as ever, a fixture in my chamber. What was to be done? He would do nothing in the office; why should he stay there? In plain fact, he had now become a millstone to me. Yet I was sorry for him. If he would but have named a single relative or friend, I would instantly have written, and urged their taking the poor fellow away to some convenient retreat. But he seemed alone, absolutely alone in the universe. At length, necessities connected with my business tyrannized over all other considerations. Decently as I could, I told Bartleby that in six days' time he must unconditionally leave the office. I warned him to take measures, in the interval, for procuring some other abode. I offered to assist him in this endeavor, if he himself would but take the first step towards a removal. "And when you finally quit me, Bartleby," added I, "I shall see that you go not away entirely unprovided. Six days from this hour, remember."

At the expiration of that period, I peeped behind the screen, and lo! Bartleby was there.

I buttoned up my coat, balanced myself, advanced slowly towards him, touched his shoulder, and said, "The time has come; you must quit this place; I am sorry for you; here is money; but you must go."

"I would prefer not," he replied, with his back still towards me.

"You *must*."

He remained silent.

"Bartleby," said I, "I owe you twelve dollars on account; here are thirty-two; the odd twenty are yours. Will you take it?" and I handed the bills towards him.

But he made no motion.

"I will leave them here, then," putting them under a weight on the table. Then taking my hat and cane and going to the door, I tranquilly turned and added, "After you have removed your things from these offices, Bartleby, you will of course lock the door and, if you please, slip your key underneath the mat, so that I may have it in the morning. I shall not see you again; so good-by to you. If, hereafter, in your new place of abode, I can be of any service to you, do not fail to advise me by letter. Good-by, Bartleby, and fare you well."

But he answered not a word; like the last column of some ruined temple, he remained standing mute and solitary in the middle of the otherwise deserted room.

As I walked home in a pensive mood, my vanity got the better of my pity. I could not but highly plume myself on my masterly management in getting rid of Bartleby. The beauty of my procedure seemed to consist in its perfect quietness. There was no vulgar bullying, no bravado of any sort. Without loudly bidding Bartleby depart—as an inferior genius might have done—I *assumed* the ground that depart he must, and upon that assumption built all I had to say. The more I thought over my procedure, the more I was charmed with it. Nevertheless, next morning, upon awakening, I had my doubts—I had somehow slept off the fumes of vanity. One of the coolest and wisest hours a man has is just after he awakes in the morning. My procedure seemed as sagacious as ever—but only in theory. How it would prove in practice—there was the rub.

After breakfast I walked downtown, arguing the probabilities pro and con. As I had intended, I was earlier than usual at my office door. I stood listening for a moment. All was still. He must be gone. I tried the knob. The door was locked. Yes, my procedure had worked to a charm; he indeed must be vanished. Yet a certain melancholy mixed with this: I was almost sorry for my brilliant success. I was fumbling under the doormat for the key, which Bartleby was to have left there for me, when accidentally my knee knocked against a panel, producing a summoning sound, and in response a voice came to me from within— "Not yet; I am occupied."

It was Bartleby.

I was thunderstruck. For an instant I stood like the man who, pipe in mouth, was killed one cloudless afternoon long ago in Virginia by summer lightning; at his own warm open window he was killed, and remained leaning out there upon the dreamy afternoon till someone touched him, when he fell.

"Not gone!" I murmured at last. But again obeying that wondrous ascendancy which the inscrutable scrivener had over me, I slowly went downstairs and out into the street and, while walking round the block, considered what I should next do in this unheard-of perplexity. Turn the man out by an actual thrusting I could not; to drive him away by calling him hard names would not do; calling in the police was an unpleasant idea; and yet, permit him to enjoy his cadaverous triumph over me—this, too, I could not think of. What was to be done? Finally, I resolved to argue the matter over with him again.

"Bartleby," said I, entering the office with a quietly severe expression, "I am seriously displeased. I am pained, Bartleby. I had thought better of you. I had imagined you of such a gentlemanly organization that in any delicate dilemma a slight hint would suffice. But it appears I am deceived. Why," I added, unaffectedly starting, "you have not even touched that money yet," pointing to it, just where I had left it the evening previous.

He answered nothing.

"Will you, or will you not, quit me?" I now demanded in a sudden passion, advancing close to him.

"I would prefer *not* to quit you," he replied, gently emphasizing the not.

"What earthly right have you to stay here? Do you pay any rent? Do you pay my taxes? Or is this property yours?"

He answered nothing.

"Are you ready to go on and write now? Are your eyes recovered? Could you copy a small paper for me this morning? Or help examine a few lines? Or step round to the post office? In a word, will you do anything at all to give a coloring to your refusal to depart the premises?"

He silently retired into his hermitage.

I was now in such a state of nervous resentment that I thought it but prudent to check myself at present from further demonstrations. I endeavored immediately to occupy myself, and at the same time to comfort my despondency. I tried to fancy that in the course of the morning, at such time as might prove agreeable to him, Bartleby, of his own free accord, would emerge from his hermitage and take up some decided line of march in the direction of the door. But no. Half past twelve o'clock came; Turkey began to glow in the face, overturn his inkstand, and become generally obstreperous; Nippers abated into quietude and courtesy; Ginger Nut munched his noon apple; and Bartleby remained standing at his window in one of his profoundest dead-wall reveries. Will it be credited? Ought I to acknowledge it? That afternoon I left the office without saying one further word to him.

Some days now passed, during which at leisure intervals I looked a little into Edwards' *Freedom of the Will* and Priestley on *Necessity*. Under the circumstances, those books induced a salutary feeling. Gradually I slid into the persuasion that Bartleby was billeted upon me for some mysterious purpose of an all-wise Providence, which it was not for a mere mortal like me to fathom. Yes, Bartleby, stay there behind your screen, thought I; I shall persecute you no more; you are harmless and noiseless as any of these old chairs. At last I see it, I feel it; I penetrate to the predestinated purpose of my life. Others may have loftier parts to enact, but my mission in this world, Bartleby, is to furnish you with office room for such period as you may see fit to remain.

I believe that this wise and blessed frame of mind would have continued with me had it not been for the unsolicited and uncharitable remarks obtruded upon me by my professional friends who visited the rooms. Sometimes an attorney, calling at my office and finding no one but the scrivener there, would undertake to obtain some sort of precise information from him touching my whereabouts; but without heeding his idle talk, Bartleby would remain standing immovable in the middle of the room. So after contemplating him in that position for a time, the attorney would depart, no wiser than he came.

Also, when a reference was going on, and the room full of lawyers and witnesses, and business driving fast, some deeply occupied legal gentleman present, seeing Bartleby wholly unemployed, would request him to run round to his office and fetch some papers for him. Thereupon, Bartleby would tranquilly decline, and yet remain idle as before. Then the lawyer would give a great stare, and turn to me. And what could I say? At last I was made aware that all through the circle of my professional acquaintance a whisper of wonder was running round, having reference to the strange creature I kept at my office. And as my friends continually intruded their relentless remarks upon this apparition, a great change was wrought in me. I resolved to gather all my faculties together, and forever rid me of this intolerable incubus.

Ere revolving any complicated project, however, I first simply suggested to Bartleby the propriety of his permanent departure. In a calm and serious tone I commended the idea to his careful and mature consideration. But, having taken three days to meditate upon it, he apprised me that his original determination remained the same; in short, that he still preferred to abide with me.

What shall I do? I now said to myself, buttoning up my coat to the last button. What shall I do? What ought I to do? What does conscience say I *should* do with this man, or, rather, ghost. Rid myself of him, I must; go, he shall. But how? You will not thrust him, the poor, pale, passive mortal—you will not thrust such a helpless creature out of your door? You will not dishonor yourself by such cruelty? No, I will not, I cannot do that. What, then, will you do? For all your coaxing, he will not budge. Bribes he leaves under your own paperweight on your table; in short, it is quite plain that he prefers to cling to you.

Then something severe, something unusual must be done. What! Surely you will not have him collared by a constable, and commit his innocent pallor to the common jail? No more, then. Since he will not quit me, I must quit him. I will change my offices; I will move elsewhere, and give him fair notice that if I find him on my new premises, I will then proceed against him as a common trespasser.

Acting accordingly, next day I thus addressed him: "I find these chambers too far from the city hall; the air is unwholesome. In a word, I propose to remove my offices next week, and shall no longer require your services. I tell you this now, in order that you may seek another place."

He made no reply, and nothing more was said.

On the appointed day I engaged carts and men, proceeded to my chambers, and, having but little furniture, everything was removed in a few hours. Throughout, the scrivener remained standing behind the screen, which I directed to be removed the last thing. It was withdrawn; and, being folded up like a huge folio, left him the motionless occupant of a naked room. I stood in the entry watching him a moment, while something from within me upbraided me.

I reentered, with my hand in my pocket—and—and my heart in my mouth.

"Good-by, Bartleby; I am going—good-by, and God someway bless you; and take that," slipping something in his hand. But it dropped upon the floor, and then—strange to say—I tore myself from him whom I had so longed to be rid of.

Established in my new quarters, for a day or two I kept the door locked, and started at every footfall in the passages. When I returned to my rooms after any little absence, I would pause at the threshold for an instant, and attentively listen, ere applying my key. But these fears were needless. Bartleby never came nigh me.

I thought all was going well, when a perturbed-looking stranger visited me, inquiring whether I was the person who had recently occupied rooms at No. —— Wall Street.

Full of forebodings, I replied that I was.

"Then, sir," said the stranger, who proved a lawyer, "you are responsible for the man you left there. He refuses to do any copying; he refuses to do anything; he says he prefers not to; and he refuses to quit the premises."

"I am very sorry, sir," said I, with assumed tranquillity, but an inward tremor, "but, really, the man you allude to is nothing to me— he is no relation or apprentice of mine, that you should hold me responsible for him."

"In mercy's name, who is he?"

"I certainly cannot inform you. I know nothing about him. Formerly I employed him as a copyist; but he has done nothing for me now for some time past."

"I shall settle him, then. Good morning, sir."

Several days passed, and I heard nothing more; and, though I often felt a charitable prompting to call at the place and see poor Bartleby, yet a certain squeamishness, of I know not what, withheld me.

All is over with him by this time, thought I at last, when, through another week, no further intelligence reached me. But, coming to my room the day after, I found several persons waiting at my door in a high state of nervous excitement.

"That's the man—here he comes," cried the foremost one, whom I recognized as the lawyer who had previously called upon me alone.

"You must take him away, sir, at once," cried a portly person among them, advancing upon me, and whom I knew to be the landlord of No. —— Wall Street. "These gentlemen, my tenants, cannot stand it any longer; Mr. B——"—pointing to the lawyer—"has turned him out of his room, and he now persists in haunting the building generally, sitting upon the banisters of the stairs by day, and sleeping in the entry by night. Everybody is concerned; clients are leaving the offices; some fears are entertained of a mob; something you must do, and that without delay."

Aghast at this torrent, I fell back before it, and would fain have locked myself in my new quarters. In vain I persisted that Bartleby was nothing to me—no more than to anyone else. In vain—I was the last person known to have anything to do with him, and they held me to the terrible account. I considered the matter, and at length said that if the lawyer would give me a confidential interview with the scrivener in his (the lawyer's) own room, I would, that afternoon, strive my best to rid them of the nuisance they complained of.

Going upstairs to my old haunt, there was Bartleby silently sitting upon the banister at the landing.

"What are you doing here, Bartleby?" said I.

"Sitting upon the banister," he mildly replied.

I motioned him into the lawyer's room; the lawyer left us.

"Bartleby," said I, "are you aware that you are the cause of great tribulation to me, by persisting in occupying the entry after being dismissed from the office?"

No answer.

"Now one of two things must take place. Either you must do something, or something must be done to you. Now what sort of business would you like to engage in? Would you like to reengage in copying for someone?"

"No; I would prefer not to make any change."

"Would you like a clerkship in a dry-goods store?"

"There is too much confinement about that. No, I would not like a clerkship; but I am not particular."

"Too much confinement!" I cried. "Why, you keep yourself confined all the time!"

"I would prefer not to take a clerkship," he rejoined, as if to settle that little item at once.

"How would a bartender's business suit you? There is no trying of the eyesight in that."

"I would not like it at all; though, as I said before, I am not particular."

His unwonted wordiness inspirited me. I returned to the charge.

"Well, then, would you like to travel through the country collecting bills for the merchants? That would improve your health."

"No; I would prefer to be doing something else."

"How, then, would going as a companion to Europe, to entertain some young gentleman with your conversation—how would that suit you?"

"Not at all. It does not strike me that there is anything definite about that. I like to be stationary. But I am not particular."

Despairing of all further efforts, I was precipitately leaving him when a final thought occurred to me—one which had not been wholly unindulged before.

"Bartleby," said I, in the kindest tone I could assume under such existing circumstances, "will you go home with me now—not to my office, but my dwelling—and remain there till we can conclude upon some convenient arrangement for you at our leisure? Come, let us start now, right away."

"No; at present I would prefer not to make any change at all."

I answered nothing; but, effectually dodging everyone by the suddenness and rapidity of my flight, rushed from the building and, jumping into the first omnibus, was soon removed from pursuit. As soon as tranquillity returned, I distinctly perceived that I had now done all that I possibly could, both in respect to the demands of the landlord and his tenants, and with regard to my own desire and sense of duty, to shield Bartleby from rude persecution. I now strove to be entirely carefree and quiescent. But so fearful was I of being again hunted out by the incensed landlord and his exasperated tenants, that, surrendering my business to Nippers for a few days, I drove in my carriage about the upper part of the town and through the suburbs, crossed over to Jersey City and Hoboken, and paid fugitive visits to Manhattanville and Astoria. In fact, I almost lived in my carriage for the time.

When again I entered my office, lo, a note from the landlord lay upon the desk. I opened it with trembling hands. It informed me that the writer had sent to the police and had Bartleby removed to the Tombs as a vagrant. Moreover, since I knew more about him than anyone else, he wished me to appear at that place and make a suitable statement of the facts. These tidings had a conflicting effect upon me. At first I was indignant; but, at last, almost approved. The landlord's energetic, summary disposition had led him to adopt a procedure which I do not think I would have decided upon myself; and yet, as a last resort, under such peculiar circumstances, it seemed the only plan.

As I afterwards learned, the poor scrivener, when told that he must be conducted to the Tombs, offered not the slightest obstacle, but, in his pale unmoving way, silently acquiesced.

Some of the compassionate and curious bystanders joined the party; and, headed by one of the constables arm in arm with Bartleby, the silent procession filed its way through all the noise and heat and joy of the roaring thoroughfares at noon.

The same day I received the note I went to the Tombs. Seeking the right officer, I stated the purpose of my call, and was informed that the individual I described was, indeed, within. I then assured the officer that Bartleby was a perfectly honest man and greatly to be pitied, however unaccountably eccentric. I narrated all I knew, and closed by suggesting the idea of letting him remain in as indulgent confinement as possible, till something less harsh might be done—though, indeed, I hardly knew what. At all events, if nothing else could be decided upon, the almshouse must receive him. I then begged to have an interview.

Being under no disgraceful charge, and quite serene and harmless in all his ways, they had permitted him freely to wander about the prison and, especially, in the enclosed grass-platted yards thereof. And so I found him there, standing all alone in the quietest of the yards, his face towards a high wall, while all around, from the narrow slits of the jail windows, I thought I saw peering out upon him the eyes of murderers and thieves.

"Bartleby!"

"I know you," he said, without looking round, "and I want nothing to say to you."

"It was not I that brought you here, Bartleby," said I, keenly pained at his implied suspicion. "And to you, this should not be so vile a place. Nothing reproachful attaches to you by being here. And see, it is not so sad a place as one might think. Look, there is the sky, and here is the grass."

"I know where I am," he replied, but would say nothing more, and so I left him.

As I entered the corridor again, a broad meatlike man in an apron accosted me and, jerking his thumb over his shoulder, said, "Is that your friend?"

"Yes."

"Does he want to starve? If he does, let him live on the prison fare, that's all."

"Who are you?" asked I, not knowing what to make of such an unofficially speaking person in such a place.

"I am the grub man. Such gentlemen as have friends here hire me to provide them with something good to eat."

"Is this so?" said I, turning to the turnkey.

He said it was.

"Well, then," said I, slipping some silver into the grub man's hands, "I want you to give particular attention to my friend there; let him have the best dinner you can get. And you must be as polite to him as possible."

"Introduce me, will you?" said the grub man, looking at me with an expression which seemed to say he was all impatience for an opportunity to give a specimen of his breeding.

Thinking it would prove of benefit to the scrivener, I acquiesced; and, asking the grub man his name, went up with him to Bartleby.

"Bartleby, this is a friend; you will find him very useful to you."

"Your sarvant, sir, your sarvant," said the grub man, making a low salutation behind his apron. "Hope you find it pleasant here, sir; nice grounds—cool apartments—hope you'll stay with us some time—try to make it agreeable. What will you have for dinner today?"

"I prefer not to dine today," said Bartleby, turning away. "It would disagree with me; I am unused to dinners." So saying, he slowly moved to the other side of the enclosure and took up a position fronting the dead wall.

"How's this?" said the grub man, addressing me with a stare of astonishment. "He's odd, ain't he?"

"I think he is a little deranged," said I sadly.

"Deranged? Deranged is it? Well, now, upon my word, I thought that friend of yourn was a gentleman forger; they are always pale and genteellike, them forgers. I can't help pity 'em—can't help it, sir," he added touchingly.

"I cannot stop longer, but look to my friend yonder. You will not lose by it. I will see you again."

Some few days after this I again obtained admission to the Tombs, and went through the corridors in quest of Bartleby, but without finding him.

"I saw him coming from his cell not long ago," said a turnkey. "Maybe he's gone to loiter in the yards."

So I went in that direction.

"Are you looking for the silent man?" said another turnkey, passing me. "Yonder he lies—sleeping in the yard there. 'Tis not twenty minutes since I saw him lie down."

The yard was entirely quiet. It was not accessible to the common prisoners. The surrounding walls, of amazing thickness, kept off all sounds behind them. The Egyptian character of the masonry weighed upon me with its gloom. But a soft imprisoned turf grew underfoot. The heart of the eternal pyramids, it seemed, wherein, by some strange magic, through the clefts, grass seed, dropped by birds, had sprung.

Strangely huddled at the base of the wall, his knees drawn up, and lying on his side, his head touching the cold stones, I saw the wasted Bartleby. But nothing stirred. I paused, then went close up to him; stooped over, and saw that his dim eyes were open; otherwise he seemed profoundly sleeping. Something prompted me to touch him. I felt his hand, when a tingling shiver ran up my arm and down my spine to my feet.

The round face of the grub man peered upon me now. "His dinner is ready. Won't he dine today, either? Or does he live without dining?"

"Lives without dining," said I, and closed the eyes.

"Eh! He's asleep, ain't he?"

"With kings and counselors," murmured I.

ERE PARTING with the reader, let me divulge one little item of rumor which came to my ear a few months after the scrivener's decease. How true it is I cannot now tell, but the report was this: that before he came to me Bartleby had been a subordinate clerk in the dead letter office at Washington, from which he had been suddenly removed by a change in the administration. Dead letters! Does it not sound like dead men? Conceive a man by nature and misfortune prone to a pallid hopelessness, can any business seem more fitted to heighten it than that of continually handling these dead letters, and assorting them for the flames? For by the cartload they are annually burned. On errands of life, these letters speed to death.

Ah, Bartleby! Ah, humanity!

CHRISTMAS IS A SAD SEASON
FOR THE POOR

JOHN CHEEVER

John Cheever

CHRISTMAS IS A SAD season. The phrase came to Charlie an instant after the alarm clock had waked him, and named for him an amorphous depression that had troubled him all the previous evening. The sky outside his window was black. He sat up in bed and pulled the light chain that hung in front of his nose. Christmas is a very sad day of the year, he thought. Of all the millions of people in New York, I am practically the only one who has to get up in the cold black of six a.m. on Christmas Day in the morning; I am practically the only one.

He dressed, and when he went downstairs from the top floor of the rooming house in which he lived, the only sounds he heard were the coarse sounds of sleep; the only lights burning were lights that had been forgotten. Charlie ate some breakfast in an all-night lunch wagon and took an elevated train uptown. From Third Avenue, he walked over to Sutton Place. The neighborhood was dark. House after house put into the shine of the streetlights a wall of black windows. Millions and millions were sleeping, and this general loss of consciousness generated an impression of abandonment, as if this were the fall of the city, the end of time.

He opened the iron-and-glass doors of the apartment building where he had been working for six months as an elevator operator, and went through the elegant lobby to a locker room at the back. He put on a striped vest with brass buttons, a false ascot, a pair of pants with a light blue stripe on the seam, and a coat. The night elevator man was dozing on the little bench in the car. Charlie woke him. The night elevator man told him thickly that the day doorman had been taken sick and wouldn't be in that day. With the doorman sick, Charlie wouldn't have any relief for lunch, and a lot of people would expect him to whistle for cabs.

CHARLIE HAD BEEN on duty a few minutes when 14 rang—a Mrs. Hewing, who, he happened to know, was kind of immoral. Mrs. Hewing hadn't been to bed yet, and she got into the elevator wearing a long dress under her fur coat. She was followed by her two funny-looking dogs. He took her down and watched her go out into the dark and take her dogs to the curb. She was outside for only a few minutes. Then she came in and he took her up to 14 again. When she got off the elevator, she said, "Merry Christmas, Charlie."

"Well, it isn't much of a holiday for me, Mrs. Hewing," he said. "I think Christmas is a very sad season of the year. It isn't that people around here ain't generous—I mean I got plenty of tips—but, you see, I live alone in a furnished room and I don't have any family or anything, and Christmas isn't much of a holiday for me."

"I'm sorry, Charlie," Mrs. Hewing said. "I don't have any family myself. It is kind of sad when you're alone, isn't it?" She called her dogs and followed them into her apartment. He went down.

It was quiet then, and Charlie lighted a cigarette. The heating plant in the basement encompassed the building at that hour in a regular and profound vibration, and the sullen noises of arriving steam heat began to resound, first in the lobby and then to reverberate up through all the sixteen stories, but this was a mechanical awakening, and it didn't lighten his loneliness or his petulance. The black air outside the glass doors had begun to turn blue, but the blue light seemed to have no source; it appeared in the middle of the air. It was a tearful light, and as it picked out the empty street he wanted to cry. Then a cab drove up, and the Walsers got out, drunk and dressed in evening clothes, and he took them up to their penthouse. The Walsers got him to brooding about the difference between his life in a furnished room and the lives of the people overhead. It was terrible.

Then the early churchgoers began to ring, but there were only three of these that morning. A few more went off to church at eight o'clock, but the majority of the building remained unconscious, although the smell of bacon and coffee had begun to drift into the elevator shaft.

At a little after nine, a nursemaid came down with a child. Both the nursemaid and the child had a deep tan and had just returned, he knew, from Bermuda. He had never been to Bermuda. He, Charlie, was a prisoner, confined eight hours a day to a six-by-eight elevator cage, which was confined, in turn, to a sixteen-story shaft. In one building or another, he had made his living as an elevator operator for ten years. He estimated the average trip at about an eighth of a mile, and when he thought of the thousands of miles he had traveled, when he thought that he might have driven the car through the mists above the Caribbean and set it down on some coral beach in Bermuda, he held the narrowness of his travels against his passengers, as if it were not the nature of the elevator but the pressure of their lives that confined him, as if they had clipped his wings.

He was thinking about this when the DePauls, on 9, rang. They wished him a merry Christmas.

"Well, it's nice of you to think of me," he said as they descended, "but it isn't much of a holiday for me. Christmas is a sad season when you're poor. I live alone in a furnished room. I don't have any family."

"Who do you have dinner with, Charlie?" Mrs. DePaul asked.

"I don't have any Christmas dinner," Charlie said. "I just get a sandwich."

"Oh, Charlie!" Mrs. DePaul was a stout woman with an impulsive heart, and Charlie's plaint struck at her holiday mood as if she had been caught in a cloudburst. "I do wish we could share our Christmas dinner with you, you know," she said. "I come from Vermont, you know, and when I was a child, you know, we always used to have a great many people at our table. The mailman, you know, and the schoolteacher, and just anybody who didn't have any family of their own, you know, and I wish we could share our dinner with you the way we used to, you know, and I don't see any reason why we can't. We can't have you at the table, you know, because you couldn't leave the elevator—could you?—but just as soon as Mr. DePaul has carved the goose, I'll give you a ring, and I'll arrange a tray for you, you know, and I want you to come up and at least share our Christmas dinner."

Charlie thanked them, and their generosity surprised him, but he wondered if, with the arrival of friends and relatives, they wouldn't forget their offer.

Then old Mrs. Gadshill rang, and when she wished him a merry Christmas, he hung his head.

"It isn't much of a holiday for me, Mrs. Gadshill," he said. "Christmas is a sad season if you're poor. You see, I don't have any family. I live alone in a furnished room."

"I don't have any family either, Charlie," Mrs. Gadshill said. She spoke with a pointed lack of petulance, but her grace was forced. "That is, I don't have any children with me today. I have three children and seven grandchildren, but none of them can see their way to coming east for Christmas with me. Of course, I understand their problems. I know that it's difficult to travel with children during the holidays, although I always seemed to manage it when I was their age, but people feel differently, and we mustn't condemn them for the things we can't understand. But I know how you feel, Charlie. I haven't any family either. I'm just as lonely as you."

Mrs. Gadshill's speech didn't move him. Maybe she was lonely, but she had a ten-room apartment and three servants and bucks and bucks and diamonds and diamonds, and there were plenty of poor kids in the slums who would be happy at a chance at the food her cook threw away. Then he thought about poor kids. He sat down on a chair in the lobby and thought about them.

They got the worst of it. Beginning in the fall, there was all this excitement about Christmas and how it was a day for them. After Thanksgiving, they couldn't miss it. It was fixed so they couldn't miss it. The wreaths and decorations everywhere, and bells ringing, and trees in the park, and Santa Clauses on every corner, and pictures in the magazines and newspapers and on every wall and window in the city told them that if they were good, they would get what they wanted. Even if they couldn't read, they couldn't miss it. They couldn't miss it even if they were blind. It got into the air the poor kids inhaled. Every time they took a walk, they'd see all the expensive toys in the store windows, and they'd write letters to Santa Claus, and their mothers and fathers would promise to mail them, and after the kids had gone to sleep, they'd burn the letters in the stove. And when it came Christmas morning, how could you explain it, how could you tell them that Santa Claus only visited the rich, that he didn't know about the good? How could you face them when all you had to give them was a balloon or a lollipop?

On the way home from work a few nights earlier, Charlie had seen a woman and a little girl going down Fifty-ninth Street. The little girl was crying. He guessed she was crying, he knew she was crying, because she'd seen all the things in the toy-store windows and couldn't understand why none of them were for her. Her mother did housework, he guessed; or maybe was a waitress, and he saw them going back to a room like his, with green walls and no heat, on Christmas Eve, to eat a can of soup. And he saw the little girl hang up her ragged stocking and fall asleep, and he saw the mother looking through her purse for something to put into the stocking— This reverie was interrupted by a bell on 11. He went up, and Mr. and Mrs. Fuller were waiting.

When they wished him a merry Christmas, he said, "Well, it isn't much of a holiday for me, Mrs. Fuller. Christmas is a sad season when you're poor."

"Do you have any children, Charlie?" Mrs. Fuller asked.

"Four living," he said. "Two in the grave." The majesty of his lie overwhelmed him. "Mrs. Leary's a cripple," he added.

"How sad, Charlie," Mrs. Fuller said. She started out of the elevator when it reached the lobby, and then she turned. "I want to give your children some presents, Charlie," she said. "Mr. Fuller and I are going to pay a call now, but when we come back, I want to give you some things for your children."

He thanked her. Then the bell rang on 4, and he went up to get the Westons.

"It isn't much of a holiday for me," he told them when they wished him a merry Christmas. "Christmas is a sad season when you're poor. You see, I live alone in a furnished room."

"Poor Charlie," Mrs. Weston said. "I know just how you feel. During the war, when Mr. Weston was away, I was all alone at Christmas. I didn't have any Christmas dinner or a tree or anything. I just scrambled myself some eggs and sat there and cried." Mr. Weston, who had gone into the lobby, called impatiently to his wife. "I know just how you feel, Charlie," Mrs. Weston said.

By NOON, THE climate in the elevator shaft had changed from bacon and coffee to poultry and game, and the house, like an enormous and complex homestead, was absorbed in the preparations for a domestic feast. The children and their nursemaids had all returned from the park. Grandmothers and aunts were arriving in limousines. Most of the people who came through the lobby were carrying packages wrapped in colored paper, and were wearing their best furs and new clothes. Charlie continued to complain to most of the tenants when they wished him a merry Christmas, changing his story from the lonely bachelor to the poor father, and back again, as his mood changed, but this outpouring of melancholy, and the sympathy it aroused, didn't make him feel any better.

At half past one, 9 rang, and when he went up, Mr. DePaul was standing in the door of their apartment holding a cocktail shaker and a glass. "Here's a little Christmas cheer, Charlie," he said, and he poured Charlie a drink. Then a maid appeared with a tray of covered dishes, and Mrs. DePaul came out of the living room. "Merry Christmas, Charlie," she said. "I had Mr. DePaul carve the goose early, so that you could have some, you know. I didn't want to put the dessert on the tray, because I was afraid it would melt, you know, so when we have our dessert, we'll call you."

"And what is Christmas without presents?" Mr. DePaul said, and he brought a large, flat box from the hall and laid it on top of the covered dishes.

"You people make it seem like a real Christmas to me," Charlie said. Tears started into his eyes. "Thank you, thank you."

"Merry Christmas! Merry Christmas!" they called, and they watched him carry his dinner and his present into the elevator. He took the tray and the box into the locker room when he got down. On the tray, there was a soup, some kind of creamed fish, and a serving of goose. The bell rang again, but before he answered it, he tore open the DePaul's box and saw that it held a dressing gown. Their generosity and their

436

cocktail had begun to work on his brain, and he went jubilantly up to 12. Mrs. Gadshill's maid was standing in the door with a tray, and Mrs. Gadshill stood behind her. "Merry Christmas, Charlie!" she said. He thanked her, and tears came into his eyes again. On the way down, he drank off the glass of sherry on Mrs. Gadshill's tray. Mrs. Gadshill's contribution was a mixed grill. He ate the lamb chop with his fingers. The bell was ringing again, and he wiped his face with a paper towel and went up to 11. "Merry Christmas, Charlie," Mrs. Fuller said, and she was standing in the door with her arms full of packages wrapped in silver paper, just like a picture in an advertisement, and Mr. Fuller was beside her with an arm around her, and they both looked as if they were going to cry. "Here are some things I want you to take home to your children," Mrs. Fuller said. "And here's something for Mrs. Leary and here's something for you. And if you want to take these things out to the elevator, we'll have your dinner ready for you in a minute." He carried the things into the elevator and came back for the tray. "Merry Christmas, Charlie!" both of the Fullers called after him as he closed the door. He took their dinner and their presents into the locker room and tore open the box that was marked for him. There was an alligator wallet in it, with Mr. Fuller's initials in the corner. Their dinner was also goose, and he ate a piece of the meat with his fingers and was washing it down with a cocktail when the bell rang. He went up again. This time it was the Westons. "Merry Christmas, Charlie!" they said, and they gave him a cup of eggnog, a turkey dinner, and a present. Their gift was also a dressing gown. Then 7 rang, and when he went up, there was another dinner and some more toys. Then 14 rang, and when he went up, Mrs. Hewing was standing in the hall, in a kind of negligee, holding a pair of riding boots in one hand and some neckties in the other. She had been crying and drinking. "Merry Christmas, Charlie," she said tenderly. "I wanted to give you something, and I've been thinking about you all morning, and I've been all over the apartment, and these are the only things I could find that a man might want. These are the only things that Mr. Brewer left. I don't suppose you'd have any use for the riding boots, but wouldn't you like the neckties?" Charlie took the neckties and thanked her and hurried back to the car, for the elevator bell had rung three times.

BY THREE O'CLOCK CHARLIE HAD fourteen dinners spread on the table and the floor of the locker room, and the bell kept ringing. Just as he started to eat one, he would have to go up and get another, and he was in the middle of the Parsons' roast beef when he had to go up and get the DePauls' dessert. He kept the door of the locker room closed, for he sensed that the quality of charity is exclusive and that his friends would have been disappointed to find that they were not the only ones to try to lessen his loneliness. There were goose, turkey, chicken, pheasant, grouse, and pigeon. There were trout and salmon, creamed scallops and oysters, lobster, crabmeat, whitebait, and clams. There were plum puddings, mince pies, mousses, puddles of melted ice cream, layer cakes, torten, éclairs, and two slices of Bavarian cream. He had dressing gowns, neckties, cuff links, socks, and handkerchiefs, and one of the tenants had asked for his neck size and then given him three green shirts. There were a glass teapot filled, the label said, with jasmine honey, four bottles of after-shave lotion, some alabaster bookends, and a dozen steak knives. The avalanche of charity he had precipitated filled the locker room and made him hesitant, now and then, as if he had touched some wellspring in the female heart that would bury him alive in food and dressing gowns. He had made almost no headway on the food, for all the servings were preternaturally large, as if loneliness had been counted on to generate in him a brutish appetite. Nor had he opened any of the presents that had been given to him for his imaginary children, but he had drunk everything they sent down, and around him were the dregs of Martinis, Manhattans, Old-Fashioneds, champagne-and-raspberry-shrub cocktails, eggnogs, Bronxes, and Side Cars.

His face was blazing. He loved the world, and the world loved him. When he thought back over his life, it appeared to him in a rich and wonderful light, full of astonishing experiences and unusual friends. He thought that his job as an elevator operator—cruising up and down through hundreds of feet of perilous space—demanded the nerve and the intellect of a birdman. All the constraints of his life—the green walls of his room and the months of unemployment—dissolved. No one was ringing, but he got into the elevator and shot it at full speed up to the penthouse and down again, up and down, to test his wonderful mastery of space.

A bell rang on 12 while he was cruising, and he stopped in his flight long enough to pick up Mrs. Gadshill. As the car started to fall, he took his hands off the controls in a paroxysm of joy and shouted, "Strap on your safety belt, Mrs. Gadshill! We're going to make a loop-the-loop!" Mrs. Gadshill shrieked. Then, for some reason, she sat down on the floor of the elevator. Why was her face so pale, he wondered; why was she sitting on the floor? She shrieked again. He grounded the car gently, and cleverly, he thought, and opened the door. "I'm sorry if I scared you, Mrs. Gadshill," he said meekly. "I was only fooling." She shrieked again. Then she ran out into the lobby, screaming for the superintendent.

The superintendent fired Charlie and took over the elevator himself. The news that he was out of work stung Charlie for a minute. It was his first contact with human meanness that day. He sat down in the locker room and gnawed on a drumstick. His drinks were beginning to let him down, and while it had not reached him yet, he felt a miserable soberness in the offing. The excess of food and presents around him began to make him feel guilty and unworthy. He regretted bitterly the lie he had told about his children. He was a single man with simple needs. He had abused the goodness of the people upstairs. He was unworthy.

Then up through this drunken train of thought surged the sharp figure of his landlady and her three skinny children. He thought of them sitting in their basement room. The cheer of Christmas had passed them by. This image got him to his feet. The realization that he was in a position to give, that he could bring happiness easily to someone else, sobered him. He took a big burlap sack, which was used for collecting waste, and began to stuff it, first with his presents and then with the presents for his imaginary children. He worked with the haste of a man whose train is approaching the station, for he could hardly wait to see those long faces light up when he came in the door. He changed his clothes, and, fired by a wonderful and unfamiliar sense of power, he slung his bag over his shoulder like a regular Santa Claus, went out the back way, and took a taxi to the Lower East Side.

The landlady and her children had just finished off a turkey, which had been sent to them by the local Democratic club, and they were stuffed and uncomfortable when Charlie began pounding on the door, shouting "Merry Christmas!" He dragged the bag in after him and dumped the presents for the children onto the floor. There were dolls and musical toys, blocks, sewing kits, an Indian suit, and a loom, and it appeared to him that, as he had hoped, his arrival in the basement dispelled its gloom. When half the presents had been opened, he gave the landlady a bathrobe and went upstairs to look over the things he had been given for himself.

NOW, THE LANDLADY'S children had already received so many presents by the time Charlie arrived that they were confused with receiving, and it was only the landlady's intuitive grasp of the nature of charity that made her allow the children to open some of the presents while Charlie was still in the room, but as soon as he had gone, she stood between the children and the presents that were still unopened. "Now, you kids have had enough already," she said. "You kids have got your share. Just look at the things you got there. Why, you ain't even played with the half of them. Mary Anne, you ain't even looked at that doll the Fire Department give you. Now, a nice thing to do would be to take all this stuff that's left over to those poor people on Hudson Street—them Deckkers. They ain't got nothing." A beatific light came into her face when she realized that she could give, that she could bring cheer, that she could put a healing finger on a case needier than hers, and—like Mrs. DePaul and Mrs. Weston, like Charlie himself and like Mrs. Deckker, when Mrs. Deckker was to think, subsequently, of the poor Shannons—first love, then charity, and then a sense of power drove her. "Now, you kids help me get all this stuff together. Hurry, hurry, hurry," she said, for it was dark then, and she knew that we are bound, one to another, in licentious benevolence for only a single day, and that day was nearly over. She was tired, but she couldn't rest, she couldn't rest.

THE BOARDED WINDOW

AMBROSE BIERCE

Ambrose Bierce.

IN 1830, ONLY a few miles away from what is now the great city of Cincinnati, lay an immense and almost unbroken forest. The whole region was sparsely settled by people of the frontier—restless souls who no sooner had hewn fairly habitable homes out of the wilderness and attained to that degree of prosperity which today we should call indigence than, impelled by some mysterious impulse of their nature, they abandoned all and pushed farther westward, to encounter new perils and privations in the effort to regain the meager comforts which they had voluntarily renounced. Many of them had already forsaken that region for the remoter settlements, but among those remaining was one who had been of those first arriving. He lived alone in a house of logs surrounded on all sides by the great forest, of whose gloom and silence he seemed a part, for no one had ever known him to smile nor speak a needless word. His simple wants were supplied by the sale or barter of skins of wild animals in the river town, for not a thing did he grow upon the land which, if needful, he might have claimed by right of undisturbed possession. There were evidences of "improvements"— a few acres of ground immediately about the house had once been cleared of its trees, the decayed stumps of which were half concealed by the new growth that had been suffered to repair the ravage wrought by the ax. Apparently the man's zeal for agriculture had burned with a failing flame, expiring in penitential ashes.

The little log house, with its chimney of sticks, its roof of warping clapboards weighted with traversing poles and its chinking of clay, had a single door and, directly opposite, a window. The latter, however, was boarded up—nobody could remember a time when it was not. And none knew why it was so closed; certainly not because of the occupant's dislike of light and air, for on those rare occasions when a hunter had passed that lonely spot the recluse had commonly been seen sunning himself on his doorstep, if heaven had provided sunshine for his need. I fancy there are few persons living today who ever knew the secret of that window, but I am one, as you shall see.

The man's name was said to be Murlock. He was apparently seventy years old, actually about fifty. Something besides years had had a hand in his aging. His hair and long, full beard were white, his gray, lusterless eyes sunken, his face singularly seamed with wrinkles which appeared to belong to two intersecting systems. In figure he was tall and spare, with a stoop of the shoulders—a burden bearer. I never saw him; these particulars I learned from my grandfather, from whom also I got the man's story when I was a lad. He had known him when living nearby in that early day.

One day Murlock was found in his cabin, dead. It was not a time and place for coroners and newspapers, and I suppose it was agreed that he had died from natural causes or I should have been told, and should remember. I know only that with what was probably a sense of the fitness of things the body was buried near the cabin, alongside the grave of his wife, who had preceded him by so many years that local tradition had retained hardly a hint of her existence. That closes the final chapter of this true story—excepting, indeed, the circumstance that many years afterward, in company with an equally intrepid spirit, I penetrated to the place and ventured near enough to the ruined cabin to throw a stone against it, and ran away to avoid the ghost which every well-informed boy thereabout knew haunted the spot. But there is an earlier chapter—that supplied by my grandfather.

When Murlock built his cabin and began laying sturdily about with his ax to hew out a farm—the rifle, meanwhile, his means of support—he was young, strong and full of hope. In that eastern country whence he came he had married, as was the fashion, a young woman in all ways worthy of his honest devotion, who shared the dangers and privations of his lot with a willing spirit and light heart. There is no known record of her name; of her charms of mind and person tradition is silent and the doubter is at liberty to entertain his doubt; but God forbid that I should share it! Of their affection and happiness there is abundant assurance in every added day of the man's widowed life; for what but the magnetism of a blessed memory could have chained that venturesome spirit to a lot like that?

One day Murlock returned from gunning in a distant part of the forest to find his wife prostrate with fever, and delirious. There was no physician within miles, no neighbor; nor was she in a condition to be left, to summon help. So he set about the task of nursing her back to health, but at the end of the third day she fell into unconsciousness and so passed away, apparently, with never a gleam of returning reason.

From what we know of a nature like his we may venture to sketch in some of the details of the outline picture drawn by my grandfather. When convinced that she was dead, Murlock had sense enough to remember that the dead must be prepared for burial. In performance of this sacred duty he blundered now and again, did certain things incorrectly, and others which he did correctly were done over and over. His occasional failures to accomplish some simple and ordinary act filled him with astonishment, like that of a drunken man who wonders at the suspension of familiar natural laws. He was surprised, too, that he did not weep—surprised and a little ashamed; surely it is unkind not to weep for the dead. "Tomorrow," he said aloud, "I shall have to make the coffin and dig the grave; and then I shall miss her, when she is no longer in sight; but now—she is dead, of course, but it is all right—it *must* be all right, somehow. Things cannot be so bad as they seem."

He stood over the body in the fading light, adjusting the hair and putting the finishing touches to the simple toilet, doing all mechanically, with soulless care. And still through his consciousness ran an undersense of conviction that all was right—that he should have her again as before, and everything explained. He had had no experience in grief; his capacity had not been enlarged by use. His heart could not contain it all, nor his imagination rightly conceive it. He did not know he was so hard struck; *that* knowledge would come later, and never go. Grief is an artist of powers as various as the instruments upon which he plays his dirges for the dead, evoking from some the sharpest, shrillest notes, from others the low, grave chords that throb recurrent like the slow beating of a distant drum. Some natures it startles; some it stupefies. To one it comes like the stroke of an arrow, stinging all the sensibilities to a keener life; to another as the blow of a bludgeon, which in crushing benumbs. We may conceive Murlock to have been that way affected, for (and here we are upon surer ground than that of conjecture) no sooner had he finished his pious work than, sinking into a chair by the side of the table upon which the body lay, and noting how white the profile showed in the deepening gloom, he laid his arms upon the table's edge, and dropped his face into them, tearless yet and unutterably weary. At that moment came in through the open window a long, wailing sound like the cry of a lost child in the far deeps of the darkening wood! But the man did not move. Again, and nearer than before, sounded that unearthly cry upon his failing sense. Perhaps it was a wild beast; perhaps it was a dream. For Murlock was asleep.

Some hours later, as it afterward appeared, this unfaithful watcher awoke and lifting his head from his arms intently listened—he knew not why. There in the black darkness by the side of the dead, recalling all without a shock, he strained his eyes to see—he knew not what. His senses were all alert, his breath was suspended, his blood had stilled its tides as if to assist the silence. Who—what had waked him, and where was it?

Suddenly the table shook beneath his arms, and at the same moment he heard, or fancied that he heard, a light, soft step—another—sounds as of bare feet upon the floor!

He was terrified beyond the power to cry out or move. Perforce he waited—waited there in the darkness through seeming centuries of such dread as one may know, yet live to tell. He tried vainly to speak the dead woman's name, vainly to stretch forth his hand across the table to learn if she were there. His throat was powerless, his arms and hands were like lead. Then occurred something most frightful. Some heavy body seemed hurled against the table with an impetus that pushed it against his breast so sharply as nearly to overthrow him, and at the same instant he heard and felt the fall of something upon the floor with so violent a thump that the whole house was shaken by the impact. A scuffling ensued, and a confusion of sounds impossible to describe. Murlock had risen to his feet. Fear had by excess forfeited control of his faculties. He flung his hands upon the table. Nothing was there!

There is a point at which terror may turn to madness; and madness incites to action. With no definite intent, from no motive but the wayward impulse of a madman, Murlock sprang to the wall, with a little groping seized his loaded rifle, and without aim discharged it. By the flash which lit up the room with a vivid illumination, he saw an enormous panther dragging the dead woman toward the window, its teeth fixed in her throat! Then there were darkness blacker than before, and silence; and when he returned to consciousness the sun was high and the wood vocal with songs of birds.

The body lay near the window, where the beast had left it when frightened away by the flash and report of the rifle. The clothing was deranged, the long hair in disorder, the limbs lay anyhow. From the throat, dreadfully lacerated, had issued a pool of blood not yet entirely coagulated. The ribbon with which he had bound the wrists was broken; the hands were tightly clenched. Between the teeth was a fragment of the animal's ear.

JUG OF SILVER

TRUMAN CAPOTE

Truman Capote

AFTER SCHOOL I used to work in the Valhalla drugstore. It was owned by my uncle, Mr. Ed Marshall. I call him Mr. Marshall because everybody, including his wife, called him Mr. Marshall. Nevertheless he was a nice man.

This drugstore was maybe old-fashioned, but it was large and dark and cool: during summer months there was no pleasanter place in town. At the left, as you entered, was a tobacco-magazine counter behind which, as a rule, sat Mr. Marshall: a squat, square-faced, pink-fleshed man with looping, manly, white mustaches.

Beyond this counter stood the beautiful soda fountain. It was very antique and made of fine, yellowed marble, smooth to the touch but without a trace of cheap glaze. Mr. Marshall bought it at an auction in New Orleans in 1910 and was plainly proud of it. When you sat on the high, delicate stools and looked across the fountain you could see yourself reflected softly, as though by candlelight, in a row of ancient, mahogany-framed mirrors. All general merchandise was displayed in glass-doored, curiolike cabinets that were locked with brass keys. There was always in the air the smell of syrup and nutmeg and other delicacies.

The Valhalla was the gathering place of Wachata County till a certain Rufus McPherson came to town and opened a second drugstore directly across the courthouse square. This old Rufus McPherson was a villain; that is, he took away my uncle's trade. He installed fancy equipment such as electric fans and colored lights; he provided curb service and made grilled cheese sandwiches to order. Naturally, though

446

some remained devoted to Mr. Marshall, most folks couldn't resist Rufus McPherson.

For a while, Mr. Marshall chose to ignore him: if you were to mention McPherson's name he would sort of snort, finger his mustaches and look the other way. But you could tell he was mad. And getting madder. Then one day toward the middle of October, I strolled into the Valhalla to find him sitting at the fountain playing dominoes and drinking wine with Hamurabi.

Hamurabi was an Egyptian and some kind of dentist, though he didn't do much business as the people hereabouts have unusually strong teeth, due to an element in the water. He spent a great deal of his time loafing around the Valhalla and was my uncle's chief buddy. He was a handsome figure of a man, this Hamurabi, being dark-skinned and nearly seven feet tall; the matrons of the town kept their daughters under lock and key and gave him the eye themselves. He had no foreign accent whatsoever, and it was always my opinion that he wasn't any more Egyptian than the man in the moon.

Anyway, there they were swigging red Italian wine from a gallon jug. It was a troubling sight, for Mr. Marshall was a renowned teetotaler. So naturally, I thought: Oh, golly, Rufus McPherson has finally got his goat. That was not the case, however.

"Here, son," said Mr. Marshall, "come have a glass of wine."

"Sure," said Hamurabi, "help us finish it up. It's store bought, so we can't waste it."

Much later, when the jug was dry, Mr. Marshall picked it up and said, "Now we shall see!" And with that disappeared out into the afternoon.

"Where's he off to?" I asked.

"Ah," was all Hamurabi would say. He liked to devil me.

A half hour passed before my uncle returned. He was stooped and grunting under the load he carried. He set the jug atop the fountain and stepped back, smiling and rubbing his hands together. "Well, what do you think?"

"Ah," purred Hamurabi.

"Gee . . ." I said.

It was the same wine jug, God knows, but there was a wonderful difference; for now it was crammed to the brim with nickels and dimes that shone dully through the thick glass.

"Pretty, eh?" said my uncle. "Had it done over at the First National. Couldn't get in anything bigger-sized than a nickel. Still, there's lotsa money in there, let me tell you."

"But what's the point, Mr. Marshall?" I said. "I mean, what's the idea?"

Mr. Marshall's smile deepened to a grin. "This here's a jug of silver, you might say—"

"The pot at the end of the rainbow," interrupted Hamurabi.

"—and the idea, as you call it, is for folks to guess how much money is in there. For instance, say you buy a quarter's worth of stuff—well, then you get to take a chance. The more you buy, the more chances you get. And I'll keep all guesses in a ledger till Christmas Eve, at which time whoever comes closest to the right amount will get the whole shebang."

Hamurabi nodded solemnly. "He's playing Santa Claus—a mighty crafty Santa Claus," he said. "I'm going home and write a book: *The Skillful Murder of Rufus McPherson*." To tell the truth, he sometimes did write stories and send them out to the magazines. They always came back.

IT WAS SURPRISING, really like a miracle, how Wachata County took to the jug. Why, the Valhalla hadn't done so much business since Stationmaster Tully, poor soul, went stark raving mad and claimed to have discovered oil back of the depot, causing the town to be overrun with wildcat prospectors. Even the pool-hall bums who never spent a cent on anything not connected with whiskey or women took to investing their spare cash in milk shakes. A few elderly ladies publicly disapproved of Mr. Marshall's enterprise as a kind of gambling, but they didn't start any trouble and some even found occasion to visit us and hazard a guess. The school kids were crazy about the whole thing, and I was very popular because they figured I knew the answer.

"I'll tell you why all this is," said Hamurabi, lighting one of the Egyptian cigarettes he bought by mail from a concern in New York City. "It's not for the reason you may imagine; not, in other words, avidity. No. It's the mystery that's enchanting. Now you look at those nickels and dimes and what do you think: Ah, so much! No, no. You think: Ah, *how* much? And that's a profound question, indeed. It can mean different things to different people. Understand?"

And oh, was Rufus McPherson wild! When you're in trade, you count on Christmas to make up a large share of your yearly profit, and he was hard pressed to find a customer. So he tried to imitate the jug; but being such a stingy man he filled his with pennies. He also wrote a letter to the editor of *The Banner*, our weekly paper, in which he said that Mr. Marshall ought to be "tarred and feathered and strung up for turning innocent little children into confirmed gamblers and sending them down the path to hell!" You can imagine what kind of laughingstock he was. Nobody had anything for McPherson but scorn. And so by the middle of November he just stood on the sidewalk outside his store and gazed bitterly at the festivities across the square.

AT ABOUT THIS time Appleseed and sister made their first appearance.

He was a stranger in town. At least no one could recall ever having seen him before. He said he lived on a farm a mile past Indian Branches; told us his mother weighed only seventy-four pounds and that he had an older brother who would play the fiddle at anybody's wedding for fifty cents. He claimed that Appleseed was the only name he had and that he was twelve years old. But his sister, Middy, said he was eight. His hair was straight and dark yellow. He had a tight, weather-tanned little face with anxious green eyes that had a very wise and knowing look. He was small and puny and high-strung; and he wore always the same outfit: a red sweater, blue denim britches and a pair of man-sized boots that went *clop-clop* with every step.

It was raining that first time he came into the Valhalla; his hair was plastered round his head like a cap and his boots were caked with red mud from the country roads. Middy trailed behind as he swaggered like a cowboy up to the fountain where I was wiping some glasses.

"I hear you folks got a bottle fulla money you fixin' to give 'way," he said, looking me square in the eye. "Seein' as you-all are givin' it away, we'd be obliged iffen you'd give it to us. Name's Appleseed, and this here's my sister, Middy."

Middy was a sad, sad-looking kid. She was a good bit taller and older-looking than her brother: a regular bean pole. She had tow-colored hair that was chopped short, and a pale, pitiful little face. She wore a faded cotton dress that came way up above her bony knees. There was something wrong with her teeth, and she tried to conceal this by keeping her lips primly pursed like an old lady.

"Sorry," I said, "but you'll have to talk with Mr. Marshall."

So sure enough he did. I could hear my uncle explaining what he would have to do to win the jug. Appleseed listened attentively, nodding now and then. Presently he came back and stood in front of the jug and, touching it lightly with his hand, said, "Ain't it a pretty thing, Middy?"

Middy said, "Is they gonna give it to us?"

"Naw. What you gotta do, you gotta guess how much money's inside there. And you gotta buy two bits' worth so's even to get a chance."

"Huh, we ain't got no two bits. Where you 'spec we gonna get us two bits?"

Appleseed frowned and rubbed his chin. "That'll be the easy part, just leave it to me. The only worrisome thing is: I can't just take a chance and guess. . . . I gotta *know*."

Well, a few days later they showed up again. Appleseed perched on a stool at the fountain and boldly asked for two glasses of water, one for him and one for Middy.

It was on this occasion that he gave out the information about his family: ". . . then there's Papa Daddy, that's my mama's papa, who's a Cajun, an' on accounta that he don't speak English good. My brother, the one what plays the fiddle, he's been in jail three times. . . . It's on accounta him we had to pick up and leave Louisiana. He cut a fella bad in a razor fight over a woman ten years older'n him. She had yellow hair."

Middy, lingering in the background, said nervously, "You oughtn't to be tellin' our personal private fam'ly business thataway, Appleseed."

"Hush now, Middy," he said, and she hushed. "She's a good little gal," he added, turning to pat her head, "but you can't let her get away with much. You go look at the picture books, honey, and stop frettin' with your teeth. Appleseed here's got some figurin' to do."

This figuring meant staring hard at the jug, as if his eyes were trying to eat it up. With his chin cupped in his hand, he studied it for a long period, not batting his eyelids once. "A lady in Louisiana told me I could see things other folks couldn't see 'cause I was born with a caul on my head."

"It's a cinch you aren't going to see how much there is," I told him. "Why don't you just let a number pop into your head, and maybe that'll be the right one."

"Uh, uh," he said, "too darn risky. Me, I can't take no sucha chance. Now, the way I got it figured, there ain't but one surefire thing and that's to count every nickel and dime."

"Count!"

"Count what?" asked Hamurabi, who had just moseyed inside and was settling himself at the fountain.

"This kid says he's going to count how much is in the jug," I explained.

Hamurabi looked at Appleseed with interest. "How do you plan to do that, son?"

"Oh, by countin'," said Appleseed matter-of-factly.

Hamurabi laughed. "You better have X-ray eyes, son, that's all I can say."

"Oh, no. All you gotta do is be born with a caul on your head. A lady in Louisiana told me so. She was a witch; she loved me and when my ma wouldn't give me to her she put a hex on her and now my ma don't weigh but seventy-four pounds."

"Ve-ry in-ter-est-ing," was Hamurabi's comment as he gave Appleseed a queer glance.

Middy sauntered up, clutching a copy of *Screen Secrets*. She pointed out a certain photo to Appleseed and said, "Ain't she the nicest-lookin' lady? Now you see, Appleseed, you see how pretty her teeth are? Not a one outa joint."

"Well, don't you fret none," he said.

After they left, Hamurabi ordered a bottle of orange Nehi and drank it slowly, while smoking a cigarette. "Do you think maybe that kid's okay upstairs?" he asked presently in a puzzled voice.

SMALL TOWNS ARE BEST for spending Christmas, I think. They catch the mood quicker and change and come alive under its spell. By the first week in December housedoors were decorated with wreaths, and store windows were flashy with red paper bells and snowflakes of glittering isinglass. The kids hiked out into the woods and came back dragging spicy evergreen trees. Already the women were busy baking fruitcakes, unsealing jars of mincemeat and opening bottles of blackberry and scuppernong wine. In the courthouse square a huge tree was trimmed with silver tinsel and colored electric bulbs that were lighted up at sunset. Late of an afternoon you could hear the choir in the Presbyterian church practicing carols for their annual pageant. All over town the japonicas were in full bloom.

The only person who appeared not the least touched by this heartwarming atmosphere was Appleseed. He went about his declared business of counting the jug money with great, persistent care. Every day now he came to the Valhalla and concentrated on the jug, scowling and mumbling to himself. At first we were all fascinated, but after a while it got tiresome and nobody paid him any mind whatsoever. He never bought anything, apparently having never been able to raise the two bits. Sometimes he'd talk to Hamurabi, who had taken a tender interest in him and occasionally stood treat to a jawbreaker or a penny's worth of licorice.

"Do you still think he's nuts?" I asked.

"I'm not so sure," said Hamurabi. "But I'll let you know. He doesn't eat enough. I'm going to take him over to the Rainbow Café and buy him a plate of barbecue."

"He'd appreciate it more if you'd give him a quarter."

"No. A dish of barbecue is what he needs. Besides, it would be better if he never was to make a guess. A high-strung kid like that, so unusual, I wouldn't want to be the one responsible if he lost. Say, it would be pitiful."

I'll admit that at the time Appleseed struck me as being just funny. Mr. Marshall felt sorry for him, and the kids tried to tease him, but had to give it up when he refused to respond. There you could see him plain as day sitting at the fountain with his forehead puckered and his eyes fixed forever on that jug. Yet he was so withdrawn you sometimes had this awful creepy feeling that, well, maybe he didn't exist. And when you were pretty much convinced of this he'd wake up and say something like, "You know, I hope a 1913 buffalo nickel's in there. A fella was tellin' me he saw where a 1913 buffalo nickel's worth fifty dollars." Or, "Middy's gonna be a big lady in the picture shows. They make lotsa money, the ladies in the picture shows do, and then we ain't gonna never eat another collard green as long as we live. Only Middy says she can't be in the picture shows 'less her teeth look good."

Middy didn't always tag along with her brother. On those occasions when she didn't come, Appleseed wasn't himself; he acted shy and left soon.

Hamurabi kept his promise and stood treat to a dish of barbecue at the café. "Mr. Hamurabi's nice, all right," said Appleseed afterward, "but he's got peculiar notions: has a notion that if he lived in this place named Egypt he'd be a king or somethin'."

And Hamurabi said, "That kid has the most touching faith. It's a beautiful thing to see. But I'm beginning to despise the whole business." He gestured toward the jug. "Hope of this kind is a cruel thing to give anybody, and I'm damned sorry I was ever a party to it."

Around the Valhalla the most popular pastime was deciding what you would buy if you won the jug. Among those who participated were: Solomon Katz, Phoebe Jones, Carl Kuhnhardt, Puly Simmons, Addie Foxcroft, Marvin Finkle, Trudy Edwards and a colored man named Erskine Washington. And these were some of their answers: a trip to and a permanent wave in Birmingham, a secondhand piano, a Shetland pony, a gold bracelet, a set of *Rover Boys* books and a life insurance policy.

Once Mr. Marshall asked Appleseed what he would get. "It's a secret," was the reply, and no amount of prying could make him tell. We took it for granted that whatever it was, he wanted it real bad.

Honest winter, as a rule, doesn't settle on our part of the country till late January, and then is mild, lasting only a short time. But in the year of which I write we were blessed with a singular cold spell the week before Christmas. Some still talk of it, for it was so terrible: water pipes froze solid; many folks had to spend the days in bed snuggled under their quilts, having neglected to lay in enough kindling for the fireplace; the sky turned that strange dull gray as it does just before a storm, and the sun was pale as a waning moon. There was a sharp wind: the old dried-up leaves of last fall fell on the icy ground, and the evergreen tree in the courthouse square was twice stripped of its Christmas finery. When you breathed, your breath made smoky clouds. Down by the silk mill where the very poor people lived, the families huddled together in the dark at night and told tales to keep their minds off the cold. Out in the country the farmers covered their delicate plants with gunnysacks and prayed; some took advantage of the weather to slaughter their hogs and bring the fresh sausage to town. Mr. R. C. Judkins, our town drunk, outfitted himself in a red cheesecloth suit and played Santa Claus at the five 'n' dime. Mr. R. C. Judkins was the father of a big family, so everybody was happy to see him sober enough to earn a dollar. There were several church socials, at one of which Mr. Marshall came face-to-face with Rufus McPherson; bitter words were passed but not a blow was struck.

Now, as has been mentioned, Appleseed lived on a farm a mile below Indian Branches; this would be approximately three miles from town, a mighty long and lonesome walk. Still, despite the cold, he came every day to the Valhalla and stayed till closing time, which, as the days had grown short, was after nightfall. Once in a while he'd catch a ride partway home with the foreman from the silk mill, but not often. He looked tired, and there were worry lines about his mouth. He was always cold and shivered a lot. I don't think he wore any warm drawers underneath his red sweater and blue britches.

It was three days before Christmas when out of the clear sky he announced, "Well, I'm finished. I mean I know how much is in the bottle." He claimed this with such grave, solemn sureness it was hard to doubt him.

"Why, say now, son, hold on," said Hamurabi, who was present. "You can't know anything of the sort. It's wrong to think so; you're just heading to get yourself hurt."

"You don't need to preach to me, Mr. Hamurabi. I know what I'm up to. A lady in Louisiana, she told me—"

"Yes yes yes—but you got to forget that. If it were me, I'd go home and stay put and forget about this damned jug."

"My brother's gonna play the fiddle at a wedding over in Cherokee City tonight and he's gonna give me the two bits," said Appleseed stubbornly. "Tomorrow I'll take my chance."

So THE NEXT day I felt kind of excited when Appleseed and Middy arrived. Sure enough, he had his quarter: it was tied for safekeeping in the corner of a red bandanna.

The two of them wandered hand in hand among the showcases, holding a whispery consultation as to what to purchase. They decided finally on a thimble-sized bottle of gardenia cologne which Middy promptly opened and partly emptied on her hair. "I smells like . . . Oh, darlin' Mary, I ain't never smelled nothin' as sweet. Here, Appleseed, honey, let me douse some on your hair." But he wouldn't let her.

Mr. Marshall got out the ledger in which he kept his records, while Appleseed strolled over to the fountain and cupped the jug between his hands, stroking it gently. His eyes were bright and his cheeks flushed from excitement. Several persons who were in the drugstore at that moment crowded close. Middy stood in the background quietly scratching her leg and smelling the cologne. Hamurabi wasn't there.

Mr. Marshall licked the point of his pencil and smiled. "Okay, son, what do you say?"

Appleseed took a deep breath. "Seventy-seven dollars and thirty-five cents," he blurted.

In picking such an uneven sum he showed originality, for the run-of-the-mill guess was a plain round figure. Mr. Marshall repeated the amount solemnly as he copied it down.

"When'll I know if I won?"

"Christmas Eve," someone said.

"That's tomorrow, huh?"

"Why, so it is," said Mr. Marshall, not surprised. "Come at four o'clock."

DURING THE night the thermometer dropped even lower, and toward dawn there was one of those swift, summerlike rainstorms, so that the following day was bright and frozen. The town was like a picture postcard of a northern scene, what with icicles sparkling whitely on the trees and frost flowers coating all windowpanes. Mr. R. C. Judkins rose early and, for no clear reason, tramped the streets ringing a supper bell, stopping now and then to take a swig of whiskey from a pint which he kept in his hip pocket. As the day was windless, smoke climbed lazily from various chimneys straightway to the still, frozen sky. By mid-morning the Presbyterian choir was in full swing; and the town kids (wearing horror masks, as at Halloween) were chasing one another round and round the square, kicking up an awful fuss.

Hamurabi dropped by at noon to help us fix up the Valhalla. He brought along a fat sack of Satsumas, and together we ate every last one, tossing the hulls into a newly installed potbellied stove (a present from Mr. Marshall to himself) which stood in the middle of the room. Then my uncle took the jug off the fountain, polished and placed it on a prominently situated table. He was no help after that whatsoever, for he squatted in a chair and spent his time tying and retying a tacky green ribbon around the jug. So Hamurabi and I had the rest to do alone: we swept the floor and washed the mirrors and dusted the cabinets and strung streamers of red and green crepe paper from wall to wall. When we were finished it looked very fine and elegant.

But Hamurabi gazed sadly at our work and said, "Well, I think I better be getting along now."

"Aren't you going to stay?" asked Mr. Marshall, shocked.

"No, oh, no," said Hamurabi, shaking his head slowly. "I don't want to see that kid's face. This is Christmas and I mean to have a rip-roaring time. And I couldn't, not with something like that on my conscience. Hell, I wouldn't sleep."

"Suit yourself," said Mr. Marshall. And he shrugged, but you could see he was really hurt. "Life's like that—and besides, who knows, he might win."

Hamurabi sighed gloomily. "What's his guess?"

"Seventy-seven dollars and thirty-five cents," I said.

"Now I ask you, isn't that fantastic?" said Hamurabi. He slumped in a chair next to Mr. Marshall and crossed his legs and lit a cigarette. "If you got any Baby Ruths I think I'd like one; my mouth tastes sour."

As the afternoon wore on, the three of us sat around the table feeling terribly blue. No one said hardly a word and, as the kids had deserted the square, the only sound was the clock tolling the hour in the courthouse steeple. The Valhalla was closed to business, but people kept passing by and peeking in the window. At three o'clock Mr. Marshall told me to unlock the door.

Within twenty minutes the place was jam full; everyone was wearing his Sunday best, and the air smelled sweet, for most of the little silk-mill girls had scented themselves with vanilla flavoring. They scrunched up against the walls, perched on the fountain, squeezed in wherever they could; soon the crowd had spread to the sidewalk and stretched into the road.

The square was lined with team-drawn wagons and Model T Fords that had carted farmers and their families into town. There was much laughter and shouting and joking—several outraged ladies complained of the cursing and the rough, shoving ways of the younger men, but nobody left. At the side entrance a gang of colored folks had formed and were having the most fun of all. Everybody was making the best of a good thing. It's usually so quiet around here: nothing much ever happens. It's safe to say that nearly all of Wachata County was present but invalids and Rufus McPherson. I looked around for Appleseed but didn't see him anywhere.

Mr. Marshall harumphed, and clapped for attention. When things quieted down and the atmosphere was properly tense, he raised his voice like an auctioneer and called: "Now listen, everybody, in this here envelope you see in my hand"—he held a manila envelope above his head—"well, in it's the *answer*—which nobody but God and the First National Bank knows up to now, ha, ha. And in this book"—he held up the ledger with his free hand—"I've got written down what you folks guessed. Are there any questions?" All was silence. "Fine. Now, if we could have a volunteer . . ."

Not a living soul budged an inch; it was as if an awful shyness had overcome the crowd, and even those who were ordinarily natural-born show-offs shuffled their feet, ashamed. Then a voice, Appleseed's, hollered, "Lemme by. . . . Outa the way, please, ma'am." Trotting along behind as he pushed forward were Middy and a lanky, sleepy-eyed fellow who was evidently the fiddling brother. Appleseed was dressed the same as usual, but his face was scrubbed rosy clean, his boots polished and his hair slicked back skin tight with Stacomb. "Did we get here in time?" he panted.

But Mr. Marshall said, "So you want to be our volunteer?"

Appleseed looked bewildered, then nodded vigorously.

"Does anybody have an objection to this young man?"

Still there was dead quiet. Mr. Marshall handed the envelope to Appleseed, who accepted it calmly. He chewed his underlip while studying it a moment before ripping the flap.

In all that congregation there was no sound except an occasional cough and the soft tinkling of Mr. R. C. Judkins' supper bell. Hamurabi was leaning against the fountain, staring up at the ceiling; Middy was gazing blankly over her brother's shoulder, and when he started to tear open the envelope she let out a pained little gasp.

Appleseed withdrew a slip of pink paper and, holding it as though it was very fragile, muttered to himself whatever was written there. Suddenly his face paled and tears glistened in his eyes.

"Hey, speak up, boy," someone hollered.

Hamurabi stepped forward and all but snatched the slip away. He cleared his throat and commenced to read when his expression changed most comically. "Well, Mother o' God . . . " he said.

"Louder! Louder!" an angry chorus demanded.

"Buncha crooks!" yelled Mr. R. C. Judkins, who had a snootful by this time. "I smell a rat and he smells to high heaven!" Whereupon a cyclone of catcalls and whistling rent the air.

Appleseed's brother whirled round and shook his fist. "Shuddup, shuddup 'fore I bust every one of your damn heads together so's you got knots the size a muskmelons, hear me?"

"Citizens," cried Mayor Mawes, "citizens—I say, this is Christmas. . . . I say . . ."

And Mr. Marshall hopped up on a chair and clapped and stamped till a minimum of order was restored. It might as well be noted here that we later found out Rufus McPherson had paid Mr. R. C. Judkins to start the rumpus. Anyway, when the outbreak was quelled, who should be in possession of the slip but me . . . don't ask how.

Without thinking, I shouted, "Seventy-seven dollars and thirty-five cents." Naturally, due to the excitement, I didn't at first catch the meaning; it was just a number. Then Appleseed's brother let forth with his whooping yell, and so I understood. The name of the winner spread quickly, and the awed, murmuring whispers were like a rainstorm.

Oh, Appleseed himself was a sorry sight. He was crying as though he was mortally wounded, but when Hamurabi lifted him onto his shoulders so the crowd could get a gander, he dried his eyes with the cuffs of his sweater and began grinning. Mr. R. C. Judkins yelled, "Gyp! Lousy gyp!" but was drowned out by a deafening round of applause.

Middy grabbed my arm. "My teeth," she squealed. "Now I'm gonna get my teeth."

"Teeth?" said I, kind of dazed.

"The false kind," says she. "That's what we're gonna get us with the money—a lovely set of white false teeth."

But at that moment my sole interest was in how Appleseed had known. "Hey, tell me," I said desperately, "tell me, how in God's name did he know there was just exactly seventy-seven dollars and thirty-five cents?"

Middy gave me this *look*. "Why, I thought he told you," she said, real serious. "He counted."

"Yes, but how—how?"

"Gee, don't you even know how to count?"

"But is that all he did?"

"Well," she said, following a thoughtful pause, "he did do a little praying, too." She started to dart off, then turned back and called, "Besides, he was born with a caul on his head."

And that's the nearest anybody ever came to solving the mystery. Thereafter, if you were to ask Appleseed "How come?" he would smile strangely and change the subject. Many years later he and his family moved to somewhere in Florida and were never heard from again.

But in our town his legend flourishes still; and, till his death a year ago last April, Mr. Marshall was invited each Christmas Day to tell the story of Appleseed to the Baptist Bible class. Hamurabi once typed up an account and mailed it around to various magazines. It was never printed. One editor wrote back and said that "if the little girl really turned out to be a movie star, then there might be something to your story." But that's not what happened, so why should you lie?

NIGHT CLUB

KATHARINE BRUSH

Katharine Brush

PROMPTLY AT quarter of ten p.m. Mrs. Brady descended the steps of the
elevated. She purchased from the news dealer in the cubbyhole beneath
them a next month's magazine and a tomorrow morning's paper and,
with these tucked under one plump arm, she walked. She walked two
blocks north on Sixth Avenue; turned and went west. But not far west.
Westward half a block only, to the place where the gay green awning
marked "Club Français" paints a stripe of shade across the glimmering
sidewalk. Under this awning Mrs. Brady halted briefly, to remark to the
six-foot doorman that it looked like rain and to await his performance
of his professional duty. When the small green door yawned open,
she sighed deeply and plodded in.

The foyer was a blackness, an airless velvet blackness like the inside
of a jeweler's box. Four drum-shaped lamps of golden silk suspended
from the ceiling gave it light (a very little) and formed the jewels: gold
signets, those, or cuff links for a giant. At the far end of the foyer there
were black stairs, faintly dusty, rippling upward toward an amber
radiance. Mrs. Brady approached and ponderously mounted the stairs,
clinging with one fist to the mangy velvet rope that railed their edge.

From the top, Miss Lena Levin observed the ascent. Miss Levin was
the checkroom girl. She had dark-at-the-roots blond hair, and slender
hips upon which, in moments of leisure, she wore her hands, like
buckles of ivory loosely attached.

This was a moment of leisure. Miss Levin waited behind her counter.
Row upon row of hooks, empty as yet, and seeming to beckon—wee
curved fingers of iron—waited behind her.

"Late," said Miss Levin, "again."

"Go wan!" said Mrs. Brady. "It's only ten to ten. *Whew!* Them *stairs!*" She leaned heavily, sideways, against Miss Levin's counter, and, applying one palm to the region of her heart, appeared at once to listen and to count. "Feel!" she cried then in a pleased voice.

Miss Levin obediently felt.

"Them stairs," continued Mrs. Brady darkly, "with my bad heart, will be the death of me. Whew! Well, dearie? What's the news?"

"You got a paper," Miss Levin languidly reminded her.

"Yeah!" agreed Mrs. Brady with sudden vehemence. "I got a paper!" She slapped it upon the counter. "An' a lot of time I'll get to *read* my paper, won't I now? On a Saturday night!" She moaned. "Other nights is bad enough, dear knows—but *Saturday* nights! How I dread 'em! Every Saturday night I say to my daughter, I say, 'Geraldine, I can't,' I say, 'I can't go through it again, an' that's all there is to it,' I say. 'I'll *quit!*' I say. An' I *will*, too!" added Mrs. Brady firmly, if indefinitely.

Miss Levin, in defense of Saturday nights, mumbled some vague something about tips.

"Tips!" Mrs. Brady hissed it. She almost spat it. Plainly money was nothing, nothing at all, to this lady. "I just wish," said Mrs. Brady, and glared at Miss Levin, "I just wish *you* had to spend one Saturday night, just one, in that dressing room! Bein' pushed an' stepped on and near knocked down by that gang of hussies, an' them orderin' an' bossin' you round like you was *black*, an' usin' your things an' then sayin' they're sorry, they got no change, they'll be back. Yeah! They *never* come back!"

"There's Mr. Costello," whispered Miss Levin through lips that, like a ventriloquist's, scarcely stirred.

"An' as I was sayin'," Mrs. Brady said at once brightly, "I got to leave you. Ten to ten, time I was on the job."

She smirked at Miss Levin, nodded, and right-about-faced. There, indeed, Mr. Costello was. Mr. Billy Costello, manager, proprietor, monarch of all he surveyed. From the doorway of the big room where the little tables herded in a ring around the waxen floor, he surveyed Mrs. Brady, and in such a way that Mrs. Brady, momentarily forgetting her bad heart, walked fast, scurried faster, almost ran.

The door of her domain was set politely in an alcove, beyond silken curtains looped up at the sides. Mrs. Brady reached it breathless, shouldered it open, and groped for the electric switch. Lights sprang up, a bright white blaze, intolerable for an instant to the eyes, like sun on snow. Blinking, Mrs. Brady shut the door.

The room was a spotless, white-tiled place, half beauty shop, half dressing room. Along one wall stood washstands, sturdy triplets in a row, with pale green liquid soap in glass balloons afloat above them. Against the opposite wall there was a couch. A third wall backed an elongated glass-topped dressing table; and over the dressing table and over the washstands long rectangular sheets of mirror reflected lights, doors, glossy tiles, lights multiplied. . . .

Mrs. Brady moved across this glitter like a thick dark cloud in a hurry. At the dressing table she came to a halt, and upon it she laid her newspaper, her magazine, and her purse—a black purse worn gray with much clutching. She divested herself of a rusty black coat and a hat of the mushroom persuasion, and hung both up in a corner cupboard which she opened by means of one of a quite preposterous bunch of keys. From a nook in the cupboard she took down a lace-edged handkerchief with long streamers. She untied the streamers and tied them again around her chunky black alpaca waist. The handkerchief became an apron's baby cousin.

Mrs. Brady relocked the cupboard door, fumbled her key ring over, and unlocked a capacious drawer of the dressing table. She spread a fresh towel on the plate glass top, in the geometrical center, and upon the towel she arranged with care a procession of things fished from the drawer. Things for the hair. Things for the complexion. Things for the eyes, the lashes, the brows, the lips, and the finger-nails. Things in boxes and things in jars and things in tubes and tins. Also an ashtray, matches, pins, a tiny sewing kit, a pair of scissors. Last of all, a hand-printed sign, a nudging sort of sign: NOTICE! THESE ARTICLES, PLACED HERE FOR YOUR CONVENIENCE, ARE THE PROPERTY OF THE MAID. And directly beneath the sign, propping it up against the looking glass, a china saucer, in which Mrs. Brady now slyly laid decoy money: two quarters and two dimes, in four-leaf clover formation.

Another drawer yielded a bottle of Bromo Seltzer, a bottle of aromatic spirits of ammonia, a tin of sodium bicarbonate, and a teaspoon. These were lined up on a shelf above the couch.

Mrs. Brady was now ready for anything. And (from the grim, thin pucker of her mouth) expecting it.

Music came to her ears. Rather, the beat of music, muffled, rhythmic, remote. *Umpa-um, umpa-um, umpa-um-umm*—Mr. "Fiddle" Baer and his band, hard at work on the first fox-trot of the night. It was teasing, foot-tapping music; but the large solemn feet of Mrs. Brady were still. She sat on the couch and opened her newspaper; and for some moments she read uninterruptedly, with special attention to the murders, the divorces, the breaches of promise, the funnies.

Then the door swung inward, admitting a blast of Mr. Fiddle Baer's best, a whiff of perfume, and a girl.

Mrs. Brady put her paper away.

The girl was petite and darkly beautiful; wrapped in fur and mounted on tall jeweled heels. She entered humming the ragtime song the orchestra was playing, and while she stood near the dressing table, stripping off her gloves, she continued to hum it softly to herself: *"Oh! I know my baby loves me, I can tell my baby loves me."* Here the dark little girl got the left glove off, and Mrs. Brady glimpsed a platinum wedding ring. *"Cause there ain't no maybe in my baby's eyes."*

The right glove came off. The dark little girl sat down in one of the chairs that faced the dressing table. She doffed her wrap, casting it carelessly over the chair back. It had a cloth-of-gold lining, and the name of a Paris house was embroidered in curlicues on the label. Mrs. Brady hovered solicitously near.

The dark little girl, still humming, looked over the articles, "placed here for your convenience," and picked up the scissors. Having cut off a very small hangnail with the air of one performing a perilous major operation, she seized and used the manicure buffer, and after that the eyebrow pencil. Mrs. Brady's mind, hopefully calculating the tip, jumped and jumped again like a taximeter.

"Oh! I know my baby loves me—" The dark little girl applied powder and lipstick belonging to herself. She examined the result searchingly in the mirror and sat back, satisfied. She cast some silver, *Klink! Klink!*

into Mrs. Brady's saucer, and half rose. Then, remembering something, she settled down again.

The ensuing thirty seconds were spent by her in pulling off her platinum wedding ring, tying it in a corner of a lace handkerchief, and tucking the handkerchief down the bodice of her tight white velvet gown.

"There!" she said.

She swooped up her wrap and trotted toward the door, jeweled heels merrily twinkling. *"Cause there ain't no maybe—"* The door fell shut.

Almost instantly it opened again, and another girl came in. A blonde, this. She was pretty in a round-eyed, doll-like way; but Mrs. Brady, regarding her, mentally grabbed the spirits of ammonia bottle. For she looked terribly ill. The round eyes were dull, the pretty, silly little face was drawn. The thin hands, picking at the fastenings of a specious beaded bag, trembled and twitched.

Mrs. Brady cleared her throat. "Can I do something for you, miss?"

Evidently the blond girl had believed herself alone in the dressing room. She started violently and glanced up, panic in her eyes. Panic, and something else. Something very like murderous hate—but for an instant only, so that Mrs. Brady, whose perceptions were never quick, missed it altogether.

"A glass of water?" suggested Mrs. Brady.

"No," said the girl, "no." She had one hand in the beaded bag now. Mrs. Brady could see it moving, causing the bag to squirm like a live thing, and the fringe to shiver. "Yes!" she cried abruptly. "A glass of water—please—you get it for me." She dropped onto the couch.

Mrs. Brady scurried to the water cooler in the corner, pressed the spigot with a determined thumb. Water trickled out thinly. Mrs. Brady pressed harder, and scowled, and thought, "Something's wrong with this thing. I mustn't forget, next time I see Mr. Costello—"

When again she faced her patient, the patient was sitting erect. She was thrusting her clenched hand back into the beaded bag again.

She took only a sip of the water, but it seemed to help her quite miraculously. Almost at once color came to her cheeks, life to her eyes. She grew young again—as young as she was. She smiled up at Mrs. Brady.

"Well!" she exclaimed. "What do you know about that!" She shook her honey-colored head. "I can't imagine what came over me."

"Are you better now?" inquired Mrs. Brady.

"Yes. Oh, yes. I'm better now. You see," said the blond girl confidentially, "we were at the theater, my boy friend and I, and it was hot and stuffy—I guess that must have been the trouble."

She paused, and the ghost of her recent distress crossed her face. "God! I thought that last act *never* would end!" she said.

While she attended to her hair and complexion, she chattered gaily to Mrs. Brady, chattered on with scarcely a stop for breath, and laughed much. She said, among other things, that she and her "boy friend" had not known one another very long, but that she was "gaga" about him. "He is about me, too," she confessed. "He thinks I'm grand."

She fell silent then, and in the looking glass her eyes were shadowed, haunted. But Mrs. Brady, from where she stood, could not see the looking glass; and half a minute later the blond girl laughed and began again. When she went out she seemed to dance out on little winged feet; and Mrs. Brady, sighing, thought it must be nice to be young . . . and happy like that.

The next arrivals were two. A tall, extremely smart young woman in black chiffon entered first, and held the door open for her companion; and the instant the door was shut, she said, as though it had been on the tip of her tongue for hours, "Amy, what under the sun *happened?*"

Amy, who was brown-eyed, brown-bobbed-haired, and patently annoyed about something, crossed to the dressing table and flopped into a chair before she made reply.

"Nothing," she said wearily then.

"That's nonsense!" snorted the other. "Tell me. Was it something she said? She's a tactless ass, of course. Always was."

"No, not anything she said. It was—" Amy bit her lip. "All right! I'll tell you. Before we left your apartment I just happened to notice that Tom had disappeared. So I went to look for him—I wanted to ask him if he'd remembered to tell the maid where we were going—Skippy's subject to croup, you know, and we always leave word. Well, so I went into the kitchen, thinking Tom might be there mixing cocktails—and there he was—and there *she* was!"

The full red mouth of the other young woman pursed itself slightly. Her arched brows lifted. "Well?"

Her matter-of-factness appeared to infuriate Amy. "He was *kissing* her!" she flung out.

"Well?" said the other again. She chuckled softly and patted Amy's shoulder, as if it were the shoulder of a child. "You're surely not going to let *that* spoil your whole evening? Amy *dear!* Kissing may once have been serious and significant—but it isn't nowadays. Nowadays it's like shaking hands. It means nothing."

But Amy was not consoled. "I hate her!" she cried desperately. "Redheaded *thing!* Calling me darling and honey, and s-sending me handkerchiefs for C-Christmas—and then sneaking off behind closed doors and k-kissing my h-h-husband—"

At this point Amy broke down, but she recovered herself sufficiently to add with venom, "I'd like to slap her!"

"Oh, oh, oh," smiled the tall young woman, "I wouldn't do that!"

Amy wiped her eyes with what might well have been one of the Christmas handkerchiefs, and confronted her friend. "Well, what *would* you do, Vera? If you were I?"

"I'd forget it," said Vera, "and have a good time. I'd kiss somebody myself. You've no idea how much better you'd feel!"

"I don't do—" Amy began indignantly; but as the door behind her opened and a third young woman—redheaded, earringed, exquisite—lilted in, she changed her tone. "Oh, hello!" she called sweetly, beaming at the newcomer via the mirror. "We were wondering what had become of you!"

The redheaded girl, smiling easily back, dropped her cigarette on the floor and crushed it out with a silver-shod toe. "Tom and I were talking to Fiddle Baer," she explained. "He's going to play 'Clap Yo' Hands' next, because it's my favorite. Lend me a comb, will you?"

"There's a comb," said Vera, indicating Mrs. Brady's business comb.

"But imagine using it!" murmured the redheaded girl. "Amy, darling, haven't you one?"

Amy produced a tiny comb from her rhinestone purse. "Don't forget to bring it when you come," she said, and stood up. "I'm going on out, I want to tell Tom something." She went.

The redheaded young woman and the tall black-chiffon one were alone, except for Mrs. Brady. The redheaded one beaded her incredible lashes. The tall one, the one called Vera, sat watching her. Presently she said, "Sylvia, look here." And Sylvia looked. Anybody, addressed in that tone, would have.

"There is one thing," Vera went on quietly, holding the other's eyes, "that I want understood. And that is, 'Hands off!' Do you hear me?"

"I don't know what you mean."

"You do know what I mean!"

The redheaded girl shrugged her shoulders. "Amy told you she saw us, I suppose."

"Precisely. And," went on Vera, gathering up her possessions and rising, "as I said before, you're to keep away." Her eyes blazed sudden white-hot rage. "Because, as you very well know, he belongs to *me*," she said, and departed, slamming the door.

BETWEEN ELEVEN o'clock and one Mrs. Brady was very busy indeed. Never for more than a moment during those two hours was the dressing room empty. Often it was jammed, full to overflowing with curled cropped heads, with ivory arms and shoulders, with silk and lace and chiffon, with legs. The door flapped in and back, in and back. The mirrors caught and held—and lost—a hundred different faces. Powder veiled the dressing table with a thin white dust; cigarette stubs, scarlet at the tips, choked the ashtray. Dimes and quarters clattered into Mrs. Brady's saucer—and were transferred to Mrs. Brady's purse. The original seventy cents remained. That much, and no more, would Mrs. Brady gamble on the integrity of womankind.

She earned her money. She threaded needles and took stitches. She powdered the backs of necks. She supplied towels for soapy, dripping hands. She removed a speck from a teary blue eye and pounded the heel on a slipper. She curled the straggling ends of a black bob and a gray bob, pinned a velvet flower on a lithe round waist, mixed three doses of bicarbonate of soda, took charge of a shed pink satin girdle, collected, on hands and knees, several dozen fake pearls that had wept from a broken string.

She served chorus girls and schoolgirls, gay young matrons and gayer young mistresses, a lady who had divorced four husbands, and a lady who had poisoned one, the secret (more or less) sweetheart of a Most Distinguished Name, and the Brains of a bootleg gang. . . . She saw things. She saw a yellow check, with the ink hardly dry. She saw four tiny bruises, such as fingers might make, on an arm. She saw a girl strike another girl, not playfully. She saw a bundle of letters some man wished he had not written, safe and deep in a brocaded handbag.

ABOUT MIDNIGHT the door flew open and at once was pushed shut, and a gray-eyed, lovely child stood backed against it, her palms flattened on the panels at her sides, the draperies of her white chiffon gown settling lightly to rest around her.

There were already five damsels of varying ages in the dressing room. The latest arrival marked their presence with a flick of her eyes and, standing just where she was, she called peremptorily, "Maid!"

Mrs. Brady, standing just where *she* was, said, "Yes, miss?"

"Please come here," said the girl.

Mrs. Brady, as slowly as she dared, did so.

The girl lowered her voice to a tense half whisper. "Listen! Is there any way I can get out of here except through this door I came in?"

Mrs. Brady stared at her stupidly.

"Any window?" persisted the girl. "Or anything?"

Here they were interrupted by the exodus of two of the damsels of varying ages. Mrs. Brady opened the door for them—and in so doing caught a glimpse of a man who waited in the hall outside, a debonair, old-young man with a girl's furry wrap hung over his arm, and his hat in his hand.

The door clicked. The gray-eyed girl moved out from the wall, against which she had flattened herself—for all the world like one eluding pursuit in a cinema.

"What about that window?" she demanded, pointing.

"That's all the farther it opens," said Mrs. Brady.

"Oh! And it's the only one—isn't it?"

"It is."

"Damn," said the girl. "Then there's *no* way out?"

"No way but the door," said Mrs. Brady testily.

The girl looked at the door. She seemed to look *through* the door, and to despise and to fear what she saw. Then she looked at Mrs. Brady. "Well," she said, "then I s'pose the only thing for me to do is to stay in here."

She stayed. Minutes ticked by. Jazz crooned distantly, stopped, struck up again. Other girls came and went. Still the gray-eyed girl sat on the couch, with her back to the wall and her shapely legs crossed, smoking cigarettes, one from the stub of another.

After a long while she said, "Maid!"

"Yes, miss?"

"Peek out that door, will you, and see if there's anyone standing there."

Mrs. Brady peeked, and reported that there was a gentleman with a little bit of a black mustache standing there. The same gentleman, in fact, who was standing there "just after you came in."

"Oh, Lord," sighed the gray-eyed girl. "Well . . . I can't stay here all *night*, that's one sure thing." She slid off the couch and went listlessly to the dressing table. There she occupied herself for a minute or two. Suddenly, without a word, she darted out.

Thirty seconds later Mrs. Brady was elated to find two crumpled one-dollar bills lying in her saucer. Her joy, however, died a premature death. For she made an almost simultaneous second discovery. A saddening one. Above all, a puzzling one.

"Now what for," marveled Mrs. Brady, "did she want to walk off with them *scissors?*"

This at twelve twenty-five.

At twelve thirty a quartet of excited young things burst in, babbling madly. All of them had their evening wraps with them; all talked at once. One of them, a Dresden-china girl with a heart-shaped face, was the center of attraction. Around her the rest fluttered like monstrous butterflies; to her they addressed their shrill exclamatory cries. "Babe," they called her.

Mrs. Brady heard snatches: "Not in this state unless . . ." "Well, you can in Maryland, Jimmy says." "Oh, there must be someplace nearer than . . ." "Isn't this marvelous?" "When did it happen, Babe? When did you decide?"

"Just now," the girl with the heart-shaped face sang softly, "when we were dancing."

The babble resumed, "But listen, Babe, what'll your mother and father . . . ?" "Oh, never mind, let's hurry." "Shall we be warm enough with just these thin wraps, do you think? Babe, will you be warm enough? Sure?"

Powder flew and little pocket combs marched through bright marcels. Flushed cheeks were painted pinker still.

"My pearls," said Babe, "are *old*. And my dress and my slippers are *new*. *Now*, let's see—what can I *borrow?*"

A lace handkerchief, a diamond bar pin, a pair of earrings were proffered. She chose the bar pin, and its owner unpinned it proudly.

"I've got blue garters!" exclaimed a shrill little girl in a silver dress.

"Give me one, then," directed Babe. "I'll trade with you. . . . There! That fixes that."

More babbling, "Hurry! Hurry up!" . . . "Listen, are you *sure* we'll be warm enough? Because we can stop at my house, there's nobody home." "Give me that puff, Babe, I'll powder your back." "And just to think a week ago you'd never even met each other!" "Oh, hurry *up*, let's get *started!*" "I'm ready." "So'm I." "Ready, Babe? You look adorable." "Come on, everybody."

They were gone again, and the dressing room seemed twice as still and vacant as before.

A minute of grace, during which Mrs. Brady wiped the spilled powder away with a damp gray rag. Then the door jumped open again. Two evening gowns appeared and made for the dressing table in a beeline. Slim tubular gowns they were, one green, one palest yellow. Yellow hair went with the green gown, brown hair with the yellow. The green-gowned, yellow-haired girl wore gardenias on her left shoulder, four of them, and a flashing bracelet on each fragile wrist. The other girl looked less prosperous; still, you would rather have looked at her.

Both ignored Mrs. Brady's cosmetic display as utterly as they ignored Mrs. Brady, producing full field equipment of their own.

"Well," said the girl with gardenias, rouging energetically, "how do you like him?"

"Oh-h—all right."

"Meaning, 'Not any,' hmm? I suspected as much!" The girl with gardenias turned in her chair and scanned her companion's profile with disapproval. "See here, Marilee," she drawled, "are you going to be a damn fool *all* your life?"

"He's fat," said Marilee dreamily. "Fat, and—greasy, sort of. I mean, greasy in his mind. Don't you know what I mean?"

"I know *one* thing," declared the other. "I know Who He Is! And if I were you, that's all I'd need to know. *Under the circumstances.*"

The last three words, stressed meaningly, affected the girl called Marilee curiously. She grew grave. Her lips and lashes drooped. For some seconds she sat frowning a little, breaking a black-sheathed lipstick in two and fitting it together again.

"She's worse," she said finally, low.

"Worse?"

Marilee nodded.

"Well," said the girl with gardenias, "there you are. It's the climate. She'll never be anything *but* worse, if she doesn't get away. Out west. Arizona or somewhere."

"I know," murmured Marilee.

The other girl opened a tin of eye shadow. "Of course," she said dryly, "suit yourself. She's not *my* sister."

Marilee said nothing. Quiet she sat, breaking the lipstick, mending it, breaking it.

"Oh, well," she breathed finally, wearily, and straightened up. She propped her elbows on the plate glass dressing-table top and leaned toward the mirror, and with the lipstick she began to make her coral-pink mouth very red and gay and reckless and alluring.

NIGHTLY AT ONE o'clock Vane and Moreno dance for the Club Français. They dance a tango, they dance a waltz; then, by way of encore, they do a Black Bottom, and a trick of their own called the Wheel. They dance for twenty, thirty minutes. And while they dance you do not leave your table—for this is what you came to see. Vane and Moreno. The new New York thrill. The sole justification for the five-dollar *couvert* extorted by Billy Costello.

From one until half past, then, was Mrs. Brady's recess. She had been looking forward to it all the evening long. When it began—when the opening chords of the tango music sounded stirringly from the room outside—Mrs. Brady brightened. With a right good will she sped the parting guests.

Alone, she unlocked her cupboard and took out her magazine—the magazine she had bought three hours before. Heaving a great breath of relief and satisfaction, she plumped herself on the couch and fingered the pages.

Immediately she was absorbed, her eyes drinking up printed lines, her lips moving soundlessly.

The magazine was Mrs. Brady's favorite. Its stories were true stories, taken from life (so the editor said); and to Mrs. Brady they were live, vivid threads in the dull, drab pattern of her night.

THE LOST PHOEBE

THEODORE DREISER

THEY LIVED together in a part of the country which was not so prosperous as it had once been, about three miles from one of those small towns that, instead of increasing in population, is steadily decreasing. The territory was not very thickly settled; perhaps a house every other mile or so, with large areas of corn- and wheatland and fallow fields that at odd seasons had been sown to timothy and clover. Their particular house was part log and part frame, the log portion being the old original home of Henry's grandfather. The new portion, of now rain-beaten, timeworn slabs, through which the wind squeaked in the chinks at times, and which several overshadowing elms and a butternut tree made picturesque and reminiscently pathetic, but a little damp, was erected by Henry when he was twenty-one and just married.

That was forty-eight years before. The furniture inside, like the house outside, was old and mildewy and reminiscent of an earlier day. You have seen the whatnot of cherry wood, perhaps, with spiral legs and fluted top. It was there. The old-fashioned four-poster bed, with its ball-like protuberances and deep curving incisions, was there also, a sadly alienated descendant of an early Jacobean ancestor. The bureau of cherry was also high and wide and solidly built, but faded-looking, and with a musty odor. The rag carpet that underlay all these sturdy examples of enduring furniture was a weak, faded, lead-and-pink-colored affair woven by Phoebe Ann's own hands, when she was fifteen years younger than she was when she died. The creaky wooden loom on which it had been done now stood like a dusty, bony skeleton, along with a broken rocking chair, a worm-eaten clothespress—heaven knows how old—a lime-stained bench that had once been used to keep flowers on outside the door, and other decrepit factors of household utility, in an east room that was a lean-to against this so-called main portion. All sorts of other broken-down furniture were about this place; an antiquated clotheshorse, cracked in two of its ribs; a broken mirror in an old cherry frame, which had fallen from a nail and cracked itself three days before their youngest son, Jerry, died; an extension hatrack, which once had had porcelain knobs on the ends of its pegs; and a sewing machine, long since outdone in its clumsy mechanism by rivals of a newer generation.

The orchard to the east of the house was full of gnarled old apple trees, worm-eaten as to trunks and branches, and fully ornamented with green and white lichens, so that it had a sad, greenish white, silvery effect in moonlight.

The low outhouses, which had once housed chickens, a horse or two, a cow, and several pigs, were covered with patches of moss as to their roofs, and the sides had been free of paint for so long that they were blackish gray as to color, and a little spongy. The picket fence in front, with its gate squeaky and askew, and the side fences of the stake-and-rider type were in an equally run-down condition. As a matter of fact, they had aged synchronously with the persons who lived here, old Henry Reifsneider and his wife Phoebe Ann.

They had lived here, these two, ever since their marriage, forty-eight years before, and Henry had lived here before that from his childhood up. His father and mother, well along in years when he was a boy, had invited him to bring his wife here when he had first fallen in love and decided to marry; and he had done so. His father and mother were the companions of himself and his wife for ten years after they were married, when both died; and then Henry and Phoebe were left with their five children growing lustily apace. But all sorts of things had happened since then. Of the seven children, all told, that had been born to them, three had died; one girl had gone to Kansas; one boy had gone to Sioux Falls, never even to be heard of after; another boy had gone to Washington; and the last girl lived five counties away in the same state, but was so burdened with cares of her own that she rarely gave them a thought. Time and a commonplace homelife that had never been attractive had weaned them thoroughly, so that, wherever they were, they gave little thought as to how it might be with their father and mother.

Old Henry Reifsneider and his wife Phoebe were a loving couple. You perhaps know how it is with simple natures that fasten themselves like lichens on the stones of circumstance and weather their days to a crumbling conclusion. The great world sounds widely, but it has no call for them. They have no soaring intellect. The orchard, the meadow, the cornfield, the pigpen, and the chicken lot measure the range of their human activities. When the wheat is headed it is reaped and threshed; when the corn is browned and frosted it is cut and shocked; when the timothy is in full head it is cut, and the haycock erected. After that comes winter, with the hauling of grain to market, the sawing and splitting of wood, the simple chores of fire building, meal getting, occasional repairing, and visiting. Beyond these and the changes of weather—the snows, the rains, and the fair days—there are no immediate, significant things. All the rest of life is a far-off, clamorous phantasmagoria, flickering like northern lights in the night, and sounding as faintly as cowbells tinkling in the distance.

Old Henry and his wife Phoebe were as fond of each other as it is possible for two old people to be who have nothing else in this life to be fond of. He was a thin old man, seventy when she died, a queer, crotchety person with coarse gray-black hair and beard, quite straggly and unkempt. He looked at you out of dull, fishy, watery eyes that had deep brown crow's-feet at the sides. His clothes, like the clothes of many farmers, were aged and angular and baggy, standing out at the pockets, not fitting about the neck, protuberant and worn at elbow and knee. Phoebe Ann was thin and shapeless, a very umbrella of a woman, clad in shabby black, and with a black bonnet for her best wear. As time had passed, and they had only themselves to look after, their movements had become slower and slower, their activities fewer and fewer. The annual keep of pigs had been reduced from five to one grunting porker, and the single horse which Henry now retained was a sleepy animal, not overnourished and not very clean. The chickens, of which formerly there was a large flock, had almost disappeared, owing to ferrets, foxes, and the lack of proper care, which produces disease. The former healthy garden was now a straggling memory of itself, and the vines and flower beds that formerly ornamented the windows and dooryard had now become choking thickets. A will had been made which divided the small tax-eaten property equally among the remaining four, so that it was really of no interest to any of them. Yet these two lived together in peace and sympathy, only that now and then old Henry would become unduly cranky, complaining almost invariably that something had been neglected or mislaid which was of no importance at all.

"Phoebe, where's my corn knife? You ain't never minded to let my things alone no more."

"Now you hush, Henry," his wife would caution him in a cracked and squeaky voice. "If you don't, I'll leave yuh. I'll git up and walk out of here someday, and then where would y' be? Y' ain't got anybody but me to look after yuh, so yuh just behave yourself. Your corn knife's on the mantel where it's allus been unless you've gone an' put it summers else."

Old Henry, who knew his wife would never leave him in any circumstances, used to speculate at times as to what he would do if she were to die. That was the one leaving that he really feared. As he climbed on the chair at night to wind the old, long-pendulumed, double-weighted clock, or went finally to the front and the back doors to see that they were safely shut in, it was a comfort to know that Phoebe was there, properly ensconced on her side of the bed, and that if he stirred restlessly in the night, she would be there to ask what he wanted.

"Now, Henry, do lie still! You're as restless as a chicken."

"Well, I can't sleep, Phoebe."

"Well, yuh needn't roll so, anyhow. Yuh kin let me sleep."

This usually reduced him to a state of somnolent ease. If she wanted a pail of water, it was a grumbling pleasure for him to get it; and if she did rise first to build the fires, he saw that the wood was cut and placed within easy reach. They divided this simple world nicely between them.

As the years had gone on, however, fewer and fewer people had called. They were well known for a distance of as much as ten square miles as old Mr. and Mrs. Reifsneider, honest, moderately Christian, but too old to be really interesting any longer. The writing of letters had become an almost impossible burden too difficult to continue or even negotiate via others, although an occasional letter still did arrive from the daughter in Pemberton County. Now and then some old friend stopped with a pie or cake or a roasted chicken or duck, or merely to see that they were well; but even these kindly minded visits were no longer frequent.

One day in the early spring of her sixty-fourth year Mrs. Reifsneider took sick, and from a low fever passed into some indefinable ailment which, because of her age, was no longer curable. Old Henry drove to Swinnerton, the neighboring town, and procured a doctor. Some friends called, and the immediate care of her was taken off his hands. Then one chill spring night she died, and old Henry, in a fog of sorrow and uncertainty, followed her body to the nearest graveyard, an unattractive space with a few pines growing in it. Although he might have gone to the daughter in Pemberton or sent for her, it was really too much trouble and he was too weary and fixed. It was suggested to him at once by one friend and another that he come to stay with them awhile, but he did not see fit. He was so old and so fixed in his notions and so accustomed to the exact surroundings he had known all his days, that he could not think of leaving. He wanted to remain near where they had put his Phoebe; and the fact that he would have to live alone did not trouble him in the least. The living children were notified and the care of him offered if he would leave, but he would not.

"I kin make a shift for myself," he continually announced to old Dr. Morrow, who had attended his wife in this case. "I kin cook a little, and, besides, it don't take much more'n coffee an' bread in the mornin's to satisfy me. I'll get along now well enough. Yuh just let me be." And after many pleadings and proffers of advice, with supplies of coffee and bacon and baked bread duly offered and accepted, he was left to himself. For a while he sat idly outside his door brooding in the spring sun. He tried to revive his interest in farming, and to keep himself busy and free from thought by looking after the fields, which of late had been much neglected. It was a gloomy thing to come in of an evening, however, or in the afternoon and find no shadow of Phoebe where everything suggested her. By degrees he put a few of her things away. At night he sat beside his lamp and read in the papers that were left him occasionally or in a Bible that he had neglected for years, but he could get little solace from these things. Mostly he held his hand over his mouth and looked at the floor as he sat and thought of what had become of her, and how soon he himself would die. He made a great business of making his coffee in the morning and frying himself a little bacon at night; but his appetite was gone. The shell in which he had been housed so long seemed vacant, and its shadows were suggestive of immedicable griefs. So he lived quite dolefully for five long months, and then a change began.

It was one night, after he had looked after the front and the back doors, wound the clock, blown out the light, and gone through all the selfsame motions that he had indulged in for years, that he went to bed not so much to sleep as to think. It was a moonlight night. The green-lichen-covered orchard just outside and to be seen from his bed where he now lay was a silvery affair, sweetly spectral. The moon shone through the east windows, throwing the pattern of the panes on the wooden floor, and making the old furniture, to which he was accustomed, stand out dimly in the room. As usual he had been thinking of Phoebe and the years when they had been young together, and of the children who had gone, and the poor shift he was making of his present days. The house was coming to be in a very bad state indeed. The bedclothes were in disorder and not clean, for he made a wretched shift of washing. It was a terror to him. The roof leaked, causing things, some of them, to remain damp for weeks at a time, but he was getting into that brooding state where he would accept anything rather than exert himself. He preferred to pace slowly to and fro or to sit and think.

By twelve o'clock of this particular night he was asleep, however, and by two had waked again. The moon by this time had shifted to a position on the western side of the house, and it now shone in through the windows of the living room and those of the kitchen beyond. A certain combination of furniture—a chair near a table, with his coat on it, the half-open kitchen door casting a shadow, and the position of a lamp near a paper—gave him an exact representation of Phoebe leaning over the table as he had often seen her do in life. It gave him a great start. Could it be she—or her ghost? He had scarcely ever believed in spirits; and still— He looked at her fixedly in the feeble half-light, his old hair tingling oddly at the roots, and then sat up. The figure did not move. He put his thin legs out of the bed and sat looking at her, wondering if this could really be Phoebe. They had talked of ghosts often in their lifetime, of apparitions and omens; but they had never agreed that such things could be. It had never been a part of his wife's creed that she could have a spirit that could return to walk the earth. Her afterworld was quite a different affair, a vague heaven, no less, from which the righteous did not trouble to return. Yet here she was now, bending over the table in her black skirt and gray shawl, her pale profile outlined against the moonlight.

"Phoebe," he called, thrilling from head to toe and putting out one bony hand, "have yuh come back?"

The figure did not stir, and he arose and walked uncertainly to the door, looking at it fixedly the while. As he drew near, however, the apparition resolved itself into its primal content—his old coat over the high-backed chair, the lamp by the paper, the half-open door.

"Well," he said to himself, his mouth open, "I thought shore I saw her." And he ran his hand strangely and vaguely through his hair, the while his nervous tension relaxed. Vanished as it had, it gave him the idea that she might return.

Another night, because of this first illusion, and because his mind was now constantly on her and he was old, he looked out of the window that was nearest his bed and commanded a hen coop and pigpen and a part of the wagon shed, and there, a faint mist exuding from the damp of the ground, he thought he saw her again. It was one of those little wisps of mist, one of those faint exhalations of the earth that rise in a cool night after a warm day, and flicker like small white cypresses of fog before they disappear. In life it had been a custom of hers to cross this lot from her kitchen door to the pigpen to throw in any scrap that was left from her cooking, and here she was again. He sat up and watched it strangely, doubtfully, because of his previous experience, but inclined, because of the nervous titillation that passed over his body, to believe that spirits really were, and that Phoebe, who would be concerned because of his lonely state, must be thinking about him, and hence returning. What other way would she have? How otherwise could she express herself? It would be within the province of her charity so to do, and like her loving interest in him. He quivered and watched it eagerly; but, a faint breath of air stirring, it wound away toward the fence and disappeared.

A third night, as he was actually dreaming, some ten days later, she came to his bedside and put her hand on his head.

"Poor Henry!" she said. "It's too bad."

He roused out of his sleep, actually to see her, he thought, moving from his bedroom into the one living room, her figure a shadowy mass of black. The weak straining of his eyes caused little points of light to flicker about the outlines of her form. He arose, greatly astonished, walked the floor in the cool room, convinced that Phoebe was coming back to him. If he only thought sufficiently, if he made it perfectly clear by his feeling that he needed her greatly, she would come back, this kindly wife, and tell him what to do. She would perhaps be with him much of the time, in the night, anyhow; and that would make him less lonely, this state more endurable.

In age and with the feeble it is not such a far cry from the subtleties of illusion to actual hallucination, and in due time this transition was made for Henry. Night after night he waited, expecting her return. Once in his weird mood he thought he saw a pale light moving about the room, and another time he thought he saw her walking in the orchard after dark. It was one morning when the details of his lonely state were virtually unendurable that he woke with the thought that she was not dead. How he had arrived at this conclusion it is hard to say. His mind had gone. In its place was a fixed illusion. He and Phoebe had had a senseless quarrel. He had reproached her for not leaving his pipe where he was accustomed to find it, and she had left. It was an aberrated fulfillment of her old jesting threat that if he did not behave himself she would leave him.

"I guess I could find yuh ag'in," he had always said.

But her cackling threat had always been, "Yuh'll not find me if I ever leave yuh. I guess I kin git someplace where yuh can't find me."

This morning when he arose he did not think to build the fire in the customary way or to grind his coffee and cut his bread, as was his wont, but solely to meditate as to where he should search for her and how he should induce her to come back. Recently the one horse had been dispensed with because he found it cumbersome and beyond his needs. He took down his soft crush hat after he had dressed himself, a new glint of interest and determination in his eye, and taking his black crook cane from behind the door, where he had always placed it, started out briskly to look for her among the nearest neighbors. His old shoes clumped soundly in the dust as he walked, and his gray-black locks, now grown rather long, straggled out in a dramatic fringe or halo from under his hat. His short coat stirred busily as he walked, and his hands and face were peaked and pale.

"Why, hello, Henry! Where're yuh goin' this mornin'?" inquired Farmer Dodge, who, hauling a load of wheat to market, encountered him on the public road. He had not seen the aged farmer in months, not since his wife's death, and he wondered now, seeing him looking so spry.

"Yuh ain't seen Phoebe, have yuh?" inquired the old man, looking up quizzically.

"Phoebe who?" inquired Farmer Dodge, not for the moment connecting the name with Henry's dead wife.

"Why, my wife Phoebe, o' course. Who do yuh s'pose I mean?" He stared up with a pathetic sharpness of glance from under his shaggy gray eyebrows.

"Wall, I'll swan, Henry, yuh ain't jokin', are yuh?" said the solid Dodge, a pursy man, with a smooth, hard, red face. "It can't be your wife yuh're talkin' about. She's dead."

"Dead! Shucks!" retorted the demented Reifsneider. "She left me early this mornin', while I was sleepin'. She allus got up to build the fire, but she's gone now. We had a little spat last night, an' I guess that's the reason. But I guess I kin find her. She's gone over to Matilda Race's; that's where she's gone."

He started briskly up the road, leaving the amazed Dodge to stare in wonder after him.

"Well, I'll be switched!" he said aloud to himself. "He's clean out'n his head. That poor old feller's been livin' down there till he's gone out'n his mind. I'll have to notify the authorities." And he flicked his whip with great enthusiasm. "Geddap!" he said, and was off.

Reifsneider met no one else in this poorly populated region until he reached the whitewashed fence of Matilda Race and her husband three miles away. He had passed several other houses en route, but these not being within the range of his illusion were not considered. His wife, who had known Matilda well, must be here. He opened the picket gate which guarded the walk, and stamped briskly up to the door.

"Why, Mr. Reifsneider," exclaimed old Matilda herself, a stout woman, looking out of the door in answer to his knock, "what brings yuh here this mornin'?"

"Is Phoebe here?" he demanded eagerly.

"Phoebe who? What Phoebe?" replied Mrs. Race, curious as to this sudden development of energy on his part.

"Why, my Phoebe, o' course. My wife Phoebe. Who do yuh s'pose? Ain't she here now?"

"Lawsy me!" exclaimed Mrs. Race, opening her mouth. "Yuh pore man! So you're clean out'n your mind now. Yuh come right in and sit down. I'll git yuh a cup o' coffee. O' course your wife ain't here; but yuh come in an' sit down. I'll find her fer yuh after a while. I know where she is."

The old farmer's eyes softened, and he entered. He was so thin and pale a specimen, pantalooned and patriarchal, that he aroused Mrs. Race's extremest sympathy as he took off his hat and laid it on his knees quite softly and mildly.

"We had a quarrel last night, an' she left me," he volunteered.

"Laws! Laws!" sighed Mrs. Race, there being no one present with whom to share her astonishment as she went to her kitchen. "The pore man! Now somebody's just got to look after him. He can't be allowed to run around the country this way lookin' for his dead wife. It's turrible."

She boiled him a pot of coffee and brought in some of her new-baked bread and fresh butter. She set out some of her best jam and put a couple of eggs to boil, lying wholeheartedly the while.

"Now yuh stay right there, Uncle Henry, till Jake comes in, an' I'll send him to look for Phoebe. I think it's more'n likely she's over to Swinnerton with some o' her friends. Anyhow, we'll find out. Now yuh just drink this coffee an' eat this bread. Yuh must be tired. Yuh've had a long walk this mornin'.'" Her idea was to take counsel with Jake, "her man," and perhaps have him notify the authorities.

She bustled about, meditating on the uncertainties of life, while old Reifsneider thrummed on the rim of his hat with his pale fingers and later ate abstractedly of what she offered. His mind was on his wife, however, and since she was not here, or did not appear, it wandered vaguely away to a family by the name of Murray, miles away in another direction. He decided after a time that he would not wait for Jake Race to hunt his wife but would seek her for himself. He must be on, and urge her to come back.

"Well, I'll be goin'," he said, getting up and looking strangely about him. "I guess she didn't come here after all. She went over to the Murrays', I guess. I'll not wait any longer, Mis' Race. There's a lot to do over to the house today." And out he marched in the face of her protests, taking to the dusty road again in the warm spring sun, his cane striking the earth as he went.

It was two hours later that this pale figure of a man appeared in the Murrays' doorway, dusty, perspiring, eager. He had tramped all of five miles, and it was noon. An amazed husband and wife of sixty heard his strange query, and realized also that he was mad. They begged him to stay to dinner, intending to notify the authorities later and see what could be done; but though he stayed to partake of a little something, he did not stay long, and was off again to another distant farmhouse, his idea of many things to do and his need of Phoebe impelling him. So it went for that day and the next and the next, the circle of his inquiry ever widening.

The process by which a character assumes the significance of being peculiar, his antics weird, yet harmless, in such a community is often involute and pathetic. This day, as has been said, saw Reifsneider at other doors, eagerly asking his unnatural question, and leaving a trail of amazement, sympathy, and pity in his wake. Although the authorities were informed—the county sheriff, no less—it was not deemed advisable to take him into custody; for when those who knew old Henry, and had for so long, reflected on the condition of the county insane asylum, a place which, because of the poverty of the district, was of staggering aberration and sickening environment, it was decided to let him remain at large; for, strange to relate, it was found on investigation that at night he returned peaceably enough to his lonesome domicile, there to discover whether his wife had returned, and to brood in loneliness until the morning. Who would lock up a thin, eager, seeking old man with iron-gray hair and an attitude of kindly, innocent inquiry, particularly when he was well known for a past of only kindly servitude and reliability? Those who had known him best rather agreed that he should be allowed to roam at large. He could do no harm. There were many who were willing to help him as to food, old clothes, the odds and ends of his daily life—at least at first. His figure after a time became not so much a commonplace as an accepted curiosity, and the replies, "Why, no, Henry; I ain't see her," or "No, Henry; she ain't been here today," more customary.

For several years thereafter then he was an odd figure in the sun and rain, on dusty roads and muddy ones, encountered occasionally in strange and unexpected places, pursuing his endless search. Undernourishment, after a time, although the neighbors and those who knew his history gladly contributed from their store, affected his body; for he walked much and ate little. The longer he roamed the public highway in this manner, the deeper became his strange hallucination; and finding it harder and harder to return from his more and more distant pilgrimages, he finally began taking a few utensils with him from his home, making a small package of them, in order that he might not be compelled to return. In an old tin coffeepot of large size he placed a small tin cup, a knife, fork, and spoon, some salt and pepper, and to the outside of it, by a string forced through a pierced hole, he fastened a plate, which could be released, and which was his woodland table. It was no trouble for him to secure the little food that he needed, and with a strange, almost religious dignity, he had no hesitation in asking for that much. By degrees his hair became longer and longer, his once black hat became an earthen brown, and his clothes threadbare and dusty.

For all of three years he walked, and none knew how wide were his perambulations, nor how he survived the storms and cold. They could not see him, with homely rural understanding and forethought, sheltering himself in haycocks, or by the sides of cattle, whose warm bodies protected him from the cold, and whose dull understandings were not opposed to his harmless presence. Overhanging rocks and trees kept him at times from the rain, and a friendly hayloft or corncrib was not above his humble consideration.

The involute progression of hallucination is strange. From asking at doors and being constantly rebuffed or denied, he finally came to the conclusion that although his Phoebe might not be in any of the houses at the doors of which he inquired, she might nevertheless be within the sound of his voice. And so, from patient inquiry, he began to call sad, occasional cries, that ever and anon waked the quiet landscapes and ragged hill regions, and set to echoing his thin "O-o-o Phoebe! O-o-o Phoebe!" It had a pathetic, albeit insane, ring, and many a farmer or plowboy came to know it even from afar and say, "There goes old Reifsneider."

Another thing that puzzled him greatly after a time and after many hundreds of inquiries was, when he no longer had any particular dooryard in view and no special inquiry to make, which way to go. These crossroads, which occasionally led in four or even six directions, came after a time to puzzle him. But to solve this knotty problem, which became more and more of a puzzle, there came to his aid another hallucination. Phoebe's spirit or some power of the air or wind or nature would tell him. If he stood at the center of the parting of the ways, closed his eyes, turned thrice about, and called "O-o-o Phoebe!" twice, and then threw his cane straight before him, that would surely indicate which way to go for Phoebe, or one of these mystic powers would surely govern its direction and fall! In whichever direction it went, even though, as was not infrequently the case, it took him back along the path he had already come, or across fields, he was not so far gone in his mind but that he gave himself ample time to search before he called again. Also the hallucination seemed to persist that at some time he would surely find her. There were hours when his feet were sore, and his limbs weary, when he would stop in the heat to wipe his seamed brow, or in the cold to beat his arms. Sometimes, after throwing away his cane, and finding it indicating the direction from which he had just come, he would shake his head wearily and philosophically, as if contemplating the unbelievable or an untoward fate, and then start briskly off. His strange figure came finally to be known in the farthest reaches of three or four counties. Old Reifsneider was a pathetic character. His fame was wide.

Near a little town called Watersville, in Green County, perhaps four miles from that minor center of human activity, there was a place or precipice locally known as the Red Cliff, a sheer wall of red sandstone, perhaps a hundred feet high, which raised its sharp face for half a mile or more above the fruitful cornfields and orchards that lay beneath, and which was surmounted by a thick grove of trees. The slope that slowly led up to it from the opposite side was covered by a rank growth of beech, hickory, and ash, through which threaded a number of wagon tracks crossing at various angles. In fair weather it had become old Reifsneider's habit, so inured was he by now to the open, to make his bed in some such patch of trees as this, to fry his bacon or boil his eggs at the foot of some tree before laying himself down for the night. Occasionally, so light and inconsequential was his sleep, he would walk at night. More often, the moonlight or some sudden wind stirring in the trees or a reconnoitering animal arousing him, he would sit up and think, or pursue his quest in the moonlight or the dark, a strange, unnatural, half-wild, half-savage-looking but utterly harmless creature, calling at lonely road crossings, staring at dark and shuttered houses, and wondering where, where Phoebe could really be.

That particular lull that comes in the systole-diastole of this earthly ball at two o'clock in the morning invariably aroused him, and though he might not go any farther he would sit up and contemplate the darkness or the stars, wondering. Sometimes in the strange processes of his mind he would fancy that he saw moving among the trees the figure of his lost wife, and then he would get up to follow, taking his utensils, always on a string, and his cane. If she seemed to evade him too easily he would run, or plead, or, suddenly losing track of the fancied figure, stand awed or disappointed, grieving for the moment over the almost insurmountable difficulties of his search.

It was in the seventh year of these hopeless peregrinations, in the dawn of a similar springtime to that in which his wife had died, that he came at last one night to the vicinity of this selfsame patch that crowned the rise to the Red Cliff. His far-flung cane, used as a divining rod at the last crossroads, had brought him hither. He had walked many, many miles. It was after ten o'clock at night, and he was very weary. Long wandering and little eating had left him but a shadow of his former self. It was a question now not so much of physical strength but of spiritual endurance which kept him up. He had scarcely eaten this day, and now exhausted he set himself down in the dark to rest and possibly to sleep.

Curiously on this occasion a strange suggestion of the presence of his wife surrounded him. It would not be long now, he counseled with himself, although the long months had brought him nothing, until he should see her, talk to her. He fell asleep after a time, his head on his knees. At midnight the moon began to rise, and at two in the morning, his wakeful hour, was a large silver disk shining through the trees to the east. He opened his eyes when the radiance became strong, making a silver pattern at his feet and lighting the woods with strange lusters and silvery, shadowy forms. As usual, his old notion that his wife must be near occurred to him on this occasion, and he looked about him with a speculative, anticipatory eye. What was it that moved in the distant shadows along the path by which he had entered—a pale, flickering will-o'-the-wisp that bobbed gracefully among the trees and riveted his expectant gaze? Moonlight and shadows combined to give it a strange form and a stranger reality, this fluttering of bog fire or dancing of wandering fireflies. Was it truly his lost Phoebe? By a circuitous route it passed about him, and in his fevered state he fancied that he could see the very eyes of her, not as she was when he last saw her in the black dress and shawl but now a strangely younger Phoebe, gayer, sweeter, the one whom he had known years before as a girl. Old Reifsneider got up. He had been expecting and dreaming of this hour all these years, and now as he saw the feeble light dancing lightly before him he peered at it questioningly, one thin hand in his gray hair.

Of a sudden there came to him now for the first time in many years the full charm of her girlish figure as he had known it in boyhood, the pleasing, sympathetic smile, the brown hair, the blue sash she had once worn about her waist at a picnic, her gay, graceful movements. He walked around the base of the tree, straining with his eyes, forgetting for once his cane and utensils, and following eagerly after. On she moved before him, a will-o'-the-wisp of the spring, a little flame above her head, and it seemed as though among the small saplings of ash and beech and the thick trunks of hickory and elm that she signaled with a young, a lightsome hand.

"O Phoebe! Phoebe!" he called. "Have yuh really come? Have yuh really answered me?" And hurrying faster, he fell once, scrambling lamely to his feet, only to see the light in the distance dancing illusively on. On and on he hurried until he was fairly running, brushing his ragged arms against the trees, striking his hands and face against impeding twigs. His hat was gone, his lungs were breathless, his reason quite astray, when coming to the edge of the cliff he saw her below among a silvery bed of apple trees now blooming in the spring.

"O Phoebe!" he called. "O Phoebe! Oh, no, don't leave me!" And feeling the lure of a world where love was young and Phoebe as this vision presented her, a delightful epitome of their quondam youth, he gave a gay cry of "Oh, wait, Phoebe!" and leaped.

Some farmer boys, reconnoitering this region of bounty and prospect some few days afterward, found first the tin utensils tied together under the tree where he had left them, and then later at the foot of the cliff, pale, broken, but elate, a molded smile of peace and delight upon his lips, his body. His old hat was discovered lying under some low-growing saplings, the twigs of which had held it back. No one of all the simple population knew how eagerly and joyously he had found his lost mate.

THE MOST DANGEROUS GAME

Richard Connell

O FF THERE TO the right—somewhere—is a large island," said Whitney. "It's rather a mystery—"

"What island is it?" Rainsford asked.

"The old charts called it Ship-Trap Island," Whitney replied. "A suggestive name, isn't it? Sailors have a curious dread of the place. I don't know why. Some superstition—"

"Can't see it," remarked Rainsford, trying to peer through the dank tropical night that pressed its thick warm blackness in upon the yacht.

"You've good eyes," said Whitney, "and I've seen you pick off a moose moving in the brown fall bush at four hundred yards, but even you can't see four miles or so through a moonless Caribbean night."

"Nor four yards," admitted Rainsford. "Ugh! It's like moist black velvet."

"It will be light enough in Rio," promised Whitney. "We should make it in a few days. I hope the jaguar guns have come from Purdey's. We should have some good hunting up the Amazon. Great sport, hunting."

"The best sport in the world," agreed Rainsford.

"For the hunter," amended Whitney. "Not for the jaguar."

"Don't talk rot, Whitney. You're a big-game hunter, not a philosopher. Who cares how a jaguar feels?"

"Perhaps the jaguar does."

"Bah! They've no understanding."

"Even so, I rather think they understand one thing—fear. The fear of pain and the fear of death."

"Nonsense." Rainsford laughed. "This hot weather is making you soft, Whitney. Be a realist. The world is made up of two classes—the hunters and the huntees. Luckily you and I are hunters. Do you think we have passed that island yet?"

"I can't tell in the dark. I hope so."

"Why?"

"The place has a reputation—a bad one."

"Cannibals?"

"Hardly. Even cannibals wouldn't live in such a godforsaken place. But it's gotten into sailor lore, somehow. Didn't you notice that the crew's nerves seemed a bit jumpy today?"

"They were a bit strange, now you mention it. Even Captain Neilson."

"Yes, even that tough-minded old Swede, who'd go up to the devil himself and ask him for a light. Those fishy blue eyes held a look I never saw there before. All I could get out of him was, 'This place has an evil name among seafaring men, sir.' Then he said gravely, 'Don't you feel anything?' Now you mustn't laugh, but I did feel a sort of chill, and there wasn't a breeze. What I felt was a—a mental chill, a dread."

"Pure imagination," said Rainsford. "One superstitious sailor can taint a whole ship's company with his fear."

"Maybe. Sometimes I think sailors have an extra sense which tells them when they are in danger. Anyhow I'm glad we are getting out of this zone. Well, I'll turn in now, Rainsford."

"I'm not sleepy. I'm going to smoke another pipe on the afterdeck."

There was no sound in the night as Rainsford sat there but the muffled throb of the yacht's engine and the swish and ripple of the propeller.

Rainsford, reclining in a steamer chair, puffed at his favorite briar. The sensuous drowsiness of the night was on him. "It's so dark," he thought, "that I could sleep without closing my eyes; the night would be my eyelids—"

An abrupt sound startled him. Off to the right he heard it, and his ears, expert in such matters, could not be mistaken. Again he heard the sound, and again. Somewhere, off in the blackness, someone had fired a gun three times.

Rainsford sprang up and moved quickly to the rail, mystified. He strained his eyes in the direction from which the reports had come, but it was like trying to see through a blanket. He leaped upon the rail and balanced himself there, to get greater elevation; his pipe, striking a rope, was knocked from his mouth. He lunged for it; a short, hoarse cry came from his lips as he realized he had reached too far and had lost his balance. The cry was pinched off short as the blood-warm waters of the Caribbean Sea closed over his head.

He struggled to the surface and cried out, but the wash from the speeding yacht slapped him in the face and the salt water in his open mouth made him gag and strangle. Desperately he struck out after the receding lights of the yacht, but he stopped before he had swum fifty feet. A certain coolheadedness had come to him, for this was not the first time he had been in a tight place. There was a chance that his cries could be heard by someone aboard the yacht, but that chance was slender and grew more slender as the yacht raced on. He wrestled himself out of his clothes and shouted with all his power. The lights of the boat became faint and vanishing fireflies; then they were blotted out by the night.

Rainsford remembered the shots. They had come from the right, and doggedly he swam in that direction, swimming slowly, conserving his strength. For a seemingly endless time he fought the sea. He began to count his strokes; he could do possibly a hundred more and then—

He heard a sound. It came out of the darkness, a high, screaming sound, the cry of an animal in an extremity of anguish and terror. He did not know what animal made the sound. With fresh vitality he swam toward it. He heard it again; then it was cut short by another noise, crisp, staccato.

"Pistol shot," muttered Rainsford, swimming on.

Ten minutes of determined effort brought to his ears the most welcome sound he had ever heard, the breaking of the sea on a rocky shore. He was almost on the rocks before he saw them; on a night less calm he would have been shattered against them. With his remaining strength he dragged himself from the swirling waters. Jagged crags appeared to jut into the opaqueness; he forced himself up hand over hand. Gasping, his hands raw, he reached a flat place at the top. Dense jungle came down to the edge of the cliffs, and, careless of everything but his weariness, Rainsford flung himself down and tumbled into the deepest sleep of his life.

When he opened his eyes he knew from the position of the sun that it was late in the afternoon. Sleep had given him vigor; a sharp hunger was picking at him.

"Where there are pistol shots there are men. Where there are men there is food," he thought; but he saw no sign of a trail through the closely knit web of weeds and trees; it was easier to go along the shore. Not far from where he had landed, he stopped.

Some wounded thing, by the evidence a large animal, had crashed about in the underwood. A small glittering object caught Rainsford's eye and he picked it up. It was an empty cartridge.

"A twenty-two," he remarked. "That's odd. It must have been a fairly large animal, too. The hunter had his nerve with him to tackle it with a light gun. It is clear the brute put up a fight. I suppose the first three shots I heard were when the hunter flushed his quarry and wounded it. The last shot was when he trailed it here and finished it."

He examined the ground closely and found what he had hoped to find—the print of hunting boots. They pointed along the cliff in the direction he had been going. Eagerly he hurried along, for night was beginning to settle down on the island.

Darkness was blacking out sea and jungle before Rainsford sighted the lights. He came upon them as he turned a crook in the coastline, and his first thought was that he had come upon a village, as there were so many lights. But as he forged along he saw that all the lights were in one building—a château on a high bluff.

"Mirage," thought Rainsford. But the stone steps were real enough. He lifted the knocker and it creaked up stiffly, as if it had never before been used.

The door, opening, let out a river of glaring light. A tall man, solidly built and black-bearded to the waist, stood facing Rainsford with a revolver in his hand.

"Don't be alarmed," said Rainsford, with a smile that he hoped was disarming. "I'm no robber. I fell off a yacht. My name is Sanger Rainsford of New York City."

The man gave no sign that he understood the words or had even heard them. The menacing revolver pointed as rigidly as if the giant were a statue.

Another man was coming down the broad marble steps, an erect slender man in evening clothes. He advanced and held out his hand.

In a cultivated voice marked by a slight accent which gave it added precision and deliberateness, he said, "It is a great pleasure and honor to welcome Mr. Sanger Rainsford, the celebrated hunter, to my home."

Automatically Rainsford shook the man's hand.

"I've read your book about hunting snow leopards in Tibet," explained the man. "I am General Zaroff."

Rainsford's first impression was that the man was singularly handsome; his second, that there was a bizarre quality about the face. The general was a tall man past middle age, for his hair was white; but his eyebrows and mustache were black. His eyes, too, were black and very bright. He had the face of a man used to giving orders. Turning to the man in uniform he made a sign. The fellow put away his pistol, saluted, withdrew.

"Ivan is incredibly strong," remarked the general, "but he has the misfortune to be deaf and dumb. A simple fellow, but a bit of a savage."

"Is he Russian?"

"A Cossack," said the general, and his smile showed red lips and pointed teeth. "So am I.

"Come," he said, "we shouldn't be chatting here. You want clothes, food, rest. You shall have them. This is a most restful spot."

Ivan had reappeared and the general spoke to him with lips that moved but gave forth no sound.

"Follow Ivan if you please, Mr. Rainsford. I was about to have my dinner, but will wait. I think my clothes will fit you."

It was to a huge beam-ceilinged bedroom with a canopied bed large enough for six men that Rainsford followed the man. Ivan laid out an evening suit and Rainsford as he put it on noticed that it came from a London tailor.

"Perhaps you were surprised," said the general as they sat down to dinner in a room which suggested a baronial hall of feudal times, "that I recognized your name; but I read all books on hunting published in

English, French and Russian. I have but one passion in life, and that is the hunt."

"You have some wonderful heads here," said Rainsford, glancing at the walls. "That cape buffalo is the largest I ever saw."

"Oh, that fellow? He charged me, hurled me against a tree and fractured my skull. But I got the brute."

"I've always thought," said Rainsford, "that the cape buffalo is the most dangerous of all big game."

For a moment the general did not reply, then he said slowly, "No, the cape buffalo is not the most dangerous." He sipped his wine. "Here in my preserve on this island I hunt more dangerous game."

"Is there big game on this island?"

The general nodded. "The biggest."

"Really?"

"Oh, it isn't here naturally. I have to stock the island."

"What have you imported, General? Tigers?"

The general grinned. "No, hunting tigers ceased to interest me when I exhausted their possibilities. No thrill left in tigers, no real danger. I live for danger, Mr. Rainsford."

The general took from his pocket a gold cigarette case and offered his guest a long black cigarette with a silver tip; it was perfumed and gave off a smell like incense.

"We will have some capital hunting, you and I," said the general.

"But what game—" began Rainsford.

"I'll tell you. You will be amused, I know. I think I may say, in all modesty, that I have done a rare thing. I have invented a new sensation. May I pour you another glass of port?"

"Thank you, General."

The general filled both glasses and said, "God makes some men poets. Some he makes kings, some beggars. Me he made a hunter. But after years of enjoyment I found that the hunt no.longer fascinated me. You can perhaps guess why?"

"No—why?"

"Simply this, hunting had ceased to be what you call a sporting proposition. I always got my quarry . . . always . . . and there is no greater bore than perfection."

The general lit a fresh cigarette.

"The animal has nothing but his legs and his instinct. Instinct is no match for reason. When I realized this, it was a tragic moment for me."

Rainsford leaned across the table, absorbed in what his host was saying.

"It came to me as an inspiration what I must do."

"And that was?"

"I had to invent a new animal to hunt."

"A new animal? You are joking."

"I never joke about hunting. I needed a new animal. I found one. So I bought this island, built this house, and here I do my hunting. The island is perfect for my purpose—there are jungles with a maze of trails in them, hills, swamps—"

"But the animal, General Zaroff?"

"Oh," said the general, "it supplies me with the most exciting hunting in the world. Every day I hunt, and I never grow bored now, for I have a quarry with which I can match my wits."

Rainsford's bewilderment showed in his face.

"I wanted the ideal animal to hunt, so I said, 'What are the attributes of an ideal quarry?' and the answer was, of course, 'It must have courage, cunning, and, above all, it must be able to reason.'"

"But no animal can reason," objected Rainsford.

"My dear fellow," said the general, "there is one that can."

"But you can't mean—"

"And why not?"

"I can't believe you are serious, General. This is a grisly joke."

"Why should I not be serious? I am speaking of hunting."

"Hunting? Good God, General Zaroff, what you speak of is murder."

The general regarded Rainsford quizzically. "Surely your experiences in the war—"

"Did not make me condone cold-blooded murder," finished Rainsford stiffly.

Laughter shook the general. "I'll wager you'll forget your notions when you go hunting with me. You've a genuine new thrill in store for you, Mr. Rainsford."

"Thank you, I am a hunter, not a murderer."

"Dear me," said the general, quite unruffled, "again that unpleasant word; but I hunt the scum of the earth—sailors from tramp ships—lascars, blacks, Chinese, whites, mongrels."

"Where do you get them?"

The general's left eyelid fluttered down in a wink. "This island is called Ship-Trap. Come to the window with me."

Rainsford went to the window and looked out toward the sea.

"Watch! Out there!" exclaimed the general, as he pressed a button. Far out Rainsford saw a flash of lights. "They indicate a channel where there's none. Rocks with razor edges crouch there like a sea monster. They can crush a ship like a nut. Oh, yes, that is electricity. We try to be civilized."

"Civilized? And you shoot down men?"

"But I treat my visitors with every consideration," said the general in his most pleasant manner. "They get plenty of good food and exercise. They get into splendid physical condition. You shall see for yourself tomorrow."

"What do you mean?"

"We'll visit my training school." The general smiled. "It is in the cellar. I have about a dozen there now. They're from the Spanish bark *Sanlucar*, which had the bad luck to go on the rocks out there. An inferior lot, I regret to say, and more accustomed to the deck than the jungle."

He raised his hand and Ivan brought thick Turkish coffee. "It is a game, you see," pursued the general blandly. "I suggest to one of them that we go hunting. I give him three hours' start. I am to follow, armed only with a pistol of smallest caliber and range. If my quarry eludes me for three whole days, he wins the game. If I find him"—the general smiled—"he loses."

"Suppose he refuses to be hunted?"

"I give him the option. If he does not wish to hunt I turn him over to Ivan. Ivan once served as official knouter to the Great White Tsar and he has his own ideas of sport. Invariably they choose the hunt."

"And if they win?"

The smile on the general's face widened. "To date I have not lost."

Then he added hastily, "I don't wish you to think me a braggart, Mr. Rainsford, and one did almost win. I eventually had to use the dogs."

"The dogs?"

"This way, please. I'll show you."

The general led the way to another window. The lights sent a flickering illumination that made grotesque patterns on the courtyard below, and Rainsford could see a dozen or so huge black shapes moving about. As they turned toward him he caught the green glitter of eyes.

"They are let out at seven every night. If anyone should try to get into my house—or out of it—something regrettable would happen to him. And now I want to show you my new collection of heads. Will you come to the library?"

"I hope," said Rainsford, "that you will excuse me tonight. I'm really not feeling at all well."

"Ah, indeed? You need a good restful night's sleep. Tomorrow you'll feel like a new man. Then we'll hunt, eh? I've one rather promising prospect—"

Rainsford was hurrying from the room.

"Sorry you can't go with me tonight," called the general. "I expect rather fair sport. A big, strong black. He looks resourceful—"

The bed was good and Rainsford was tired, but nevertheless he could not sleep, and had only achieved a doze when, as morning broke, he heard, far off in the jungle, the faint report of a pistol.

General Zaroff did not appear till luncheon. He was solicitous about Rainsford's health. "As for me," he said, "I do not feel so well. The hunting was not good last night. He made a straight trail that offered no problems at all."

"General," said Rainsford, "I want to leave the island at once."

He saw the dead black eyes of the general studying him. The eyes suddenly brightened. "Tonight," said he, "we will hunt—you and I."

Rainsford shook his head. "No, General," he said, "I will not hunt."

The general shrugged his shoulders. "As you wish. The choice rests with you, but I would suggest that my idea of sport is more diverting than Ivan's."

"You don't mean—" cried Rainsford.

"My dear fellow," said the general, "have I not told you I always mean what I say about hunting? This is really an inspiration. I drink to a foeman worthy of my steel at last."

The general raised his glass, but Rainsford sat staring at him. "You'll find this game worth playing," the general said enthusiastically. "Your brain against mine. Your woodcraft against mine. Your strength and stamina against mine. Outdoor chess! And the stake is not without value, eh?"

"And if I win—" began Rainsford huskily.

"If I do not find you by midnight of the third day, I'll cheerfully acknowledge myself defeated," said General Zaroff. "My sloop will place you on the mainland near a town."

The general read what Rainsford was thinking.

"Oh, you can trust me," said the Cossack. "I will give you my word as a gentleman and a sportsman. Of course, you, in turn, must agree to say nothing of your visit here."

"I'll agree to nothing of the kind."

"Oh, in that case—but why discuss that now? Three days hence we can discuss it over a bottle of Veuve Cliquot, unless—"

The general sipped his wine.

Then a businesslike air animated him. "Ivan," he said, "will supply you with hunting clothes, food, a knife. I suggest you wear moccasins; they leave a poorer trail. I suggest, too, that you avoid the big swamp in the southeast corner of the island. We call it Death Swamp. There's quicksand there. One foolish fellow tried it. The deplorable part of it was that Lazarus followed him. You can't imagine my feelings, Mr. Rainsford, I loved Lazarus; he was the finest hound in my pack. Well, I must beg you to excuse me now. I always take a siesta after lunch. You'll hardly have time for a nap, I fear. You'll want to start, no doubt. I shall not follow until dusk. Hunting at night is so much more exciting than by day, don't you think? *Au revoir*, Mr. Rainsford, *au revoir*."

As General Zaroff with a courtly bow strolled from the room, Ivan entered by another door. Under one arm he carried hunting clothes, a haversack of food, a leathern sheath containing a long-bladed hunting knife; his right hand rested on a cocked revolver thrust in the crimson sash about his waist. . . .

RAINSFORD HAD FOUGHT HIS WAY through the bush for two hours, but at length he paused, saying to himself through tight teeth, "I must keep my nerve."

He had not been entirely clearheaded when the château gates closed behind him. His first idea was to put distance between himself and General Zaroff, and to this end he had plunged along, spurred by the sharp rowels of something approaching panic. Now, having got a grip on himself, he had stopped to take stock of himself and the situation.

Straight flight was futile, for it must inevitably bring him to the sea. Being in a picture with a frame of water, his operations, clearly, must take place within that frame.

"I'll give him a trail to follow," thought Rainsford, striking off from the path into trackless wilderness. Recalling the lore of the fox hunt and the dodges of the fox, he executed a series of intricate loops, doubling again and again on his trail. Night found him leg-weary, with hands and face lashed by the branches. He was on a thickly wooded ridge. As his need for rest was imperative, he thought, "I have played the fox, now I must play the cat of the fable."

A big tree with a thick trunk and outspread branches was nearby, and, taking care to leave no marks, he climbed into the crotch and stretched out on one of the broad limbs. Rest brought him new confidence and almost a feeling of security.

An apprehensive night crawled slowly by like a wounded snake. Toward morning, when a dingy gray was varnishing the sky, the cry of a startled bird focused Rainsford's attention in its direction. Something was coming through the bush, coming slowly, carefully, coming by the same winding way that Rainsford had come. He flattened himself against the bough and, through a screen of leaves almost as thick as tapestry, watched.

It was General Zaroff. He made his way along, with his eyes fixed in concentration on the ground. He paused, almost beneath the tree, dropped to his knees and studied the ground. Rainsford's impulse was to leap on him like a panther, but he saw that the general's right hand held a small automatic.

The hunter shook his head several times as if he were puzzled. Then, straightening himself, he took from his case one of his long black cigarettes; its pungent incenselike smoke rose to Rainsford's nostrils.

Rainsford held his breath. The general's eyes had left the ground and were traveling inch by inch up the tree. Rainsford froze, every muscle tensed for a spring. But the sharp eyes of the hunter stopped before they reached the limb where Rainsford lay. A smile spread over his brown face. Very deliberately he blew a smoke ring into the air; then he turned his back on the tree and walked carelessly away along the trail he had come. The swish of the underbrush against his hunting boots grew fainter and fainter.

The pent-up air burst hotly from Rainsford's lungs. His first thought made him feel sick and numb. The general could follow a trail through the woods at night; he could follow an extremely difficult trail; he must have uncanny powers; only by the merest chance had he failed to see his quarry.

Rainsford's second thought was more terrible. It sent a shudder through him. Why had the general smiled? Why had he turned back?

Rainsford did not want to believe what his reason told him was true—the general was playing with him, saving him for another day's sport. The Cossack was the cat; he was the mouse. Then it was that Rainsford knew the meaning of terror.

"I will not lose my nerve," he told himself, "I will not."

Sliding down from the tree, he set off into the woods. Three hundred yards from his hiding place he stopped where a huge dead tree leaned precariously on a smaller, living one. Throwing off his sack of food, he took his knife from its sheath and set to work.

When the job was finished, he threw himself down behind a fallen log a hundred feet away. He did not have to wait long. The cat was coming back to play with the mouse.

Following the trail with the sureness of a bloodhound came General Zaroff. Nothing escaped those searching black eyes, no crushed blade of grass, no bent twig, no mark, no matter how faint, in the moss. So intent was the Cossack on his stalking that he was upon the thing Rainsford had made before he saw it. His foot touched the protruding bough that was the trigger. Even as he touched it, the general sensed his danger, and leaped back with the agility of an ape. But he was not quite quick enough; the dead tree, delicately adjusted to rest on the cut living one, crashed down and struck the general a glancing blow on the shoulder as it fell; but for his alertness he must have been crushed beneath it. He staggered, but he did not fall; nor did he drop his revolver. He stood there, rubbing his injured shoulder, and Rainsford, with fear again gripping his heart, heard the general's mocking laugh ring through the jungle.

"Rainsford," called the general, "if you are within sound of my voice let me congratulate you. Not many men know how to make a Malay man catcher. Luckily for me, I too have hunted in Malacca. You are proving interesting, Mr. Rainsford. I am now going to have my wound dressed; it is only a slight one. But I shall be back. I shall be back."

When the general, nursing his wounded shoulder, had gone, Rainsford again took up his flight. It was flight now, and it carried him on for some hours. Dusk came, then darkness, and still he pressed on. The ground grew softer under his moccasins; the vegetation grew ranker, denser; insects bit him savagely. He stepped forward and his foot sank into ooze. He tried to wrench it back, but the mud sucked viciously at his foot as if it had been a giant leech. With a violent effort he tore his foot loose. He knew where he was now. Death Swamp and its quicksand.

The softness of the earth had given him an idea. Stepping back from the quicksand a dozen feet, he began, like some huge prehistoric beaver, to dig.

Rainsford had dug himself in, in France, when a second's delay would have meant death. Compared to his digging now, that had been a placid pastime. The pit grew deeper; when it was above his shoulders he climbed out and from some hard saplings cut stakes, sharpening them to a fine point. These stakes he planted at the bottom of the pit with the points up. With flying fingers he wove a rough carpet of weeds and branches and with it covered the mouth of the pit. Then, wet with sweat and aching with tiredness, he crouched behind the stump of a lightning-blasted tree.

By the padding sound of feet on the soft earth he knew his pursuer was coming. The night breeze brought him the perfume of the general's cigarette. It seemed to the hunted man that the general was coming with unusual swiftness; that he was not feeling his way along, foot by foot. Rainsford, from where he was crouching, could not see the general, neither could he see the pit. He lived a year in a minute. Then he heard the sharp crackle of breaking branches as the cover of the pit gave way; heard the sharp scream of pain as the pointed stakes found their mark. Then he cowered back. Three feet from the pit a man was standing with an electric torch in his hand.

"You've done well, Rainsford," cried the general. "Your Burmese tiger pit has claimed one of my best dogs. Again you score. I must now see what you can do against my whole pack. I'm going home for a rest now. Thank you for a most amusing evening."

At daybreak Rainsford, lying near the swamp, was awakened by a distant sound, faint and wavering, but he knew it for the baying of a pack of hounds.

Rainsford knew he could do one of two things. He could stay where he was. That was suicide. He could flee. That was postponing the inevitable. For a moment he stood there thinking. An idea that held a wild chance came to him, and, tightening his belt, he headed away from the swamp.

The baying of the hounds drew nearer, nearer. Rainsford climbed a tree. Down a watercourse, not a quarter of a mile away, he could see the bush moving. Straining his eyes, he saw the lean figure of General Zaroff. Just ahead of him Rainsford made out another figure, with wide shoulders, which surged through the jungle reeds. It was the gigantic Ivan and he seemed to be pulled along. Rainsford realized that he must be holding the pack in leash.

They would be on him at any moment now. His mind worked frantically, and he thought of a native trick he had learned in Uganda. Sliding down the tree, he caught hold of a springy young sapling and to it fastened his hunting knife, with the blade pointing down the trail. With a bit of wild grapevine he tied back the sapling . . . and ran for his life. As the hounds hit the fresh scent, they raised their voices and Rainsford knew how an animal at bay feels.

He had to stop to get his breath. The baying of the hounds stopped abruptly, and Rainsford's heart stopped, too. They must have reached the knife.

Shinning excitedly up a tree, he looked back. His pursuers had stopped. But the hope in Rainsford's brain died, for he saw that General Zaroff was still on his feet. Ivan, however, was not. The knife, driven by the recoil of the springing tree, had not wholly failed.

Hardly had Rainsford got back to the ground when, once more, the pack took up the cry.

"Nerve, nerve, nerve!" he panted to himself as he dashed along. A blue gap showed through the trees dead ahead. The hounds drew nearer. Rainsford forced himself on toward that gap. He reached the sea, and across a cove could see the gray stone of the château. Twenty feet below him the sea rumbled and hissed. Rainsford hesitated. He heard the hounds. Then he leaped far out into the water.

When the general and his pack reached the opening, the Cossack stopped. For some moments he stood regarding the blue-green expanse of water. Then he sat down, took a drink of brandy from a silver flask, lit a perfumed cigarette, and hummed a bit from *Madama Butterfly*.

GENERAL ZAROFF ATE an exceedingly good dinner in his great paneled hall that evening. With it he had a bottle of Pol Roger and half a bottle of Chambertin. Two slight annoyances kept him from perfect enjoyment. One was that it would be difficult to replace Ivan; the other, that his quarry had escaped him. Of course—so thought the general, as he tasted his after-dinner liqueur—the American had not played the game.

To soothe himself, he read in his library from the works of Marcus Aurelius. At ten he went to his bedroom. He was comfortably tired, he said to himself, as he turned the key of his door.

There was a little moonlight, so before turning on the light he went to the window and looked down on the courtyard. He could see the great hounds, and he called, "Better luck another time." Then he switched on the light.

A man who had been hiding in the curtains of the bed was standing before him.

"Rainsford!" screamed the general. "How in God's name did you get here?"

"Swam. I found it quicker than walking through the jungle."

The other sucked in his breath and smiled. "I congratulate you. You have won the game."

Rainsford did not smile. "I am still a beast at bay," he said in a low, hoarse voice. "Get ready, General Zaroff."

The general made one of his deepest bows. "I see," he said. "Splendid. One of us is to furnish a repast for the hounds. The other will sleep in this very excellent bed. On guard, Rainsford. . . ."

He had never slept in a better bed, Rainsford decided.

THE MAGIC BARREL
BERNARD MALAMUD

Bernard Malamud

Not long ago there lived in uptown New York, in a small, almost meager room, though crowded with books, Leo Finkle, a rabbinical student in the Yeshivah University. Finkle, after six years of study, was to be ordained in June and had been advised by an acquaintance that he might find it easier to win himself a congregation if he were married. Since he had no present prospects of marriage, after two tormented days of turning it over in his mind, he called in Pinye Salzman, a marriage broker whose two-line advertisement he had read in the *Forward*.

The matchmaker appeared one night out of the dark fourth-floor hallway of the gray stone rooming house where Finkle lived, grasping a black, strapped portfolio that had been worn thin with use. Salzman, who had been long in the business, was of slight but dignified build, wearing an old hat, and an overcoat too short and tight for him. He smelled frankly of fish, which he loved to eat, and although he was missing a few teeth, his presence was not displeasing, because of an amiable manner curiously contrasted with mournful eyes. His voice, his lips, his wisp of beard, his bony fingers were animated, but give him a moment of repose and his mild blue eyes revealed a depth of sadness, a characteristic that put Leo a little at ease although the situation, for him, was inherently tense.

He at once informed Salzman why he had asked him to come, explaining that his home was in Cleveland, and that but for his parents, who had married comparatively late in life, he was alone in the world. He had for six years devoted himself almost entirely to his studies, as a result of which, understandably, he had found himself without time for a social life and the company of young women. Therefore he thought it the better part of trial and error—of embarrassing fumbling—to call in an experienced person to advise him on these matters. He remarked in passing that the function of the marriage broker was ancient and honorable, highly approved in the Jewish community, because it made practical the necessary without hindering joy. Moreover, his own parents had been brought together by a matchmaker. They had made, if not a financially profitable marriage—since neither had possessed any worldly goods to speak of—at least a successful one in the sense of their everlasting devotion to each other. Salzman listened in embarrassed surprise, sensing a sort of apology. Later, however, he experienced a glow of pride in his work, an emotion that had left him years ago, and he heartily approved of Finkle.

The two went to their business. Leo had led Salzman to the only clear place in the room, a table near a window that overlooked the lamplit city. He seated himself at the matchmaker's side but facing him, attempting by an act of will to suppress the unpleasant tickle in his throat. Salzman eagerly unstrapped his portfolio and removed a loose rubber band from a thin packet of much-handled cards. As he flipped through them, a gesture and sound that physically hurt Leo, the student pretended not to see and gazed steadfastly out the window. Although it was still February, winter was on its last legs, signs of which he had for the first time in years begun to notice. He now observed the round white moon, moving high in the sky through a cloud menagerie, and watched with half-open mouth as it penetrated a huge hen, and dropped out of her like an egg laying itself. Salzman, though pretending, through eyeglasses he had just slipped on, to be engaged in scanning the writing on the cards, stole occasional glances at the young man's distinguished face, noting with pleasure the long, severe scholar's nose, brown eyes heavy with learning, sensitive yet ascetic lips, and a certain almost hollow quality of the dark cheeks. He gazed around at shelves upon shelves of books and let out a soft, contented sigh.

When Leo's eyes fell upon the cards, he counted six spread out in Salzman's hand.

"So few?" he asked in disappointment.

"You wouldn't believe me how much cards I got in my office," Salzman replied. "The drawers are already filled to the top, so I keep them now in a barrel, but is every girl good for a new rabbi?"

Leo blushed at this, regretting all he had revealed of himself in a curriculum vitae he had sent to Salzman. He had thought it best to acquaint him with his strict standards and specifications, but in having done so, felt he had told the marriage broker more than was absolutely necessary.

He hesitantly inquired, "Do you keep photographs of your clients on file?"

"First comes family, amount of dowry, also what kind promises," Salzman replied, unbuttoning his tight coat and settling himself in the chair. "After comes pictures, rabbi."

"Call me Mr. Finkle. I'm not yet a rabbi."

Salzman said he would, but instead called him doctor, which he changed to rabbi when Leo was not listening too attentively.

Salzman adjusted his horn-rimmed spectacles, gently cleared his throat and read in an eager voice the contents of the top card:

"Sophie P. Twenty-four years. Widow one year. No children. Educated high school and two years college. Father promises eight thousand dollars. Has wonderful wholesale business. Also real estate. On the mother's side comes teachers, also one actor. Well known on Second Avenue."

Leo gazed up in surprise. "Did you say a widow?"

"A widow don't mean spoiled, rabbi. She lived with her husband maybe four months. He was a sick boy, she made a mistake to marry him."

"Marrying a widow has never entered my mind."

"This is because you have no experience. A widow, especially if she is young and healthy like this girl, is a wonderful person to marry. She will be thankful to you the rest of her life. Believe me, if I was looking now for a bride, I would marry a widow."

Leo reflected, then shook his head.

Salzman hunched his shoulders in an almost imperceptible gesture of disappointment. He placed the card down on the wooden table and began to read another:

"Lily H. High school teacher. Regular. Not a substitute. Has savings and new Dodge car. Lived in Paris one year. Father is successful dentist thirty-five years. Interested in professional man. Well-Americanized family. Wonderful opportunity.

"I knew her personally," said Salzman. "I wish you could see this girl. She is a doll. Also very intelligent. All day you could talk to her about books and theyater and whatnot. She also knows current events."

"I don't believe you mentioned her age?"

"Her age?" Salzman said, raising his brows. "Her age is thirty-two years."

Leo said after a while, "I'm afraid that seems a little too old."

Salzman let out a laugh. "So how old are you, rabbi?"

"Twenty-seven."

"So what is the difference, tell me, between twenty-seven and thirty-two? My own wife is seven years older than me. So what did I suffer? Nothing. If Rothschild's daughter wants to marry you, would you say on account her age, no?"

"Yes," Leo said dryly.

Salzman shook off the no in the yes. "Five years don't mean a thing. I give you my word that when you will live with her for one week you will forget her age. What does it mean five years—that she lived more and knows more than somebody who is younger? On this girl, God bless her, years are not wasted. Each one that it comes makes better the bargain."

"What subject does she teach in high school?"

"Languages. If you heard the way she speaks French, you will think it is music. I am in the business twenty-five years, and I recommend her with my whole heart. Believe me, I know what I'm talking, rabbi."

"What's on the next card?" Leo said abruptly.

Salzman reluctantly turned up the third card:

"Ruth K. Nineteen years. Honor student. Father offers thirteen thousand cash to the right bridegroom. He is a medical doctor. Stomach specialist with marvelous practice. Brother-in-law owns own garment business. Particular people."

Salzman looked as if he had read his trump card.

"Did you say nineteen?" Leo asked with interest.

"On the dot."

"Is she attractive?" He blushed. "Pretty?"

Salzman kissed his fingertips. "A little doll. On this I give you my word. Let me call the father tonight and you will see what means pretty."

But Leo was troubled. "You're sure she's that young?"

"This I am positive. The father will show you the birth certificate."

"Are you positive there isn't something wrong with her?" Leo insisted.

"Who says there is wrong?"

"I don't understand why an American girl her age should go to a marriage broker."

A smile spread over Salzman's face.

"So for the same reason you went, she comes."

Leo flushed. "I am pressed for time."

Salzman, realizing he had been tactless, quickly explained. "The father came, not her. He wants she should have the best, so he looks around himself. When we will locate the right boy he will introduce him and encourage. This makes a better marriage than if a young girl without experience takes for herself. I don't have to tell you this."

"But don't you think this young girl believes in love?" Leo spoke uneasily.

Salzman was about to guffaw but caught himself and said soberly, "Love comes with the right person, not before."

Leo parted dry lips but did not speak. Noticing that Salzman had snatched a glance at the next card, he cleverly asked, "How is her health?"

"Perfect," Salzman said, breathing with difficulty. "Of course, she is a little lame on her right foot from an auto accident that it happened to her when she was twelve years, but nobody notices on account she is so brilliant and also beautiful."

Leo got up heavily and went to the window. He felt curiously bitter and upbraided himself for having called in the marriage broker. Finally, he shook his head.

"Why not?" Salzman persisted, the pitch of his voice rising.

"Because I detest stomach specialists."

"So what do you care what is his business? After you marry her do you need him? Who says he must come every Friday night in your house?"

Ashamed of the way the talk was going, Leo dismissed Salzman, who went home with heavy, melancholy eyes.

Though he had felt only relief at the marriage broker's departure, Leo was in low spirits the next day. He explained it as arising from Salzman's failure to produce a suitable bride for him. He did not care for his type of clientele. But when Leo found himself hesitating whether to seek out another matchmaker, one more polished than Pinye, he wondered if it could be—his protestations to the contrary, and although he honored his father and mother—that he did not, in essence, care for the matchmaking institution? This thought he quickly put out of mind yet found himself still upset. All day he ran around in the woods—missed an important appointment, forgot to give out his laundry, walked out of a Broadway cafeteria without paying and had to run back with the ticket in his hand; had even not recognized his landlady in the street when she passed with a friend and courteously called out, "A good evening to you, Doctor Finkle." By nightfall, however, he had regained sufficient calm to sink his nose into a book and there found peace from his thoughts.

Almost at once there came a knock on the door. Before Leo could say enter, Salzman, commercial cupid, was standing in the room. His face was gray and meager, his expression hungry, and he looked as if he would expire on his feet. Yet the marriage broker managed, by some trick of the muscles, to display a broad smile.

"So good evening. I am invited?"

Leo nodded, disturbed to see him again, yet unwilling to ask the man to leave.

Beaming still, Salzman laid his portfolio on the table. "Rabbi, I got for you tonight good news."

"I've asked you not to call me rabbi. I'm still a student."

"Your worries are finished. I have for you a first-class bride."

"Leave me in peace concerning this subject." Leo pretended lack of interest.

"The world will dance at your wedding."

"Please, Mr. Salzman, no more."

"But first must come back my strength," Salzman said weakly. He fumbled with the portfolio straps and took out of the leather case an oily paper bag, from which he extracted a hard seeded roll and a small smoked whitefish. With a quick motion of his hand he stripped the fish out of its skin and began ravenously to chew. "All day in a rush," he muttered.

Leo watched him eat.

"A sliced tomato you have maybe?" Salzman hesitantly inquired.

"No."

The marriage broker shut his eyes and ate. When he had finished he carefully cleaned up the crumbs and rolled up the remains of the fish in the paper bag. His spectacled eyes roamed the room until he discovered, amid some piles of books, a one-burner gas stove. Lifting his hat he humbly asked, "A glass tea you got, rabbi?"

Conscience-stricken, Leo rose and brewed the tea. He served it with a chunk of lemon and two cubes of lump sugar, delighting Salzman.

After he had drunk his tea, Salzman's strength and good spirits were restored.

"So tell me, rabbi," he said amiably, "you considered some more the three clients I mentioned yesterday?"

"There was no need to consider."

"Why not?"

"None of them suits me."

"What then suits you?"

Leo let it pass because he could give only a confused answer.

Without waiting for a reply, Salzman asked, "You remember this girl I talked to you—the high school teacher?"

"Age thirty-two?"

But, surprisingly, Salzman's face lit in a smile. "Age twenty-nine."

Leo shot him a look. "Reduced from thirty-two?"

"A mistake," Salzman avowed. "I talked today with the dentist. He took me to his safety-deposit box and showed me the birth certificate. She was twenty-nine years last August. They made her a party in the mountains where she went for her vacation. When her father spoke to me the first time I forgot to write the age and I told you thirty-two, but now I remember this was a different client, a widow."

"The same one you told me about? I thought she was twenty-four?"

"A different. Am I responsible that the world is filled with widows?"

"No, but I'm not interested in them, nor for that matter, in schoolteachers."

Salzman pulled his clasped hands to his breast. Looking at the ceiling he devoutly exclaimed, "*Yiddishe kinder*, what can I say to somebody that he is not interested in high school teachers? So what then you are interested?"

Leo flushed but controlled himself.

"In what else will you be interested," Salzman went on, "if you not interested in this fine girl that she speaks four languages and has personally in the bank ten thousand dollars? Also her father guarantees further twelve thousand. Also she has a new car, wonderful clothes, talks on all subjects, and she will give you a first-class home and children. How near do we come in our life to paradise?"

"If she's so wonderful, why wasn't she married ten years ago?"

"Why?" said Salzman with a heavy laugh. "Why? Because she is *partikiler*. This is why. She wants the *best*."

Leo was silent, amused at how he had entangled himself. But Salzman had aroused his interest in Lily H., and he began seriously to consider calling on her. When the marriage broker observed how intently Leo's mind was at work on the facts he had supplied, he felt certain they would soon come to an agreement.

LATE SATURDAY afternoon, conscious of Salzman, Leo Finkle walked with Lily Hirschorn along Riverside Drive. He walked briskly and erectly, wearing with distinction the black fedora he had that morning taken with trepidation out of the dusty hatbox on his closet shelf, and the heavy black Saturday coat he had thoroughly whisked clean. Leo also owned a walking stick, a present from a distant relative, but quickly put temptation aside and did not use it. Lily, petite and not unpretty, had on something signifying the approach of spring. She was *au courant*, animatedly, with all sorts of subjects, and he weighed her words and found her surprisingly sound—score another for Salzman, whom he uneasily sensed to be somewhere around, hiding perhaps high in a tree along the street, flashing the lady signals with a pocket mirror; or perhaps a cloven-hoofed Pan, piping nuptial ditties as he danced his invisible way before them, strewing wild buds on the walk and purple grapes in their path, symbolizing fruit of a union, though there was of course still none.

Lily startled Leo by remarking, "I was thinking of Mr. Salzman, a curious figure, wouldn't you say?"

Not certain what to answer, he nodded.

She bravely went on, blushing, "I for one am grateful for his introducing us. Aren't you?"

He courteously replied, "I am."

"I mean," she said with a little laugh—and it was all in good taste, or at least gave the effect of being not in bad—"do you mind that we came together so?"

He was not displeased with her honesty, recognizing that she meant to set the relationship aright, and understanding that it took a certain amount of experience in life, and courage, to want to do it quite that way. One had to have some sort of past to make that kind of beginning.

He said that he did not mind. Salzman's function was traditional and honorable—valuable for what it might achieve, which, he pointed out, was frequently nothing.

Lily agreed with a sigh. They walked on for a while and she said after a long silence, again with a nervous laugh, "Would you mind if I asked you something a little bit personal? Frankly, I find the subject fascinating." Although Leo shrugged, she went on half embarrassedly, "How was it that you came to your calling? I mean, was it a sudden passionate inspiration?"

Leo, after a time, slowly replied, "I was always interested in the Law."

"You saw revealed in it the presence of the Highest?"

He nodded and changed the subject. "I understand that you spent a little time in Paris, Miss Hirschorn?"

"Oh, did Mr. Salzman tell you, Rabbi Finkle?" Leo winced, but she went on, "It was ages ago and almost forgotten. I remember I had to return for my sister's wedding."

And Lily would not be put off. "When," she asked in a trembly voice, "did you become enamored of God?"

He stared at her. Then it came to him that she was talking not about Leo Finkle, but of a total stranger, some mystical figure, perhaps even passionate prophet that Salzman had dreamed up for her—no relation to the living or dead. Leo trembled with rage and weakness. The trickster had obviously sold her a bill of goods, just as he had him, who'd expected to become acquainted with a young lady of twenty-nine, only to behold, the moment he laid eyes upon her strained and anxious face, a woman past thirty-five and aging rapidly. Only his self-control had kept him this long in her presence.

"I am not," he said gravely, "a talented religious person," and in seeking words to go on, found himself possessed by shame and fear. "I think," he said in a strained manner, "that I came to God not because I loved Him, but because I did not."

This confession he spoke harshly because its unexpectedness shook him.

Lily wilted. Leo saw a profusion of loaves of bread go flying like ducks high over his head, not unlike the winged loaves by which he had counted himself to sleep last night. Mercifully, then, it snowed, which he would not put past Salzman's machinations.

HE WAS INFURIATED with the marriage broker and swore he would throw him out of the room the minute he reappeared. But Salzman did not come that night, and when Leo's anger had subsided, an unaccountable despair grew in its place. At first he thought this was caused by his disappointment in Lily, but before long it became evident that he had involved himself with Salzman without a true knowledge of his own intent. He gradually realized—with an emptiness that seized him with six hands—that he had called in the broker to find him a bride because he was incapable of doing it himself. This terrifying insight he had derived as a result of his meeting and conversation with Lily Hirschorn. Her probing questions had somehow irritated him into revealing—to himself more than her—the true nature of his relationship to God, and from that it had come upon him, with shocking force, that apart from his parents, he had never loved anyone. Or perhaps it went the other way, that he did not love God so well as he might, because he had not loved man. It seemed to Leo that his whole life stood starkly revealed and he saw himself for the first time as he truly was—unloved and loveless. This bitter but somehow not fully unexpected revelation brought him to a point of panic, controlled only by extraordinary effort. He covered his face with his hands and cried.

The week that followed was the worst of his life. He did not eat and lost weight. His beard darkened and grew ragged. He stopped attending seminars and almost never opened a book. He seriously considered leaving the Yeshivah, although he was deeply troubled at the thought of the loss of all his years of study—saw them like pages torn from a book, strewn over the city—and at the devastating effect of this decision upon his parents. But he had lived without knowledge of himself, and never in the Five Books and all the Commentaries—*mea culpa*—had the truth been revealed to him. He did not know where to turn, and in all this desolating loneliness there was no *to whom*, although he often thought of Lily but not once could bring himself to go downstairs and make the call. He became touchy and irritable, especially with his landlady, who asked him all manner of personal questions; on the other hand, sensing his own disagreeableness, he waylaid her on the stairs and apologized abjectly, until mortified, she ran from him. Out of this, however, he drew the consolation that he was a Jew and that a Jew suffered. But gradually, as the long and terrible week drew to a close, he regained his composure and some idea of purpose in life: to go on as planned. Although he was imperfect, the ideal was not. As for his quest of a bride, the thought of continuing afflicted him with anxiety and heartburn, yet perhaps with this new knowledge of himself he would be more successful than in the past. Perhaps love would now come to him, and a bride to that love. And for this sanctified seeking who needed a Salzman?

The marriage broker, a skeleton with haunted eyes, returned that very night. He looked, withal, the picture of frustrated expectancy—as if he had steadfastly waited the week at Miss Lily Hirschorn's side for a telephone call that never came.

Casually coughing, Salzman came immediately to the point: "So how did you like her?"

Leo's anger rose and he could not refrain from chiding the matchmaker: "Why did you lie to me, Salzman?"

Salzman's pale face went dead white, the world had snowed on him.

"Did you not state that she was twenty-nine?" Leo insisted.

"I give you my word—"

"She was thirty-five, if a day. *At least* thirty-five."

"Of this don't be too sure. Her father told me—"

"Never mind. The worst of it was that you lied to her."

"How did I lie to her, tell me?"

"You told her things about me that weren't true. You made me out to be more, consequently less than I am. She had in mind a totally different person, a sort of semimystical Wonder Rabbi."

"All I said, you was a religious man."

"I can imagine."

Salzman sighed. "This is my weakness that I have," he confessed. "My wife says to me I shouldn't be a salesman, but when I have two fine people that they would be wonderful to be married, I am so happy that I talk too much." He smiled wanly. "This is why Salzman is a poor man."

Leo's anger left him. "Well, Salzman, I'm afraid that's all."

The marriage broker fastened hungry eyes on him.

"You don't want anymore a bride?"

"I do," said Leo, "but I have decided to seek her in a different way. I am no longer interested in an arranged marriage. To be frank, I now admit the necessity of premarital love. That is, I want to be in love with the one I marry."

"Love?" said Salzman, astounded. After a moment he remarked, "For us, our love is our life, not for the ladies. In the ghetto they—"

"I know, I know," said Leo. "I've thought of it often. Love, I have said to myself, should be a by-product of living and worship rather than its own end. Yet for myself I find it necessary to establish the level of my need and fulfill it."

Salzman shrugged but answered, "Listen, rabbi, if you want love, this I can find for you also. I have such beautiful clients that you will love them the minute your eyes will see them."

Leo smiled unhappily. "I'm afraid you don't understand."

But Salzman hastily unstrapped his portfolio and withdrew a manila packet from it.

"Pictures," he said, quickly laying the envelope on the table.

Leo called after him to take the pictures away, but as if on the wings of the wind, Salzman had disappeared.

March came. Leo had returned to his regular routine. Although he felt not quite himself yet—lacked energy—he was making plans for a more active social life. Of course it would cost something, but he was an expert in cutting corners; and when there were no corners left he would make circles rounder. All the while Salzman's pictures had lain on the table, gathering dust. Occasionally as Leo sat studying, or enjoying a cup of tea, his eyes fell on the manila envelope, but he never opened it.

The days went by and no social life to speak of developed with a member of the opposite sex—it was difficult, given the circumstances of his situation. One morning Leo toiled up the stairs to his room and stared out the window at the city. Although the day was bright his view of it was dark. For some time he watched the people in the street below hurrying along and then turned with a heavy heart to his little room. On the table was the packet. With a sudden relentless gesture he tore it open. For a half hour he stood by the table in a state of excitement, examining the photographs of the ladies Salzman had included. Finally, with a deep sigh he put them down. There were six, of varying degrees of attractiveness, but look at them long enough and they all became Lily Hirschorn: all past their prime, all starved behind bright smiles, not a true personality in the lot. Life, despite their frantic yoo-hooings, had passed them by; they were pictures in a briefcase that stank of fish. After a while, however, as Leo attempted to return the photographs into the envelope, he found in it another, a snapshot of the type taken by a machine for a quarter. He gazed at it a moment and let out a cry.

Her face deeply moved him. Why, he could at first not say. It gave him the impression of youth—spring flowers, yet age—a sense of having been used to the bone, wasted; this came from the eyes, which were hauntingly familiar, yet absolutely strange. He had a vivid impression that he had met her before, but try as he might he could not place her although he could almost recall her name, as if he had read it in her own handwriting. No, this couldn't be; he would have remembered her. It was not, he affirmed, that she had an extraordinary beauty—no, though her face was attractive enough; it was that *something* about her moved him. Feature for feature, even some of the ladies of the photographs could do better; but she leaped forth to his heart—had *lived*, or wanted to—more than just wanted, perhaps regretted how she had lived—had somehow deeply suffered: it could be seen in the depths of those reluctant eyes, and from the way the light enclosed and shone from her, and within her, opening realms of possibility: this was her own. Her he desired. His head ached and eyes narrowed with the intensity of his gazing, then as if an obscure fog had blown up in the mind, he experienced fear of her and was aware that he had received an impression, somehow, of evil. He shuddered, saying softly, it is thus with us all. Leo brewed some tea in a small pot and sat sipping it without sugar, to calm himself. But before he had finished drinking, again with excitement he examined the face and found it good: good for Leo Finkle. Only such a one could understand him and help him seek whatever he was seeking. She might, perhaps, love him. How she had happened to be among the discards in Salzman's barrel he could never guess, but he knew he must urgently go find her.

Leo rushed downstairs, grabbed up the Bronx telephone book, and searched for Salzman's home address. He was not listed, nor was his office. Neither was he in the Manhattan book. But Leo remembered having written down the address on a slip of paper after he had read Salzman's advertisement in the "personals" column of the *Forward*. He ran up to his room and tore through his papers, without luck. It was exasperating. Just when he needed the matchmaker he was nowhere to be found. Fortunately Leo remembered to look in his wallet. There on a card he found his name written and a Bronx address. No phone number was listed, the reason—Leo now recalled—he had originally communicated with Salzman by letter. He got on his coat, put a hat on over his skullcap and hurried to the subway station. All the way to the far end of the Bronx he sat on the edge of his seat. He was more than once tempted to take out the picture and see if the girl's face was as he remembered it, but he refrained, allowing the snapshot to remain in his inside coat pocket, content to have her so close. When the train pulled into the station he was waiting at the door and bolted out. He quickly located the street Salzman had advertised.

The building he sought was less than a block from the subway, but it was not an office building, nor even a loft, nor a store in which one could rent office space. It was a very old tenement house. Leo found Salzman's name in pencil on a soiled tag under the bell and climbed three dark flights to his apartment. When he knocked, the door was opened by a thin, asthmatic, gray-haired woman in felt slippers.

"Yes?" she said, expecting nothing. She listened without listening. He could have sworn he had seen her, too, before but knew it was an illusion.

"Salzman—does he live here? Pinye Salzman," he said, "the matchmaker?"

She stared at him a long minute. "Of course."

He felt embarrassed. "Is he in?"

"No." Her mouth, though left open, offered nothing more.

"The matter is urgent. Can you tell me where his office is?"

"In the air." She pointed upward.

"You mean he has no office?" Leo asked.

"In his socks."

He peered into the apartment. It was sunless and dingy, one large room divided by a half-open curtain, beyond which he could see a sagging metal bed. The near side of the room was crowded with rickety chairs, old bureaus, a three-legged table, racks of cooking utensils, and all the apparatus of a kitchen. But there was no sign of Salzman or his magic barrel, probably also a figment of the imagination. An odor of frying fish made Leo weak to the knees.

"Where is he?" he insisted. "I've got to see your husband."

At length she answered, "So who knows where he is? Every time he thinks a new thought he runs to a different place. Go home, he will find you."

"Tell him Leo Finkle."

She gave no sign she had heard.

He walked downstairs, depressed.

But Salzman, breathless, stood waiting at his door.

Leo was astounded and overjoyed. "How did you get here before me?"

"I rushed."

"Come inside."

They entered. Leo fixed tea, and a sardine sandwich for Salzman. As they were drinking he reached behind him for the packet of pictures and handed them to the marriage broker.

Salzman put down his glass and said expectantly, "You found somebody you like?"

"Not among these."

The marriage broker turned away.

"Here is the one I want." Leo held forth the snapshot.

Salzman slipped on his glasses and took the picture into his trembling hand. He turned ghastly and let out a groan.

"What's the matter?" cried Leo.

"Excuse me. Was an accident this picture. She isn't for you."

Salzman frantically shoved the manila packet into his portfolio. He thrust the snapshot into his pocket and fled down the stairs.

Leo, after momentary paralysis, gave chase and cornered the marriage broker in the vestibule. The landlady made hysterical outcries but neither of them listened.

"Give me back the picture, Salzman."

"No." The pain in his eyes was terrible.

"Tell me who she is then."

"This I can't tell you. Excuse me."

He made to depart, but Leo, forgetting himself, seized the matchmaker by his tight coat and shook him frenziedly.

"Please," sighed Salzman. *"Please."*

Leo ashamedly let him go. "Tell me who she is," he begged. "It's very important for me to know."

"She is not for you. She is a wild one—wild, without shame. This is not a bride for a rabbi."

"What do you mean wild?"

"Like an animal. Like a dog. For her to be poor was a sin. This is why to me she is dead now."

"In God's name, what do you mean?"

"Her I can't introduce to you," Salzman cried.

"Why are you so excited?"

"Why, he asks," Salzman said, bursting into tears. "This is my baby, my Stella, she should burn in hell."

LEO HURRIED UP to bed and hid under the covers. Under the covers he thought his life through. Although he soon fell asleep he could not sleep her out of his mind. He woke, beating his breast. Though he prayed to be rid of her, his prayers went unanswered. Through days of torment he endlessly struggled not to love her; fearing success, he escaped it. He then concluded to convert her to goodness, himself to God. The idea alternately nauseated and exalted him.

He perhaps did not know that he had come to a final decision until he encountered Salzman in a Broadway cafeteria. He was sitting alone at a rear table, sucking the bony remains of a fish. The marriage broker appeared haggard, and transparent to the point of vanishing.

Salzman looked up at first without recognizing him. Leo had grown a pointed beard and his eyes were weighted with wisdom.

"Salzman," he said, "love has at last come to my heart."

"Who can love from a picture?" mocked the marriage broker.

"It is not impossible."

"If you can love her, then you can love anybody. Let me show you some new clients that they just sent me their photographs. One is a little doll."

"Just her I want," Leo murmured.

"Don't be a fool, doctor. Don't bother with her."

"Put me in touch with her, Salzman," Leo said humbly. "Perhaps I can be of service."

Salzman had stopped eating and Leo understood with emotion that it was now arranged.

Leaving the cafeteria, he was, however, afflicted by a tormenting suspicion that Salzman had planned it all to happen this way.

LEO WAS INFORMED by letter that she would meet him on a certain corner, and she was there one spring night, waiting under a streetlamp. He appeared, carrying a small bouquet of violets and rosebuds. Stella stood by the lamppost, smoking. She wore white with red shoes, which fitted his expectations, although in a troubled moment he had imagined the dress red, and only the shoes white. She waited uneasily and shyly. From afar he saw that her eyes—clearly her father's—were filled with desperate innocence. He pictured, in her, his own redemption. Violins and lit candles revolved in the sky. Leo ran forward with flowers outthrust.

Around the corner, Salzman, leaning against a wall, chanted prayers for the dead.

IF GRANT HAD BEEN
DRINKING AT APPOMATTOX

JAMES THURBER

[signature: James Thurber]

THE MORNING of the ninth of April, 1865, dawned beautifully. General
Meade was up with the first streaks of crimson in the eastern sky.
General Hooker and General Burnside were up, and had breakfasted, by
a quarter after eight. The day continued beautiful. It drew on toward
eleven o'clock. General Ulysses S. Grant was still not up. He was asleep
in his famous old navy hammock, swung high above the floor of his
headquarters' bedroom. Headquarters was distressingly disarranged:
papers were strewn on the floor; confidential notes from spies scurried
here and there in the breeze from an open window; the dregs of an
overturned bottle of wine flowed pinkly across an important mili-
tary map.

Corporal Shultz, of the Sixty-fifth Ohio Volunteer Infantry, aide to
General Grant, came into the outer room, looked around him, and
sighed. He entered the bedroom and shook the General's hammock
roughly. General Ulysses S. Grant opened one eye.

"Pardon, sir," said Corporal Shultz, "but this is the day of surrender.
You ought to be up, sir."

"Don't swing me," said Grant, sharply, for his aide was making the
hammock sway gently. "I feel terrible," he added, and he turned over
and closed his eye again.

"General Lee will be here any minute now," said the Corporal
firmly, swinging the hammock again.

"Will you cut that out?" roared Grant. "D'ya want to make me sick,
or what?" Shultz clicked his heels and saluted. "What's he coming here
for?" asked the General.

"This is the day of surrender, sir," said Shultz. Grant grunted bitterly.

"Three hundred and fifty generals in the Northern armies," said Grant, "and he has to come to *me* about this. What time is it?"

"You're the Commander-in-Chief, that's why," said Corporal Shultz. "It's eleven twenty-five, sir."

"Don't be crazy," said Grant. "Lincoln is the Commander-in-Chief. Nobody in the history of the world ever surrendered before lunch. Doesn't he know that an army surrenders on its stomach?" He pulled a blanket up over his head and settled himself again.

"The generals of the Confederacy will be here any minute now," said the Corporal. "You really ought to be up, sir."

Grant stretched his arms above his head and yawned.

"All right, all right," he said. He rose to a sitting position and stared about the room. "This place looks awful," he growled.

"You must have had quite a time of it last night, sir," ventured Shultz.

"Yeh," said General Grant, looking around for his clothes. "I was wrassling some general. Some general with a beard."

Shultz helped the commander of the Northern armies in the field to find his clothes.

"Where's my other sock?" demanded Grant. Shultz began to look around for it. The General walked uncertainly to a table and poured a drink from a bottle.

"I don't think it wise to drink, sir," said Shultz.

"Nev' mind about me," said Grant, helping himself to a second, "I can take it or let it alone. Didn' ya ever hear the story about the fella went to Lincoln to complain about me drinking too much? 'So-and-So says Grant drinks too much,' this fella said. 'So-and-So is a fool,' said Lincoln. So this fella went to What's-His-Name and told him what Lincoln said and he came roarin' to Lincoln about it. 'Did you tell So-and-So I was a fool?' he said. 'No,' said Lincoln, 'I thought he knew it.'" The General smiled, reminiscently, and had another drink. "*That's* how I stand with Lincoln," he said, proudly.

The soft thudding sound of horses' hooves came through the open window. Shultz hurriedly walked over and looked out.

"Hoof steps," said Grant, with a curious chortle.

"It is General Lee and his staff," said Shultz.

"Show him in," said the General, taking another drink. "And see what the boys in the back room will have."

Shultz walked smartly over to the door, opened it, saluted, and stood aside. General Lee, dignified against the blue of the April sky, magnificent in his dress uniform, stood for a moment framed in the doorway. He walked in, followed by his staff. They bowed, and stood silent. General Grant stared at them. He only had one boot on and his jacket was unbuttoned.

"I know who you are," said Grant. "You're Robert Browning, the poet."

"This is General Robert E. Lee," said one of his staff, coldly.

"Oh," said Grant. "I thought he was Robert Browning. He certainly looks like Robert Browning. There was a poet for you, Lee: Browning. Did ja ever read 'How They Brought the Good News from Ghent to Aix'? 'Up Derek, to saddle, up Derek, away; up Dunder, up Blitzen, up Prancer, up Dancer, up Bouncer, up Vixen, up—' "

"Shall we proceed at once to the matter in hand?" asked General Lee, his eyes disdainfully taking in the disordered room.

"Some of the boys was wrassling here last night," explained Grant. "I threw Sherman, or some general a whole lot like Sherman. It was pretty dark." He handed a bottle of Scotch to the commanding officer of the Southern armies, who stood holding it, in amazement and discomfiture. "Get a glass, somebody," said Grant, looking straight at General Longstreet. "Didn't I meet you at Cold Harbor?" he asked. General Longstreet did not answer.

"I should like to have this over with as soon as possible," said Lee. Grant looked vaguely at Shultz, who walked up close to him, frowning.

"The surrender, sir, the surrender," said Corporal Shultz in a whisper.

"Oh sure, sure," said Grant. He took another drink. "All right," he said. "Here we go." Slowly, sadly, he unbuckled his sword. Then he handed it to the astonished Lee. "There you are, General," said Grant. "We dam' near licked you. If I'd been feeling better we *would* of licked you."

THE LEGEND
OF SLEEPY HOLLOW

WASHINGTON IRVING

Washington Irving

IN THE BOSOM of one of those spacious coves which indent the eastern shore of the Hudson, at that broad expansion of the river denominated by the ancient Dutch navigators the Tappan Zee, and where they always prudently shortened sail and implored the protection of Saint Nicholas, there lies a small market town which is generally known by the name of Tarry Town. This name was given by the good housewives of the adjacent country from the inveterate propensity of their husbands to linger about the village tavern on market days. Not far from this village, perhaps about two miles, there is a little valley among high hills which is one of the quietest places in the whole world. A small brook murmurs through it and, with the occasional whistle of a quail or tapping of a woodpecker, is almost the only sound that ever breaks the uniform tranquillity.

From the listless repose of the place, this sequestered glen has long been known by the name of Sleepy Hollow. Some say that the place was bewitched during the early days of the Dutch settlement; others, that an old Indian chief, the wizard of his tribe, held his powwows there before the country was discovered by Master Hendrick Hudson. Certain it is, the place still continues under the sway of some witching power that holds a spell over the minds of the descendants of the original settlers. They are given to all kinds of marvelous beliefs, are subject to trances and visions, and frequently hear music and voices in the air. The whole neighborhood abounds with local tales, haunted spots, and twilight superstitions.

The dominant spirit that haunts this enchanted region is the apparition of a figure on horseback without a head. It is said to be the ghost of a Hessian trooper, whose head had been carried away by a cannonball in some nameless battle during the Revolutionary War, and who is ever seen by the countryfolk, hurrying along in the gloom of the night as if on the wings of the wind. Historians of those parts allege that the body of the trooper having been buried in the yard of a church at no great distance, the ghost rides forth to the scene of battle in nightly quest of his head; and that the rushing speed with which he sometimes passes along the Hollow is owing to his being in a hurry to get back to the churchyard before daybreak. The specter is known, at all the country firesides, by the name of the Headless Horseman of Sleepy Hollow.

It is remarkable that this visionary propensity is not confined to native inhabitants of this little retired Dutch valley, but is unconsciously imbibed by everyone who resides there for a time. However wide-awake they may have been before they entered that sleepy region, they are sure, in a little time, to inhale the witching influence of the air and begin to grow imaginative, to dream dreams, and see apparitions.

In this by-place of nature there abode, some thirty years since, a worthy wight of the name of Ichabod Crane, a native of Connecticut, who "tarried" in Sleepy Hollow for the purpose of instructing the children of the vicinity. He was tall and exceedingly lank, with narrow shoulders, long arms and legs, hands that dangled a mile out of his sleeves, and feet that might have served for shovels. His head was small, and flat at top, with huge ears, large green glassy eyes, and a long snipe nose, so that it looked like a weathercock perched upon his spindle neck, to tell which way the wind blew. To see him striding along on a windy day, with his clothes bagging and fluttering about him, one might have mistaken him for some scarecrow eloped from a cornfield.

His schoolhouse was a low building of one large room, rudely constructed of logs. It stood in a rather lonely but pleasant situation, just at the foot of a woody hill, with a brook running close by, and a formidable birch tree growing at one end of it. From hence the low murmur of his pupils' voices, conning over their lessons, might be heard on a drowsy summer's day, interrupted now and then by the voice of the master in a tone of menace or command; or by the appalling sound of the birch as he urged some wrongheaded Dutch urchin along the flowery path of knowledge. All this he called "doing his duty," and he never inflicted a chastisement without following it by the assurance, so consolatory to the smarting urchin, that "he would remember it, and thank him for it the longest day he had to live."

When school hours were over, Ichabod was even the companion and playmate of the larger boys; and on holiday afternoons would convoy some of the smaller ones home, who happened to have pretty sisters, or good housewives for mothers, noted for the comforts of the cupboard. Indeed it behooved him to keep on good terms with his pupils. The revenue arising from his school would have been scarcely sufficient to furnish him with daily bread, for he was a huge feeder and, though lank, had the dilating powers of an anaconda. To help out his maintenance he was, according to custom in those parts, boarded and lodged at the homes of his pupils a week at a time; thus going the rounds of the neighborhood, with all his worldly effects tied up in a cotton handkerchief.

That this might not be too onerous for his rustic patrons, he assisted the farmers occasionally by helping to make hay, mending the fences, and driving the cows from pasture. He laid aside, too, all the dominant dignity with which he lorded it in the school, and became wonderfully gentle and ingratiating. He found favor in the eyes of the mothers by petting the children, particularly the youngest, and he would sit with a child on one knee, and rock a cradle with his foot for whole hours together.

In addition to his other vocations, he was the singing master of the neighborhood, and picked up many bright shillings by instructing the young folks in psalmody. Thus, by divers little makeshifts, the worthy pedagogue got on tolerably enough and was thought, by all who understood nothing of the labor of headwork, to have a wonderfully easy life of it.

The schoolmaster is generally a man of some importance in the female circle of a rural neighborhood, being considered a kind of idle, gentlemanlike personage, of vastly superior taste and accomplishments to the rough country swains. How he would figure among the country damsels in the churchyard, between services on Sundays!—gathering grapes for them from the wild vines that overran the surrounding trees; reciting for their amusement all the epitaphs on the tombstones; while the more bashful bumpkins hung sheepishly back, envying his superior elegance and address.

He was, moreover, esteemed by the women as a man of great erudition, for he had read several books quite through, and was a perfect master of Cotton Mather's *History of New England Witchcraft*. His appetite for the marvelous was extraordinary. It was often his delight, after his school was dismissed, to stretch himself on the clover bordering the little brook and there con over old Mather's direful tales in the gathering dusk. Then, as he wended his way to the farmhouse where he happened to be quartered, every sound of nature, the boding cry of the tree toad, the dreary hooting of the screech owl, fluttered his excited imagination. His only resource on such occasions was to sing psalm tunes; and the good people of Sleepy Hollow were often filled with awe at hearing his nasal melody floating along the dusky road.

Another of his sources of fearful pleasure was to pass long winter evenings with the old Dutch wives, as they sat spinning by the fire, with a row of apples roasting and spluttering along the hearth, and listen to their marvelous tales of ghosts and goblins, haunted bridges and haunted houses, and particularly of the headless horseman. But if there was a pleasure in all this while snugly cuddling in the chimney corner, it was dearly purchased by the terrors of his subsequent walk homeward. How often did he shrink with curdling awe at some rushing blast, howling among the trees of a snowy night, in the idea that it was the Galloping Hessian of the Hollow!

All these, however, were mere phantoms of the dark. Daylight put an end to all these evils. He would have passed a pleasant life of it if his path had not been crossed by a being that causes more perplexity to mortal man than ghosts, goblins, and the whole race of witches put together, and that was—a woman.

Among the musical disciples who assembled, one evening in each week, to receive his instructions in psalmody was Katrina Van Tassel, the only child of a substantial Dutch farmer. She was a blooming lass of fresh eighteen, plump as a partridge, ripe and melting and rosy-cheeked as one of her father's peaches, and universally famed, not merely for her beauty, but her vast expectations. She was withal a little of a coquette, as might be perceived in her dress. She wore ornaments of pure yellow gold to set off her charms, and a provokingly short petticoat to display the prettiest foot and ankle in the country round.

Ichabod Crane had a soft and foolish heart toward the sex; and it is not to be wondered at that so tempting a morsel soon found favor in his eyes, more especially after he had visited her in her paternal mansion. Old Baltus Van Tassel was a perfect picture of a thriving, contented, liberal-hearted farmer. He seldom, it is true, sent either his eyes or his thoughts beyond the boundaries of his own farm; but within those everything was snug, happy, and abundant.

The Van Tassel stronghold was situated on the banks of the Hudson, in one of those green, sheltered, fertile nooks in which the Dutch farmers are so fond of nestling. A great elm tree spread its broad branches over it, at the foot of which bubbled up a spring of the softest and sweetest water. Hard by the farmhouse was a vast barn, every window and crevice of which seemed bursting forth with the treasures of the farm. Rows of pigeons were enjoying the sunshine on the roof. Sleek unwieldy porkers were grunting in the repose and abundance of their pens. A stately squadron of snowy geese were riding in an adjoining pond, convoying whole fleets of ducks; regiments of turkeys were gobbling through the farmyard.

The pedagogue's mouth watered as he looked upon this sumptuous promise of luxurious winter fare. In his devouring mind's eye he pictured to himself every roasting pig running about with an apple in his mouth; the pigeons were snugly put to bed in a comfortable pie, and tucked in with a coverlet of crust.

As the enraptured Ichabod fancied all this, and as he rolled his great green eyes over the fat meadowlands, the rich fields of wheat, rye, buckwheat, and Indian corn, and the orchard, burdened with ruddy fruit, which surrounded the warm tenement of Van Tassel, his heart yearned after the damsel who was to inherit these domains, and his imagination expanded with the idea how they might be readily turned into cash, and the money invested in immense tracts of wild land, and shingle palaces in the wilderness. His busy fancy already presented to him the blooming Katrina, with a whole family of children, mounted on the top of a wagon loaded with household trumpery; and he beheld himself bestriding a pacing mare, with a colt at her heels, setting out for Kentucky, Tennessee, or the Lord knows where.

When he entered the house, the conquest of his heart was complete. It was one of those spacious farmhouses, with high-ridged but low-sloping roofs, built in the style handed down from the first Dutch settlers, the projecting eaves forming a piazza along the front. From the piazza the wondering Ichabod entered the hall, which formed the center of the mansion. Here, rows of resplendent pewter, ranged on a long dresser, dazzled his eyes. In one corner stood a huge bag of wool ready to be spun; ears of Indian corn and strings of dried apples and peaches hung in gay festoons along the walls; and a door left ajar gave him a peep into the best parlor, where the claw-footed chairs and dark mahogany tables shone like mirrors. Mock oranges and conch shells decorated the mantelpiece; strings of various colored birds' eggs were suspended above it, and a corner cupboard, knowingly left open, displayed immense treasures of old silver and well-mended china.

From the moment Ichabod laid his eyes upon these regions of delight, the peace of his mind was at an end, and his only study was how to win the heart of the peerless daughter of Van Tassel. In this enterprise, however, he had to encounter a host of rustic admirers, who kept a watchful and angry eye upon each other, but were ready to fly out in the common cause against any new competitor. Among these the most formidable was a burly, roaring, roistering blade of the name of Brom Van Brunt, the hero of the country round, which rang with his feats of strength and hardihood. He was broad-shouldered, with short curly black hair, and a bluff but not unpleasant countenance, having a mingled air of fun and arrogance. From his Herculean frame, he had received the nickname of "Brom Bones." He was famed for great skill in horsemanship; he was foremost at all races and cockfights; and, with the ascendancy which bodily strength acquires in rustic life, was the umpire in all disputes. He was always ready for either a fight or a frolic, but had more mischief and good humor than ill will in his composition. He had three or four boon companions who regarded him as their model, and at the head of whom he scoured the country, attending every scene of feud or merriment for miles round. Sometimes his crew would be heard dashing along past the farmhouses at midnight, with whoop and halloo, and the old dames would exclaim, "Aye, there goes Brom Bones and his gang!"

This hero had for some time singled out the blooming Katrina for the object of his uncouth gallantries; and though his amorous toyings were something like the gentle caresses of a bear, yet it was whispered that she did not altogether discourage his hopes. Certain it is, his advances were signals for rival candidates to retire; insomuch that, when his horse was seen tied to Van Tassel's paling on a Sunday night, all other suitors passed by in despair.

Such was the formidable rival with whom Ichabod Crane had to contend. Considering all things, a stouter man than he would have shrunk from the competition. Ichabod had, however, a happy mixture of pliability and perseverance in his nature; he was in form and spirit like a supplejack—though he bent, he never broke.

To have taken the field openly against his rival would have been madness. Ichabod, therefore, made his advances in a quiet and gently insinuating manner. Under cover of his character of singing master, he had made frequent visits at the farmhouse, carrying on his suit with the daughter by the side of the spring under the great elm, while Balt Van Tassel sat smoking his evening pipe at one end of the piazza and his little wife plied her spinning wheel at the other.

I profess not to know how women's hearts are wooed and won. To me they have always been matters of riddle and admiration. But certain it is that from the moment Ichabod Crane made his advances, the interests of Brom Bones declined; his horse was no longer seen tied at the palings on Sunday nights, and a deadly feud gradually arose between him and the schoolmaster of Sleepy Hollow. Brom would fain have carried matters to open warfare, and Ichabod had overheard a boast by Bones that he would "double the schoolmaster up, and lay him on a shelf of his own schoolhouse"; but Ichabod was too wary to give him an opportunity. Brom had no alternative but to play off boorish practical jokes upon his rival. Bones and his gang of rough riders smoked out Ichabod's singing school by stopping up the chimney; broke into the schoolhouse at night and turned everything topsy-turvy. But what was still more annoying, Brom took opportunities of turning him to ridicule in presence of his mistress, and had a scoundrel dog whom he taught to whine in the most ludicrous manner, and introduced as a rival of Ichabod's to instruct Katrina in psalmody.

In this way matters went on for some time. On a fine autumnal afternoon, Ichabod, in pensive mood, sat enthroned on the lofty stool whence he usually watched all the concerns of his little schoolroom. His scholars were all busily intent upon their books, or slyly whispering behind them with one eye kept upon the master; and a kind of buzzing stillness reigned. It was suddenly interrupted by the appearance of a Negro, mounted on the back of a ragged colt. He came clattering up to the school door with an invitation to Ichabod to attend a merrymaking to be held that evening at Mynheer Van Tassel's.

All was now bustle and hubbub in the lately quiet schoolroom. The scholars were hurried through their lessons, without stopping at trifles; those who were tardy had a smart application now and then in the rear to quicken their speed, and the whole school was turned loose an hour before the usual time.

The gallant Ichabod now spent at least an extra half hour at his toilet, brushing and furbishing up his only suit, of rusty black. That he might make his appearance in the true style of a cavalier, he borrowed a horse from the farmer with whom he was staying. The animal was a broken-down plow horse that had outlived almost everything but his viciousness. He was gaunt and shaggy, with a ewe neck and a head like a hammer; his rusty mane and tail were tangled and knotted with burrs; one eye had lost its pupil, and was glaring and spectral, but the other had the gleam of a genuine devil. In his day he must have had fire and mettle, if we may judge from the name he bore of Gunpowder.

Ichabod was a suitable figure for such a steed. He rode with short stirrups, which brought his knees nearly up to the pommel of the saddle; his sharp elbows stuck out like grasshoppers'; he carried his whip perpendicularly in his hand, like a scepter, and, as his horse jogged on, the motion of his arms was not unlike the flapping of a pair of wings. A small wool hat rested nearly on the top of his nose, and the skirts of his black coat fluttered out almost to the horse's tail.

Around him nature wore that rich and golden livery which we always associate with the idea of abundance. As he jogged slowly on his way, his eye ranged with delight over the treasures of jolly autumn. On all sides he beheld vast stores of apples gathered into baskets and barrels for the market, others heaped up in rich piles for the cider press. Farther on he beheld great fields of Indian corn, and the yellow pumpkins lying beneath them, turning up their fair round bellies to the sun. He passed the fragrant buckwheat fields, and as he beheld them, soft anticipations stole over his mind of dainty slapjacks, well buttered and garnished with honey by the delicate little dimpled hand of Katrina Van Tassel.

It was toward evening that Ichabod arrived at the castle of the Heer Van Tassel, which he found thronged with the pride and flower of the adjacent country. Old farmers, a spare leathern-faced race, in homespun coats and breeches, blue stockings, huge shoes, and magnificent pewter buckles. Their brisk withered little dames, in close crimped caps, long-waisted short gowns, homespun petticoats, and gay calico pockets hanging on the outside. Buxom lasses, almost as antiquated in dress as their mothers, excepting where a straw hat, a fine ribbon, or perhaps a white frock gave symptoms of city innovation. The sons, in short square-skirted coats with rows of stupendous brass buttons, and their hair generally queued with an eelskin in the fashion of the times, eelskins being esteemed as a potent nourisher and strengthener of the hair. Brom Bones, however, was the hero of the scene, having come to the gathering on his favorite steed, Daredevil, a creature, like himself, full of mettle and mischief, and which no one but himself could manage.

Ichabod was a kind and thankful creature, whose spirits rose with eating as some men's do with drink. He could not help rolling his large eyes round him on the ample charms of a genuine Dutch country tea table in the sumptuous time of autumn. Such heaped-up platters of cakes and crullers of various kinds, known only to experienced Dutch housewives! And then there were apple pies and peach pies and pumpkin pies, besides slices of ham and smoked beef; and, moreover, delectable dishes of preserved plums, and peaches, and pears, and quinces, not to mention broiled shad and roasted chickens; together with bowls of milk and cream, with the motherly teapot sending up its clouds of vapor from the midst. Ichabod chuckled with the possibility that he might one day be lord of all this scene of almost unimaginable luxury and splendor. Then, he thought, how soon he'd turn his back upon the old schoolhouse and snap his fingers in the face of every niggardly patron!

And now the sound of the music from the hall summoned to the dance. The musician was an old gray-headed Negro, who had been the itinerant orchestra of the neighborhood for more than half a century. His instrument was as old and battered as himself. He accompanied every movement of the bow with a motion of the head, bowing almost to the ground and stamping with his foot whenever a fresh couple were to start.

Ichabod prided himself upon his dancing as much as upon his vocal powers. Not a limb, not a fiber about him was idle as his loosely hung frame in full motion went clattering about the room. How could the flogger of urchins be otherwise than animated and joyous? The lady of his heart was his partner in the dance, and smiling graciously in reply to all his amorous oglings; while Brom Bones, sorely smitten with love and jealousy, sat brooding by himself in one corner.

When the dance was at an end, Ichabod was attracted to a knot of the sager folks, who, with old Van Tassel, sat smoking at one end of the piazza, gossiping over former times, and drawing out long stories about ghosts and apparitions, mourning cries and wailings, seen and heard in the neighborhood. Some mention was made of the woman in white, who haunted the dark glen at Raven Rock, and was often heard to shriek on winter nights before a storm, having perished there in the snow. The chief part of the stories, however, turned upon the favorite specter of Sleepy Hollow, the Headless Horseman, who had been heard several times of late near the bridge that crossed the brook in the woody dell next to the church; and, it was said, tethered his horse nightly among the graves in the churchyard.

The tale was told of old Brouwer, a most heretical disbeliever in ghosts, how he met the horseman returning from his foray into Sleepy Hollow, and was obliged to get up behind him; how they galloped over hill and swamp until they reached the church bridge. There the horseman suddenly turned into a skeleton, threw old Brouwer into the brook, and sprang away over the treetops with a clap of thunder.

This story was matched by Brom Bones, who made light of the Galloping Hessian as an arrant jockey. He affirmed that, on returning one night from a neighboring village, he had been overtaken by this midnight trooper; that he had offered to race with him for a bowl of punch, and should have won it, too; but just as they came to the church bridge, the Hessian bolted, and vanished in a flash of fire.

The revel now gradually broke up. The old farmers gathered together their families in their wagons, and were heard for some time rattling along over the distant hills. Some of the damsels mounted behind their favorite swains, and their lighthearted laughter, mingling with the clatter of hoofs, echoed along the silent woodlands. Ichabod only lingered behind, according to the custom of country lovers, to have a tête-à-tête with the heiress, fully convinced that he was now on the highroad to success. Something, however, I fear me, must have gone wrong, for he sallied forth, after no very great interval, with an air quite desolate and chopfallen. Oh, these women! these women! Was Katrina's encouragement of the poor pedagogue all a mere trick to secure her conquest of his rival? Let it suffice to say, Ichabod stole forth with the air of one who had been sacking a henroost, rather than a fair lady's heart. Without looking to the right or left, he went straight to the stable, and with several hearty cuffs and kicks, roused his steed most uncourteously.

It was the very witching time of night that Ichabod, heavyhearted and crestfallen, pursued his travel homeward. Far below, the Tappan Zee spread its dusky waters. In the dead hush of midnight he could hear the faint barking of a watchdog from the opposite shore. The night grew darker and darker; the stars seemed to sink deeper in the sky, and driving clouds occasionally hid them from his sight. He had never felt so lonely and dismal.

All the stories of ghosts and goblins that he had heard earlier now came crowding upon his recollection. He would, moreover, soon be approaching the very place where many of the scenes of the ghost stories had been laid.

Just ahead, where a small brook crossed the road, a few rough logs lying side by side served for a bridge. A group of oaks and chestnuts, matted thick with wild grapevines, threw a cavernous gloom over it. Ichabod gave Gunpowder half a score of kicks in his starveling ribs, and attempted to dash briskly across the bridge; but instead of starting forward, the perverse old animal only plunged to the opposite side of the road into a thicket of brambles. He came to a stand just by the bridge, with a suddenness that nearly sent his rider sprawling over his head. Just at this moment, in the dark shadow on the margin of the brook, Ichabod beheld something huge, misshapen, black, and towering. It stirred not, but seemed gathered up in the gloom, like some gigantic monster ready to spring upon the traveler.

The hair of the affrighted schoolteacher rose upon his head, but, summoning up a show of courage, he demanded in stammering accents, "Who are you?" He received no reply. He repeated his demand in a still more agitated voice. Still there was no answer. Once more he cudgeled the sides of the inflexible Gunpowder and, shutting his eyes, broke forth with involuntary fervor into a psalm tune. Just then the shadowy object of alarm put itself in motion and, with a scramble and a bound, stood at once in the middle of the road. He appeared to be a horseman of large dimensions, and mounted on a black horse of powerful frame. He kept aloof on one side of the road, jogging along on the blind side of old Gunpowder, who had now got over his waywardness.

Ichabod quickened his steed, in hopes of leaving this midnight companion behind. The stranger, however, quickened his horse to an equal pace. Ichabod pulled up, and fell into a walk, thinking to lag behind—the other did the same. His heart began to sink within him. There was something in the stranger's moody silence that was appalling. It was soon fearfully accounted for. On mounting a rising ground, which brought the figure of his fellow traveler in relief against the sky, gigantic in height, and muffled in a cloak, Ichabod was horror-struck on perceiving that he was headless! But his horror was still more increased on observing that the stranger's head was carried before him on the pommel of the saddle.

Ichabod's terror rose to desperation; he rained a shower of kicks and blows upon Gunpowder, hoping to give his companion the slip, but the specter started full jump with him. Away then they dashed, stones flying and sparks flashing at every bound. Ichabod's flimsy garments fluttered in the air, as he stretched his long lank body away over his horse's head in the eagerness of his flight.

They had now reached that stretch of the road which descends to Sleepy Hollow, shaded by trees for about a quarter of a mile, where it crosses the famous church bridge just before the green knoll on which stands the church.

Gunpowder, who seemed possessed with a demon, plunged headlong downhill. As yet his panic had given his unskillful rider an apparent advantage in the chase; but just as he had got halfway through the hollow, the girths of the saddle gave way, and Ichabod felt it slipping from under him. He had just time to save himself by clasping old Gunpowder round the neck when the saddle fell to the earth. He had much ado to maintain his seat, sometimes slipping on one side, sometimes on another, and sometimes jolted on the high ridge of his horse's backbone, with a violence that he feared would cleave him asunder.

An opening in the trees now cheered him with the hopes that the church bridge was at hand. He saw the whitewashed walls of the church dimly glaring under the trees beyond. He recollected the place where Brom Bones's ghostly competitor had disappeared. "If I can but reach that bridge," thought Ichabod, "I am safe." Just then he heard the black steed panting and blowing close behind him; he even fancied that he felt his hot breath. Another convulsive kick in the ribs, and old Gunpowder sprang upon the bridge; he thundered over the resounding planks; he gained the opposite side; and now Ichabod cast a look behind to see if his pursuer should vanish, according to rule, in a flash of fire and brimstone. Just then he saw the goblin rising in his stirrups, in the very act of hurling his head at him. Ichabod endeavored to dodge the horrible missile, but too late. It encountered his cranium with a tremendous crash—he was tumbled headlong into the dust, and Gunpowder, the black steed, and the goblin rider passed by like a whirlwind.

The next morning old Gunpowder was found without his saddle, and with the bridle under his feet, soberly cropping the grass at his master's gate. Ichabod did not make his appearance at breakfast; dinner hour came, but no Ichabod. The boys assembled at the schoolhouse, and strolled idly about the banks of the brook; but no schoolmaster. An inquiry was set on foot, and after diligent investigation they came upon the saddle trampled in the dirt. The tracks of horses' hoofs deeply dented in the road were traced to the bridge, beyond which, on the bank of a broad part of the brook, was found the hat of the unfortunate Ichabod, and close beside it a shattered pumpkin. The brook was searched, but the body of the schoolmaster was not to be discovered.

The mysterious event caused much speculation at the church on the following Sunday. Knots of gazers were collected in the churchyard, at the bridge, and at the spot where the hat and pumpkin had been found. They shook their heads, and came to the conclusion that Ichabod had been carried off by the Galloping Hessian. As he was a bachelor, and in nobody's debt, nobody troubled his head anymore about him.

It is true, an old farmer who had been down to New York on a visit several years after brought home the intelligence that Ichabod Crane was still alive; that he had only changed his quarters to a distant part of the country, had kept school and studied law at the same time, had turned politician, and finally had been made a justice of the Ten Pound Court. Brom Bones too, who shortly after his rival's disappearance conducted the blooming Katrina to the altar, was observed to look exceedingly knowing whenever the story of Ichabod was related, and always burst into a hearty laugh at the mention of the pumpkin, which led some to suspect that he knew more about the matter than he chose to tell.

The old country wives, however, who are the best judges of these matters, maintain to this day that Ichabod was spirited away by supernatural means. The bridge became more than ever an object of superstitious awe, and that may be the reason why the road has been altered of late years, so as to approach the church by the border of the millpond. The schoolhouse, being deserted, soon fell to decay, and was reported to be haunted by the ghost of the unfortunate teacher; and the plowboy, loitering homeward of a still summer evening, has often fancied Ichabod's voice at a distance, chanting a melancholy psalm tune among the tranquil solitudes of Sleepy Hollow.

THE MUSIC
OF ERICH ZANN

H. P. LOVECRAFT

I HAVE EXAMINED maps of the city with the greatest care, yet have never again found the Rue d'Auseil. These maps have not been modern maps alone, for I know that names change. I have, on the contrary, delved deeply into all the antiquities of the place, and have personally explored every region, of whatever name, which could possibly answer to the street I knew as the Rue d'Auseil. But despite all I have done, it remains a humiliating fact that I cannot find the house, the street, or even the locality, where, during the last months of my impoverished life as a student of metaphysics at the university, I heard the music of Erich Zann.

That my memory is broken I do not wonder; for my health, physical and mental, was gravely disturbed throughout the period of my residence in the Rue d'Auseil, and I recall that I took none of my few acquaintances there. But that I cannot find the place again is both singular and perplexing; for it was within a half hour's walk of the university and was distinguished by peculiarities which could hardly be forgotten by anyone who had been there. I have never met a person who has seen the Rue d'Auseil.

The Rue d'Auseil lay across a dark river bordered by precipitous brick blear-windowed warehouses and spanned by a ponderous bridge of dark stone. It was always shadowy along that river, as if the smoke of neighboring factories shut out the sun perpetually. The river was also odorous with evil stenches which I have never smelled elsewhere, and which may someday help me to find it, since I should recognize them at once. Beyond the bridge were narrow cobbled streets with rails; and then came the ascent, at first gradual, but incredibly steep as the Rue d'Auseil was reached.

I have never seen another street as narrow and steep as the Rue d'Auseil. It was almost a cliff, closed to all vehicles, consisting in several places of flights of steps, and ending at the top in a lofty ivied wall. Its paving was irregular, sometimes stone slabs, sometimes cobblestones, and sometimes bare earth with struggling greenish gray vegetation.

The houses were tall, peaked-roofed, incredibly old, and crazily leaning backward, forward, and sidewise. Occasionally an opposite pair, both leaning forward, almost met across the street like an arch; and certainly they kept most of the light from the ground below. There were a few overhead bridges from house to house across the street.

The inhabitants of that street impressed me peculiarly. At first I thought it was because they were all silent and reticent; but later decided it was because they were all very old. I do not know how I came to live on such a street, but I was not myself when I moved there. I had been living in many poor places, always evicted for want of money; until at last I came upon that tottering house in the Rue d'Auseil kept by the paralytic Blandot. It was the third house from the top of the street, and by far the tallest of them all.

My room was on the fifth story; the only inhabited room there, since the house was almost empty. On the night I arrived I heard strange music from the peaked garret overhead, and the next day asked old Blandot about it. He told me it was an old German viol player, a strange dumb man who signed his name as Erich Zann, and who played evenings in a cheap theater orchestra; adding that Zann's desire to play in the night after his return from the theater was the reason he had chosen this lofty and isolated garret room, whose single gable window was the only point on the street from which one could look over the terminating wall at the declivity and panorama beyond.

Thereafter I heard Zann every night, and although he kept me awake, I was haunted by the weirdness of his music. Knowing little of the art myself, I was yet certain that none of his harmonies had any relation to music I had heard before; and concluded that he was a composer of highly original genius. The longer I listened, the more I was fascinated, until after a week I resolved to make the old man's acquaintance.

One night as he was returning from his work, I intercepted Zann in the hallway and told him that I would like to know him and be with him when he played. He was a small, lean, bent person, with shabby clothes, blue eyes, grotesque, satyr-like face, and nearly bald head; and at my first words seemed both angered and frightened. My obvious friendliness, however, finally melted him; and he grudgingly motioned to me to follow him up the dark, creaking, and rickety attic stairs.

His room, one of only two in the steeply pitched garret, was on the west side, toward the high wall that formed the upper end of the street. Its size was very great, and seemed the greater because of its extraordinary barrenness and neglect. Of furniture there was only a narrow iron bedstead, a dingy washstand, a small table, a large book-case, an iron music rack, and three old-fashioned chairs. Sheets of music were piled in disorder about the floor. The walls were of bare boards, and had probably never known plaster; while the abundance of dust and cobwebs made the place seem more deserted than inhab-ited. Evidently Erich Zann's world of beauty lay in some far cosmos of the imagination.

Motioning me to sit down, the dumb man closed the door, turned the large wooden bolt, and lighted a candle to augment the one he had brought with him. He now removed his viol from its moth-eaten covering, and taking it, seated himself in the least uncomfortable of the chairs. He did not employ the music rack, but, offering no choice and playing from memory, enchanted me for over an hour with strains I had never heard before; strains which must have been of his own devising. To describe their exact nature is impossible for one unversed in music. They were a kind of fugue, with recurrent passages of the most captivating quality, but to me were notable for the absence of any of the weird notes I had overheard from my room below on other occasions.

Those haunting notes I had remembered, and had often hummed and whistled inaccurately to myself, so when the player at length laid down his bow I asked him if he would render some of them. As I began my request the wrinkled satyr-like face lost the bored placidity it had possessed during the playing, and seemed to show the same curious mixture of anger and fright which I noticed when first I accosted the old man. For a moment I was inclined to use persuasion, regarding rather lightly the whims of senility; and even tried to awaken my host's weirder mood by whistling a few of the strains to which I had listened the night before. But I did not pursue this course for more than a moment; for when the dumb musician recognized the whistled air his face grew suddenly distorted with an expression wholly beyond analysis, and his long, cold, bony right hand reached out to stop my mouth and silence the crude imitation. As he did this he further demonstrated his eccentricity by casting a startled glance toward the lone curtained window, as if fearful of some intruder—a glance doubly absurd, since the garret stood high and inaccessible above all the adjacent roofs, this window being the only point on the steep street, as the concierge had told me, from which one could see over the wall at the summit.

The old man's glance brought Blandot's remark to my mind, and with a certain capriciousness I felt a wish to look out over the wide and dizzying panorama of moonlit roofs and city lights beyond the hilltop, which of all the dwellers in the Rue d'Auseil only this crabbed musician could see. I moved toward the window and would have drawn aside the nondescript curtains, when with a frightened rage even greater than before, the dumb lodger was upon me again; this time motioning with his head toward the door as he nervously strove to drag me thither with both hands. Now thoroughly disgusted with my host, I ordered him to release me, and told him I would go at once. His clutch relaxed, and as he saw my disgust and offense, his own anger seemed to subside. He tightened his relaxing grip, but this time in a friendly manner, forcing me into a chair; then with an appearance of wistfulness crossing to the littered table, where he wrote many words with a pencil, in the labored French of a foreigner.

The note which he finally handed me was an appeal for tolerance and forgiveness. Zann said that he was old, lonely, and afflicted with strange fears and nervous disorders connected with his music and with other things. He had enjoyed my listening to his music, and wished I would come again and not mind his eccentricities. But he could not play to another his weird harmonies, and could not bear hearing them from another; nor could he bear having anything in his room touched by another. He had not known until our hallway conversation that I could overhear his playing in my room, and now asked me if I would arrange with Blandot to take a lower room where I could not hear him in the night. He would, he wrote, defray the difference in rent.

As I sat deciphering the execrable French, I felt more lenient toward the old man. He was a victim of physical and nervous suffering, as was I; and my metaphysical studies had taught me kindness. In the silence there came a slight sound from the window—the shutter must have rattled in the night wind, and for some reason I started almost as violently as did Erich Zann. So when I had finished reading, I shook my host by the hand, and departed as a friend.

The next day Blandot gave me a more expensive room on the third floor, between the apartments of an aged moneylender and the room of a respectable upholsterer. . . . There was no one on the fourth floor.

It was not long before I found that Zann's eagerness for my company was not as great as it had seemed while he was persuading me to move down from the fifth story. He did not ask me to call on him, and when I did call he appeared uneasy and played listlessly. This was always at night—in the day he slept and would admit no one. My liking for him did not grow, though the attic room and the weird music seemed to hold an odd fascination for me. I had a curious desire to look out of that window, over the wall and down the unseen slope at the glittering roofs and spires which must lie outspread there. Once I went up to the garret during theater hours, when Zann was away, but the door was locked.

What I did succeed in doing was to overhear the nocturnal playing of the dumb old man. At first I would tiptoe up to my old fifth floor, then I grew bold enough to climb the last creaking staircase to the peaked garret. There in the narrow hall, outside the bolted door with the covered keyhole, I often heard sounds which filled me with an indefinable dread—the dread of vague wonder and brooding mystery. It was not that the sounds were hideous, for they were not; but that they held vibrations suggesting nothing on this globe of earth, and that at certain intervals they assumed a symphonic quality which I could hardly conceive as produced by one player. Certainly, Erich Zann was a genius of wild power. As the weeks passed, the playing grew wilder, while the old musician acquired an increasing haggardness and furtiveness pitiful to behold. He now refused to admit me at any time, and shunned me whenever we met on the stairs.

Then one night as I listened at the door, I heard the shrieking viol swell into a chaotic babel of sound; a pandemonium which would have led me to doubt my own shaking sanity had there not come from behind that barred portal a piteous proof that the horror was real—the awful, inarticulate cry which only a mute can utter, and which rises only in moments of the most terrible fear or anguish. I knocked repeatedly at the door, but received no response. Afterward I waited in the black hallway, shivering with cold and fear, till I heard the poor musician's feeble effort to rise from the floor by the aid of a chair. Believing him just conscious after a fainting fit, I renewed my rapping, at the same time calling out my name reassuringly. I heard Zann stumble to the window and close both shutter and sash, then stumble to the door, which he falteringly unfastened to admit me. This time his delight at having me present was real; for his distorted face gleamed with relief while he clutched at my coat as a child clutches at its mother's skirts.

Shaking pathetically, the old man forced me into a chair while he sank into another, beside which his viol and bow lay carelessly on the floor. He sat for some time inactive, nodding oddly, but having a paradoxical suggestion of intense and frightened listening. Subsequently he seemed to be satisfied, and crossing to a chair by the table wrote a brief note, handed it to me, and returned to the table, where he began to write rapidly and incessantly.

The note implored me in the name of mercy, and for the sake of my own curiosity, to wait where I was while he prepared a full account in German of all the marvels and terrors which beset him. I waited, and the dumb man's pencil flew.

It was perhaps an hour later, while I still waited and while the old musician's feverishly written sheets still continued to pile up, that I saw Zann start as from the hint of a horrible shock. Unmistakably he was looking at the curtained window and listening shudderingly. Then I half fancied I heard a sound myself; though it was not a horrible sound, but rather an exquisitely low and infinitely distant musical note, suggesting a player in one of the neighboring houses, or in some abode beyond the lofty wall over which I had never been able to look. Upon Zann the effect was terrible, for, dropping his pencil, suddenly he rose, seized his viol, and commenced to rend the night with the wildest playing I had ever heard from his bow save when listening at the barred door.

It would be useless to describe the playing of Erich Zann on that dreadful night. It was more horrible than anything I had ever overheard, because I could now see the expression of his face, and could realize that this time the motive was stark fear. He was trying to make a noise; to ward something off or drown something out—what, I could not imagine, awesome though I felt it must be. The playing grew fantastic, delirious, and hysterical, yet kept to the last the qualities of supreme genius which I knew this strange old man possessed. I recognized the air—it was a wild Hungarian dance popular in the theaters, and I reflected for a moment that this was the first time I had ever heard Zann play the work of another composer.

Louder and louder, wilder and wilder, mounted the shrieking and whining of that desperate viol. The player was dripping with an uncanny perspiration and twisted like a monkey, always looking frantically at the curtained window. In his frenzied strains I could almost see shadowy satyrs and bacchanals dancing and whirling insanely through seething abysses of clouds and smoke and lightning. And then I thought I heard a shriller, steadier note that was not from the viol; a calm, deliberate, purposeful, mocking note from far away in the west.

At this juncture the shutter began to rattle in a howling night wind which had sprung up outside as if in answer to the mad playing within. Zann's screaming viol now outdid itself, emitting sounds I had never thought a viol could emit. The shutter rattled more loudly, unfastened, and commenced slamming against the window. Then the glass broke shiveringly under the persistent impacts, and the chill wind rushed in, making the candles sputter and rustling the sheets of paper on the table where Zann had begun to write out his horrible secret. I looked at

Zann, and saw that he was past conscious observation. His blue eyes were bulging, glassy and sightless, and the frantic playing had become a blind, mechanical unrecognizable orgy that no pen could even suggest.

A sudden gust, stronger than the others, caught up the manuscript and bore it toward the window. I followed the flying sheets in desperation, but they were gone before I reached the demolished panes. Then I remembered my old wish to gaze from this window, the only window in the Rue d'Auseil from which one might see the slope beyond the wall, and the city outspread beneath. It was very dark, but the city's lights always burned, and I expected to see them there amid the rain and wind. Yet when I looked from that highest of all gable windows, looked while the candles sputtered and the insane viol howled with the night wind, I saw no city spread below, and no friendly lights gleamed from remembered streets, but only the blackness of space illimitable; unimagined space alive with motion and music, and having no semblance of anything on earth. And as I stood there looking in terror, the wind blew out both the candles in that ancient peaked garret, leaving me in savage and impenetrable darkness with chaos and pandemonium before me, and the demon madness of that night-baying viol behind me.

I staggered back in the dark, without the means of striking a light, crashing against the table, overturning a chair, and finally groping my way to the place where the blackness screamed with shocking music. To save myself and Erich Zann I could at least try, whatever the powers opposed to me. Once I thought some chill thing brushed me, and I screamed, but my scream could not be heard above that hideous viol. Suddenly out of the blackness the madly sawing bow struck me, and I knew I was close to the player. I felt ahead, touched the back of Zann's chair, and then found and shook his shoulder in an effort to bring him to his senses.

He did not respond, and still the viol shrieked on without slackening. I moved my hand to his head, whose mechanical nodding I was able to stop, and shouted in his ear that we must both flee from the unknown things of the night. But he neither answered me nor abated the frenzy of his unutterable music, while all through the garret strange currents of wind seemed to dance in the darkness and babel. When my hand touched his ear I shuddered, though I knew not why—knew not why till I felt of the still face; the ice-cold, stiffened, unbreathing face whose glassy eyes bulged uselessly into the void. And then, by some miracle, finding the door and the large wooden bolt, I plunged wildly away from that glassy-eyed thing in the dark, and from the ghoulish howling of that accursed viol whose fury increased even as I plunged.

Leaping, floating, flying down those endless stairs through the dark house; racing mindlessly out into the narrow, steep, and ancient street of steps, and tottering houses; clattering down steps and over cobbles to the lower streets and the putrid canyon-walled river; panting across the dark bridge to the broader, healthier streets and boulevards we know; all these are terrible impressions that linger with me. And I recall that there was no wind, and that the moon was out, and that all the lights of the city twinkled.

Despite my most careful searches and investigations, I have never since been able to find the Rue d'Auseil. But I am not wholly sorry; either for this or for the loss in undreamable abysses of the closely written sheets which alone could have explained the music of Erich Zann.

ENOCH
AND THE GORILLA
FLANNERY O'CONNOR

Flannery O'Connor

Enoch Emery had borrowed his landlady's umbrella and he discovered as he stood in the entrance of the drugstore, trying to open it, that it was at least as old as she was. When he finally got it hoisted, he pushed his dark glasses back on his eyes and reentered the downpour.

The umbrella was one his landlady had stopped using fifteen years before (which was the only reason she had lent it to him) and as soon as the rain touched the top of it, it came down with a shriek and stabbed him in the back of the neck. He ran a few feet with it over his head and then backed into another store entrance and removed it. Then to get it up again, he had to place the tip of it on the ground and ram it open with his foot. He ran out again, holding his hand up near the spokes to keep them open and this allowed the handle, which was carved to represent the head of a fox terrier, to jab him every few seconds in the stomach. He proceeded for another quarter of a block this way before the back half of the silk stood up off the spokes and allowed the storm to sweep down his collar. Then he ducked under the marquee of a movie house. It was Saturday and there were a lot of children standing more or less in a line in front of the ticket box.

Enoch was not very fond of children, but children always seemed to like to look at him. The line turned and twenty or thirty eyes began to observe him with a steady interest. The umbrella had assumed an ugly position, half up and half down, and the half that was up was about to come down and spill more water under his collar. When this happened the children laughed and jumped up and down. Enoch glared at them and turned his back and lowered his dark glasses. He found himself facing a life-size four-color picture of a gorilla. Over the gorilla's head, written in red letters was "GONGA! Giant Jungle Monarch and a Great Star! HERE IN PERSON!!!" At the level of the gorilla's knee, there was more that said, "Gonga will appear in person in front of this theater at 12 A.M. *TODAY!* A free pass to the first ten brave enough to step up and shake his hand!"

Enoch was usually thinking of something else at the moment that Fate began drawing back her leg to kick him. When he was four years old, his father had brought him home a tin box from the penitentiary. It was orange and had a picture of some peanut brittle on the outside of it and green letters that said, "A NUTTY SURPRISE!" When Enoch had opened it, a coiled piece of steel had sprung out at him and broken off the ends of his two front teeth. His life was full of so many happenings like that that it would seem he should have been more sensitive to his times of danger. He stood there and read the poster twice through carefully. To his mind, an opportunity to insult a successful ape came from the hand of Providence.

He turned around and asked the nearest child what time it was. The child said it was twelve ten and that Gonga was already ten minutes late. Another child said that maybe the rain had delayed him. Another said, no not the rain, his director was taking a plane from Hollywood. Enoch gritted his teeth. The first child said that if he wanted to shake the star's hand, he would have to get in line like the rest of them and wait his turn. Enoch got in line. A child asked him how old he was. Another observed that he had funny-looking teeth. He ignored all this as best he could and began to straighten out the umbrella.

In a few minutes a black truck turned around the corner and came slowly up the street in the heavy rain. Enoch pushed the umbrella under his arm and began to squint through his dark glasses. As the truck approached, a phonograph inside it began to play "Tarara Boom Di Aye," but the music was almost drowned out by the rain. There was a large illustration of a blonde on the outside of the truck, advertising some picture other than the gorilla's.

The children held their line carefully as the truck stopped in front of the movie house. The back door of it was constructed like a paddy wagon, with a grate, but the ape was not at it. Two men in raincoats got out of the cab part, cursing, and ran around to the back and opened the door. One of them stuck his head in and said, "Okay, make it snappy, willya?" The other jerked his thumb at the children and said, "Get back willya, willya get back?"

A voice on the record inside the truck said, "Here's Gonga, folks. Roaring Gonga and a great star! Give Gonga a big hand, folks!" The voice was barely a mumble in the rain.

The man who was waiting by the door of the truck stuck his head in again. "Okay willya get out?" he said.

There was a faint thump somewhere inside the van. After a second a dark furry arm emerged just enough for the rain to touch it and then drew back inside.

"Damn," the man who was under the marquee said; he took off his raincoat and threw it to the man by the door, who threw it into the wagon. After two or three minutes more, the gorilla appeared at the door, with the raincoat buttoned up to his chin and the collar turned up. There was an iron chain hanging from around his neck; the man grabbed it and pulled him down and the two of them bounded under the marquee together. A motherly-looking woman was in the glass ticket box, getting the passes ready for the first ten children brave enough to step up and shake hands.

The gorilla ignored the children entirely and followed the man over to the other side of the entrance where there was a small platform raised about a foot off the ground. He stepped up on it and turned facing the children and began to growl. His growls were not so much loud as poisonous; they appeared to issue from a black heart. Enoch was terrified and if he had not been surrounded by the children, he would have run away.

"Who'll step up first?" the man said. "Come on come on, who'll step up first? A free pass to the first kid stepping up."

There was no movement from the group of children. The man glared at them. "What's the matter with you kids?" he barked. "You yellow? He won't hurt you as long as I got him by this chain." He tightened his grip on the chain and jangled it at them to show he was holding it securely.

After a minute a little girl separated herself from the group. She had long wood-shaving curls and a fierce triangular face. She moved up to within four feet of the star.

"Okay okay," the man said, rattling the chain, "make it snappy."

The ape reached out and gave her hand a quick shake. By this time there was another little girl ready and then two boys. The line re-formed and began to move up.

The gorilla kept his hand extended and turned his head away with a bored look at the rain. Enoch had got over his fear and was trying frantically to think of an obscene remark that would be suitable to insult him with. Usually he didn't have any trouble with this kind of composition but nothing came to him now. His brain, both parts, was completely empty. He couldn't think even of the insulting phrases he used every day.

There were only two children in front of him by now. The first one shook hands and stepped aside. Enoch's heart was beating violently. The child in front of him finished and stepped aside and left him facing the ape, who took his hand with an automatic motion.

It was the first hand that had been extended to Enoch since he had come to the city. It was warm and soft.

For a second he only stood there, clasping it. Then he began to stammer. "My name is Enoch Emery," he mumbled. "I attended the Rodemill Boys' Bible Academy. I work at the city zoo. I seen two of your pictures. I'm only eighteen years old but I already work for the city. My daddy made me come . . ." and his voice cracked.

The star leaned slightly forward and a change came in his eyes: an ugly pair of human ones moved closer and squinted at Enoch from behind the celluloid pair. "You go to hell," a surly voice inside the ape suit said, low but distinctly, and the hand was jerked away.

Enoch's humiliation was so sharp and painful that he turned around three times before he realized which direction he wanted to go in. Then he ran off into the rain as fast as he could.

IN SPITE OF himself, Enoch couldn't get over the expectation that something was going to happen to him. The virtue of hope, in Enoch, was made up of two parts suspicion and one part lust. It operated on him all the rest of the day. He had only a vague idea what he wanted, but he was not a boy without ambition: he wanted to become something. He wanted to better his condition. He wanted, someday, to see a line of people waiting to shake his hand.

All afternoon he fidgeted and fooled in his room, biting his nails and shredding what was left of the silk off the landlady's umbrella. Finally he denuded it entirely and broke off the spokes. What was left was a black stick with a sharp steel point at one end and a dog's head at the other. It might have been an instrument for some specialized kind of torture that had gone out of fashion. Enoch walked up and down his room with it under his arm and realized that it would distinguish him on the sidewalk.

About seven o'clock in the evening he put on his coat and took the stick and headed for a little restaurant two blocks away. He had the sense that he was setting off to get some honor, but he was very nervous, as if he were afraid he might have to snatch it instead of receive it.

He never set out for anything without eating first. The restaurant was called the Paris Diner; it was a tunnel about six feet wide, located between a shoeshine parlor and a dry-cleaning establishment. Enoch slid in and climbed up on the far stool at the counter and said he would have a bowl of split-pea soup and a chocolate malted milk shake.

The waitress was a tall woman with a big yellow dental plate and the same color hair done up in a black hairnet. One hand never left her hip; she filled orders with the other one. Although Enoch came in every night, she had never learned to like him.

Instead of filling his order, she began to fry bacon; there was only one other customer in the place and he had finished his meal and was reading a newspaper; there was no one to eat the bacon but her. Enoch reached over the counter and prodded her hip with the stick. "Listen here," he said, "I got to go. I'm in a hurry."

"Go then," she said. Her jaw began to work and she stared into the skillet with a fixed attention.

"Lemme just have a piece of theter cake yonder," he said, pointing to a half of pink and yellow cake on a round glass stand. "I think I got something to do. I got to be going. Set it up there next to him," he said, indicating the customer reading the newspaper. He slid over the stools and began reading the outside sheet of the man's paper.

The man lowered the paper and looked at him. Enoch smiled. The man raised the paper again. "Could I borrow some part of your paper that you ain't studying?" Enoch asked. The man lowered it again and stared at him; he had muddy unflinching eyes. He leafed deliberately through the paper and shook out the sheet with the comic strips and handed it to Enoch. It was Enoch's favorite part. He read it every evening like an office. While he ate the cake that the waitress had torpedoed down the counter at him, he read and felt himself surge with kindness and courage and strength.

When he finished one side, he turned the sheet over and began to scan the advertisements for movies that filled the other side. His eye went over three columns without stopping; then it came to a box that advertised Gonga, Giant Jungle Monarch, and listed the theaters he would visit on his tour and the hours he would be at each one. In thirty minutes he would arrive at the Victory on Fifty-seventh Street and that would be his last appearance in the city.

If anyone had watched Enoch read this, he would have seen a certain transformation in his countenance. It still shone with the inspiration he had absorbed from the comic strips, but something else had come over it: a look of awakening.

The waitress happened to turn around to see if he hadn't gone. "What's the matter with you?" she said. "Did you swallow a seed?"

"I know what I want," Enoch murmured.

"I know what I want too," she said with a dark look.

Enoch felt for his stick and laid his change on the counter. "I got to be going."

"Don't let me keep you," she said.

"You may not see me again," he said, "the way I am."

"Any way I don't see you will be all right with me," she said.

Enoch left. It was a pleasant damp evening. The puddles on the sidewalk shone and the store windows were steamy and bright with junk. He disappeared down a side street and made his way rapidly along the darker passages of the city, pausing only once or twice at the end of an alley to dart a glance in each direction before he ran on. The Victory was a small theater, suited to the needs of the family, in one of the closer subdivisions; he passed through a succession of lighted areas and then on through more alleys and back streets until he came to the business section that surrounded it. Then he slowed up. He saw it about a block away, glittering in its darker setting. He didn't cross the street to the side it was on but kept on the far side, moving forward with his squint fixed on the glary spot. He stopped when he was directly across from it and hid himself in a narrow stair cavity that divided a building.

The truck that carried Gonga was parked across the street and the star was standing under the marquee, shaking hands with an elderly woman. She moved aside and a gentleman in a polo shirt stepped up and shook hands vigorously, like a sportsman. He was followed by a boy of about three who wore a tall Western hat that nearly covered his face; he had to be pushed ahead by the line. Enoch watched for some time, his face working with envy. The small boy was followed by a lady in shorts, she by an old man who tried to draw extra attention to himself by dancing up instead of walking in a dignified way. Enoch suddenly darted across the street and slipped noiselessly into the open back door of the truck.

The handshaking went on until the feature picture was ready to begin. Then the star got back in the van and the people filed into the theater. The driver and the man who was master of ceremonies climbed in the cab part and the truck rumbled off. It crossed the city rapidly and continued on the highway, going very fast.

There came from the van certain thumping noises, not those of the normal gorilla, but they were drowned out by the drone of the motor and the steady sound of wheels against the road. The night was pale and quiet, with nothing to stir it but an occasional complaint from a hoot owl and the distant muted jarring of a freight train. The truck sped on until it slowed for a crossing, and as the van rattled over the tracks, a figure slipped from the door and almost fell, and then limped hurriedly off toward the woods.

Once in the darkness of a pine thicket, he laid down a pointed stick he had been clutching and something bulky and loose that he had been carrying under his arm, and began to undress. He folded each garment neatly after he had taken it off and then stacked it on top of the last thing he had removed. When all his clothes were in the pile, he took up the stick and began making a hole in the ground with it.

The darkness of the pine grove was broken by paler moonlit spots that moved over him now and again and showed him to be Enoch. His natural appearance was marred by a gash that ran from the corner of his lip to his collarbone and by a lump under his eye that gave him a dulled insensitive look. Nothing could have been more deceptive for he was burning with the intensest kind of happiness.

He dug rapidly until he had made a trench about a foot long and a foot deep. Then he placed the stack of clothes in it and stood aside to rest a second. Burying his clothes was not a symbol to him of burying his former self; he only knew he wouldn't need them anymore. As soon as he got his breath, he pushed the displaced dirt over the hole and stamped it down with his foot. He discovered while he did this that he still had his shoes on, and when he finished, he removed them and threw them from him. Then he picked up the loose bulky object and shook it vigorously.

In the uncertain light, one of his lean white legs could be seen to disappear and then the other, one arm and then the other: a black heavier shaggier figure replaced his. For an instant, it had two heads, one light and one dark, but after a second, it pulled the dark back head over the other and corrected this. It busied itself with certain hidden fastenings and what appeared to be minor adjustments of its hide.

For a time after this, it stood very still and didn't do anything. Then it began to growl and beat its chest; it jumped up and down and flung its arms and thrust its head forward. The growls were thin and uncertain at first but they grew louder after a second. They became low and poisonous, louder again, low and poisonous again; then stopped altogether. The figure extended its hand, clutched nothing, and shook its arm vigorously; it withdrew the arm, extended it again, clutched nothing, and shook. It repeated this four or five times. Then it picked up the pointed stick and placed it at a cocky angle under its arm and left the woods for the highway. No gorilla anywhere, Africa or California or New York, was happier than he.

A man and woman sitting close together on a rock just off the highway were looking across an open stretch of valley at a view of the city in the distance and they didn't see the shaggy figure approaching. The smokestacks and square tops of buildings made a black uneven wall against the lighter sky and here and there a steeple cut a sharp wedge out of a cloud. The young man turned his neck just in time to see the gorilla standing a few feet away, hideous and black, with its hand extended. He eased his arm from around the woman and disappeared silently into the woods. She, as soon as she turned her eyes, fled screaming down the highway. The gorilla stood as though surprised and presently its arm fell to its side. It sat down on the rock where they had been sitting and stared over the valley at the uneven skyline of the city.

THE UNTOLD LIE

SHERWOOD ANDERSON

R AY PEARSON AND Hal Winters were farmhands employed on a farm three miles north of Winesburg. On Saturday afternoons they came into town and wandered about through the streets with other fellows from the country.

Ray was a quiet, rather nervous man of perhaps fifty with a brown beard and shoulders rounded by too much and too hard labor. In his nature he was as unlike Hal Winters as two men can be unlike.

Ray was an altogether serious man and had a little sharp-featured wife who had also a sharp voice. The two, with half a dozen thin-legged children, lived in a tumbledown frame house beside a creek at the back end of the Wills farm where Ray was employed.

Hal Winters, his fellow employee, was a young fellow. He was not of the Ned Winters family, who were very respectable people in Winesburg, but was one of the three sons of the old man called Windpeter Winters who had a sawmill near Unionville, six miles away, and who was looked upon by everyone in Winesburg as a confirmed old reprobate.

People from the part of northern Ohio in which Winesburg lies will remember old Windpeter by his unusual and tragic death. He got drunk one evening in town and started to drive home to Unionville along the railroad tracks. Henry Brattenburg, the butcher, who lived out that way, stopped him at the edge of the town and told him he was sure to meet the down train but Windpeter slashed at him with his whip and drove on. When the train struck and killed him and his two horses a farmer and his wife who were driving home along a nearby road saw the accident. They said that old Windpeter stood up on the seat of his wagon, raving and swearing at the onrushing locomotive, and that he fairly screamed with delight when the team, maddened by his incessant slashing at them, rushed straight ahead to certain death. Boys like young George Willard and Seth Richmond will remember the incident quite vividly because, although everyone in our town said that the old man would go straight to hell and that the community was better off without him, they had a secret conviction that he knew what he was doing and admired his foolish courage. Most boys have seasons of wishing they could die gloriously instead of just being grocery clerks and going on with their humdrum lives.

But this is not the story of Windpeter Winters nor yet of his son Hal who worked on the Wills farm with Ray Pearson. It is Ray's story. It will, however, be necessary to talk a little of young Hal so that you will get into the spirit of it.

Hal was a bad one. Everyone said that. There were three of the Winters boys in that family, John, Hal, and Edward, all broad-shouldered big fellows like old Windpeter himself and all fighters and woman chasers and generally all-around bad ones.

Hal was the worst of the lot and always up to some devilment. He once stole a load of boards from his father's mill and sold them in Winesburg. With the money he bought himself a suit of cheap, flashy clothes. Then he got drunk and when his father came raving into town to find him, they met and fought with their fists on Main Street and were arrested and put into jail together.

Hal went to work on the Wills farm because there was a country schoolteacher out that way who had taken his fancy. He was only twenty-two then but had already been in two or three of what were spoken of in Winesburg as "women scrapes." Everyone who heard of his infatuation for the schoolteacher was sure it would turn out badly. "He'll only get her into trouble, you'll see," was the word that went around.

And so these two men, Ray and Hal, were at work in a field on a day in late October. They were husking corn and occasionally something was said and they laughed. Then came silence. Ray, who was the more sensitive and always minded things more, had chapped hands and they hurt. He put them into his coat pockets and looked away across the fields. He was in a sad distracted mood and was affected by the beauty of the country. If you knew the Winesburg country in the fall and how the low hills are all splashed with yellows and reds you would understand his feeling. He began to think of the time, long ago when he was a young fellow living with his father, then a baker in Winesburg, and how on such days he had wandered away to the woods to gather nuts, hunt rabbits, or just to loaf about and smoke his pipe. His marriage had come about through one of his days of wandering. He had induced a girl who waited on trade in his father's shop to go with him and something had happened. He was thinking of that afternoon and how it had affected his whole life when a spirit of protest awoke in him. He had forgotten about Hal and muttered words. "Tricked, by Gad, that's what I was, tricked by life and made a fool of," he said in a low voice.

As though understanding his thoughts, Hal Winters spoke up. "Well, has it been worthwhile? What about it, eh? What about marriage and all that?" he asked and then laughed. Hal tried to keep on laughing but he too was in an earnest mood. He began to talk earnestly. "Has a fellow got to do it?" he asked. "Has he got to be harnessed up and driven through life like a horse?"

Hal didn't wait for an answer but sprang to his feet and began to walk back and forth between the corn shocks. He was getting more and more excited. Bending down suddenly he picked up an ear of the yellow corn and threw it at the fence. "I've got Nell Gunther in trouble," he said. "I'm telling you, but you keep your mouth shut."

Ray Pearson arose and stood staring. He was almost a foot shorter than Hal, and when the younger man came and put his two hands on the older man's shoulders they made a picture. There they stood in the big empty field with the quiet corn shocks standing in rows behind them and the red and yellow hills in the distance, and from being just two indifferent workmen they had become all alive to each other. Hal sensed it and because that was his way he laughed. "Well, old daddy," he said awkwardly, "come on, advise me. I've got Nell in trouble. Perhaps you've been in the same fix yourself. I know what everyone would say is the right thing to do, but what do you say? Shall I marry and settle down? Shall I put myself into the harness to be worn out like an old horse? You know me, Ray. There can't anyone break me but I can break myself. Shall I do it or shall I tell Nell to go to the devil? Come on, you tell me. Whatever you say, Ray, I'll do."

Ray couldn't answer. He shook Hal's hands loose and turning walked straightaway toward the barn. He was a sensitive man and there were tears in his eyes. He knew there was only one thing to say to Hal Winters, son of old Windpeter Winters, only one thing that all his own training and all the beliefs of the people he knew would approve, but for his life he couldn't say what he knew he should say.

At half past four that afternoon Ray was puttering about the barnyard when his wife came up the lane along the creek and called him. After the talk with Hal he hadn't returned to the cornfield but worked about the barn. He had already done the evening chores and had seen Hal, dressed and ready for a roistering night in town, come out of the farmhouse and go into the road. Along the path to his own house he trudged behind his wife, looking at the ground and thinking. He couldn't make out what was wrong. Every time he raised his eyes and saw the beauty of the country in the failing light he wanted to do something he had never done before, shout or scream or hit his wife with his fists or something equally unexpected and terrifying. Along the path he went scratching his head and trying to make it out. He looked hard at his wife's back but she seemed all right.

She only wanted him to go into town for groceries and as soon as she had told him what she wanted began to scold. "You're always puttering," she said. "Now I want you to hustle. There isn't anything in the house for supper and you've got to get to town and back in a hurry."

Ray went into his own house and took an overcoat from a hook back of the door. It was torn about the pockets and the collar was shiny. His wife went into the bedroom and presently came out with a soiled cloth in one hand and three silver dollars in the other. Somewhere in the house a child wept bitterly and a dog that had been sleeping by the stove arose and yawned. Again the wife scolded. "The children will cry and cry. Why are you always puttering?" she asked.

Ray went out of the house and climbed the fence into a field. It was just growing dark and the scene that lay before him was lovely. All the low hills were washed with color and even the little clusters of bushes in the corners by the fences were alive with beauty. The whole world seemed to Ray Pearson to have become alive with something just as he and Hal had suddenly become alive when they stood in the cornfield staring into each other's eyes.

The beauty of the country about Winesburg was too much for Ray on that fall evening. That is all there was to it. He could not stand it. Of a sudden he forgot all about being a quiet old farmhand and throwing off the torn overcoat began to run across the field. As he ran he shouted a protest against his life, against all life, against everything that makes life ugly. "There was no promise made," he cried into the empty spaces that lay about him. "I didn't promise my Minnie anything and Hal hasn't made any promise to Nell. I know he hasn't. She went into the woods with him because she wanted to go. What he wanted she wanted. Why should I pay? Why should Hal pay? Why should anyone pay? I don't want Hal to become old and worn out. I'll tell him. I won't let it go on. I'll catch Hal before he gets to town and I'll tell him."

Ray ran clumsily and once he stumbled and fell down. "I must catch Hal and tell him," he kept thinking and although his breath came in gasps he kept running harder and harder. As he ran he thought of things that hadn't come into his mind for years—how at the time he married he had planned to go west to his uncle in Portland, Oregon—how he hadn't wanted to be a farmhand, but had thought when he got out west he would go to sea and be a sailor or get a job on a ranch and ride a horse into western towns, shouting and laughing and waking the people in the houses with his wild cries. Then as he ran he remembered his children and in fancy felt their hands clutching at him. All of his thoughts of himself were involved with the thoughts of Hal and he thought the children were clutching at the younger man also. "They are the accidents of life, Hal," he cried. "They are not mine or yours. I had nothing to do with them."

Darkness began to spread over the fields as Ray Pearson ran on and on. His breath came in little sobs. When he came to the fence at the edge of the road and confronted Hal Winters, all dressed up and smoking a pipe as he walked jauntily along, he could not have told what he thought or what he wanted. Ray Pearson lost his nerve and this is really the end of the story of what happened to him. It was almost dark when he got to the fence and he put his hands on the top bar and stood staring. Hal Winters jumped a ditch and coming up close to Ray put his hands into his pockets and laughed. He seemed to have lost his own sense of what had happened in the cornfield and when he put up a strong hand and took hold of the lapel of Ray's coat he shook the old man as he might have shaken a dog that had misbehaved.

"You came to tell me, eh?" he said. "Well, never mind telling me anything. I'm not a coward and I've already made up my mind." He laughed again and jumped back across the ditch. "Nell ain't no fool," he said. "She didn't ask me to marry her. I want to marry her. I want to settle down and have kids."

Ray Pearson also laughed. He felt like laughing at himself and all the world.

As the form of Hal Winters disappeared in the dusk that lay over the road that led to Winesburg, he turned and walked slowly back across the fields to where he had left his torn overcoat. As he went some memory of pleasant evenings spent with the thin-legged children in the tumbledown house by the creek must have come into his mind, for he muttered words. "It's just as well. Whatever I told him would have been a lie," he said softly, and then his form also disappeared into the darkness of the fields.

HORSE THIEF

ERSKINE CALDWELL

I DIDN'T steal Lud Moseley's calico horse.

People all over have been trying to make me out a thief, but anybody who knows me at all will tell you that I've never been in trouble like this before in all my life. Mr. John Turner will tell you all about me. I've worked for him, off and on, for I don't know exactly how many years. I reckon I've worked for him just about all my life, since I was a boy. Mr. John knows I wouldn't steal a horse. That's why I say I didn't steal Lud Moseley's, like he swore I did. I didn't grow up just to turn out to be a horse thief.

Night before last, Mr. John told me to ride his mare, Betsy. I said I wanted to go off a little way after something, and he told me to go ahead and ride Betsy, like I have been doing every Sunday night for going on two years now. Mr. John told me to take the Texas saddle, but I told him I didn't care about riding saddle. I like to ride with a bridle and reins, and nothing else. That's the best way to ride, anyway. And where I was going I didn't want to have a squeaking saddle under me. I wasn't up to no mischief. It was just a little private business of my own that nobody has got a right to call me down about. I nearly always rode saddle Sunday nights, but night before last was Thursday night, and that's why I didn't have a saddle when I went.

Mr. John Turner will tell you I'm not the kind to go off and get into trouble. Ask Mr. John about me. He has known me all my life, and I've never given him or anybody else trouble.

When I took Betsy out of the stable that night after supper, Mr. John came out to the barnyard and asked me over again if I didn't want

564

to take the Texas saddle. That mare, Betsy, is a little rawboned, but I didn't mind that. I told Mr. John I'd just as lief ride bareback. He said it was all right with him if I wanted to get sawn in two, and to go ahead and do like I pleased about it. He was standing right there all the time, rubbing Betsy's mane, and trying to find out where I was going, without coming right out and asking me. But he knew all the time where I was going, because he knows all about me. I reckon he just wanted to have a laugh at me, but he couldn't do that if I didn't let on where I was headed. So he told me it was all right to ride his mare without a saddle if I didn't want to be bothered with one, and I opened the gate and rode off down the road toward Bishop's crossroads.

That was night before last—Thursday night. It was a little after dark then, but I could see Mr. John standing at the barnyard gate, leaning on it a little, and watching me ride off. I'd been plowing that day, over in the new ground, and I was dog-tired. That's one reason why I didn't gallop off like I always did on Sunday nights. I rode away slow, letting Betsy take her own good time, because I wasn't in such a big hurry, after all. I had about two hours' time to kill, and only a little over three miles to go. That's why I went off like that.

EVERYBODY KNOWS I've been going to see Lud Moseley's youngest daughter, Naomi. I was going to see her again that night. But I couldn't show up there till about nine thirty. Lud Moseley wouldn't let me come to see her but once a week, on Sunday nights, and night before last was Thursday. I'd been there to see her three or four times before on Thursday nights that Lud Moseley didn't know about. Naomi told me to come to see her on Thursday nights. That's why I had been going there when Lud Moseley said I couldn't come to his house but once a week. Naomi told me to come anyway, and she had been coming out to the swing under the trees in the front yard to meet me.

I haven't got a thing in the world against Lud Moseley. Mr. John Turner will tell you I haven't. I don't especially like him, but that's to be expected, and he knows why. Once a week isn't enough to go to see a girl you like a lot, like I do Naomi. And I reckon she likes me a little, or she wouldn't tell me to come to see her on Thursday nights, when Lud Moseley told me not to come. Lud Moseley thinks if I go to see her more than once a week that maybe we'll take it into our heads to go get married without giving him a chance to catch on. That's why he said I couldn't come to his house but once a week, on Sunday nights.

He's fixing to have me sent to the penitentiary for twenty years for stealing his calico horse, Lightfoot. I reckon he knows good and well I didn't steal the horse, but he figures he's got a chance to put me out of the way till he can get Naomi married to somebody else. That's the way I figure it all out, because everybody in this part of the country who ever heard tell of me knows I'm not a horse thief. Mr. John Turner will tell you that about me. Mr. John knows me better than that. I've worked for him so long he even tried once to make me out as one of the family, but I wouldn't let him do that.

So, night before last, Thursday night, I rode off from home bareback, on Betsy. I killed a little time down at the creek, about a mile down the road from where we live, and when I looked at my watch again, it was nine o'clock sharp. I got on Betsy and rode off toward Lud Moseley's place. Everything was still and quiet around the house and barn. It was just about Lud's bedtime then. I rode right up to the barnyard gate, like I always did on Thursday nights. I could see a light up in Naomi's room, where she slept with her older sister, Mary Lee. We had always figured on Mary Lee's being out with somebody else, or maybe being ready to go to sleep by nine thirty. When I looked up at their window, I could see Naomi lying across her bed, and Mary Lee was standing beside the bed talking to her about something. That looked bad, because when Mary Lee tried to make Naomi undress and go to bed before she did, it always meant that it would take Naomi another hour or more to get out of the room, because she had to wait for Mary Lee to go to sleep before she could leave. She had to wait for Mary Lee to go to sleep, and then she had to get up and dress in the dark before she could come down to the front yard and meet me in the swing under the trees.

I SAT THERE on Betsy for ten or fifteen minutes, waiting to see how Naomi was going to come out with her sister. I reckon if we had let Mary Lee in on the secret she would have behaved all right about it, but on some account or other Naomi couldn't make up her mind to run the risk of it. There was a mighty chance that she would have misbehaved about it and gone straight and told Lud Moseley, and we didn't want to run that risk.

After a while I saw Naomi get up and start to undress. I knew right away that that meant waiting another hour or longer for her to be able to come and meet me. The moon was starting to rise, and it was getting to be as bright as day out there in the barnyard. I'd been in the habit of opening the gate and turning Betsy loose in the yard, but I was scared to do it night before last. If Lud Moseley should get up for a drink of water or something, and happen to look out toward the barn and see a horse standing there, he would either think it was one of his and come out and lock it in the stalls, or else he would catch on it was me out there. Anyway, as soon as he saw Betsy, he would have known it wasn't his mare, and there would have been the mischief to pay right there and then. So I opened the barn door and led Betsy inside and put her in the first empty stall I could find in the dark. I was scared to strike a light, because I didn't know but what Lud Moseley would be looking out the window just at that time and see the flare of the match. I put Betsy in the stall, closed the door, and came back outside to wait for Naomi to find a chance to come out and meet me in the swing in the yard.

It was about twelve thirty or one o'clock when I got ready to leave for home. The moon had been clouded, and it was darker than everything in the barn. I couldn't see my hand in front of me, it was that dark. I was scared to strike a light that time, too, and I felt my way in and opened the stall door and stepped inside to lead Betsy out. I couldn't see a thing, and when I found her neck, I thought she must have slipped her bridle like she was always doing when she had to stand too long to suit her. I was afraid to ride her home without a lead of some kind, because I was scared she might shy in the barnyard and start tearing around out there and wake up Lud Moseley. I felt around on the ground for the bridle, but I couldn't find it anywhere. Then I went back to the stall door and felt on it, thinking I might have taken it off myself when I was all excited at the start, and there was a halter hanging up. I slipped it over her head and led her out. It was still so dark I couldn't see a thing, and I had to feel my way outside and through the barnyard gate. When I got to the road, I threw a leg over her, and started for home without wasting any more time around Lud Moseley's place. I thought she trotted a little funny, because she had a swaying swing that made me slide from side to side, and I didn't have a saddle pommel to hold on to. I was all wrought up about getting away from there without getting caught up with, and I didn't think a thing about it. But I got home all right and slipped the halter off and put her in her stall. It was around one or two o'clock in the morning then.

The next morning after breakfast, when I was getting ready to catch the mules and gear them up to start plowing in the new ground again, Lud Moseley and three or four other men, including the sheriff, came riding lickety-split up the road from town and hitched at the rack. Mr. John came out and slapped the sheriff on the back and told him a funny story. They carried on like that for nearly half an hour, and then the sheriff asked Mr. John where I was. Mr. John told him I was getting ready to go off to the new ground, where we had planted a crop of corn that spring, and then the sheriff said he had a warrant for me. Mr. John asked him what for, a joke or something? And the sheriff told him it was for stealing Lud Moseley's calico horse, Lightfoot. Mr. John laughed at him, because he still thought it just a joke, but the sheriff pulled out the paper and showed it to him. Mr. John still wouldn't believe it, and he told them there was a mix-up somewhere, because, he told them, I wouldn't steal a horse. Mr. John knows I'm not a horse thief. I've never been in any kind of trouble before in all my life.

They brought me to town right away and put me in the cell room at the sheriff's jail. I knew I hadn't stole Lud Moseley's horse, and I wasn't scared a bit about it. But right after they brought me to town, they all rode back and the sheriff looked in the barn and found Lud Moseley's calico horse, Lightfoot, in Betsy's stall. Mr. John said things were all mixed up, because he knew I didn't steal the horse, and he knew I wouldn't do it. But the horse was there, the calico one, Lightfoot, and his halter was hanging on the stall door. After that they went back to Lud Moseley's and measured my foot tracks in the barnyard, and then they found Betsy's bridle. Lud Moseley said I had rode Mr. John's mare over there, turned her loose, and put the bridle on his Lightfoot and rode off. They never did say how come the halter to get to Mr. John's stable, then. Lud Moseley's stall door was not locked, and it wasn't broken down. It looks now like I forgot to shut it tight when I put Betsy in, because she got out someway and came home of her own accord sometime that night.

Lud Moseley says he's going to send me away for twenty years, where I won't have a chance to worry him over his youngest daughter, Naomi. He wants her to marry a widowed farmer over beyond Bishop's crossroads who runs twenty plows and who's got a big white house with fifteen rooms in it. Mr. John Turner says he'll hire the best lawyer in town to take up my case, but it don't look like it will do much good, because my footprints are all over Lud Moseley's barnyard, and his Lightfoot was in Mr. John's stable.

I reckon I could worm out of it someway, if I made up my mind to do it. But I don't like to do things like that. It would put Naomi in a bad way, because if I said I was there seeing her, and had put Betsy in the stall to keep her quiet, and took Lightfoot out by mistake in the dark when I got ready to leave—well, it would just look bad, that's all. She would have to say she was in the habit of slipping out of the house to see me after everybody had gone to sleep, on Thursday nights, and it would just look bad all around. She might take it into her head someday that she'd rather marry somebody else than me, and by that time she'd have a bad name for having been mixed up with me—and slipping out of the house to meet me after bedtime.

Naomi knows I'm no horse thief. She knows how it all happened— that I rode Lud Moseley's calico horse, Lightfoot, off by mistake in the dark, and left the stall door unfastened, and Betsy got out and came home of her own accord.

Lud Moseley has been telling people all around the courthouse as how he is going to send me away for twenty years so he can get Naomi married to that widowed farmer who runs twenty plows. Lud Moseley is right proud of it, it looks like to me, because he's got me cornered in a trap, and maybe he will get me sent away sure enough before Naomi gets a chance to tell what she knows is true.

But, somehow, I don't know if she'll say it if she does get the chance. Everybody knows I'm nothing but a hired man at Mr. John Turner's, and I've been thinking that maybe Naomi might not come right out and tell what she knows, after all.

I'd come right out and explain to the sheriff how the mix-up happened, but I sort of hate to mention Naomi's name in the mess. If it had been a Sunday night, instead of night before last, a Thursday, I could—well, it would just sound too bad, that's all.

If Naomi comes to town and tells what she knows, I won't say a word to stop her, because that'll mean she's willing to say it and marry me.

But if she stays at home, and lets Lud Moseley and that widowed farmer send me away for twenty years, I'll just have to go, that's all.

I always told Naomi I'd do anything in the world for her, and I reckon this will be the time when I've got to prove whether I'm a man of my word or not.

THE HAUNTED BOY

CARSON McCULLERS

Carson McCullers [signature]

H<small>UGH LOOKED</small> for his mother at the corner, but she was not in the yard. Sometimes she would be out fooling with the border of spring flowers—the candytuft, the sweet william, the lobelias (she had taught him the names)—but today the green front lawn with the borders of many-colored flowers was empty under the frail sunshine of the mid-April afternoon. Hugh raced up the sidewalk, and John followed him. They finished the front steps with two bounds, and the door slammed after them.

"Mama!" Hugh called.

It was then, in the unanswering silence as they stood in the empty, wax-floored hall, that Hugh felt there was something wrong. There was no fire in the grate of the sitting room, and since he was used to the flicker of firelight during the cold months, the room on this first warm day seemed strangely naked and cheerless. Hugh shivered. He was glad John was there. The sun shone on a red piece in the flowered rug. Red-bright, red-dark, red-dead—Hugh sickened with a sudden chill remembrance of "the other time." The red darkened to a dizzy black.

"What's the matter, Brown?" John asked. "You look so white."

Hugh shook himself and put his hand to his forehead. "Nothing. Let's go back to the kitchen."

"I can't stay but just a minute," John said. "I'm obligated to sell those tickets. I have to eat and run."

The kitchen, with the fresh checked towels and clean pans, was now the best room in the house. And on the enameled table there was a lemon pie that she had made. Assured by the everyday kitchen and the pie, Hugh stepped back into the hall and raised his face again to call upstairs.

"Mother! Oh, Mama!"

Again there was no answer.

"My mother made this pie," he said. Quickly he found a knife and cut into the pie—to dispel the gathering sense of dread.

"Think you ought to cut it, Brown?"

"Sure thing, Laney."

They called each other by their last names this spring, unless they happened to forget. To Hugh it seemed sporty and grown and somehow grand. Hugh liked John better than any other boy at school. John was two years older than Hugh, and compared to him the other boys seemed like a silly crowd of punks. John was the best student in the sophomore class, brainy but not the least bit a teacher's pet, and he was the best athlete too. Hugh was a freshman and didn't have so many friends that first year of high school—he had somehow cut himself off, because he was so afraid.

"Mama always has me something nice for after school." Hugh put a big piece of pie on a saucer for John—for Laney.

"This pie is certainly super."

"The crust is made of crunched-up graham crackers instead of regular pie dough," Hugh said, "because pie dough is a lot of trouble. We think this graham-cracker pastry is just as good. Naturally, my mother can make regular pie dough if she wants to."

Hugh could not keep still; he walked up and down the kitchen, eating the pie wedge he carried on the palm of his hand. His brown hair was mussed with nervous rakings, and his gentle gold-brown eyes were haunted with pained perplexity. John, who remained seated at the table, sensed Hugh's uneasiness and wrapped one gangling leg around the other.

"I'm really obligated to sell those Glee Club tickets."

"Don't go. You have the whole afternoon." He was afraid of the empty house. He needed John, he needed someone; most of all he needed to hear his mother's voice and know she was in the house with him. "Maybe Mama is taking a bath," he said. "I'll holler again."

The answer to his third call too was silence.

"I guess your mother must have gone to the movie or gone shopping or something."

"No," Hugh said. "She would have left a note. She always does when she's gone when I come home from school."

"We haven't looked for a note," John said. "Maybe she left it under the doormat or somewhere in the living room."

Hugh was inconsolable. "No. She would have left it right under this pie. She knows I always run first to the kitchen."

"Maybe she had a phone call or thought of something she suddenly wanted to do."

"She *might* have," he said. "I remember she said to Daddy that one of these days she was going to buy herself some new clothes." This flash of hope did not survive its expression. He pushed his hair back and started from the room. "I guess I'd better go upstairs. I ought to go upstairs while you are here." He stood with his arm around the newel-post; the smell of varnished stairs, the sight of the closed white bathroom door at the top revived again "the other time." He clung to the newel-post, and his feet would not move to climb the stairs. The red turned again to whirling, sick dark. Hugh sat down. *Stick your head between your legs,* he ordered, remembering scout first aid.

"Hugh," John called. "Hugh!"

The dizziness clearing, Hugh accepted a fresh chagrin—Laney was calling him by his ordinary first name; he thought he was a sissy about his mother, unworthy of being called by his last name in the grand, sporty way they used before. The dizziness cleared when he returned to the kitchen.

"Brown," said John, and the chagrin disappeared. "Does this establishment have anything pertaining to a cow? A white, fluid liquid. In French they call it *lait.* Here we call it plain old milk."

The stupidity of shock lightened. "Oh. Laney, I am a dope! Please excuse me. I clean forgot." Hugh fetched the milk from the refrigerator and found two glasses. "I didn't think. My mind was on something else."

"I know," John said. After a moment he asked in a calm voice, looking steadily at Hugh's eyes: "Why are you so worried about your mother? Is she sick, Hugh?"

Hugh knew now that the first name was not a slight; it was because John was talking too serious to be sporty. He liked John better than any friend he had ever had. He felt more natural sitting across the kitchen table from John, somehow safer. As he looked into John's gray, peaceful eyes, the balm of affection soothed the dread.

John asked again, still steadily: "Hugh, is your mother sick?"

Hugh could have answered no other boy. He had talked with no one about his mother, except his father, and even those intimacies had been rare, oblique. They could approach the subject only when they were occupied with something else, doing carpentry work or the two times they hunted in the woods together—or when they were cooking supper or washing dishes.

"She's not exactly sick," he said, "but Daddy and I have been worried about her. At least, we used to be worried for a while."

John asked: "Is it a kind of heart trouble?"

Hugh's voice was strained. "Did you hear about that fight I had with that slob Clem Roberts? I scraped his slob face on the gravel walk and nearly killed him sure enough. He's still got scars or at least he did have a bandage on for two days. I had to stay in school every afternoon for a week. But I nearly killed him. I would have if Mr. Paxton hadn't come along and dragged me off."

"I heard about it."

"You know why I wanted to kill him?"

For a moment John's eyes flickered away.

Hugh tensed himself; his raw boy hands clutched the table edge; he took a deep, hoarse breath. "That slob was telling everybody that my mother was in Milledgeville. He was spreading it around that my mother was crazy."

"The dirty bastard."

Hugh said in a clear, defeated voice: "My mother *was* in Milledgeville. But that doesn't mean that she was crazy," he added quickly. "In that big state hospital there are buildings for people who are crazy, and there are other buildings for people who are just sick. Mama was sick for a while. Daddy and me discussed it and decided that the hospital in Milledgeville was the place where there were the best doctors and she would get the best care. But she was the furtherest from crazy than anybody in the world. You know Mama, John." He said again: "I ought to go upstairs."

John said: "I have always thought that your mother is one of the nicest ladies in this town."

"You see, Mama had a peculiar thing happen, and afterward she was blue."

Confession, the first deep-rooted words, opened the festered secrecy of the boy's heart, and he continued more rapidly, urgent and finding unforeseen relief. "Last year my mother thought she was going to have a little baby. She talked it over with Daddy and me," he said proudly. "We wanted a girl. I was going to choose the name. We were so tickled. I hunted up all my old toys—my electric train and the tracks. . . . I was going to name her Crystal—how does that name strike you for a girl? It reminds me of something bright and dainty."

"Was the little baby born dead?"

Even with John, Hugh's ears turned hot; his cold hands touched them. "No, it was what they call a tumor. That's what happened to my mother. They had to operate at the hospital here." He was embarrassed and his voice was very low. "Then she had something called change of life." The words were terrible to Hugh. "And afterward she was blue. Daddy said it was a shock to her nervous system. It's something that happens to ladies; she was just blue and run-down."

Although there was no red, no red in the kitchen anywhere, Hugh was approaching "the other time."

"One day, she just sort of gave up—one day last fall." Hugh's eyes were wide open and glaring: again he climbed the stairs and opened the bathroom door—he put his hand to his eyes to shut out the memory. "She tried to—hurt herself. I found her when I came in from school."

John reached out and carefully stroked Hugh's sweatered arm.

"Don't worry. A lot of people have to go to hospitals because they are run-down and blue. Could happen to anybody."

"We had to put her in the hospital—the best hospital." The recollection of those long, long months was stained with a dull loneliness, as cruel in its lasting unappeasement as "the other time"— how long had it lasted? In the hospital Mama could walk around and she always had on shoes.

John said carefully: "This pie is certainly super."

"My mother is a super cook. She cooks things like meat pie and salmon loaf—as well as steaks and hot dogs."

"I hate to eat and run," John said.

Hugh was so frightened of being left alone that he felt the alarm in his own loud heart.

"Don't go," he urged. "Let's talk for a little while."

"Talk about what?"

Hugh could not tell him. Not even John Laney. He could tell no one of the empty house and the horror of the time before. "Do you ever cry?" he asked John. "I don't."

"I do sometimes," John admitted.

"I wish I had known you better when Mother was away. Daddy and me used to go hunting nearly every Saturday. We *lived* on quail and dove. I bet you would have liked that." He added in a lower tone: "On Sunday we went to the hospital."

John said: "It's kind of a delicate proposition selling those tickets. A lot of people don't enjoy the high school Glee Club operettas. Unless they know someone in it personally, they'd rather stay home with a good TV show. A lot of people buy tickets on the basis of being public-spirited."

"We're going to get a television set real soon."

"I couldn't exist without television," John said.

Hugh's voice was apologetic. "Daddy wants to clean up the hospital bills first, because as everybody knows sickness is a very expensive proposition. Then we'll get TV."

John lifted his milk glass. "Skoal," he said. "That's a Swedish word you say before you drink. A good-luck word."

"You know so many foreign words and languages."

"Not so many," John said truthfully. "Just 'kaput' and 'adios' and 'skoal' and stuff we learn in French class. That's not much."

"That's *beaucoup*," said Hugh, and he felt witty and pleased with himself.

Suddenly the stored tension burst into physical activity. Hugh grabbed the basketball out on the porch and rushed into the backyard. He dribbled the ball several times and aimed at the goal his father had put up on his last birthday. When he missed he bounced the ball to John, who had come after him.

It was good to be outdoors and the relief of natural play brought Hugh the first line of a poem. "My heart is like a basketball." Usually when a poem came to him he would lie sprawled on the living-room floor, studying to hunt rhymes, his tongue working on the side of his mouth. His mother would call him Shelley-Poe when she stepped over him, and sometimes she would put her foot lightly on his behind. His mother always liked his poems; today the second line came quickly, like magic. He said it out loud to John: " 'My heart is like a basketball, bounding with glee down the hall.' How do you like that for the start of a poem?"

"Sounds kind of crazy to me," John said. Then he corrected himself hastily. "I mean it sounds—odd. Odd, I meant."

Hugh realized why John changed the word, and the elation of play and poems left him instantly. He caught the ball and stood with it cradled in his arms. The afternoon was golden and the wisteria vine on the porch was in full, unshattered bloom. The wisteria was like lavender waterfalls. The fresh breeze smelled of sun-warmed flowers. The sunlit sky was blue and cloudless. It was the first warm day of spring.

"I have to shove off," John said.

"No!" Hugh's voice was desperate. "Don't you want another piece of pie? I never heard of anybody eating just one piece of pie."

He steered John into the house and this time he called only out of habit because he always called on coming in. "Mother!" He was cold after the bright, sunny outdoors. He was cold not only because of the weather but because he was so scared.

"My mother has been home a month and every afternoon she's always here when I come home from school. Always, always."

They stood in the kitchen looking at the lemon pie. And to Hugh the cut pie looked somehow—odd. As they stood motionless in the kitchen the silence was creepy and odd too.

"Doesn't this house seem quiet to you?"

"It's because you don't have television. We put on our TV at seven o'clock and it stays on all day and night until we go to bed. Whether anybody's in the living room or not. There're plays and skits and gags going on continually."

"We have a radio, of course, and a vic."

"But that's not the company of a good TV. You won't know when your mother is in the house or not when you get TV."

Hugh didn't answer. Their footsteps sounded hollow in the hall. He felt sick as he stood on the first step with his arm around the newel-post. "If you could just come upstairs for a minute—"

John's voice was suddenly impatient and loud. "How many times have I told you I'm obligated to sell those tickets. You have to be public-spirited about things like glee clubs."

"Just for a second—I have something important to show you upstairs."

John did not ask what it was and Hugh sought desperately to name something important enough to get John upstairs. He said finally: "I'm assembling a hi-fi machine. You have to know a lot about electronics—my father is helping me."

But even when he spoke he knew John did not for a second believe the lie. Who would buy a hi-fi when they didn't have television? He hated John, as you hate people you have to need so badly. He had to say something more and he straightened his shoulders.

"I just want you to know how much I value your friendship. During these past months I had somehow cut myself off from people."

"That's okay, Brown. You oughtn't to be so sensitive because your mother was—where she was."

John had his hand on the door and Hugh was trembling. "I thought if you could come up for just a minute—"

John looked at him with anxious, puzzled eyes. Then he asked slowly: "Is there something you are scared of upstairs?"

Hugh wanted to tell him everything. But he could not tell what his mother had done that September afternoon. It was too terrible and—odd. It was like something a *patient* would do, and not like his mother at all. Although his eyes were wild with terror and his body trembled he said: "I'm not scared."

"Well, so long. I'm sorry I have to go—but to be obligated is to be obligated."

John closed the front door and he was alone in the empty house. Nothing could save him now. Even if a whole crowd of boys were listening to TV in the living room, laughing at funny gags and jokes, it would still not help him. He had to go upstairs and find her. He sought courage from the last thing John had said, and repeated the words aloud: "To be obligated is to be obligated." But the words did not give him any of John's thoughtlessness and courage; they were creepy and strange in the silence.

He turned slowly to go upstairs. His heart was not like a basketball but like a fast, jazz drum, beating faster and faster as he climbed the stairs. His feet dragged as though he waded through knee-deep water and he held on to the banisters. The house looked odd, crazy. As he looked down at the ground-floor table with the vase of fresh spring flowers that too looked somehow peculiar. There was a mirror on the second floor and his own face startled him, so crazy did it seem to him. The initial of his high school sweater was backward and wrong in the reflection and his mouth was open like an asylum idiot. He shut his mouth and he looked better. Still the objects he saw—the table downstairs, the sofa upstairs—looked somehow cracked or jarred because of the dread in him, although they were the familiar things of every day. He fastened his eyes on the closed door at the right of the stairs and the fast, jazz drum beat faster.

He opened the bathroom door and for a moment the dread that had haunted him all that afternoon made him see again the room as he had seen it "the other time." His mother lay on the floor and there was blood everywhere. His mother lay there dead and there was blood everywhere, on her slashed wrist, and a pool of blood had trickled to the bathtub and lay dammed there.

Hugh touched the doorframe and steadied himself. Then the room settled and he realized this was not "the other time." The April sunlight brightened the clean white tiles. There was only bathroom brightness and the sunny window. He went to the bedroom and saw the empty bed with the rose-colored spread. The lady things were on the dresser. The room was as it always looked and nothing had happened . . . nothing had happened and he flung himself on the quilted rose bed and cried from relief and a strained, bleak tiredness that had lasted so long. The sobs jerked his whole body and quieted his jazz, fast heart.

Hugh had not cried all those months. He had not cried at "the other time," when he found his mother alone in that empty house with blood everywhere. He had not cried but he made a scout mistake. He had first lifted his mother's heavy, bloody body before he tried to bandage her. He had not cried when he called his father. He had not cried those few days when they were deciding what to do. He hadn't even cried when the doctor suggested Milledgeville, or when he and his father took her to the hospital in the car—although his father cried on the way home. He had not cried at the meals they made—steak every night for a whole month, so that they felt steak was running out of their eyes, their ears; then they had switched to hot dogs, and ate them until hot dogs ran out of their ears, their eyes. They got in ruts of food and were messy about the kitchen, so that it was never nice except the Saturday the cleaning woman came. He did not cry those lonesome afternoons after he had the fight with Clem Roberts and felt the other boys were thinking queer things of his mother. He stayed at home in the messy kitchen, eating Fig Newtons or chocolate bars. Or he went to see a neighbor's television—Miss Richards, an old maid who saw old-maid shows. He had not cried when his father drank too much, so that it took his appetite and Hugh had to eat alone. He had not even cried on those long, waiting Sundays when they went to Milledgeville and he twice saw a lady on a porch without any shoes on and talking to herself. A lady who was a patient and who struck at him with a horror he could not name. He did not cry when at first his mother would say: *Don't punish me by making me stay here. Let me go home.* He had not cried at the terrible words that haunted him—"change of life"—"crazy"— "Milledgeville"—he could not cry all during those long months strained with dullness and want and dread.

He still sobbed on the rose bedspread, which was soft and cool against his wet cheeks. He was sobbing so loud that he did not hear the front door open, did not even hear his mother call or the footsteps on the stairs. He still sobbed when his mother touched him and burrowed his face hard in the spread. He even stiffened his legs and kicked his feet.

"Why, Loveyboy," his mother said, calling him a long-ago child name. "What's happened?"

He sobbed even louder, although his mother tried to turn his face to her. He wanted her to worry. He did not turn around until she had finally left the bed, and then he looked at her. She had on a different dress—blue silk it looked like in the pale spring light.

"Darling, what's happened?"

The terror of the afternoon was over, but he could not tell it to his mother. He could not tell her what he had feared, or explain the horror of things that were never there at all—but had once been there.

"Why did you do it?"

"The first warm day I just suddenly decided to buy myself some new clothes."

But he was not talking about clothes; he was thinking about "the other time" and the grudge that had started when he saw the blood and horror and felt *why did she do this to me.* He thought of the grudge against the mother he loved the most in the world. All those last, sad months the anger had bounced against the love with guilt between.

"I bought two dresses and two petticoats. How do you like them?"

"I hate them!" Hugh said angrily. "Your slip is showing."

She turned around twice and the petticoat showed terribly. "It's supposed to show, goofy. It's the style."

"I still don't like it."

"I ate a sandwich at the tearoom with two cups of cocoa and then went to Mendel's. There were so many pretty things I couldn't seem to get away. I bought these two dresses and look, Hugh! The shoes!"

His mother went to the bed and switched on the light so he could see. The shoes were flat-heeled and *blue*—with diamond sparkles on the toes. He did not know how to criticize. "They look more like evening shoes than things you wear on the street."

"I have never owned any colored shoes before. I couldn't resist them."

His mother sort of danced over toward the window, making the petticoat twirl under the new dress. Hugh had stopped crying now, but he was still angry. "I don't like it because it makes you look like you're trying to seem young, and I bet you are forty years old."

His mother stopped dancing and stood still at the window. Her face was suddenly quiet and sad. "I'll be forty-three years old in June."

He had hurt her and suddenly the anger vanished and there was only love. "Mama, I shouldn't have said that."

"I realized when I was shopping that I hadn't been in a store for more than a year. Imagine!"

Hugh could not stand the sad quietness and the mother he loved so much. He could not stand his love or his mother's prettiness. He wiped the tears on the sleeve of his sweater and got up from the bed. "I have never seen you so pretty, or a dress and slip so pretty." He crouched down before his mother and touched the bright shoes. "The shoes are really super."

"I thought the minute I laid eyes on them that you would like them." She pulled Hugh up and kissed him on the cheek. "Now I've got lipstick on you."

Hugh quoted a witty remark he had heard before as he scrubbed off the lipstick. "It only shows I'm popular."

"Hugh, why were you crying when I came in? Did something at school upset you?"

"It was only that when I came in and found you gone and no note or anything—"

"I forgot all about a note."

"And all afternoon I felt— John Laney came in but he had to go sell Glee Club tickets. All afternoon I felt—"

"What? What was the matter?"

But he could not tell the mother he loved about the terror and the cause. He said at last: "All afternoon I felt—odd."

AFTERWARD WHEN his father came home he called Hugh to come out into the backyard with him. His father had a worried look—as though he spied a valuable tool Hugh had left outside. But there was no tool and the basketball was put back in its place on the back porch.

"Son," his father said, "there's something I want to tell you."

"Yes, sir?"

"Your mother said that you had been crying this afternoon." His father did not wait for him to explain. "I just want us to have a close understanding with each other. Is there anything about school—or girls—or something that puzzles you? Why were you crying?"

Hugh looked back at the afternoon and already it was far away, distant as a peculiar view seen at the wrong end of a telescope.

"I don't know," he said. "I guess maybe I was somehow nervous."

His father put his arm around his shoulders. "Nobody can be nervous before they are sixteen years old. You have a long way to go."

"I know."

"I have never seen your mother look so well. She looks so gay and pretty, better than she's looked in years. Don't you realize that?"

"The slip—the petticoat is supposed to show. It's a new style."

"Soon it will be summer," his father said. "And we'll go on picnics—the three of us." The words brought an instant vision of glare on the yellow creek and the summer-leaved, adventurous woods. His father added: "I came out here to tell you something else."

"Yes, sir?"

"I just want you to know that I realize how fine you were all that bad time. How fine, how damn fine."

His father was using a swear word as if he were talking to a grown man. His father was not a person to hand out compliments—always he was strict with report cards and tools left around. His father never praised him or used grown words or anything. Hugh felt his face grow hot and he touched it with his cold hands.

"I just wanted to tell you that, son." He shook Hugh by the shoulder. "You'll be taller than your old man in a year or so." Quickly his father went into the house, leaving Hugh to the sweet and unaccustomed aftermath of praise.

Hugh stood in the darkening yard after the sunset colors faded in the west and the wisteria was dark purple. The kitchen light was on and he saw his mother fixing dinner. He knew that something was finished; the terror was far from him now, also the anger that had bounced with love, the dread and guilt. Although he felt he would never cry again—or at least not until he was sixteen—in the brightness of his tears glistened the safe, lighted kitchen, now that he was no longer a haunted boy, now that he was glad somehow, and not afraid.

THE VALIANT WOMAN

J. F. POWERS

J.T. Powers

THEY HAD come to the dessert in a dinner that was a shambles. "Well, John," Father Nulty said, turning away from Mrs. Stoner and to Father Firman, long gone silent at his own table. "You've got the bishop coming for confirmations next week."

"Yes," Mrs. Stoner cut in, "and for dinner. And if he don't eat any more than he did last year—"

Father Firman, in a rare moment, faced it. "Mrs. Stoner, the bishop is not well. You know that."

"And after I fixed that fine dinner and all." Mrs. Stoner pouted in Father Nulty's direction.

"I wouldn't feel bad about it, Mrs. Stoner," Father Nulty said. "He never eats much anywhere."

"It's funny. And that new Mrs. Allers said he ate just fine when he was there," Mrs. Stoner argued, and then spit out, "but she's a damned liar!"

Father Nulty, unsettled but trying not to show it, said, "Who's Mrs. Allers?"

"She's at Holy Cross," Mrs. Stoner said.

"She's the housekeeper," Father Firman added, thinking Mrs. Stoner made it sound as though Mrs. Allers were the pastor there.

"I swear I don't know what to do about the dinner this year," Mrs. Stoner said.

Father Firman moaned. "Just do as you've always done, Mrs. Stoner."

"Huh! And have it all to throw out! Is that any way to do?"

"Is there any dessert?" Father Firman asked coldly.

Mrs. Stoner leaped up from the table and bolted into the kitchen, mumbling. She came back with a birthday cake. She plunged it in the center of the table. She found a big wooden match in her apron pocket and thrust it at Father Firman.

"I don't like this bishop," she said. "I never did. And the way he went and cut poor Ellen Kennedy out of Father Doolin's will!"

She went back into the kitchen.

"Didn't they talk a lot of filth about Doolin and the housekeeper?" Father Nulty asked.

"I should think they did," Father Firman said. "All because he took her to the movies on Sunday night. After he died and the bishop cut her out of the will, though I hear he gives her a pension privately, they talked about the bishop."

"I don't like this bishop at all," Mrs. Stoner said, appearing with a cake knife. "Bishop Doran—there was the man!"

"We know," Father Firman said. "All man and all priest."

"He did know real estate," Father Nulty said.

Father Firman struck the match.

"Not on the chair!" Mrs. Stoner cried, too late.

Father Firman set the candle burning—it was suspiciously large and yellow, like a blessed one, but he could not be sure. They watched the fluttering flame.

"I'm forgetting the lights!" Mrs. Stoner said, and got up to turn them off. She went into the kitchen again.

The priests had a moment of silence in the candlelight.

"Happy birthday, John," Father Nulty said softly. "Is it fifty-nine you are?"

"As if you didn't know, Frank," Father Firman said, "and you the same but one."

Father Nulty smiled, the old gold of his incisors shining in the flickering light, his collar whiter in the dark, and raised his glass of water, which would have been wine or better in the bygone days, and toasted Father Firman.

"Many of 'em, John."

"Blow it out," Mrs. Stoner said, returning to the room. She waited by the light switch for Father Firman to blow out the candle. Mrs. Stoner, who ate no desserts, began to clear the dishes into the kitchen, and the priests, finishing their cake and coffee in a hurry, went to sit in the study.

Father Nulty offered a cigar.

"John?"

"My ulcers, Frank."

"Ah, well, you're better off." Father Nulty lit the cigar and crossed his long black legs. "Fish Frawley has got him a Filipino, John. Did you hear?"

Father Firman leaned forward, interested. "He got rid of the woman he had?"

"He did. It seems she snooped."

"Snooped, eh?"

"She did. And gossiped. Fish introduced two town boys to her, said, 'Would you think these boys were my nephews?' That's all, and the next week the paper had it that his two nephews were visiting him from Erie. After that, he let her believe he was going east to see his parents, though both are dead. The paper carried the story. Fish returned and made a sermon out of it. Then he got the Filipino."

Father Firman squirmed with pleasure in his chair. "That's like Fish, Frank. He can do that." He stared at the tips of his fingers bleakly. "You could never get a Filipino to come to a place like this."

"Probably not," Father Nulty said. "Fish is pretty close to Minneapolis. Ah, say, do you remember the trick he played on us all in Marmion Hall!"

"That I'll not forget!" Father Firman's eyes remembered. "Getting up New Year's morning and finding the toilet seats all painted!"

"*Happy Circumcision!* Hah!" Father Nulty had a coughing fit.

When he had got himself together again, a mosquito came and sat on his wrist. He watched it a moment before bringing his heavy hand down. He raised his hand slowly, viewed the dead mosquito, and sent it spinning with a plunk of his middle finger.

"Only the female bites," he said.

"I didn't know that," Father Firman said.

"Ah, yes . . ."

Mrs. Stoner entered the study and sat down with some sewing—Father Firman's black socks.

She smiled pleasantly at Father Nulty. "And what do you think of the atom bomb, Father?"

"Not much," Father Nulty said.

Mrs. Stoner had stopped smiling. Father Firman yawned.

Mrs. Stoner served up another: "Did you read about this communist convert, Father?"

"He's been in the Church before," Father Nulty said, "and so it's not a conversion, Mrs. Stoner."

"No? Well, I already got him down on my list of Monsignor's converts."

"It's better than a conversion, Mrs. Stoner, for there is more rejoicing in heaven over the return of . . . uh, he that was lost, Mrs. Stoner, is found."

"And that congresswoman, Father?"

"Yes. A convert—she."

"And Henry Ford's grandson, Father. I got him down."

"Yes, to be sure."

Father Firman yawned, this time audibly, and held his jaw.

"But he's one only by marriage, Father," Mrs. Stoner said. "I always say you got to watch those kind."

"Indeed you do, but a convert nonetheless, Mrs. Stoner. Remember, Cardinal Newman himself was one."

Mrs. Stoner was unimpressed. "I see where Henry Ford's making steering wheels out of soybeans, Father."

"I didn't see that."

"I read it in *The Reader's Digest* or someplace."

"Yes, well . . . " Father Nulty rose and held his hand out to Father Firman. "John," he said. "It's been good."

"I heard Hirohito's next," Mrs. Stoner said, returning to converts.

"Let's wait and see, Mrs. Stoner," Father Nulty said.

The priests walked to the door.

"You know where I live, John."

"Yes. Come again, Frank. Good night."

Father Firman watched Father Nulty go down the walk to his car at the curb. He hooked the screen door and turned off the porch light. He hesitated at the foot of the stairs, suddenly moved to go to bed. But he went back into the study.

"Phew!" Mrs. Stoner said. "I thought he'd never go. Here it is after eight o'clock."

Father Firman sat down in his rocking chair. "I don't see him often," he said.

"I give up!" Mrs. Stoner exclaimed, flinging the holey socks upon the horsehair sofa. "I'd swear you had a nail in your shoe."

"I told you I looked."

"Well, you ought to look again. And cut your toenails, why don't you? Haven't I got enough to do?"

Father Firman scratched in his coat pocket for a pill, found one, swallowed it. He let his head sink back against the chair and closed his eyes. He could hear her moving about the room, making the preparations; and how he knew them—the fumbling in the drawer for a pencil with a point, the rip of page from his daily calendar, and finally the leg of the card table sliding up against his leg.

He opened his eyes. She yanked the floor lamp alongside the table, setting the bead fringe tinkling on the shade, and pulled up her chair on the other side. She sat down and smiled at him for the first time that day. Now she was happy.

She swept up the cards and began to shuffle with the abandoned virtuosity of an old riverboat gambler, standing them on end, fanning them out, whirling them through her fingers, dancing them halfway up her arms, cracking the whip over them. At last they lay before him tamed into a neat deck.

"Cut?"

"Go ahead," he said. She liked to go first.

She gave him her faint, avenging smile and drew a card, cast it aside for another which he thought must be an ace from the way she clutched it face down.

She was getting all the cards, as usual, and would have been invincible if she had possessed his restraint and if her cunning had been of a higher order. He knew a few things about leading and lying back that she would never learn. Her strategy was attack, forever attack, with one baffling departure: she might sacrifice certain tricks as expendable if only she could have the last ones, the heartbreaking ones, if she could slap them down one after another, shatteringly.

She played for blood, no bones about it, but for her there was no other way; it was her nature, as it was the lion's, and for this reason he found her ferocity pardonable, more a defect of the flesh, venial, while his own trouble was all in the will, mortal. He did not sweat and pray over each card as she must, but he did keep an eye out for reneging and demanded a cut now and then just to aggravate her, and he was always secretly hoping for aces.

With one card left in her hand, the telltale trick coming next, she delayed playing it, showing him first the smile, the preview of defeat. She laid it on the table—so! She held one more trump than he had reasoned possible. Had she palmed it from somewhere? No, she would not go that far; that would not be fair, was worse than reneging, which so easily and often happened accidentally, and she believed in being fair. Besides he had been watching her.

God smote the vines with hail, the sycamore trees with frost, and offered up the flocks to the lightning—but Mrs. Stoner! What a cross Father Firman had from God in Mrs. Stoner! There were other housekeepers as bad, no doubt, walking the rectories of the world, yes, but . . . yes. He could name one and maybe two priests who were worse off. One, maybe two. Cronin. His scraggly blonde of sixty—take her, with her everlasting banging on the grand piano, the gift of the pastor; her proud talk about the goiter operation at the Mayo Brothers', also a gift; her honking the parish Buick at passing strange priests because they were all in the game together. She was worse. She was something to keep the home fires burning. Yes sir. And Cronin said she was not a bad person really, but what was he? He was quite a freak himself.

For that matter, could anyone say that Mrs. Stoner was a bad person? No. He could not say it himself, and he was no freak. She had her points, Mrs. Stoner. She was clean. And though she cooked poorly, could not play the organ, would not take up the collection in an emergency, and went to card parties, and told all—even so, she was clean. She washed everything. Sometimes her underwear hung down beneath her dress like a paratrooper's pants, but it and everything she touched was clean. She washed constantly. She was clean. She had her other points, to be sure—her faults, you might say. She snooped—no mistake about it—but it was not snooping for snooping's sake; she had a reason. She did other things, always with a reason. She overcharged on rosaries and prayer books, but that was for the sake of the poor. She censored the pamphlet rack, but that was to prevent scandal. She pried into the baptismal and matrimonial records, but there was no other way if Father was out, and in this way she had once uncovered a bastard and flushed him out of the rectory, but that was the perverted decency of the times. She held her nose over bad marriages in the presence of the victims, but that was her sorrow and came from having her husband buried in a mine. And he had caught her telling a bewildered young couple that there was only one good reason for their wanting to enter into a mixed marriage—the child had to have a name, and that—that was what?

She hid his books, kept him from smoking, picked his friends (usually the pastors of her colleagues), bawled out people for calling after dark, had no humor, except at cards, and then it was grim, very grim, and she sat hatchet-faced every morning at Mass. But she went to Mass, which was all that kept the church from being empty some mornings. She did annoying things all day long. She said annoying things into the night. She said she had given him the best years of her life. Had she? Perhaps—for the miner had her only a year. It was too bad, sinfully bad, when he thought of it like that. But all talk of best years and life was nonsense. He had to consider the heart of the matter, the essence. The essence was that housekeepers were hard to get, harder to get than ushers, than willing workers, than organists, than secretaries—yes, harder to get than assistants or vocations.

And she was a *saver*—saved money, saved electricity, saved string, bags, sugar, saved—him. That's what she did. That's what she said she did, and she was right, in a way. In a way, she was usually right. In fact, she was always right—in a way. And you could never get a Filipino to come way out here and live. Not a young one anyway, and he had never seen an old one. Not a Filipino. They liked to dress up and live.

Should he let it drop about Fish having one, just to throw a scare into her, let her know he was doing some thinking? No. It would be a perfect cue for the one about a man needing a woman to look after him. He was not up to that again, not tonight.

Now she was doing what she liked most of all. She was making a grand slam, playing it out card for card, though it was in the bag, prolonging what would have been cut short out of mercy in gentle company. Father Firman knew the agony of losing.

She slashed down the last card, a miserable deuce trump, and did in the hapless king of hearts he had been saving.

"Skunked you!"

She was awful in victory. Here was the bitter end of their long day together, the final murderous hour in which all they wanted to say—all he wouldn't and all she couldn't—came out in the cards. Whoever won at honeymoon won the day, slept on the other's scalp, and God alone had to help the loser.

"We've been at it long enough, Mrs. Stoner," he said, seeing her assembling the cards for another round.

"Had enough, huh!"

Father Firman grumbled something.

"No?"

"Yes."

She pulled the table away and left it against the wall for the next time. She went out of the study carrying the socks, content and clucking. He closed his eyes after her and began to get under way in the rocking chair, the nightly trip to nowhere. He could hear her brewing a cup of tea in the kitchen and conversing with the cat. She made her way up the stairs, carrying the tea, followed by the cat, purring.

He waited, rocking out to sea, until she would be sure to be through in the bathroom. Then he got up and locked the front door (she looked after the back door) and loosened his collar going upstairs.

In the bathroom he mixed a glass of antiseptic, always afraid of pyorrhea, and gargled to ward off pharyngitis.

When he turned on the light in his room, the moths and beetles began to batter against the screens, the lighter insects humming. . . .

Yes, and she had the guest room. How did she come to get that? Why wasn't she in the back room, in her proper place? He knew, if he cared to remember. The screen in the back room—it let in mosquitoes, and if it didn't do that she'd love to sleep back there, Father, looking out at the steeple and the blessed cross on top, Father, if it just weren't for the screen, Father. Very well, Mrs. Stoner, I'll get it fixed or fix it myself. Oh, could you now, Father? I could, Mrs. Stoner, and I will. In the meantime you take the guest room. Yes, Father, and thank you, Father, the house ringing with amenities then. Years ago, all that. She was a pie-faced girl then, not really a girl perhaps, but not too old to marry again. But she never had. In fact, he could not remember that she had even tried for a husband since coming to the rectory, but, of course, he could be wrong, not knowing how they went about it. God! God save us! Had she got her wires crossed and mistaken him all these years for *that? That!* Him! Suffering God! No. That was going too far. That was getting morbid. No. He must not think of that again, ever. No.

But just the same she had got the guest room and she had it yet. Well, did it matter? Nobody ever came to see him anymore, nobody to stay overnight anyway, nobody to stay very long . . . not anymore. He knew how they laughed at him. He had heard Frank humming all right—before he saw how serious and sad the situation was and took pity—humming, "Wedding Bells Are Breaking Up That Old Gang of Mine." But then they'd always laughed at him for something—for not being an athlete, for wearing glasses, for having kidney trouble . . . and mail coming addressed to Rev. and Mrs. Stoner.

Removing his shirt, he bent over the table to read the volume left open from last night. He read, translating easily, *"Eisdem licet cum illis* . . . Clerics are allowed to reside only with women about whom there can be no suspicion, either because of a natural bond (as mother, sister, aunt) or of advanced age, combined in both cases with good repute."

Last night he had read it, and many nights before, each time as though this time to find what was missing, to find what obviously was not in the paragraph, his problem considered, a way out. She was not mother, not sister, not aunt, and *advanced age* was a relative term (why, she was younger than he was) and so, eureka, she did not meet the letter of the law—but, alas, how she fulfilled the spirit! And besides it would be a slimy way of handling it after all her years of service. He could not afford to pension her off, either.

He slammed the book shut. He slapped himself fiercely on the back, missing the wily mosquito, and whirled to find it. He took a magazine and folded it into a swatter. Then he saw it—oh, the preternatural cunning of it!—poised in the beard of Saint Joseph on the bookcase. He could not hit it there. He teased it away, wanting it to light on the wall, but it knew his thoughts and flew high away. He swung wildly, hoping to stun it, missed, swung back, catching Saint Joseph across the neck. The statue fell to the floor and broke.

Mrs. Stoner was panting in the hall outside his door.

"What is it!"

"Mosquitoes!"

"What is it, Father? Are you hurt?"

"Mosquitoes—damn it! And only the female bites!"

Mrs. Stoner, after a moment, said, "Shame on you, Father. She needs the blood for her eggs."

He dropped the magazine and lunged at the mosquito with his bare hand.

She went back to her room, saying, "Pshaw, I thought it was burglars murdering you in your bed."

He lunged again.

THE MINISTER'S BLACK VEIL

NATHANIEL HAWTHORNE

THE SEXTON stood in the porch of Milford meetinghouse, pulling busily at the bell rope. The old people of the village came stooping along the street. Children, with bright faces, tripped merrily beside their parents, or mimicked a graver gait, in the conscious dignity of their Sunday clothes. Spruce bachelors looked sidelong at the pretty maidens, and fancied that the Sabbath sunshine made them prettier than on weekdays. When the throng had mostly streamed into the porch, the sexton began to toll the bell, keeping his eye on the Reverend Mr. Hooper's door. The first glimpse of the clergyman's figure was the signal for the bell to cease its summons.

"But what has good Parson Hooper got upon his face?" cried the sexton in astonishment. All within hearing immediately turned about and beheld Mr. Hooper, pacing slowly his meditative way toward the meetinghouse.

"Are you sure it is our parson?" inquired Goodman Gray.

"Of a certainty it is good Mr. Hooper," replied the sexton.

Mr. Hooper, a gentlemanly person of about thirty, still a bachelor, was dressed with due clerical neatness. There was but one thing remarkable in his appearance. Swathed about his forehead and hanging down over his face, so low as to be shaken by his breath, Mr. Hooper had on a black veil. On a nearer view it seemed to consist of two folds of crape, which entirely concealed his features except the mouth and chin, but probably did not intercept his sight further than to give a darkened aspect to all things. With this gloomy shade before him, good Mr. Hooper walked at a slow pace, nodding kindly to those of his parishioners who still waited on the meetinghouse steps. But so wonder-stricken were they that his greeting hardly met with a return.

"I can't really feel as if good Mr. Hooper's face was behind that piece of crape," said the sexton.

"I don't like it," muttered an old woman as she hobbled into the meetinghouse. "He has changed himself into something awful, only by hiding his face."

"Our parson has gone mad!" cried Goodman Gray, following him across the threshold.

A rumor had preceded Mr. Hooper into the meetinghouse and set all the congregation astir. Few could refrain from twisting their heads toward the door; many stood upright, while several little boys clambered upon the seats, and came down again with a terrible racket. There was a general bustle, a rustling of the women's gowns and shuffling of the men's feet. But Mr. Hooper appeared not to notice. He entered with an almost noiseless step, bent his head mildly to the pews on each side, and bowed as he passed his oldest parishioner, a white-haired great-grandsire, who occupied an armchair in the center of the aisle.

Mr. Hooper ascended the pulpit and came face-to-face with his congregation. The veil shook with his measured breath as he gave out the psalm; it threw its obscurity between him and the holy page as he read the Scriptures; and while he prayed, the veil lay heavily on his uplifted countenance. Such was the effect of this simple piece of crape that more than one woman of delicate nerves was forced to leave the meetinghouse.

Mr. Hooper had the reputation of a good preacher, though he strove to win his people heavenward by mild, persuasive influences, rather than to drive them by the thunders of the Word. But in the sermon which he now delivered there was something which made it the most powerful effort that they had ever heard from their pastor's lips. The subject had reference to secret sin, and those sad mysteries which we hide from our nearest and dearest and would conceal from our own consciousness, forgetting that the Omniscient can detect them. A subtle power was breathed into his words. The most innocent girl and the man of hardened breast felt as if the preacher had crept up on them and discovered their hoarded iniquity of deed or thought. There was nothing terrible in what Mr. Hooper said, and yet, with every tremor of his melancholy voice, the hearers quaked.

At the close of the services, the people hurried out with indecorous confusion, and were conscious of lighter spirits the moment they lost sight of the black veil. Some gathered in little circles, huddled closely together, whispering. Some went homeward alone, wrapped in silent meditation. A few shook their heads, intimating that they could penetrate the mystery; while one or two affirmed that there was no mystery at all, but only that Mr. Hooper's eyes were so weakened by the midnight lamp as to require a shade. After a brief interval, forth came good Mr. Hooper also. Turning his veiled face from one group to another, he paid due reverence to the hoary heads, saluted the middle-aged with kind dignity, and greeted the young with mingled authority and love. Strange and bewildered looks repaid him for his courtesy. None, as on former occasions, aspired to the honor of walking by their pastor's side. Old Squire Saunders, doubtless by an accidental lapse of memory, neglected to invite Mr. Hooper to his table, where the clergyman had been wont to bless the food almost every Sunday. He returned to the parsonage and, at the moment of closing the door, looked back upon the people. A sad smile gleamed faintly from beneath the black veil and flickered about his mouth as he disappeared.

"How strange," said a lady, "that a simple black veil, such as any woman might wear on her bonnet, should become such a terrible thing on Mr. Hooper's face!"

"Something must surely be amiss with Mr. Hooper's mind," observed her husband, the physician of the village. "But the strangest part is the effect of this vagary, even on a sober-minded man like myself. The black veil, though it covers only our pastor's face, throws its influence over his whole person, and makes him ghostlike from head to foot. Do you not feel it so?"

"Truly do I," replied the lady, "and I would not be alone with him for the world. I wonder he is not afraid to be alone with himself!"

"Men sometimes are so," said her husband.

The afternoon service was attended with similar circumstances. At its conclusion, the bell tolled for the funeral of a young lady. The relatives and friends were assembled in the house, when their talk was interrupted by the appearance of Mr. Hooper, still covered with his black veil. It was now an appropriate emblem. The clergyman stepped into the room where the corpse was laid and bent over the coffin, to take a last farewell of his deceased parishioner. As he stooped, the veil hung straight down from his forehead, so that if her eyelids had not been closed forever, the dead maiden might have seen his face. Could Mr. Hooper have been fearful of her glance that he so hastily caught back the black veil? The only witness, a superstitious old woman, later affirmed that at the instant when the clergyman's features were disclosed, the corpse had slightly shuddered, rustling the shroud and muslin cap.

From the coffin Mr. Hooper passed to the head of the staircase, to make the funeral prayer. It was a tender prayer, full of sorrow, yet so imbued with celestial hopes that the music of a heavenly harp seemed faintly to be heard. The people trembled, though they but darkly understood him when he prayed that they, and himself, and all of mortal race, might be ready, as he trusted this young maiden had been, for the dreadful hour that should snatch the veil from their faces. The bearers went heavily forth, and the mourners followed, saddening all the street, with the dead before them and Mr. Hooper in his black veil behind.

"Why do you look back?" said one in the procession to his partner.

"I had a fancy," replied she, "that the minister and the maiden's spirit were walking hand in hand."

"And so had I, at the same moment," said the other.

That night, the handsomest couple in Milford village were to be joined in wedlock. Though reckoned a melancholy man, Mr. Hooper had a placid cheerfulness for such occasions. There was no quality of his disposition which made him more beloved than this. The company at the wedding awaited his arrival with impatience, trusting that the strange awe which had gathered over him throughout the day would now be dispelled. But when Mr. Hooper came, the first thing that their eyes rested on was the same horrible black veil, which could portend nothing but evil to the wedding. Such was its immediate effect on the guests that a cloud seemed to have dimmed the light of the candles.

The bridal pair stood up before the minister. But the bride's cold fingers quivered in the tremulous hand of the bridegroom, and her deathlike paleness caused a whisper that the maiden who had been buried a few hours before was come from her grave to be married. After performing the ceremony, Mr. Hooper raised a glass of wine, wishing happiness to the new-married couple in a strain of mild pleasantry that ought to have brightened the features of the guests. At that instant, catching a glimpse of his figure in the looking glass, the black veil involved his own spirit in the horror with which it overwhelmed all others. His frame shuddered, his lips grew white, he spilled the untasted wine upon the carpet, and rushed forth into the darkness.

The next day, the whole village of Milford talked of little else than Parson Hooper's black veil. But of all the busybodies and impertinent people in the parish, not one ventured to put the plain question to Mr. Hooper, wherefore he did this thing. There was a feeling of dread which caused each to shift the responsibility upon another, till at length it was found expedient to send a deputation of the church, in order to deal with Mr. Hooper about the mystery before it should grow into a scandal.

Never did an embassy so ill discharge its duties. The minister received them with friendly courtesy, but became silent after they were seated. They sat a considerable time, speechless, confused, and shrinking uneasily from Mr. Hooper's eye, which they felt to be fixed upon them with an invisible glance. Finally, the deputies returned abashed to their constituents, pronouncing the matter too weighty to be handled, except by a council of the churches.

But there was one woman in the village who determined to chase away the strange cloud that appeared to be settling around Mr. Hooper. As his plighted wife, it should be her privilege to know what the black veil concealed. At the minister's first visit, therefore, she entered upon the subject with a direct simplicity, which made the task easier both for him and her. After he had seated himself, she fixed her eyes steadfastly upon the veil, but could discern nothing of the dreadful gloom that had so overawed the multitude.

"No," said she aloud, and smiling, "there is nothing terrible in this piece of crape, except that it hides a face which I am always glad to look upon. Come, let the sun shine from behind the cloud. First lay aside your black veil; then tell me why you put it on."

Mr. Hooper's smile glimmered faintly. "There is an hour to come," said he, "when all of us shall cast aside our veils. Take it not amiss if I wear this piece of crape till then."

"Your words are a mystery, too," returned the young lady. "Take away the veil from them, at least."

"Elizabeth, I will," said he, "so far as my vow may suffer me. This veil is a symbol, and I am bound to wear it ever, both in light and darkness, in solitude and before the gaze of multitudes. No mortal eye will see it withdrawn. Even you, Elizabeth, can never come behind it!"

"What grievous affliction hath befallen you," she earnestly inquired, "that you should thus darken your eyes forever?"

"If it be a sign of mourning," replied Mr. Hooper, "I, perhaps like most other mortals, have sorrows dark enough to be typified by a black veil."

"But what if the world will not believe that it is the symbol of an innocent sorrow?" urged Elizabeth. "There may be whispers that you hide your face under the consciousness of secret sin. For the sake of your holy office, do away this scandal!"

The color rose into her cheeks as she intimated the nature of the rumors that were already abroad in the village. But Mr. Hooper smiled that same sad smile.

"If I hide my face for sorrow, there is cause enough," he replied; "and if I cover it for secret sin, what mortal might not do the same?"

For a few moments Elizabeth appeared lost in thought, considering, probably, what new methods might be tried to withdraw her lover from so dark a fantasy which, if it had no other meaning, was perhaps a symptom of mental disease. The tears rolled down her cheeks. But in an instant a new feeling took the place of sorrow; her eyes were fixed insensibly on the black veil when, like a sudden twilight in the air, its terrors fell around her. She arose, and stood trembling before him.

"And do you feel it then, at last?" said he mournfully.

She made no reply, but covered her eyes with her hand and turned to leave the room. He rushed forward and caught her arm.

"Have patience with me, Elizabeth!" cried he, passionately. "Do not

599

desert me, though this veil must be between us here on earth. Be mine, and hereafter there shall be no darkness between our souls! It is but a mortal veil—it is not for eternity! Oh, you know not how lonely I am, and how frightened, to be alone behind my black veil. Do not leave me in this miserable obscurity forever!"

"Lift the veil but once, and look me in the face," said she.

"Never! It cannot be!" replied Mr. Hooper.

"Then farewell!" said Elizabeth.

She withdrew her arm from his grasp and slowly departed, pausing at the door to give one long shuddering gaze.

From that time no attempts were made to remove Mr. Hooper's black veil or, by a direct appeal, to discover its secret. By persons who claimed a superiority to popular prejudice, it was reckoned merely an eccentric whim. But with the multitude, good Mr. Hooper was irreparably a bugbear. He could not walk the street with any peace of mind, so conscious was he that the gentle and timid would turn aside to avoid him, and that others would make it a point of hardihood to throw themselves in his way. The impertinence of the latter compelled him to give up his customary walk at sunset to the burial ground; for when he leaned pensively over the gate, there would always be faces behind the gravestones, peeping at his black veil. A fable went the rounds that the stare of the dead people drove him thence.

It grieved him, to the very depth of his kind heart, to observe how the children fled from his approach. Their instinctive dread caused him to feel more strongly than aught else, that a preternatural horror was interwoven with the threads of the black crape. In truth, his own antipathy to the veil was known to be so great that he never willingly passed before a mirror, nor stooped to drink at a still fountain, lest he should be affrighted by himself. This was what gave plausibility to the whispers that Mr. Hooper's conscience tortured him for some great crime too horrible to be entirely concealed. Thus, from beneath the black veil there rolled a cloud into the sunshine, an ambiguity of sin or sorrow, which enveloped the poor minister, so that love or sympathy could never reach him. It was said that ghost and fiend consorted with him there. Even the lawless wind, it was believed, respected his dreadful secret, and never blew aside the veil.

Among all its bad influences, the black veil had the one desirable effect of making its wearer a very efficient clergyman. By the aid of his mysterious emblem—for there was no other apparent cause—he became a man of awful power over souls that were in agony for sin. Dying sinners cried aloud for Mr. Hooper, and would not yield their breath till he appeared, though as he stooped to whisper consolation they shuddered at the veiled face so near their own. Strangers came long distances to attend service at his church, with the mere idle purpose of gazing at his figure, because it was forbidden them to behold his face.

In this manner Mr. Hooper spent a long life, irreproachable in outward act, yet shrouded in dismal suspicions; kind and loving, though unloved, and dimly feared; a man apart from men, shunned in their health and joy, but ever summoned to their aid in mortal anguish. Nearly all his parishioners, who were of mature age when he was settled, had been borne away by many a funeral: he had one congregation in the church, and a more crowded one in the churchyard; and having done his work so well, it was now good Mr. Hooper's turn to rest.

Several persons were visible by the shaded candlelight in the death chamber of the old clergyman. There was the grave physician, seeking to mitigate the last pangs of the patient whom he could not save. There were the deacons, and other pious members of his church. There, also, was a minister, who had ridden in haste to pray by the bedside. There was a nurse, whose calm affection had endured in secrecy and would not perish even at the dying hour. Who but Elizabeth! And there lay the hoary head of good Mr. Hooper upon the death pillow, with the black veil still reaching down over his face, so that each gasp of his faint breath caused it to stir.

For some time his mind had been confused, wavering between the past and the present, and hovering forward into the indistinctness of the world to come. There had been feverish turns, which tossed him from side to side and wore away what little strength he had. But in his struggles, he still showed an awful solicitude lest the black veil should slip aside.

At length the death-stricken old man lay quietly in the torpor of exhaustion, with an imperceptible pulse, and breath that grew fainter and fainter. The minister approached the bedside. "Venerable Parson Hooper," said he, "the moment of your release is at hand. Are you ready for the lifting of the veil that shuts in time from eternity?"

Mr. Hooper at first replied merely by a feeble motion of his head; then, apprehensive, perhaps, that his meaning might be doubted, he exerted himself to speak.

"Yea," said he, in faint accents, "my soul hath a patient weariness until that veil be lifted."

"And is it fitting," resumed the minister, "that a man so given to prayer, holy in deed and thought, should leave a shadow on his memory that may seem to blacken a life so pure? I pray you, my venerable brother, before the veil of eternity be lifted, let me cast aside this black veil from your face!"

And thus speaking, the minister bent forward to reveal the mystery of so many years. But, exerting a sudden energy that made all the beholders stand aghast, Mr. Hooper snatched both his hands from beneath the bedclothes and pressed them strongly on the black veil.

"Never!" he cried. "On earth, never!"

"Dark old man!" exclaimed the affrighted minister, "with what horrible crime upon your soul are you now passing to the judgment?"

Mr. Hooper's breath heaved; it rattled in his throat; but with a mighty effort he raised himself in bed; and there he sat, shivering with the arms of death around him, while the black veil hung down, awful, at that last moment, in the gathered terrors of a lifetime. And yet the faint, sad smile, so often there, now seemed to glimmer from its obscurity and linger on his lips.

"Why do you tremble at me alone?" cried he, turning his veiled face round the circle of pale spectators. "Tremble also at each other! Have men avoided me, and women shown no pity, and children screamed and fled, only for my black veil? What has made this piece of crape so awful? When the friend shows his inmost heart to his friend, the lover to his best beloved; when man does not shrink from the eye of his Creator, loathsomely treasuring up the secret of his sin; then deem me a monster, for the symbol beneath which I have lived, and die! I look around me, and, lo! On every visage a Black Veil!"

Mr. Hooper fell back upon his pillow, a veiled corpse, with a faint smile lingering on the lips. Still veiled, they laid him in his coffin, and a veiled corpse they bore him to the grave. The grass of many years has sprung up and withered on that grave, and good Mr. Hooper's face is dust; but awful still is the thought that it mouldered beneath the Black Veil!

THE ROCKPILE

JAMES BALDWIN

James Baldwin

Across the street from their house, in an empty lot between two houses, stood the rockpile. It was a strange place to find a mass of natural rock jutting out of the ground; and someone, probably Aunt Florence, had once told them that the rock was there and could not be taken away because without it the subway cars underground would fly apart, killing all the people. This, touching on some natural mystery concerning the surface and the center of the earth, was far too intriguing an explanation to be challenged, and it invested the rockpile, moreover, with such mysterious importance that Roy felt it to be his right, not to say his duty, to play there.

Other boys were to be seen there each afternoon after school and all day Saturday and Sunday. They fought on the rockpile. Surefooted, dangerous, and reckless, they rushed each other and grappled on the heights, sometimes disappearing down the other side in a confusion of dust and screams and upended, flying feet. "It's a wonder they don't kill themselves," their mother said, watching sometimes from the fire escape. "You children stay away from there, you hear me?" Though she said "children," she was looking at Roy, where he sat beside John on the fire escape. "The good Lord knows," she continued, "I don't want you to come home bleeding like a hog every day the Lord sends." Roy shifted impatiently, and continued to stare at the street, as though in this gazing he might somehow acquire wings. John said nothing. He had not really been spoken to: he was afraid of the rockpile and of the boys who played there.

Each Saturday morning John and Roy sat on the fire escape and watched the forbidden street below. Sometimes their mother sat in the room behind them, sewing, or dressing their younger sister, or nursing the baby, Paul. The sun fell across them and across the fire escape with a high, benevolent indifference; below them, men and women, and boys and girls, sinners all, loitered; sometimes one of the church members passed and saw them and waved. Then, for the moment that they waved decorously back, they were intimidated. They watched the saint, man or woman, until he or she had disappeared from sight. The passage of one of the redeemed made them consider, however vacantly, the wickedness of the street, their own latent wickedness in sitting where they sat; and made them think of their father, who came home early on Saturdays and who would soon be turning this corner and entering the dark hall below them.

But until he came to end their freedom, they sat, watching and longing above the street. At the end of the street nearest their house was the bridge which spanned the Harlem River and led to a city called the Bronx, which was where Aunt Florence lived. Nevertheless, when they saw her coming, she did not come from the bridge, but from the opposite end of the street. This, weakly, to their minds, she explained by saying that she had taken the subway, not wishing to walk, and that, besides, she did not live in *that* section of the Bronx. Knowing that the Bronx was across the river, they did not believe this story ever, but, adopting toward her their father's attitude, assumed that she had just left some sinful place which she dared not name, as, for example, a movie palace.

In the summertime boys swam in the river, diving off the wooden dock, or wading in from the garbage-heavy bank. Once a boy, whose name was Richard, drowned in the river. His mother had not known where he was; she had even come to their house, to ask if he was there. Then, in the evening, at six o'clock, they had heard from the street a woman screaming and wailing; and they ran to the windows and looked out. Down the street came the woman, Richard's mother, screaming, her face raised to the sky and tears running down her face. A woman walked beside her, trying to make her quiet and trying to hold her up. Behind them walked a man, Richard's father, with Richard's body in his arms. There were two white policemen walking in the gutter, who did not seem to know what should be done. Richard's father and Richard were wet, and Richard's body lay across his father's arms like a cotton baby. The woman's screaming filled the street; cars slowed down and the people in the cars stared; people opened their windows and looked out and came rushing out of doors to stand in the gutter, watching. Then the small procession disappeared within the house which stood beside the rockpile. Then, *"Lord, Lord, Lord!"* cried Elizabeth, their mother, and slammed the window down.

One Saturday, an hour before his father would be coming home, Roy was wounded on the rockpile and brought screaming upstairs. He and John had been sitting on the fire escape and their mother had gone into the kitchen to sip tea with Sister McCandless. By and by Roy became bored and sat beside John in restless silence; and John began drawing into his schoolbook a newspaper advertisement which featured a new electric locomotive. Some friends of Roy passed beneath the fire escape and called him. Roy began to fidget, yelling down to them through the bars. Then a silence fell. John looked up. Roy stood looking at him.

"I'm going downstairs," he said.

"You better stay where you is, boy. You know Mama don't want you going downstairs."

"I be right *back*. She won't even know I'm gone, less you run and tell her."

"I ain't *got* to tell her. What's going to stop her from coming in here and looking out the window?"

"She's talking," Roy said. He started into the house.

"But Daddy's going to be home soon!"

"I be back before *that*. What you all the time got to be so *scared* for?" He was already in the house and he now turned, leaning on the windowsill, to swear impatiently, "I be back in *five* minutes."

John watched him sourly as he carefully unlocked the door and disappeared. In a moment he saw him on the sidewalk with his friends. He did not dare to go and tell his mother that Roy had left the fire escape, because he had practically promised not to. He started to shout, *Remember, you said five minutes!* but one of Roy's friends was looking up at the fire escape. John looked down at his schoolbook; he became engrossed again in the problem of the locomotive.

When he looked up again he did not know how much time had passed, but now there was a gang fight on the rockpile. Dozens of boys fought each other in the harsh sun: clambering up the rocks and battling hand to hand, scuffed shoes sliding on the slippery rock; filling the bright air with curses and jubilant cries. They filled the air, too, with flying weapons: stones, sticks, tin cans, garbage, whatever could be picked up and thrown.

John watched in a kind of absent amazement—until he remembered that Roy was still downstairs, and that he was one of the boys on the rockpile. Then he was afraid; he could not see his brother among the figures in the sun; and he stood up, leaning over the fire-escape railing. Then Roy appeared from the other side of the rocks; John saw that his shirt was torn; he was laughing. He moved until he stood at the very top of the rockpile.

Then something, an empty tin can, flew out of the air and hit him on the forehead, just above the eye. Immediately, one side of Roy's face ran with blood; he fell and rolled on his face down the rocks. Then for a moment there was no movement at all, no sound; the sun, arrested, lay on the street and the sidewalk and the arrested boys. Then someone screamed or shouted; boys began to run away, down the street, toward the bridge. The figure on the ground, having caught its breath and felt its own blood, began to shout. John cried, "Mama! Mama!" and ran inside.

"Don't fret, don't fret," panted Sister McCandless as they rushed down the dark, narrow, swaying stairs, "don't fret. Ain't a boy been born don't get his knocks every now and again. *Lord!*" They hurried into the sun.

A man had picked Roy up and now walked slowly toward them. One or two boys sat silent on their stoops; at either end of the street there was a group of boys watching. "He ain't hurt bad," the man said. "Wouldn't be making this kind of noise if he was hurt real bad."

Elizabeth, trembling, reached out to take Roy, but Sister McCandless, bigger, calmer, took him from the man and threw him over her shoulder as she once might have handled a sack of cotton. "God bless you," she said to the man, "God bless you, son." Roy was still screaming. Elizabeth stood behind Sister McCandless to stare at his bloody face.

"It's just a flesh wound," the man kept saying, "just broke the skin, that's all." They were moving across the sidewalk, toward the house. John, not now afraid of the staring boys, looked toward the corner to see if his father was yet in sight.

Upstairs, they hushed Roy's crying. They bathed the blood away, to find, just above the left eyebrow, the jagged, superficial scar.

"Lord, have mercy," murmured Elizabeth, "another inch and it would've been his eye." And she looked with apprehension toward the clock. "Ain't it the truth," said Sister McCandless, busy with bandages and iodine.

"When did he go downstairs?" his mother asked at last.

Sister McCandless now sat fanning herself in the easy chair, at the head of the sofa where Roy lay, bound and silent. She paused for a moment to look sharply at John. John stood near the window, holding the newspaper advertisement and the drawing he had done.

"We was sitting on the fire escape," he said. "Some boys he knew called him."

"When?"

"He said he'd be back in five minutes."

"Why didn't you tell me he was downstairs?"

He looked at his hands, clasping his notebook, and did not answer.

"Boy," said Sister McCandless, "you hear your mother a-talking to you?"

He looked at his mother. He repeated:

"He said he'd be back in five minutes."

"He said he'd be back in five minutes," said Sister McCandless with scorn; "don't look to me like that's no right answer. You's the man of the house, you supposed to look after your baby brothers and sisters—you ain't supposed to let them run off and get half killed. But I expect," she added, rising from the chair, dropping the cardboard fan, "your Daddy'll make you tell the truth. Your Ma's way too soft with you."

He did not look at her, but at the fan where it lay in the dark red, depressed seat where she had been. The fan advertised a pomade for the hair and showed a brown woman and her baby, both with glistening hair, smiling happily at each other.

"Honey," said Sister McCandless, "I got to be moving along. Maybe I drop in later tonight. I don't reckon you going to be at Tarry Service tonight?" Tarry Service was the prayer meeting held every Saturday night at church to strengthen believers and prepare the church for the coming of the Holy Ghost on Sunday.

"I don't reckon," said Elizabeth. She stood up; she and Sister McCandless kissed each other on the cheek. "But you be sure to remember me in your prayers."

"I surely will do that." She paused, with her hand on the doorknob, and looked down at Roy and laughed. "Poor little man," she said, "reckon he'll be content to sit on the fire escape *now*."

Elizabeth laughed with her. "It sure ought to be a lesson to him. You don't reckon," she asked nervously, still smiling, "he going to keep that scar, do you?"

"Lord, no," said Sister McCandless, "ain't nothing but a scratch. I declare, Sister Grimes, you worse than a child. Another couple of weeks and you won't be able to *see* no scar. No, you go on about your housework, honey, and thank the Lord it weren't no worse." She opened the door; they heard the sound of feet on the stairs. "I expect that's the Reverend," said Sister McCandless placidly. "I *bet* he going to raise cain."

"Maybe it's Florence," Elizabeth said. "Sometimes she get here about this time." They stood in the doorway, staring, while the steps reached the landing below and began again climbing to their floor. "No," said Elizabeth then, "that ain't her walk. That's Gabriel."

"Well, I'll just go on," said Sister McCandless, "and kind of prepare his mind." She pressed Elizabeth's hand as she spoke and started into the hall, leaving the door behind her slightly ajar. Elizabeth turned slowly back into the room. Roy did not open his eyes, or move; but she knew that he was not sleeping; he wished to delay until the last possible moment any contact with his father. John put his newspaper and his notebook on the table and stood, leaning on the table, staring at her.

"It wasn't my fault," he said. "I couldn't stop him from going downstairs."

"No," she said, "you ain't got nothing to worry about. You just tell your Daddy the truth."

He looked directly at her, and she turned to the window, staring into the street. What was Sister McCandless saying? Then from her bedroom she heard Delilah's thin wail and she turned, frowning, looking toward the bedroom and toward the still open door. She knew that John was watching her. Delilah continued to wail; she thought, angrily, *Now that girl's getting too big for that*, but she feared that Delilah would awaken Paul and she hurried into the bedroom. She tried to soothe Delilah back to sleep. Then she heard the front door open and close—too loud; Delilah raised her voice; with an exasperated sigh Elizabeth picked the child up. Her child and Gabriel's, her children and Gabriel's: Roy, Delilah, Paul. Only John was nameless and a stranger, living, unalterable testimony to his mother's days in sin.

"What happened?" Gabriel demanded. He stood, enormous, in the center of the room, his black lunch box dangling from his hand, staring at the sofa where Roy lay.

John stood just before him, it seemed to her astonished vision just below him, beneath his fist, his heavy shoe. The child stared at the man in fascination and terror—when a girl down home she had seen rabbits stand so paralyzed before the barking dog. She hurried past Gabriel to the sofa, feeling the weight of Delilah in her arms like the weight of a shield, and stood over Roy, saying:

"Now, ain't a thing to get upset about, Gabriel. This boy sneaked downstairs while I had my back turned and got hisself hurt a little. He's all right now."

Roy, as though in confirmation, now opened his eyes and looked gravely at his father. Gabriel dropped his lunch box with a clatter and knelt by the sofa.

"How you feel, son? Tell your Daddy what happened?"

Roy opened his mouth to speak and then, relapsing into panic, began to cry. His father held him by the shoulder.

"You don't want to cry. You's Daddy's little man. Tell your Daddy what happened."

"He went downstairs," said Elizabeth, "where he didn't have no business to be, and got to fighting with them bad boys playing on that rockpile. That's what happened and it's a mercy it weren't nothing worse."

He looked up at her. "Can't you let this boy answer me for hisself?"

Ignoring this, she went on, more gently: "He got cut on the forehead, but it ain't nothing to worry about."

"You call a doctor? How you know it ain't nothing to worry about?"

"Is you got money to be throwing away on doctors? No, I ain't called no doctor. Ain't nothing wrong with my eyes that I can't tell whether he's hurt bad or not. He got a fright more'n anything else, and you ought to pray God it teaches him a lesson."

"You got a lot to say *now*," he said, "but I'll have *me* something to say in a minute. I'll be wanting to know when all this happened, what you was doing with your eyes *then*." He turned back to Roy, who had lain quietly sobbing, eyes wide open and body held rigid; and who now, at his father's touch, remembered the height, the sharp, sliding rock beneath his feet, the sun, the explosion of the sun, his plunge into darkness and his salty blood; and recoiled, beginning to scream, as his father touched his forehead. "Hold still, hold still," crooned his father, shaking, "hold still. Don't cry. Daddy ain't going to hurt you, he just wants to see this bandage, see what they've done to his little man." But Roy continued to scream and would not be still and Gabriel dared not lift the bandage for fear of hurting him more. And he looked at Elizabeth in fury: "Can't you put that child down and help me with this boy? John, take your baby sister from your mother—don't look like neither of you got good sense."

John took Delilah and sat down with her in the easy chair. His mother bent over Roy and held him still, while his father, carefully— but still Roy screamed—lifted the bandage and stared at the wound. Roy's sobs began to lessen. Gabriel readjusted the bandage. "You see," said Elizabeth, finally, "he ain't nowhere near dead."

"It sure ain't your fault that he ain't dead." He and Elizabeth considered each other for a moment in silence. "He came mighty close to losing an eye. Course, his eyes ain't as big as your'n, so I reckon you don't think it matters so much." At this her face hardened; he smiled. "Lord, have mercy," he said, "you think you ever going to learn to do right? Where was you when all this happened? Who let him go downstairs?"

"Ain't nobody let him go downstairs, he just went. He got a head just like his father, it got to be broken before it'll bow. I was in the kitchen."

"Where was Johnnie?"

"He was in here."

"Where?"

"He was on the fire escape."

"Didn't he know Roy was downstairs?"

"I reckon."

"What you mean, you reckon? He ain't got your big eyes for nothing, does he?" He looked over at John. "Boy, you see your brother go downstairs?"

"Gabriel, ain't no sense in trying to blame Johnnie. You know right well if you have trouble making Roy behave, he ain't going to listen to his brother. He don't hardly listen to me."

"How come you didn't tell your mother Roy was downstairs?"

John said nothing, staring at the blanket which covered Delilah.

"Boy, you hear me? You want me to take a strap to you?"

"No, you ain't," she said. "You ain't going to take no strap to this boy, not today you ain't. Ain't a soul to blame for Roy's lying up there now but you—you because you done spoiled him so that he thinks he can do just anything and get away with it. I'm here to tell you that ain't no way to raise no child. You don't pray to the Lord to help you do better than you been doing, you going to live to shed bitter tears that the Lord didn't take his soul today." And she was trembling. She moved, unseeing, toward John and took Delilah from his arms. She looked back at Gabriel, who had risen, who stood near the sofa, staring at her. And she found in his face not fury alone, which would not have surprised her; but hatred so deep as to become insupportable in its lack of personality.

His eyes were struck alive, unmoving, blind with malevolence—she felt, like the pull of the earth at her feet, his longing to witness her perdition. Again, as though it might be propitiation, she moved the child in her arms. And at this his eyes changed, he looked at Elizabeth, the mother of his children, the helpmeet given by the Lord. Then her eyes clouded; she moved to leave the room; her foot struck the lunch box lying on the floor.

"John," she said, "pick up your father's lunch box like a good boy."

She heard, behind her, his scrambling movement as he left the easy chair, the scrape and jangle of the lunch box as he picked it up, bending his dark head near the toe of his father's heavy shoe.

THE
ENCHANTED BLUFF

WILLA CATHER

Willa Cather [signature]

We had our swim before sundown, and while we were cooking our supper the oblique rays of light made a dazzling glare on the white sand about us. The translucent red ball itself sank behind the brown stretches of cornfield as we sat down to eat, and the warm layer of air that had rested over the water and our clean sandbar grew fresher and smelled of the rank ironweed and sunflowers growing on the flatter shore. The river was brown and sluggish, like any other of the half dozen streams that water the Nebraska cornlands. On one shore was an irregular line of bald clay bluffs where a few scrub oaks with thick trunks and flat, twisted tops threw light shadows on the long grass. The western shore was low and level, with cornfields that stretched to the skyline, and all along the water's edge were little sandy coves and beaches where slim cottonwoods and willow saplings flickered.

The turbulence of the river in springtime discouraged milling, and, beyond keeping the old red bridge in repair, the busy farmers did not concern themselves with the stream; so the Sandtown boys were left in undisputed possession. In the autumn we hunted quail through the miles of stubble and fodderland along the flat shore, and, after the winter skating season was over and the ice had gone out, the spring freshets and flooded bottoms gave us our great excitement of the year. The channel was never the same for two successive seasons. Every spring the swollen stream undermined a bluff to the east, or bit out a few acres of cornfield to the west and whirled the soil away to deposit it in spumy mudbanks somewhere else. When the water fell low in midsummer, new sandbars were thus exposed to dry and whiten in the

August sun. Sometimes these were banked so firmly that the fury of the next freshet failed to unseat them; the little willow seedlings emerged triumphantly from the yellow froth, broke into spring leaf, shot up into summer growth, and with their mesh of roots bound together the moist sand beneath them against the batterings of another April. Here and there a cottonwood soon glittered among them, quivering in the low current of air that, even on breathless days when the dust hung like smoke above the wagon road, trembled along the face of the water.

It was on such an island, in the third summer of its yellow green, that we built our watch fire; not in the thicket of dancing willow wands, but on the level terrace of fine sand which had been added that spring; a little new bit of world, beautifully ridged with ripple marks, and strewn with the tiny skeletons of turtles and fish, all as white and dry as if they had been expertly cured. We had been careful not to mar the freshness of the place, although we often swam to it on summer evenings and lay on the sand to rest.

This was our last watch fire of the year, and there were reasons why I should remember it better than any of the others. Next week the other boys were to file back to their old places in the Sandtown High School, but I was to go up to the Divide to teach my first country school in the Norwegian district. I was already homesick at the thought of quitting the boys with whom I had always played; of leaving the river, and going up into a windy plain that was all windmills and cornfields and big pastures; where there was nothing willful or unmanageable in the landscape, no new islands, and no chance of unfamiliar birds—such as often followed the watercourses.

Other boys came and went and used the river for fishing or skating, but we six were sworn to the spirit of the stream, and we were friends mainly because of the river. There were the two Hassler boys, Fritz and Otto, sons of the little German tailor. They were the youngest of us; ragged boys of ten and twelve, with sunburned hair, weather-stained faces, and pale blue eyes. Otto, the elder, was the best mathematician in school, and clever at his books, but he always dropped out in the spring term as if the river could not get on without him. He and Fritz caught the fat, horned catfish and sold them about the town, and they lived so much in the water that they were as brown and sandy as the river itself.

There was Percy Pound, a fat, freckled boy with chubby cheeks, who took a half dozen boys' story papers and was always being kept in for reading detective stories behind his desk. There was Tip Smith, destined by his freckles and red hair to be the buffoon in all our games, though he walked like a timid little old man and had a funny, cracked laugh. Tip worked hard in his father's grocery store every afternoon, and swept it out before school in the morning. Even his recreations were laborious. He collected cigarette cards and tin tobacco tags indefatigably, and would sit for hours humped up over a snarling little scroll saw which he kept in his attic. His dearest possessions were some little pill bottles that purported to contain grains of wheat from the Holy Land, water from the Jordan and the Dead Sea, and earth from the Mount of Olives. His father had bought these dull things from a Baptist missionary who peddled them, and Tip seemed to derive great satisfaction from their remote origin.

The tall boy was Arthur Adams. He had fine hazel eyes that were almost too reflective and sympathetic for a boy, and such a pleasant voice that we all loved to hear him read aloud. Even when he had to read poetry aloud at school, no one ever thought of laughing. To be sure, he was not at school very much of the time. He was seventeen and should have finished the high school the year before, but he was always off somewhere with his gun. Arthur's mother was dead, and his father, who was feverishly absorbed in promoting schemes, wanted to send the boy away to school and get him off his hands; but Arthur always begged off for another year and promised to study. I remember him as a tall, brown boy with an intelligent face, always lounging among a lot of us little fellows, laughing at us oftener than with us, but such a soft, satisfied laugh that we felt rather flattered when we provoked it. In afteryears people said that Arthur had been given to evil ways even as a lad, and it is true that we often saw him with the gambler's sons and with old Spanish Fanny's boy, but if he learned anything ugly in their company he never betrayed it to us. We would have followed Arthur anywhere, and I am bound to say that he led us into no worse places than the cattail marshes and the stubble fields. These, then, were the boys who camped with me that summer night upon the sandbar.

After we finished our supper we beat the willow thicket for

driftwood. By the time we had collected enough, night had fallen, and the pungent, weedy smell from the shore increased with the coolness. We threw ourselves down about the fire and made another futile effort to show Percy Pound the Little Dipper. We had tried it often before, but he could never be got past the big one.

"You see those three big stars just below the handle, with the bright one in the middle?" said Otto Hassler. "That's Orion's belt, and the bright one is the clasp." I crawled behind Otto's shoulder and sighted up his arm to the star that seemed perched upon the tip of his steady forefinger. The Hassler boys did seine fishing at night, and they knew a good many stars.

Percy gave up the Little Dipper and lay back on the sand, his hands clasped under his head. "I can see the North Star," he announced contentedly, pointing toward it with his big toe. "Anyone might get lost and need to know that."

We all looked up at it.

"How do you suppose Columbus felt when his compass didn't point north anymore?" Tip asked.

Otto shook his head. "My father says that there was another North Star once, and that maybe this one won't last always. I wonder what would happen to us down here if anything went wrong with it?"

Arthur chuckled. "I wouldn't worry, Ott. Nothing's apt to happen to it in your time. Look at the Milky Way! There must be lots of good dead Indians."

We lay back and looked, meditating, at the dark cover of the world. The gurgle of the water had become heavier. We had often noticed a mutinous, complaining note in it at night, quite different from its cheerful daytime chuckle, and seeming like the voice of a much deeper and more powerful stream. Our water had always these two moods: the one of sunny complaisance, the other of inconsolable, passionate regret.

"Queer how the stars are all in sort of diagrams," remarked Otto. "You could do most any proposition in geometry with 'em. They always look as if they meant something. Some folks say everybody's fortune is all written out in the stars, don't they?"

"They believe so in the old country," Fritz affirmed.

But Arthur only laughed at him. "You're thinking of Napoleon,

Fritzey. He had a star that went out when he began to lose battles. I guess the stars don't keep any close tally on Sandtown folks."

We were speculating on how many times we could count a hundred before the evening star went down behind the cornfields, when someone cried, "There comes the moon, and it's as big as a cartwheel!"

We all jumped up to greet it as it swam over the bluffs behind us. It came up like a galleon in full sail; an enormous, barbaric thing, red as an angry heathen god.

"When the moon came up red like that, the Aztecs used to sacrifice their prisoners on the temple top," Percy announced.

"Go on, Perce. You got that out of *Golden Days*. Do you believe that, Arthur?" I appealed.

Arthur answered, quite seriously, "Like as not. The moon was one of their gods. When my father was in Mexico City he saw the stone where they used to sacrifice their prisoners."

As we dropped down by the fire again someone asked whether the Mound Builders were older than the Aztecs. When we once got upon the Mound Builders we never willingly got away from them, and we were still conjecturing when we heard a loud splash in the water.

"Must have been a big cat jumping," said Fritz. "They do sometimes. They must see bugs in the dark. Look what a track the moon makes!"

There was a long, silvery streak on the water, and where the current fretted over a big log it boiled up like gold pieces.

"Suppose there ever *was* any gold hid away in this old river?" Fritz asked. He lay like a little brown Indian, close to the fire, his chin on his hand and his bare feet in the air. His brother laughed at him, but Arthur took his suggestion seriously.

"Some of the Spaniards thought there was gold up here somewhere. Seven cities chuck-full of gold, they had it, and Coronado and his men came up to hunt it. The Spaniards were all over this country once."

Percy looked interested. "Was that before the Mormons went through?"

We all laughed at this.

"Long enough before. Before the Pilgrim Fathers, Perce. Maybe they came along this very river. They always followed the watercourses."

"I wonder where this river really does begin?" Tip mused. That was an old and a favorite mystery which the map did not clearly explain. On the map the little black line stopped somewhere in western Kansas; but since rivers generally rose in mountains, it was only reasonable to suppose that ours came from the Rockies. Its destination, we knew, was the Missouri, and the Hassler boys always maintained that we could embark at Sandtown in floodtime, follow our noses, and eventually arrive at New Orleans. Now they took up their old argument. "If us boys had grit enough to try it, it wouldn't take no time to get to Kansas City and St. Joe."

We began to talk about the places we wanted to go to. The Hassler boys wanted to see the stockyards in Kansas City, and Percy wanted to see a big store in Chicago. Arthur was interlocutor and did not betray himself.

"Now it's your turn, Tip."

Tip rolled over on his elbow and poked the fire, and his eyes looked shyly out of his queer, tight little face. "My place is awful far away. My Uncle Bill told me about it."

Tip's Uncle Bill was a wanderer, bitten with mining fever, who had drifted into Sandtown with a broken arm, and when it was well had drifted out again.

"Where is it?"

"Aw, it's down in New Mexico somewheres. There aren't no railroads or anything. You have to go on mules, and you run out of water before you get there and have to drink canned tomatoes."

"Well, go on, kid. What's it like when you do get there?"

Tip sat up and excitedly began his story.

"There's a big red rock there that goes right up out of the sand for about nine hundred feet. The country's flat all around it, and this here rock goes up all by itself, like a monument. They call it the Enchanted Bluff down there, because no white man has ever been on top of it. The sides are smooth rock, and straight up, like a wall. The Indians say that hundreds of years ago, before the Spaniards came, there was a village away up there in the air. The tribe that lived there had some sort of steps, made out of wood and bark, hung down over the face of the bluff, and the braves went down to hunt and carried water up in big jars swung on their backs. They kept a big supply of water and dried meat up there, and never went down except to hunt. They were a peaceful tribe that made cloth and pottery, and they went up there to get out of the wars. You see, they could pick off any war party that tried to get up their little steps. The Indians say they were a handsome people, and they had some sort of queer religion. Uncle Bill thinks they were Cliff Dwellers who had got into trouble and left home. They weren't fighters, anyhow.

"One time the braves were down hunting and an awful storm came up—a kind of waterspout—and when they got back to their rock they found their little staircase had been all broken to pieces, and only a few steps were left hanging away up in the air. While they were camped at the foot of the rock, wondering what to do, a war party from the north came along and massacred 'em to a man, with all the old folks and women looking on from the rock. Then the war party went on south and left the village to get down the best way they could. Of course they never got down. They starved to death up there, and when the war party came back on their way north, they could hear the children crying from the edge of the bluff where they had crawled out, but they didn't see a sign of a grown Indian, and nobody has ever been up there since."

We exclaimed at this dolorous legend and sat up.

"There couldn't have been many people up there," Percy demurred. "How big is the top, Tip?"

"Oh, pretty big. Big enough so that the rock doesn't look nearly as tall as it is. The top's bigger than the base. The bluff is sort of worn away for several hundred feet up. That's one reason it's so hard to climb."

I asked how the Indians got up in the first place.

"Nobody knows how they got up or when. A hunting party came along once and saw that there was a town up there, and that was all."

Otto rubbed his chin and looked thoughtful. "Of course there must be some way to get up there. Couldn't people get a rope over someway and pull a ladder up?"

Tip's little eyes were shining with excitement. "I know a way. Me and Uncle Bill talked it all over. There's a kind of rocket that would take a rope over—lifesavers use 'em—and then you could hoist a rope ladder and peg it down at the bottom and make it tight with guy ropes on the other side. I'm going to climb that there bluff, and I've got it all planned out."

Fritz asked what he expected to find when he got up there.

"Bones, maybe, or the ruins of their town, or pottery, or some of their idols. There might be most anything up there. Anyhow, I want to see."

"Sure nobody else has been up there, Tip?" Arthur asked.

"Dead sure. Hardly anybody ever goes down there. Some hunters tried to cut steps in the rock once, but they didn't get higher than a man can reach. The bluff's all red granite, and Uncle Bill thinks it's a boulder the glaciers left. It's a queer place, anyhow. Nothing but cactus and desert for hundreds of miles, and yet right under the bluff there's good water and plenty of grass. That's why the bison used to go down there."

Suddenly we heard a scream above our fire, and jumped up to see a dark, slim bird floating southward far above us—a whooping crane, we knew by her cry and her long neck. We ran to the edge of the island, hoping we might see her alight, but she wavered southward along the river course until we lost her. The Hassler boys declared that by the look of the heavens it must be after midnight, so we threw more wood on our fire, put on our jackets, and curled down in the warm sand. Several of us pretended to doze, but I fancy we were really thinking about Tip's bluff and the extinct people. Over in the wood the ringdoves were calling mournfully to one another, and once we heard a dog bark, far away. "Somebody getting into old Tommy's melon patch," Fritz murmured sleepily, but nobody answered him. By and by Percy spoke out of the shadows.

"Say, Tip, when you go down there will you take me with you?"

"Maybe."

"Suppose one of us beats you down there, Tip?"

"Whoever gets to the bluff first has got to promise to tell the rest of us exactly what he finds," remarked one of the Hassler boys, and to this we all readily assented.

Somewhat reassured, I dropped off to sleep. I must have dreamed about a race for the bluff, for I awoke in a kind of fear that other people were getting ahead of me and that I was losing my chance. I sat up in my damp clothes and looked at the other boys, who lay tumbled in uneasy attitudes about the dead fire. It was still dark, but the sky was blue with the last wonderful azure of night. The stars glistened like crystal globes, and trembled as if they shone through a depth of clear water. Even as I watched, they began to pale and the sky brightened. Day came suddenly, almost instantaneously. I turned for another look at the blue night, and it was gone. Everywhere the birds began to call, and all manner of little insects began to chirp and hop about in the willows. A breeze sprang up from the west and brought the heavy smell of ripened corn. The boys rolled over and shook themselves. We stripped and plunged into the river just as the sun came up over the windy bluffs.

When I came home to Sandtown at Christmastime, we skated out to our island and talked over the whole project of the Enchanted Bluff, renewing our resolution to find it.

ALTHOUGH THAT WAS twenty years ago, none of us has ever climbed the Enchanted Bluff. Percy Pound is a stockbroker in Kansas City and will go nowhere that his red touring car cannot carry him. Otto Hassler went on the railroad and lost his foot, braking; after which he and Fritz succeeded their father as the town tailors.

Arthur sat about the sleepy little town all his life—he died before he was twenty-five. The last time I saw him, when I was home on one of my college vacations, he was sitting in a steamer chair under a cottonwood tree in the little yard behind one of the two Sandtown saloons. He was very untidy and his hand was not steady, but when he rose, unabashed, to greet me, his eyes were as clear and warm as ever. When I had talked with him for an hour and heard him laugh again, I wondered how it was that when Nature had taken such pains with a man, from his hands to the arch of his long foot, she had ever lost him in Sandtown. He joked about Tip Smith's bluff, and declared he was going down there just as soon as the weather got cooler; he thought the Grand Canyon might be worthwhile, too.

I was perfectly sure when I left him that he would never get beyond the high plank fence and the comfortable shade of the cottonwood.

And, indeed, it was under that very tree that he died one summer morning.

Tip Smith still talks about going to New Mexico. He married a slatternly, unthrifty country girl, has been much tied to a perambulator, and has grown stooped and gray from irregular meals and broken sleep. But the worst of his difficulties are now over, and he has, as he says, come into easy water. When I was last in Sandtown I walked home with him late one moonlight night, after he had balanced his cash and shut up his store. We took the long way around and sat down on the schoolhouse steps, and between us we quite revived the romance of the lone red rock and the extinct people. Tip insists that he still means to go down there, but he thinks now he will wait until his boy Bert is old enough to go with him. Bert has been let into the story, and thinks of nothing but the Enchanted Bluff.

O HOW
SHE LAUGHED!

CONRAD AIKEN

[signature: Conrad Aiken]

IT WAS A minor episode in my life—happened when I was taking my examinations for college—and I will tell it briefly.

My family—which consisted of my father, my mother, and my brother Phil—had just moved to a rather shabby little boardinghouse in Oxford Street. It was one of our recurring periods of poverty: the "old man" was always impractical; just as we had really got our heads once more above water he would buy a lot of worthless securities, and down we would go again, from a house to a flat, from a flat to a boardinghouse. Phil and I never understood these remarkable alternations of fortune: but I suppose my mother did—poor thing—well enough. Anyway, when my father died, a few years ago, we found that he had accumulated, during his life, a good-sized trunkful of beautifully engraved and embossed securities which weren't worth a penny. There were enough of them to paper the walls of a house, and they would have looked very well.

Neither my father nor mother were particularly "social," and it was therefore all the more surprising that, in the Oxford Street lodgings, they should so suddenly have made friends of the Lyntons. We all sat at one long table, of course, like a Last Supper—and some sort of acquaintance with the other boarders was inevitable; but we had survived many such exposures before, without making any friends. The Lyntons, however, seemed from the outset to amuse my father (who was rather a shy man) inordinately. I think my mother was not so convinced—for she was a queer, bitter sort of frustrated "highbrow," and very critical—but even she, for once, unbent a little. In a very short time an extraordinary intimacy had sprung up between the Lyntons and the Beebes, which, if it involved my mother and father more than Phil and myself, nevertheless involved us too.

In fact, almost the first thing I remember about the life at Oxford Street was going to a circus with the Lyntons—a party so incredibly gay and frivolous that Phil and I, who were more accustomed to seeing the old people play cribbage, or now and then, in a wild moment, poker (the chips being broken matches, the stakes nil), were absolutely staggered. And Mrs. Lynton was the life of the party. Mr. Lynton was a good laugher—a very good laugher. His foxy eyes would close themselves up into watery slits, his beautifully pointed Vandyke beard would prod at his necktie, he would wriggle to and fro and emit far-off falsetto cries, and become quite helpless—especially when it was Mrs. Lynton who had provided the cause.

But Mrs. Lynton was better still. O how she laughed! She laughed at the elephants, she laughed at the kangaroos, she laughed at the monkeys, at the clowns—she had only to roll her brown horse-chestnut eyes at Mr. Lynton, and he too collapsed almost into the sawdust—even my father succumbed, and my staid intellectual mother. It was only Phil and myself who got rather tired of this surprising and sudden and motiveless gaiety. Eventually we struck rather a false note in the party by adopting (in taciturn unison) a stubborn silence. . . . The older people thought we were prigs.

And that circus lasted us for days. No meal passed without three or four hilarious passages devoted to it. A mere word sufficed to set them off.

"And *do* you remember that little monkey with the pink behind?" Mrs. Lynton would say, and it would all begin over again.

"And the kangaroo skipping in and out under that little door!"

"And the smells! the smells! the smells!"

"And the way that clown would spit into the bottle!"

Whereupon Mr. Lynton would shut up his eyes and bury his little brown beard in his chest, and Mrs. Lynton would become extraordinarily girlish, and my poor father would become positively foolish. And Phil and I, exchanging covert sorrows, would decide to be glum, if only for the preservation of decency.

625

Apparently, the Lyntons were as poor as we were. Mr. Lynton was an architect, with an office of his own, but no business. Mrs. Lynton was an artist, with a little studio in Joy Street, to which she went every day, always bringing back with her a new sunset or landscape. I thought her pictures were terrible, and never was in the least surprised that she couldn't sell them. So far as I know, she never *did* sell them—not one. But every night when she returned to Oxford Street, there would be a new canvas under her arm; and every night, just before dinner, we all had to file into the Lyntons' room, where the new masterpiece would be tilted on a chair, or on the carefully propped pillows of the bed, and with an air of mystery and secrecy we would have to put our heads on one side and say, "Wonderful! Marvelous! That effect of shadow among the trees! The delicious sense of distance! . . . Was it an actual scene somewhere? Oh, done from a note? from memory? It's beautiful!" And I could feel my father uneasily wondering whether the Lyntons expected him to buy it, and how much it would cost, and groping for phrases about painting (of which he didn't know a thing), and then we would have a cup of fruit punch, and go down to dinner.

Both my father and mother thought Mrs. Lynton was captivating— simply captivating! My father perhaps a little more than my mother. Now and then it seemed to me I detected a note of faint skepticism on the part of my mother. "Isn't she charming? ridiculous?" my father would say, "she's like a child. She's never grown up. . . ."

Which was perfectly true. She was nothing if not playful. Playful was her middle name. She had more facial tricks than I ever remember to have seen in a single creature. She rolled those great conscious eyes to every point in the compass—arched her careful eyebrows singly or together, blushed at will—to give a touch of girlish modesty to some outrageous statement—pouted, frowned, or looked hurt like a spanked baby—and all with an air of entire assurance. She assumed that she was the best be-all and end-all of existence. Not that she wasn't pretty!—she was. Her small face was really quite charming. But that she should consider it necessary to behave like a girl of ten, and take it for granted that everyone would be enslaved to her, as her husband was—this increasingly infuriated both Phil and myself. It was evident that she thought herself a great artist, and that her husband thought so too.

But did he?

One night after dinner Phil burst into my room, where I was pegging away at a problem in specific gravity, and said, with a scared face, "Come upstairs, boy. Say, they're having the hell of a row!"

"Who?"

"The laughing hyenas."

We sprinted up the stairs and listened. Phil's room adjoined the Lyntons'. Sure enough, I could hear Mrs. Lynton—not laughing, for once—but actually crying. I was astounded. I was embarrassed. She was crying hysterically, and trying to talk at the same time, her voice rising and falling with extraordinary fluctuations and breaks and changes.

"No—no—no—no—" she said, "go away from me, don't touch me! You've broken my spirit! I'll never paint again! I hate you, go away, go away!" And then more sobs, and unintelligible murmurs, and then Mr. Lynton's voice, quite surprisingly harsh and loud—as if he suddenly turned, as it were, "at bay":

"Shut up! . . . I'm tired of having to treat you like a child! Why in God's name don't you grow up? Stop being a damned kitten!"

"I'm *not* a kitten. You know it's just my nature!"

"Nature? It isn't *human* nature!"

We could hear Mr. Lynton's footsteps pacing the floor, to and fro, to and fro, and it was as if we could actually see him, with his hands in his pockets, and his beard pressed firmly down on his necktie.

"Why are you so cruel to me? You know I only try to be happy!"

"Idiot! . . . You're driving me mad. Your happiness is just plain selfishness, that's what it is! What in *hell* do you ever think of but yourself? Not *me*, certainly. All I exist for is to appreciate you. I have to be amused by you. Good God, I've had to flirt with you publicly for fifteen years, and I'm sick of it. Your whole life has just been one long promiscuous flirtation with the whole damned Western Hemisphere! . . . What kind of a life is that for *me*?"

"You're a brute, that's what you are; you're a sadist! You don't love me anymore, that's what it is! And you want to stop me from painting! And you want to get rid of me!"

There was a silence, as if both of them were standing still. Then abruptly the door slammed, and we heard steps rushing down the stairs.

In a moment Mrs. Lynton began to sob, more loudly than ever; and Phil and I crept back to my room to discuss this amazing turn of events. Words failed us. The event stupefied us. We decided that all was not well in Denmark, and let it go at that.

And the very next night—as if nothing at all had happened—we were all invited to go to Mrs. Lynton's studio in Joy Street for a Patriot's Day party.

At dinner the Lyntons were as hilarious as ever. Mrs. Lynton was bubbling over with her comic misadventures in the preparations for the celebration—Chinese lanterns had caught fire, a beer bottle had exploded frothily over the fireplace, two of the eggs had been bad and had smelled like Roman catacombs, mice had eaten half the sardines, and so on, and so on. She rolled her brown eyes, grimaced, was arch and moody by turns, became almost tearful as she told us of the sardines—poor little things—and my father and Mr. Lynton fairly crowed with delight. Phil and I looked at her with renewed wonder.

And the whole party went off in that fashion. Never was a studio so consciously arty. There were no chairs at all—only black cushions on a scarlet floor—and we had to squat round the hearth and toast marshmallows at the wood fire (though it was a very warm night) and another lantern blazed up, and the sardines (what remained of them) were rancid—but everything was made into one huge, uproarious, continuous joke. Paintings were stacked everywhere; and it seemed to me that a little—perhaps commercial?—pressure was being put upon my poor ignorant father to look at every one of them. In fact, we all had to look at them. They were stood for us in every conceivable light: autumn trees, violet sunsets, marshes in moonlight, haystacks on Cape Cod, cranberry bogs, wharves, dories hauling up nets—watercolors, oils, crayons, every damned kind of picture that I ever heard of. And all of them atrocious. We went through the vocabulary of praise till it was worn to a fiber. "Wonderful! Marvelous! . . . Did you do this one recently? . . . It seems to me your sense of color has deepened. . . . And that aerial perspective, that effect of fog!" Though I myself ventured only a few scared words, my throat began to feel as parched as if I'd been ten days on a desert. And all the while Mrs. Lynton was coquettish and playful, laughed girlishly, wrung her hands, was so pleased with everything—wasn't it a sweet little studio? A sweet view over the river and the bridge? And what a lark to have to sit on the floor like Indians! And to eat rotten little fishes! . . .

It was then that the shock, the terrible shock, of pure hard reality occurred, and from the most unexpected quarter.

My mother was looking at a painting of a sandy beach, with grass-covered dunes and lobster pots, all done in a purple light that never was, thank God, on land or sea.

"But isn't that a little gem?" said Mr. Lynton. "Isn't it a *marvel?*"

"I particularly like the sand," crowed Mrs. Lynton. "And do you know why it's so good, so sandlike?"

"Just feel it, Mrs. Beebe," said Mr. Lynton, positively purring through his beard, "it even *feels* like sand!"

My mother felt of the beach, skeptically.

"Now, doesn't it?" cried Mrs. Lynton. "And do you know why?"

"No," said my mother, a little coldly, and drawing back from the easel. "Why?" Her voice was curiously flat.

"Because I mixed sand with the paint!"

This was a dramatic moment: we were expected to be impressed. It was, as it were, the very last word in aestheticism. The Lyntons glowed at us. They waited with delighted eagerness for our praise, our astonishment. But instead my mother became all at once quite acid.

"I'm afraid," she said, "I think that's just sentimental nonsense. Do you want to scratch matches on it?"

It was as if a torpedo had been exploded in the room. Mr. Lynton walked toward the window and blew his nose. My father looked sheepish. And in an instant the whole party had obviously come to an end—the gaiety seemed false, the studio looked tawdry, we all felt poor and miserable, there was nothing to say. We drank the bad coffee, which Mrs. Lynton presently brought us, vainly endeavored to make her talk or laugh again, and then, a little later, went home.

That was the end of the curious intimacy between the Lyntons and the Beebes. A week later, the Lyntons moved away from Oxford Street. And six months later, we learned from the *Herald* one morning that Mrs. Lynton had died of pneumonia. I believe a note of condolence was written, and was never answered—and we never saw Mr. Lynton again.

BIOGRAPHICAL NOTES

CONRAD AIKEN *1889-1973*
Born in Savannah, Georgia, of New England parents, orphaned at eleven, Aiken was raised by a great-grandaunt in New Bedford, Massachusetts. A graduate of Harvard, he devoted most of his time thereafter to writing, and finally produced some fifty volumes of short stories, novels, poetry and literary criticism. From 1950 to 1952 he held the chair of poetry at the Library of Congress. Among his many honors and awards are a Pulitzer Prize, a National Book Award, a Bollingen Prize and the Gold Medal of the National Institute of Arts and Letters. Page 624

SHERWOOD ANDERSON *1876-1941*
After receiving a spotty education and working at a number of jobs in his native Ohio, Anderson went to Chicago. Earning his living as an advertising copywriter, he also produced his first novels. When in 1919 he published a collection of unified short stories, *Winesburg, Ohio,* its simple, straightforward style was so new and forceful that it created a sensation. In 1927 he turned to newspaper editing in Marion, Virginia, where, in a cabin near his home, he continued to write of life in small-town America. Page 558

JAMES BALDWIN *1924—*
Son of a pastor in Harlem, New York City, Baldwin thought briefly of studying for the ministry. In his early twenties he went to Paris, where he began to write short stories deeply rooted in the black experience. Recognition, especially of his importance as a com-

mentator on the plight of black America, came in 1953 with his first novel, *Go Tell It on the Mountain.* Besides his short stories, collected in *Going to Meet the Man,* and six well-received novels, he has written magazine articles, a number of brilliant essays and three plays. Page 604

STEPHEN VINCENT BENÉT *1898-1943*
A published poet while still a student at Yale, Benét later was awarded a Pulitzer Prize for his long and brilliant narrative poem on the Civil War, "John Brown's Body." He was also an established novelist as well as author of many fine short stories, such as "A Tooth for Paul Revere," dealing with the American experience. "The Devil and Daniel Webster," published in 1937, remains one of the best-known, best-loved tales in American literature. Some of his finest pieces have been collected in *Tales Before Midnight.* Page 380

AMBROSE BIERCE *1842-?1914*
Starting as a newspaperman in San Francisco, Bierce was almost fifty before he gained national recognition with a collection of stories called *In the Midst of Life and Other Stories.* The theme that awakened the full range of his talent was the Civil War, and he returned to it repeatedly. His sharp wit, darkened by a real bitterness toward life, found permanent expression in his publication *The Devil's Dictionary,* full of cynical definitions. Visiting Mexico while the revolution of Pancho Villa was in progress, he simply disappeared. Page 441

KAY BOYLE *1903—*
Born in St. Paul, Minnesota, into a household where books were a staple, Boyle began writing early. Prolific, even while working as a college teacher, she has produced novels, novelettes, short stories, war correspondence, poetry, magazine articles and children's books. But she is best known for her short stories, many dealing with the infinitely subtle ways in which the human need for love reveals itself. Her stories are collected in more than half a dozen volumes, including *The Smoking Mountain* and *Nothing Ever Breaks Except the Heart.*   Page 395

RAY BRADBURY *1920—*
Since his earliest writing Bradbury has concentrated with remarkable success on fantasy and science fiction. Such imaginative works as *The Martian Chronicles, The Illustrated Man* and *Something Wicked This Way Comes* have gained new readers for the field, and new respect. He was born in Waukegan, Illinois, and moved with his family to Los Angeles, where he still resides.   Page 230

HEYWOOD BROUN *1888-1939*
A native of Brooklyn, New York, Broun became a journalist while a student at Harvard, writing for the old New York *Morning Telegraph.* A brilliant essayist, he soon became America's favorite newspaper writer. Whether commenting on sports, theater, social injustice, books, ideas or simply the first robin of spring, he was read avidly. In 1938 his Christmas column was broadcast by Franklin Roosevelt in the President's Christmas message to the nation.   Page 294

KATHARINE BRUSH *1902-1952*
A best-selling novelist of the 1930s, Brush was known for her deft, caustic portraits of café society in the Prohibition era. Born in Middletown, Connecticut, at sixteen she was writing for the Boston *Traveler.* Her literary career began with light verse and short fiction contributed to leading magazines. Later she became a scriptwriter in Hollywood. Her permanent home was in New York City, the setting of many of her stories.   Page 460

PEARL S. BUCK *1892-1973*
Growing up in China, Pearl Buck early acquired a love of that country which found expression in the Pulitzer Prize–winning novel *The Good Earth,* as well as in many other distinguished books. A person of great causes, she worked long and tirelessly in behalf of retarded and displaced children. She is the only American woman to have won the Nobel Prize in literature.   Page 363

ERSKINE CALDWELL *1903—*
A minister's son, Caldwell was born and educated in Georgia and at the universities of Pennsylvania and Virginia. He worked as a mill hand, farm laborer, soda jerk and newspaperman before the huge success in 1932 of his novel *Tobacco Road,* which also became a successful play and movie. A year later came the equally sensational *God's Little Acre.* His varied early experience and extensive travel provided the penetrating knowledge of Southern life that is the foundation of his voluminous work, part of which has achieved worldwide popularity.   Page 564

TRUMAN CAPOTE *1924—*
A native of New Orleans, Capote lists writing only after conversation, reading and travel as a "preferred pastime." A writer of extraordinary versatility, he has won international acclaim. His novel *Breakfast at Tiffany's* was made into both a Broadway musical and a movie. With *In Cold Blood* he created a journalistic nonfiction style that reads like suspense fiction.   Page 446

WILLA CATHER *1876-1947*
Though born in Virginia, Willa Cather grew up in Nebraska among the immigrant settlers about whom she later wrote so movingly. After graduating from the University of Nebraska, she worked first as a teacher, then as an editor. The publication of *O Pioneers!* in 1913 established her as a major novelist. Among her other books at least two, *My Ántonia* and *Death Comes for the Archbishop,* are now accepted as classics. She wrote few short stories. "The Enchanted Bluff" is one of her earliest.   Page 614

JOHN CHEEVER *1912—*
When at seventeen Cheever was expelled from Thayer Academy in Massachusetts, his schooling ended. Born in Quincy, Massachusetts, of old New England stock, he later spent four years in the army. He wrote scripts for radio and eventually for television and became a teacher of advanced composition at Barnard College, New York City. His elegant prose, shrewd observation and wry humor have won him a distinguished place in contemporary literature. His honors include a National Book Award for his novel *The Wapshot Chronicle* and a Pulitzer Prize. Page 431

WALTER VAN TILBURG CLARK
1909–1971
Most of Clark's early life was spent in Reno, Nevada, where his father served as president of the University of Nevada. That state also gave him the setting for his best-known novel, *The Ox-Bow Incident*, the book in which the Western came suddenly of age. He attended schools in Nevada, Vermont and New York, where he was a teacher and a coach of athletics. He wrote two other novels and more than twenty short stories. Page 207

RICHARD CONNELL *1893–1949*
Author of about three hundred short stories, Connell was also a successful writer of advertising copy and Hollywood screenplays. Born in Poughkeepsie, New York, where his father edited a newspaper, he attended Harvard, and served in France during World War I. After living in New York, he moved permanently to California. Page 489

MARC CONNELLY *1890–1980*
While working as a columnist for a Pittsburgh newspaper, Connelly began writing musical-comedy lyrics. Visiting New York in 1915 to hear his words set to music, he fell in love with the theater and stayed on to become one of its most notable authors and directors, writing short stories and verse as well. His greatest Broadway hit, *Green Pastures*, is as widely beloved today as when it won a Pulitzer Prize in 1930. Page 254

STEPHEN CRANE *1871–1900*
The fourteenth child of a New Jersey Methodist minister, Crane died before his thirtieth year. Yet within that short span he wrote novels, short stories and poetry that fill fourteen volumes. Best known for *The Red Badge of Courage* (a classic novel of combat experience in the Civil War that he wrote without ever having seen battle), Crane was one of the earliest and among the greatest of the realistic school of American writers. Page 338

THEODORE DREISER *1871–1945*
A big, slow-moving man with blazing gray eyes, Dreiser was born in Indiana. He attended Indiana University but left after his freshman year. In Chicago, at twenty-one, he began a newspaper career. From then on he was steadily occupied with journalism, magazine editing and his own writing, much of it social protest. His two best-known novels, *Sister Carrie* and *An American Tragedy*, are powerful examples of the new realism he brought to fiction. Page 473

WILLIAM FAULKNER *1897–1962*
One of America's foremost novelists, Faulkner was born and raised in Mississippi, the son of an aristocratic tradition. In a series of distinguished novels set in his hometown of Oxford and the surrounding county, fictionalized as Yoknapatawpha, he mirrored the decline of the old South under the onslaught of technology. In World War I he served with the Royal Air Force. Later he worked as a newspaperman and screenwriter before earning international fame with such novels as *The Sound and the Fury*, *Light in August* and *Sanctuary*. In 1950 he received the Nobel Prize in literature. Page 176

F. SCOTT FITZGERALD *1896–1940*
Only twenty-four when his first book, *This Side of Paradise*, brought him fame, the flamboyant Fitzgerald soon became the living symbol of America's raucous Jazz Age. Then, in mid-career, came tragedy. His wife, Zelda, suffered a mental breakdown, more or less permanent. He fell ill, took heavily to drink and was plunged into financial trouble. In

Hollywood, where he wrote movie scripts, the downward slide accelerated. *The Last Tycoon*, the novel left unfinished at his death, was published in 1941. His masterpiece, *The Great Gatsby*, had appeared in 1925. Page 9

CHARLOTTE PERKINS GILMAN
1860–1935
That haunting study of insanity, "The Yellow Wall Paper," published in 1892, was one of Gilman's few works of fiction. An early campaigner for women's rights, she devoted most of her time to writing and lecturing on social reform. Her book, *Women and Economics*, published in 1898, was translated into six languages. Born in Hartford, Connecticut, she died in Pasadena, California. Page 195

SUSAN GLASPELL *1876–1948*
A leader in the revolt against the romanticism of the World War I era, Glaspell turned repeatedly to her native Midwest as a setting for her novels and plays. She was known for her delicate skill in portraying rounded, down-to-earth characters, and one of her plays, *Alison's House*, received a Pulitzer Prize. Born in Davenport, Iowa, she began her career as a reporter for the Des Moines *Daily News*. Later she lived with her husband, George Cook, in Provincetown, Massachusetts, where she was prominent in the famous colony of artists and writers. Page 52

SHIRLEY ANN GRAU *1929–*
In all her novels and short stories Grau writes of the South she knows so well in a style that is distinctly and hauntingly her own. Born and educated in New Orleans, Louisiana, she still resides there with her husband, a professor at Tulane University, and her three children. In 1965 she was awarded a Pulitzer Prize for *The Keepers of the House*. Her recent collection of stories is *The Wind Shifting West*. Page 285

BRET HARTE *1836–1902*
During the Gold Rush, young Harte moved with his family from New York State to California. A writer even as a child, he soon found colorful subjects for short stories about the earthily human, rough-and-tumble lives of the hordes of men and women who had swarmed west to get rich quick. While literary fame came to him early, it soon ebbed away. He continued to write after leaving California for New York and Europe, but unlike his friend Mark Twain, he could never recapture his early success. Page 274

NATHANIEL HAWTHORNE *1804–1864*
The son of a sea captain, Hawthorne was born in Salem, Massachusetts. He worked variously as an editor and customs collector, and in 1853 was appointed American consul in Liverpool by his old school friend, President Franklin Pierce. With the publication in 1837 of a volume of his short stories, *Twice-Told Tales*, dealing with the effect of the Puritan conscience on America, his writing had begun to attract attention. Apart from the stories, his fame rests on two powerful novels, *The House of the Seven Gables* and *The Scarlet Letter*. Page 594

ERNEST HEMINGWAY *1899–1961*
A believer in the vigorous life, himself seeming a little larger than life, Hemingway's first thirty years of writing were capped in 1954 with the Nobel Prize in literature. He had richly earned the honor with his many compelling short stories and his world-famous novels, *The Sun Also Rises*, *A Farewell to Arms* and *The Old Man and the Sea*. Born in Oak Park, Illinois, he began his career as a newsman in Kansas City. After service in World War I, he lived for a time in Paris, where his first book was published. His deceptively simple style has had a large influence on modern writers. Page 113

O. HENRY *1862–1910*
One of the most prolific, and once the most popular, of America's short-story writers, William Sydney Porter was born in Greensboro, North Carolina. At twenty he went to Texas, where he wrote for a Houston newspaper after having been employed as a teller in an Austin bank. Convicted later of embezzlement, he served a jail term, then went to New York. There, in the lives of ordinary people,

he found the themes for a host of memorable stories. His most famous collection, *The Four Million* (the opposite of high society's Four Hundred), appeared in 1906. One of his stories was successfully dramatized as *Alias Jimmy Valentine*.   Page 95

WASHINGTON IRVING *1783–1859*
Known for his gentle nature, charm and courtesy, Irving was a personal as well as a literary success in both the young United States and Europe. Born in New York, he briefly practiced law and for a time represented the family mercantile business in England. But most of his life was spent in travel, in diplomatic missions, and in the writing which earned him a permanent place as America's earliest author of importance. Sunnyside, his lovely Hudson River estate not far from the scene of "The Legend of Sleepy Hollow," is still preserved.   Page 526

SHIRLEY JACKSON *1919–1965*
Novelist, writer of short stories and radio and television scripts, Jackson's work reveals a preoccupation with the darker regions of human consciousness. Her novel *The Haunting of Hill House* was made into a successful movie, and her story "The Lottery" became a play. But she could also write delightfully about ordinary life, as in *Life Among the Savages*, a series of essays on her children. She was born in San Francisco and lived most of her adult life in rural Vermont.   Page 322

HENRY JAMES *1843–1916*
Though born an American, in New York City, James's major works are set in Europe, where he lived for most of his life. Brother of William James, the psychologist and philosopher, and son of Henry James, Sr.—the eminent theologian and friend of Emerson and Carlyle—Henry James, Jr., was reared in privileged circumstances. Hailed for such classically probing novels as *The Portrait of a Lady* and *The Ambassadors*, he was also known for his short stories and criticism. After war broke out in 1914, he disapproved of America's neutrality and became a British citizen in the year before his death. Page 302

RING LARDNER *1885–1933*
Author of eight volumes of short stories and a novel, *The Big Town*, and co-author with George S. Kaufman of a comedy, *June Moon*, Lardner's full recognition did not come until he was forty. Before that he was widely known and celebrated as a sportswriter of unusual talent. A gregarious man who mixed with all sorts of people from prizefighters to stockbrokers, his subtle command of colloquial American speech became a trademark. Much of his writing was done in hotel rooms, rented for the purpose, where he worked in seclusion behind drawn shades.   Page 102

JACK LONDON *1876–1916*
By the age of twenty-two London had been a cannery worker in San Francisco (his birthplace), an oyster pirate, a deckhand on a sealing vessel, a hobo, a Socialist agitator, a college student and finally a gold miner in the Klondike. It was this trip to the far North that inspired his most famous novel, *The Call of the Wild*, and many of his best stories. His vivid adventure tales became so popular that by 1913 he was said to be the world's highest-paid author. At forty, in despair over his health, finances and deteriorating talents, he died by an overdose of drugs, thought to have been deliberate.   Page 36

H. P. LOVECRAFT *1890–1937*
Recognition as a master of horror and fantasy tales came to Lovecraft only after he had been writing for twenty years, publishing in such specialized periodicals as *Weird Tales* and *Amazing Stories*. He was writing newspaper articles on science at the early age of sixteen, but frail health kept him from attending college, and most of his life was spent in Providence, Rhode Island, his birthplace. Much of his work anticipates the modern vogue of science fiction.   Page 540

CARSON McCULLERS *1917–1967*
Author of such modern classics as *The Member of the Wedding* and *The Ballad of the Sad Café*, McCullers belongs to that school of writing known as Southern Gothic. All of her novels and short stories are laid in the

South, evoking a world of loneliness and alienation. Born in Columbus, Georgia, she began writing at sixteen, and for a time had an ambition to become a concert pianist. She studied creative writing at New York University and when only twenty-three achieved wide fame with her first novel, *The Heart is a Lonely Hunter*.   Page 571

BERNARD MALAMUD *1914—*
Like many of the characters he created, Malamud was born into the Jewish immigrant world of Brooklyn, New York. Graduating from The City College of New York, he taught English in the city's evening high schools, later joined the faculty of Bennington College, in Vermont. With publication of the novel *The Assistant* in 1957, he was quickly recognized as an important delineator of the American immigrant experience. He has twice won a National Book Award—first in 1959 for a volume of short stories, *The Magic Barrel*, and then in 1967 for *The Fixer*, a novel.   Page 505

HERMAN MELVILLE *1819–1891*
Until fairly recently Melville was the most ignored of America's great writers. Born in New York City of Scotch-Dutch parents, he was one of eight children. After working as a bank clerk, farmer and teacher, he went to sea on a merchantman, and later took part in a whaling cruise. Two accounts of his experiences in the South Seas, *Typee* and *Omoo*, were immensely successful, launching him on a writing career. When, however, his monumental novel, *Moby Dick*, appeared, it was misunderstood and condemned by the critics and ignored by the public, and his fame was eclipsed. The last years of his life were spent in obscurity, twenty of them as a customs inspector.   Page 406

FLANNERY O'CONNOR *1925–1964*
Born and educated in Georgia, O'Connor knew at an early age that she had inherited the rare fatal disease that ran in her family. Perhaps it was this knowledge, combined with a deep religious sense and keen humor, that gave her work its harsh moral objectivity

and ferocious comedy. *Wise Blood*, her first novel, earned favorable comparison with the work of Franz Kafka. Her short stories have been collected in two volumes, *A Good Man Is Hard to Find and Other Stories* and *Everything That Rises Must Converge*. Shy and reticent, she spent most of her life on the family farm in Milledgeville, Georgia.   Page 549

JOHN O'HARA *1905–1970*
The eldest of eight children, O'Hara was born in Pottsville, Pennsylvania. Prevented from going to college by the death of his doctor father, he worked as everything from ship steward to movie critic. In 1934 the success of his first novel, *Appointment in Samarra*, established him as a writer. His novels regularly made the best-seller lists and at least three of them—*Pal Joey*, *Ten North Frederick* and *Butterfield 8*—were made into popular films. But many critics prefer the clean, sure style of his short stories.   Page 83

EDGAR ALLAN POE *1809–1849*
One of America's first important writers, Poe was born in Boston. Orphaned at three, he was reared by foster parents in Richmond, Virginia. Working as an editor, critic, and writer of short stories, he first gained attention in 1833 with his tale "MS. Found in a Bottle." There followed a series of world-renowned short stories, including "The Murders in the Rue Morgue," the first true detective story. His poem "The Raven" remains one of the most popular in American literature.   Page 165

J. F. POWERS *1917—*
Coming of age during the Depression in Jacksonville, Illinois, his birthplace, Powers later went to Chicago. There he wrote in his spare time while supporting himself with a variety of odd jobs. Publication in 1943 of his short story "Lions, Harts, Leaping Does" brought enthusiastic recognition, and his tales have since been widely anthologized. Two well-received collections of them are *Prince of Darkness and Other Stories* and *The Presence of Grace*. A novel, *Morte d'Urban*, won a National Book Award in 1963.   Page 584

DAMON RUNYON *1884-1946*
Born in Manhattan, Kansas, and reared in Colorado, Runyon as a young man served with the U.S. Army in the Philippines. He later became a highly paid sportswriter, then a star reporter whose assignments took him to France in World War I. But it is on his colorful tales about the antics of Broadway's *Guys and Dolls*—the title of his first collection of stories, on which a musical comedy was based—that his fame rests. Page 240

JOHN STEINBECK *1902-1968*
At the age of sixty, for his contribution to American and world literature, Steinbeck was awarded a Nobel Prize. His first novel, published in 1929, was a traditional romance, but he soon turned to the earthy realism of such moving works as *The Grapes of Wrath* and *Of Mice and Men*. Born in the Salinas Valley of California, he wrote with graphic power of a wide variety of people and places, drawing his most unforgettable portrayals from the life of his native state. In 1962 his account of a memorable nationwide tour, companioned by his dog, became a best seller, *Travels with Charley*. Page 154

JESSE STUART *1907—*
Still living in W-Hollow, Kentucky, on the land where he was born, Stuart populates his writings with the hill people he knows so well. The first of his family to go as far as high school, he worked his way through Lincoln Memorial University in Tennessee, attended graduate school at Vanderbilt University, then returned home as a teacher. Since 1930 he has published more than three dozen well-received volumes of poetry, fiction and non-fiction. Page 74

JAMES THURBER *1894-1961*
A gifted cartoonist before he began to write, Thurber won an international audience for his special brand of humor. Born in Columbus, Ohio, he attended Ohio State University, then began work as a newspaperman. Both "The Secret Life of Walter Mitty," one of his best-known stories, and *The Male Animal*, a stage hit of 1940 written with

Elliott Nugent, were also successful movies. There exist nearly a dozen collections of his essays and stories. Page 523

MARK TWAIN *1835-1910*
Like many other American writers, Samuel Langhorne Clemens began his career writing for newspapers. Born in Florida, reared in the Mississippi River town of Hannibal, Missouri, he left school at twelve, when his father died. Later he became a steamboat pilot, then went west, where he worked as a miner, prospector and reporter. Fame arrived with his story "The Celebrated Jumping Frog of Calaveras County." Marrying in 1870 into an old Connecticut family, he lived the rest of his life in Hartford, writing steadily and achieving world fame with such masterworks as *The Adventures of Tom Sawyer* and *The Adventures of Huckleberry Finn*. Page 31

JOHN UPDIKE *1932—*
At twenty-six Updike published his first book, a collection of light verse entitled *The Carpentered Hen*. A number of distinguished short-story collections followed, then several best-selling novels—*Rabbit, Run; The Centaur*, which won a National Book Award; and *Couples*. A Harvard graduate, Updike draws in much of his writing on the background with which he is most familiar, the area around his birthplace, Shillington, Pennsylvania. Page 358

EUDORA WELTY *1909—*
Most of Welty's writing has been in the short-story form, but she has also produced three well-received novels, *Delta Wedding; The Ponder Heart*, which was dramatized in 1957; and *Losing Battles*. She was born in Jackson, Mississippi. Her penetrating evocations of southern life have won her a Pulitzer Prize, a National Medal for Literature and wide acclaim. Page 219

EDITH WHARTON *1862-1937*
An interest in literature was thought an eccentricity in the wealthy world of Edith Newbold Jones's childhood. There were governesses, homes in New York and Newport,

and travel abroad. At twenty-three she was married to Edward Wharton, who proved mentally unstable. Perhaps as an escape she turned to writing, and made her permanent home in Paris. There she wrote the distinguished novels and short stories that brought her fame, including *Ethan Frome* and *The Age of Innocence*. She was twice honored with a Pulitzer Prize.   Page 260

MARY E. WILKINS *1852–1930*
Toward the close of the nineteenth century, when sentiment and happy endings were the fashion in fiction, Wilkins won popularity with her realistic vignettes of life in New England villages. She lived with her family in Randolph, Massachusetts (her birthplace), until she married Dr. Charles Freeman, when she moved to her husband's home in New Jersey. Her published work comprises a play, two volumes of verse, twelve novels and over two hundred short stories.   Page 145

RICHARD WRIGHT *1908–1960*
With the publication in 1940 of his powerful novel, *Native Son*, Wright took an early lead in the black people's struggle against poverty and prejudice, bringing a new and disturbing light to bear on the problem. Born on a plantation near Natchez, Mississippi, in his mid-twenties he drifted to Chicago and New York. Writing for anyone who would publish his work, he supported himself with odd jobs. After the success of *Native Son*, in protest against segregation in the United States, he moved first to Mexico and then to Paris, where he lived as an expatriate until his death.   Page 170

ACKNOWLEDGMENTS

WINTER DREAMS, copyright 1922 by Frances Scott Fitzgerald Lanahan, is from *All the Sad Young Men* by F. Scott Fitzgerald. Used by permission of Charles Scribner's Sons and of The Bodley Head, Ltd. WHAT STUMPED THE BLUEJAYS is from *A Tramp Abroad* by Mark Twain, published by Harper & Row, Publishers, Inc. A JURY OF HER PEERS, copyright 1950, is used by permission of the estate of Susan Glaspell: THE STORM, from *Tales from the Plum Grove Hills* by Jesse Stuart, was published by E. P. Dutton and Co., Inc., 1946. Used by permission of the author. THE PIONEER HEP-CAT, copyright © 1960, 1961 by John O'Hara, is from *Assembly* by John O'Hara. Used by permission of Random House, Inc., and of Curtis Brown Ltd. Page 92, line 30: excerpt from "Poor Butterfly," copyright 1916 by Harms, Inc., copyright renewed, all rights reserved, is used by permission of Warner Bros. Music. I CAN'T BREATHE, copyright 1926 by International Magazine Co., Inc., is from *Round Up* by Ring Lardner. Used by permission of Charles Scribner's Sons. Page 103, lines 24-25: excerpt from "Always" by Irving Berlin, copyright 1925 by Irving Berlin, copyright renewed, all rights reserved, is used by permission of Irving Berlin Music Corporation, New York, and of J. Albert and Son Pty. Ltd., Sydney. Page 105, lines 27-28: excerpt from "Just a Cottage Small," copyright 1925 by Harms, Inc., copyright renewed, all rights reserved, is used by permission of Warner Bros. Music. THE SHORT HAPPY LIFE OF FRANCIS MACOMBER, copyright 1936 by Ernest Hemingway, is from *The Short Stories of Ernest Hemingway*. Used by permission of Charles Scribner's Sons, of the Executors of the Hemingway Estate and of Jonathan Cape Limited. A NEW ENGLAND NUN, copyright 1891 by Mary E. Wilkins, is from *The New England Nun and Other Stories* by Mary E. Wilkins. Used by permission of Harper & Row, Publishers, Inc. THE CHRYSANTHEMUMS, copyright 1937, copyright © renewed 1964 by John Steinbeck, is used by permission of The Viking Press, Inc., and of McIntosh and Otis, Inc. THE MAN WHO SAW THE FLOOD, copyright 1940, copyright © 1961 by Richard Wright, is from *Eight Men* by Richard Wright. Used by permission of Thomas Y. Crowell Co., Inc., and of Paul R. Reynolds, Inc. BARN BURNING, copyright 1939, copyright © renewed 1967 by Estelle Faulkner and Jill Faulkner Summers, is from *Collected Stories of William Faulkner*. Used by permission of Random House, Inc., of the Author's Literary Estate and of Chatto & Windus, Ltd. THE YELLOW WALL PAPER, copyright 1892 by New England Magazine Corporation, copyright 1899 by Small Maynard & Co., was reproduced from the *New England Magazine* by Rockwell & Churchill Press, 1901, by permission of the publisher. HOOK, copyright 1940, copyright © 1968 by Walter Van Tilburg Clark, is used by permission of International Creative Management. THE KEY, copyright 1941, copyright © renewed 1969 by Eudora Welty, is from *A Curtain of Green and Other Stories* by Eudora Welty. Used by permission of Harcourt Brace Jovanovich, Inc., and of Russell & Volkening, Inc. THE SHORE LINE AT SUNSET, copyright © 1959 by Ray Bradbury, is used by permission of Harold Matson Company, Inc. THE IDYLL OF MISS SARAH BROWN by Damon Runyon, copyright 1933, copyright © renewed 1960 by Damon Runyon, Jr., and Mary Runyon McCann as Children of the Deceased Author, is used by permission of American Play Company, Inc. CORONER'S INQUEST, copyright 1930, copyright © renewed 1958, is used by permission of Marc Connelly. ROMAN FEVER, copyright 1934 by *Liberty Magazine*, copyright © renewed 1962 by William R. Tyler, is from *The Collected*

639